HACKED

THE FIRST SIMCAVALIER TRILOGY

Published in paperback in 2021 by Sixth Element Publishing
on behalf of Kate Baucherel

Sixth Element Publishing
Arthur Robinson House
13-14 The Green
Billingham TS23 1EU
www.6epublishing.net

Bitcoin Hurricane (SimCavalier Book One)
First published in Great Britain in 2017 by Sixth Element Publishing
Copyright © 2017 by Kate Baucherel

Hacked Future (SimCavalier Book Two)
First published in Great Britain in 2018 by Sixth Element Publishing
Copyright © 2018 by Kate Baucherel

Tangled Fortunes (SimCavalier Book Three)
First published in Great Britain in 2020 by Sixth Element Publishing
Copyright © 2020 by Kate Baucherel

ISBN 978-1-914170-13-3

British Library Cataloguing in Publication Data. A catalogue record for this book is
available from the British Library.

HACKED
THE FIRST SIMCAVALIER TRILOGY

SIMCAVALIER BOOK ONE: BITCOIN HURRICANE

SIMCAVALIER BOOK TWO: HACKED FUTURE

SIMCAVALIER BOOK THREE: TANGLED FORTUNES

KATE BAUCHEREL

Books by Kate Baucherel

The SimCavalier series
Book 1: Bitcoin Hurricane
Book 2: Hacked Future
Book 3: Tangled Fortunes
Book 4: Critical Nexus

Short stories in the Harvey Duckman Presents... series
Gridlock (Vol. 1, 2019)
White Christmas (Xmas Special, 2019)
Finch (Vol. 5, 2020)
Parrot Radio (Pirate Special, 2020)
Xanthe (A SimCavalier Origins story)
Firebird (A Finch story)
The Eagle's Flight (A Finch story)

Non-Fiction
Blockchain Hurricane:
Origins, Applications and Future of Blockchain and Cryptocurrency
Poles Apart: Challenges for Business in the Digital Age
What's Hot in Blockchain and Crypto Volumes 1&2

CONTENTS

BITCOIN HURRICANE
SIMCAVALIER BOOK ONE

HACKED FUTURE

SIMCAVALIER BOOK TWO

TANGLED FORTUNES
SIMCAVALIER BOOK THREE

BITCOIN HURRICANE
SIMCAVALIER BOOK ONE

1: THE WORM

The worm crept through the virtual spaces of the world, threading itself imperceptibly through fibres and circuits, spreading silently across networks. It travelled patiently, carefully, a parasite replicating by laying eggs in host after host, spreading its presence exponentially around the globe. Its larvae would lie dormant for days, waiting for the opportunity to leap a new void, until the file in which the code slept was emailed to an unsuspecting recipient, and the journey continued.

Sometimes the worm landed in the lush breeding ground of a large institution, spreading across all the interconnected devices, taking advantage of gaps in outdated operating systems and in ancient software that unsuspecting users had clung to over the years. It slid unnoticed through ecosystems of unsecured smart devices, household appliances falling prey to the intruder thanks to manufacturers who cut corners and costs in the race to expand the Internet of Things. It crept into software companies, hitching a ride on downloads, and from there spread outwards like feathery seeds, riding on the wind of upgrades installed by trusting users.

At other times, it came up short, storming bastions protected by strong firewalls, passcodes, and the constant patrolling of the virtual ramparts by competent, conscientious cyber security troops; the worm kept probing for an opening, persisting in its attack until a slip, a trip, a minor human error, the simple click of an email, compromised even the best procedures and protocols.

A malicious little bundle of binary code, the worm was no empathetic artificial intelligence: it had no conscious sense of purpose, but was doing its job well. The surrogate offspring of a power in the shadows, carried to term by a scratch team of hungry developers commissioned on the Dark Web, it was born of greed and poverty. The only way out of the slums created by the fall of traditional industry, the devaluation of hard currency, the rising of the seas, the migration from extreme heat, and global economic upheaval was to embrace the digital world and code your way to freedom. The best underground developers commanded the highest fees; their employers played for the highest stakes.

Now, the worm was on the move. Its owners could not track its progress in its dormant state. They simply had to be patient and make their plans around the predetermined moment of activation.

•

Sir Simon Winchester glowered at the wall of blank monitors for a moment, cursing under his breath, then turned to face his board members who had gathered hurriedly in the sumptuous and ancient oak-panelled room. In his decades of service to the bank, he had watched the fallout from wave upon wave of cyber attacks: the calls for robust systems, the horror at loss of data, the scramble of rivals to salvage their reputations as they went to the wall. As chief executive, one of his first and strongest commitments had been to reinforce and stabilise protection. Attacks never ceased: the bank simply had to be prepared.

"Current status, Bill?" he enquired levelly of the chief technology officer.

"Ransomware attack, activated twelve minutes ago," replied the CTO. "Pretty standard stuff, I think. We're still identifying the point of entry to our systems. There are global reports coming in over tech networks but nothing has gone public on the news channels yet."

"It helps that it's late in the day in the UK and Europe. That'll reduce the immediate impact," replied Sir Simon.

Bill nodded. "Good timing for us tonight, although it's starting to hit the States now. That'll cause a lot more trouble, and it's only Wednesday."

The bank's head of trading spoke up. "Cryptocurrency trading showed a spike in the minutes before the first reports came through, so there are some theories that it could be a targeted attack on the banking sector. Bill, what's your take on that?"

"Not sure. There is some reported fallout in other industries, but there's no clear indication of what weakness is being exploited yet."

Bill looked worried. He turned to Sir Simon. "This one's spreading like wildfire internally, faster than we can close the gates. It's digging into some of the older software right at the heart of our operations. I need backup on this; we have our specialist team on standby."

Sir Simon nodded. They needed to react fast to neutralise the threat and get back to full operations. "Bring them in now, Bill. We need this virus closed down and cleaned out as fast as possible. Make the call."

Make the call? Bill winced at the anachronism, then nodded and pressed his thumb to a biometric scanner on his smartscreen.

Accessing a private, uncompromised network, he sent a single word alert to a blockchain. A response dropped into the same block in seconds, completing the transaction and sealing the contract. The team was on the way.

Less than an hour later, two strangers were ushered into the boardroom. A young man in a grey hoodie stepped forwards and shook the hand of the CEO. "Good evening, Sir Simon. Ross White." He indicated his silent companion. "My colleague, Cameron Silvera."

Cameron stepped forward. "Sorry to hear about this disruption, sir. We'll tackle the security breach in due course; that's history. Our priority is to neutralise the threat. The team is setting up downstairs. We'll keep you in the loop."

Sir Simon nodded. "Anything you need, just ask."

•

An unassuming, middle-aged man sat alone at a round metal table outside a small coffee shop, slowly sipping an Americano. It was late morning. The pavements were quiet, and all the other tables at the café empty. The early rush of Thursday's commuters was over, and lunchtime was not far away. A shaft of weak sunlight glinted off the metal chairs under the café's awning.

His gaze fell on a harassed-looking woman, slightly overweight, her smart skirt straining at the waist and an ID badge dangling carelessly on a red lanyard, as she crossed the road towards the café and headed for the counter inside, pulling a smartscreen from her pocket.

"Gotcha!" exclaimed the observer as he fingered the scanning device tucked under his table. Any moment now, his mark would be firing up her network.

The latest cyber attack was causing havoc around the globe. There were rumours of a banking system crisis. Crypto transactions were running slow, with the more volatile digital currencies suspended altogether. The small network of legacy ATMs had been reporting problems dispensing old bank notes, which were still in use in some quarters where the digital world had not been fully embraced. Cyber security teams worldwide had been fighting to arrest the spread of the latest virus since it first hit the news last night. It looked like the attack had been slowed, but not in time for the businesses or the man in the street caught up in the mess. Shame for them, he thought, but this was the opportunity he'd been waiting for. They finally had a solid tip-off. They were going to find the man, this time. The next thing he needed in the hunt was an inside view, and the key was within reach.

Rushing into the café, the woman barely noticed another city worker grabbing a well-earned few minutes of peace on his break. All hell was breaking loose in the bank, and now she had to deal with an urgent message from the kids' school as well. Returning to work after a few years' break had seemed like a good idea at the time. So much had changed, and she was struggling to keep up. She ordered a skinny latte and a triple chocolate muffin, refuelling for the next few hours of her shift. The machine behind the counter whirred into action, and a roboserver selected her cake from a display and placed it on a waiting tray. Heading to a comfortable sofa and small wooden table in the corner, she thumbed her screen to life and scanned for a connection. Stretching to relieve aching muscles, she smiled tiredly at the friendly human waiter as her coffee and cake arrived. There was a discreet 'ping!' from her screen as the wifi connection opened. She logged back in to the work network and settled down to deal with her personal emails.

A discreet Bluetooth speaker chirruped in the watcher's ear. "She's picked up the connection... into the network... delivering the package now... okay, Andy, all clear."

Slipping the hidden device into his pocket, the man abandoned the dregs of his coffee and strolled nonchalantly away towards a waiting autocar.

•

Cameron groaned as the radio sparked into life. Woken from deep sleep in the darkness, disoriented, it took a few moments to come to. An activity sensor embedded in the still dark lightbulb automatically set the kettle on the other side of the wall to boil. Coffee was more essential to Cameron than light in the morning.

Hearing movement, a small black and white cat hopped up onto the bed and began kneading ecstatically, purring with the delight of a pet who knows its meal ticket has been roused and breakfast is not far away. Cameron stroked its head idly; the purring redoubled.

Snatches of news tumbled from the speakers in the wall by the bed, making no sense yet. It had been a tough thirty-six hours for Cameron, delivering payback in the form of sore eyes, dry mouth, and an aching back. The most recent cyber attack had caught yet another legacy system with its pants down, hidden deep and half-forgotten inside an apparently ultra-modern bank. Cameron's team had been working round the clock to limit the spread of infection. Who cared where it had come from – Asian tigers, Slavic trolls, the favelas of Rio de Janeiro, or bored high school dropouts – the ripples of disruption were slowing, thanks to a flash of classic Cameron intuition marking the first significant win of the battle, and the combined efforts of threat intelligence teams around the world to neutralise the virus. Snatching a few hours' sleep might have seemed to be an ill-afforded luxury, but it was a necessity. Tired teams made mistakes. Everyone had to be rested and ready to make leaps of logic in containing, defusing, and mopping up after the threat.

The sounds from the radio gradually formed themselves into words. "I come to pick up my money and they said I can't, there's been a cyber attack. I don't know what one of them even is," complained a strident voice. "Why isn't it working? Why don't they do something?"

Cameron flung back the covers in disgust, eliciting a mutter of protest from a slumbering form, and a startled squeak from the cat, dislodged from its cosy nest. Cameron was already half way to the kitchen as the kettle steamed.

Cameron reached into the cupboard to select a clean bowl, grabbed the nearest box of cereal, and turned to the tiny but serviceable refrigerator to find some milk. Despite embracing all things digital and working in tech, Cameron held the very clear opinion that while a smart kettle might be utterly essential in the provision of timely coffee, a smart fridge was just a ridiculous concept. Sniffing suspiciously at the carton, the milk passed the test. Cameron splashed it over the cereal and part of the table, cursed, and reached for a cloth.

The cat circled its food bowl, mewing as if it was half starved. Cameron had no idea if it had been fed two days or two hours ago. No matter: an extra meal wouldn't bother a cat the way it might bother a human who constantly monitored calorie intake, weight gain, daily steps, and heart attack risk factors, in an effort to keep medical costs to a minimum.

Munching on cereal, Cameron glanced at a discreet cylinder tucked on the shelf. "Can you read out my emails?"

"I'm sorry, I didn't understand that. Did you want to read about snails?" replied a smooth voice.

Cameron swallowed. "Read out my emails."

The 'bot paused. "You have one hundred and thirty-six unread messages. You have seventy-eight automated mailings. You have three priority messages from Ross White, four messages from Charlie Silvera, two messages from…"

"Delete the automated messages," snapped Cameron. "Volume down, and play the priority emails." Another spoonful of cereal, another swig of coffee, and the latest updates from the past few hours unfolded.

"Hi Cameron," came Ross's voice. "Enjoy your rest? We've been working our butts off here. We've pretty much dealt with the surface disruption, but the older stuff in this bloody banking system is wide open and needs patching. There are still a few reports of compromised servers in the wider world but the decrypt you developed is fixing those. The antidote that's circulating seems to have stopped virus transmission dead in its tracks." Ross sounded almost cheerful. "Now we're trying to settle the currency systems. We've had to close down all the ATMs country-wide for a short while, so there will be hell on when the public gets wind of this. Cryptocurrency trading is all suspended. We may be looking at a soft fork to upgrade protection, which will take days to organise, and that could get ugly if someone decides to dig their heels in. I'm knackered and I need to get some fresh air. See you when you get back."

"Hi Cameron, me again. The guys want some breakfast. Can you grab a few things on the way in?"

"Cameron, we've picked up a really odd subroutine embedded in this virus. Nothing I've seen before. I need you to take a look. See you shortly."

•

Mystified, Cameron dropped the cereal bowl in the sink, and crept quietly into the bedroom to fetch some clothes: clean underwear, jeans, casual sports shoes, t-shirt, and a respectable long-sleeved top. Spring weather in England could be unpredictable from hour to hour; best to be prepared for all eventualities. 'Cast ne'er a clout till May be out' had been one of their grandmother's favourite sayings, trotted out every time either Cameron or Charlie dared to leave the house without a jumper. Cameron smiled at the memory of the tiny, rotund woman who had baked the most exquisite cakes for her treasured grandchildren, terrified her own offspring, and ruled the whole family with an iron will. The saying was becoming redundant these days; climate change had eliminated the spring frosts, although the rain still fell, and the nights could be cool.

Closing the apartment door carefully, Cameron bounded down the three flights of stairs with the renewed energy of someone with a mystery to solve, greeting neighbours as they too headed out for work. A familiar gaggle of young people, they were not exactly friends, but nodding acquaintances, occasional drinking partners, fellow fitness enthusiasts, part of the landscape. They knew very little about each other's lives or backgrounds, and co-existed in those happy, prosperous golden years between the intense undergraduate rite of passage at university, and settling down to family life in the suburbs.

"Hey Cameron," called Jasvinder as they met on the second-floor landing, "How's it going? Didn't see you at training last night – out for a works do, were you?"

"Something like that," grinned Cameron. "Long day and a hot date." Jasvinder had no idea what Cameron actually did for a living – some sort of robotics training thing, wasn't it? – and it was best to keep it that way. Fighting cyber crime seemed so exotic but there were dangers to being identified. Modern-day spies, Charlie had once dubbed the team. As soon as an identity got out there, it was retirement– or worse.

They streamed out of the revolving main doors of the small apartment block into fresh air and early morning sunshine. A haze of blossom had appeared on the cherry trees lining the pavement. One of the guys yawned, and sneezed violently.

"Dammit, forgot to get hayfever meds. Starting so early this year." He set off in the direction of the nearby underground station.

Cameron started to follow then hesitated, deciding to walk instead. Traffic was busy, the underground would be heaving, and it would probably be quicker on foot. Could do with some extra steps in the fitness log, too, after a day and half of sitting at a screen in the depths of the bank. The bright weather was unlikely to last in any case: better make the most of it.

With four lanes of traffic crawling silently down the main road, and deep in thought, Cameron was unaware of a car pulling out from the side street in pursuit of its quarry. The route north to the river was automatic and familiar. Turning onto the High Street, Cameron walked briskly past brightly painted shop fronts, ducking instinctively as a delivery drone flew down and through the archway of an ancient coaching inn that had once welcomed horse-drawn carriages bound for the south. The smell of warm bread broke the reverie. Diving into the bakery in a small row of shops, Cameron quickly selected the team's favourite pastries from a tempting display. The owner bagged them up, spots of buttery translucence appearing on the paper, a rich scent rising from the bag.

Cameron followed the main road towards the river, avoiding the busy market today, and passing under the shadow of the Shard, its gleaming mirrored flanks reflecting the distorted images of a mass of drones rising from the market on their way to deliver fresh food across the city, and its pointed tip breaking the wispy clouds high above. A fresh breeze rustled the paper bag as Cameron crossed the Thames, Tower Bridge standing proud to the east. A river ferry hooted as it passed under the bridge on its way to the pier. The tide was out, exposing mudflats and beaching small boats. The smell that wafted up on the breeze was musty but not unpleasant; pollution in the river had improved immeasurably since Cameron was a child. Entering the busy City district, Cameron disappeared into the crowds that bustled through the maze of bleached white stone buildings, heading for the bank.

•

The two men went unnoticed as they sat in their autocar in a side street, drinking endless cardboard cups of coffee, and watching the apartment door revolve as it disgorged its chattering residents in all directions. Few families; these were mainly young professionals able to pay the price of living close to the action in the capital. Property prices were notoriously high this close to the river, and across London as a whole. The old north-south divide had been repaired when Parliament sat for a few years in the wilderness of Northern England during refurbishments to the Palace of Westminster, although with the return to the bright lights of London some of the old competitiveness between regions had resurfaced. Now, the economic battle was drawn along digital lines: the haves, with their smartscreens and fibre connections and biometrics; the have nots, relying on paper forms and paper money, resistant to the digital skills that pave the pathway from poverty to success.

A short blonde girl in high heels and bright colours emerged, chatting to a young black guy with a phone in his hand and a sweater slung over his arm. A tall, unconsciously elegant, dark-haired woman, dressed down in jeans with a smart leather backpack, blinking as she stepped into the sunlight. A slim Asian lad in a smart suit and blue turban who headed straight for the small car park. A pale young man, muscled and fit, scowling at the world, casual in a grey hoodie, stumbled out through the door.

"I don't believe it, that's our boy," exclaimed Giles, dropping his empty cup behind the seat and grabbing his camera.

"Are you sure?" asked his companion.

Giles sighed. "Matches the most likely person on the CCTV images from the bank. Right place. I'm guessing he hasn't slept much for the past couple of days, and this guy certainly looks pretty tired. You'll need to direct. Switch off the autonav."

Traffic was heavy and slow on the main road. Giles had no problem snapping image after image as his companion teased the car along. The young man approached a row of shops, and disappeared momentarily from view. The autocar stopped at a set of traffic lights long enough for Giles to see him emerge carrying a bag, before the one-way system swept all the traffic away to the east, and they could see him no more.

"Get any good ones?"

"Think so," replied Giles. "Clearer than the CCTV, anyway. Hardly the Laughing Cavalier, is he? Who'd have thought he's the brains behind saving the world?"

2: SIMCAVALIER

Ross was the first to arrive at the bank after the alert came in. Young, fit and athletic, his favourite grey hoodie always gave his pale features a drawn look. He loped into the bank's sumptuous marble hallway, dark wood staircases sweeping away to upper floors, and chandeliers sparkling in the late afternoon light.

Approaching the long reception desk under the gaze of its CCTV cameras, he gave a code word to the smart receptionist and was swiftly issued with his security pass. A PA hurried down the broad staircase, his brogues silent on the thick pile of the carpet, and ushered Ross through the barriers and up to a small, empty meeting room.

Ross paced around the room, ignoring the six high-backed wooden chairs set neatly around a polished table. He paused to gaze down from the tall window to the street below. The pavements were less crowded than before, and the odd streetlight flicked into life as the sun dipped down below the rooftops. He spotted several familiar figures approaching the bank from different directions, called away from family and friends, work and play, to go into battle.

Cameron appeared at the door fifteen minutes later. "Team's all here, Ross. Ready to roll."

The PA reappeared and guided them up another floor to the boardroom. Oak panels spoke of the bank's history, a wall of monitors of its future, and a sense of controlled concern emanating from the gathered men and women spoke of its immediate present. Ross glanced at Cameron, then stepped forward and shook the hand of the bank's chief executive. They were underway.

•

Bill the CTO showed Ross and Cameron down to the heart of the building.

"We've set your team up in the main operations room." He gestured to an open door. "Coffee, water, snacks in this kitchen, breakout space for you too. Bathrooms are just down the hall, I'll get some towels and freshen up packs into the showers. You have full access to everything in this section using your passes. There are security personnel in reception and I'll stick around for as long as you need me."

Cameron smiled. "Many thanks, Bill, appreciate it. We'll get started straight away, need to stop the beastie spreading before we do anything else. I'll want your help when we zip the systems back up and patch the holes, but right now I think you can leave us to it."

Bill nodded. "I think you have all the access codes you need. Call me at any time if you need something. Here's my number." He headed wearily for the stairs, as Cameron and Ross entered the operations room.

Six pairs of eyes turned towards them.

"All set, boss," said a short, chubby man in jeans and a garish rock band t-shirt, nodding at Cameron.

"Thanks Sandeep." Cameron paused. "Okay. Joel, see if you can get hold of a clean copy of this virus. Check the tech communities, dig into that last NSA dump on the Dark Web, there has to be a copy circulating somewhere. You and I can work on rebutting the attack externally. Ross, you, Pete and Ella get into the bank system and quarantine that critter. Close it down, stop it spreading further through the network than it already has. Noor, I want you to keep track of other compromised systems and open communications with the teams working on them. Sandeep, you and Susie work with Noor, and have a look at possible breaches too. See if there are any systematic failures or if it's just an ID 10-T error." Cameron grinned. "I love a challenge. Let's go."

•

Andy was tired. He ran a hand through his untidy brown hair, sighed, and leaned his elbows on the desk, thinking. His editor was getting impatient. After three years of chasing whispers and mirages, he still had to produce the cyber security scoop he'd promised. He was a good tech journalist, but one story kept eluding him. Who were the people behind the fight against cyber crime? He felt like the frustrated hacks in the superhero films his dad had loved, trying to unmask a hero, while the alter ego hid in plain sight.

Right now, though, there was a more urgent story to cover. There were ripples on the forums, a sudden upsurge of activity, distant whispers of a new cyber attack. Andy took a slug of coffee and shook his head, refocusing. He scoured his network, seeking confirmation and clarity before writing his piece for the hungry rolling news that broadcast all day, every day. As he searched, a notification appeared in the corner of his screen. An anonymous message, which immediately grabbed his attention.

"The SimCavalier rides into battle. This one's spreading like the Great Fire."

His heart was racing. This was unprecedented. He'd been following this shadowy figure through several years of high profile cyber security alerts. The name appeared on tech forums, quoted in awed discussions among the top echelons of the threat intelligence community. This – person? entity? group? – seemed to be at the forefront of combating the increasingly steady waves of cyber crime, hacking, and ransomware. Disrupted by the failure of traditional encryption less than a decade ago, the world was still struggling to manage digital security. Andy's painstaking research showed clearly that without the diligent and inspired work of the SimCavalier, it might have descended further into anarchy. He was a true modern hero, and should be celebrated. Andy couldn't understand why he sought to stay in the shadows.

It looked as if years of gradual infiltration into the cyber security community had finally paid off. Someone was on Andy's side, ready to help.

"Call Giles," he barked at the portal.

A moment later the voice call connected. "What's up, boss?"

"You've picked up this latest cyber attack, yes?"

"Sure. Kicked off around an hour, hour and a half ago by all accounts. Most reports coming from the United States, but I guess that's because they've been hit in the middle of the day. A few from Europe. Getting ready to break it on the news channels."

"It's here. There's a case right here in London. And he's on it."

"Wow. Shit. Sorry. I mean, how do you know? There are no confirmed reports of infection here in the UK yet."

"We've just had a tipoff. *'The SimCavalier rides into battle.'* Can't get much clearer than that. The guy is mobilising against the latest threat. And as for location, this says *'spreading like the Great Fire'.* Great Fire of London? Nothing else it can be."

Giles was sceptical. "That's incredible. But where do we take it from here? London's a bloody big place. He'll have it killed in short order and be gone before we get close to him."

Andy laughed. "I think it's a bit easier than that. Where's the Monument to the Great Fire of London? It's smack in the middle of the City. I reckon we're looking at a bank."

Cameron laughed as the ransom demand appeared on Ross's monitor. A dancing cocktail gif dominated the screen with a flashing neon message: '*Welcome to the Speakeasy. Bitcoin Accepted Here*'. "Hah, brilliant. At least the bastards have a sense of humour."

"Doesn't make it any easier to crack," grumbled Ross. He was aching after a day's hard training, and regretted missing out on a recuperative massage and a relaxing evening. "Fairly standard stuff, though. Do we know what it looks like in the wild?"

Joel shook his head, dreadlocks swaying. "Nothing yet. Plenty of reports coming through but we don't have a dump of the code. Watching the usual channels."

Noor piped up from her desk. "I'm in touch with a team in New York, and another in Sydney. They're seeing a lot of hits in the financial sector."

Cameron thought for moment. "Interesting, Noor, stay on top of that. Ella, can you run some models on trading over the past week. It could be just coincidence that this is the first wave of reports, but we'd better eliminate all possibilities."

"Right you are." Ella slipped on her headphones and opened a secure, anonymous browser. Her hands glided across the screen as she captured data from pools across the world and began the painstaking process of analysis.

Ross settled into his seat. "Okay, Pete, let's roll. What's tonight's playlist? Better pick something to keep us awake."

Pete scrolled through the options. "You said it. Melissa Mix?" Solid bass lines and fast rhythms kicked into life, quickly muffled as the two of them pulled their headsets on and got to work.

Cameron turned to Sandeep and Susie. "Okay Susie, in at the deep end. Your first big job. How are you feeling?"

Susie smiled nervously. "I'll be fine. It'll be interesting to see where the breach was. I thought this place was as tight as a drum. I guess I was wrong."

"The bigger they are, the harder they fall. There's always a way in. Sandeep will keep you straight. Can you both make sure you do a wide sweep for all potential gaps and compromises? We need to leave this place sewn up properly. There'll be other penetrations no one knows about."

Sandeep and Susie nodded. Cameron turned back to Joel. "Anything yet?"

"Still digging. I'm keeping an eye on that Bitcoin wallet, too. There've been a handful of ransom payments already. You'd think people would learn there's no point paying."

Cameron sighed. "Me too. If no one paid there'd be no point writing viruses and we'd have a quiet life. I had plans this evening." Joel raised a questioning eyebrow; Cameron refused to be drawn. "I'd better make my excuses. I don't mind, really. This is too interesting. I do love my job."

Joel laughed. "You're quite the hero, Cameron. I'm happy, I got out of rugby training tonight; I won't be so sore now when we play on Saturday. It's coming up to the end of the season, anyway, so it'll soon be time for a proper rest." He turned back to the scrolling screen. "Aha! We've got our first look. Here we go, Speakeasy code dump. Nice work. Let's see what this one's made of."

•

Midnight chimes rang out across London, from the rolling boom of Big Ben to the distinctive sounds of the ancient towers of the city. The bells of St Clements, Shoreditch and Old Bailey sang out their tunes, passed down the generations in the old nursery rhyme for three hundred years. Deep in the bank, the bells went unheard; the team was taking a well-earned break.

"Land it on the top," squealed Ella, as Pete expertly guided a small drone around the room and up towards a hanging light fitting.

Susie was doubled up with laughter. "I can't believe you guys."

The little drone, a toy modelled on a spaceship from the latest Hollywood blockbuster, dropped down on the light and a ragged round of applause rang out.

Pete swore. "I can't get it to lift off again – that light's blocking the signal. Hold on." He moved his chair to the wall, clambered up and stretched high on tiptoe to achieve the right angle. Pete rocked precariously on his perch, and the drone wobbled and swooped off the light. Ella ducked as it went overhead.

"Pizza in the kitchen," called Ross. Pete jumped off his chair and parked the drone as they all trooped out, inviting smells wafting from the corridor. Greasy cardboard boxes were open on the table, and the hungry team members grabbed a couple of slices each. Ross sat apart, munching on chicken and salad, making at least some effort to stick to the nutrition required of his punishing training regime.

Cameron sat at the head of the table, devouring a slice piled high with meat and chillies. "Good work so far, guys. Let's take stock. Ross, over to you. How far have you got?"

"We've started to dismantle the cage. I'll need you to get your head around a decrypt over the next few hours. The ransom is masking a couple of subroutines. It's like a bloody Russian Doll, every time we dig deeper we come across another element. It's not particularly complex but it's taking time. Most of the systems are untouched, particularly the newer, more transparent software. Blockchains are okay. It's the older stuff where we're finding weaknesses."

"Hmm. We need to have a chat with Bill about legacy systems. That can wait until the morning, though. Sandeep?"

Sandeep, lounging on a bright orange beanbag, glanced at Susie. "Nothing so far, boss. The security protocols are pretty tight, which is what we expected. We're combing through mail servers and reverse engineering from Ross's work. We'll find it."

Noor looked up. "Go back in time. A couple of folks I'm chatting to who've found their breaches have mentioned a long lag between penetration and execution, anything up to eight weeks so far. We'd expect that in a phishing attack, compromising the network then gradually digging deep over time, but this looks and acts like a simple worm."

The group fell silent, reflecting. Cameron absent-mindedly reached for another slice of pizza. "Anyone else?"

The others stepped up the table and refilled their plates.

"The thing I don't understand," continued Cameron after a pause, "is that this looks like ransomware, and it's certainly collecting a bit of dosh, but it's not making them rich, and it has these extra bells and whistles attached. Why? What's going on?"

Ross shrugged, left the table, and flopped onto an empty beanbag. "Dunno. Don't care right now. I'm tired. Let's get it nailed and then you can worry about motives."

Ella looked up at Cameron. "I may have an idea. I think I'm getting somewhere with the financial modelling. It's hard to spot, but I've confirmed what the bank indicated. There's a spike in cryptocurrency futures trading just before the attack."

Cameron's eyes widened. The others looked confused.

"So?" asked Sandeep.

Ella turned to him, looking serious. "Okay, so people who buy and sell stocks, shares, money, they hope that if they can buy something now, then the price will go up so they can sell it and make a profit. Yeah?"

Sandeep nodded. "Sure, that makes sense."

Ella continued. "So, futures work a bit differently. People make money when the price goes down. They say, I'll short sell that thing, I don't know, like a thousand of those shares for twenty coins each. So, the trader 'lends' them a thousand shares to sell, and they get twenty thousand coins in their wallet from the buyer. A bit later on, they have to buy a thousand shares to give back to the trader – do you follow? So, if the shares are still worth twenty coins, they've broken even, if it's gone up they've lost money. If the price has dropped, though, it might only cost ten coins a share to re-buy, so boom! Profit of ten thousand coins."

Sandeep blinked. "That's pretty fucked up. This really happens?"

"Sure," replied Ella. "Common practice, been around for centuries, literally. It was all stocks and shares and hard currency back then, obviously, but people have been shorting cryptocurrency for thirty years, especially in the early days when Bitcoin first took off and the price was bouncing up and down. Lots of winners, lots of losers. Fun times."

Ross frowned. "Are you saying there could be some connection?"

"Not sure," replied Ella. "It's a tiny spike, could be a coincidence, but if I'd given up on making money from ransoms, I'd look at other options."

Cameron looked at the clock. "We need to get back to work. Ella, can you develop those models. See what you can find in terms of location and timing of trades, any trackback to the parties involved, and if there've been any unusual profits taken. It'll be interesting to see how that pans out. You may be onto something."

Standing up and stretching, Cameron stacked the empty pizza boxes, while Joel collected the plates and dropped them into the dishwasher. The team returned to their desks, headphones back on, concentration restored.

Cameron's fingers flexed and dived onto the keyboard with renewed energy, seeking a route to decryption, and an antidote to stop the virus spreading.

•

Bill arrived at the bank just before 8am and headed downstairs. All was quiet. Poking his head around the door of the breakout room, he saw a pile of pizza boxes on the table and three figures sprawled, asleep, on the beanbags. The sound of running water betrayed a fourth person taking a shower.

Opening the door to the operations room, Bill found Cameron, Ross,

Susie and Noor deep in conversation. The animated discussion broke off as soon as they saw Bill arrive.

"Morning all. No midnight calls so I guess you're making progress?" Bill sounded hopeful. "The Board meets at nine. What can I tell them? Are you coming up to brief them?"

Cameron stood up. "Come and have a look at this, Bill. See what we've been up to. Ross, Susie, can you sort out some breakfast for the troops?"

As Ross and Susie closed the door behind them, Noor returned to her desk, watching the flurry of new forum posts as IT staff across the country arrived at work and discovered new instances of the infection. They were logging into the threat intelligence forums, comparing notes, seeking fixes. Cameron took Bill across to a bank of monitors.

"Internal stuff first. Here's the first thing every infected user sees…" The dancing cocktails appeared on the screen. "It's been dubbed the Speakeasy virus, for obvious reasons. Now, that's a mask using old encryption technology, and the data behind it is still sound. I know we don't encrypt for high security these days, it's too easy for hackers to crack, but it still foxes the man in the street, which is why ransomware trojans haven't stopped doing the rounds. It's taken us most of the night to develop the decrypt for this bit, but it's done. We were the first to release that part of the solution worldwide, I'm well chuffed. Great team effort."

Bill smiled at the pride in Cameron's voice. "So, we're up and running again?"

"No, still a fair way to go for you, I'm afraid. This encryption was hiding a couple of subroutines, bits of hidden code. They don't affect the newer systems but they've got their suckers into an SQL database with dodgy security. First question, Bill, what the hell is something that archaic doing down there in your bank servers?"

Shamefaced, Bill explained. "We inherited a mess. After Brexit when the Euro traders moved out, the City had to innovate, and they went deep into cryptocurrency to survive. We needed to keep the original systems running for hard currencies, at least until consumers caught up, and some of those dated back even further, pre-2000. Investment was all channelled into cryptocurrency trading and the old systems were left behind. Eventually, support ran out, no new security updates. Twenty years on, enough customers still insist on using hard currencies that we have to maintain the service. All the effort we've put in to get them up to speed on digital and they treat bank notes like a bloody comfort blanket. We never thought we'd still be running these systems now."

Cameron felt sorry for him. The work the bank had done to secure their old network against generic attack was pretty good, truth be told. Another patch would do the trick – until the next cyber criminal innovation.

"Do you know where it got in?" he asked.

"Closing in on it," replied Cameron. "We know it's an email penetration, just have to identify the exact route. For now, we're concentrating on sorting those hidden subroutines, and identifying an antidote to halt the spread of the virus. It's no use decrypting when it'll just re-infect. I think we're pretty close."

Bill nodded. "Okay. I'll advise the Board that we're offline today but we're getting close to complete repair. Good job. I'll leave you to it." He turned to the door as Ella walked in, coffee and muffin in hand, hair tousled and damp. "Looks like breakfast's arrived."

"Bye, Bill, see you later. We'll keep you posted."

•

The train glided silently up to the platform, wheels clicking on the rails. Swept through the doors in a crowd of commuters, Andy found a seat and pulled out his smartscreen. He checked the news channels for the latest public announcements about the ongoing cyber attack. It had a name: Speakeasy. Businesses around the world were reporting compromised networks. Advice was being repeated to sit tight, pay no ransom, wait for the tech guys to work their magic. All very bland.

He needed the inside dish. Logging on to a threat intelligence community under a long-held assumed identity, it was immediately evident that the decrypt had been developed, verified, and was rippling out to the world. He dipped in and out of discussions, dropping the odd comment to maintain his cover: *'High five, guys.' 'Looks sound to me.' 'Great work! Deploying now, I'll let you know how it goes.'* Weaving through the threads, he was looking for one handle in particular – and there it was. 6.20am UK time. Post author: @SimCavalier. *'Tested and running, Speakeasy decrypt process and batch file attached.'* A string of virtual applause from hundreds of forum members, and several verifications of the fix, showed up as replied to the simple post.

Andy sat back, satisfied, as the train dived into the tunnels beneath North London and slowed as it approached its destination.

The net was closing.

Andy's surveillance guy was waiting for him in a meeting room just off the bustling office floor. A small coffee machine in the corner sparked into life as it detected Andy's arrival, delivering exactly the right dose of caffeine to match his recorded sleep patterns from the previous night. This morning, it was one strong cup.

"Hi, Andy, good run in this morning?"

Andy took a swig of coffee and winced. "Very smooth, thanks – not the coffee, the commute. Long night though."

"Saw the news. I guess your boy is in the middle of it all?"

"Oh yes. We're as close as we've ever been to this guy and we have the next piece of the puzzle. Our tipoff indicates that he's operating somewhere in the City of London. It's still a big place, and we can't cover the whole lot, especially as we still can't identify him by sight. Stroke of luck, though: it looks like he's first to figure out the decrypt, as usual, and we've got the original post on this forum."

The monitor on the wall glowed as Andy brought up the discussion thread for his colleague to see.

"Can we pinpoint where that was sent from? There's a good chance he was still on site."

The surveillance expert nodded. "We can dig around in the background of the forum. The IP addresses for each post are in there somewhere. It's a private community sitting on generic software, and the admins will have access for moderation and management. Shouldn't be too hard to crack."

"Get onto it," said Andy. "As soon as we know where he is, we'll have a chance to get a good look at him, at last."

•

It was late morning when the final strike of the battle was delivered. Noor turned excitedly to the rest of the team. "We did it! Cameron, it's stopped. No new reports. The antidote is holding."

A ragged cheer went up from the exhausted group. Cameron lounged back in the soft leather chair – only the finest furniture, even here in the depths of the bank – and smiled broadly. "Brilliant work guys. Just fantastic."

Ross stood up and stretched. "Looking good here, too. Not spread any further in the network. System is still compromised, but we've contained the subroutines in those deep databases. One's executed, but the other's dormant for now. Odd. Anyway, next step, kill the activated code and clean up."

"No," countered Cameron. "Next step, you go and get some rest. Ross, Susie, Noor, Ella, Pete, get your heads down. We'll probably need you back here, not before early evening, though. Joel, Sandeep, let's grab some lunch and then we'll make a start on the subroutines. We'll stay in close touch with external teams, make sure we really have neutralised it out there, and share anything we crack here."

Ross nodded gratefully and shuffled to the door, exhausted. He'd had no time to recover from the previous day's training session and he was stiff and aching all over. He didn't expect to find it hard to sleep today, regardless of the bright spring sunshine that would be illuminating his bedroom. "Goodnight, folks. See you later."

The other four followed him out, eager to get some rest.

Cameron turned to the remaining two team members. "Sorry guys, I know you're tired too, at least you managed a snooze through the night. We'll go steady this afternoon and we'll all be in our beds before we know it. Right. Lunch. Let's get out of here."

The coffee shop opposite the bank was full to bursting; it was the busiest time of the day. The crowd swept the three of them, unresisting, along the wide pavement towards a pedestrian area full of small boutiques, cafes and restaurants. The spring day was still cool in the shade of the surrounding buildings, so there were plenty of spaces at outdoor tables. Cameron, Joel and Sandeep flopped onto vacant chairs in the fresh air, relieved to be outside.

•

Andy leaned over to look closer at the monitor. The CCTV images were grainy, following the to-ing and fro-ing of several hundred people as they passed through the bank's reception. "Have you picked any likely leads up yet?"

The surveillance man nodded. "We have a live feed right now, which isn't telling us much, but we've been able to access the archives for the last twenty-four hours. They're much more interesting. Look here." He scrolled back and froze the frame. "Okay. Your tipoff came in at 6.15pm. About twenty minutes before this, there's a flurry of activity. Some big suits have arrived, straight through security. The rest of the traffic is going the other way." He tapped the screen. "Now, look, I think this is our man. Arrives on his own, against the flow, barely waits, they're obviously expecting him. About ten minutes later we see a couple more coming in. There's a hiccup in the recording, you can only just see them arriving and we can't tell how many are in the group, or where they went."

Andy nodded. "Got anything else?"

"Yep." He fast forwarded, and pointed at the screen. "We spotted him again, with a girl, we think, leaving the building just after eight this morning. Fifteen minutes later, and here they both are coming back in. Loads of bags. Breakfast for the troops? I think they've been in there all night."

"That fits," said Andy. "The communities we've been tracking have a bunch of comments overnight from our boy, and he released that Speakeasy decrypt early this morning. Is he still there?"

"No. Here, this is some of the first live footage we accessed. There's our guy in the hoodie, four others with him, walking out with the rest of the bank staff for an early lunch. I'm still watching, but he hasn't come back. Missed him again, huh?"

Andy slammed his hand on the desk in irritation. "It's got to be him. Okay, if nothing else, we know what he looks like. That's a big step forward. Keep an eye on any more movement. If he comes back in, I want to know."

A thought struck him. "He has to sleep sometime. He's got to have a home. Can you get back into that forum, identify @SimCavalier posts for say the last three months, pick out any residential locations? He arrived pretty fast last night, so he's based in London somewhere. If we can place this guy in the hoodie at the right location, we've got our man."

3: A WARNING

Charlie closed the heavy front door behind him with a sigh of relief. Mornings were never peaceful in the Silvera household, with three kids getting ready for school and a bouncy Labradoodle anticipating a long walk. The sound of Sameena directing the children from the breakfast table, to the bathroom, and to find their bags and shoes, faded as he strode across the gravel to the car. He'd lost track of whether they needed guitars, violins, swimming kit, or all three on Thursdays; hopefully his wife had the timetable in hand. Right now, his focus was on the business, on the cusp of completing a major car components order. Pulling out of their drive and up the leafy lane out of the village, he set the route to the factory, and flicked on the news channel.

"…said the Prime Minister. Returning to our main story: organisations across the globe are battling an ongoing cyber attack, dubbed the Speakeasy Virus. The majority of incidents have been reported in the banking sector, with disruption to currency trading, although the attack has not been confined to financial institutions. Several established global businesses have announced network failures, and small companies are equally badly hit. The authorities are advising those affected not to pay any ransom demand. Over now to our correspondent in the City of London."

"Initial reports of this attack came in yesterday evening, just after 6pm UK time," announced a reporter. "Threat intelligence professionals across the world have been battling to crack the codes throughout the night, but the first major breakthrough came here, in central London, with the development of a decryption programme by an as yet unknown British specialist. There are continued reports of infection, but it would appear the threat is diminishing. Now, back to the studio."

Charlie sighed. He suspected Cameron was right in the middle of it all, and would be pretty busy mopping up the mess. Hopefully it would all be over by the weekend; Cameron was due to visit, to celebrate Sameena's birthday.

"*Incoming call,*" announced the car.

"Answer," said Charlie, gazing out at the familiar passing scenery.

"Morning Charlie," came the voice of his second in command. "Are you on your way in? We've had a bit of problem."

Charlie's heart sank. "What's up, Holly?"

There was a pause, and Charlie heard Holly calling indistinctly to someone else in the office. "Sorry Charlie, just sorting out Production. The network went down at our host around 3am. Looks like they got caught by this latest cyber attack on one of their shared servers. The remote backups should have kicked in by now, but they're holding off to check that the ransomware hasn't spread to connected facilities."

Charlie's good mood evaporated. "What's happening in the factory, Holly? We shouldn't be affected. There are all sorts of service agreements in place."

Holly sounded annoyed. "All we're getting is blank screens, and the printers are on standby. As far as we know our dedicated servers are okay, and we understand the host company has gotten hold of the decryption software now, but all comms have been shut down as a precaution. Not a lot we can do, but wanted to let you know before you walk into a silent building."

"Okay. Thanks. Forewarned is forearmed, huh. See what you can find out about expected restore time. I'll see you shortly." Great start to the day, thought Charlie, as the call terminated. The company was hot on minimising human failures in cyber security – they'd had Cameron's team in to do the training, of course – but having an external breach affect the host of their supposedly secure cloud was another matter. The hosting company must be beside themselves, their previously spotless reputation on the line. How had this snuck through their defences?

Whatever malicious code had compromised the cloud wasn't Charlie's greatest problem right now. They needed the printers back online in the factory; those components had to be out on deadline, and they were already skating close to contract penalties for going over time.

"Call Matt at Owens and York." The voice call connected. "Morning Matt, sorry to bother you. Bit of a hiccup – we're on standby in the factory, waiting for our host to decrypt their servers. We're okay, but there's been a breach somewhere up the line and all our systems are dormant as a precaution. Can you check the cyber attack clauses in this contract and drop a marker into the blockchain? Just need to cover ourselves in case the delay takes us into penalties."

"Sure, Charlie, I'll get onto that now." The lawyers were good at their job.

Sometimes Charlie yearned for the factory floor he recalled as a youngster, fresh out of university and learning the ropes in the family firm. He'd been so keen to jump on the emerging technology bandwagon back in 2025, and it was true that his enthusiasm for change and shrewd application of the right solutions had sealed the future of the business where less agile competitors had gone to the wall. Right now, though, he'd trade the expanse of 3D printers nurtured by his modern workforce for the skilled machine tooling teams that had retired years before.

The car paused at the junction and turned on to the dual carriageway, stopping and starting in the queue of autocars that crawled towards the town. Charlie sighed and leaned back in his seat. "I never could get the hang of Thursdays," he muttered to himself, with an ironic half-smile.

A message pinged: eleven year old Nina's face appeared on the monitor. "Dad, don't forget to pick me up from netball tonight. See you later. Bye." Charlie knew one of the advantages of living so close to work was the luxury of seeing his kids grow up, picking them up from school, being part of their daily lives. Tonight, though, Nina would have to rely on her mother.

•

Refreshed, Cameron, Sandeep and Joel got back to work. Light streamed in to the basement through skylights from ground level, illuminating dust motes in the air.

"Sandeep, on the comms please, see how that decrypt is going down and check that the spread of the virus has really stopped. Joel, let's dig into these subroutines."

Picking a path through the archaic operating systems, Cameron stalked the first subroutine as it whirled around the database. Once identified, it was a simple matter to isolate the code and pull it out onto a separate quarantined machine. Bringing the code up onto the monitor, Joel and Cameron ran through each line. It was tiny, repetitive thing, programmed to pick up data and move it around, scrambling the database, wiping any meaning from the information that had been stored there.

Cameron pointed to a short line of code. "See here, it's searching for a file. I thought that was a data dump, but check this later instruction. If it finds it, the routine terminates."

"Ah, you genius," breathed Joel. "Let's give it what it wants, shall we?" He turned to the main interface and navigated to the right directory. "No, nothing there. Here goes." Quickly and efficiently, he created a new file and dropped it in. The two of them watched the activity of the SQL database on a separate monitor. Moments later, the queries stopped.

Cameron and Joel high fived each other. Sandeep looked up, grinning.

"Let's get that out to the web," said Cameron. "Anyone else picked it up yet?"

Sandeep laughed. "Sorry boss, the guys on the East Coast beat you to it by a few minutes. I'll drop a confirmation of the fix to them. I guess it's only a temporary thing?"

Cameron nodded. "We'll make sure it's in the full patch when we restore the databases from backup. The operating system down there is so old there'll be nothing coming out from the big tech companies, I guess. We'll need to be prepared for more of the same now this is vulnerability is out in the open. At least we'll know the first place to look, another time."

Joel looked up at the skylights. Daylight was fading. "That took longer than I thought. It's already five o'clock. Shall we take a break?" He looked at Cameron, who nodded in agreement.

"The databases look stable. Definitely time for a coffee."

The three of them sat on beanbags, conserving energy. Cameron had been working for almost twenty-four hours and was coming up to the wall of endurance. Sandeep and Joel were barely less tired, having snatched only a couple of hours' rest during the night.

"Let's leave the second subroutine for Ross," suggested Joel. "As far as I can see, it's not doing any damage at the moment, and I'm knackered."

"Fair enough," replied Cameron. "I'll go and debrief Bill. The whole lot should be back up and running tomorrow. Do you guys want to do another sweep for breaches? Just make sure nothing's happened while we've been down here?"

Sandeep and Joel brightened.

"That's always fun to do," said Joel. "Okay, we'll get started."

•

Chief executive Sir Simon Winchester joined Cameron and Bill in the small meeting room that Cameron had first entered a full day earlier.

"I understand from Bill here that the worst is over."

"Yes, Sir Simon," replied Cameron. "As you already know, we managed to deliver the first global decryption for the visible ransomware overnight. This morning we assisted a team overseas to develop an antidote to the spread of the virus, effectively stopping it from downloading to new host computers. However, we have reason to believe the attack was tailing off already.

"Since then, we've isolated the first of two subroutines that were hidden behind the ransomware shell and which directly attacked the older operating systems in your bank."

Sir Simon looked from Cameron to Bill. "That all sounds good, although most of it is beyond me. How long until we're up and running again?"

Cameron glanced at Bill and ploughed on. "Ross and the rest of the team will be back in shortly to work on isolating the second subroutine, tidy up the system, and compare the corrupted databases with the most recent clean backups. We'll then look to restore data to the most current version available. You should be good to boot up the whole network again early tomorrow morning, and we anticipate minimal loss of data overall."

Bill grinned, relieved, and Sir Simon nodded approvingly.

Cameron continued. "After that point, we can apply patches to the live system to protect against any recurrence of this specific threat and potentially stop similar routines in their tracks. We also need to identify the route of the original penetration and work with Bill to minimise future threats from the same source."

Cameron strongly suspected that the breach was due to human error, which meant there would be some retraining to be carried out for the staff: time to remind them of the implications of getting lax with emails. Bill caught Cameron's eye. He was obviously of the same opinion.

"We're indebted to you, Silvera," said Sir Simon. "Good job. Keep me in the loop on the reboot, Bill." He walked out of the meeting room and closed the door.

Cameron sighed. "I'll hand over to Ross at eight o'clock and go get some R&R. I need to be on my game for those patches, make sure we close up nice and tight." Pushing the heavy chair back on the carpet, Cameron stood up wearily.

Bill opened the door and the two of them strolled down the stairs.

As soon as they arrived in the operations room, there was a commotion. Sandeep called Cameron over to his monitor. "Good thinking running a new security scan. What prompted that, boss?"

Cameron blinked, and Bill looked puzzled. "Why, what have you found?"

Joel stepped forward, a bright white grin flashing across his dark features. "We picked up a new breach. It was very straightforward but occurred well after the attack started, around 10am today, and wasn't targeted at the background operating systems. We only caught it by chance. External login to the bank network, looks like an unsecured connection, and a sneaky little trojan slipped through. It's been broadcasting images from your CCTV, Bill. We closed it down straight away. We know whose account was compromised – a bit of security retraining needed there – but we haven't identified where those images have been sent. Not sure we ever will. Probably a little autocar around the corner that no one would notice. Now that the connection is down, they'll be long gone."

"I'll check the CCTV... Oh." Bill paused.

Sandeep finished his sentence for him. "If they could see your CCTV feeds, they'd make sure they couldn't be seen by the cameras."

Bill nodded, resigned. "We could approach other networks locally but it's a busy district, and whoever they are they won't be obvious. Might even be in one of the adjoining buildings, out of sight. I wonder what they were after?"

•

Andy swore loudly as the CCTV feeds went blank. "Dammit. No more sightings. Have we got enough to go on?"

"Possibly." Andy looked up, hopeful. "We've sifted through the forum posts. Had to go back a lot longer than three months. This guy's careful. The business IP addresses match with the physical locations of known victims of cyber attacks over time; he hasn't tried to hide those. Interesting to see the range of places he's been working, though. Really high-profile stuff. Banks, data centres, power installations, all sorts."

Andy nodded. "This guy is the dog's. Top bloke. What about residential?"

"Nothing. The rest of the IP addresses are all over the place. Looks like he's simply been gaming them in the last year or so, changing to all sorts of mad locations from Patagonia to Iceland. Prior to that he was using one of the last VPNs to cloak his address, but the encryption on those is next to useless now. I guess he had to find a new way of hiding his whereabouts when going online."

"That makes sense. He goes out of his way to stay hidden, huh."

"Yes, Andy. It's almost as if he doesn't want you to find him." The surveillance guy sighed. He had his own opinions of the ethics of this investigation, but business was business.

"Okay, during the changeover from the VPN, we've picked up three posts, over a year ago, from a location just the other side of the river, near Borough tube station. That'll be your starting point."

Andy sat back, satisfied. "Okay, it's starting to come together. We think we know where this SimCavalier lives, or lived. We think we know what he looks like. Let's see if the pieces join up. Get Giles to stake him out."

•

Friday morning dawned, cool and clear. At the bank, Ross was ready to drop. Normally fit and on his game, the combination of long hours and the intense concentration needed to clean the databases had taken its toll. The strange anomaly in this worm worried him, too. There was something odd about the second subroutine, and try as he might he'd failed to crack it. He was looking forward to handing the reins back to the boss and getting some more sleep; maybe he'd be ready for a run later.

Ross admired his boss's talent, but resented playing second fiddle while his own career went nowhere. Cameron's flashes of insight and intuitive strategy were extraordinary, but there was a lot of hard graft from the whole team underneath. Ross believed he didn't always get the credit he deserved. Cameron's insistence on complete anonymity riled him. They were saving the world, weren't they? Surely he deserved a pat on the back, just occasionally? Some public recognition for a job well done?

"Another cuppa, Ross?" asked Susie, the new girl on the team.

Ross rubbed his face and ran a hand through his ginger hair. His grey eyes were bloodshot, his naturally pale skin looking wan in the artificial light. No more coffee. There was a limit to how much caffeine his system could take, especially with another race just two weeks away: the sensor on his wrist showed he was close to the maximum. Too much disruption too close to the start line, he reflected. Back in the day, cyber threats at this scale had appeared very rarely; the business generally ticked over doing steady nine to five digital training contracts, consultancy, and innocent security work to futureproof clients. That was perfect to keep his triathlon preparation steady. The last couple of years had been busier, and interruptions to his routine were increasingly unwelcome. With Cameron insisting on absolute discretion from the team, he had trouble concocting reasonable excuses time after time for his training partners.

"No," he replied curtly, feeling irritated and taking it out on the nearest person. He sighed. "Sorry Susie, tired out. Cameron and the other guys are on the way. They're bringing breakfast. Almost time for a kip. How's it going?"

"Baptism of fire, Ross," grinned Susie. "It's been a challenge but I love it. Really tired though. Can't think straight any longer."

The door opened. Ross looked up as Cameron strolled in, looking refreshed and carrying an inviting, greasy paper bag, the smell of warm croissants drifting across the desk. "Breakfast as ordered, folks. Stand down, you've done a great job."

There was a scattered round of applause and a rustling of paper as five hungry pairs of hands made a grab for the pastries. Cameron let Ross enjoy the croissant, knowing it was one of his guilty pleasures in an otherwise strict regime. Once he'd reduced it to scant crumbs, the two of them slid out to talk in private in a meeting room on the other side of the hall.

"What's the anomaly you picked up in this code, then? There's not much you haven't seen before, Ross. What's got you so rattled?"

Ross slumped in his chair. "I'm not sure. It's what we thought was a second subroutine set to attack the systems. It doesn't appear to be executable – or rather, there is a piece of executable code in there, but it's completely unrelated to the original virus and is not triggered by any of the existing routines. It's code within code. It's almost as if the developer has annotated the virus code and then bundled it up in some obscure encryption to conceal the annotation. I can't get into it at all."

"Wow. That's pretty deep. You're absolutely sure it's not a secondary subroutine waiting to be triggered? Or something that's been released half-built?"

"Doesn't feel like it. It looks like a complete unit, no loose ends. There isn't anything I can find in the original code which would set it off. It categorically would not launch on its own as part of this attack." He paused, reflecting. "I think it needs human intervention. We don't have the key; somehow we need to get through the encryption. Run a quantum decryption, maybe?"

"Hmmm." Cameron thought for a moment. "If it's not part of this virus, what's its purpose? The Speakeasy creators would want the code to be as light as possible to avoid detection as it spread. There should be nothing in there that isn't functional. Most users won't pick up on this subroutine at all. The only people who'd ever see it would be teams like ours. No one else would be digging this deep into the virus. It's odd."

"I have a bad feeling about this." Ross stood up and stretched his back.

"I'm going home to sleep on it. We're done. Susie's found the most likely penetration source and she can hand over to Sandeep. The database is clean and ready to restore. Good luck securing these godawful old systems. Over to you, boss."

Cameron smiled lopsidedly. "Sleep well. Back here for four to wrap up with the client. We should get our weekend after all."

•

Giles marched into the crowded office and headed for his desk. He plugged in his camera and set the images to upload, then walked across to the kitchen alcove where the coffee machine stood. A steaming cup of Americano was waiting for him. Technology was wonderful sometimes. He turned to see Andy approaching, and heard the machine behind him whirr into life again.

"How did you get on?"

"Some decent pics, I think," replied Giles. "Nice place he lives in. Must be doing okay for himself."

Andy laughed. "I think our 'SimCavalier' is hot property right now. Could probably afford to live at the Ritz judging by the volume of transactions going to that crypto wallet. Threat intelligence is big business."

The coffee machine sputtered as it dispensed a shot of espresso and diluted it with boiling water. Andy picked up his cup and the two men wandered over to Giles' desk. The monitor showed the first of the morning's images: a group of young professionals emerging from a building, smiling and talking. Slightly blurred to begin with, the focus sharpened as more images loaded.

Andy tapped the screen, indicating the young man in the grey hoodie. "Nice job, Giles." They scrolled through the series of images of the man, showing him walking to the main road, entering a shop, emerging with a bag in his hand.

"That's the lot. We got caught in the one-way system. Couldn't stop again. I think we have enough."

Andy flicked through the images again, zooming in on the target. He frowned. "Let's compare these with the CCTV from the bank. Something doesn't look quite right." He shook his head. "No. It's got to be him. The IP trace for @SimCavalier definitely leads to that apartment block. Too much of a coincidence to get the same guy in two places."

"Want me to dig around the other occupants?" Andy shook his head.

"No, that's too random. We need to find out who his friends are. We can't risk frightening him off. He's been tough to pin down; thank goodness for that tipoff about the latest job. I don't understand why he doesn't come right out and take the credit. Me, I'd be shouting from the rooftops if I saved the world."

•

Deep in the bank, while Ross and his team were all home in bed, Cameron, Joel and Sandeep were ready to roll on the final phase. It was time to restore and secure the legacy systems.

Bill had joined them, keen to get the network back to life. He held his breath as the restored data flowed into the system, lines of records scrolling up the monitors faster than eye could follow.

"That's a beautiful sight," he sighed. "Ready to boot?"

"Yes. Go for it." Bill's own staff stepped in to bring the network back online, as Cameron turned to the team.

"Right, let's have a look at the source of infection, then we can close up. What are the likely routes? What have we got so far? Sandeep?"

"Okay, Cameron, Susie pieced together most of this, and I've followed it up. She's done a good job. We've traced a file that came in on an email around six weeks ago. Bill and I have spoken to the guy who received it, first thing this morning. He can't really remember, but thinks he opened an attached document and found there was no content. Just assumed there was an error with the mail system. He expected the sender to fire it over again but never received anything and forgot all about it."

Bill continued. "We've had a look back through his mailbox. It was an executable file alright, and the sender wasn't who he thought it was. Phishing mail masquerading as a known contact from his address book. He's been with the bank for decades, and his HR record shows he's done the security training, but he simply didn't act on it. There's likely to be a disciplinary. He's been slack before. One of the old guard who doesn't always see the point of thinking before they click."

Cameron shrugged. "Human error. Always. Whether it's the individual, or the management not picking it up. So that was our virus? Are we sure?"

Sandeep nodded, confidently. "Yes, we've been over the rest of it with a fine-toothed comb. Apart from that odd little trojan yesterday morning, nothing else." He turned to Bill. "Really impressed. Great security. Pure bad luck on this one, I think."

Relieved, Bill stood up. "I'll go and let the Board know that we're back up and running, and leave you to patch the rest."

•

It was done. Cameron sat in the silent room, satisfied. The archaic operating system was once more as tight as a drum. Out in the real world, people were charging wallets and drawing money as normal, the attack already forgotten as the weekend approached. Joel and Sandeep had already left; there was talk of a team night out to celebrate a job well done.

Cameron heard a knock at the door, and looked up as Ross walked in to the room. He seemed refreshed and much less pale, cheeks flushed from exercise, hair damp, casual in tracksuit and trainers.

"Good sleep? Good run?" asked Cameron.

Ross grinned. "Much better, thanks. Did the towpaths up to the Olympic Park, down the Lea and then round to Limehouse. I jumped on the train there, and took advantage of the showers here in the bank. Blew the cobwebs away nicely. How's it going?"

"Pretty much sorted. Back end secure and we know how it got in. Some training to do over the next few weeks. I haven't touched that hidden code, just surgically removed it. Let's go and wrap up with the Board. It's payday."

•

Cameron and Ross once again shook hands with Sir Simon Winchester, handed back their security passes, and walked out of the building.

"Another one bites the dust," said Ross with satisfaction.

Cameron nodded. "Could have been whole lot worse. It was a pretty straightforward takedown once we cracked the routine."

"Once you cracked it," corrected Ross.

Cameron looked wryly at him. "Team effort, man. Couldn't do it without you."

They were silent for a moment. It had been an odd job. The malicious code had been unusually simple to disable, in the end. The hidden routine was still a mystery, despite cleaning up the rest of the virus. Cameron had isolated the odd code and planned to work on it in quarantine. First, however, there were more important things to deal with. Time to get back into normal life.

"What've you got planned for the weekend, then? Racing?"

Ross shook his head. "Next big one is two weeks away. I need to get back on track with my training. This job came along at the wrong time. Can't be helped. You?"

"Family calls. Big brother throwing a knees-up. It's Sameena's fortieth and everyone is descending on the village. It'll be good to take a break."

Ross laughed. "That'll be a first. You never switch off. Taking the new fella along?"

Cameron reddened. "Nope. I think it would be too much of a shock to the system. And anyway, he's strictly recreational right now. I don't want Charlie to think I'm settling down."

Ross dragged his grey hoodie over his head as the afternoon air cooled. The two of them strolled towards the station. From the shadows, a figure watched them until they turned out of sight.

•

Cameron opened the apartment door and the cat miaowed an ecstatic greeting. Otherwise, all was silent.

"Lights." The glow illuminated a tidy kitchen/diner, washing up done and put away, and a note on the table next to a bowl of fresh apples. "Cam, hope the training went well, enjoy your weekend – Ben. PS. I fed the cat."

Cameron sighed, and glared at the cat which was protesting starvation. It would have been good to have Ben along this weekend, but letting the whole tribe loose on him at once would be unfair. The kids were curious enough but Aunt Vicky was another matter. Mandisa would be sorry not to meet him, though. She was dying for news of her best friend's latest conquest and had been badgering Cameron for the last two weeks for an introduction. It would have to wait.

Too tired to meet up with the rest of the team, but not in the mood to travel this evening, Cameron threw country clothes and smarts into a bag and set an early alarm. Lying on the bed in the dark, the cat purring, that hidden code continued to niggle.

It was no use. The mystery had to be solved.

The cyber communities were abuzz with speculation. Cameron set the apartment's IP address mask to a random point on the globe, and logged in to join the chatter. As much as their work was serious, these professionals scattered across the world were all friends, and they provided each other with a lot of light relief through snide observations and clever in-jokes. Today's posts ranged from the serious work of sorting the Speakeasy attack, through a long discussion of the sleeping habits of cats, to the mystery of the second subroutine.

Cameron skimmed the thread about cats, laughed out loud at couple of posts, uploaded a picture of the little black and white cat curled up in an impossibly tortuous position with a toy mouse clutched between its paws, and then turned to the hidden code discussion.

"Hey guys, what've we got so far?"

There was a chorus of welcome.

"SimCavalier, you back! How you doing?"

"Where've you been hiding?"

"You cracked it already?"

"Been busy, guys. Thought you'd have broken it by now. You been asleep? Spend all your time taking pictures of cats? I leave you alone for a few hours and look what happens."

A gale of laughter was accompanied by posted snippets of film, old gifs that still made users laugh. "We've been waiting for you to ride in and fix it, SimCavalier. We brought popcorn."

Cameron grinned broadly. "Seriously guys, where are we? I promise not to take all the credit."

There was a ripple of amusement. "Yeah, you're not RunningManTech. You play fair. Where's he got to, anyway? Haven't seen him on here for days. He's not answering threads."

"RunningManTech is running, what did you think he'd be doing? He's got a race coming up. Training before pleasure. C'mon, let's have a look at this. I'm tired."

Cameron pushed the code dump up to the forum. "Say what you see. Looks pretty straightforward from here, you useless lot. Line 24 refers back to a web address, liberatorseven.com, anything there?"

"Yeah, it exists, but it's parked. The ICANN listing's pretty funny."

Cameron brought the details of the rogue domain up on the screen, and laughed.

"It's a homage to old-school sci-fi. Well, I thought they had a sense of humour when I saw the Speakeasy gif. Look at this… '*Registrant J-L Picard, 1701 Tribble Street, Enterprise Town, Nevada… Phone 702-474-571*'. That's classic."

"Keep reading," came a post. "It gets better."

Cameron scanned further down the listing.

"Whaaa…? 'Tech contact Z Beeblebrox' – seriously? This got through ICANN? – '42 Magratheasgata, Trondheim… Phone 72-26-7709'. Love it."

Cameron paused. "This is all a lot of fun, but why? Why go to all this trouble? Let's have a look at the source code again."

The chatter died down as the forum members pored over the lines of code. Cameron was thinking hard: it made no sense. The little programme did not appear to hide anything, and had not run in the attack.

It hadn't run.

What would happen if it ran?

"Has anyone tried running this routine?"

"Yeah, of course, it's a dead end. Check it out." Cameron turned to the quarantine computer, a stripped-back operating system linked to nothing at all. The code was already loaded there for examination.

'*Run.*'

On screen, a single box appeared. '*Password?*' it said.

Cameron snapped an image of the monitor with the smartscreen camera, and uploaded it to the forum.

"This what you all got?"

"Yeah. Pretty odd stuff for a bundle of malicious code."

"Is that what it is? It didn't attack anything. Sure, it was delivered as part of an attack, but it stayed dormant. We are the only people who have seen it. Maybe we are the people who were meant to run it."

"So what's the password, genius?"

"That's the big question, isn't it, guys," replied Cameron. "Okay. I'm sure this routine has been written for us to find. The only people who'd see it and get this far are nerds like us. Look at all the references. The password has to be something that links us all. Chuck me some ideas."

"More sci-fi references? Spaceships?"

"TARDIS, Rocinante, Heart of Gold, Sleeper Service…"

"Millennium Falcon," came another post.

"Red Dwarf. Serenity…"

"Nope, nothing yet. Give me a second, just pulling a routine together to test all possibilities in that genre. What other terms would all of us know? It can't be too random, it's relying on shared context in the threat intelligence field."

"Cyberattacks, viruses, worms? Speakeasy. WannaCry. ILoveYou. Chairmaker. EternalPetya. Mirai. Morris…"

"Running those now… No, nothing."

"How about us?"

"What do you mean?"

"Our handles. Feed all our handles in and see what you get." There was a wave of chatter, and then silence, a virtual in-drawing of breath.

Cameron ran the routine, testing the names of all the forum members faster than human eye could follow.

Nothing.

No, wait. One name would not be on the list. The user who generated it.

Barely breathing, Cameron typed slowly into the box on the screen: '*SimCavalier*'.

The box flashed green and disappeared. The screen went dark. Plain white text appeared.

'Batten down the hatches for hurricane season.'

4: HOMECOMING

Another early morning, but this time Cameron felt relaxed, if not particularly well rested. After the revelations of the hidden subroutine, the release of sleep had been slow to come, with disturbing dreams of giant worms and server stacks, swirling storms, and the shining sword of a cavalier.

Rain had fallen overnight, and the air was damp and cool. Leaving the cat with enough food to feed a feline army, Cameron grabbed the overnight bag and walked steadily down the deserted staircase to the quiet, pre-dawn dark of the street, heading straight to the underground station. The Northern Line shuttle to Euston was just pulling in to the platform. Fifteen minutes later, Cameron emerged onto the station concourse and scanned the departure listings. The next train out towards Milton Keynes and Birmingham was leaving in a quarter of an hour; plenty of time to buy a coffee before heading down the ramp to board.

The train emerged into the early morning daylight, slowly winding through North London towards Watford and beyond, passing Wembley Stadium, its famous arch dominating the skyline, white metal shining against the rich, dark colours of the dawn sky. As buildings gave way to trees and fields, the carriage picked up speed, a short crescendo in the steady electric hum. Cameron leant against the window, hypnotised by the familiar rhythm of the wheels on the tracks. The sun was rising; it cast a pale, yellow light over the countryside. Small towns and farms, fields and villages, flew by, a patchwork of countryside that Cameron knew by heart. The train crossed a bridge over the Grand Union Canal; there was little pleasure boat traffic at this time of day, but plenty of freight barges were already on the move, shipping goods slowly up the country on the ancient network of waterways.

Purring to a stop, the train disgorged a handful of passengers. Cameron strolled through the small station and out of the main doors, where a fleet of autocars waited patiently at charging points. The For Hire sign on a small autocar lit up as it sensed passing trade. Cameron climbed in, stowed the bag, told the taxi the address, and thumbed its payment button. The little cab waited until the seatbelt locked, then pulled out towards the road.

Cameron relaxed, enjoying the ride. They crossed the river and left the town behind, skirting the hill where Iron Age man once built his fort, and Twentieth Century man built dormitory suburbs. The empty dual carriageway crossed a silent motorway, and for a while followed the line of a branch of the canal, white-painted locks in motion as deliveries arrived at local depots. A few kilometres further on, the cab turned off the main road and drove steadily down a leafy village lane to the house Cameron had grown up in, which was now home to Charlie and his lively family.

Cameron climbed out of the vehicle, retrieved her bag, and sent the little autocar back to its lair. Straightening up, she braced herself as a whirlwind of children and an excitable dog arrived at speed.

"Aunty Cam! Aunty Cam! Daddy, Daddy, Aunty Cam's here!"

Charlie ambled up and extricated Cameron from the sea of hugs. "Hi little sis, good trip?" He kissed her warmly on the cheek, took her bag and they walked together towards the house. "Sorry you couldn't get here last night – busy time at work, I guess." Cameron nodded, and Charlie grimaced. "We got a hit from the same virus. No – don't worry," he continued hurriedly, as she looked concerned, "our own systems weren't compromised; you've done a great job there. Lost our printers for almost a day thanks to a breach at the main data centre, took a while for them to be sure they could restore backups safely. Luckily, we're covered for cyber attack interruption. No problem with the insurers, especially as the in-house systems are so tight."

Cameron smiled. "Good to hear our defences are holding. Nasty little virus, did a fair bit of short-term damage, but we caught it at our end and it looks like the fix we developed neutralised the threat globally. Great work from Ross and the team."

"How's Ross doing?" asked Charlie. "And why would Mandisa be asking me if you're bringing someone to the party? New boyfriend?"

"Ross is fine, his usual grumpy self, does a good job, but only happy when he's running, swimming, biking or all three. Any rumours of a new boyfriend are strictly unconfirmed and not to reach Aunt Vicky under any circumstances, okay?"

Charlie laughed. Aunt Vicky was their mother's only sister. In her seventies now, she still lived in the village, and had kept a close eye on her niece and nephew since their parents' untimely passing. Cameron was hoping to keep Ben off her radar for now.

40

Entering the old farmhouse kitchen, the tail end of breakfast was evident. Plates, spoons, jars of jam, cartons of milk, and empty cups were scattered on the wooden table in the centre of the kitchen. The children had scampered off as soon as there was a hint of a chore to be done, and Sameena was alone, stacking the dishwasher and gradually clearing the table.

Cameron walked over to her sister-in-law and gave her a hug. "Happy Birthday, Sameena. Are you all set for the party?"

Sameena put down a jam-covered plate and laughed. "Nowhere near ready, Cam, neither for the party nor for being forty. I just want to pretend I am thirty again. Is that allowed?" She shook her head ruefully for a moment, then smiled broadly. "You are in your usual room, we haven't kicked you out yet. Waiting for you to settle down first. Nina is after that attic, mind. She is growing up far too fast. Secondary school next year – can you believe it?"

Cameron could. Nina had shot up over the past couple of years, obviously bestowed with the long legs and slim build of the Silvera women. Bright and academic, she had Charlie and Cameron's dark hair, and her mother's coffee-coloured skin and brown eyes. Her precocious intelligence was being matched by emerging beauty.

"There may be trouble ahead," sang Cameron under her breath.

Dilan and Tara marched into the kitchen, squabbling over a toy. "Mum, it's my turn. Tara grabbed it off me!"

Sameena sighed and turned to deal with the fight.

Cameron took her chance to grab a slice of toast from the table, and spread it with jam, suddenly hungry after the last few days of disrupted routine.

Charlie laughed as he came into the room. "You have jam all over your face, Cam. Nothing changes. Want a coffee?"

Cameron shook her head. "Toast will do, thanks. What's the plan for today? Can I do anything?"

"I think we're organised, love. Caterers will be here by noon, they'll do all the heavy lifting. You relax. You've had a hard week. I've put your bag upstairs."

"Thanks, Charlie. I said I'd meet Mandisa for a drink before lunch. I'll take Roxy out for a walk, keep her out from under everyone's feet. Is that okay?"

Charlie smiled gratefully. "Good plan. Say hi to Mandisa. She's coming this afternoon, isn't she?"

"Oh yes," replied Cameron, nodding, "but we need a good gossip without Aunt Vicky listening in." She winked at Charlie, who laughed knowingly.

Cameron finished her toast, and headed upstairs to unpack her bag. Climbing a hidden staircase to the top floor, she emerged into her attic domain, which extended almost the full length of the house. Walls angled inwards with the steep pitch of the roof, low to the floor at the skirting boards. Three bright dormer windows faced south. The view over the green fields was as breath-taking as ever; a line of dark trees and hedges showed where the brook babbled between fields, and in the distance sheep were grazing. Cameron's bedroom was partitioned off at one end. Faded, once brightly patterned, wallpaper still decorated the attic. Real paper books were ranged on low shelves under the sloping eaves. A threadbare teddy sat by the bed, framed, printed photographs and a scrap metal salamander hung on the wall. A PC sat on an old desk, with twin monitors mounted on brackets. A router stood on a small cabinet next to the desk, dormant, no lights flashing. In the corner, a pile of older hardware and jumbled wires was gathering dust. On a shelf, in pride of place, lay her mother's old ZX81, the family's first home computer, useless without its monitor and cassette player. Those were lurking in a cupboard, and hadn't seen the light of day for over a decade.

Cameron unpacked her bag, hanging her dress in the small wardrobe ready for the afternoon's celebrations. She unearthed a treat for the kids, and the gift she'd bought for Sameena weeks ago; she was so glad she hadn't left shopping until the last minute.

Next, she plugged in the PC and router, changing the admin passwords as a matter of course, using a new combination from the generator on her smartscreen. Checking her mailbox, there were no urgent messages to deal with.

The forums were filled with speculation on the strange result of cracking the hidden code, but Cameron chose not to log on just now. That could wait. The best brains in the world were puzzling over its significance. For Cameron, a greater challenge awaited. It was time to face the children. She took a deep breath and headed downstairs into the fray.

Sameena looked relieved when Cameron allowed the kids to bear her off to the family room. Dilan and Tara headed straight for the computer. The monitor hung on the wall, facing the room. Anything they did, every site they accessed, could be seen by passing adults. There was little temptation to disappear down online rabbit holes, and plenty of scope to show off.

"Cameron, look what I did." Tara tapped on a file and the screen was suddenly full of tumbling unicorns, turning cartwheels across the pink background as stars and sparkles flew. "I made it all by myself."

Dilan snorted with derision. At eight, the simple programming his little sister loved was beneath him, although Cameron clearly remembered his own similar early attempts, featuring dancing dinosaurs and exploding meteors.

Nina had followed them in, but was sitting apart, sulking, a smartscreen dangling in her hand. "Mum won't let me have today's wifi password."

"Come and sit with us," offered Cameron. "I've got a challenge for you. And anyway, it's the party this afternoon, your mum doesn't want you creeping off to a corner with that screen and ignoring everyone." Nina grumbled, but put down the screen and joined her aunt and siblings at the computer.

Cameron dropped a pre-prepared file from her smartscreen over to the PC. "Right kids, code cracking time. There's a hidden message in this graph – what treat have I brought for you? There's also a key to what each of the points in the graph could mean. Trouble is, there are 256 possibilities for each one. Do you think you can crack the message before lunch?"

Tara looked worried, but Nina rolled her eyes. "Aunty Cam, that's way too easy. Just need to process all the possibilities and watch the spikes."

Cameron laughed. "It's one thing to know the theory, another to run it. Get going. Get the answer, and you'll get the treat. And it has to be all three of you working as a team."

She sat back, smiling, as her nieces and nephew fought for position in front of the monitor. Gradually they settled to work together, Nina explaining the process to Dilan, and Tara watching the patterns. That'll keep them out of Sameena's hair for an hour or so, she thought.

Relaxing on the familiar old sofa, Cameron gazed around the walls at family photos, printed and framed treasures as well as scrolling digital displays. High up, away from direct sunlight, were the black and white portraits of her own grandparents and great-grandparents, stiff and formal, holding still for the photographer to avoid blurring the precious negative. The pictures of her parents were more relaxed, smiling on holiday, smart at a wedding, and laughing in a family portrait with Cameron as a toddler and Charlie aged about ten.

Lower down were informal images of Cameron and Charlie, and of Sameena with her brothers and sisters, every moment of their childhoods captured in digital colour. Digital screens scrolled pictures from the last decade of the three dark-haired youngsters now huddled around the monitor. So many changes in the past century, reflected Cameron. Even her own grandmother had barely scratched the surface of the burgeoning digital world. Now, the world was almost entirely digital, just fifty years after the World Wide Web came into existence.

She dozed in her warm nest on the old sofa, relaxing properly for the first time in days.

A cheer went up from the children. Cameron started awake and checked her watch. "Seventy-three minutes. Not bad at all. What's the answer?"

"Chocolate," squealed Tara.

Cameron grinned, and produced a small parcel.

"Off you go. Enjoy." She yawned and stretched, clambered off the sofa, and closed down the screen as the kids ran outside. Time to go and meet Mandisa. It would be good to see her friend again.

•

Cameron escaped out of the back door and walked around the side of the house, feeling the crunch of familiar gravel beneath her feet. Roxy the Labradoodle bounced around her madly, wagging her blonde tail so hard that her hindquarters danced, anticipating a proper walk. The early spring snowdrops and crocuses in the lawn were over, a few sad green spikes all that remained of the colourful display. A host of bright yellow daffodils nestled under the hedge and surrounded the base of the lilac trees. No blossom yet; spring was further ahead in the city. The bleat of lambs carried on a light breeze from the fields opposite the house. Cameron clipped Roxy's leash to her collar and set off out of the gate.

The village had hardly changed since her childhood, and probably very little since her mother's childhood, either. There had been a village here for a millennium. In 1068, the Domesday Book recorded two households, five ploughlands and seven acres of woodland, farmed by Saxon lords under the tenancy of Count Robert of Mortain. It had grown since those times, but remained small.

Rounding the corner, Cameron skirted a limestone wall and passed the neat gardens of a row of cottages, once home to the workers at a nearby farm. The street opened up onto the village green, bordered on the far side by the same small brook, and deserted but for another distant dog walker. Cameron smiled as she remembered the hot summers of her childhood. She and her friends spent days dressed in swimming costumes and sandals, playing in the clear shallow water, trying to catch young sticklebacks which slipped through their fingers and away downstream. The green still hosted sports day for the tiny village school that stood opposite, where Charlie, then Cameron, and now the three children, had first studied their reading, writing, 'rithmetic, and Ruby. Eight years older than his sister, Charlie had spent those summers acting cool rather than staying cool, hanging out with his older friends well away from the embarrassing little kids.

The road meandered up a small rise, topped by the ancient square tower of a pretty limestone church. Cameron gave a passing nod to the place; her parents and grandparents had been laid to rest in that churchyard, and she would pay her respects later. Behind the church she could see workers in the vineyard checking the buds for emerging flower clusters. A small private vineyard had once thrived there, but as the world warmed, vines became big business, changing the focus of centuries of local agriculture. Now the fields were all planted in thin, dark rows, providing Chardonnay and Pinot Gris to the great champagne houses whose traditional lands were increasingly barren.

The road narrowed, and Cameron shivered slightly in the shadow of a row of great horse-chestnut trees. Up ahead she could see the welcoming sign of the village pub, the social hub for everything from Friday nights to funerals. Cameron reached the old white building, opened the gate, and crossed the small beer garden, exchanging greetings in passing with a couple of pre-lunch drinkers. She tied Roxy up to an empty wooden picnic table and entered the porch of the pub, stepping down, blinking, into a small wooden-beamed bar. Sitting on a stool, gossiping with the landlord, was Mandisa.

"Caaaaaameron," she squealed. "Where's the new boyfriend then?" Mandisa hopped off the stool and gave her friend a hug, peering behind her at the door, hoping to see another figure entering.

Cameron laughed ruefully. "I'm sorry. I didn't think he was ready for the Spanish Inquisition. We'll have to get together in London instead. I'm less busy now, thank goodness. All quiet on the Western Front." She tapped her nose conspiratorially. After ten years in the business, she still managed to keep her front-line role a secret from all but her closest friends and family. Even Ben, bless him, thought she simply delivered training and advice on cyber security. She wondered what he'd made of the last few days, and their broken dates, early mornings, and late nights.

"I'll have a half, please, and a bowl of water for the dog." Cameron sighed. "Total chaos at home. Last minute organisation and caterers everywhere. Madness. It's great to get out for an hour; I used the dog as an excuse."

Mandisa laughed. "I bet the kids aren't helping at all."

"Well, they think they are. Nina's not so bad, she has her head screwed on and she's growing up fast, but Dilan and Tara are driving Sameena mad. I've done my morning shift as the good aunt and this is my statutory break. At least I'll have you as reinforcements this afternoon."

Nodding to the landlord, Cameron and Mandisa took their drinks out to the beer garden, Cameron ducking as she stepped through the door. "Number of times I've banged my head coming up that step…" she grumbled.

"Your fault for growing so tall," chided Mandisa. "I told you to stop when we were eleven. Is the weather good up there? Can you reach the high shelf for me?"

Cameron good-naturedly flicked a drop of beer at her friend. "Not fair. Not my fault. Short arse."

The dog walker from the green had made it all the way up the village. Off her leash, Roxy's tail wagged like a demented metronome, spying a friend. The two dogs snuffled at each other and splashed as they drank their water. Cameron and Mandisa said hello to the new arrival; not someone they knew, an incomer to the village, but apparently long enough established for the dogs to be acquainted.

"You're Charlie's sister, aren't you? Down from London for the party, eh?"

Cameron nodded.

"Andrew. Andrew Taylor. I live up the hill. Nice to meet you. Shame you're not here more often. I commute up, it's just as easy as trying to cross London."

"Ah, too quiet here. Much more fun in the capital for now, Andrew. So, you know Charlie, then? Are you coming along this afternoon?"

"Call me Andy. I think the whole village is invited." He looked enquiringly at Mandisa. "Sorry, you are…?"

"Old schoolfriend. I only live the other side of the town. Mandisa Menzi. I'll be there too." She extended her hand.

Andy shook Mandisa's hand, and looked curiously at Cameron. "I'm sure we've met before, somewhere."

Cameron shrugged. "I don't think so, Andy."

Andy frowned, something niggling at the back of his mind. "Must be the family resemblance. Young Nina is the double of you, Cameron."

Cameron smiled. "Yes, she's growing up fast." She finished her drink.

46

"We'd better get going. I promised to wear this beastie out and she needs a good run on the field. Nice to meet you, Andy. See you this afternoon." Roxy trotted over obediently and Cameron re-attached her leash. Mandisa took the glasses back in to the bar, and they set off out of the garden again and turned to go further up the lane.

Andy watched them go, puzzled, then ducked into the pub.

•

The party was in full swing. Long tables laden with food lined a shady stone terrace in the angle of the house. Discreet caterers passed among the crowd on the terrace and lawn, replenishing glasses and collecting plates. Children ran around squealing, playing in the longer grass away from the adults. Nina had forgotten her grown-up pose and lack of smartscreen, and was joining in the fun with visiting cousins and local friends. Cameron and Mandisa exchanged gossip with villagers they had known from school days, gathering news of old friends who had moved away. A couple of Charlie and Sameena's university friends were gamely chatting up the two girls, amused that the little sister they remembered had grown into an elegant, self-confident woman.

Cameron glanced across the lawn and spotted her elderly aunt. She was holding forth with tales of bygone times and the latest village gossip, fuelled by local fizz, but Cameron could tell even from a distance that Aunt Vicky was not on her usual sparkling form. Excusing herself from the laughing group, Cameron caught her aunt at the groaning buffet table in search of more nibbles. "What's up, Aunt Vicky?"

"Oh Cameron, darling, it's the cat." She sounded upset. Cameron wondered what had happened to the evil fluffball this time. The old cat that Cameron grew up with had been a sleek, elegant, black tom with impeccable manners. You could leave a slice of ham on the table and the cat would not so much as sniff at it. There was an easy truce with all the neighbouring cats, and he spent sunny days outside on the porch making friends with every visitor and every passer-by.

That was years ago, and Bob the cat was long gone. Aunt Vicky had subsequently acquired a long-haired ginger beast of dubious provenance by the name of Donald. Donald stalked the garden, dug up the seedlings in the vegetable patch, fought with Boris the tabby next door, and regularly got himself stuck up trees in pursuit of feathered prey, from where his loyal staff would rescue him.

"The poor baby is ill," (oh that's a shame, thought Cameron) "and when I contacted the vet, they said they could treat him, but it sounded like a pre-existing condition, and his pet insurance won't cover the costs. He may need an operation – it could be thousands. What am I going to do?"

Cameron could think of several answers to this question, none of which were particularly diplomatic or comforting. She discarded 'Good riddance' and 'Don't waste your money' for the kinder option.

"Poor Donald. He's had a wonderful pampered life. What is he, fourteen? That's well over seventy in cat years. I'm sure he'll be fine. You can't expect him to be on top form at that age – present company excepted, of course." Cameron had her fingers crossed behind her back. Had she managed to navigate the fine line?

Aunt Vicky snuffled sadly. "Yes dear, I suppose you're right. When I adopted him, he was in such a state I didn't expect him to last four years, let alone eight. Oh, the worry he's caused me."

"Come on, Aunt Vicky, chin up. This is Sameena's day. You can worry about Donald tomorrow. Have another glass of fizz. Can't believe the weather, can you? Lovely for the time of year."

Cameron steered her aunt to the nearest smiling caterer and picked up two glasses. She thought about providing some distraction from cat woes by dropping a hint about the new boyfriend, but before she could put her foot firmly in her mouth, she heard a voice behind her.

"Afternoon Vicky, how are you? Haven't seen your Donald over our fence recently. Boris thinks all his Christmases have come at once."

Aunt Vicky's face lit up. "Andy, how lovely to see you. Have you met my niece, Cameron? Cameron, this is my next-door neighbour. He works up in London too."

"I met your lovely niece this morning, Vicky, when I was out walking Jasper. Hello Cameron. We've definitely met before somewhere, just can't place it." He smiled broadly, but his eyes were narrowed and searching.

"Hello Andy," replied Cameron cautiously. "I'm still sure we haven't met. I didn't realise you were Aunt Vicky's new neighbour. When did you move in?"

"Arrived at the end of last year. Beautiful spot. Easy distance to the city. Of course, I can work here at home too, so convenient since they upgraded the village connections."

Aunt Vicky nodded enthusiastically. "Oh yes, it's lovely to have neighbours in the village during the day. In the old days, unless you worked on the farm, everyone commuted. The place was deserted. Much more fun now."

Andy was not to be deterred. "What is it you do down in London, Cameron?"

"Oh – I work in robotics – nothing exciting – training and so on. I have to be there in person, no chance of doing it from here. What about you?" Cameron smiled sociably, but something didn't feel right. There was nothing outwardly threatening about this unassuming man, but he was watching her a little too closely for a casual acquaintance. She glanced around for an escape, and saw Mandisa coming across the lawn towards her. As Andy opened his mouth to reply, Cameron hurriedly butted in.

"Sorry, Aunt Vicky, Andy, we have something to sort out for the birthday girl." She stepped forward to meet Mandisa, and they turned around to head for the house. Cameron could feel Andy's eyes boring into her back.

"He gives me the creeps," said Mandisa. "I don't know what it is, but I don't like him."

Cameron nodded. She trusted her sixth sense. It was what made her good at her job, after all. She needed to know more about this Andrew Taylor. Leaving Mandisa in the kitchen, she dashed up to the attic and fired a quick encrypted message to Ross. *"Andrew Taylor, late forties, average everything, lives in my village, moved here last summer, works in London, cat Boris, dog Jasper, no family. Might be tough to track, common name, but any dirt?"* If there was any basis to her gut instinct, Ross would find out.

Cameron slipped back downstairs clutching the gift for Sameena, just as a splendid birthday cake was being positioned on a small table in the middle of the lawn. Staying well away from the mysterious Mr Taylor, she and Mandisa joined a cluster of friends and family to sing Happy Birthday. Glowing, Sameena cut into the cake, Charlie proposed a toast to his wife, glasses clinked, and the cake was whisked away for cutting. Mandisa disappeared into the kitchen again and acquired two slices, handing one to Cameron.

Cameron sighed. "Ah, a slice won't hurt. I feel like I've eaten enough for the whole weekend already this afternoon. After the last few days I need to get back to training."

Mandisa laughed. "No, girl, what you need is a holiday. You work too hard. What say we have a week away? Go and find some sunshine?"

Cameron brightened. "That's a nice idea. I have a bunch of training booked in, and there is a loose end to tidy from this latest job. If it's quiet after that then yes, take me away."

The cool spring evening was growing dark as the sun set behind the house. Guests were starting to take their leave, and the crowd thinned out as they left in twos and threes, most on foot, some by autocar back to other villages, the local town, and the station. The chattering voices of other children faded. Nina appeared, carrying a tired Tara, and followed by Dilan dragging a large stick.

Cameron took charge of them, gently persuading Dilan to give up his stick and leave it on the terrace for the night. She hustled the younger two to their bedrooms while Nina wandered off to join her parents for an hour or so, claiming the privilege of a later bedtime. Tara, resplendent in Tigger pyjamas and clutching a cuddly panda, snuggled up in her bed, asleep before her head hit the pillow. Dilan insisted he wasn't tired, resisting every effort to tuck him in, but when Cameron checked on him a few minutes later, he was out for the count.

•

Andrew Taylor frowned as he climbed the hill towards his house. Where had he seen that girl before? It wasn't simply the family resemblance to Charlie and Nina that had triggered this half-baked recollection. He had seen her recently, this week, in another context.

Boris the cat arrived at the door with him, yowling for food after a day protecting his territory, or sleeping in the warmest spot in the garden, more like. Inside, Jasper trotted up to greet him, tail wagging. Andy fed them both, distracted, puzzling over the mystery. He thought through his week. Had he seen her out in London? Had she been in the office? Sitting on the same train? No, he couldn't place her anywhere. Why was this niggling so much?

Frustrated, Andy switched on his computer and glanced at the job he'd been working on this morning. Two sets of photographs, one grainy and almost monochrome, one high resolution colour. Images of the same man, his quarry.

Andy scrolled through the CCTV images. He could see the man entering a lobby, walking to reception. In the next image, his back was to the camera, the hood of his sweatshirt hanging down, as he spoke to the receptionist. A later image picked up his features as he left the building: white, pale, short hair. Dark? Hard to tell.

Andy flicked to the other set of images. The same man walking away from the camera in the morning sunlight. Height, build, hoodie the same. Blond hair. Hmm. That could be a trick of the light. Scrolling back through the photos for a full-face image, Andy cursed at he realised the first three or four snaps of the man leaving the apartment were just out of focus. He really wasn't having any luck.

Suddenly, something caught his eye. He zoomed in to the group of young people leaving the apartment, his quarry's face blurred, but others clear.

Andy sat back, stunned. That was where he'd seen her before. Charlie's sister lived in the same apartment block as the man he was stalking. She had left home at the same time yesterday morning, and had been caught on camera by Andy's staff. Finally, he had a lead to the SimCavalier.

5: RUN AND HIDE

Cameron woke early again. The morning sun was streaming through the blinds that hung on the dormer window. She yawned and stretched, luxuriating in the pleasure of a rare morning where nothing needed to be done. The house was quiet, the children still asleep, exhausted after the fun of the party.

An old red dressing gown hung on a hook by the wardrobe. Cameron threw it on over her pyjamas and padded down the attic stairs, opening the door to the main landing quietly. The click of the latch alerted Roxy, and Cameron heard the dog's claws tapping on the old flagstones of the hallway below, as she too stretched and rose from sleep.

The kitchen was a mess. No one had bothered to tidy at the end of the night, although the debris of the afternoon's catering had been neatly removed. Cameron filled the kettle and clicked it on to boil. The switch was stiff with lack of use, the kettle tuned in to the activity and biorhythms and apps of the household.

She opened the fridge, and jumped as a disembodied voice addressed her. "Good morning. The milk is almost out of date. Shall I order some more? You have an offer to change brand, would you like to hear it?"

Cameron paused, then replied clearly, "Order four litres, same brand."

"Order placed," came the reply. "Delivery in eighteen minutes."

Cameron lifted out the old milk carton and sniffed at it anyway. Seems fine, she thought. The kettle boiled. Cameron threw a teabag into the large mug that Nina had printed for her when she was little, poured in the water, and let the bag stew for a few minutes while she absent-mindedly stacked plates and glasses by the dishwasher. Adding a splash of milk, Cameron returned the carton to the fridge, closing the door quickly to stop it talking.

She opened the back door to let Roxy run out in the garden. It was cloudy, and too cold to settle down outside, so Cameron wandered through to the family room and curled up on the sofa. A movement caught her eye at the window; the milk drone had arrived. She got up quickly and went to the front door to collect the cartons and put them away, hoping that Charlie and Sameena wouldn't be disturbed by the delivery drone's arrival.

It was peaceful in the sleeping house, and Cameron's mind wandered as she reflected on the events of the past week. The job at the bank had ultimately been simple, but the long hours had taken more out of her than she expected. The mystery of the message hidden in the subroutine of the Speakeasy virus added a layer of concern, a niggle at the back of her mind.

She would head back to London this afternoon, she decided, and spend some time with Ben. He was a sweet guy, and funny, and great in bed: she liked him a lot. She would plan the next round of training with Bill at the bank, and organise her diary to get a girls' week away very soon with Mandisa. She would stop worrying about the mysterious Mr Taylor, and the meaning of the cryptic message. Life would settle into its normal routine, until the next time.

Fine intentions. But Cameron's competitive streak and love of a mystery would ultimately win. She needed to know what the message meant. She wanted to get there before everyone else. However hard she tried to relax, it would draw her back in the end.

She sighed. Today she would reserve for herself, her family, and her friends. Tomorrow was another matter.

The door opened, and Charlie wandered in. "You're up early. I heard the milk come. Another cuppa?"

Cameron smiled. "Go on, then." She handed Charlie her empty mug.

"News channel," muttered Charlie into thin air as he wandered back out towards the kitchen. A screen on the wall glowed, and the mellifluous tones of the hosts of the Sunday morning news and discussion programmes washed over Cameron as she sat, deep in thought. Snippets of news stories drifted in and out of her consciousness. "...*last breeding pair of polar bears in the wild... earliest recorded full melt of Arctic floes...*" "*...thirty-eighth annual drone racing championship underway at Alexandra Palace...*" "*...sterling strengthens against the Bitcoin... cyber hero applauded following successful code cracking...*"

Charlie reappeared with tea and toast. He put the tray down on the small table, straightened, and looked at screen, astonished. "Cameron – isn't that Ross?"

Cameron looked up, open-mouthed, as the newscaster continued.

"...foiled the so-called 'Speakeasy' cyberattack this week. These first pictures show the threat intelligence operative known only as the SimCavalier riding to the rescue when the virus struck on Wednesday. He has been hailed as a hero, and there are calls to recognise his contribution to maintaining the security of…"

"Pause," shouted Cameron. "Go back thirty seconds." She stared at the screen. The first grainy picture clearly showed Ross standing alone in the foyer of the bank.

Cameron laughed incredulously. "That's where we were this week. That's Ross, you're right, but they're talking about me." She was suddenly sober. "Charlie, this is really bad. No one has ever gotten close to identifying any of us. I've been doing this for almost ten years. And now, they've found the team – if not me – and they know my handle. What the hell is going on?"

"Cam, love, that's manageable. I know you want to stay anonymous, but if they haven't identified you then you're in the clear. Find the breach and move on."

Cameron shook her head. "We did find a breach, just didn't think anything of it. Joel swept the systems and found a hack into the CCTV systems after the attack started. Never considered for a moment that they've be looking for us. But how would they know where to hack – unless they've attacked every compromised business." She paused. "No, that doesn't make sense. Too many options, and anyway the breach occurred before the bank went public, I'm sure of it." She frowned, thinking hard.

Charlie was worried. He knew his little sister was dabbling in some dangerous networks. She was part of the thin green line at the forefront of the cyber security battle, and the foe was in the shadows. Organised crime? The remnants of hostile regimes? Nothing good.

"Play," ordered Charlie, and the broadcast resumed. The first picture faded and a second was displayed. "Hah, not to worry, there's another picture and it definitely isn't Ross this time. Colour shot, no ginger hair. Stab in the dark. You're in the clear, Cam."

Cameron looked up at him, feeling nauseous, suddenly pale. "No, Charlie. I'm not. Look at that picture again. Where are they?"

Charlie peered at the screen, and turned back to his sister, appalled.

"Oh, dear god, Cameron, that's outside your apartment."

She nodded silently, and her head swam.

•

Ross paced himself between splits, the monitor on his wrist counting down three minutes of recovery before his next four hundred metre sprint. He was sweating despite the cool morning, back on course with his training plan, but suffering from the interruption of the cyber attack. Two more weeks to the race, two more splits to finish today. Most of his training partners were already cooling down on the bikes, some pulling on compression leggings.

The monitor pinged and he accelerated, pushing himself hard as he pounded around the track. He should be faster than race pace. At the end of the lap, he spat in disgust at his time. One more to go, he thought, as he jogged slowly along.

Lucy whizzed past him in her racing chair, completing her final training lap. "Hey, Ross, smile, you grumpy sod."

He scowled, staying focused.

A passer-by leaned on the fence, watching him run. Ross took no notice, retreating into himself, drawing from a reserve of inner strength for the final lap.

He accelerated once more, pushing again as he rounded the first bend, and feeling released as his legs finally obeyed and carried him around the track to a strong finish. He punched the air and slowed to a jog, relieved. He followed Lucy towards the cooldown area next to a small stand that had been built along the straight, empty of spectators on a cloudy Sunday morning.

As he relieved his aching muscles on the static bike, the team coach approached him.

"Not bad, Ross, but you're cutting it fine for the race. I'm looking at final selections for the elite team next weekend, and there are some hungry youngsters snapping at your heels. I'm sorry to hear about your grandmother. I guess that couldn't be helped, but it really messed up the last week, didn't it? You need to pull something good out of the bag; you don't want to waste all that training."

Ross started guiltily. He needed to keep track of how many grandmothers' funerals he used as excuses to cover his increasingly erratic work commitments.

"Thanks, coach. She'd been ill for a while, but it's tough when they finally go. We've arranged the funeral so it doesn't clash with training."

The coach nodded sympathetically, and Ross felt like a fraud. Too many lies. He was starting to get out of his depth.

Ross headed for the showers, avoiding the rest of the team. His performance hadn't been up to scratch, and he knew they were all watching. The older ones, afraid he might let them down. The younger ones, sensing a chance for glory.

The Olympic selectors would be there at the race, putting the building blocks in place for Reykjavik 2048. Ross craved recognition; this might be his last shot as an amateur sportsman. He was anonymous despite all his efforts at work, and likely to remain anonymous despite all his sacrifices for training.

Boiling with frustration and anger, he stayed a long time under the cooling jets of water until the changing room fell silent.

Ginger hair still dark and damp from the shower, Ross walked out into the warming air. The door fell closed behind him, biometric locks securing the building until a registered club member came to open them again. He wasn't the last person to leave, though. Ross looked up as the club's groundsman rounded the corner.

"Hey, Ross, is the coach still around?"

"No, mate, you've missed him. Just locking up."

The groundsman looked crestfallen, and indicated the box he was carrying. "Ah bugger. This package just arrived for him. What am I going to do?"

Ross shrugged. "He won't be back until tomorrow. What've you got?"

"Dunno." He scanned the box. "Er, it looks like it's from the supplement suppliers. Yeah, here, look: *'Silent Running nutrition boost'*. Hold on, it says it's been made up for you. There's stroke of luck. You may as well take it now."

"Thanks mate, I will," replied Ross, his mind racing.

The groundsman handed Ross the box, gave him a cheery smile, and waved as he returned to his work.

Ross stowed the box in his kit bag, pulled out his smartscreen, and switched it on. Within moments it lit up with alerts. Cameron. Ross connected a voice call as he strolled towards the station.

"Ross, I've been trying to reach you for hours." She sounded flustered. "Have you seen the public news channels?"

"No, of course not, I've been at training. What's wrong?"

"Someone's doxed us. The news has got hold of our details and we're all over the headlines. Ross, they've got pictures, pictures of you at the bank."

Ross took a deep breath, trying to contain his excitement. Maybe, just maybe, his luck was turning. He fought to keep his voice light.

"Hey, Cameron, don't panic, it was going to happen one day, wasn't it? What have they said?"

"Ross, sod it, I am panicking, this is serious. There are some bad guys out there who may not be too happy about the work we do. They've picked up on my handle, but they've linked it with the team. They're saying you're me, which is pretty funny I suppose, but it potentially puts us all in danger."

He was taken aback by how concerned she was. Ross had never been convinced of her arguments about the dangers of their profession. There were probably thousands of people doing what they did. One threat intelligence group out of hundreds around the world. Okay, so Cameron – or her avatar, the SimCavalier – was well known; she'd cracked some big attacks, stopped them in their tracks, leaped to the solution with some fey intuition and no little skill. She deserved the public kudos. The whole team did. They'd be celebrities.

"Cameron, calm down. Most people in the business know the SimCavalier, same as they see me, RunningManTech, out there on the forums. Is it so bad to get some real publicity? I know you've always been hiding, but maybe it's time we were recognised for the work we do?"

Cameron took a deep breath at the other end of the call. She was furious. She needed to step back and deal with this professionally. Ross was a long-standing colleague and partner, but not a friend, she reminded herself.

"No, Ross. The position of this team is unchanged. We stay in the shadows. If you want to take advantage of this and move into the light, you do it alone. Your contract is very clear."

Ross kicked a pebble hard against the fence. It made a satisfying clang. Bugger Cameron and her obsession about secrecy. He said nothing.

Cameron paused. "Ross, they appear to have traced back to my home as well as hacking the bank cameras. We need a full investigation into the breach, and we have to close it down. Are you with me?"

That was a surprise. How the hell could anyone have found her home? Ross had thought even finding the right bank would be a long shot. They were dealing with hacks, not hackers.

"Yeah, of course I'm with you, Cameron, always," he lied.

"Team meeting, face to face, 10am tomorrow."

The call went dead. Ross scowled. It was going to be one hell of a meeting.

At the house, Cameron put the screen down, a knot of worry growing in her stomach. She realised that she no longer trusted her business partner. His reaction to the breach had changed everything.

•

The children were now up and in full voice, careering around the house with Roxy in happy pursuit. Tara was giggling hysterically as Nina caught her and tickled her under the arms. Dilan chased the girls, growling, in his dinosaur pyjamas. Cameron jumped aside to avoid being swept up in the tangle of children and dog as they crossed the upstairs landing. It was hard to be serious with this amount of laughter in the house, she reflected, grinning broadly. Today was her time; stop worrying.

Sameena came out of Dilan's bedroom carrying a pile of clothes. "Dilan Silvera," she called, "get your bedroom tidied! I have just found all your dirty school uniform under your bed. It needs washing for tomorrow. Go and put the rest of your things away."

Grumbling, Dilan turned away from the chase. "But Muuum…"

"Don't argue, young man, get organised. And you, Nina. Are you ready for school tomorrow? You have tests coming up. Make sure your room is tidy and you have everything you need. Tara, come and help me."

Cameron watched, impressed, as the children went about their chores. Sameena had them in hand, there was no doubt. She made a mental note to tidy her own room before she left.

"Sameena," she called, bounding down the stairs with Roxy, "I'm heading back to London this afternoon. Is there anything you need me to do?"

"So soon, Cameron? I had hoped you would stay until tomorrow morning. You are always welcome, you know. And the children will be sorry not to spend more time with you."

Cameron was tempted to change her mind, but no, it would be a rush to get back if she stayed until the morning, and besides, she didn't want to break another date with Ben.

"I'm so sorry, Sameena, I promised a friend I would meet them tonight. I'll stay for lunch, of course, but I'll catch the train about four."

Mollified, Sameena smiled at her sister-in-law. "Vicky is coming for lunch. We will have some nice family time after all that fuss yesterday. Would Mandisa like to come over as well?"

"Great idea, Sameena," said Cameron happily. "I'll call her now."

•

The eight of them were crowded around the large table in the dining room. Nina was holding court at one end, with Dilan and Tara to either side of her. Sameena served the children from the large steaming bowls in the centre of the table, ignoring complaints of 'but I don't like onion'. Aunt Vicky, sitting between Sameena and Charlie at the other end, was in a much better mood.

"How's Donald?" asked Cameron, between mouthfuls of delectable chicken curry.

"Oh, he's much better, thank you, Cameron. I'm sure he'll be fine. He seems to have pulled round. He went out this morning and was back to his usual self. He dug up next door's bedding plants." Aunt Vicky sounded almost proud.

Cameron glanced at Mandisa, who was sitting next to her, and tried not to laugh.

"Was that next-door-Andrew-Taylor or the other neighbour, Aunt Vicky?"

"Oh no, not Andy. Henry, on the other side." A shadow passed across Aunt Vicky's face. "He doesn't much like Donald. And his dog keeps trying to get into my garden. The new wall makes no difference. Do you know, he wouldn't pay a penny towards it?" She paused as a thought struck her. "Oh, Cameron, Andy was asking after you this morning. He wanted to know about the training you do. I think his company in London wants to talk to you."

Cameron blinked. "Uh, okay, I don't turn down work… What's his business?"

"Oh, darling, no idea. Shall I give him your mailbox address?"

"Not the private one, Aunt Vicky. Ask him to contact Argentum – here, I'll write it down for you – and tell him I work for them."

Cameron exchanged a look with Mandisa. She was not happy about this at all. She changed the subject rapidly.

"Mandisa and I are thinking of a girls' week away. Get some sunshine. We've collected enough carbon offset credits for flights. Where shall we go?"

Aunt Vicky piped up, "We always went to Spain. Most of the big resorts in the south are under water but the northern coast is still lovely." She paused, and grinned naughtily. "Oh, we had such fun. The Canaries should be alright, surely, they have mountains?"

Charlie shook his head. "The weather there can be terrible. It's warm but it's wet. A last-minute trip when you know the weather forecast might work. How many flights do they have now?"

"Oh, not many these days," replied Mandisa. "The weather's caused problems for regular tourism and there are barely any scheduled flights. I'm thinking about the Emirates – they have a good flight quota because of their international trade and connecting routes, and it's just about cool enough at this time of year – it won't go over fifty. The hotels will still be open."

"That sounds like fun." Sameena's eyes were dancing. "Charlie, we should take the kids on a long-distance holiday. It would be lovely to fly again. We must be close to having enough carbon points for us all to travel?"

"Not far off," agreed Charlie. "Maybe next year? Let's start looking at what we could do. Shame most of the equatorial belt is out of bounds. Cam, do you remember going to Singapore with mum and dad when we were kids? The Gardens by the Bay? You must have been, what, eight?"

"Wow, yes, just. The photos are in the cloud somewhere. That was the last long-haul holiday we had all together." Cameron fell silent, remembering another time and place, another world, and the blissful ignorance of childhood.

Charlie coughed. "Anyone fancy a walk?"

The chatter picked up again as the children cleared the table and stacked the dishwasher, under protest. Roxy gambolled around, anticipating a trip round the fields. Aunt Vicky excused herself, but the six Silveras and Mandisa headed out along a footpath around the outskirts of the village. The clouds had started to clear, with patches of sunlight filtering through. The children and the dog jumped in puddles and squelched through mud, washing their boots and paws in the running water of the brook. Mandisa and Cameron strolled behind, at a precise safe distance calculated to keep them dry and free of mud.

"So, tell me more about this new squeeze?"

Cameron blushed. "Oh, he's just a guy I met at training. I liked him the moment I saw him, but he had a girlfriend. That was a while ago. Then he turns up, we're talking, I find out they've split up… The rest is history."

"Does he know what you do?"

"Not yet. Not exactly. Although I had to break a date last week, and then he came over on Thursday night and I got back so late that he must be wondering. It's not always a nine to five job."

"I need to meet him, Cam. I'm in the lab all of this week, but I'll be coming down to London for a conference the week after next. Drinks?"

Cameron gave in gracefully. "Of course. You can give him the third degree. You'll like him."

Mandisa smiled, victorious.

"The taxi's here." Dilan had been looking out for it. The tiny autocar pulled up in the entrance to the driveway and the door swung open invitingly. Cameron emerged from the front door of the house with Tara hanging onto her hand. "Aunty Cam, don't go."

"I'll be back soon. You behave yourself."

Nina sidled up to her. "Aunty Cam, can I do my homework in your attic? Please?"

The invasion begins, thought Cameron.

"Sure, babe. The computer won't switch on for you, though. You'll need your screen. And be careful with my things, won't you?" She treated Nina to a mock scowl, which Nina returned in kind. They glared at each other for a moment, and Nina cracked first, laughing. Cameron grinned and tousled her hair.

Charlie joined them, carrying Cameron's bag. "Be careful, little sis. We're here if you need any help at all. Let me know how you get on with Ross tomorrow."

Cameron nodded gratefully. The taxi beeped insistently.

"Better go – I don't want to miss my train." Bag stowed and seatbelt fastened, the autocar purred off up the hill. The roads were quiet, and Cameron reached the station without incident. As she boarded the train, her screen pinged, and a handsome face appeared: dark eyes, black hair, and a cheeky grin.

"Hey, you, I'm on my way home. Want to meet me at the station?"

Ben smiled, his eyes twinkling. "Sure. See you soon."

•

The last rays of the evening sun illuminated the terracotta tiling of the small restaurant, giving it a rich, Mediterranean glow. A waiter appeared at their table by the window, which looked out onto the street and a small city park beyond. There was more blossom on the cherry trees, and daffodils nodded in hosts on the grass, bright as dusk fell. "Would you like to see the dessert menu?"

Cameron looked up, glass of wine in hand.

Ben grinned broadly. "Always."

The waiter produced two small headsets, each with a clear glass viewer. They slipped them on, and gazed at the menu. Here, a tempting slice of chocolate fudge cake, icing glistening, whipped cream sliding slowly down the angle of the slice. There, a rich crème brulée, the caramelised top cracked, revealing the custard beneath. A portion of tiramisu in a tall glass, the layers of sponge, cream and chocolate moist with coffee and marsala. Lemon cheesecake sat on a plate, garnished with strawberries. Nutrition labels hovered over each choice, defining calories and sugar content.

Cameron pulled off her headset and the menu vanished. "Tiramisu, please."

Ben took one last, longing look at the delicious selection and handed his viewer back, too. "Crème brulée."

The order was in progress in the kitchen before the waiter turned away from the table.

Ben gazed outside at the light evening traffic as it flowed silently by. "Do you remember when we still had petrol engines?" he asked.

Cameron nodded. "Oh yes, I grew up a few miles from the race track. I remember the sound of the engines on Grand Prix day, those Formula One beasts, even at home in the garden. We had air force planes overhead from time to time, too. Although they still fly, of course."

Ben sighed. "My dad loved cars, and racing, and everything about them. He was devastated when the last of the petrol cars were forced off the road. We used to go to rallies. I drove, sometimes, I learned how to fix things – things the on-board computer didn't handle. In fact, some of the cars we worked on didn't even have computers."

There are still some old cars around, thought Cameron. Out in the countryside, where no one was looking. There were at least three such cars garaged in the village, that she knew of. Probably more.

Ben continued. "He goes to the electric Grand Prix, and it's exciting, but he says he misses the roar and the smell and the danger. I don't miss the pollution in the city, though." That was true enough. Respiratory disease was at an all-time low thanks to the clean air.

"Is that how you ended up in engineering?" Cameron was curious to know more about him. "What kind of things do you work on now?"

"I design for printers. It's all very well saying you can print anything you want, but the blueprints have to be absolutely right in the first place. No use printing a bicycle that's missing a wheel, or makes the frame out of rubber and the tyres out of metal, is it." Ben laughed. "There are some terrible tales about that kind of mistake. A whole batch of whistles with no hole in the middle." Cameron giggled. "Chairs with three legs. Car doors with no handle or hinge." He shrugged, grinning. "Engineers have never gone away. We just changed the way we work."

Their food arrived, and Cameron took another slug of wine. She really didn't have room for pudding, but the augmented reality menu had been too good to resist. Ben tucked into his crème brulée with gusto. Cameron reckoned he'd be able to finish of the tiramisu if she struggled.

"So how did you get into tech, then?" he asked, as he scraped the last remnants of caramel cream from the side of the dish.

"My mum, I guess. She was always into computers. Bits of programming here and there, always up to date, made sure my brother and I knew the basics of coding and security right from primary school. I think I was six when I coded my first web page. It was very pink." She paused, reminiscing. "I was nine or ten when the first wave of big cyber attacks came. Lots of fuss about hidden 'bots, systems falling over, data breaches, people losing money through hard currency account scams and huge raids on the early cryptocurrency wallets. I remember thinking, surely this can be stopped. It's so easy to get it right, why do so many people get it wrong? That evolved into the work I do now. Training. Bringing people up to speed for their own good. Patching and fixing security systems. It's fun."

"Yeah, getting it right counts for everything," reflected Ben. "We're quite alike, aren't we?" He smiled at her, and her stomach did a backflip. "So that cyber attack, last week, is that why you had to break our date?"

Cameron dropped her gaze to the table. She really didn't want to involve Ben in the hidden part of her world, not just yet. "Yes. There were a few things to sort out. Don't worry about it. It's very rare."

The waiter approached and Cameron looked up, relieved at a chance to change the subject.

"Would you care for coffee?" he asked.

"No thanks," replied Cameron. "Can we get the bill?"

The waiter nodded and handed Cameron a screen. She approved the tab and tip, and thumbed a payment authority. The coins left her account instantly and credited the restaurant. The waiter smiled and retrieved his screen. "Thank you very much, you have a nice evening, now."

Ben gave two swift taps on the autocar call screen on the wall as they left the restaurant. A minute later, a small two-seater vehicle pulled up by the kerb. "Your carriage awaits, ma'am," joked Ben, executing a sweeping bow and guiding Cameron to the door. The taxi bore them back towards her apartment, and as Cameron settled in Ben's arms she was content. Cyber crime could just wait, tonight.

6: FOLLOW THE MONEY

Ben watched as Cameron gradually awoke, disturbed by the morning sun coming through the open blinds. She blinked her green eyes and they caught the light, clear and emerald bright. Ben smiled and gave her a playful poke in the ribs.

"Hey," she protested.

"Time to get up, sleepyhead. I have to get to work, and so do you."

Cameron yawned and looked around at the clock; Ben was right. She heard the faint sound of the cat mewing pathetically for attention, shut out of the bedroom. Cameron clambered out from an entanglement of covers and let the little animal in. She could hear the kettle automatically warming up in the kitchen, but coffee could wait for a few more moments. Snuggling back into bed with boyfriend on one side and purring cat on the other, Cameron was enjoying the calm before the storm.

Ben finally eased himself out of bed and walked towards the bathroom. Cameron heard the shower start to run. Spreading herself across the full width of the mattress without disturbing the cat, Cameron thought through the day ahead.

Team meeting. Sandeep, Ella and Pete had all seen the news reports and had messaged her before she'd tried to contact them, absolutely raging. Susie didn't quite follow the extent of the crisis that had occurred. Still no word from Joel or Noor who'd both been out of connected range all weekend, but they'd get the message in time for the meeting. Cameron had no idea how it would go. Ross could be unpredictable and fiery, and his reaction to the broadcast images had been completely unexpected. She thought back through the time they'd worked together. Had he ever expressed this deep need for recognition? If that was really how he felt, he'd kept it very quiet.

Whatever the outcome, she would go the bank in the afternoon to work with Bill on planning training. The day to day work patrolling the borders of cyber security was her bread and butter, the life blood of the business she had built over the past decade. That said, the visit would be a good chance to dig deeper into the CCTV hack and try to get some leads.

She was fascinated by the message hidden in the Speakeasy subroutine. What did it mean? Where had the attack originated? Cameron quickly scanned the forums on her smartscreen. The community was still discussing its source and meaning, with no clear consensus. There were a lot of talented folk out there; between them, they could generally guarantee to take down, dissect, and trace the perpetrators of any attack in just a few days. There was a distinct feeling of frustration across the network that this mystery was foiling the best of them.

The best of them? Cameron knew she was at the top of her game and commanded a lot of respect from her peers. It was no false modesty to say that she probably was the best they had, right now. They would be starting to look to her for answers. Time to get to work.

She sighed, and as the sound of running water ceased in the bathroom, she threw back the covers and stood up.

•

The offices of Argentum Associates lay behind a plain entrance in an anonymous side street a few hundred metres from Cameron's apartment. Sandeep was the first to arrive. He checked the coffee machine: supplies were running low. "Order a full set of coffee refills please, two litres of milk, and some fresh muffins."

"Order received, delivery in four minutes," replied a disembodied voice.

Sandeep opened the dishwasher and retrieved eight mugs which he placed on the table, along with a plate for the muffins. The delivery hatch beeped; he walked across to the wall and collected the order. The muffins were slightly squashed. Sandeep tapped the 'three out of five stars' option on the delivery hatch touchpad, muttering under his breath. He tipped the misshapen cakes onto the plate and looked up as Ella and Susie walked in.

"Good weekend?" Ella and Susie glanced fleetingly at each other, and Sandeep raised an eyebrow. "Really? Hah, you devils. Thought you were having fun on Friday."

Susie blushed. Ella deadpanned, and hurriedly changed the subject. "Yeah, great thanks, until we saw the news report. What the hell happened?"

Sandeep sighed. "You know that second breach that Joel and I picked up while you lot were asleep on Wednesday? The hack into the CCTV? That's where some of the pictures came from. They had access to the live feed for around eight hours, maybe ten hours tops, but I wondered if they'd been into the archives. I guess this confirms the older records were compromised, after all."

Pete came through the door as Sandeep was speaking. "What I don't get," he said, "is why the hell were they in those records on that day in that bank? How did they know what they were looking for?"

"That's the million-coin question, isn't it, guys?" Cameron had arrived. She grabbed a mug from the table – another gift from the kids, with a cartoon dog on it – and placed it under the coffee dispenser. "Cappuccino." Turning away, she smiled as she saw the plate. "Muffins, good call. Where are the others?"

"Joel's running late, power outage on the Northern Line. I guess Ross'll be stuck in the same place unless he's cycling. Noor's on her way."

"Great, while we're waiting, let's have another look at that breach, Sandeep. Did you isolate the original trojan?"

"Yes, boss." Sandeep brought it up on the screen. "Very simple, dropped straight into the network past their two-factor authentication. Easy to identify the culprit, an employee on an unsecured wifi network outside the building."

Pete stepped up to the screen. "I've seen this style of code before. It's a real quick and dirty routine. Nothing sophisticated."

"Where have you come across it? We need some context, Pete. Sandeep, did you get details of where the employee was, what the circumstances were?"

"Sure, Cameron. Bill and I spoke to her. She went out for a break to check emails from her kids' school in the coffee shop over the road. That's a regular haunt of bank staff."

"City Coffee? I know it," interjected Susie. "In my last job, we did some work there, tightening up their access point. They were keen to be seen as a safe place for city staff to relax. I'd be surprised if anything got through. That was a year ago, but they're good with updates."

"Interesting. Sandeep, did you check the device? Smartscreen, was it?" Sandeep shook his head. "Never thought."

"That's fine, it's been a busy week. I'm back there this afternoon to speak to Bill about training plans. Come along with me and do some digging." Cameron turned to Pete. "Where have you seen this before?"

"Not this exact thing, but the style's familiar. I think – and I could be wrong – it's old-school surveillance stuff. I'll run it by a couple of my contacts on the forums, see where it's popped up since military days."

The door opened and Ross marched in. "Sorry I'm late. Looks like there was a power outage on the tube. Bloody autocar swarm closed the road, couldn't even get through on the bike. Cleared now."

Cameron nodded. "Joel was stuck on the shuttle. I guess it's all recharged now, if the swarm has cleared." Sure enough, Cameron caught sight of Joel in the street view camera, approaching the door, closely followed by Noor. "I'm not convinced that commandeering autocars to recharge power failures is a great idea in the city. There'll be commuters and tourists stuck all over London wondering why their lift spat them out onto the street. More disruption than it's worth."

Ross laughed nervously. He hated the small talk. It was time to get down to business. "Yeah, it was a bit of a mess out there," he muttered.

All eight of them were now assembled, coffee and muffins in hand. No point delaying the main discussion. Cameron took on a serious tone. "Okay everyone." She took a deep breath. "You've all seen the footage that was broadcast on the news channels. How the team was compromised is something we will get to the bottom of later. Right now, we have to agree our position going forwards."

She paused, and looked around at her team.

"Your contracts all have a secrecy clause. I set up this business with my eyes open. We tackle the worst of cyber crime, we put up defences against perpetrators across the globe. We're not dealing with innocents. We're stopping not just idiots but determined criminals.

"Take your bit of sleuthing last week, Ella: you found the spike in futures trading. We have a good estimate of how much money was creamed off the markets thanks to the Speakeasy attack. Ross, I see you put the details on the forums, thank you."

Ross looked shamefaced for a moment; he hadn't credited Ella with the find.

"Other teams have looked into the model and confirmed Ella's findings. Someone out there has made a decent profit, but it could have been a lot more. I bet they're not your average investor. It's very likely they commissioned the build of Speakeasy to create that artificial drop in value. I imagine they'll be a little pissed off that we stopped the attack in its tracks so quickly. What happens if they decide they need us out of the way so they can try again?"

Ross snorted. "I think you're blowing it out of all proportion, Cameron. This is central London, not the Rio favelas or the Macau underworld. You have more chance of being crushed by swarming autocars than being taken out by a Cosa Nostra hit man."

Cameron turned to him, face like thunder. "I hope you're right, Ross, for your sake, because it's your face that's plastered all over the internet, and your handle that's linked with the futures model."

Ross just glared at her, unable to respond.

Susie interjected. "I'm sorry, Cameron, I know we have the secrecy clause here, and I'm happy to abide by it, but we didn't have anything like that in my last job."

Pete shook his head. "Susie, you were out in the open doing prevention work, brilliantly I might add. Now you're on the front line. It's different. It's more like the military intelligence environment that I used to work in. There are some dangerous people out there, and we're a hair's breadth from them."

Joel nodded in agreement. "I'm ex-army too, Susie. Pete's right. You can't underestimate the threat level." He looked at Cameron, and across to Ross. "I know they have Ross's face, so he's running the biggest risk, but they have your name too, boss. Judging by the other photos, they have an idea where you live, too. Who's the poor schmuck that looks like Ross, anyway? Do we have a responsibility to him? How do we protect you all?"

Cameron started to speak, but Ross cut her off. "What if I don't want protecting, Joel? What if, for once, for bloody once, we get some kudos from the public for saving their hides? For fuck's sake, Joel, you got a medal for sitting on your arse in a tent in the desert. We stop the whole banking system from crashing round our ears, the man in the street gets his pay credit and lives to spend another day, and not a whisper. The news channel's all over us because they want to thank us."

He was standing now, his face flushed with anger.

"Don't you see that? We're heroes. If we really are targets, hiding away puts us in more danger. Go public, and we'll get any protection we need, police, security, whatever." Ross slammed his hand against the wall in frustration. The monitor wobbled.

"Calm down, man." Sandeep put a hand on his shoulder. Ross shrugged it off angrily. The group was silent.

Noor spoke up tentatively. "I'm with Cameron. I don't want publicity. I just want to do my job."

Ross glared at her.

Ella rounded on him. "Ross, do you really understand what happened with those cryptocurrency futures? It looked like nothing much, a tiny blip, but it was a major manipulation of the markets. The timing had to be precise, the targets were carefully chosen – we're not dealing with amateurs. I don't know how we're going to do it now, but we have to protect our identities." She sat back in her chair, and glanced at Susie, who looked shell-shocked.

Cameron sighed. "Pete, Joel, I know your positions. Noor, Ella, thanks for your support."

Sandeep raised his hand. "I'm with you. Anonymity as far as the general public is concerned."

Susie looked at Cameron and nodded. "Me too."

Ross was shaking. "So, what now? You're out in the open, SimCavalier, 'I Cam Silvera'? Won't take them long to crack that, for all your stupid secrecy. '*I don't want publicity*'," he mocked. "You've got it, what are you going to do?"

"They don't have me," replied Cameron icily. "They have you. Your face. My name, sure, but your face. They've done some real digging. Yes, they've photographed my apartment block, but they are looking for you. God help you if the wrong people find you first."

Joel looked at them both. "Ross, you're outnumbered seven to one. No publicity. We can get our lawyers to force the images offline. Pete and I can tighten up security for both of you. God knows how they found your apartment, Cameron, I know how much you do to hide that address."

Ross grabbed his bag and headed for the door. "Fuck you, Joel, I'm not interested. I'll step into the light. I'm not afraid. I'll deflect them from Cameron though. How about credit for Speakeasy going to RunningManTech as far as the public's concerned? Make them forget the SimCavalier. You can stay in your hidey-hole."

The rest of the group sat, stunned, as he left the room, slamming the door behind him. They could hear him clattering down the stairs and out of the door.

Cameron felt sick to her stomach. She turned to Pete, and her voice shook. "Suspend all of Ross's access to Argentum Associates systems. We redouble our efforts to trace the breach back to source. We keep this team secure."

She leaned onto the table and put her head in her hands.

•

Bill met them at the bank's reception just after lunch. "Hi Cameron, good to see you." He shook her hand. "Sandeep, you too." Another handshake. He ushered them through the barriers and upstairs to the now-familiar meeting room. "Let's get the diaries on screen and organise these training sessions. How does next Tuesday look for you? We can run four short sessions. That'll cover the bulk of the staff for a quick refresher. And Wednesday for a run-through with my team?"

"That's fine with me, Bill." Cameron reiterated the dates and times to her calendar. "You should get a confirmation through in a moment."

Bill's screen pinged. "Got it. That was easy enough. Anything else I can do for you now?"

Cameron looked him directly in the eyes. "We have another errand, I'm afraid. Did you see the news channels over the weekend?"

Bill nodded soberly. "Yes. That CCTV footage. Thank goodness you picked up on the breach at the time. Nasty stuff. What do you need from me?"

Sandeep spoke up. "We need to know more about the breach. We have to trace the source. Can I get a look at the device which was compromised? Do you have it?"

"Sure, the staff member concerned has been reprimanded but she's at work today. I'll get her in. Reception!"

The monitor came to life. "Yes, Bill?"

"Get me Tracy Gardner."

A momentary pause, and another face appeared on the screen. "Tracy, hi, can you bring Grace to the first-floor meeting room. Get her to bring her smartscreen with her." The face on the screen nodded assent and turned away to the bank of monitors behind her as the picture faded.

A few minutes later came a knock at the door. A nervous looking woman in her early forties, small and overweight, was ushered in. She was clutching a smartscreen.

"Hi Grace, just sit down, nothing to worry about. You've met Sandeep Tahir before, and this is Cameron Silvera. You're not in any trouble, we just need a little more information from you."

The woman nodded nervously.

Cameron smiled at her, and spoke calmly. "We know it was an easy mistake to make, Grace. It's possible that someone went out of their way to trick you and you simply wouldn't have known. Well done for following all the security rules for authentication." Grace gave a cautious smile. "Sandeep here would like to have a look at your smartscreen, and I'd like you to tell me exactly what happened in that coffee shop."

Grace glanced at Bill, who nodded encouragingly. "Uh... I went out for my break early. I had a message from my kids' school. I've only just come back to work here, I'm normally working from home so I can sort things out straight away. Tracy let me go ten minutes before everyone else."

"Do you usually go there on break?"

Grace nodded. "Yes, a lot of us do, it's really handy and the cake's lovely. I've logged on in there before, loads of times, is that wrong? Everyone does it."

Bill backed her up. "Yes, I've done it myself. The café owner has always made a real effort to provide a secure environment, it helps trade. Bank policy is that two-factor authentication over a secure network is fine for remote access. How else would everyone work from home?"

Fair point, thought Cameron. But all the protocols and policies in the world could not secure systems against the lethal combination of determined hacking and human error. That was what paid her wages, and it would never end.

Sandeep looked up. "The café network is on there, properly secured from what I can see. It's been in regular use, but it wasn't accessed by this device on Wednesday morning."

Grace looked confused. "But... I picked the usual network and it connected straight away. They always change the password on Thursdays, and it was Wednesday, so I didn't even think."

"No, Grace, it picked up a signal alright, but not the secure café network. Look, here..." Sandeep turned the smartscreen around so everyone could see. "There's the café network, GreatCityCoffee, last access Friday, Thursday, Tuesday. You're certainly keeping them in business, aren't you. Wednesday morning, you were connected to this one – GraetCityCoffee. Looks almost the same. It would be the first to appear on an alphabetical list. If it was being generated within the café it may have been the strongest signal. It's completely unsecured so you'd go straight on."

Grace stared at him, wide eyed.

"You were unlucky, Grace. Whoever it was knew that staff spent their breaks in that café, and you were simply the first to arrive."

"Was there anyone else in there?" Cameron interjected. "Were you alone?"

"No one else was inside. I had the whole place to myself. Well, the waiter was there, obviously. There might have been someone at the tables on the pavement, I'm not sure."

Sandeep looked at Cameron. "Would that have been close enough to generate a strong signal from a mobile relay?"

Cameron shrugged. "It's our best guess. Go and pay them a visit.

Get a feel for the distance the signal would have to travel. Grace, where exactly were you sitting?"

•

Sandeep stepped into the café. They were already cleaning up ready to close. The lunchtime rush had been over for an hour or so. A few chairs had been stacked on the tables. Sure enough, there in the far corner against the wall, furthest from the door, was the little sofa Grace had described.

The waiter glanced at him. "Can I help you?"

"Just an espresso, please." The machine behind the counter flicked into life as water began to boil. The waiter lounged on a solitary chair, watching the news channel on a wall monitor, and glancing at both the coffee maker and the little vacuum 'bot that hummed around under the tables gathering up the crumbs and debris of the day.

Sandeep sat down on the sofa and stretched out casually, gauging the distance to the other side of the café. It was a small space, and it wouldn't take a powerful relay to cover the whole area. But Grace had been alone in here. Could a signal get through the thick walls?

Looking closer, he noticed that part of the front wall had been knocked through at some time in its history. The inconspicuous partition that filled the void was designed to open, presumably to take advantage of the few days of English summer. This material was likely to be thin enough that a signal would not be obstructed. The theory was holding up.

His coffee arrived, a thick crema hiding potent dark liquid in the tiny cup. He drank it in one gulp, wincing at the caffeine hit. Good espresso, rich flavour, very smooth. Too many people confused bitterness for strength. He'd come back here, if he was passing.

Thumbing the payment, he nodded to the waiter and strolled back outside. Sure enough, there was a table set right next to the exterior of the partition wall. Any signal broadcast from there would deliver perfect coverage to the rest of the café.

Sandeep glanced around for cameras. There had been none in the café itself, but he spotted a familiar shiny globe on a lamp-post a few metres away. Public CCTV to the rescue. With luck, the last week's recordings would still be available, and Argentum Associates was one of the few private agencies who had official access to them.

•

Back at the office, Cameron logged on to the secure public CCTV archive. It wouldn't be hard to track the target. They had the location, and the time must be in a window of only a few hours. Sandeep's hands swept across the birds-eye view of London that was displayed on the screen, searching for the right camera, zooming down with precise little taps.

"Okay, there's the bank. Is that the café awning over the road? Yep. I see the tables. Ah! This is the one." Homing in on the camera position, the screen seamlessly changed to show the current view from the lens, and a timeline. Sandeep scrolled carefully along the timeline as the image flickered from light to dark and back, day and night. "Wednesday… 4pm, 2pm, noon, ten, eight… What time did the system breach occur?"

Cameron dug back into the files. "Uh… 10.32. Grace's office access record shows she went out for her break at 9.49. They worked fast, didn't they?"

Sandeep gently moved the images forwards, frame by frame. "The place is open… bit of a rush, must be breakfast time…" He counted the customers in, and counted them out again. "Okay, it's empty right now, that's 8.45am. Two, three, four people going in… two straight back out again with takeaway cups. Here's someone else… Sitting at the table nearest the door… Waiter comes out..." He kept scrolling. "9.25… two people leaving from indoors, they're the ones who arrived just before nine… Okay, another bod's arrived, sitting at the table next to the partition. Could be our mark. Waiter comes back, delivers to the new table. The person by the door's finished their breakfast… they've moved off… he clears the table… There. Nine fifty-two. Grace has arrived. So, the only other person at the café is this guy on the central table."

"Zoom in as far as you can," ordered Cameron.

"Can't get close enough to see in detail." Sandeep shook his head.

Cameron peered at the screen. Something about the figure looked familiar. It triggered the memory of a dog walker in the distance.

"You're not going to believe this," she said with mounting horror. "I think I know who that is. How the hell is he mixed up in this?"

Sandeep turned to her in surprise, but both of them were suddenly startled by an incoming call alert.

"Argentum Associates, can I help you?" Ella answered.

"Hi, I'm trying to reach Cameron Silvera," came a man's voice. "Is she available?"

Cameron waved frantically at Ella to stay off camera and keep the company logo on-screen, and shook her head violently.

"I'm sorry, she's with a client. May I say who called?"

"Sure," said the voice, jovial and friendly. "It's Andrew. Andrew Taylor."

●

Cameron returned to her apartment just after six, drained by the day's drama. She fed the cat and checked the fridge. Time to do some shopping. The discreet cylinder on the kitchen shelf relayed a list back to her, things she'd noted over the past week that had been used up. She added a couple of extra treats and placed her order.

Doing her shopping manually felt good. People tended to rely on their household tech to the extent they no longer noticed it. Her fridge did not do product promotion, or place orders automatically for direct drop to the shelves. For that matter, her portal was still an old model, sitting visible on the shelf, not integrated into the smart lightbulbs in every room. It wasn't the same as walking to a shop with a written list, but Cameron felt she was as much in control as she could be, without compromising comfort.

The cat skated through the apartment, its tail bushy with adrenaline. Drone on the balcony. Cameron opened the glass doors and collected her order from the little machine. To keep her hand in, and relieve some stress, she intended to cook. Fresh ingredients had come straight from the market stalls. She dug out her mother's old recipe book, heavily annotated, and searched for a skillet and saucepan, a chopping board, and a sharp knife. Most important of all, she picked a glass from the cupboard and opened a bottle of Yorkshire claret.

The sauce bubbling and pasta boiling, Cameron poured another glass of wine and turned to the computer. Gaming her IP address again, she logged in to the forums.

Most of the buzz was around the strange message they'd cracked on Friday, and the weekend's revelations on the news channel. She ignored the gossip around the news, other than posting a quick disclaimer to say that the pictures were not of her. No one on the forum knew her gender or location for sure; it would soon be written off as a hoax.

There was some activity around Ella's cryptocurrency futures analysis, posted by Ross. She frowned. He hadn't explicitly claimed the credit for that breakthrough, but neither had he given Ella, or the rest of the team, any mention. He was a funny creature. She wondered what he was up to. There had been no message since he stormed out of the office. Better to leave him be, leave him to train, get the fight out of his system. He'd either come back round, or the lawyers would silence him.

•

Ross eyed the encroaching storm clouds. Night was falling as he cycled home, and a chill wind heralded rain. He was still furious. Furious with Cameron and the rest of the team for their obsession with secrecy. Furious, if he dared admit it, with himself. He craved recognition, but always sabotaged his own efforts.

Two weeks before a big race, and he'd dropped his training to fix the cyber attack. Yes, it was his job, but deep inside he admitted that Cameron was a sympathetic boss, and would have made allowances for him, changed the shifts, accommodated his needs.

Ross pushed harder up Crouch Hill. His legs felt good. This wonder supplement could be helping to give him an edge. Of course, that could just be his imagination – these things took time to build up – but it was a nice gesture from the coach.

The rain began as he crested the hill, clattering on his helmet and soaking quickly through his jerkin. Sweeping into the estate, he stowed his bike safely and made it through the door as the storm hit.

Ross dripped his way to through to the bathroom and pulled off his wet clothes. He lay naked on his bed for a few minutes, staring at the ceiling, cooling gradually. Conscious that he was stiffening up, he made his way to the shower, enjoying the warmth of the water.

Clean and rested, he ordered the next meal in his nutrition pack. It dropped into the delivery hatch, hot from the kitchens, thirty minutes later. Protein and carbohydrates balanced to perfection, antioxidants boosting his immune system, and delicious too. Back on track. Only the race mattered now.

Supper over, glass of water in hand, Ross sat back and relaxed. He swiped idly at his smartscreen, and glanced at the forums, setting his status to Away, browsing and avoiding comment. He didn't want to talk to anyone. Posts full of bloody cats again. Honestly, they were supposed to be professionals. Cameron showed as active. Where did she claim to be posting from today? Tokyo? Hah. Total paranoia.

There was a flurry of activity on the thread around the hidden message. What the hell was 'hurricane season' anyway? Cameron would be in the middle of that, taking all the glory, no doubt. He had no wish to see her.

He glanced at the thread he'd started with Ella's theory on cryptocurrency futures. A few comments, curious to know more, but nothing had been posted for a while. They could wait. He logged off again, and loaded an old game. Lost in the challenge, making longer and longer links of coloured blocks, time passed quickly. When the alarm sounded for bed time, it startled him.

The lights of the main room faded with his footsteps as he trudged wearily to the bedroom. He still felt like a failure. For all his bluster this morning, he'd done nothing to make contact with the news channels. They were still searching in vain. Underneath his bravado, there was a tiny knot of worry. Perhaps Cameron was right, after all.

7: EXPOSURE

"'Batten down the hatches for hurricane season?' That's bizarre." Noor looked puzzled as Cameron demonstrated the cracked routine to the group.

"We know there's always another threat around the corner. Why bother to warn us? It's not specific enough to make any difference." Pete was equally confused.

"What's hurricane season?" asked Susie.

"The time of year when there used to be a lot of storms around the Caribbean," replied Cameron, reading from a wiki on the monitor. "Says here it used to run June through November, lots of big storms one after the other." She turned to Joel. "That's where your mum and dad came from, isn't it? Any insights?"

Joel leaned back in his chair and stared at the ceiling. "Haven't been back there for years. Still got cousins on the high ground. Not enough carbon credits for regular family visits. But yeah, hurricanes. Wow, there were some bad times when they made landfall. My dad was a kid when the big one hit the island. Ripped through the place. He and my aunts and uncles all ended up sleeping in one room in their grandparent's place, little more than a shack. That was before drones and 3D printers and shit. They had to rebuild the place themselves. That's why my dad left, in the end. Economic disaster. More jobs over here."

Sandeep chipped in. "They used to name them, didn't they, all the tropical storms?"

"Yeah, man, they're still doing it. There are just more small storms for longer, and then a couple of really big ones make landfall each year." Joel paused. "Don't you remember the big storm that hit Cayman last year? They called it Hurricane Usain, I don't think they'd been so far down the alphabet before. Wrecked the main financial district. All those offshore bank accounts were disrupted for days. Drone relief couldn't get through because of the winds. Took weeks to recover, and some of the last low-lying parts of the islands completely disappeared into the sea."

Sandeep and Ella nodded, recalling the news reports.

"Wow," said Susie. "Is it that bad every year?"

"Pretty much. If they're lucky, the storm blows itself out at sea, just some bad weather and waves. If it makes landfall – if it becomes a real hurricane - there's a lot of destruction. Nice analogy for a cyber attack. The attack hits its target, there's chaos. If not, if there's just a daft worm floating round, or a short-lived Distributed Denial of Service attack, there's much less disruption. We have to tackle both."

Sandeep turned to Cameron. "So, what does this all tell us? I guess the Speakeasy crew have other things in the pipeline."

"We know they can time attacks," Ella chipped in. "The financial analysis showed the timing had to be precise for them to hit payday this time."

"If we work to the traditional 'hurricane season', June through November, I guess we have to assume there's something coming any time from a month from now to six months." Cameron shrugged, and Sandeep snorted with ironic laugher.

"Well, that really helps," he said sarcastically.

"Hold on though," said Joel, "hurricane season isn't one storm. This sounds more like they're throwing a whole bunch of things at us."

"Yeah, that's what we all thought last night on the forums," confirmed Cameron. "It won't change our normal defensive behaviour at all. If anything, we'll be advising our clients to tighten up. We stay right on top of updates. We put pressure on the software providers. We warn the powers that be. We'll have to, because if we don't, and an attack, or a series of attacks, happens, and they find out the whole threat intelligence community sat on their hands, didn't react to a warning, there will be hell to pay."

"Damned if we do, and damned if we don't." Joel frowned.

"I don't get it," said Ella, flatly. "What's in it for them? If we close them down, if we're watching for the next attacks, then won't they lose out?"

"Vanity?" suggested Pete. "Mad cyber criminal, James Bond style, telling us the plan because they're sure we won't live to tell the tale?"

Cameron shook her head. "I don't know what's going on here, but I do know we have absolutely no choice but to redouble defensive efforts." She gathered her thoughts. Time to make a start. "Noor, can you analyse the last, say, fifty years of hurricane records and see if there's a pattern, a peak? That may give us a better feel for the timing of a major attack. Sandeep, Susie, check through client records, see if we can bring forward security reviews, highlight any sensitive systems."

Ella interjected. "What about that enquiry yesterday? Andrew Taylor? He was asking about training."

Cameron scowled. "I don't know what he wants, but I'm willing to bet it's not training."

She glanced at Sandeep and raised an eyebrow. They had kept their findings quiet until now; it was time to share them with the team. "I met him at Charlie's this weekend. There is a chance that he has something to do with the CCTV breach. I don't know if this call is pure coincidence and a genuine enquiry, or he's put two and two together and linked Argentum with the pictures." She paused, considering her options. "Tell you what, Joel, Pete, can you pick this one up? Get a feel for the situation. Find out where he's coming from. We'll take the business if it's genuine, of course, otherwise scare him off if need be. Keep me out of it for now."

The two men nodded, and went into the small alcove reserved for training calls, careful to position the camera so that the other party would see only the two men, and the company's logo on the wall behind.

Cameron called over to them. "I messaged Ross on Saturday to dig around and find out about him, but he never came back to me. Not enough data, I guess. But here's what I know already." She flipped his name, address, and description over to their screen.

"Cheers, Cameron. We're on it."

"Ella, can you go back to your cryptocurrency futures. If that's the best way for the Speakeasy crew to make money, can you model some likely scenarios for profit? We can keep an eye on the markets and possibly steal a march on them."

Ella smiled, and bent to her work. Cameron knew where the strengths of her team lay. She also knew she was missing Ross, for all his moods and fury. He might change his mind. She hoped so.

•

Andy abandoned the London office in favour of home. They'd had no contact from the mysterious SimCavalier, nor from the anonymous source of the tipoff that had led him to the bank. His attempts to speak to Cameron had met with a brick wall. Two brick walls, to be precise.

"Mr Taylor? My name is Joel Bardouille, this is my colleague Peter Iveson. We've received your enquiry about a cyber security review and training."

Even on the screen, Andy could tell these were big lads.

"If we can run over a few details about the business, and we can arrange a site visit to discuss in more detail. What's the company name?"

Andy panicked slightly, and obfuscated as best he could. "Oh… it's not my business, I'm enquiring for a friend. It's just that I met Cameron, Cameron Silvera, at a social event and she said she did training…?"

"That's correct, Mr Taylor," replied the bald man, Peter. "I'm afraid Ms Silvera is occupied on another contract. Would you like us to contact your friend directly?"

"Uh, no, I mean, uh, I can take details for now. He has, uh, a manufacturing business. Just a small operation. What kind of things do you offer?"

"The standard service, Mr Taylor," Joel explained smoothly. "We conduct penetration tests on the network and servers, identify any weakness that may be vulnerable to direct attack, review your friend's software for the most recent security updates, and deliver staff training. It's normally human error that compromises any installation."

Not much different to my job, thought Andy. Human weakness brings in the stories. He reflected on the tipoff he'd received. What weakness had prompted that exposure?

Odd, though. Cameron had said she worked in robotics training. Had these two gorillas gotten the wrong end of the stick? Or was she closer to the world of the SimCavalier than he'd anticipated? Was her presence at the apartment block no coincidence?

"So, I guess Cameron would handle the training? Could I possibly have a chat with her when she's available? I'm sure we can arrange the other things with my friend, but I would love to find out about…"

"I'm sorry, Mr Taylor, but Cameron is completely committed for the next few weeks with existing contracts and a planned vacation. I am sure that Joel and I will be able to complete whatever is required. It's not something that should be left for long."

Andy admitted defeat gracefully. "That's fine, thank you, gentlemen. I will speak to my friend and come back to you with his answer." He terminated the call, puzzling over the new twist.

At the other end, Joel and Pete, sat back and laughed. "Round one to us, Cameron. He didn't know where to look. He's determined to get to you, isn't he?"

"Find out who he is, will you? Aunt Vicky was clueless. She thinks he's great. I don't reckon there's anything sinister going on with him, but he may be mixed up in something bigger. It really doesn't feel right."

Sitting in his study at home, looking out towards the village street,

Andy reflected on the call. Although he was no closer to Cameron herself, he knew she had lied about her work. She was concealing something. Protecting a boyfriend? Time to do some digging with his neighbour.

Andy brightened up as he heard a drone arriving. One of the big advantages of living in the country was the access to fresh food straight from the farms round about. As the world warmed, the supply grew of local fruit and vegetables that once had to be imported. He stood up and went to the front door to collect the delivery.

The drone slowed, approaching its destination. At that moment, a ginger streak flew out of the bushes in his neighbour's garden. Jumping and twisting in the air, Donald brought the drone down, skilfully dodging its rotor. Andy howled with rage, watching his fresh avocados bounce down the hill. Donald sat, purring loudly, one paw on the crippled machine as it struggled weakly to fly.

Aunt Vicky rushed out of her house, as fast as her legs could carry her. "Donald! Donald! Bad cat! Bad!" She flapped at him ineffectively with her hands. He ignored her, and rolled over, toying with his catch.

Andy had a better idea. Whistling for Jasper, the dog came bounding out and Donald took fright, belting back into the bushes at high speed. Andy picked up the remaining produce, and pressed the breakdown button on the drone. Within the hour a recovery drone would arrive to pick up its fallen fellow and bear it away for repair.

Aunt Vicky wrung her hands and stumbled out an apology. "Andy, I'm so sorry, naughty Donald, he hasn't been well, you know."

"He looks perfectly healthy to me, Vicky." Andy softened. Here was a golden opportunity. "I was about to put the kettle on. Care to join me?"

•

Cameron and her team settled down to the familiar routine of contract work, the Speakeasy threat averted and the ripples of that initial disruption fading. With the hurricane warning uncovered, and a man down on the team, there was more urgency to their delivery. Ross had sent a curt message asking for two weeks off to focus on his race. Cameron granted it instantly.

"Hey, Noor, how's that pen test going? Want a coffee?" Ella looked over at her colleague, hard at work digging through the servers of a small insurance group.

"Love one, thanks Ella. This system is like a sieve. It took me less than an hour to get through. The developers should be shot. I've managed to get hold of some of their stored hashes, I've dropped some scripts into the existing code and they haven't been pushed back, and the session information is wide open. Going to be fun tightening it all up." Noor smiled, satisfied at a job well done.

"Wow, that's bad. So, if you were up to no good, you could identify data in their blockchain, drop a mine in there to collect information whenever you wanted it, and keep an eye on who's accessing the system? Nasty."

The door opened, and Sandeep and Joel appeared. "Coffee time? Perfect."

"How did the training go, guys?" asked Ella. "You were over at the university today, yeah?"

"Oh wow," sighed Joel. "They may be the brains of the country, but some of them really haven't a clue about cyber security. The amount of legacy software they hang on to is appalling. The IT guys know their stuff, but they're fighting a losing battle. The academics have settled into a nice routine of teaching the same thing year after year, so they keep an old device with a defunct operating system to run their out of date materials, then they hook it up to the network, and the whole place is wide open. No clue."

Sandeep grinned. "Joel was pretty surprised. I've seen it before. They're all wrapped up in their own worlds. Takes a lot of careful nudges from us to bring them up to speed. We're getting there, though. Managed to prize an old Windows 20 laptop off someone today, their IT girl said she owes me, she's been trying for years."

Cameron, Pete and Susie trooped in, returning from a patch-and-update job. "Bang up to date. All finished." Cameron turned to the accounts controller. "Complete signoff for SussexGrid and issue invoice."

A disembodied voice replied. "Invoice transmitted. Can I help you with anything else?"

"No, that's all for now." Cameron turned to the rest of the team. "Hey, I'm meeting some friends later, want to join us for a drink? I know it's a school night, but we're doing well. We've earned a break."

They gathered at a big table in the window of the busy pub. Pete tapped out their orders on his smartscreen and they thumbed their individual payments over to his account. A few minutes later, the drinks were delivered to their table.

"No drones?" asked Susie.

The waiter laughed. "The wooden beams play havoc. Kept catching the rotors. Beer showers for the punters. Much easier to deliver by hand."

"Cheers." Pete raised his pint to his colleagues and Cameron's friends.

"Introductions," said Cameron, taking a drink. "Most of you know Mandisa. Mandisa, this is Susie, she's just started with us. And this is Ben." No further details. Joel raised an eyebrow discreetly at Ella, who grinned, guessing that this must be the mysterious boyfriend.

Pete glanced over at the monitor on the wall, showing the latest news. "Hey, guys, the latest Mars mission is taking off. Look – live shots from Kazakhstan."

Ben spoke up. "I got involved with this, a bit anyway. Engineering for the 3D printers they're taking. They literally have to print all the tools and equipment they need. Much easier to take a hold full of extruded raw materials ready for the printer than the actual items, especially if they have to deal with unexpected situations on-planet. It's sustainable, too. They can recycle and reprint."

The others around the table looked impressed.

"Wow, that's really something," said Noor. "You're part of the expansion of the galactic empire."

Ben laughed, embarrassed. "I guess so. In a really small way. Amazing though, that printing was the breakthrough for colonisation. Who knew?"

Mandisa grinned at Cameron. "I like him," she whispered. "If he can hold his own with this crew, he's a keeper. Are you bringing him on holiday?"

Cameron shook her head, and whispered back. "Not enough flight credits, and anyway, it's our break."

Ben spotted them conspiring together, and smiled affectionately across at Cameron. She grinned back, smitten. Mandisa could be right.

•

Race day arrived, grey and damp. Ross rose with the murky dawn just after five, and made his way to the start to meet the team. Race pack full of energy gels, invigorated by a strong ten days of training, he proudly pulled on the elite team colours.

The coach gave him a slap on the back. "Brilliant work the last couple of weeks, Ross. You've really focused, and it's paid off. You're in the shape of your life."

"Couldn't have done it without your support. I appreciate you going the extra mile for me."

The coach gave him a curious look. "All your own work, Ross. Now, go and show them what you're made of."

Ross adjusted his wetsuit and made his way to the pontoon on the north side of the lake, poised to dive into the chill waters of the Serpentine. He could see the bikes lined up in the distance, ready for the second leg. He held his nerves steady, and bumped fists with his team-mates. They were ready to go. The whistle sounded, and he dived, thinking of nothing else but his race, focused completely on his task.

•

"Bloody hell, Ross, you knocked it out of the park!" "Well done, mate, fantastic race!" "Knew you had it in you, you grumpy sod."

Ross couldn't control the grin that spread across his face. Personal best time, in front of the Olympic selectors. Right up there as part of the elite team, keeping the youngsters at bay.

The coach arrived, congratulating all his athletes. "You've all come on massively. That was a hell of a performance all round. Some brilliant personal best times. Dave, Adebayo, Ross, Tomasz, top class showing for the elite today. I'm proud of you all."

Ross was happier than he'd been for months. The exercise high and the buzz of recognition coursed through his veins. This was what he wanted, this was worth the sacrifices.

Maybe walking away from Cameron had been the key to focusing on his training. Had he overreacted? Perhaps. It would be time to take stock next week. He still hadn't followed up the news channel broadcasts. With nothing to add to their first revelation, the story had faded. He was old news.

Was it time to offer an olive branch, try to regain Cameron's trust? Once the celebrations were over, he'd think about it.

He and his team-mates were borne off to cool down and collect their gear. Tomasz and Dave drew the short straw for post-match testing along with the placed competitors, and disappeared to the officials' tent. Ross slowly packed up his wetsuit and bike, changing back into his regular grey hoodie. The cheers were still ringing in his ears. Most of the spectators had now drifted away, although one middle-aged, balding man still stood by the finish line, his unblinking gaze focused on the athletes as they as they left the park.

•

Andy was getting frustrated. It was more than two weeks since the pictures broke, and he hadn't had a sniff of the real identity of the SimCavalier. The forums he prowled under an anonymous handle were silent; the subject had been discussed, rebutted and dropped. The SimCavalier himself had posted a clear statement that the pictures were not of him. Andy suspected this was purely a smokescreen.

He needed Cameron to join the dots, but she would not respond to his calls. The muscle from her company, the two ex-forces lads, had made it very clear that she was unavailable, unless this was a genuine sales enquiry. His appeals to Aunt Vicky seemed to have fallen on deaf ears – she was more concerned about that awful cat, and although after Donald's attack on the drone she had promised to speak to her niece, nothing had come of it.

"No choice, Giles. Let's go and pick him up. I don't want to tip my hand to Cameron, it'll get me into too much trouble at home. Total discretion, okay?"

Giles laughed. "Aunt Vicky sounds formidable."

They walked towards the cluster of autocars that sat waiting outside the office block, nose-in to their charging stations like a row of multi-coloured suckling piglets.

Andy winced. "Oh yes. She keeps me in order. She keeps most of the village in order. Her cat's another matter. Furry bloody liability."

"How are we going to do this?"

"Can't risk Cameron spotting me, if she's there, so we'll keep away from the apartment itself. If you play the lost tourist, get him to the car, I'll be waiting. Just want to confirm his ID, see if he wants to play ball. If so we bring him in."

A large blue autocar detached itself from the cluster and rolled silently to a stop at the kerb. "Borough Underground Station," Giles ordered. The car waited for their seatbelts to click, and pulled off towards the main road. "Looked like he was heading that way the morning we photographed him. With luck, we'll pick him up on the way home."

Positioning himself outside a busy chain café, midway between the station and the turn to the apartment, Giles sipped coffee and water and scanned the passers-by for his mark. Mothers with pushchairs crowded the café and pavement tables, meeting friends for a chat and a break before collecting older children from school. Looking up for a moment, Giles saw heavy-laden delivery drones flying along the street high above the silent traffic. Sunlight glinted off solar panels, some static, others jutting from the rooflines, turning constantly to catch the rays as the sun moved across the sky.

He re-focused on the swelling commuter crowd coming from the direction of the station, and after almost an hour he spotted the distinctive grey hoodie. Thank goodness it was another cool day.

Leaving his seat, to the delight of the mums who immediately took over his table, he hurried further down the road and crossed over, perfectly timing his walk to intercept the man. Digging his smartscreen out of his pocket, he unrolled it and brought up a tourist map, pretending to study it as he struggled against the flow. He bumped artfully into the man in the grey hoodie, and dropped the screen. The man stopped and apologised.

"No problem, pal, my fault. Hey, do you know how to get to the market?" He pointed vaguely at the map, and the man frowned.

"You're going completely the wrong way. Here, follow me."

They set off northwards, Giles thanking the stranger profusely.

A few blocks later, the man paused. "I'm going this way, you just carry straight on, you can't miss it."

Giles thanked him again, and made to walk off. He could see Andy out of the corner of his eye approaching his mark on the side street. Andy drew the stranger aside and out of view. Neatly done, thought Giles.

He turned back and listened, out of sight. The man's voice was protesting, confused. "I don't know what you're talking about. My name's Rory MacPherson, I'm a researcher, I work at City University, I'm doing politics." He pulled out an ID card, and Andy studied it.

"Could you tell me where you were on Thursday 13th April?"

"Yes. I was at the university all day. Conference for external students. Presented a paper in the morning. There's footage on the university site."

Andy blinked. It was a cast-iron alibi. There was no way this could be the SimCavalier; no way he'd have been in the bank that day to be caught by the CCTV. He'd been over and over those pictures for two weeks, and he'd known all along that something didn't feel right.

He had the wrong man.

"I'm so sorry, Rory. This appears to be a case of mistaken identity," he said smoothly, handing back the ID card. "Please accept my apologies for bothering you."

Andy walked off up the main road, catching Giles before he was seen. Rory stared after him, shook his head, and walked on towards his apartment.

Andy slammed his fist against the wall in frustration. "The wrong guy. It's not him. I'm as sure as I can be that the SimCavalier lives right here. Maybe the guy on the bank footage isn't our man either. What have we missed? Let's get back to the office."

•

The two of them pored over the stolen CCTV images, frame by frame.

"Here's our man arriving on his own. Yes, I see now, the logo on his sweatshirt is a different shape, larger. Rory's in the clear. I knew there was something wrong. How did we not pick that up?"

Giles ignored him. Frustration and hindsight were not going to help. "There's another group coming in, but there's a glitch in the recording – look, it jumps, just there. Can't see much."

"Hmmm." Andy paused the playback and peered at the screen from every angle. "One tall guy with dreadlocks. That's odd, now, he looks familiar. I'm sure that's the muscle from Argentum. Joel Bardouille. Almost definite." There was a cold feeling in the pit of his stomach.

"Short dark-haired girl."

"Big solid bloke with no hair." Andy was sweating now. That could be other guy who'd been obstructing him for the last two weeks. Had he accidentally stumbled on the right group through Cameron?

"I can't make any of the rest out… Fast forward. Didn't we pick the original guy leaving around eight the next morning?"

Giles scrolled through the footage quickly, swiping the time bar sideways until he reached the morning. There was an influx of people running jerkily through the hall as the recording speeded forwards. Giles stopped it quickly. "Yeah, here we go, battling against the flow, our man with what looks like the same short dark-haired girl."

"And here they come back. Breakfast run. Okay, what was our next sighting?"

"Lunchtime. That was the last time we picked him up on camera before the feed was closed down. Look… here he goes. The dark-haired girl too. Your big bald guy, wouldn't argue with him. What about those two? The girls? Blondie in a short skirt, dark girl in trousers."

"Possibly. Yes, look, they've caught up with the other three in this next shot."

"So far so good," said Andy, still mystified. "So, there's five of them. Did you pick up any of the other guys over at the apartments? Mind you," he laughed, "could be one of the girls. You never know."

Giles shook his head. "Definitely not seen them before. The girls don't look…" Andy sat forward suddenly, cutting him off.

"Hold on. Where's the guy with the dreadlocks. He didn't leave with the others."

Giles turned back to the screen and scrolled through slowly. "Nothing yet… Ah, there. On his way out. There's three of them."

Andy took one look, and put his head in his hands.

"Oh god. It's her. It's Cameron. She's the one. She's our SimCavalier."

•

Ross slept late. When he woke, he was still on a high from the race. He dressed quickly and left the house, ignoring the chatter of the coffee machine. Making his way to a favourite café, he looked forward to the rare treat of eating a forbidden pastry and watching the world go by.

Sitting on a stool at the window, he watched idly as people passed by on the narrow street. Colleagues on their way to work, chattering in twos and threes, exchanging tales about the weekend. Solitary figures listening through earbuds to their personal soundtrack for a Monday morning, or focused on their smartscreens. Some were quite unaware of their surroundings, moving on autopilot. Others were scanning the world around them through an augmented reality lens, on screen or built into glasses, picking up advertising and offers from stores as they passed.

Music played in the café, and a monitor showed the news channels, presenters mouthing silently. Ross ignored both. Flipping through the latest news on his smartphone, watching occasional videos of the race, he didn't notice the stranger until he sat on a stool beside him.

"Good morning, Ross."

Ross started and looked round, confused. A fan? Where had he seen him before?

"You had a good race yesterday. Congratulations. Lucky you weren't picked up for testing, isn't it?"

The truth slowly dawned. "I don't know what you're talking about. I'm clean."

The man shook his head sadly. "Oh Ross, 'Silent Running' supplements? Did you really think your coach had ordered those for you?"

Ross's mouth went dry. "But… but… they came from the usual place…?"

"You understood what you wanted to believe. You took the help that was offered. You achieved your goal. As did I. RunningManTech, my employers would like your help. And you are in no position to refuse."

8: SALVAGED HONOUR

Ross's world came crashing down around him. He could feel his heart thumping in his chest. He looked at the stranger in horror. How could he have been so stupid?

"Come with me."

Ross stumbled out of the café. The man guided him to an autocar that waited nearby. "Get in."

They travelled in silence for almost an hour.

The autocar stopped in the middle of an anonymous industrial park in the suburbs. Blank office windows reflected the light. A small grove of wind turbines whirled in the light breeze. Every building had a south-facing pitch with solar tiling, drawing energy for the workers below. A few patches of scraggy grass attested to attempts to landscape the park, but they had fallen into neglect.

The stranger led Ross, still stunned and unresisting, through secure doors to a featureless, cream-tiled lobby. He gestured to a windowless office off the hall, which held a monitor, two chairs, and a table. Ross sat down heavily on the thin fabric cushion of the furthest chair, and leaned on the table, his head in his hands. The stranger took the seat nearest the door, demonstrably blocking Ross's exit.

The monitor on the wall hummed into life, a camera lens waking above the screen. Ross looked up, but the screen, though lit, stayed blank. Ross had no doubt that the camera, on the other hand, was actively broadcasting his reactions to the party on the other end of this call.

"Good morning, RunningManTech." The voice was synthesised. Could it be an artificial intelligence? Ross suspected not; this was simply a way of remaining anonymous and hidden.

"We have been following your career with interest. Unlike others in your field, you make no attempt to hide yourself."

Ross blinked. This had to be a joke. They were playing a trick on him, taking the mick over his attitude to privacy.

The voice continued. "The insights you have published show a comprehensive grasp of the mechanics of cyber manipulation. However, your most recent postings touch on the motivation of agencies like ourselves. We are concerned."

Ross found his voice. "Guys? Is that you? What the fuck are you doing?"

"This is not a joke, RunningManTech."

He knew that. The sting was serious. There was no way his workmates could be involved.

"Okay, I'll play along for now," replied Ross with false bravado, trying to keep the tremble from his voice. "How do you know who I am?"

"As I say, you make no attempt to hide. We have been following the activities of all leading threat intelligence specialists for many years. One by one, they have hidden themselves away. They conceal themselves behind anonymous nicknames. They mask their locations. They know we are watching. You, however, can be easily traced. From your home to your club to the businesses in which you operate, your location is always known. As you posture and brag online, you act as if you are immune."

Ross licked his dry lips. "So you know about RunningManTech in cyberspace. Who's to say that's me? Check the news channels. Seen the pictures two weeks ago? They say I'm the SimCavalier. You sure you got the right man?"

"Yes. Those reports are a distraction. We have known you for a long time." Images appeared on the screen: Ross at his home, last summer, in the garden. Ross with training partners at his running club, wrapped in a tracksuit, in winter. Ross and Cameron leaving the bank together, probably when they finished the recent job.

"We have a job for you, and you cannot refuse our request. You know that your sporting career depends upon it."

Ross put his head in his hands. He felt sick. What the hell had his hubris dropped him into?

The voice continued. "First, you recently posted your theory that the Speakeasy creators profited from the manipulation of cyptocurrency. Have you shared this theory elsewhere?"

"No." Warning bells were clanging, too late. He had to hold back from revealing the team's involvement, and the detail of Ella's work, for which he had claimed credit on the forum.

"Good. We have suspended new posts to that thread, reducing interest and speculation. We will resume these online discussions and provide our own proofs to discredit your findings. You will confirm that your analysis was inaccurate, and that your claims were pure speculation."

"Yes," said Ross quietly.

"Second, we are aware that you have close connections with the specialist known as the SimCavalier. We require you to update us on all his progress and insights as our next wave of attacks is deployed. If he becomes aware that you are working for us, it will be more than your sporting career that suffers. Do you understand?"

Ross stared in horror. The room swam around him as he tried to stand. The stranger at the door pushed him back into his seat.

"Your tacit agreement is not required." The monitor clicked off, and Ross allowed the stranger to guide him outside. He stopped and vomited violently onto the patch of thin grass by the door. The stranger waited until he had finished, then unceremoniously pushed him into the autocar, and it glided away.

•

Another hazy day in the desert, sand masking the blue sky. Mandisa shrieked with delight as the vintage land cruiser crested another tall dune, her stomach leaping as they swept down a near-impossible gradient. The line of preserved, petrol-powered 4x4s snaked across the undulating sand, each driver carefully following the tracks of the leader and throwing up a localised sandstorm in their wake. In the distance, the sun glinted off an expanse of solar farms. Closer at hand, they could see more solar panels on a stationary roof, the only clue to their destination. Tourists from Dubai and Abu Dhabi were taking an adrenaline-fuelled journey towards this shining star in the east, eager for the 'authentic Bedouin experience', buffet barbecue, and belly dancers.

Mandisa glanced across the seat at Cameron. "Isn't this cool? Best way to get you to relax."

Cameron flashed a broad grin, green eyes masked by designer sunglasses, clinging to the armrest on the door as they were flung around like riders on a rollercoaster.

The passengers in the two seats behind them looked less comfortable. These old vehicles running on fossil fuel were a novelty, but the smell of exhaust fumes and the noise of the engine, coupled with the violent movement, was making the other occupants look rather green.

To the relief of their companions, the land cruiser slowed to a halt, parking up with the rest of the fleet, disgorging gaggles of tourists at the camp. Several rushed for the toilets, others climbed a nearby dune, sliding down on makeshift sledges. Camels were tethered close by for short rides, once stomachs were settled from the drive.

Mandisa and Cameron climbed the dune, feet slipping as they struggled to gain purchase in the sand. Reaching the crest triumphantly, they gazed to the west as the sun dipped towards the horizon.

"Great to be off-grid for a few days, huh?" Mandisa looked sidelong at her friend.

Cameron grinned. "I'll still be checking the net when we get back to the hotel, but yes, it's a novelty alright. Anyway, the team has everything under control. Nothing urgent. No problems that they can't deal with."

True seclusion was getting difficult to find in an ever-more connected world. Some corners of the north of England and the Scottish Highlands had kept their dark skies and deliberate no-coverage stance. National Parks across the world were also, as a rule, havens of peace.

Gazing at the endless expanse of dunes and solar farms that stretched into the distance, Mandisa sighed with pleasure. She missed the warmth and big skies of her native South Africa, even though she had only returned to visit her grandparents a handful of times since emigrating at the age of eleven. This rare trip to the desert seemed to be a suitable panacea.

There was a general movement towards the compound as the sun finally set, and the evening's entertainment began: food, drink, and dancing. They tucked into barbecued meat and salads, seated on low cushions around the stage, relaxing in the desert warmth as the dancers performed traditional routines in flowing, cool costumes. Even in early May, the evening temperature was close to thirty degrees Celsius. No wonder the summers were now too hot for tourists.

The darkness around the compound had become total, and the entertainment ended. The host called for quiet, and one by one the lights in the compound dimmed. Lying flat on their cushions, Cameron and Mandisa's eyes adjusted to the blackness, and they stared at the myriad stars which revealed themselves. There were gasps around them. Dark skies were a rare treat.

"Where's Mars?" whispered Mandisa under her breath.

"It's really faint at the moment," Cameron answered quietly, careful not to disturb others who lay in silent awe. "It's coming back from its furthest point from Earth. There… I think it's there… see the red dot? It doesn't twinkle like the stars."

"I see it… so the mission is on its way to intercept it at its closest. That's neat. Hey, do you think we could see the rocket?"

Cameron laughed softly. "Hardly. It's more than a week out, it'll have passed the moon by now and be on its way."

There was a hum of low voices around the compound as people pointed out constellations, planets, and distant galaxies to each other.

"Just imagine," reflected Cameron, thinking of her boyfriend and wishing he had been able to come with them, "Ben's 3D printer programs are on board. I wonder what the first thing they'll print will be?"

"A bottle opener, no question, celebrate the landing." Mandisa giggled, then groaned and squinted as the lights began to glow again. The evening was at an end. They got up slowly and reluctantly gathered their belongings. joining the other tourists who were shuffling towards the parked land cruisers for the return trip.

The journey back was much shorter and smoother. The theatre of crossing the dunes like adventurers seeking a remote oasis masked the fact that there was a perfectly serviceable metalled road close to the compound, which ran straight back to town. Climbing out of the archaic vehicle at the door of the hotel, Cameron gazed up at the curved flanks of the majestic building, LEDs bathing it in ever-changing coloured light. The window of their room looked down on the old race track, the hotel forming a bridge. There were still cyclists training, or simply having fun, under floodlights in the relative cool of the night. She thought about Ben and the high-octane Formula One races of years ago. It must have been spectacular here when those races were running, engines howling and echoing under the hotel bridge as the drivers battled for position. Electric races were as fast, but the visceral thrill of the sheer noise had gone.

The next morning, the two girls discussed plans for their final couple of days over a leisurely breakfast.

"We could go to the waterpark again," suggested Mandisa. "Loads of fun, and it's going to be a hot day."

"Could go this afternoon... I fancy a trip into town, do some sightseeing. We haven't really left the island yet, apart from the desert trip."

Settled on their plans, the two of them hailed an autocar at the door to take them to downtown. The road swept past the huge development at Masdar, planned as the world's first zero-carbon city. Abandoned for years, it now had a new lease of life as renewable power generation technology caught up with the dream. After all, the country which had been built on the riches from fossil fuel now had to rely on the sun for its wealth, and it was succeeding against popular resistance, gradually winning round its people.

Passing the splendid white domes and minarets of the Grand Mosque, Cameron was surprised to see crowds. A demonstration? There was a sense of anger and noise, and more autocars were arriving from all directions. What could have sparked such a gathering? Mandisa shrugged; there had been nothing on the news channels.

Onwards to the downtown area, and the air of menace still hung around them. Cameron started to see posters in Arabic plastered on walls and on ad screens. Raising her smartscreen, the translation subtitles appeared. *"Modesty for women!" "Bring back the hijab!"*

Cameron frowned at Mandisa. "This is strange. Why would that argument be rearing its head again? It's years since the change, even here."

Mandisa was equally taken aback. "I don't like it. Something feels wrong. Let's just go back to the island… I'm not comfortable."

Cameron nodded. They took the cowards' way out, returning to their safe tourist haven and forgetting the troubles of their hosts as they squealed and screamed their way down flumes and slides like children in the bright sunshine.

The next day, sadly, they took their leave of the hotel, and made their way back to the nearby airport. Here, too, there was trouble.

"Fuel is not just for planes!" translated her smartscreen. "Fuel is our right!"

The two women skirted the protest and made it into the departure hall, crowded despite the handful of flights that were scheduled. The queue moved slowly, and Mandisa anxiously checked the time. "I don't understand the delay – we're cutting it fine."

Sure enough, a harassed-looking staff member came up and down the line. "Passengers for London? Passengers for London? Straight through here please."

They were ushered to a new desk to check their credentials and luggage. "I'm sorry ma'am, I can't retrieve your booking." Cameron glowered at the desk clerk and presented her screen with all the details on it. The poor man poked ineffectively at the keyboard, glancing at his colleagues who were all struggling too. "I will have to label manually… here is your reference… please proceed to the border controls."

"I smell a cyber attack," whispered Cameron to Mandisa. "I want to get home. I'll have a look at the forums when I get the chance."

Border control was no better. Where systems had become increasingly smooth over the years, easing from paper passports and rubber stamps to distributed, verified credentials held in the identity blockchain, there were border police milling around in confusion.

"Looks like they can't access the blockchain from here. Everyone is having to present verification manually, and that takes forever. I haven't seen this level of chaos close up for years."

"At least they're holding the flight," Mandisa pointed at the departure listings. "We'll be on it."

Curled up at the departure gate with her smartscreen, Cameron navigated quickly to the forums. A login from the Emirates wouldn't give her away. She'd used this location as a mask before; it should be lost in the noise. "Hey guys, what's going down?"

"Hey SimCavalier, good to see you. You've been quiet recently."

"Busy, guys, don't think I've been ignoring you on purpose. Need to know about any reports of compromised systems in the aviation sector and across the credentialing blockchain. Acting on a tipoff from a friend." She raised her eyebrows at Mandisa, who grinned.

Another member chipped in. "Reported glitches in credentialing, nothing major, the blockchain isn't compromised but there's been a DDoS attack on some key servers."

A distributed denial of service attack? Interesting, thought Cameron. That was an easy way to cause a lot of disruption, preventing normal queries from the border staff but without accessing or damaging the data.

"Several airlines are reporting failures in flight administration systems," came a second contributor, "but not across the board. Low level stuff, generally where updates haven't been applied."

"Thanks everyone. Catch you later." Cameron turned to Mandisa. "Nothing major. Some security loopholes being exploited, and a DDoS attack. It'll all be back online before we get home. More updates to do."

Boarding had finally started. Cameron and Mandisa took their seats for the long flight back to London.

•

Andrew Taylor had a lot on his mind. Once he had joined the dots between Cameron and the SimCavalier, he was lost for what to do next. His journalistic instincts cried out for the story. His basic human decency – rare in the profession – was pushing to protect her. She was Charlie's sister. Vicky's niece. She had battled to protect her identity for years, certainly for longer than he had been pursuing the story. Could he bring himself to compromise that for his own short-term glory? He suspected he'd be chased out of the village with flaming brands and pitchforks – or worse, with Donald on his tail.

Decency prevailed.

Andy tried calling her office again. Feigning continued interest in their services from the fictional manufacturing business, he enquired after Cameron. Away on holiday, he was told.

He approached Aunt Vicky. She was in a sulk after Boris had won a significant battle against Donald to reclaim control of the roof of the garden shed. Stop bothering my niece. She's too young for you.

Finally, Andy had no choice. He went to see Charlie.

Sameena opened the front door with a welcoming smile. "Charlie should be back soon. He's collecting Nina from swimming club. Come on in, Andy."

She showed him into the family room, where Dilan was working on the computer. As his mother came in, he started.

She looked at the screen and sighed. "Dilan, you said you were doing your homework. That is a game. Have you finished your maths?"

"Yes, mum. I promise. Can I keep playing?"

"Hmm, okay, but now Andy is here you should log out. Go and play outside. It's a nice day."

Andy laughed. "I was the same at his age. Let me think, what did we always slope off to play? Minecraft, was it? Yes, that's right. Great fun."

Sameena shook her head. "I couldn't get into that. My brothers enjoyed it, though. You should compare notes with Charlie on Minecraft, he and Nasser are always laughing about something called 'Stampy Longnose'. Ah, here he comes now." She went back into the hall. "Charlie, Andy is here. Shall I make some coffee?"

Charlie came in, jovial and relaxed. "Coffee sounds like a plan. Nina, go and hang out your swimming kit. Hi, Andy. What's up? Did Sameena mention Minecraft just then? Don't tell me you played that too?"

"A bit," replied Andy, relieved at the small talk. "I was a teenager when it came out. Great way to relax when I should have been doing homework."

Sameena reappeared with coffees, as Charlie reached over to an old bookshelf, dusty and untouched for years. "Hey, have a look at this. My Official Construction Handbook. I was, what, ten when I got this. Rollercoasters and diamond fortresses and pixelated pigs. Loved it."

His wife laughed as she left the room.

Andy swallowed. "Look, Charlie, I'm sorry. I need to talk to you about Cameron."

Charlie looked intently at him, suddenly concerned.

"No, nothing bad, at least… It's complicated. I've been trying to reach her. I need to talk to her. It's to do with my work. And hers. I need your help."

"What do you mean?" asked Charlie, puzzled. "Researching? Interviews? What interest does the news-watching public have in robotics training?"

Andy couldn't meet his eyes. "I'm sorry, Charlie. I know that's not what she does. I've been following the SimCavalier for years, detailed investigative work, trying to find what I thought was the man behind all this great security stuff. I even had a tipoff about the last cyber attack. I had no idea…"

"Jesus, Andy…" Charlie looked stunned as the pieces clicked into place. "Don't tell me those news reports last month came from you?"

Andy nodded miserably. "We thought we had him. Then I met Cameron here in the village. I knew I'd seen her before somewhere. It took me a long time to put two and two together." He grinned weakly at Charlie. "She's bloody brilliant, you know. A real superhero. She's saved the country's bacon more than a few times. Nothing but respect for her in the industry."

Deep down, Charlie was raging, furious that the sister he still unconsciously protected had been so close to exposure and danger. He couldn't really blame Andy, though; this was his job, and it was pure chance that Cameron had fallen into the path of his investigations.

"She won't talk to you. She won't step out of the shadows. It's too dangerous. Didn't the possible repercussions ever occur to you? Why do you think she was so hard for you to track down?"

"I know. I've told my editor we've lost the SimCavalier for now, that the tipoff was a hoax, and I'm still looking. I couldn't do it to her – to you – to Vicky." Andy looked across at Charlie. "I'd like her to work with me. If I can deliver cyber security scoops, it'll be a payoff for the years of research, keep my editor happy. I give you my solemn word that I won't compromise her identity."

Charlie looked thoughtful. "I can't speak for her, but I'll call her. She's away, due back this evening. I can't promise how she'll react, but thanks for coming clean. I appreciate it."

The two men stood up, and Andy shook Charlie's hand firmly. "Thanks Charlie. I'm sorry. I'll see you later at the pub?"

Charlie gave him a genuine smile. "You will. Thanks, Andy."

The first day back in the office is always stressful, Cameron reminded herself, as she settled back into the daily routine. A couple of smaller payments remained outstanding from clients: that was rare. Most contracts now triggered a coin transfer as soon as completion was confirmed by all parties. Debt collection was a job for Sandeep at his most persuasive. The human accountant at the other end of their AI interface reported steady cashflow, all salaries paid, and sales performing to target. It was a good time to be in the cyber security business. Cameron smiled wryly. She and her peers were probably the most consistent beneficiaries of cyber crime over time. The thought made her pause: park that intuition for another time.

Noor gave her a summary of news over the last week. "We're starting to see updates coming through from major software suppliers for the weaknesses that were identified through Speakeasy. I've done an initial review of all our clients and we're booking them in for visits, tests and training. There've been a lot of new enquiries through, too. It'll be good to have Ross back."

Cameron looked up quizzically. "He's been in touch?"

"Oh yes, he asked for a meeting with Pete, Ella and the lawyers. He's very contrite. He says he completely understands the concern over privacy, he's taken no action over the news reports, and he would like to come back to work."

That was good news, thought Cameron. For all his moods, he was thorough and worked hard.

"Great, I'll check things through with the legal team and get him back in the office. Looks like we have a busy summer ahead. He'll have plenty to keep him occupied."

She was still scrolling through reports when a call alert came through on her private screen. Charlie.

"Hey Charlie, what's up?"

"Hey Cam, couldn't get hold of you last night. Good holiday?"

"Fantastic, back in harness now though. Flight was delayed so we got back pretty late." She giggled. "Cyber attack on the airport systems. How ironic."

"Cam, I've been talking to Andy Taylor. No – wait," he continued hurriedly, as Cameron glared at him. "You need to hear this."

"Charlie, I know he's your friend, but…"

"Cam, listen. Do you know what he does?"

"No. He's been telling people he works with some manufacturing company, wanted training, I don't believe him."

"Oh shit, okay, I should have told you weeks ago but it didn't seem important. He's a journalist."

Cameron gasped in shock. "What? I didn't see that coming. Why the hell didn't you tell me, Charlie? You know the score."

"I know, I didn't realise he'd been trying to speak to you. He's been talking to Aunt Vicky too, but it never occurred to her to mention it. But Cam, it's okay."

Cameron snorted in derision.

"Let me finish," insisted Charlie. "He's made the connection between you and your public handle. He's been working on the story for years. As soon as he realised it was you, he pulled the plug. He wants to talk to you, but he won't expose you. I trust him. Why don't you meet? You could come here?"

"Too busy to come up right now, but I'll think about a meeting. Do you know what he wants?"

"I think so. He's looking for a story, of course, but what if you worked together? Give him some good cyber tales to write about?"

"Keep your enemies close."

"That's the spirit, Cam. So, shall I pass a message back to Andy? And what about this mystery boyfriend? Mandisa seems to think a lot of him."

•

Cameron arrived early on the terrace outside a bustling café by the river. She picked a table on the fringes, conscious that she wanted an easy exit. Joel lounged on a chair few metres away, browsing on his smartscreen. He raised it slightly, squinted, and laughed. Cameron caught sight of the logo of the latest craze in augmented reality games. She wondered what mythical beast he'd spotted floating down the Thames.

A cleaner 'bot arrived, all arms, and quickly tidied the debris of the last customers' refreshments onto a tray, before rolling away to the kitchen. A human waiter appeared and took her order; the café chain prided itself on these personal touches.

As the girl turned away, a voice called out. "And an Americano, please." Andy slid into the seat opposite Cameron.

She looked daggers at him.

He had the grace to look embarrassed. "I'm sorry."

Cameron sighed. "You're sorry that it was me, or you're sorry for trying to expose a completely innocent party to potential danger and end their career?"

"I'm sorry it was you. I knew the consequences of the investigation could be difficult, but I was following the story." He looked rueful. "Ethics and consequences are not always at the forefront of news gathering."

"You're right there." Cameron laughed despite herself. "So, where do we go from here?"

"I gave my word to Charlie, we are not running the story. My editor is furious with me, thinks I've given up, and so close to the prize. I'd love to put someone on a pedestal to recognise the work you do, even if it can't be you. Who was the guy we filmed, anyway?"

"Oh, he'd lap up the attention, he would. But he wouldn't have a job any more. Strict secrecy clauses. No hero for you, unless he goes out on his own, and he wouldn't last five minutes." She paused. "Okay, you don't have a story. What do you want from me?"

Andy leaned forward, keen to get her on side.

"Okay, there are plenty of good tech journalists following the scene, sources who help out when there are attacks, that sort of thing. I'd like you to be my source. Get the real story out there from a top threat intelligence operative – heavily disguised, of course."

"Dark glasses and a false nose, that'll do it."

Andy grinned.

Cameron looked thoughtful. "There's a lot of daft stuff gets written. It could be good to have a public voice that doesn't compromise our position."

This was looking promising. Andy ploughed on. "This could be a partnership, Cameron. I bet there are things we work on that could help you do your job. Stories that come to us, advance warnings, news that hasn't broken. We had an anonymous tipoff that you would be in the City of London during Speakeasy – would it have helped you to know about that?"

"So that's how you found us. Interesting. You moved pretty quickly."

Andy blinked, startled.

Cameron laughed at his confusion. "We did our own investigations, Andy. Why do you think I've been avoiding you? Saw you bugging the café that Thursday morning. We didn't have to hack anything to find you, either. Sloppy."

Andy gave her a sideways look and she grinned at him. "I guess we'd better alert the bank they've got a mole. What time did you get word?"

Andy thought for a moment. "Late on the Wednesday afternoon. Took us a while to figure out where exactly we were looking. Had to narrow it down through reports of outages."

"That early, huh. That's pretty much when the attack started. The leak must be high up."

"Actually," replied Andy, "we can't be sure that it came from the bank. In fact, as it specifically mentioned the SimCavalier, I'm certain it's originated from the cyber security community. Could that be the case?"

It was Cameron's turn to be wrong-footed. "That never occurred to me, Andy. Not something I'd expect from our side." She paused, reflecting. "Andy, I accept your apology, and I trust Charlie's judgement. I think we can work together. I'll help you with good stories, you help me with an eye on the wider world."

"Thank you, Cameron." Andy was enormously relieved. "Look, there is one other guy at work who knows who you are. My colleague Giles. He's been with me on this story. I'd like to bring him into my confidence. Don't want him accidentally blowing your cover. Is that okay with you?"

Cameron nodded. "Yes, as long as you can trust him. You know that if he causes any trouble, the deal is off, and Charlie will know about it."

Andy winced. "It's your Aunt Vicky who scares me more, Cameron. I would hate to cross her."

He looked up as Joel wandered over in response to a wave from Cameron. "Andy, Joel, I know you've met before." The two men shook hands. "We're going to do some work together. I'll brief the team this afternoon." She turned to Andy. "Let's set up a more formal meeting, get your man Giles in too, and see exactly where we can help each other." Cameron drained the last of her coffee and stood up. "Better get back to work. Thanks, Andy. See you soon."

Andy watched the two of them as they left the terrace, and waved as they turned the corner. Relieved, light-headed, he felt as if a weight had been lifted from his shoulders. He had played fair by Charlie and Vicky, and salvaged his own career.

9: HURRICANE SEASON

Ross looked downright miserable as he sat facing his colleagues in the Argentum Associates office. Cameron had cleared his return with the lawyers, and his access to the company's systems had been restored. Nevertheless, he felt as if he was on probation. In the back of his mind, he tried to suppress the horror he felt at the betrayal he was undertaking. It's the only way, he reminded himself. The only way to keep his reputation as an athlete intact. Possibly the only way to stay alive. He was under no illusions that the stranger and his associates were deadly serious.

"Nice to see you, Ross," ventured Susie. "How are you doing?"

"Great run in the qualifiers," said Sandeep encouragingly. "That's you with a shot at the next Olympics, is that right?" He sounded impressed.

"Good to see you got down to some solid training when you had the chance," added Joel. "Cleared your head, yeah?"

"Thanks, guys. Yes, it was a good race." Ross's voice was flat, despite trying to sound pleased. A good race, perhaps, but at such a price.

"I'm glad to be back," he continued. "I'm sorry. I misjudged the mood around publicity. I didn't mean to fly off the handle like that. The whole fuss has died down, anyway. No more news reports."

"Cheer up, you grumpy sod. It's water under the bridge now." Cameron continued, brisk and business like. "You need to hit the ground running, RunningManTech. We have a lot of work to do."

"'Batten down the hatches for hurricane season.' Yes, I guess we do. What do you want me to cover?"

Cameron pulled up a work schedule on the nearest monitor.

"We've got some patching and updates to do for a raft of clients. New security updates have been released by some of the major software providers for internal server operating systems and the big utilities installations. Standard stuff. Noor, Sandeep, Pete, Joel, can you make sure they are applied across the board."

The four of them nodded. "Sure, Cameron, in hand."

"Ella, can you and Susie keep digging on those financial models." Cameron paused. "Ross, you know you dropped some info about the futures trading scam onto the forums? I notice that there's been a bit of activity there recently, and the work has been widely discredited. Even you chipped in on the thread to say you're not sure it's genuine after all. What's going on?"

Ella, startled, protested. "What the hell? Those figures are good…"

Ross started to apologise. "Ella. I know your work's sound. I'm sorry, but I thought it would be better to downplay the findings."

Ella had a face like thunder.

Ross rushed on. "Isn't it a good thing, though, with this focus on secrecy and everything? Not playing our hand publicly? I thought it would help "

Cameron shrugged. "Forums are hardly public. We need other teams to know what they might be facing. Ella, keep working. We'll publish insights as we go along, and keep our banking contacts informed."

Ella looked happier.

"Okay, Ross, I need your analytical brain. Work with the others client by client, get into any old, patched, custom systems, chase down the vulnerabilities that you find. Sweep for phishing emails. I'll handle the ID 10-T factor. Identify obsolete software that really should have been replaced. Refresher training across the board, try and minimise human error. Ella, Susie, when you're not crunching numbers you can get involved with the training too."

There was a flurry of movement as the eight of them got up from the table and moved to separate screens around the walls of the office. The level of noise rose as calls were placed to clients, appointments booked, and plans made. Cameron glanced across at Ross, who was coding up a scanning routine for deployment in email servers. He looked pale and drawn, but was absorbed in his task. He should be happy, she reflected. He'd been desperate to return to work, and he'd posted a fantastic time in his last race. Everything should be coming up roses. What could be bothering him?

Ah well, that was Ross. She dismissed the thought, and went back to her work.

•

It began slowly. The powers in the shadows gently teased the public networks, their untraceable 'bots provoking arguments, fuelling divisions, and spreading falsehoods across vulnerable communities. Uncorroborated statements and provocative posts were shared and spread like wildfire, as people shared whatever accorded with their world view, disregarding evidence and experts. Sources went unverified as memes and fake news gathered millions of followers, polarising communities and stirring up conflict.

Andy was the first to notice the trend as he monitored post sentiment across the world.

"This is odd," he called over to Giles. "Have you seen the latest global mood scores?"

Giles looked up, and a few other heads appeared over their monitors. There was a hum in the newsroom. "What's going on, Andy?"

Casting the graphs to the big screen, Andy explained. "This is a live feed tracking the moods of posts on all the public communities on the web. The tone of posts, the content, the frequency, the use of language; all together these indicate whether people are happy with what's occurring in their lives."

"Clever stuff," observed Giles, impressed.

"Oh yes. We keep tabs on moods. It's very interesting around election time, gives us a heads-up on national reaction to political statements during campaigns. Some governments are finally getting wise to tracking sentiment around policy statements, too."

Giles nodded. "I remember seeing these when we covered the presidential election two years ago. No one expected Bruno Mars to clinch the nomination; we spotted it before it happened."

Andy grinned. "Yeah, that was a good one. We've been staying right up to date with these stats ever since. Never know what we'll pick up next. So, the last couple of years in the US have been generally pretty stable. There's always discrepancy between rural and city mood ratings depending on policy emphasis but it's not too abrasive. We see a nice sweep of polarised moods country-wide around Superbowl time, but that's all good-natured stuff, to be honest.

"In England and Wales it's the same picture, generally. You get the occasional blip with big sporting events. Scotland depends on the time of year: happier when the days are longer. Weather patterns have an impact on mood, which is always a laugh but hindsight's no use in that business; the weather channel scoops us every time." There was a ripple of laughter round the room.

"Europe, steady patterns of happiness, occasional sweep of common misery as against pockets of delight when the extreme right wing are agitating. Russian bloc, still assimilating the re-absorbed nations and sketchy connectivity, but moving around a steady average."

"What about the southern hemisphere?" called an Australian reporter from the other side of the office.

"Southern hemisphere? You're all mad as a box of frogs. Says so here."

"No change there, then," chuckled the heckler.

"Moving on..." Andy grinned. "Latin America and Africa are really diverse but mood patterns hold regardless of individual national cultures. Asia, now, that's a tough one. China's a nightmare to track. So many different platforms; we get some decent data from Renren, Weibo and Fenda but it's not enough to draw inferences..."

Giles interrupted. "Okay Andy, we get the point. You know your way round these trends, and they're normally pretty steady within their own cultures and political systems. So, what's going on?"

"Unfounded polarisation is what's going on, Giles. Have a look at the last week for – what's this first one – Europe. Okay, we've had steady fluctuations as we'd anticipate for most of the year. There've been no significant policy announcements or major incidents. No sporting events on a national scale. But look: over the last month we've seen greater extremes of happiness and dissatisfaction."

Giles nodded. "I see that. Are you sure there's no local variation around, I dunno, weather, like you say, or kids being off school. That'll affect the happiness rating for parents." There were a few knowing laughs from their colleagues. Andy shook his head.

"No, we've adjusted for those. Some of the trends are actually reversing the expected social mood for the time. Bank holiday in the UK, no rain, everyone's grumpy. Where's the sense in that?"

"Fair point," Giles nodded. "What about the others?"

"Here's the US stats. You can see the big blip for the Superbowl back in January. Then everything settles back to where it should be. Now, all of a sudden: boom. Polarising sentiment. No reason for it.

"Look at England and Wales again: there's a blip around the local elections in May, and the FA Cup Final, but those have settled, and to be honest there were no real surprises." He flipped quickly through the remaining pages. "They're all the same. Something's going down and we don't know what it is. Fortunately, I know someone who will." He grinned at Giles. "Let's go and see our friend."

•

Cameron was alone in the office when the entrance alert buzzed. Glancing up at the screen, she saw Andy and Giles hovering on the street. "Let them in," she ordered, and then watched as Giles followed Andy out of street view and onto the hallway cameras.

"Morning, Cameron. How are you?"

Cameron shrugged. "All the usual stuff, Andy. Training idiots to change their passwords and remember them, and reminding them not to trust email clickbait. Patching systems that haven't been updated because there were more important things to do. Gently teasing obsolete software out of the hands of people who are convinced they don't need an upgrade. Same old stuff." She looked up and smiled wryly. "What can I do for you?"

"I've got a puzzle for you to solve," declared Andy. He yawned suddenly.

Cameron glanced at him. "Late night? Get yourselves a coffee." She nodded at the machine in the corner.

Andy looked grateful and barked, "Americano. Double," in its general direction. He laughed. "That bloody cat of your aunt's, Donald, was scrapping all night. Wrestling with the noisy black cat over the road. I ended up chucking a bucket of water over them. That soon shut them up."

Andy collected his coffee and sat down opposite Cameron. He gestured for Giles to join them, and brought out his screen. "Okay. Cut to the chase, we're seeing some bizarre polarisation of opinion and sentiment worldwide. We don't know where it's coming from. We think you might."

Cameron nodded approvingly. "Good. I think I have an idea. I started noticing this when Mandisa and I were on holiday. The country's stable despite all the changes over the last decade, but there was something kicking off under the surface. Demonstrations at the airport against the aviation exclusivity on fossil fuel. Protests in the city calling for the return of the hijab for women. As you say, polarisation. I got Noor to have a detailed look at the local web activity, as her Arabic is way better than mine, and she identified an increased output of downright inflammatory stuff from sources that are almost certainly chatbots."

Giles leaned forwards. "What do you mean?"

"Okay," said Cameron. "Chatbot 101. At any time, at least a fifth of the accounts across web communities are not human. We've known that for more than twenty years and we still can't find a way to stop it. They just keep springing up. Most of the time they just tick over, automatically spewing whatever poisonous viewpoint they've been programmed to reflect."

Giles raised his eyebrows. "That many? Really?"

Cameron looked at him. "Check your own accounts. Do you know everyone you talk to? Do you know the source of everything you read and share?"

Giles thought for a moment, blushed, and shook his head. Cameron continued. "From time to time, we get a spike in chatbot activity which can directly influence human behaviour. We saw this back in 2016 with elections that took place at the time. In societies where closed communities formed online, chatbots reinforced consensus reality, created online echo chambers, and polarised public opinion."

Giles was looking confused again. "Consensus reality? Echo chambers?"

"Honestly, Giles. You must have come across this. Where everyone in your group thinks the same, so you believe the whole world works like that? Call yourself a journalist... jeez."

Andy jumped to Giles' defence. "He's too young to remember all of that. I'm surprised you remember it yourself, Cameron."

She laughed. "I remember it, all right. It's what first got me interested in this whole area. Apparently, these polarisation strategies, helped by a fair bit of malicious hacking and some seriously biased news reporting..." Cameron gave Andy a mock scowl. "They worked okay in Britain and the US where there were large online communities reinforcing each other's opinions, but were picked up when the French didn't play ball. Not so much reliance on those online communities, so less of an echo chamber for extremism. Different cultures, you see."

Andy nodded. "I see. But if that kind of thing only worked in certain cultures, what's behind this new spike?"

"Well, the world has moved on, we're more reliant on the web than ever, so the influence will be greater. If it really is impacting worldwide, then from what Noor found in her research, the provocation is very specifically targeted to prey on different national sensitivities. Let's have a look at the kind of things that have been trending."

Andy pulled up the first set of results. "Unites States. What've we got? Uh... okay, there's a bunch of stuff on gun law, calls to repeal the 2029 automatic weapons ban. Anti-vaccination propaganda, going after the ovarian cancer vaccine this time, blaming it for every birth defect they can think of. And some fossil fuel activists, same as you saw in the Emirates. They're always ranting on somewhere, but right now there's a real flurry of activity."

Giles was working through the files. "Here's another one, some agitation in Spain against foreign pensioners using all the healthcare resources." He laughed in disbelief. "That's crazy, it's their disposable income that's keeping the economy afloat since cheap holiday flights ended. Oh, and there's also a wave of protests from Catalan nationalists over the resettlement of refugees from the south."

Cameron was listening intently. This was going far further then she'd suspected. "Looks like there's some fairly sophisticated manipulation going on. I wonder, what's the rationale? Any indication of who's behind it?"

"As far as I can see," replied Andy, "there's no obvious regime leader looking smug out there, everyone's been affected to some degree. There are no significant elections coming up. Who's going to benefit?"

"That's the key, isn't it? Follow the money." They were all silent for a moment. "I'm going to get Ella to run some models. I wonder how this could impact on the markets?"

"Do you think this is significant, then?" asked Andy. "Has it started?"

"I think so. We may be into hurricane season."

•

Pete and his buddy checked each other's scuba equipment and prepared themselves to jump off the small boat as it bobbed, out of sight of land, over the site of an old shipwreck. "Ready?" "Ready."

Pete jumped first, holding his mask and valves tight to his face. His fins hit the water, spread one in the front of the other, slowing his entry into the chilly sea. He felt the pressure of water on his body as he dipped briefly under the surface, then emerged again, buoyant. He could feel cold water penetrating his neoprene gloves and hood, trickling across his hairless scalp, although his body stayed dry, the suit sealed tightly at his wrists and neck. He turned towards the boat and raised his hand to signal the skipper. His buddy jumped in nearby with a splash, and the two of them swam around to the boat's anchor line and prepared to descend.

They exchanged thumbs-down signals and pressed the release valves on their suits, venting as much air as possible. Pete clearly remembered his early days of diving when he was learning to manage his dry suit, and the embarrassment of hanging upside down in the water, helpless, as the legs and boots of the suit filled with air and his buddies laughed.

No mishaps this time: with over five hundred dives in his logbook, Pete rarely made mistakes. Suits and jackets vented, following the line of the anchor rope, the two divers inverted and finned downwards, feeling the pressure mount as they descended towards the sea floor. Pete's ears popped as they reached double the surface pressure, then three times, then four. At thirty metres deep, the sea floor was a mixture of rock and silt, with clumps of kelp waving to and fro. Colours had faded, but the light of Pete's torch brought vivid reds and pinks to life, urchins and sunstars. A large silver fish swam idly by, ignoring the pair.

Floating gently above the sea bed, Pete looked his buddy in the eye and shrugged. Signing to each other, they set out to search the surrounding area, finning side by side as they surveyed the silt in a careful pattern radiating from the anchor.

There was nothing. Where they had expected to find a well-known shipwreck, some of the hull and boilers intact, there were only rocks. Disappointed, the two divers amused themselves for a short while chasing lobsters and crabs down a small gully, and collected an empty urchin shell, before slowly ascending by the anchor line again. They rose steadily, the pressure on their limbs reducing gradually, eyes on their dive computers, managing the gas absorption and expansion in their bodies.

From the boat, the skipper looked down and frowned as he saw clusters of bubbles breaking the surface close to the boat.

"They're on their way back up. Didn't expect them so early." He turned to the other member of the crew. "Stand by with oxygen in case there's something wrong."

Pete's hand was the first to break the surface, giving the boat the OK signal. The skipper breathed a sigh of relief, and the crewman dropped a ladder over the side. Pete handed his weights and fins up to the boat and climbed over the side. Pulling his mask off, he glared at the skipper.

"Nothing there. Not a single speck of rust. Wreck of a wooden ship carrying kelp, maybe?"

The skipper was taken aback. "No, we're right over it. The GPS co-ordinates are spot on. Look for yourself."

Pete shrugged out of his buoyancy jacket and switched off the air supply from his cylinders, stowing them securely on a rack in the middle of the boat. Joining the skipper in the tiny cabin, not much more than a box designed to shield the driver and instruments from the elements and support the boat's solar panels, they re-checked their positioning. Sure enough, the co-ordinates appeared correct.

"I don't understand. I haven't had any bother with this site before. Mind you, it's not like we have any marks to follow, out here. GPS could be on the blink, I suppose. Look, we'll waive the dive fee for today, is that alright? Let's get back to shore."

The passengers settled on benches as the boat hauled anchor and set off, cutting silently through the waves, propellers powered on this trip by the bright sun overhead. Pete was sweating in his dry suit now, the contrast between air and sea temperatures taking its toll. Gazing vacantly at the blue horizon as he swigged from a water bottle, he was perfectly placed to see the ship.

It sailed steadily towards them, a huge cargo vessel stacked with containers. Pete turned to the skipper, suddenly concerned. "We're nowhere near the main shipping lanes, are we?"

The skipper had his eyes forwards, searching for distant marks to the port. He was struggling to reconcile the GPS navigation with his knowledge of the coast. Something wasn't right.

"No, a couple of miles off." He turned briefly, and his eyes widened in horror as he saw the container ship bearing down towards them, heading for the shoreline.

"What the hell?" He grabbed the radio, still the most reliable method of communication at sea. "Red container vessel eastbound at 51.22 / 01.50, this is Manta IV on Channel 13, over."

"Manta IV, this is MV Barnard, switch to Channel 68."

"Manta switching Channel 68."

"Barnard, be advised, you have strayed from the shipping lane, over."

"Manta, our GPS shows no course deviation, over."

Pete was listening intently. "Skip, tell them the GPS may be faulty. Quickly."

"Barnard, GPS may be inaccurate, check your marks, you're heading towards the sand bars, repeat, sand bars. Over." He turned to Pete. "Is that possible? The satellites can't have moved."

Before Pete could reply, the radio squawked again. "Manta, thank you, adjusting course, over and out." They heard the distant rumble of the huge ship's emergency fossil fuel engines starting up, adding a rush of energy as it struggled to turn away from danger. The radio sounded again as the airwaves were flooded with emergency calls, and overhead they heard the clattering rotors of a coastguard drone, heading out to sea.

•

Susie was the last one into the office on Monday morning. Pete was in the middle of recounting his dramatic tale from the weekend.

"...this great big red hull bearing down on us, its engines screaming

110

– never heard those emergency motors kick in before. We're heading backwards at fast as we can, trying to avoid the wash, boat rocking all over the place. We're off course for the port too, GPS is haywire, trying to follow the old marks into the harbour…" He paused as Susie flew through the door.

"Sorry I'm late. There was a lost drone in my street, buzzing everywhere. Navigation systems must have gone down."

"Same problem, I guess." Pete continued. "So anyway, we hear the coastguard overhead, and thought they'd sent a mayday signal, but no, it's another ship, beached on the sand bars further up the coast. All sorts of panic on the radio. Big red manages to turn and heads back to the shipping lanes, we got back to harbour and went for a stiff drink."

"Normal quiet Sunday, then, Pete," teased Joel. "A few new shipwrecks for you to dive?"

"Nah, most of them are beached on the sandbars, so they'll be re-floated. The only sinking was in the middle of the channel, too deep for me to play with. All hands safe, thank goodness."

Ross turned to Susie. "You had a lost drone this morning, huh? Pete's right, it sounds like the same problem. But why only one? If the GPS scramble has affected shipping at such a scale, why isn't every drone in London chasing its tail?"

"Probably older versions of software in some equipment. I didn't see which delivery company that drone came from. Should be able to find out. There'll be a vulnerability in there, which has hit shipping as well. Any reports from airlines?"

Noor shook her head. "Nothing on the major carriers. Military are keeping quiet, but I haven't picked up any reports of crashes or planes off course."

"That points even more clearly to a hole in some older software, then. Flight instrumentation is top priority for updates. Can't have planes falling from the sky."

"Odd target for a cyber attack, though," said Ella. "This is just mischief. There's no financial gain to be had."

Cameron shook her head. "No, this is just another disruption in the chain. More chaos building. I think we can be sure that the hurricanes have started." She thought for a moment. "Let's work out a shorthand for each attack so we're clear where we are. Joel, they use common names for the tropical storms, don't they? What shall we use?"

"Coffee brands," joked Sandeep.

"Rugby players," suggested Joel.

"Film stars," said Ella.

"Bands," said Susie.

"Has to be something international," said Cameron. "I'll be running this through the forums."

"Can't use brand names or countries," replied Joel. "That would be too confusing. How about authors. Politicians. Scientists?"

"Scientists. I like scientists. What've we got?" Cameron pulled up a wiki on screen.

"A – Ayrton? Hertha Ayrton. Electric arcs and sand ripples. Nice. Okay, the first 'storm' was this business with the chatbots, all that propaganda stirring up the crowds." Cameron opened her forum account, cloaking the location out of habit. "I'll publish these live. Next?"

"B – Becquerel?" suggested Noor. "Henri Becquerel. Nobel prize for evidence of radioactivity. What was the second attack?"

"I guess it would be the Distributed Denial of Service attack on the credentialing blockchain," replied Pete. "That was a bit of a mess. What was it again, a botnet of smart fridges? I'll never trust mine again. Lucky the team over in Beijing sorted it out quickly."

"Okay, DDoS attack is Storm Becquerel." Cameron added a line to her forum post. "What was the third one? Do we count the hack on the airline flight management systems?"

"Oh, I think so," replied Ross. "It was simple and short lived, but it was high profile. I'm surprised you got back from the Emirates with your luggage. People were stranded for days, and there are still bags circling the world, from what I hear. That's our C. Who's it going to be?"

"Marie Curie. Got to be," said Susie.

"Two Nobel prizes, can't fault that," replied Ross with a rare grin. "Storm Curie for the flights."

"So this GPS problem is our fourth attack, then? Our D."

"Has anyone worked out the vulnerability yet?" asked Pete.

"Plenty of people working on it. Susie, we need to get a lead on that drone's delivery company, we should be able to get the details of the attack from their systems. Pete, could you find out the software used on your dive boat. By all accounts there was a huge panic at NASA and Roscosmos," continued Cameron, "but as there wasn't a universal effect, they're pretty sure there are no compromises with the satellites. Looks like some sort of glitch in the receivers."

"Okay, definitely our D. Darwin?" suggested Ella. She grinned sidelong at Pete. "Although with you reversing the evolutionary path, Pete, land back to water, it's a strange choice."

Pete threw a table tennis ball at her. She caught it and threw it back with a deft flick of the wrist. Pete mishandled the catch, and the ball ricocheted off the wall behind and bounced in the middle of the table. Joel snatched it out of the air, laughing.

Cameron glanced at the time. "Okay folks, we have clients to see. Ross, you and I can have a look at those GPS vulnerabilities when we get our hands on the software. See if we can get the fix out first, maintain our good reputation."

They scattered, eager to get on with their work.

•

The team worked late through the summer evening, analysing the delivery drone's navigation system and the download from Pete's dive boat charter. As the day wore on, reports of more serious accidents had emerged over the news channels and through online communities, the effects rippling out worldwide.

In the end, the breakthrough came. The Argentum team were first to the finishing line, another feather in their caps. The grateful courier service retrieved its lost drones. The software company behind the flawed systems rapidly updated its clients' systems. Cameron uploaded the patch for the other teams battling the same challenge.

"Even the most up to date software has holes in it, if you look carefully," sighed Sandeep. "It's wide open."

"We'll recommend urgent updates. Get some details out there, Sandeep. Push the whole industry to get their house in order."

Ross finally left the office at dusk, collecting his bike, and waving briefly to Cameron and Sandeep as he rode towards the river and home. He cycled far enough to be sure he was out of sight, and turned off his normal route, dismounting at the gate to a secluded green space. Propping his bike against a tree, he wandered along a path, his feet crunching on the gravel. The little park was deserted. Perfect.

Pulling out a burner smartscreen – a cheap device that could be disposed of, thrown away at the first sign of detection – he initiated a call. Moments later, it was answered: still no face on the screen. The other party remained anonymous. The synthesised voice grated on his nerves.

"We have noticed new speculation around the manipulation of cryptocurrencies."

Ross winced. "Uh, I haven't seen that. Look, there are plenty of good people working on these threats. Someone else will have come up with the same theory independently."

There was no response.

He blustered on. "That's how it works, you know that. Lots of teams, lots of experts all over the world. Sometimes we get the first fix, sometimes other people. We all work together."

"Accepted. You have something to report?"

"Uh, yes. We're looking at the recent navigation system failures. We've identified a vulnerability in older software that was compromised to scramble GPS signals. It was an easy breach. The fix is out there and confirmed by other teams. We're recommending updates across the board for all navigation systems going forward, as there seem to be a number of other bits of dodgy code where attacks could be initiated."

"Good."

Ross was puzzled. "I don't understand where you're coming from. Every time we find a fix for an attack, we make sure updates are rolled out to close down the route to future hacks. Every time I report in, you're pleased, you tell me to recommend more updates. How does this benefit you?"

"You do not need to know. You have done well. Continue."

The connection terminated. Ross was left standing alone in the encroaching darkness of the park.

10: TURNING UP THE HEAT

Charlie could hear the commotion from the top of the stairs. Hurrying down to the kitchen, he found the children in uproar.

"I told the screen to put cartoons on and it said it doesn't like them. It won't switch over from the news," wailed Tara.

"My school forum's all messed up. My friends have disappeared and I can see all the teachers' messages. There's swearing!" declared an appalled Nina.

Dilan said nothing; he was getting on with his breakfast.

Charlie tried ineffectively to calm his daughters down. "Don't worry, it'll just be a little glitch in the system. These things happen."

The wailing redoubled.

"You've all got holiday club today, aren't you excited? Visit to the canal museum? A ride through the tunnel?"

Nina rolled her eyes. "Oh dad, really? I've been before. It's going to be so dull."

Sameena came bustling in. "Come on, you three, aren't you ready yet? The bus will be here soon. Dilan, no, you can't have thirds, go and clean your teeth. Nina, have you drunk your milk? Tara, why are you wearing that dress? I said shorts and a t-shirt. Go and get changed, quickly." She threw her hands up in mock horror. "Children. It's like herding cats."

They all jumped as the screen changed and started blasting out rock music, strobe lights flashing.

"Who did that?" cried Charlie. "Off! Off!"

The screen was unresponsive. Sameena marched over and fiddled around the back of the device, searching for a manual override. Finally, she found it, and the room fell mercifully silent.

"Well, that was a wake-up call. Must get Cameron to have a look at it when she comes up this weekend."

"Oh, don't bother her, Charlie. She's supposed to be relaxing. I'm looking forward to meeting Ben. I'm so glad she's bringing him to meet us at last."

Charlie grinned. "It'll be good if she's found someone who can keep up with her. She won't mind looking at the screen, though. Especially if it keeps the kids quiet."

A hoot from the road outside heralded the otherwise silent arrival of the bus. Sameena rushed out of the kitchen, chivvying the children up and shepherding them out of the front door. "Have a lovely day." She watched and waved as they took their seats and the bus pulled off up the hill, then she turned back to the house.

"Peace at last."

Charlie swigged the last of his coffee. "Right, I'll be off. Quarterly board meeting today. Should be pretty smooth, we've had a few good months." He kissed Sameena and picked up his bag. His wife reached for the dog's leash, and an excited Roxy joined them as they left the house together.

•

Ross tossed and turned. He was having trouble sleeping. Was it the pressure of work, the pressure of training, or the terrible feelings of failure and betrayal that gnawed at his guts? He had lost weight since the high of his last, triumphant, race. The summer sun never touched his pale complexion, making his gaunt visage stand out even more. He did not know how this might end.

Tangled in the twisted sheet, sweating profusely, he struggled to free himself and went to open a window, desperate for air. This was the hottest night he could remember. The sun was already up, but it was still very early. There was no sound of footsteps on the street, no whirr of drone rotors to be heard. Flinging open the window, he gasped as cool air hit him. How strange. Turning back towards his bed, he brushed against a radiator. It was burning hot.

"Heating off." There was no acknowledgement from the house portal. "Heating off." Swearing, Ross pulled on a pair of underpants and opened his bedroom door. Where the hell were the kill switches? He tried the portal again. "Heating off."

Feeling his way down the wall of the hall, he racked his brains. When his mum redecorated, they'd taken out all the ugly, obsolete light switches and plastered over the holes. For years now, sensors in lightbulbs simply switched them on when you entered a room, and off when you left. With the heating on voice control, and reacting intelligently to the environment, there was no need for a manual switch. Somewhere, though, there had been the original controls, the override for the heating system. They had been too complex to remove, still connected to the circuits that were not controlled by the portal, so instead they'd carved a hole for it in the wall, pushed it deep inside, and papered over the gap.

His hands glided over the paper, much shabbier than it had been ten years ago. Fingertips explored dips in the plaster beneath. It had been around here somewhere…

Success. Ross felt a regular rectangular dip in the wall. After another desperate shout at the portal which elicited no response, he took a deep breath of the stifling air and tore into the paper, trying to make a neat flap with his fingers, hoping to cause as little mess as possible. The control panel appeared. Flipping its cover off, he saw lights beneath. There was the slider, the kill switch that he sought. Stiff with years of neglect, it took Ross some effort to push it to the off position, but finally it clicked into place. Ross sighed and closed the control panel cover, then ineffectively tried to fold back the torn flap of wallpaper. Hopefully that would kill the heating.

He shook his head ruefully. Well, he was up now. Time for a cold shower. He'd be in the office early.

•

"Have we all been following the reports of portal and screen failures?" asked Cameron as the team met for their morning catch-up.

There was a chorus of assent.

"There's been some disruption to a few private communities, too. Some software they use in the education sector," added Ella. "We've had a call from the developers to give them a hand finding the fix."

"That's good," grinned Cameron. Charlie had been on the phone before his meeting. "My niece got caught up in that. I'm not sure she was ready to find out how her teachers think."

"The bloody heating was the one that got me," complained Ross. "Barely slept. Ridiculous trick in the middle of summer. And now the aircon's off in here. Where's this come from?"

"Same place as the rest, what do you think?" Joel was getting more and more irritated by Ross's attitude.

"Is this our E then? Storm Edison, anyone?" Noor tried to keep the peace.

"Whatever." They were all fractious with the heat. There was something simmering in the air.

"Let's crack on with our contracts." Cameron realised splitting them up would reduce the friction. "Get some fresh air, get out to see clients, make the most of the nice weather."

They didn't take much persuading. Only Ella and Susie opted to stay in the stifling office, working on their financial models. Ross made his way east to see the delivery company and check up on their drone navigation updates. Joel and Noor made their way north to the community software developers, to help unscramble their user accounts. Pete had an appointment at Lloyds of London to discuss insurance claims arising from the GPS receiver failures.

Sandeep followed up a call to the airport, working with an airline that was still tidying up from the flight information hack. Although the team had identified the system weakness, a new breach had exploited the vulnerability they'd discovered before they had a chance to deploy their fix. It had been frustrating for Sandeep and for the client, and continued to disrupt passengers across the world.

Cameron made it her business to call on the national portal provider. She needed some insights into the latest attack. Leaving the office, she walked the short distance to the river, where a ferry was just pulling in. That would be a cool way to travel, out in the middle of the Thames. She boarded the broad, flat vessel and joined a group of tourists at the stern for the short journey upriver to Westminster pier.

As they approached the bridge, Cameron could hear shouting. A large demonstration was taking place outside Parliament. She climbed up from the pier towards Big Ben. The square in front of the Palace of Westminster was crowded with people waving placards as statues of Churchill, Mandela, Lincoln, Gandhi and other great statesmen gazed impassively upon them. The protestors were agitated, the police presence heavy. As Cameron watched, the demonstrators broke the police cordon, rushing towards the palace. Shouting, sirens, and the sound of taser drones filled the air. Cameron started to run towards Whitehall and Trafalgar Square, the crowd surging towards her. She changed direction and turned down a side street, back towards the river, adrenaline pumping.

The cumulative effect of social media propaganda and polarisation of society, the annoyance of failures of flights and deliveries, the inconvenience of failing portals, and the extreme heat, had pushed the city to the limit. The fallout had just begun.

•

"…Business news now, and the pound has fallen sharply against the Bitcoin today after further concerns over the government's reactions to recent far-right demonstrations. The pound remains stable against the Dollar, Euro, Yen and Yuan which have also seen falls due to political unrest. All cryptocurrencies remain strong…"

Sir Simon Winchester, the bank's chief executive, turned away from the screens on the wall of the boardroom and glowered at his team of analysts.

"So, after posting the best quarter on record, a few hard-right idiots are mucking about with the markets. There's talk of downgrading the country's credit rating. What's kicked all this off?"

The analysts glanced at each other nervously. One of them spoke up.

"This movement wasn't predicted by any of our models. We haven't seen a swing like this for two decades. You have to go back to pre-crypto days to find any fiscal upheaval on this scale. It takes a major external influence to have this kind of effect. Even the terrorist activity in the early part of the millennium didn't cause this much disruption."

Sir Simon sighed. "These things are always transitory. No one can destabilise a whole currency system, and god knows they've tried for decades. I don't think anyone's gotten close since Soros shorted the market in '92. Made him millions, though." For a moment, he was lost in thought. "Okay, thanks for the heads up, keep monitoring the situation. Any unusual trades on hard or cryptocurrency, I need to know straight away. Pay particular attention to futures."

The analysts trooped out, and Sir Simon turned to the screen. "Reception. Get Bill up here."

A few minutes later, Bill appeared at the door. The chief executive was alone, lounging in a tan leather chair, watching the monitors as waves of green and red swept across the central screens, showing the rise and fall of stocks and shares. To the side, another feed showed currency movements, the value of the pound against hard and cryptocurrencies, in real time.

The central screens were, in the main, green. Some of the graphs to the right were dropping.

Bill took in the scene and frowned. "What's up?"

The Sir Simon swung upright and gestured for him to sit. "Your cyber security team. Ms Silvera and her crew. Good operatives."

Bill nodded in agreement, wondering where this was going.

"They've been in and out updating the systems, haven't they? And they did a good job on the ransomware attack back in the Spring."

"Yes, as you know there's been a tipoff about a wave of attacks. Looking at the chaos out there, I think they may have started. Cameron and her team have patched and strengthened all of our older systems, we've completed a full round of training, and our software upgrades are bang up to date."

Sir Simon smiled, approvingly. "Good. They are a talented group, and farsighted. I was particularly interested in their findings around currency manipulation and profits from Bitcoin futures. Who identified this element of the last attack?"

"Ah, yes, that would be Ella Stanford." Bill smiled. "She's good. Used to work in the City, professionally qualified, knows her stuff."

"I think she's onto something. These market movements are unusual. The value of cryptocurrencies is rising, more quickly and more smoothly than the economic conditions would suggest. I can't unilaterally suspend trading, but I can be ready, and make sure my peers are also prepared. Can you contact the Argentum team? I want to speak to her."

"Yes, sir. I'll place a call now."

"Good. And have your staff on alert for anything unusual in the markets or on our systems. There's a storm coming. I can feel it in my bones."

•

Cameron was back in the office when Ben called. "Hey, babe. You busy?"

"Ah, crikey, I nearly got caught in that fuss over at Parliament Square. Very scary."

"Are you okay?" Ben sounded concerned.

"Yeah, calmed down now, thanks. Looking forward to getting out of London for the weekend. What are you after? You getting second thoughts about coming up to the village? Charlie's not that scary."

Ben laughed. "From what I've heard, it's Aunt Vicky and her cat I should be more frightened of. No, this is work related. Something you might know more about than me. There's something odd going on with our systems. We have a big network of intelligent sensors feeding back data to our design centre, and they're all going offline. There's no problems reported on the network. All connections good."

Cameron sat up straight, concerned. "That's odd. You're right. Tell me a bit more about these sensors."

"Most of the stuff we design has sensors built into the print. For instance, a component may have a way of tracking wear and tear and the data comes back to us. If there's a problem, we can improve the design, or the spec of the materials."

Cameron knew the type of feedback loop he described. Simple, unobtrusive use of what was once called 'the Internet of Things' to optimise manufacturing processes and service customers more effectively. Commendable stuff.

She thought carefully. "So, let me get this right, the sensors look as if they are offline at your end. They're not sending data back, although the network is sound."

"That's right."

"Can you test any sensors? See what they're processing?"

"We don't touch them. The manufacturing companies take our designs and the sensors are printed along with the components. Pretty neat, huh? But no, I can't get hold of any easily."

"They're part of the 3D printing process, you say? That's interesting. I'll have a chat with Charlie. See whether any of the components they produce have a similar feature."

"Good idea. This is pretty standard in the industry. There'll be some sort of equivalent in his designs. What are you thinking? I bet you've come up with the answer already."

"Hmm. Maybe. Those little sensors may not be much, but put them together and you have a lot of processing power. Could be nothing, but after the last few weeks I don't know what's coming next. The Speakeasy crew have some imagination, I'll give them that."

"Okay babe, thanks, I have to go. I'll see you tonight." Ben terminated the call, and Cameron sat, thoughtful, her eyes unfocused. Her flash of intuition was disturbing. What storm had been unleashed this time?

•

Ella and Susie arrived at the bank in response to Bill's call. They were ushered straight up to the boardroom where he was waiting. "Sir Simon Winchester – Ella Stanford, Susie Lu."

"Good afternoon, Ms Stanford, Ms Lu. Thank you for coming so promptly." The chief executive paused. "I believe that in your investigations into the Speakeasy cyber attack in April, you identified a pattern of market behaviour that enable the perpetrators to profit."

Ella nodded. "Yes, sir, I've modelled that period completely and I've been watching the markets since then. Cryptocurrency is rising again. Of course, it has a history of fluctuations. It's not necessarily the precursor to an attack."

Sir Simon shook his head. "This feels different. Yes, cryptocurrency is rising against the pound and dollar, and fluctuations are not unknown. But every hard currency is falling. This is unprecedented."

Susie stepped forwards. "We have serious concerns." She glanced at Ella, and continued. "We have identified a series of different styles of attack which have cumulatively weakened the global economy and standing of incumbent political parties. The cyber security community has named them in the style of tropical storms."

Sir Simon nodded. "Very good. Please continue."

"The first one we noted was Storm Ayrton: social media manipulation. There was a sharp increase in 'bot traffic across social networks worldwide in May, and the high level of interference has been sustained. People think they're talking to other humans when they're actually talking to machines. The machines have been trained to provoke disruption and polarisation of opinion. That's the origin of this build-up of demonstrations and political fuss over the last three months."

"That makes a lot of sense," Bill interjected. "This unrest puts pressure on the government to resolve it, uses up resources." He looked closer at the flickering green and red numbers on the stocks screen. "Interesting, some of the highest valued London stocks at the moment are in defence and infrastructure. That fits."

"What else have you observed, Ms Lu?" asked Sir Simon.

"Okay, around the time that Storm Ayrton began, there was a low-level Distributed Denial of Service attack on some credentialing servers. Cameron picked up on this when she flew back from the Emirates. We called this Storm Becquerel. A simultaneous exploitation of vulnerable flight management software caused delays and upheaval worldwide: that's Storm Curie. Then there were the shipwrecks and drones going astray after the GPS hack: Darwin. We're up to Storm Edison so far with the reported portal failures. They still haven't been resolved."

"Thank you, yes, I see." Sir Simon paused. "A steady wave of attacks. Very interesting. Do you anticipate these continuing? Do you have any insight into the source?"

Ella looked resigned and worried. "We have some idea of where this is coming from, but other than fighting each wave and making sure that defences are solid, there is very little we can do. As Susie says, if this currency movement is genuinely down to manipulation of society through social networks and environmental irritations, then it's highly possible we are seeing the start of something bigger."

Stepping forward, Bill sought to reassure them all. "Systems are as tight as a drum down there. All the upgrades are complete. If we start seeing unusual trades, is there any way we can stop them?"

Sir Simon shook his head. "All we can hope is that the movements are steady. If there's a run on futures, and the prices hold, there's no profit to be taken. Ms Stanford, what is your view on possible manipulation in the opposite direction."

Ella composed herself. She'd run the scenarios with Cameron.

"Hard currency is falling because of a loss of confidence in the sovereign states," she said. "There are threats to reduce national credit ratings, for instance. It's taken weeks to get to this stage, drip-feeding polarising propaganda and provoking unrest."

"Yes," agreed Sir Simon. "Only a sustained campaign of this type could have such a significant effect. However, is it not true that a reversal of sentiment will also take time?"

Ella nodded in agreement. "If this manipulation is the work of our Speakeasy perpetrators, they can't artificially reverse sentiment quickly enough to have an acute effect on valuations. However, if they have a way of suddenly reducing confidence in cryptocurrency, that's a different matter. It worked in April because there was a single attack that induced loss of confidence in the whole system for a very short period of time. I can't see a way for them to do this globally unless they have another worm ready to roll, and our industry has worked hard to tighten up all the critical systems. Unless…" she tailed off.

"Unless what?" prompted Bill.

"Unless… there is a compromise already built in."

Susie put her hand to her mouth. She was pale. "Oh god. Is that why they gave us the warning? They knew we would strengthen defences. We had to."

The chief executive looked from one to the other. "What are you saying? Surely if you've built defences then the attackers have to rely on human error to exploit new vulnerabilities."

Ella shook her head. "Quite the opposite. They are relying on professionals like us to do their jobs. What if the updates we've applied were already compromised? What if the work we've done – all of us, worldwide – has thrown the systems wide open?"

•

The summer weather had set in for August. While London was suffering from the heat, with pockets of protest and unrest disrupting the capital and stretching the police to the limit, the countryside basked calmly in glorious warmth.

The vines growing around the village had ripened, and tall tractors with impossibly thin wheels rolled through the fields, shaking grapes from the plants and delivering them to the sorting shed. There, high-speed cameras again took the place of centuries of human expertise, detecting the precise ripeness and sugar content of each fruit, choosing only the best for the ancient champagne houses. This year's crop had the look of a vintage, a rare millésime; even the local fizz produced from the poorer quality grapes was expected to be excellent.

Cameron and Ben strolled hand in hand down the footpath that skirted the vines, as Roxy strained on her leash. She knew there was a run coming and dragged her dawdling humans along the familiar route as fast as possible. Reaching the stile to an empty field, Cameron let the dog off her leash. Roxy wriggled through under the fence, as Ben and Cameron climbed up the protruding cross-pieces of the stile and over to the other side. They watched as Roxy scampered here and there, chasing her tail, poking her nose down rabbit holes, and leaving her mark on the fences and hedgerows. Cameron could see white wind turbines in the distance, barely moving, bright against the cloudless blue sky. Today the country's electricity came from the power of the sun.

Barbecue smoke wafted on a light breeze from a nearby garden. Ben sniffed appreciatively. "Smells good."

Cameron gave him a playful punch on the arm. "You've just had breakfast, you can't be hungry again. We'll get our barbecue this evening." She looked around the fields and sighed. "I love this place. I miss the steady pace of life."

"Bit quiet for me," admitted Ben. "I can see how you ended up spending all your time with computers. I was always out doing things with my hands, born engineer. It's nice to be here, though," he added quickly, dodging another poke, as Cameron laughed.

A large drone flew overhead, laden with goods. Startled, Roxy barked at it until it disappeared between houses and into the village.

"It's nice to see you relax," Ben continued. "You've had a hellish few weeks. All sorted now?"

"It never ends." Cameron looked ruefully at him. "We're running to keep up with security updates for clients, there are phishing emails flying everywhere, and these random attacks are just getting more and more intense. No sooner have we defused one than another pops up. It's the same all over the world."

"Surely the defensive work you're doing is having some impact?" Ben was concerned. Cameron was under a lot of stress.

"Hard to tell. We're finding weaknesses and patching them, but we've had repeat attacks that come along straight away and exploit the weakness we found before the patch goes in. It's almost as if there's someone watching and reacting to what we do, pushing us to get security updates in as fast as possible."

She was thoughtful for a moment. The idea that someone in the cyber security community was involved in the attacks had occurred to her before. She pushed it to the back of her mind again. Something to address later.

She was brought back to earth suddenly by a crash of metal from the direction of the village. Startled, she looked up, and heard shouting.

"The drone's gone down. Roxy! Roxy!" she whistled frantically. "Here, Roxy!"

They ran down a path towards the village, Roxy at their heels, and arrived at a scene of devastation. The delivery drone had veered off course, crashing into a passing autocar. Villagers were working together to try and free the trapped passenger, the car's wheels spinning as it tried to continue on its way. Boxes, glass and debris were scattered on the road, and the drone was embedded in the side of the car, its rotors warped and bent. Ben stepped in and helped to disable the autocar's power system. The wheels stopped whirring, locks holding the far door clicked open, and the shocked passenger climbed out, shaking, and bleeding from myriad tiny glass shards.

Cameron triggered the recovery alert on the drone, looking anxiously into the sky.

Ben joined her. "I know what you're thinking. Is this a one-off? Or are there more."

She nodded. "It's very unusual for a drone to fail. There were a few navigation problems with the GPS attack that caused all those ships to run aground."

"Storm Darwin?" interjected Ben.

"Yes, that's the one. The affected drones just flew around in circles, completely lost. Ross and I found the fix for that particular vulnerability. I wonder what this is. Interference with the local signal, maybe?" She pulled out her smartscreen and scanned the net for news.

"Nothing else reported, yet, but it's only been a few minutes. Let's go and see Andy. He may have more information."

The two of them headed up the hill towards Andy's house. Aunt Vicky met them half way up.

"Cameron, darling, what was that noise? Oh... this must be Ben, how lovely to meet you." Distracted from the crash, Aunt Vicky's attention was focused on the young man. "I'm looking forward to a nice long chat with you at the barbecue this afternoon."

Ben shook her hand warmly and smiled. Aunt Vicky looked pleased.

Cameron took Ben's arm. "We were just popping up to see Andy. Is he in, Aunt Vicky?"

"I think so, darling, I saw him come back from walking Jasper about half an hour ago."

"Great, thanks. We'll see you at the barbecue." Cameron ushered Ben up the hill, and knocked on Andy's door.

Andy's welcome was effusive. "Cameron. Good to see you. What was that racket earlier? And who is this young man?"

"Ben – Andy. Drone crashed down on the high street. Took out an autocar. Any other reports like that?"

Andy looked startled. "That's unusual." He snapped his fingers at the screen on the wall and it sprang to life, displaying the raw news feeds that formed the building blocks of reporting. Selecting map view and narrowing down the report time to the current day, clusters of incidents appeared on the screen.

"There you go. Reports from today. Let's have a look." He drilled down into a cluster pinpointed on the Midlands. "There's the crash in the village. Look, four more reported within a ten-kilometre radius." He zoomed back out.

Cameron and Ben watched, fascinated, as more pinpoints popped onto the screen, each one a reported incident. Andy drilled into a few clusters at random. "All drones."

Cameron put her head in her hands. "I don't believe it. We've just rolled out drone software updates. How the hell have they been attacked so quickly? We just can't keep up."

"Another storm?" asked Andy quietly.

Cameron nodded. "I guess that's our F. We agreed on Franklin. I'd better get online." She looked at Ben soberly. "That wasn't what I'd planned for this weekend."

He hugged her. "Don't worry. I understand. It can't be helped. You get to work. I'll keep Aunt Vicky at bay and play with the kids for you. At least you can do this from here. You don't need to go back to London."

Andy looked concerned. "Is there anything I can do to help?"

"Get something out on the news, Andy. Warn people to keep watch for drones out of control. Ask for the public to be vigilant for anything else unusual. This is building up to something huge."

11: INTO THE BLUE

The worm had been roused from its slumber. Parameters deep in its code found their mark, matching, against a pre-ordained date string, the heartbeat of the servers in which it slept. It had travelled the world, spreading its progeny into every corner of the web, into every network it could penetrate.

Its creators watched in the shadows. They had nudged their master plan forward in real life while the worm spread in the virtual world. Their bots were trolling public sentiment in every country, in every language, across every community forum. Lightning attacks from their Dark Web contractors had increased unrest and destabilised political powers. Operatives on the ground enabled them to gain control of people who could help to ensure the malicious code reached its mark. Compromised threat intelligence operatives were doing their bidding, appearing to strengthen cyber defences while inadvertently assisting the spread of the worm.

It was time.

•

Bill was surprised when the call alert sounded; he was enjoying his weekend off. He was even more shocked to see his chief executive's face on the screen.

"Sir Simon, how can I help you?"

"Bill, the activity we anticipated has begun. Could you alert Ms Stanford and Ms Silvera. No more discussion over open networks."

The call went dead.

Futures trading. Bill hauled himself out of the deckchair in which he had been lounging, and went into his house. He flicked on the wall screen and pulled up the live cryptocurrency market details. Sure enough, the volume of futures trades had risen above its normal level. Broadening the date range, the graphs they had been following suddenly made sense. The gradual climb in volume, with hindsight, had started weeks before, but had been carefully disguised.

Bill called Ella Stanford first. "Good afternoon, Ella, apologies for the weekend call. The activity we discussed has reached the warning threshold." On the other end of the call, Ella's eyes widened, and she nodded. "Understood. I'll be there in an hour. I'll bring Susie as well."

Bill, Ella and Susie arrived at the bank within a few minutes of each other. Sir Simon's plush autocar stood at the door. The streets were deserted. A combination of concern over drone accidents, damage from the last few days' unrest, and businesses being closed as normal for the weekend meant that there were few people out in the city.

The three of them passed through the security checks and the barrier in the foyer, and made their way up the sweeping, carpeted stairs to the now-familiar boardroom. Sir Simon was sitting in his usual leather chair, gazing ruefully at the monitors on the wall. An untouched cup of coffee sat in front of him of the table. He turned towards the door as Bill, Ella and Susie entered.

"Bill, Ms Stanford, Ms Lu, thank you for coming so promptly. Do you have any word from Ms Silvera?"

Ella stepped forwards. "I've spoken to her. She's not in London this weekend; she's out in the country visiting family. She's busy looking into what we've dubbed Storm Franklin, the latest drone malfunctions that are causing major incidents."

Sir Simon nodded. "That's fine, she doesn't need to be here. I've alerted my counterparts in the industry. We are endeavouring to suspend cryptocurrency futures, but the timing could not be neater. Although we are all aware that crypto markets never close, the mere fact that this has reached a peak at a weekend has caught many institutions off guard."

"Not you, though," said Bill.

Sir Simon smiled.

"If it were I who planned this strategy, and I had the ability to time its execution precisely, I would ensure that it happened at the most inconvenient point for those who may try to stop me."

Susie gave him an irreverent grin. "Very good. You may have a future in cyber security, Sir Simon."

The bank's chief executive laughed. "This has certainly been an eye-opener." He adopted a more serious tone. "This is just the start, though. It's the next step that worries me. How are they going to force the price back down and take their profits? That's the real challenge."

He sighed. "Suspending trading may reduce their profits, but it's a drop in the ocean. Where the hell will it go from here?"

Ross stared at the news channel, horrified. The information he had passed on about drone weaknesses had seemed innocent at the time. The speed at which the second attack had hit all the drone systems was astounding. He was absolutely certain that the failures being reported could only have come from a fast exploit of the vulnerability he'd exposed.

How the hell had they managed to deploy the attack, though? How could the malicious code have dropped so fast? It was one thing writing a quick exploit to take down the drones, but quite another to make sure it appeared in their operating systems. They would have to have access to the servers that controlled the drones. Either they already did – in which case, why did the GPS scramble not hit everyone? – or something had changed recently.

Ross went cold. The updates. They'd recommended security updates. The strangers in the shadows had pushed for them to happen. What if the updates themselves were compromised?

He scrambled for his smartscreen and placed a call to Cameron. She answered quickly. Behind her on the screen, he could see faded, brightly patterned wallpaper, and bright sunshine coming through a dormer window.

"Ross? What's up? Aren't you training?"

"Training's finished. Cameron, these drone crashes…"

"Storm Franklin, Ross. They're all over the place."

"I know, I've seen the news."

"Yeah, Andy's done a good job getting that out there."

"Look, Cameron, you know that vulnerability we picked up when we were analysing the GPS scramble? Is this attack exploiting that exact code error?"

"Yes, I think so. I'm working on it now. I've managed to get hold of a copy of the operating system. The thing I don't get, is that we advised security updates and they seem to have been applied. The one I'm looking at had the latest version."

Ross took a deep breath. "What if the updates were compromised? Cameron, what if the malicious code was delivered direct from the update servers?"

Cameron stared at him, horrified. "Ella and Susie had the same thought about updates at the bank. We had no evidence. Ross, we need to get upstream to the main drone operating system providers. Can you follow that up?" She paused. "What I don't understand is how they could have found and reacted to that vulnerability so quickly? No one on the forums had picked it up before us. We haven't published the details. What are we up against?"

Ross swallowed hard. "Cameron... I need to talk to you..." He shook his head. "No, it's alright. I'll get on with the drone people."

The call terminated.

Cameron sat back, startled.

Breathing hard, Ross put down his smartscreen and buried his head in his hands. The lies and deceit were catching up with him.

Thinking fast, he placed a call to Joel, phrasing it carefully. "I'm coming over to your place. Get the kettle on." He grabbed a rucksack and filled it with some spare clothes, a few packs of energy gels, and a bottle of water. He left the two smartscreens, his own and the burner device, on the table. Helmet on, he collected his bike, and the house door locked behind him. Ross pedalled away steadily towards Joel's neighbourhood.

He had been gone for almost twenty minutes when the stranger's autocar pulled up outside the house.

•

Ella, Susie, Bill and Sir Simon were still deep in discussion in the bank's boardroom.

Sir Simon turned to Ella. "How could the value of cryptocurrency be destabilised rapidly and accurately, without also closing down trading? That's the question. It's all very well making the value fall, but these people will want to complete their trades and take their profits."

Ella pulled her notes up on her screen. "During the Speakeasy attack, there was a brief loss of confidence in banking systems. That caused the small drop in cryptocurrency values that we saw after the trading peak."

"Do you think they'd try that again?" asked Bill. "A bit obvious, isn't it? They know we're watching this time."

"Hmm, not so sure," replied Ella. "There was some odd activity on the forums, apparently, when Ross published my original findings. The consensus in the end was that there was not enough evidence to back up the assumptions. I disagree."

"How interesting," said Sir Simon. "Your analysis was perfectly accurate and well supported. There would be no reason to discredit it. However, that may explain the difficulty I have had persuading my counterparts elsewhere to take the suspension of trading seriously."

Susie chipped in. "I'm still concerned about the motivation behind

131

their warning. It gave us the opportunity to strengthen defences, but what if there was something already planted to enable an attack?"

"Yes, you thought there may have been a vulnerability in the updates that have been rolled out, didn't you," agreed Bill. "Why don't you have a look at the code that came down the line? I can set you up a quarantine machine to work on."

"Good idea," replied Ella. "I'll see if Sandeep can join us. He's got a good eye for this sort of thing." She went to place a call on her screen, but Sir Simon held up a warning hand.

"Wait. If they have planned this so carefully, I have no doubt that some communications networks are unsafe. In fact, I would trust very few things right now. Use my personal screen." He unrolled a small device from his pocket and handed it to Ella. "That may be safer. Be careful what you say."

He turned to Bill. "We're going to need provisions. This team can't work on an empty stomach. Go and do some shopping, Bill. No drone deliveries."

Bill nodded and left the room, closing the heavy oak door behind him.

Sir Simon looked at the two girls. "How many other systems have been updated? Could this be a blanket disruption of many things to impact overall confidence in anything automated? That strategy would also afford the perpetrators cover, create enough chaos to make good their escape, as it were."

Ella looked helpless. "Well, everything. We have clients in transport. Drone systems, obviously. Utilities and power. All sorts. Multiply that by every threat team across the world – it's huge."

"We can expect some major disruption, then." Sir Simon sighed. "Ms Stanford, while your colleagues start on the analysis, would you accompany me to Downing Street? The Prime Minister needs to hear this."

•

Cameron looked drawn and pale when she finally descended from her attic. The family, and Ben, were out in the garden enjoying the sunshine. As she wandered, blinking, out of the patio doors onto the terrace, Charlie looked up. "How's it going, Cam?"

She smiled wanly. "It's getting serious. I think I know why the drones have gone down. That's the easy part. The tough bit is, we don't know exactly how the code was delivered. And Ross... something odd's going on with Ross..." Cameron shook her head.

Ben beckoned her over. "Come and sit down. You need a break."

She smiled, and joined him on a little bench seat in the shade of a large tree. Charlie poured her a glass of wine and brought a plate of snacks. She felt the stress recede.

Stretching her aching back, she yawned. "I'm going to have to get back to London. I think this is going to explode. We've been waiting for the big one. It feels like we're close."

Ben gave her shoulders a squeeze. "We can get the train tonight, if you like."

Cameron nodded. Charlie and Sameena were quiet.

Over the sound of the children and their friends playing in a remote corner of the garden, they heard a voice calling.

"Cameron? Charlie?" Around the corner of the house came Jasper, straining on his leash, closely followed by Andy. He bent down and released the dog, who rushed off to find his friend.

"Glass of wine, Andy?" Charlie grabbed another garden seat and pulled it into the shade.

"Thanks, Charlie. That'd be lovely. Cameron, something you should see." He pulled out his smartscreen. "This just came through. We have a permanent camera monitoring Number Ten Downing Street. On normal Sundays, we just get the cat going out for a walk. Today, the Prime Minister has visitors. Look. Isn't that Ella?"

Cameron gasped. "Yes. And that's Sir Simon Winchester."

Andy stared. "Of course. I recognise him now."

Charlie looked from his sister to his friend, concerned. "Who?"

"He's the chief executive of the bank. This can mean only one thing. The trading patterns we anticipated have started. The hurricane's coming." She stood up, suddenly distressed.

"Why hasn't Ella called? What's going on?" She reached for her screen.

Andy held out a warning hand. "Is it safe to call? Forum manipulation, hacks, drones, and now the bank. How far does this spread?"

Cameron grinned at him. "Yes, you're right, but I have an idea. There's something I want to try. Andy, I may need your help."

"What for?"

"I'm going to build our own end-to-end messaging system, but it will mean disrupting some of the public networks. Can you get something out on the news channels? Tell people not to panic, that normal service will be resumed, say it's scheduled maintenance overrunning or something."

"Wow. That's heavy-handed, isn't it?"

"Not really, Andy, in the circumstances. And I'm only talking about the Bluetooth network." She smiled. "I'm going to build a mesh network. Better let the team know – they're probably expecting it." She bent over her screen. "Right. Careful wording…"

'Hi Ella, are you lunching with Simon? Get your teeth into a good blue steak.' She hit send.

"Let's see if that works." The reply came almost by return.

"Aha! Let's see. 'Yes, Susie and Sandeep here too. Chatting about the future. Speak to you shortly.'" Cameron grinned.

"Excellent, that's three of them already at the bank, and we know that Sir Simon has taken this seriously enough to alert the authorities. Let's see what the others are up to. I've already spoken to Ross; he's off to talk to the drone systems people. I'll just let him know about the mesh."

She quickly sent a message to Ross: 'Hope you're not still feeling blue.' It bounced back.

"Hmm, that's odd. His screen's switched off. I'll worry about that later. Let's try the others."

Three times she sent, 'How's your Sunday going? Isn't this blue sky incredible?'

She sat back down on the bench and took a bite from a small piece of quiche, waiting for a response.

Joel's came first. 'Coffee with Ross. He's droning on as usual.'

"Hah, brilliant, so Ross has pulled Joel in to help him. Good thinking." Noor's reply beeped. 'Pretty quiet. How's Franklin?'

Cameron thought for a moment and sent a reply. 'Had to see a specialist. Not sure about the root of the problem. I'll speak to you soon.' She crossed her fingers that Noor could work through the tortuous phrasing and understand what was happening.

Pete hadn't responded. "He's probably out diving. He'll be in touch when he surfaces." She picked up her wine glass and looked at Andy. "Anything else going on that I should know about?"

"Maybe. There are some reports coming through from the US about rogue security bots on the rampage. Some shootings. Reports possible fatalities."

"Oh no, that's awful." Sameena looked horrified. "Is it widespread? I have family in Texas."

Andy nodded, sombre. "Yes, nothing breaking on the news channels just yet. We're verifying sources, but at least twelve states appear to be involved."

"I need to get on the forums. Give me a minute." Cameron chose to use her private connection in the attic, bounding back up the stairs again.

She set the location to a town in California, and logged on. Sure enough, there was chaos.

"SimCavalier, glad you're here."

"What are we up to so far, Storm Franklin?"

"You think this is part of the pattern? In that case it's Galileo," typed Cameron. "I'm so sorry to see this, guys, it's dreadful."

"Sunday morning. Lots of people out and about, kids going to sports clubs, folk going to church. Just awful."

"Do you need help with a fix?"

"No. We're good, thanks, SimCavalier. Uploaded it already, and it seems to be stopping them in their tracks."

"Anyone isolated the cause?"

"Well, we're not sure. A bunch of us rolled out security updates on the robocops last week. Thought they were tight. Guess we were wrong."

Cameron sighed. "Same thing we're seeing. There's a chance of a compromise at update level. Get into the source servers, see what you can find."

"Really? That's mad."

"How far ahead was this planned, anyway?"

"What the hell are we dealing with?"

"No idea, guys, just know that it's everywhere. Listen, I'm going to try something here. We may need tighter security. Keep your Bluetooth devices to hand. Stay safe. Be vigilant."

Cameron went to sign off the group, then hesitated. What was going on with the crypto futures thread? She navigated over to it. There was a buzz around the topic. After weeks of dismissing the ideas Ross had posted, a few analysts were reporting similar trends. Good to see others picking up on it independently. They might still have a chance to minimise profiteering from this wave of attacks. She dropped a post onto the thread.

"Can the cryptocurrency be destabilised quickly?"

Responses came back swiftly.

"Denial of Service attacks on banking systems?"

"Yes, a run on currency when the banks came back online would do it. Wouldn't a DDoS stop them from realising their trades, though? Any more?"

"Power outages, same effect?"

"Security fork adoption conflicts?"

"The community would have to pretty badly divided to stop a genuine security fork being applied. We're all friends here, aren't we?"

There was a chorus of virtual assent and amused chatter.

"Anything that takes away people's trust in machines, SimCavalier. Power outages, sure, but trust is eroding already."

"Fair point. Robocops, drones, credentialing… The disturbances have all helped to raise the crypto value against hard currency, but there may be a tipping point."

"We're looking out for development, SimCavalier."

"Thanks guys. Stay safe."

She logged off and sat staring at the blank screen.

Ben came upstairs to find her deep in thought. "You okay? What's the news from America?"

"It's grim. Rogue robocops. Same story, the updates were applied and malicious code has been dropped in at the same time. I think there will be a lot of fatalities. They've managed to close them down, thank goodness." She sighed, reflecting on the horror of this latest attack.

"What now?"

Cameron shook herself. "I think we're reaching a peak. The things that have happened over the past few hours or so have gone beyond causing unrest. Now they're challenging our reliance on machines. They're ready to take their profits." She looked up at her boyfriend. "Ben, you know what you were saying about data sensors in components? Let me get on with building this mesh, and then we need to talk to Charlie."

She took a deep breath and started typing. The virus she was creating would spread from one Bluetooth device to the next, harnessing speakers and headsets, signage and adverts, building an alternative internet. Their communications would be hidden from view.

Gradually, the mesh network took shape.

•

Pete and his friends clambered off the dive boat, lugging their gear onto the pier. They gave the skipper a cheery wave as he cast off and headed for his berth.

"Great dive." The GPS had not betrayed them this time. The skipper had put them straight over the wreck they'd been looking for, in perfect conditions.

Pete unzipped his buddy's dry suit and turned so his friend could do the same. He felt the top of his head gingerly. "I think I caught the sun out there."

There was a gale of laughter.

"That'll teach you," said one of the other divers sternly. "I offered you sunblock, but no. Honestly, men." She grinned.

The group gradually stripped off their layers and changed into shorts and t-shirts. Their gear was carefully stowed in bags and boxes, and Pete summoned an autotrailer to carry the heavy load back along the harbour.

"Who's coming for a pint?" asked his buddy, as they followed the trailer to the car park.

"Not me, sorry," replied Pete. "I have to get back." He hailed an autocar and transferred his kit into it. "See you all next week. Train station, please." The little car's motor strained as it carted the heavy equipment up a short hill, settling as it reached the main road. They trundled towards the main line station; there was a train to London due in a few minutes. Perfect timing.

As they approached the station car park, the vehicle ground to a halt. The doors popped open and Pete started with surprise. "Oh. Autocar swarm." He jumped out and grabbed his gear before the little car swept off to join its fellows on a recharging mercy mission. The platform was only a short walk away; he wouldn't miss the train.

Settling into his seat, bags carefully stowed, Pete finally switched on his smartscreen. A message popped straight up for his attention. *'How's your Sunday going? Isn't this blue sky incredible?'*

He was immediately on alert – and impressed. There must be something serious going down if Cameron had acted on the emergency plan they'd put together years ago. He scanned the news channels. Reports of rogue robocops in America. Nothing more on the drone crashes. What was happening under the radar? Ah, the last item on the bulletin, a scheduled maintenance warning for Bluetooth. Clever girl.

Pete sent a quick reply: *'Nice dive. Swarming all over the wreck. Some pretty blue fish down there too.'* He switched off his smartscreen and went to his bag. In an inside pocket, rarely used but always charged, lay his Bluetooth headset. He sat back down in his seat and waited patiently for the call, looking out of the window.

The train was rattling on towards London. Fast run this afternoon, he thought. It looked as if the train wasn't stopping at its usual stations. They passed through one, and he caught glimpses of a crowded platform, and shocked faces as people jumped backwards. That wasn't right.

A mutter of concern and disbelief rose in the carriage. Pete looked around, then stood up and started to walk towards the front of the train. He could see the track curving away ahead of them, and another station just visible in the distance. They passed green signals at speed, some of the old lights still operating despite the automated carriages that had been running for years. To his horror, Pete saw another train at the station, and realised they were on the same tracks.

He threw himself into a seat, bellowing "we're going to crash," at the top of his voice. He put his feet flat on the floor, pressed his head and body against the high seat back, and clutched the armrests. The impact came, and he fell into blackness.

•

Cameron's screen beeped just as Ben appeared to check on her progress. "I was right, Pete was diving. Hmm, he says there's been a car swarm. Probably a local outage. Hope so."

She replied quickly. 'Sounds great. Hope you're doing some research.'

"There we go. He'll come back with details on that swarm for us. Probably nothing to worry about."

"How's it going?" asked Ben.

"Done. It'll take a little while to spread. Let's go downstairs."

Returning to the shady garden and flopping back in her seat, Cameron turned to Charlie. "Ben was telling me about sensors that are built into components." She glanced at Ben. "You can explain it better than me."

"Uh, okay. I produce designs for 3D printing. We've got some up on the Mars mission. Anyway, some of these include sensor elements that send feedback to our systems so we can refine the design, materials mix, and so on."

Charlie nodded. "I know the type of thing. Yes, a lot of our larger components have feedback loops in. All the prototype stuff too. Valuable data. We don't collect ourselves, of course. We just produce the physical items." He looked at Cameron. "Why?"

"Ben tells me there's been a hiatus in data capture. Nothing arriving at the servers, but the network is showing no errors. Can you check with your designers that their data is arriving cleanly? I'm hoping it's just a local problem."

"Sure," replied Charlie, "but what do design sensors have to do with your line of work?"

"Not sure yet. Just a feeling I have. Charlie, Ben, how much processing power would an average component sensor have? How many components are we talking about? And can you control them?"

"They're very small, but quite powerful for their size, I guess... and millions, maybe billions of them in circulation. As for control... yeah, there is a way to interrogate them, refine the data capture in an existing sensor."

"Oh, that's great," said Cameron, her voice dripping with sarcasm. "An old-school Mirai botnet ready to roll."

Ben and Charlie looked at her blankly.

"What's a Mirai…?" asked Ben.

"Botnet. It's a clever little trick. We've been looking for something like this. It's one of the most likely attack scenarios. A botnet can harness the processing power of a huge network of devices and flood a site with traffic."

She looked at Charlie soberly. "I'm sorry, I really can't stay. I have to get back. This is going haywire." She stood up. "I'll order a taxi."

Cameron walked into the house and turned to the nearest screen. The news channel was running.

"Breaking: train services across the UK have been suspended pending urgent investigations, following a serious crash between a stationary carriage waiting at a platform, and an out of control train which had jumped several stop points at high speed." Images of twisted metal and a damaged station frontage showed on the screen, human and robot paramedics attending to casualties.

Cameron swore.

"We're going to have to get an auto car all the way back to London. Trains are off."

"Cars are off too," said Charlie, following her in. "There was a report earlier of a swarm; all cars out of action."

"Dammit, that'll be the swarm Pete saw. I hoped it was local. I guess it wasn't. Looks like I'm stranded."

"There are worse places," reminded her brother. "And you can work from here. Let me know if there's anything you need. Think about it, if this carries on, I'm stranded too. I'm not fit enough to cycle to work tomorrow, and there's probably no point if none of the staff can get in either."

Cameron couldn't help giggling at the thought of her brother on his bike. "It'd do you good. Right, I'm going to finish off that mesh network. Send coffee and snacks." She climbed back up to her attic, and set to work.

•

At the bank, Ella, Susie, and Sandeep were trawling through the latest updates they'd made to the systems, looking for any clue to compromises, any hint of malicious code. Sir Simon and Bill were watching the crypto futures market like a hawk, jumping at any blip.

"Trading's slowed right down. We must be close to the peak."

"How's the value looking?"

"Still artificially high. It's got to drop. This is like the thick air before a storm hits. Any moment now, we're going to get drenched. Well, metaphorically speaking," added Bill, as Sir Simon looked sidelong at him.

Ella's screen pinged.

'*All set*,' it said, followed by a link.

"Oh, good girl. Okay, we have open comms with Cameron."

They all donned their headsets.

"Afternoon, everyone. Hi Ella, you have Susie and Sandeep with you?" The other two said hello.

"Noor, you at home?"

"No, Cameron, I'm in the office. I thought I'd be more useful here."

"Good thinking. Joel, you have Ross?"

"No, he headed off an hour ago. Said he had some things to sort out. Haven't you heard from him?"

"Not a word since we spoke earlier. He hasn't replied to any messages either." Odd, she thought. What had he wanted to tell her this morning?

"Where's Pete?" asked Ella.

"He's been diving. He'll be on his way back from the coast. Probably stuck waiting for a train. I'm sure he'll join us as soon as he can."

Bill sat in the background, grinning. He loved watching this team work. They were a great unit.

"Let's roll," said Cameron. "First off, it looks like there is a Mirai botnet taking shape out there. It won't be a coincidence. We all need to be vigilant for a DDoS attack."

"Is that the attack you anticipate will cause a drop in cryptocurrency values?" asked Sir Simon.

"Possibly," answered Ella. "Although it could mask something else. It's a tough attack to defend against. But something doesn't quite fit. If they block the servers, they won't be able to complete their trades. Something else has to give first. I think they'll take their profits, and then use a DDoS attack to mask their escape."

"No unusual traffic reported, Cameron, but we'll keep our eyes peeled," replied Sandeep.

"What have we got so far? Joel – drones? Anything?"

"Yeah. There's a nasty bit of code attached to one of the recent update files. Ross and I cobbled together a patch and that's on its way out now."

"Nice one. Fast work. Can you transmit copy?"

"Sure." There was a pause. "There you go. Cameron, something odd though. I checked out the work that the guys in the US have been doing on the rogue robocops. There are a lot of similarities with the patch, but I haven't seen the code they found yet."

Cameron was taken aback. "You're saying it's the same attack?"

"It's not impossible. The first reports came in very early this morning, US time. Around the same time as the drones went haywire."

Noor broke in to the conversation. "You know this train crash? There were reports of service glitches all over the place from around the same time. Coincidence?"

"Hmm, maybe not. What else has happened today?"

"Autocar swarm?"

"That was later. That started this afternoon."

"Yes… but it's still going, and it's country-wide. What are they swarming to fix?"

They were all silent for a moment, before the horrifying truth swept over them.

"Power distribution. The power distributors are down. Forget bots and drones and trains… this is it. This is where the country loses confidence in tech."

There was a shout from Bill. "It's dropping."

They watched as the value of cryptocurrency went into freefall, before the lights flickered and went out.

12: BLACKOUT

Ella gave a startled cry as the lights went out. "What happened?"

"Power's gone," replied Bill. "The priority for the bank's emergency power generation is keeping those servers running, nothing else. Is your network still running?"

"Yes, no problem. These are very low power devices, and won't need charging for a while." Ella did a quick rollcall.

"Noor here. I'm fine here in the office. The solar panels are at top production, and the batteries are full."

"I'm still here," Joel called, "but I don't have batteries. All our excess generation goes straight to the grid, and we're purely solar too. I won't have power after nightfall."

"I think we're alright. Roof full of panels and batteries in the cellar," replied Cameron. "But that's autocars and trains out of action. No one can go anywhere."

"What do we do now?" asked Noor. "If this was a call from a client, what would we be doing?"

"We'd be heading to their site ready to quarantine, fix and patch," replied Joel, "or we'd be straight on the net advising their people what to do. We can't do either right now."

Cameron paused as a thought struck her. "Actually, we can. I bet I can get there. And I think it'll be fun."

•

Deep in the bank, Ella and Susie looked at each other in the dim light that streamed in from the ground level skylights. They held their breath, and to their relief heard the gentle whirr of the servers, still running.

"Emergency power saving," explained Sir Simon. "We have full batteries which keep the servers and security systems online in the event of an outage. The roof panels will keep the batteries topped up."

"You can keep working, but we don't have any additional comms," explained Bill.

"Let's get cracking, then," said Sandeep. "You captured Joel's fix, didn't you, Ella? If he's right, then the same worm has infected all systems. That'll help us find any compromise here and fix it."

"Brilliant, Sandeep. Good thinking."

"What about the scenarios we ran? We know the cryptocurrency price has started falling. We can't see how far this spreads, or if they've started taking profits, but we can be ready for when the power comes back."

"What do you mean, Ms Stanford?"

"Well, Sir Simon, this attack should send clear signals around your industry that there really is something wrong. You've laid the foundations, your voice is one they listen to, and you got the Prime Minister to support you. I'd be surprised if trading hasn't been suspended already."

Bill nodded. "But what do we have to prepare for?" he asked.

"Cameron says there was a botnet out there. A DDoS attack would tie the systems up, and could mask other things. These people may have robbed the bank, but they haven't made it out of the door yet."

Realisation dawned.

"If we're ready for them, we can block the exits? Is that what you're saying?"

Ella nodded. "Let's get to work."

•

Ross cycled steadily south through the London suburbs towards the Thames from Joel's home. He had no real idea where to go. The roads were deserted, quieter than a normal Sunday. A few drones were flying; the fix he and Joel had delivered had been tested and deployed. He found himself heading for the small city airport. For a moment it crossed his mind to jump on a plane, leave the country, hide himself. But no. Passing through the border would flag his location straight up to anyone who was watching – and he had no doubt that someone was.

He reached the river. Was this the end of the road? As he stared into the sluggish current, he caught sight of an old Victorian brick building, perfectly round, incongruous in its modern setting: the Woolwich foot tunnel.

Ross pulled himself from the brink, and wheeled his bike towards the entrance and down the old stairs. The tunnel was dingy, lights flickering, water dripping. He cycled where he could, and trudged the rest of the half-kilometre down under the Thames and up to the south bank. As he reached the end, the lights behind him were suddenly extinguished. He shivered. He didn't know what had caused it, but he was glad to be out in the sunlight.

Cycling onwards, he passed a cluster of local shops, and realised he was hungry. He propped his bike against a wall, and approached the door of a general store, hesitating when he saw that although the door was open, the lights were off.

"You open?" he called.

"Yeah, mate, but we got no power. About to shut up shop."

Ross stepped in to the gloom. "Just wanted a sandwich? Any food left?"

The shopkeeper shrugged. "All the fresh stuff'll have to be chucked if the power don't come back. Help yourself. Can't take your money anyways." He ambled over towards Ross, scowling. "Should've bought into that solar network when I had the chance."

"This has got to be the first blanket outage since… oh… 2034?" said Ross, as he picked up some cold meat, cheese and bread. "Remember that? I was still at school, just. Took a few hours to fix. Chaos."

"World's gone crazy today, innit. Drones, trains, and what about America, eh? Thought they'd seen the last of their mass shootings, and then the 'bots get them."

Ross muttered in agreement, thanked the shopkeeper, and took his leave. A plan was starting to form in his head. The problem had to be at the distribution centres. There was enough power being generated, he reflected, as the sun beat down, a light breeze blew, and the river flowed. SussexGrid was one of their clients. Maybe he had a chance to redeem himself. Could he make it there before dark? He retrieved his bike, and turned away from the river, heading south with renewed purpose.

•

Cameron's eyes were dancing as she explained her plan to Charlie, Sameena, Ben and Andy.

"…if I get to the plant, I think the fix we already have will solve the problem. Where did Aunt Vicky stow it?"

"It's at the back of one of the barns on Jack's farm down the village," said Charlie.

"You'd better ask your aunt before you borrow it," joked Andy. "And be home before midnight."

Ben laughed.

"But Cameron," said Sameena, worriedly, "you can't drive."

"That's okay," replied Cameron. She grinned at Ben. "I know a man who can."

Andy, Cameron and Ben trooped up the hill. Donald was lounging on the path in front of Aunt Vicky's door, a mound of ginger fur. Jasper growled at him. Donald took no notice. Boris the tabby was sitting on Andy's doorstep, not taking his eyes from his rival.

"Bit of a fight, I reckon," sighed Andy. "Boris keeps trying to take back control but Donald rides roughshod over him. Cats. Honestly." He skirted around the lurking felines and called into the back garden. "Vicky? Are you home?"

An indistinct reply came, and the three of them crowded round the side of the house to find Aunt Vicky calmly tidying her flowerbeds. She stood up, brushing down her skirt.

"Hello Andy. Oh, Cameron, darling, and Ben. How lovely. I'd offer you a cup of tea but I can't get anything to work. What can I do for you?"

Cameron glanced at Ben. "Um, Aunt Vicky, can I borrow your car?"

She had never before seen her aunt lost for words.

"Oh, really?" she finally stammered. "But... It's been covered in hay for years. It will need a wash. And I don't even know if it will work."

Cameron laughed. "Oh, Aunt Vicky. I'm sure it'll be fine." She crossed her fingers behind her back. "So, do you have a key?"

"Yes, dear." She pulled herself together. "But do you have a driver? I'm sure I can remember..."

"It's fine," interjected Ben. "I can drive. My dad was a real petrolhead. I haven't done it for a few years, but I know what I'm doing." Aunt Vicky looked relieved. Scurrying into the dark interior of the house, she scuffled around in a drawer, and finally extracted a key fob.

"I don't think there'll be any charge in the battery, but the car isn't locked. You know where it is?"

Cameron nodded, and threw her arms round her aunt. "Thank you so much." She and Ben dashed back out of the garden, and made their way up the village street to the farm.

Jack showed them to the barn, which lay at the top of a long track that sloped down towards the road. "It's that yellow one, at the back. This one here's mine. That one belongs to the lad at the pub..."

Ben stared. "You have quite a collection."

"Aye, it seemed a shame to scrap them. Good memories."

"Can we get hold of any fuel?" Jack frowned.

"I'm not so sure. There used to be a service station up at the junction, but I don't think there's much left in the tanks under that concrete. How far do you need to go?"

"At least two hundred kilometres, possibly more."

Jack shook his head. "There's your problem. You won't have the range."

Ben was thinking hard. "What did all these run on?"

"Well, that yellow car of your aunt's was petrol. Nippy little thing. She used to frighten the life out of me, and my stock, bombing round the lanes. My old pickup truck's diesel, all the farm vehicles were until we switched to electric. Don't know about the other ones."

"Cameron, how far away is Mandisa? She's a scientist, isn't she? Could she get hold of enough ethanol to fill a tank?"

"She lives right on the other side of the town, and her lab is further away again. Is there anything else we could use? Something we'd be able to make here?"

"Not for a petrol engine," Ben shook his head. "But diesel, now… Jack, could we use your pickup, instead?"

Jack nodded. "Certainly. I'll get the key." He turned away towards the house. Cameron looked puzzled.

"Why does that make a difference?"

Ben laughed. "Totally different engines. The truck will run on vegetable oil. There's no shortage of that."

Jack came back and proffered and old key at Ben. "There you go, son. All yours. Let's get her running. There's enough fuel left in there to get you a few miles, charge up the battery. I sneak her out for a spin from time to time, but not enough to keep a charge. That's why she's parked on top of a hill. Have you done this before?" Ben shook his head. "Right, you push."

The farmer clambered into the cab and turned the key. There was a click, but nothing more. "Dead as a dodo. Now, if this happens again, put her in second gear and roll her. Try and hold the clutch right at the biting point. It'll catch. Now, push."

Ben and Cameron pushed the truck laboriously out of the barn. As it hit the gradient, it gathered its own momentum. They stood and watched as it rolled down the hill, and cheered when the engine coughed into life, a cloud of smoke bursting from the exhaust. Jack drove onto the main road and out of sight. He returned a few minutes later, pulling up at the gate, the engine idling.

"Right, son, hop in. She's all yours. Take care to park at the top of a hill. Bring her back in one piece."

Stammering out their thanks, Ben took Jack's place at the wheel, and Cameron climbed up beside him in the passenger seat. Ben drove cautiously along the street to Charlie's house.

"I'll wait here. We're at the bottom of a hill. Get some oil. And a map. Do you know where we're going?"

Cameron jumped out and ran around to the garden. "We're sorted. Come and look. We've got Jack's old pickup working."

The whole family rushed to the road, the children distracted from playing.

"Ewww, it smells," complained Tara, pinching her nose.

"Cool," said Dilan, impressed.

Nina took several photographs with her screen, recording the pickup from all angles and Ben grinning in the driver's seat.

Cameron drew her sister-in-law aside. "Sameena, I need as many bottles or cans of vegetable oil as you can find. And some water would be good too. I'm just going to get a map." She rushed upstairs, and brought a map up on the computer screen. Transferring it to her smartscreen, she checked it could be viewed offline. All good. She did the same with the fix file that Joel had sent.

An idea occurred to her; she made a quick call. "Joel, you live just off the M25, don't you? We have transport. We'll collect you in an hour. We're going to SussexGrid. I'll call you when we get close for directions."

"That's great, Cameron. Nice one," replied Joel. "I'll see you shortly."

Turning her attention to Noor, she thought through her plans. "Keep trying to get hold of Pete. I lost contact with him. Could be a faulty Bluetooth device."

Noor nodded. "I hope so, Cameron."

"Get onto the forums and see who is still live, try and get some direct connections established, and find out what's happening globally. Get Joel's drone fix out as far as possible and see if it works for other reported failures. I bet it will. If you can, start a movement to suspend cryptocurrency trading, and warn people to watch out for a DDoS attack. I'm sure that's the next step, something to help them get their money out."

"Okay, Cameron, I'm on it. Good luck."

Cameron rushed back downstairs. Sameena had loaded several bottles of water and a bag with cake and sandwiches into the truck, along with couple of cans of vegetable oil. Ben was cautiously filling the tank with a third. He looked up. "Ready?"

"Ready." She jumped into the cab and pulled on her sunglasses. "Ready as I'll ever be."

•

Sir Simon Winchester was frustrated. Isolated in the bank, the tech experts were working hard to prepare for the next storm. That might protect his small part of the financial world, but it would not be enough to stop this threat in the shadows. It had to be a team effort.

He reflected on the skilful planning that had gone into this unprecedented series of attacks. First, destabilise hard currency through unrest. Next, unleash a worm to flip the market, destroying confidence in tech. That must have been a long time in the making, he realised, to penetrate so completely, and to execute simultaneously. The power outage triggered by the same worm isolates the decision makers, keeps trades running long enough to realise a handsome profit. Then, if Cameron's team were right, another wave to ensure the perpetrators made good their escape. Extraordinary. Unprecedented.

How could he spread the word?

"Ms Stanford?"

Ella looked up, startled.

"Your offices are nearby, are they not?"

"About twenty minutes' walk, yes."

"I presume that you have a number of communication channels that you can access from those offices? Power, too? I would expect no less."

Ella nodded. "Yes. It's well set up."

"What if I were to go in person to your offices and attempt to contact my counterparts in the industry? That may be a step towards minimising the damage from this market manipulation."

Sandeep blinked. "What a great idea. We're very close to completing this fix, it's taken no time thanks to Joel's input. Do we really need to stay down here, Ella? Can we run the possible attack scenarios from the office?"

"Can't see why not. Susie, why don't you go over with Sir Simon. Sandeep, Bill and I can stay here. When the power comes back, we'll need to be ready to fight."

Susie gratefully grabbed her bag and flashed a grin at Ella. "It'll be good to get out in the fresh air. I'll call you when we get there." She positively scampered out of the door, followed by Sir Simon.

They walked down to London Bridge. There were no cars on the streets. They were all still attached to their swarm hosts, feeding in every Joule they could generate in a fruitless attempt to keep the city's infrastructure running. Bicycles whizzed freely over the bridge, and a river ferry, running under its own solar power, hooted mournfully. The city still functioned, after a fashion.

Wind turbines all up the Thames were whirring gently as a light breeze blew, but the power they generated remained untapped. Passing the market, quiet on a lazy Sunday afternoon, they turned into a side street and arrived at the door of Argentum Associates. Susie presented her credentials and the door slid open: no problem with the power or the network here. Climbing the stairs, Susie and Sir Simon entered the office, to find Noor busy on a monitor, a Bluetooth speaker on the table beside her, and a cup of hot coffee in her hand.

"Hi Susie. Oh – hello, Sir Simon."

"Ah, coffee, what a great idea. The only things on at the bank are the servers and the security systems. Coffee machines are non-essential."

Susie slipped a mug into place. "Cappuccino."

Sir Simon smiled. "You're right, Ms Lu. I must review those protocols. Good evening, Ms Khawaja. I'll have a double espresso, please."

Susie gave Noor a quick status update. "Ella and Sandeep have almost finished cleaning the systems and they're standing by for the next challenge. How are you getting on here?"

"I still can't raise Pete, and Ross has simply disappeared. But Cameron – oh my word – she and Ben have managed to get an old car running, and they're on their way to SussexGrid. They've just picked up Joel. It's brilliant."

"How marvellous," said Sir Simon. "She's a very resourceful woman, isn't she?"

"I'm in touch with as many teams as I can find," continued Noor. "There are a lot of people offline, but those of us that are able are working towards fixing the outage worldwide."

"This is the reason I've joined you here," explained Sir Simon. "If you can help me to connect with fellow decision makers in the currency markets, I hope we can come to an agreement to suspend trading as soon as the power is restored. That would limit the profits for this group, whoever they are, to the money they have already made. If thereafter they are prevented from withdrawing those funds, so much the better. However, we must take steps to mitigate our losses immediately."

Noor understood perfectly. "Take this monitor." She indicated a blank screen, which glowed into life at her touch. "Susie, can you keep an eye on the forums. Let's get to work."

•

The ancient pickup truck pulled, wheezing, into the car park at SussexGrid. Ben looked around frantically for a good place to park, and spotted a service road sloping down behind the offices that fronted the distribution plant.

"That'll do." He stopped the truck at the top of the slope, ready to roll if its battery died. "I'm going to give this engine a bit of TLC. You go and save the world." He gave Cameron a kiss as she shouldered her bag and headed for the door.

Joel reached out and shook Ben's hand. "Awesome drive, man. Reminded me of being back in the army. Nice work." He grinned, and followed his boss towards the offices.

The door opened, and a startled security guard let them in. The company's chief technology officer came running to the foyer. "Cameron! We weren't expecting you, but you are a sight for sore eyes. Have you fixed it already?"

Cameron laughed. "Nice to see you too, Julia. I love your confidence. It's actually possible that we have fixed it. Let's see what we're dealing with."

Cameron and Joel followed her to the nerve centre of the installation, and started work.

A short time later, the security guard opened the door again to a dishevelled-looking young man with ginger hair. "Your colleagues have already arrived. You know where you're going. Let me take care of your bike."

•

Stranded by his swarming autocar, the stranger had given up on Ross returning to his home. In frustration, he prowled around the outside of the house, and found a window ajar. After several attempts, he managed to force it fully open. It was a struggle to get through, especially without alerting any neighbours, although the overgrown trees in the garden shielded his efforts from most casual gazes. Must lose some weight, he muttered to himself.

Inside, he started to search, room by room, for any clues to the disappearance of his prey. On a table he found two screens, abandoned and switched off. One he managed to open: the only data on it showed communication with the hub, and with the stranger himself. The other was impenetrably sealed with biometric markers. He threw it to the floor in disgust.

As he walked back along the hall towards the bedroom where he had entered, the daylight cast a shadow around a regular tear in the wallpaper. Pausing, he ripped at the flap. The tear had been made deliberately, and recently. What had been hidden under there? He tore the paper off and dug with his fingers into the hole in the wall, past the obsolete control panel, feeling his way.

At SussexGrid, Julia triumphantly flipped a switch, and there was a rush of glorious light. A ragged cheer went up from the assembled team.

The stranger felt an overwhelming sharp pain travel from his hand into his body. There was bang, and he fell backwards to the carpet. He did not move.

•

"The power's back on," cried Ella as the lights flicked back on and screens lit up.

In the office, Susie and Sir Simon jumped at the sound of Ella's voice emanating from the speaker.

"Bill, get up to the boardroom, check the market feeds," Sir Simon's voice sounded over the speaker in the operations room. "I think we've managed to close it down."

Bill rushed out of the room.

Ella turned to Sandeep. "Right, I guess we'd better brace ourselves. Keep an eye on the traffic."

Sure enough, as they watched, the traffic to the bank's servers started rising steadily.

"I can't believe it's started so quickly," said Sandeep.

"It makes sense," replied Ella. "If they really have managed to stop trading, then whoever is behind this knows we've rumbled them. They'll be trying to get their profits out now. Noor, did you catch that? We believe the DDoS attack has been initiated."

"Confirming that," replied Noor. "Reports coming in from all over the place. At least we were all ready. What do you think it's masking?"

Bill came flying back through the door. "Futures trading on cryptocurrency markets is suspended, but there's something else going on. Alerts on all the client accounts. Balances are yoyoing up and down. There are transfers happening, but we can't tell where they're going to."

"That's it!" yelled Ella. "They're taking the scenic route through other people's accounts. Noor, check whether this pattern is holding elsewhere. We've closed down all the vulnerabilities in the servers, but they're obfuscating the real transactions. Covering their tracks. I think it's just a smokescreen."

Noor was frantically keeping track of all the forum activity. "That hot team on the east coast have picked up on it. They're working on it."

"I'm tracking the paths… there's a clear line emerging towards a set of wallets. Noor, transmit these wallet addresses… see what people come up with."

There was a shout of triumph across the office. "East Coast confirmed, one of the wallet addresses matches Speakeasy."

"Unbelievable," cried Ella. "Why would they do that?"

"Showing off? Reminding us all who started this? It's pretty much empty. I think that's their signature flourish."

"DDoS has slowed. Traffic falling back to normal levels," reported Sandeep.

Ella sagged in her chair. "They took their money, then. We failed in the end."

Sir Simon's voice was strong and positive. "No, Ms Stanford, you did not fail. The amounts they got away with were tiny compared to the possible profits. They haven't had the payoff they'd expect from all this effort. You should be proud of yourselves. All of you."

•

In the critical care ward of Southern Infirmary, Dr Roberts perked up as the main lighting flickered back on. Her patient was breathing quietly, monitors steady, condition stable.

"Do we have any ID yet?" she asked her colleague.

"Possibly," he responded. "When he was brought in, he only had the clothes on his back and a Bluetooth headset. Transport police have found an unclaimed set of bags further back in the train." He looked round as the curtain twitched and a uniformed newcomer entered the cubicle.

"Can we try this smartscreen, doctor?"

Dr Roberts nodded. She picked up the patient's limp hand and pressed his thumb to the screen. It lit up instantly.

"Brilliant. And a lot of messages waiting. Someone is missing this lad."

The policeman smiled. "I'll go and give them the good news, shall I?"

"Yes please." The doctor turned as her patient stirred. "Hello, Pete.

How are you feeling? I'm Dr Roberts. You've been involved in a train crash. Everything is going to be just fine."

•

The pickup truck trundled along the motorway. Ross's bike lay in the back, and Joel, Cameron and Ross were crammed together in the cab while Ben drove steadily home. The power restored, cars were moving on the road again. Very few had passengers. Most were empty, returning from their swarm hosts to their usual charging points, job done. Those people who were travelling looked up in amazement as the battered old vehicle made its stately way along the carriageway.

Joel jumped out at his home, and Ross clambered out too and hauled his bike over the tailgate. "I'm going to crash in Joel's spare room tonight. Thanks, Ben. And thank you, Cameron." He paused. "Cameron... I need to tell you something." He hung his head. "The tipoff to the news channels. I'm so sorry. It was me."

He was close to tears.

Stunned, Cameron jumped out of the cab and hugged him awkwardly. "I had no idea, Ross. Don't worry. No harm done in the end. Let's talk properly tomorrow."

Ross nodded. There was going to be a lot to cover.

"We'd better get going," warned Ben. "I don't trust these headlights." He coaxed the idling engine into life. Cameron took her place at his side again and they continued on their way.

The lights were still on at Charlie's house as the truck pulled up at the gate. Cameron clambered down from the cab as her brother emerged from the front door, alerted by the throaty growl of the engine.

"I don't believe it. You made it."

Andy was close behind him. "Cameron, I swear, I would give anything to run that story. You bloody marvel."

Cameron grinned at him. "It is quite a story, isn't it? And it deserves to be told, if only to warn people what could happen, what is likely to happen again. I'll give you your scoop, but I stay in the shadows."

The truck horn beeped behind her.

"We'd better get this beauty back to Jack. He'll want to know we've taken care of her." Taking her seat in the cab for the last time, Cameron waved. "Andy, we'll talk tomorrow. Charlie, we'll be back in a jiffy."

•

Monday morning dawned, unseasonably cold and drizzly. Cameron curled up tight against Ben's back, ignoring the light that had disturbed her sleep.

Ben, too, was stirring. "Ohh, I am aching all over. Driving hurts. My shoulders. My back." He stretched, and Cameron protested.

"If you're going to kick me out of bed, I may as well go and get some coffee."

She grabbed the red bathrobe and padded down the stairs, heading for the kitchen, where she found Charlie already up and watching the news channels.

"All credit for the fast resolution of these unprecedented attacks must go to the talented teams of threat intelligence operatives with whom it has been my pleasure to work," said Sir Simon to the interviewer.

"Can you give us details of the agency the bank has worked with, Sir Simon?"

"I'm sorry, I can't identify them. It's best if they remain anonymous; their role at the forefront of the war against cyber crime is extremely sensitive."

Cameron smiled. "Andy will get his story, no problem. I may have to reconsider our blanket secrecy. It might be better to be a little open. It may even give us more protection and help in the long term."

The kettle boiled, and Charlie filled four mugs with strong coffee.

"Are you staying another day?"

"No," Cameron sighed. "There's a lot of clearing up to do. Everyone's in the office this morning. I should go and visit Pete in hospital. The cat will be going loopy and she'll need feeding. And Ben has to get back to work."

Charlie took a good look at his little sister. "He's a keeper, Cam. You know that, don't you?"

She nodded. "Yes, Charlie. I know."

ACKNOWLEDGEMENTS

This book would not have been written without months of persuasion from David Morton of itsw.co (http://itsw.co/), who eventually convinced me to put the first five hundred words down on paper. Lorraine Ellison's howls of laughter at an early snippet of the adventures of Donald the Cat finally pushed me to write the rest. Further thanks to David for curbing the wilder improbable tech scenarios that tumbled from my imagination, chapter by chapter, to Rosie Brent and Vicky Burke who each read the first complete draft, enjoyed it, and suggested some key changes, and to my remarkably patient family. Most of the tech in this book already exists in some form or another, and I'm looking forward to seeing how our lives change over the next few decades.

HACKED FUTURE
FUTURE
SIMCAVALIER BOOK TWO

PROLOGUE

The man stepped out of the autocar and it sped away into the night. He walked purposefully towards the unassuming brick building that housed the data centre, his progress illuminated by a cluster of streetlights which flicked on as they sensed his approach. The security guard on duty watched his screens, showing the man from several angles as circling security drones and hidden CCTV cameras recorded his arrival. As he approached the discreet pedestrian gateway, the visitor fished in his pocket and presented a card to the sensor.

Not chipped, then, thought the guard, one of the traditionalists who relied on wearables and portables. He'd noticed that a lot of the technicians who passed through the door chose physical security measures as well as the more common wave of a hand implanted with a programmable microchip. There must be a lesson there.

The guard went to his terminal and pulled up the visitor records. On a cursory check at the start of his nightshift he had been sure no one was expected, but faults could occur at any time. Sure enough there it was: server playing up, an urgent callout to tech support properly recorded on the calendar.

The new arrival crossed the few metres of landscaped grounds to the building's main entrance. He tapped his access card on the door and it sprang open obediently. He stepped through and smiled at the guard.

"Late one tonight," he said.

The guard grunted and held out his hand for the card. He examined it, looking critically at the young man. Quite young, early thirties. A touch under six feet tall. Slim. Dark skin and brown eyes. Expensive trousers and shoes slightly out of keeping with the cheap work shirt bearing the support company's logo. Not someone he'd seen before, but there were always people coming and going.

"Evening…" he glanced at the card again, "…Aman. First time here?"

"No, no," replied the visitor. "I normally do callouts through the day. Swapped shifts this evening."

There was a pause as the guard checked the details on the card against the callout record. All in order. He handed the card back and pulled a small scanner across the desk.

"Need to run you through biometrics," he said. "Right hand thumbprint, please."

The visitor placed his thumb to the screen, but the light stayed red. He looked worried for a moment, then his face cleared. He held his hand up to the guard.

"Burned my fingers getting a dish out of the oven a couple of days ago," he said apologetically. "I've been off work. That's why I've ended up with this late shift."

Sure enough, there was a red weal across the pad of the visitor's thumb and blisters on two of his fingers, deep enough to obliterate temporarily the swirls and ridges of his prints. The guard scowled.

"Well, Aman," he said finally, "everything else checks out, but you need to get a retina scan on file as soon as you get back to base."

The visitor nodded earnestly. "Yes, of course," he replied. "I should have thought of that. I'm sorry."

The guard stepped out of his office through a door on the other side of the barrier. He beckoned at Aman. "Bag on the conveyor, please, and empty your pockets."

Aman had already started to place his belongings on the belt. He stepped through the arch of the scanner. No alarms sounded. His bag reappeared from the x-ray machine and the guard gestured to him to open it, revealing a selection of cables, tools and spare parts. All in order.

"Screen?" asked the guard.

Aman pulled his smartscreen out of his pocket and thumbed the lock, smiling apologetically.

"I've disabled the signal," he said, "but I'll need it to check the repair."

The guard turned it over in his hands and swiped through the settings. The support company's familiar logo was emblazoned on the home screen. He nodded and handed it back, satisfied.

"You're good to proceed," said the guard at last. He returned to his office and released the final lock on the inner door. "You know where you're going?"

"Sure," said the visitor. "Like the back of my hand."

The door slid open and he walked off confidently down the corridor. The security guard watched until he turned, without any hesitation, in the direction of the main data hall. He nodded to himself and returned to his cubbyhole. All was well.

The visitor exhaled, relieved. Losing concentration for a moment, he almost tripped on one of the little cleaner bots that travelled the corridors out of hours. He smiled. So far so good.

Printing a company identity card with his own photograph had been straightforward: the holograms wouldn't stand up to scrutiny, but he had been right to assume that if the card was seen to hold the correct access codes to enter the site there would be no problem. The real owner of the access card was drinking in a bar a mile away. The card was still safe in his pocket and he was enjoying the attentions of an attractive new colleague. He was quite unaware that a device in her handbag was reading the data from his card and transmitting it straight to its clone.

The callout record had been surprisingly easy to create. He'd expected far more security around the system, however this data centre hosted servers for many clients. The calendar was held outside the virtually watertight firewalls to enable multiple parties to access it. Finding a small client who was complacent about security had taken only a few hours. An intercepted email, a tiny package of malware deposited on a busy salesperson's laptop, and the little company's network had opened like a flower in the sun. From there, it was straightforward to hop onto the shared calendar to announce his arrival. The appointment record wouldn't stand up to forensic scrutiny if the trail reached the compromised client, but it was enough to get past the data centre's gatekeepers, and he would be long gone when, or even if, the breach was detected.

The visitor had memorised the layout of the building. Not only did the website of the hosting company feature a 360° virtual tour of the place, but within its old, listed exterior it was a standard data centre design and the plans were readily available. Sending the managers an innocent enquiry, posing as a new customer, had helped to gather more detail on the layout of the servers themselves in the data hall. Loading the plans into a virtual reality simulator had allowed him to walk through this visit a hundred times. His target was one of the only large stacks owned by a single organisation.

He kept moving, aware that the CCTV would be recording his progress and that he had to look natural. It was time to ensure that the coast was clear in the data hall.

A sophisticated phishing attack that he'd initiated several weeks ago had finally succeeded in delivering a package of malware to an unsuspecting admin assistant. The malware had been quickly deleted by the in-house IT security staff, but not before he'd succeeded in gaining access to some unsecured devices on the fringes of the network. Undetected, the software had remained dormant until it was needed, hiding in the connected public-address system. Prior to setting out for the centre this evening, he had switched on the loudspeakers in the building. Normally quiescent unless an announcement was in progress, the speakers were all currently live, and his little software package was pinging out signals beyond the range of hearing. He glanced discreetly at the smartscreen in his hand. It showed the results of echolocation from the speakers located in the server room. There was someone moving around. It might be a technician working late or a patrolling security bot. Either way, he had no wish to meet it.

He slowed his pace fractionally, but it wasn't enough. Thinking fast, he stopped and put his bag on the floor, rummaging through it as if concerned he'd forgotten a vital component for the repair. The dot on his screen moved towards the edge of the display and disappeared. The threat seemed to have receded. He feigned relief, picked up his bag again, and moved off down the corridor.

He entered the huge data hall and glanced around. Around the edge of the walls he spotted the dark dots of the helpful speaker and several watching cameras. The ceiling was unusual: slick and shiny. Was it glass? Server stacks rose around him in neat rows, humming gently. It was warm despite the cooling systems that ran constantly in the background. Aman pulled off his jacket and slung it over his arm. Despite careful preparation, it took a few heart-stopping moments for him to identify the server stack that was his primary target. This unremarkable cabinet was bursting with commercial secrets. After fruitless months of trying to get through the data centre's firewalls, he had finally reached his goal.

He set to work, carefully passing through physical controls before linking his screen to the server. An app he'd created scrolled through possible passcodes faster than the eye could follow. He was rewarded with access in less than a minute, a command line appearing on the screen. He made a show of checking the installation, then opened his bag and pulled out a spare part: an innocent-looking network card. He slipped it into the server. It would go unnoticed to casual eyes, even during routine maintenance, but the circuits within it would give him all the access he needed. The client had been very specific about the design files they wanted. There was a good payday to come.

For the sake of the unblinking cameras, he tapped at the screen, peered at imaginary readouts, fiddled with wires, and rubbed his chin. A run-of-the-mill tech support operative checking his work. He glanced at his echolocation displays: someone was approaching. Time up.

He cautiously disconnected his screen and closed up the stack.

Hearing footsteps, he moved smoothly to the door and back down the corridor, dodging another herd of cleaner bots, and skirting around a larger maintenance bot that emerged from the ladies' restrooms. He pulled his jacket back on, ready for the cool of the night.

Reaching the main door, he rang for the guard. The lock clicked open, and he dropped his bag back on the conveyor belt for examination. Stepping through the scanner, he waited while the guard made a cursory search of the contents. There would be nothing to find. He calmly handed his screen to the security guard, hoping the hammering of his heart could not be heard.

"All sorted," he said cheerily. "Could you sign my work chit?"

The guard barely looked up as he scribbled his signature.

Out in the fresh air, the visitor felt a rush of adrenaline and relief. His autocar was waiting. He climbed in and sat back heavily, breathing deeply as the tension dissipated. As the car sped away into the darkness, he pulled out his screen and a second basic device. Time to tie up some loose ends.

First, a call on the second device to the young lady who had been so helpful in capturing and transmitting the access codes. He thanked her sincerely and assured her that, as agreed, he would destroy the records he held. They proved her involvement in petty theft from her employer: the threat of discovery had made her extremely useful to him. However, her services would not be required again, and he was an honourable criminal.

Second, a call on his main smartscreen. A grin spread over his face as he waited to connect.

"Done," he said as soon as the call connected. He couldn't keep the smug tone out of his voice. The team had an all-star reputation among the digital mercenaries of the dark web, and he'd just earned them another great review.

1: SECRETS AND LIES

The smell was all too familiar. Joel pushed the door open cautiously and peered into the gloomy kitchen. The blinds across the windows were closed and very little light penetrated the room. He could hear the refrigerator running, but no other sounds emanated from the house. Two chairs were tucked tidily away under a small table. A selection of shorts, t-shirts and underwear hung on a drying rack in the corner, bright luminescent logos puncturing the half-darkness. There was no sign of a disturbance. Stepping across the threshold, Joel motioned to Ross to stay back. The younger man nodded hurriedly, gagging as the sweet scent of death drifted from the house. Ross moved away from the doorway and onto an unkempt square of grass that served as a small front garden, taking a few deep breaths of fresh evening air in a vain attempt to quell his rising nausea.

As Joel moved into the room, the light automatically flicked on, illuminating the small kitchen and a corridor beyond. At the edge of the light was the unmistakable shape of a pair of immobile feet. Taking a deep breath, Joel moved forward, careful to tread lightly and touch nothing. The man was lying flat on his back, sightless eyes fixed on the ceiling. Unassuming, unremarkable, and undoubtedly dead.

Joel retraced his steps, pushed the door closed, and joined Ross in the garden.

"What the hell happened here?" asked Joel.

Ross was even paler than usual and shaking slightly. "I have no idea," he replied. He stared fixedly at the ground.

Joel peered at him keenly. "Ross, what part of your shady past has caught up with you?"

Ross shrugged, embarrassed, and remained silent.

Joel sighed and plucked his smartscreen from an inside pocket. He tapped the 'Emergency Call' icon and a chatbot immediately responded.

"Emergency services. Please describe the incident," said the bot.

"Unexplained death, we found a body," replied Joel.

"Thank you. Please stay calm. Are you at the incident location?" asked the voice.

"Yeah," replied Joel.

There was a pause, and the voice continued. "Your location services appear to be disabled on this device. Please confirm your location by activating your device or scanning your chip."

Joel activated the app's location service and a green box appeared on the screen with a countdown timer.

"Law enforcement services have been alerted and will reach you shortly," said the bot. The call terminated, and the countdown timer began to tick. A second notification popped up asking for feedback on the bot's handling of the call. Joel swiped the survey request away, irritated, and turned back to Ross.

"They'll be here in four minutes. Is there anything you need to tell me before they get here?" Ross shook his head firmly and said nothing. Joel continued. "Could be a straightforward burglary, I suppose. Petty criminal going after your computers and your grandmother's jewellery."

"I guess," replied Ross. "And he was unlucky enough to have a heart attack in the middle of the job?"

Joel nodded. "It's plausible. Let's see what the professionals say."

The pair of them stood silently in the garden. Ross was wrapped in his own thoughts, still feeling sick, occasionally kicking at a tuft of grass. Joel checked his messages, then tapped out a quick note to say he would be late home. The sun was going down slowly, and trees cast long shadows in the golden light. The hot summer had come to an abrupt end and there was a distinct autumnal feel to the air. It was remarkably peaceful, at odds with the grisly find indoors.

They both jumped, startled, as a large police drone swooped around the side of the house. Joel glanced at his screen.

"Twenty seconds early. Not bad," he said approvingly.

The drone completed its sweep of the exterior of the building and landed at the door. Its warning beacon began to flash the message *'Police Line: Do Not Cross.'*

A few moments later the first human response arrived, vehicles gliding silently to a halt outside the house. A petite black woman in neat plain clothes, hair plaited tight and close to her head, stepped out of the leading autocar. She exuded an air of quiet authority as she walked smartly towards Joel and Ross.

"Detective Inspector Mercer," she said crisply. There was a hint of a northern accent in her voice. "And you are?"

"Joel Bardouille," replied Joel, extending his hand, "and this is Ross White. It's Ross's house," he added.

DI Mercer briefly shook Joel's hand and then passed a scanner across his hand. "Thank you, Mr Bardouille. Mr White?"

Ross reluctantly extended his arm. The scanner beeped happily. Ross scowled.

DI Mercer replaced the scanner in her pocket. "Would you like to tell me what has happened here?" she asked.

Joel glanced at Ross, who was tight-lipped and pale. He turned back to the officer.

"Ross stayed at my place last night. We'd been working late," Joel explained, "dealing with the power distribution failure. His bike was over at my house, so I left the office early today and went to fetch it. We arrived at about the same time. There was a horrible smell as soon as Ross opened the door."

The officer nodded. "Did you call us immediately?"

Joel continued. "Almost, I mean, only a couple of minutes. I'm ex-army so I knew what we were dealing with straight away. I've been in, but I didn't touch anything. There's a body in the corridor through there." He waved vaguely towards the door of the house. "I'd guess it's a burglary gone wrong. We work in tech; we're both part of Argentum Associates. There's some valuable computer equipment in there."

"And all my racing gear," interjected Ross. "I'm a triathlete. This isn't my only bike." He gestured at a bicycle that was leaning on the wall of the house.

DI Mercer nodded. "Thank you. That's very helpful. My team will start setting up now, but we will need your assistance to build a complete picture of the incident."

"Of course," replied Joel. "I'm not sure how much help we can be, though."

DI Mercer smiled thinly. "Every detail, however small, could assist. If you could step into the office, we'll take initial statements." She indicated a tall vehicle parked at the kerb, the door opening to reveal a self-contained pod with a reassuringly comfortable chair and a small drinks dispenser. "Mr White, you first, please. It's a full AI suite. The bots will run through the process and you can approve and seal the recording before you leave. Help yourself to coffee."

Mercer turned to Joel. "Mr Bardouille, please show my colleagues what you found." A trio of white-suited officers joined them, and they approached the house together.

•

Ross, shoulders hunched, walked slowly towards the pod and through the door, which slid smoothly shut behind him. He threw himself into the chair and looked sourly at the coffee machine.

"Cappuccino," he muttered.

Water began to boil in the depths and a cup slid into place.

"Welcome to the Mobile Interview Suite," came a disembodied, calming voice. "Please relax. You can call me Missy." Ross grunted out a greeting. Missy continued. "Please look directly into the camera and state your full name."

On the wall in front of Ross a green light blinked rapidly above a camera lens. Ross stared levelly at it. "Ross Edmund White," he said clearly. The lens scanned his retina and facial contours. The light stopped blinking but remained on.

"Thank you, Ross," said Missy.

Ross sat back, then started upright again as the coffee machine beside him began to hiss and bubble loudly. Dark jets of coffee poured into the cup, followed by superheated foamy milk. White bubbles threatened to escape over the lip of the cup, suspended on the edge by surface tension alone. As Ross reached towards the cup, Missy's voice distracted him again.

"Please present your chip to the scanner."

An amber light blinked on a raised pad below the camera, and Ross waved his hand towards it. The scanner beeped, and the light turned green, then winked out.

Ross turned back to the coffee machine and retrieved his drink, formalities complete.

"Documenting case number SJ slash 360287 slash 13," continued Missy's mellifluous voice. "I will now run through some routine questions to build your initial witness statement. Once complete, you can review the recording and edit any answer before giving your full approval."

Ross nodded automatically. He had stopped shaking after the gruesome discovery, but still felt unsettled, the interview suite bringing back memories he would rather forget. He took a cautious sip of his coffee. It was too hot to drink. He focused on calming his breathing, relaxing his muscles, and making his reactions as natural as possible. The camera would be taking note of everything. A rueful smile played over his lips as he felt himself falling back into old habits.

"Please tell me how and when you arrived at the scene," said Missy.

"I left the Argentum office near London Bridge at about four," said Ross carefully. "I took an autocar to the end of the road here and walked down to the house. Joel – Joel Bardouille – arrived right after I did, with my bike."

So far so good, thought Ross. Factually correct, so nothing would flag up to the monitoring systems. He continued. "I unlocked the door and as soon as I opened it we could smell... you know..." He gagged at the memory. That was genuine enough, at least.

A short rail popped swiftly out of the wall, the paper bag that hung from it rocking slightly with the speed of movement. It was so incongruous that it distracted Ross from the resurging feelings of nausea. He straightened up and resisted the urge to laugh.

"Thank you, Ross, please take your time," said Missy. "Did you enter the scene?"

"No. I looked in from the doorway and saw there was someone... something... on the other side of the kitchen, in the corridor," replied Ross. "Joel went in to look properly while I stayed in the garden. When he came back out we called the police."

"Does anyone else live at this property?" asked Missy.

"No." Ross sighed. "Not since my grandmother died two years ago."

"Do you have any idea who this person may be?" the voice continued.

Ross shook his head, buying time before speaking. "I don't get many visitors," he replied. His voice was steady. "I have a lot of valuable gear in the house. Computers, racing bikes, that sort of thing. It's no secret. People see me going out training from here."

"What security do you have in place?" asked Missy.

"Nothing fancy," replied Ross. "This is a pretty safe neighbourhood. The front door has personalised locks" At this he raised his hand, indicating the embedded microchip. "Plus an old-school key."

"When were you last in the property?"

"Yesterday morning, but I left very early." Missy was silent, so Ross continued. "I work in threat intelligence. My team were tackling that big power outage that hit the city. I went to a client site and took my bike as there were no cars running. I went back to Joel's afterwards. Stayed there last night." He paused and grinned despite himself. "His girlfriend's an amazing cook."

"Thank you, Ross," replied Missy after a pause. "That concludes your initial statement." A screen glowed into life on the wall. "Please review the video and tap to edit or approve."

Ross watched the recording back, relieved, and tapped the green button. A single line of text appeared in its place.

Missy spoke again. "Please read the statement on the screen out loud for the recording."

"I believe the facts stated in this witness statement are true," said Ross clearly.

The screen faded, and the door of the little vehicle opened. Ross clambered out, still carrying his coffee, and blinked as a shaft of light from the setting sun caught him directly in the eyes. He stepped forwards into the shadow of one of the trees that lined the street, and saw Joel approaching from the house.

"My turn, then," he said. "Found where he got in, mate. There's a window open round the back. That's not like you."

"Dammit, I'd forgotten that window," said Ross. "It was a warm night and I couldn't sleep at all. The heating was full on. The whole house environment system was buggered. I ended up digging out the old manual thermostat controls from behind the wallpaper to kill it." He winced. "Sorry. Bad choice of words."

Joel gave him a mirthless grin. "I'd better get this statement done. Is the coffee any good?" He nodded at Ross's full cup.

"Yeah… but scalding hot," said Ross. "I'll see you out here when you're done. Can I crash at your place again tonight? Not much chance of staying in my own bed."

Joel shrugged. "I guess so. Martha should be fine with it. She likes you, for some reason." Ross scowled, and Joel laughed. "Of course you can stay, you daft sod," he said with a broad grin. He stepped into the Mobile Interview Suite and the door closed behind him.

Ross sat on the low wall that separated the small garden from the road, sipping his cooling coffee. Every nerve in his body was telling him to run. Outwardly, he was calm. The nausea that had plagued him since first finding the body had receded. He could hear the footsteps and chatter of crowds on the main road, and music drifting out from a local bar. Autocars made no noise as they sped past, taking people home after a day's work. Drones of all sizes flew overhead, carrying packages and fresh food for hungry households. An unexpected movement caught Ross's eye and he looked up at the sky. An Olsen drone had rounded the corner, attracted by the police presence. It hovered over the garden, assessing the activity against pre-programmed criteria to see if it warranted an alert to the news channels. Startled, Ross pulled the grey hood over his head and held still. He usually courted publicity and craved recognition for his successes, but he really didn't want the press getting hold of this story. He watched silently as an officer waved it away. Nothing to see here.

A neighbour walked by on the other side of the street, staring at the police vehicles and the official drone still flashing at the door. Ross nodded to the man, who acknowledged the greeting nervously and hurried on. There was no need to stop and look. If something really interesting had happened, he'd see it on his news feed.

Ross waited patiently for Joel to finish in the mobile unit, watching the sun sink lower on the horizon.

"Mr White?" Ross turned to see DI Mercer approaching. "Thank you for your statement. How are you feeling?"

"Better, thanks," he replied. He paused, wondering what the right thing was for him to say. "Uh, how are you doing?"

"The forensics team have everything in hand," said Mercer. "Now, obviously you won't be able to come back here until the scene is cleared, and it's getting late. Do you have somewhere to stay tonight?"

"Yeah. I can stay with Joel again. I need to get some things, though. A change of clothes for starters. And I'm due at training in the morning so I'll need my gear."

DI Mercer nodded. "I understand. We can't bring you through the scene, though." She thought for a moment, then called to a junior officer. "John? Can you get a list from Mr White of the things he will need and their location in the house?" The young policeman nodded. "We'll deliver them to Mr Bardouille's address," continued Mercer. "You should be able to return home tomorrow evening once the clean-up teams have finished their job."

The Mobile Interview Suite door slid open and Joel hopped out, tossing his empty coffee cup in the pod's recycling bin. He heard the hiss of sterilising steam as the cup was cleaned and returned to the dispenser, ready for a new interviewee.

"All done. Are we free to go?" he asked.

"Yes, and thank you both for your co-operation," replied Mercer. She turned to Ross. "We'll let you know as soon as we're finished up here."

Ross hesitated. "What shall I do with my bike? No point dragging it back to your place, is there, Joel?"

"We'll look after it," offered DI Mercer. "John, can you get this bike locked away please?"

"Thanks," said Ross. "That makes life easier. You ready, Joel?" He stood up and dropped his own cup into the pod's recycling receptor. He extended his hand to DI Mercer, who shook it firmly. Joel also shook the officer's hand and followed Ross towards the main road.

DI Mercer watched them until they were out of sight, then turned and went back to the house.

She entered the kitchen again and closed the door. Her nose wrinkled in disgust.

The head of the forensics team glanced over at her sympathetically and stepped away from the scene in the corridor, pulling his face mask clear of his mouth and nose.

"You get used to it, Sara," he said. "This isn't a bad one. We're quite lucky he was found so quickly in this warm weather."

"Too much information, Ivan," replied Mercer, wincing.

"We'll be clearing up soon," he continued. "There are no visible injuries. We're going to need a post mortem, but it looks like a heart attack."

"Burglary gone wrong, then," mused Mercer. "Do we know who he is? Face doesn't ring any bells. He's not on my radar."

"No clue yet." The white-suited officer shook his head. "He's not carrying any ID, not even a smartscreen, and he's not chipped. We haven't run biometrics yet: we'll do that back at the morgue. We're pretty certain he entered through the open window to the rear. The drone picked up recently crushed vegetation close to the wall there, and the pressure exerted is more in line with the weight of this individual rather than the resident."

Mercer nodded. "I've reviewed the lad's statement. The doors are chip-responsive with a physical double-lock and there's no sign of forced entry. That window is the only possibility." She frowned. "Odd that he left it open though, being so security-conscious."

"I think we have the answer to that question," replied Ivan. He gestured towards a small machine sitting on the kitchen table. It pinged intermittently. "We've scanned all the smart devices in the building and run a few tests. There seems to have been a fault with the environmental controls. The heating went up very high – we can confirm that from a spike in the fridge's cooling system – and the whole system was shut down manually."

"Manually?" asked Mercer, curious.

"Yes," said Ivan. "The records show an attempt to reboot the system by verbal command, which failed. Then it was disconnected completely from the power supply." He beckoned Mercer to the corridor. "Look there. The original thermostat was behind this wallpaper, and someone's torn their way in to switch it off." He laughed. "For a tech guy's house, it's a very old system."

"That chain of events makes sense," reflected Mercer. "It's possible that he opened the window for some fresh air and forgot to shut it when he was called out to work. We'll confirm his version and the timings when we take our follow-up statements." She glanced at a clock on the kitchen wall. "Are you quite sure the body wasn't here before he left the house?"

Ivan began to answer but broke off as a flurry of movement from caught his attention.

"Boss?" A suited figure stood up, voice muffled by the mask. "You need to see this." Ivan bent to examine the body. Mercer stood still, quietly alert, listening to the exchange.

"We thought it was odd that he's not wearing gloves. I went to take fingerprints for the scene analysis," continued the muffled voice, "and he doesn't have any."

"What?" Ivan's voice echoed through the house, and DI Mercer felt a cold chill run down her spine.

"No fingerprints at all, boss." The voice sounded confused. "Could be, what's it called, that genetic thing where they don't have any?"

"Adermatoglyphia," growled Ivan. "It's highly unlikely, although I suppose it'd be useful in his line of work. Let's have a look." Mercer heard rustling as he knelt to examine the hand.

"This is interesting," he called to his colleagues. "Slight discolouration on the fingers. Looks like a burn, possibly an electrical burn. The kind of thing you'd see if someone was struck by lightning or stuck their fingers in a socket."

"Could be a coincidence," called Mercer from the kitchen. "See what the post mortem comes up with. What about these fingerprints?"

Ivan bent closer to the corpse. "Nothing. First time I've seen this." He touched the hand lightly, turning the fingers out of the shadow into the penetrating spotlight that illuminated the forensic site. "Wait," he continued, "look here. Is that scar tissue?"

"You think they may have been deliberately removed?" asked the masked officer.

"It's possible," replied Ivan. He stood up again and sighed. "Sara?"

"I hear you," replied DI Mercer from the kitchen. "Not your average burglar after all. Keep digging."

•

Ross sprawled in an armchair, letting the commentary from the evening's world league rugby game wash over him. The announcer's voice was steady, his tone reflecting the slow progress of Joel's favourite virtual rugby union team as they pushed laboriously up the pitch.

"Groves waiting, waiting… got to use it… the ball is out, and the pass goes short to Davison and out to Wise on the blind side. There's no way through, Wise can't offload and is taken down by Taylor. Turnover ball."

Joel, who was glued to the screen, groaned in disgust.

"Did you see that? They had players out wide begging for the pass." He turned to Ross and looked him up and down for a reaction. "Not your sport, really, is it? Shame. In real life you'd be quick on the wing." Joel took a swig of beer from the small green bottle that was clutched in his huge hand.

Ross mustered a bleak smile and shook his head. "Never fancied rugby, in the real world or not. I was the skinny nerd at school. The team used me as the ball at lunchtimes. The girls' team."

"That's funny," laughed Joel. "Sorry, mate. You did alright for yourself, though. How did the skinny nerd end up as a triathlete?"

"I had some time on my hands," replied Ross, looking decidedly uncomfortable. "I got the chance to train and I liked it and I was good at it. Still am, I guess. Keeps me out of trouble."

Joel knew when to drop a subject. He turned back to the rugby game just in time to see the opposing team sweep in for a try under the posts. The try scorer's avatar jumped high in delight.

"She's a good player," said Joel grudgingly. "Romanian girl. She's only nineteen. The Accra Aces outbid the rest of the league by miles when she went pro."

The game view swept across virtual stands of cheering supporters and then cut to the fly-half's avatar lining up for a kick at goal.

"That's enough of that," said Joel with a grin. "Off." The screen faded. He stood up and stretched, then paused and sniffed appreciatively at the scent of cooking coming from the kitchen.

"I'll go and help Martha," he said. "Want anything, Ross?"

Ross shook his head and raised his still full glass of water. "I'm fine. Need some help?"

"No, you're okay. Relax. You've had a bit of a shock." Joel left the room, and a moment later Ross heard the door of the kitchen close behind him. He took a sip of water and leaned back in the armchair, staring at the ceiling, eyes unfocused.

Enough. Ross took a deep breath, and with one eye on the door he fumbled in the capacious inside pocket of his jacket. He pulled out two smartscreens and two cheap screens that weren't designed to be all that smart. Burners. Devices for brief use and disposal. Devices for secrecy.

Ross shuddered and fought to quell a new bout of nausea as he recalled his first sight of the body. Contrary to his statement, he had discovered the scene alone. His own smartscreen and one of the burner phones he had retrieved from the kitchen. The other two devices he had recovered after a frantic, horrifying search of the dead man's jacket pockets.

Ross was relieved when his own smartscreen lit up on command, displaying a picture of himself dressed in athletics club strip, standing proud on a podium in the sun. He had found it on the floor, probably cast aside by the intruder, but it seemed to be undamaged. Detecting the chip close by in his wrist, the screen unlocked. Notifications began to stream across the display as it connected to the network, a riot of coloured text bubbles and dancing icons. Messages, missed calls, news alerts, game notifications, calendar reminders, weather warnings. Ross put his screen aside without responding to any of them.

The second smartscreen remained blank. It was a new model, smaller than the one Ross owned. It had amassed a few scratches, one quite deep across the top left corner of the screen. The casing was a plain dark grey, and it was dirty. Ross tried to wipe it clean with a corner of his hoodie sleeve, but the muck was ingrained. He tapped the screen cautiously and it glowed for a moment before sinking back into standby mode, waiting for the right biometric cue to spill its secrets.

Next, Ross turned to the two burner phones. They were identical: small, silver, featureless. He picked the cleaner of the two and tapped a simple code to unlock it. The screen lit up. There was one number in the memory, but he had no intention of calling it. He put the device aside. Picking up the second phone, he examined it carefully. To his surprise there was no keypad lock. There were several numbers recorded on the device. One he knew would connect direct to the burner phone that he had once carried. The others he did not recognise. He tapped one out of curiosity, but the line was dead, trying to connect to a device that was no longer in use. He switched of the phone and tucked both of the stranger's devices back into his jacket pocket out of sight. Hearing the kitchen door open, Ross sat back casually and began to check through the endless stream of information on his own screen.

Joel reappeared carrying plates and cutlery. He looked curiously over at Ross.

"When did you get your screen back?" he asked.

"That nice policeman dropped it off with my underpants and training gear," lied Ross. "It had slid under my bed." He felt he needed to say more. "Plenty of missed messages." Ross made a show of scrolling through the notifications.

Joel laughed. "Serves you right for losing it in the first place." He put the plates on the large table at the other side of the room. "Dinner's ready." He went back towards the kitchen but turned around smartly as Martha arrived with a steaming hotpot. The three of them took their places at the table, and Martha ladled out generous portions of spicy fish and vegetable stew.

"Did the police say when they'd be finished," asked Joel between mouthfuls.

Ross nodded, unable to speak as he savoured the stew. He swallowed. "I can go back tomorrow afternoon. They've secured the house and removed… you know…" Ross took a drink of water. "Anyway, they're doing a final forensic sweep in daylight and then the cleaners will do their thing. I'm training in the morning, so I'll go home after that. Cameron said she doesn't need us tomorrow, didn't she?"

"Yeah, we all need a break after this weekend's job," reflected Joel. "I might have a lie-in myself."

Martha laughed. "Some of us have to work! There are a few things that need doing if you have the time." Joel raised an eyebrow at Ross, who laughed. Martha joined in, not offended in the slightest.

"What's gone wrong now?" asked Joel.

"The mirror in the wardrobe is defaulting to winter," complained Martha, "when I need summer clothes. The bathroom scales are all over the place and they're sending alerts to the fridge. Every time I touch the dessert shelf I get a warning on my smartscreen to confirm my BMI with the insurers."

Joel nodded sympathetically. "Losing access to desserts is serious business." He ducked as a bread roll sailed over his head.

"I think the whole house needs rebooting," Martha continued, without skipping a beat. "The batteries aren't registering power input from the floor tiles, and the shutters are jammed open on the spare bedroom window."

Ross nodded. "They are, but don't worry. I'll be away early tomorrow." He took another mouthful of stew, suddenly hungry.

"The power outages must have knocked it all out of sync," sighed Joel. "I'll give the system a once-over tomorrow and boot it back up properly."

He gave Martha a mock frown. "Spending my day off debugging my own house. It's not fair."

"Just be glad I don't bring my work home with me," said Martha. "A fish farm in the basement could get complicated."

Ross snorted with laughter, hand over his mouth, and swallowed the last of his stew. "At least you bring some of your work home, Martha. This is delicious."

The three of them finished their plates in companionable silence. The fish was very good, fresh from the farms that jostled for space in the Thames estuary. The challenge of providing good local nutrition for the sprawling city had been met as the world warmed. Wide shallow flood plains provided the ideal habitat for fish, while the original human population had been displaced to higher ground. Swarms of chilled transport drones collected the silvery bounty each day, dropping direct to the markets and restaurants and food outlets of the capital.

Ross loved the ready availability of fish, and particularly Martha's skill at transforming it into some of the best food he'd had in months. Staying here with Joel was a far cry from his lonely existence at home, relying on meal-drops and eating for one. Checking his fitness monitor, Ross also appreciated how well the fresh food was keeping his nutrition in balance. His coach would be happy. Maybe it was time to do some work on the house, upgrade the kitchen, and learn to cook like Martha.

Joel's chair scraped on the warm tiled floor as he stood up and began to gather plates. Every movement on the tiles generated tiny amounts of electricity, feeding into the power supply for the whole apartment complex, and earning a few coins for excess production when the electricity generated was used by the neighbours.

Ross got up to help him, and they carried the debris of the meal back to the kitchen.

"Thanks for all of this, mate," said Ross. "I really appreciate it."

"No problem," replied Joel. "You going to be okay, going home?"

"I think so," replied Ross. "It's a good incentive to clear the place out, have a real tidy up. I've been meaning to fix up the house since my gran died. Just never got around to it."

"How come you lived with your grandma?" asked Joel, intrigued. "I didn't realise you'd lost your parents."

"I haven't," replied Ross. "At least, I don't think so." He sighed. "You know I had some bother when I was younger. I got into trouble and I served my time. My mum wanted nothing to do with me when I came out, so I was stuck in a hostel for a while. When she moved away with her new boyfriend, my gran took me in. I've seen her once since then, at gran's funeral. As for my dad, he left when I was little."

Joel looked at his colleague sympathetically. "I never knew. I'm sorry to hear it, man. If there's anything I can do...?"

Ross shook his head. "You've done so much already." He grinned, naturally and easily, feeling comfortable for the first time in days. "And you've got your hands full debugging this place." Ross pointed to the kettle, which was flashing red.

Joel sighed. "Busman's holiday," he growled. He pressed the reset button on the base of the kettle and it stopped flashing. He pushed the button again, trying unsuccessfully to set it to boil. It was quite unresponsive. "Another one for the list."

"Once one thing goes, the rest follow," said Ross sympathetically. "How old's your network?"

"This place was a new build six years ago," replied Joel. "And of course, I've gotten my hands dirty upgrading it. You'd be amazed how fast the security goes out of date. I hate to think of the holes in the other apartment systems in this complex."

"Hacker heaven," agreed Ross. "I'd have had a field day back when I was younger."

"You still could." Joel looked sidelong at him. "I can think of a couple of neighbours I'd like to shake up a bit."

"What, turn their music down?"

"Definitely. They have terrible taste," replied Joel.

"Could set the cleaner bots running in the middle of the night?" said Ross

"Nice. Or how about scrambling their streaming schedules?" suggested Joel.

"Nah, too easy," replied Ross. "Could switch off the hot water mid-shower?"

"Ah, that's more like it," replied Joel. "I like it. Can I book you in?"

"If you're serious, I'd be up for a bit of fun," said Ross. He began to laugh and discovered he couldn't stop. He felt a welcome, cathartic release. Joel joined in with a deep guffaw, and the two of them were howling with laughter when Martha appeared at the kitchen door.

"What are you plotting?" she asked, amused.

"Nothing," replied Joel innocently, recovering his composure as Ross choked back another laugh and wiped tears from his eyes. "Just discussing work."

Martha looked unconvinced.

"I'll head to bed and leave you two alone," said Ross. "I need to be up early for training, anyway." He put the last plate in the dishwasher and walked towards the door.

"Night, mate," said Joel.

"Goodnight, Ross," said Martha. "Sleep well."

"Goodnight." Ross went back to the other room and picked up his jacket from the armchair. He climbed the stairs to the spare room and closed the door behind him. He dug into the jacket pocket for the collection of screens and dropped them onto the bed. Pulling off his jeans and t-shirt, he added them and the jacket to a pile on a small chair at the side of the room.

Ross stepped into the small ensuite and the lights flicked on. He looked at himself critically in the mirror, his reflection lit by the warm glow of the LEDs in the ceiling. Pale skin and ginger hair, legacy of a Scottish father he could not remember. Golden stubble on his chin, in need of a shave. Muscled and toned thanks to years of athletics training. Cynical grey-green eyes that seemed much older than his twenty-eight years.

He shook his head to clear his thoughts. Too much contemplation. He didn't want to spend time searching his soul tonight. That would be quite a job, something to keep for later.

Ross cleaned his teeth and flopped into bed. The lights dimmed automatically, and he lay in the dark, his eyes adjusting to the shadow. The shutter was still open on the window, and Ross could see the stars above the dark city. He fixed his eyes on Orion, the bright glow of Betelgeuse at one corner and a brilliant line of stars forming the hunter's belt. The familiar constellation moved slowly across the sky, and eventually he slept.

2: EDEN

Cameron Silvera leaned against the wall of the gym studio and took a gulp of water. She was sweating despite the air conditioning and had to stop herself from drinking too much of the welcome cool liquid at once. Looking around the room, she was relieved to see that her training partners were equally tired. Snatches of chatter reached her ears as the twenty or so white-suited students took advantage of a two-minute break.

"Mitts and pads on!" called a voice. There was a flurry of activity as everyone rushed to obey the instructor's command.

Cameron dug through her bag and pulled out a bulky pair of gloves, two soft shin pads, and a gumshield. She sat wearily on the wooden floor and pulled the pads over her feet and up towards her knees. Next to her, Jasvinder groaned.

"I'm going to feel this tomorrow," he muttered.

Cameron laughed mirthlessly. "You're going to feel it? I've barely trained for weeks." She stood up, straightened her white jacket, and tightened the knot of the black belt which was wrapped around her waist. She slipped her gumshield into her mouth and pulled her gloves on to take the sting out of her punches

The students paired off and lined up along the centre of the hall. Opposite Cameron, Jasvinder fiddled with his own gumshield, his eyes unfocused. The instructor barked a command and the pairs bowed to each other. Cameron stepped back into stance and prepared to spar.

"Hajime," said the instructor sharply, and the room exploded into movement.

Jasvinder approached, light on his feet, hands held ready to guard against his partner's strikes. Cameron smiled to herself, focusing on nothing but the challenge in front of her. She assessed her opponent's approach carefully and spotted a familiar undefended opening. With a twist of her hips she jabbed a fist through Jasvinder's arms to his solar plexus, then skipped back out of range. Jasvinder grimaced.

"What's up with you?" asked Cameron as she circled. "It's been a while since I caught you that easily."

"Ah, sorry, Cameron. I'm not concentrating," replied Jasvinder. He shook his head and reset his guard firmly. The two of them circled for a moment and Cameron came forward again. This time Jasvinder was ready. His knee lifted, hips turning imperceptibly, and his foot curved out and caught Cameron full in the stomach with a side kick as her punch floated in thin air.

"Oof! Thanks very much," laughed Cameron. She redoubled her efforts, moving sideways to dodge a second kick arcing towards her head, firing back with a solid punch to the ribs. The two old sparring partners traded blows, challenging each other's technique and skill. When the instructor called the class to stop, they laughed and tapped fists, tired but happy.

Stowing her pads back in her bag, Cameron turned to Jasvinder.

"How are you getting home?" she asked.

"I'm walking," replied Jasvinder. "I can't get an autocar. My chip's on the blink."

"Do you want a lift?" offered Cameron. "It's not like it's out of my way."

"Thanks, that'd be great," said Jasvinder, relieved.

"I'm going to get a shower first," said Cameron. "I won't be long. Meet you in the lobby?"

Cameron strolled through the gym to the changing room, idly watching people working out on treadmills and weight machines. She was unconsciously looking for a familiar face, but Ben wouldn't be training tonight, as he had been called out of town for work. The changing room door slid open as she approached. She dropped her kit bag on the bench and took another swig of water. A bank of lockers stood against the wall. She waved her hand vaguely across the line of doors and one sprang open, revealing her street clothes, shoes, towel and toiletries. Cameron folded her belt carefully and stripped off her sweaty karate gi. Wrapped in the towel, she headed for the showers.

As Cameron luxuriated in the jets of warm water, snatches of conversation drifted through the changing room, mingled with the sound of the news channel which rolled permanently on the wall screens.

"…hard session, my legs are so sore…"

"…reports from South East Asia of an outbreak of Grasshopper Flu…"

"…you going out on Saturday? There's a new club open…"

"…police have refused to comment on the incident where it is thought a man died…"

"…this weather's terrible, honestly, it's turned so quickly…"

"…data breach is now thought to have affected more than eighteen million customers…"

"Cameron?" A voice close by startled her.

"Yes?" she replied.

"We're all heading for a drink," continued the voice. "Want to come along?"

Cameron stepped out of the shower and grabbed her towel. Behind her, the jets of water closed off, sensing that the stall was empty. She peered round the tiled wall to the main changing room where a knot of girls from her class were dressing.

"Not tonight," she said, apologetically. "I'm broken. I need a rest. Next time?"

"Definitely," said the young woman who had spoken before, pulling on her shoes.

Dry and dressed in jeans and a jumper, Cameron followed the group out of the changing room and met Jasvinder in the lobby. He was still wearing his karate gi under a padded jacket. They stepped outside into a gust of biting wind and Cameron hugged herself to stay warm, regretting the lack of a coat despite the glow of training. Autumn was coming in with a vengeance.

A row of charging stations in a bay outside the gym stood empty, the autocars that normally rested there absent. Cameron thumbed a call button on the stand, and moments later a little car rounded the corner, its For Hire light shining. They jumped in, and Cameron gave the address of the apartment block where both she and Jasvinder lived.

"That's better," said Jasvinder, settling into the car seat. "It beats walking on a night like this. Thanks, Cameron. I appreciate it."

"No problem," she replied. "What's up with your chip?"

"It's been glitchy on and off for days," he sighed. "You forget how much you rely on it. You have one, don't you?"

Cameron nodded. "I've had it for years. It was quite an early one, but it's up to date. I don't use it often. It's handy for going through border control when I travel." She laughed. "And for gym lockers, of course."

"Yeah, right," said Jasvinder. "The trouble is, my clothes got stuck in there the other night." He looked down at his white trousers.

"You didn't risk it this evening, then?" said Cameron.

"No chance!" replied Jasvinder. "But I hope my room-mate's at home or I'll be camping in the stairwell." He laughed despite himself. "I should be okay. There's an override system. I just hope I can remember the password."

The autocar swept silently down the main road, turning into a side street and pulling up outside a large brick apartment building with an elegant glass entrance. Cameron thumbed the payment to the car and scrambled out with her kit bag. She flashed her wrist at a sensor on the wall by the entrance and the lock clicked in response. Jasvinder followed her through the rotating door and into the warm hallway. Lights flickered on, guiding them to the stairwell. They climbed steadily together, their legs weary from a good class.

At the second-floor landing, Jasvinder turned towards his apartment, waving his hand at the sensors by his door without much hope. The door remained firmly shut, but the sound of music drifted through to the landing. He knocked loudly, and a moment later his room-mate appeared, laughing. Jasvinder gave Cameron a cheery wave and went inside.

Cameron climbed higher to her own apartment. She pulled a slim metal key from her pocket and inserted it into the well-oiled lock. The door opened. She heard the patter of eager paws and a little black and white cat emerged from the gloom, chirruping a welcome. As Cameron stepped over the threshold, the lights turned smoothly on. She closed the door, dropped her bag, and threw herself gratefully onto the sofa. The cat clambered onto her knee, circling and purring.

"Missed me, baby?" She ruffled the fur on the cat's head and its nose pushed wetly against her hand. "Hungry?"

The cat hopped down and trotted towards an empty bowl. Cameron hauled herself upright and went to the cupboard, measuring out a portion of kibbles. The cat settled to its meal and Cameron opened the refrigerator.

"Good evening," came a cheery disembodied voice. "Your food inventory is low. Would you like to place an order?"

Cameron cursed and hurriedly closed the fridge door.

"Bloody software updates," she muttered under her breath. She pulled her smartscreen from a pocket of the kit bag and logged on to the apartment's environment control centre. With a few swipes and taps she disabled all the fridge's smart functions. She put her screen down on the kitchen counter and cautiously opened the door again. The light came on, but the only sound was the gentle humming of the cooling system. Cameron grabbed a half-empty wine bottle and a box of leftover spaghetti bolognese from the shelf. She picked a plate and a glass from a nearby cupboard, set the pasta to heat through, and poured herself some wine. Leaning against the kitchen counter, she took a sip from her glass, and wondered what was going on in the world.

"On," she called to the monitor set into the opposite wall. The screen glowed into life and the familiar news channel announcer appeared.

"…A spokesperson for Calton Global said that the breach had been identified quickly and systems secured to prevent any further incidents. The company insists that only a small percentage of customer records have been accessed, and they will be contacting all of those affected."

Cameron laughed mirthlessly. "I bet there's more to it," she muttered under her breath. She took another sip of her drink as the announcer moved on to the next piece of headline news, and the image on the screen switched to lush rainforests and gleaming high-rise buildings.

"…the virus is spreading rapidly, with reports of cases in major population centres…"

"Off!" Cameron shivered despite the warmth of the room. Talk of viruses and epidemics brought back bad memories. People she had loved, people she had lost.

She needed some distraction. Not music, or streaming: real humans to talk to.

"Call Ben," she ordered the smartscreen. It placed the call, but there was no answer. Cameron frowned. He must be working late again. Not for the first time, she wondered what crisis had pulled him away from London to the company's overseas offices. She missed him, although in his absence she was glad to have fallen back into the routine of training after a busy few weeks.

The oven beeped. Cameron put on a heatproof mitt and carried the hot plate of steaming pasta to the table. She sat down to eat but her appetite had gone. She toyed listlessly with her food and sipped her wine in silence.

An alert from her smartscreen made her jump. Glancing at the message, Cameron grinned. Activity on her threat intelligence forum. People to chat to. She moved over to her computer, pausing to refill her wine glass as she passed the fridge. Choosing a random IP address to conceal her real location, she connected to the forum, and immersed herself in chatter.

"Hey, SimCavalier, glad you could join us."

"How you doing?"

"Fine, guys," typed Cameron. "What's going on?"

"Calton Global in big trouble with this latest breach," replied a member known to Cameron only as 'Bordegiciel'. She had a feeling the handle was slightly vulgar.

"News say eighteen million accounts accessed," continued the post, "my source says ten, twenty times that."

"Wow," typed Cameron, "that's a decent haul for a little hacker. Calton has fingers in every pie, doesn't it, from health to agritech? Any idea what was compromised?"

"No idea yet," replied her contact. "No data dumps, no news from inside, just spin doctors saying all okay."

Cameron sat deep in thought, running through possible scenarios in her head, alive to the challenge. She watched as other forum members added comments to the thread, speculating about the data that had been stolen and the identity of the thief. She took another sip of wine and leaned back on her chair, stretching her back which was starting to ache from training. The cat hopped up onto her knee again, startling her out of her reverie. She shook her head and returned to the screen, scrolling through the thread to catch up with the most recent speculation, while scratching the purring cat behind the ears with her free hand.

"Friend of mine worked on their algorithms for the product lifecycle blockchain," chipped in one member. "She said they were tight as a drum for security. Close monitoring of access rights. Physical separation of data on the servers. All kinds of application firewalls restricting volume queries."

That rang a familiar warning bell in Cameron's head. "Firewalls with volume conditions," she typed. "Not always as good as people make out. If you can get into the conditional programming, it's an easy route."

"You would need to know the system well," replied Bordegiciel. "Inside job. Human error."

"Always," typed Cameron, sighing to herself. "People are so much trouble."

"Bots too," came another comment. "Artificial intelligence is getting craftier all the time."

"Seriously, though," typed Cameron, "this isn't the first hack where access-limiting firewalls have been mentioned. Remember the TrustCentre break-in a few years ago? They got in to the server farm through a security camera on default settings, reprogrammed the firewall to accept infinite queries, went straight through the security on the servers like a dose of salts, and casually downloaded a bunch of data before they were picked up."

"I remember that," replied one of the older forum members. "It made all the headlines."

"The hackers were found, weren't they?" asked Bordegiciel. "They put the data up for sale without covering their tracks too well, and the UN cyber defence squads landed on them."

"They were sent down, if I recall," replied Cameron. "They're probably out for hire again now, though. I wonder what they're up to."

I bet Ross knows, she thought.

"Does RunningManTech have any ideas?" asked another forum member. "Haven't seen him for a few days."

"You read my mind," replied Cameron. "And he's fine, we've all been busy."

"All of us been busy, SimCavalier," said Bordegiciel. "Say, is your HackerTracker up to date?"

Cameron started to reply to the new question, then looked up as her smartscreen chirruped, alerting her to an incoming call.

"I'll add this latest one to it and take a look at trends," she typed quickly. "Got to go, guys."

She logged off quickly, dislodged the cat as she jumped up from her chair, and lunged at the smartscreen to accept before the caller rang off. There was a pause, and then the welcome sound of a familiar voice.

"Hi gorgeous."

"Hi Ben." Cameron felt a warmth spreading in her core and butterflies twisting in her stomach. She smiled into the dark eyes on the screen. "It's getting late."

At the other end of the call, Ben sighed. "Bit of an emergency at work. I'm sorry."

"All okay now?" asked Cameron, brightly, hoping for good news.

"I'm not sure," replied Ben. "I may be stuck here in the Paris office for longer than I expected." He looked upset. "I miss you. I wish you were here. I can't even get back this weekend."

Cameron's heart sank. "Are you still okay for next week?" she asked. "Nina was hoping you'd be able to come. It's a big day for her."

"I know it is. I'll do my best," said Ben earnestly. "I want to be there."

"What's going on?" asked Cameron. "Can you tell me?"

"I don't really know myself," replied Ben. "But reading between the lines, there may be something here which is related to your line of work. I can't say much more."

Interesting, thought Cameron. She didn't press for details. If there had been a security breach or cyberattack at Ben's company, then it would come across her radar soon enough. Best not to compromise his position.

"Don't worry," she replied. "I'm sure it'll be sorted soon, and then you'll be home."

"You could come over here," suggested Ben. "If it drags on, you could try and get the train this weekend."

"Really?" said Cameron. "I'll check my visa status. I might have to renew."

"Do it," said Ben. "Even if I've finished up, we can spend the weekend here together."

"I will. That would be fantastic," said Cameron, excited.

Ben grinned broadly. "I can't wait to see you." He leaned back from the screen, and Cameron could see in the background the generic décor of an international hotel chain: Too-bright lighting, charging pods at the side of the bed, and a picture wall shifting gradually from local landmarks to night scenes and stars.

"Cheers," said Ben, lifting a glass towards her.

"Cheers yourself," said Cameron, lifting her own wine glass in reply. They shared a moment of quiet as each took a sip.

"I have to go," said Ben. "Another early start in the morning."

"Me too," replied Cameron. "Sleep well."

Ben blew her a kiss and the call disconnected. Cameron sighed, and sat back heavily on the sofa. The cat snuggled closer to her, purring, and Cameron felt herself dozing off. It was time for bed.

•

The office door opened.

"Morning," said Cameron from behind her screen.

Sandeep jumped. "You gave me a shock. I'm normally in first. Do you want a coffee?"

"I've got one, thanks," replied Cameron. "You could order some breakfast, though."

"Already done," said Sandeep. He walked over to the delivery hatch and pulled it open. The croissants were still warm, dropped fresh from the bakery. "Here." He proffered the bag, and Cameron took one of the flaky pastries gratefully.

"I thought I heard the drone," said Cameron indistinctly, through a mouthful of crumbs.

"What brings you in here so early?" asked Sandeep. "I thought our meeting wasn't until nine."

Cameron shrugged. "I couldn't sleep." She beckoned Sandeep over. "Here, take a look at this."

Sandeep bent to peer at the data scrolling upwards in front of his eyes. Cameron tapped once on the screen and the scrolling stopped.

"Okay, here," she said. "I'm on the Eden network. This is the auction for the Calton Global hack. There's a big bundle of swag for sale and the usual sharks are circling."

"Yes, seen that," said Sandeep. "I had a peek at Eden ready for this morning. Some interesting data sets. Calton has been well and truly filleted."

Cameron grinned. "The guys on the east coast are at the group headquarters looking for the leaks now. I'll be briefing everyone this morning. We've got a busy time ahead of us auditing local clients." She paused and tapped her screen again. "But look here. There are several sales going on. I can match up most of the datasets to what we know of Calton's activities, plus there are a few bundles which look to be in a similar field, and a couple of unrelated breaches we've already heard about. But then there's this dataset." She sat back, frowning. "Who do you think it could be?"

Sandeep looked closer at Cameron's screen, surprised. "I see what you mean." He pointed at a line of characters. "There's some IP data, but the rest of it... I'm not sure. Is that something to do with engineering designs?" He straightened up, thinking hard. "Have you heard anything about a factory hack? Commercial espionage? I haven't seen anything on the forums or official notifications."

"Nothing," replied Cameron. "Either it's very old data from before I set up my HackerTracker, or they don't know it's happened."

"I don't think it's that old," said Sandeep. "Look at these file extensions. That's recent design software."

"Huh? Yes, you're right," replied Cameron. "Someone's in trouble." She frowned, thinking. Something was niggling at the back of her mind. "I wonder if they genuinely have no idea, or if there's been a cover-up?"

Sandeep strolled over to the coffee machine, which started to boil as it sensed his approach. Sliding a cup into place, he waited for the steaming black liquid to finish pouring. He carried his drink over to another screen and reached for a croissant from the bag. Taking a bite, he tapped the screen with his free hand and it glowed into life.

"Okay, let's have a look at this." Sandeep checked the incognito settings on his connection and navigated carefully to the hidden auction site. "You've dumped everything you've seen so far, yes?"

"Got it all," replied Cameron.

The two of them bent to work, seeking clues in the patterns that danced across their screens. They were so absorbed in their task that they barely noticed Ross, Joel and Noor arriving for the morning's meeting.

The hiss of the coffee machine boiling again brought Cameron back to reality, her head spinning with tantalising possibilities. She looked up, blinking. "Morning folks."

There was a chorus of greetings in reply.

"Coffee's brewing and the croissants are fresh," said Sandeep, standing and stretching. "Cameron, want another drink?"

She nodded and passed her empty cup over. Sandeep followed the others to the coffee machine and refilled their mugs.

A screen on the wall glowed into life and Pete's face appeared.

"Hi everyone, sorry I can't be there in the flesh," he said. He looked tired, and in the background Cameron could see medical equipment and clean white walls.

"Glad you could join us, Pete," she said. "How are you feeling?"

"On the mend, thanks," replied Pete. "Bored, more than anything. Have you got anything fun for me to do?"

"Maybe," said Cameron with a grin.

Ross, Joel, Noor, Sandeep and Cameron gathered around the table in the centre of the room. Sandeep glanced at the clock.

"Huh? Susie and Ella are late," he said. "Anyone heard from them?"

Joel shrugged, Ross shook his head, and Noor looked concerned. At that moment the door opened, and the two girls rushed in.

"Sorry," panted Ella. "There was a car crash on the bridge. Traffic's backed up and there are crowds of people watching." She collected a coffee, refusing the croissant that Joel offered, and sat down.

"Really?" said Pete from the screen. "That's rare. What happened?"

"We didn't see it," replied Susie, "but apparently there was a kid who ran onto the road in front of an autocar."

"The car's ethical decision program kicked in," continued Ella, as Susie's coffee brewed, "so it swerved to hit the nearest empty vehicle."

"'Minimise Danger to Life and Limb'," quoted Noor. "Was anyone hurt?"

"I don't think so," replied Susie. "The car was full of cushion foam, so its passenger was probably fine. The first response drones arrived before we got across the bridge, and I saw a couple flying away again. They can't have been needed." She took her place at the table and reached for one of the remaining croissants.

Cameron called the group to order. "We've got a busy few weeks ahead of us," she said. "The spoils of the Calton Global hack are out there now on Eden and the bidding is fierce. We have some idea of the real scale of the breach, and the east coast team is working with Calton to find and seal the hole."

"How far does the fallout spread?" asked Ross.

"Global reach," replied Cameron. "The hackers managed to access some of the data repositories behind the blockchain at several points. There's supply chain information on sale which is commercially sensitive, and health data for tens of millions of end users, at the very least."

"That's bad," said Ross. "Do we know what happened? Where was the breach?"

Cameron laughed drily. "It's bad, alright. I think they got complacent. I don't know, but I suspect they spent so much time keeping the whole product lifecycle transparent that they diverted resources from securing the data beneath it."

"That's more common than you know," said Pete from the screen. "People forget that the blockchain doesn't hold all the underlying databanks. It simply records changes of state in the ledger. Whatever you've got in the background is still vulnerable."

Susie spoke up. "Fairly standard hacking, then."

"Looks like it," replied Cameron. "Right now, the guys on the east coast are focusing on Calton Global's servers and any phishing attacks that have crept through to key systems." She sighed. "Most of the time it's still down human error."

"What about the breach itself?" asked Ross insistently. "From what you say there could be multiple points of access. More than just Calton's servers."

"That struck me too when I was looking at the data bundles," said Sandeep. "There are several bundles that seem to hold similar data, but they're configured differently. Not the same source."

"If so, it implies a co-ordinated attack on several actors in the blockchain," chipped in Pete. "That takes some doing."

"It's possible," said Cameron. "Good thinking. We haven't gotten in to the detail of their ledger yet; it's a private system for Calton's own supply chain. Noor, could you see if the east coast guys working at Calton have looked at the whole product lifecycle on the blockchain? Have they come to the same conclusion?"

Noor glanced at the clock. "It's three in the morning with them. I'll see who's awake." She pinged a message out to her contact; there was no immediate reply. "Guess they're sleeping."

"Try them again later," said Cameron decisively. "We have a list of Calton Global partners to see; we can keep our eyes open for related breaches when we audit their systems. In the meantime, we have another puzzle." She pulled up her screen dump of the second data auction. "Check this out. There's no official report of this breach as far as I can tell. It's possible the source doesn't even know."

There was silence as the group studied the details.

Ross let out a low whistle. "Nice haul," he said. "I'm surprised this is out for auction. It looks more like a theft-to-order."

Sandeep looked up as an alert beeped on his screen. "Hold on," he said. He got up from the table and moved over to his workstation. "You may be right. It's gone." He tapped at the screen, interrogating the transactions. "One bid, settlement complete." Sandeep turned to his colleagues. "I think we caught that by chance."

"Does that mean the hackers offloaded to the people who commissioned them on the open market?" asked Cameron. "Risky. Unless..."

Ross finished her sentence. "Unless the buyers are so paranoid about anonymity that the hackers have no idea who they were working for."

"That's very clever," said Noor, nodding. "Deliberately obfuscating the trail. The target may not know they've been compromised. The hackers may be middle-men, too."

"I wonder if we can trace the files back to source?" mused Joel. "Did you capture enough information to try that?"

Sandeep nodded. "I think so. It'll take some digging, but it should be possible."

"What about the sale itself?" asked Joel. "What do we know about it?"

Sandeep pulled the Eden records up on a screen. "Let's have a look... There are a lot of transactions on this ledger, but I have the time of the sale... let's see... here are the possible blocks timestamped within a minute either side." He opened the first set of records. "We can't see the values but there are only a few thousand wallet addresses involved."

Noor peered over his shoulder. "That is a lucky break, catching the sale as it happened. You'd never have a chance to find this otherwise. Not on Eden, anyway."

From the wallscreen, Pete laughed. "Eden, full of snakes. Garden of criminality."

"It does have quite a reputation," observed Sandeep, "But Eden has the most secure cryptocurrency system out there right now. It's very useful for people who value their privacy."

Ella turned to Cameron. "Do you want me to work through what you've found today and see if I can match up earlier transactions going to the same wallets on the ledger?"

Cameron stood up. "Definitely. Find the money, Ella. Get cracking on that analysis. Pete, do you want to feed in to Ella if you get any ideas?"

"Sure," said Pete. "And remember, if there's anything to deal with on health data leaks, I am in a hospital right now."

"Good point," laughed Cameron. "Not sure they'd like a patient wheeling themselves down to IT and getting their hands dirty, though."

"You know what I mean," muttered Pete. He sounded deflated. "It's pretty dull here. I'll keep my eyes and ears open. It's amazing how much you learn just listening to the staff."

"Thanks, Pete," replied Cameron. "I appreciate it. Keep yourself busy."

Pete smiled, and reached forward to tap his screen off. "Bye for now," he said. "I'll be in touch after the ward rounds." The feed went off.

Cameron turned to the others. "Here's the list of local Calton partners. We're contracted to audit them all, and I guess we need to be looking out for secondary breaches now, too."

Susie scanned quickly down the screen. "Oh, no," she groaned. "Hardy's are on there."

"Who are they?" asked Cameron.

"I did some work for them a couple of years ago," replied Susie. "Old man Hardy is a tough client. He founded the business way back, and he's coming up for retirement. He always thinks he knows best, and he's not keen on women."

Cameron grinned. "First on the list, then. I love a challenge."

•

"Why shouldn't my assistants have oversight of the workings of this organisation?" said Joseph Hardy. "It's the best way for them to learn. It's no business of yours, young lady."

Cameron bristled, and behind Hardy she could see Sandeep stifling a

191

laugh. He bit his fist and made a terrified face. Cameron worked hard to keep her face composed.

"The protocols for individual logins are not just for show, Mr Hardy," Cameron replied. "I believe that it's a requirement in your staff regulations that you keep login details private."

"You believe?" fired back Hardy. "Check your facts. It's perfectly normal to extend access for effective training."

"I'm not disagreeing with that, Mr Hardy," replied Cameron, her voice low and steady. "However, there are ways for your staff to do what they need to do without compromising your security."

Hardy snorted. "My dear, I am the chairman. I am the company's founder, and because I am all but retired I don't get personally involved in day to day operations." He drew himself up to his full height in an attempt to look Cameron in the eye. He failed, but did not let his disappointment show. "For the last eight years, decision making has increasingly been deferred to my doppelganger."

Cameron raised an eyebrow. "Your digital twin is running the company? You have an artificial intelligence at the head of the organisation?"

"Exactly," replied Hardy. "It keeps the business focused on my founding principles and provides consistent leadership."

There were so many reasons why this was a bad idea, thought Cameron. The management levels below must be seething, unable to put their stamp on the business and lead it forwards. She hoped for their sake that the doppelganger was a good learner, able to react to the rapidly changing world.

"You see, Miss Silvera, there is nothing to compromise," continued Hardy. "You need to be looking elsewhere for your supposed breach."

Cameron was furious but could not let it show. Hardy would take any anger as a sign of weakness.

"Mr Hardy, I don't think you understand the severity of this matter," she said. "Not only have we found commercially sensitive data that traces back to your business, but there has been no data breach officially notified from this company."

"Wind your censorious neck back in, Miss Silvera," Hardy shot back. "I built this business from nothing almost fifty years ago, and I have dealt with cyberattacks from global powers, restless teenage hackers, and our own competitors. We were one of the first companies in our industry to use blockchains to protect our data and manage our supply chain. We have always been exemplars of good security. You assume I know nothing about cyber security: you are very wrong. There is nothing to find here."

Cameron took a deep breath and tried not to rise to the bait. There would be no value in contesting the details. She needed to focus on the job in hand.

"You have built an enviable reputation in the market," she responded levelly, hoping a little flattery would disarm him. "Nevertheless, my team has been engaged to audit Calton Global partners, and I must insist on access to your devices, and to your doppelganger, in order to eliminate you and your staff from our enquiry."

Hardy glowered at her, a look of disdain on his face. "You are wasting your time."

Not a direct no, then, thought Cameron in triumph. "May I introduce my colleague, Sandeep Tahir," she said, relieved. "He will run through the forensic tests." Cameron turned on her heel and walked towards the door. As she passed Sandeep, he grinned sympathetically, and she raised her eyebrows. "Nail him," she whispered.

Out in the corridor, Cameron leaned against the wall and took a deep breath. Whatever the man thought, there was a serious problem in his business. As a talented young entrepreneurial star back before Cameron was born, Joseph Hardy must have been formidable. He had been an archetypal arrogant millennial with his eyes on the prize and a genuine understanding of day to day business challenges. Close to retirement, he had taken his hand off the tiller, acting as the company's figurehead and a stalwart of the business community. Susie had been right in that he was hard to deal with, but Cameron hadn't been prepared for that level of arrogance and aggression.

She shook her head. There was a job to do.

"How's it going, Cameron?" The head of IT appeared around the corner, accompanied by Ross. "You've just had both barrels of the Hardy special, haven't you?" she said, smiling sympathetically. "He can be a bit difficult."

Cameron pulled herself together. "He's on top form, Jessie. Sandeep is checking through the whole setup now." She turned to Ross. "How are you doing?"

"All good, thanks," replied Ross. "Jessie's given me a full access to the in-house network logs and oversight of the channels Hardy's have access to on the Calton Global blockchain. I've set the diagnostics running. We were just going for a coffee."

"Please, join us," said Jessie.

The three of them strolled down the wide corridor towards the factory canteen. Doors at intervals led to quality control, design, accounts and

HR. Screens and old-school cork boards lined the walls, busy with notices of news and events, on paper and on scrolling video presentations. A series of fire doors opened seamlessly as they approached, triggered by the chip embedded in Jessie's hand. Scanners running alongside the traditional CCTV cameras recorded their movements around the building.

As they neared the canteen, a scent of coffee mingled with lunch drifted through the air. Cameron paused at a display that showed all the staff and their place in the business. She found Joseph Hardy's picture was at the top of the hierarchy but set to the side of the main organisation tree. Sidelined, sliding away to retirement, clinging to power through his doppelganger. She tapped on the tile that held a generic photograph of a young woman, presumably the intern, and it flipped to show a few lines of text. "Yasmin Hardy, Chairman's assistant…"

"A distant cousin, I think," said Jessie. "She's only been here a few weeks."

Cameron looked at him. "Jessie, did you know that he's being free and easy with his access codes? It looks like he's bypassed the biometric controls so that his interns can see a lot more than they ought."

Jessie swore, annoyed. "Dammit, again? I reset everything when Yasmin joined us. He keeps doing it."

"A little knowledge is a dangerous thing, huh?" Ross chipped in. "Knows enough to give himself an easy life and thinks it doesn't matter."

Jessie nodded. "They're all short-term contracts for work experience, and he's too impatient to get profiles properly set up. As half of them are nieces and nephews and the other half are related to his business chums, he doesn't treat it seriously."

"To be fair," said Ross, "he isn't there day to day, is he? Could the breach really have come from his office?" He grinned. "Or are you just making a point, Cameron?"

Cameron flashed him a smile as she followed Jessie to the canteen counter. "Well, Sandeep will be extremely thorough. It would be a shame if that annoyed him."

"What can I get you?" asked the chatbot on the counter.

"Latte, please," replied Jessie. "Cameron? Ross?"

"Same here," said Cameron.

"I'll stick to water, thanks," said Ross. "No! Wait. Espresso."

The canteen manager bustled out of the kitchen. "Hello, Jessie dear, how are you? I'll bring your drinks over."

"Thanks, Olivia," replied Jessie. "We'll be over in the booth." She nodded towards the far side of the large, airy room to a cluster of enclosed, circular pods with high backs for privacy.

The three of them crossed the room and settled in to a light blue pod with a wide, comfortable seat circling around the edge and a small coffee table in the centre. Cameron pulled out her smartscreen and slid it into a handy charging dock under the table. Ross did the same. Footsteps outside heralded the arrival of their drinks. Olivia placed a tray of steaming cups and a plate of cookies on the table and withdrew.

Cameron picked up a cookie. She took a bite, savouring the sweetness and the sticky, soft interior. She brushed a few crumbs from her chin and reached for her coffee.

"Okay, let's recap," she said.

Jessie took a deep breath. "Obviously we heard about the problems at Calton Global. We've been working with them for the last seven years. They notified us as soon as they knew about the security breach and data theft at their end. That's routine."

"You had no idea that there had been a similar breach here, at that stage," asked Cameron.

"Not at all," replied Jessie, her brows furrowed. "There was no reason to presume lightning would strike twice in the same supply chain."

Ross nodded. "It's unusual to see a multi-location attack."

Cameron turned to Ross. "What have you got on the breach so far?"

"I've matched one of the datasets we identified back to the database here," he replied. "The path of the theft isn't clear but we're doing the usual device sweeps and activity audits." Ross turned to Jessie. "Are you sure nothing flagged up at all?"

"No, definitely not," said Jessie firmly. She bent to pick up her coffee, and Cameron shot a puzzled glance at Ross. How could the Hardy's head of IT have missed the signs? Ross raised an eyebrow in reply. They could talk over this later. For now, Cameron was sure that there had been a security breach, and she couldn't shake the feeling that Jessie was lying.

3: TEAMWORK

"I can't make it down this weekend, Charlie," said Cameron apologetically. Her brother, at the other end of the call, gave her a quizzical look.

"You'll be here for Nina's do next week though, won't you?" he asked.

"Of course I will," replied Cameron. "I'd be a bad aunt if I missed that."

"I know you'll be there for Nina," replied Charlie, "but you'll have to answer to Aunt Vicky if you show up without Ben. He is the apple of her eye."

"Oh, stop it, Charlie," groaned Cameron. "I think she likes Ben almost as much as that cat of hers. Well, not quite…"

"Donald?" laughed Charlie. "He's a bloody liability. You won't believe the latest story."

Cameron braced herself. Aunt Vicky's scruffy ginger cat, Donald, was notorious for his antics. "Enlighten me," she said drily.

"Donald went hunting," said Charlie. "He must have dragged his catch back through the door without Aunt Vicky spotting him. He proudly laid his prey at the foot of her bed and went off to do something else unspeakable."

"So, she found a dead – a dead what? – in her bedroom?" said Cameron, at once amused and disgusted.

"Oh, better than that," replied Charlie, "it was a rabbit, and it was still alive. It hopped away under her bed and she knew nothing about it until Donald decided to come and play with it at three in the morning."

"No! That's brilliant," replied Cameron. "What happened?"

"Plenty of screaming by all accounts," said Charlie, trying not to laugh. "Donald and the rabbit were summarily ejected, but the whole street was awake by then."

"I'm surprised Andy didn't broadcast the footage on the news channel," said Cameron drily. Aunt Vicky's next-door neighbour was a journalist who was always on the lookout for the next scoop.

"Andy saw the funny side eventually," said Charlie. "He wasn't impressed. He is not a big supporter of Donald."

"Poor thing," joked Cameron. "He's been working hard for the last few weeks. He needs the sleep."

"I know," said Charlie. "I've barely seen him. He did an excellent job on that wave of cyberattacks, and he managed to keep you out of the limelight."

"Oh yes," replied Cameron. "It was well done. I think Ross enjoyed working with him. I must call him on Monday when I'm back in the office."

"I'll let him know if I see him. So, little sis, what are you up to this weekend that drags you away from your loving brother and his wonderful family?" asked Charlie with a smile. "Spill the beans, Cam."

Cameron grinned happily. "I'm off to Paris. Ben's over there with work. He can't get back home so he arranged for me to come and stay with him."

Charlie laughed. "Good lad. I approve."

"It wasn't planned," said Cameron. "It's just pure luck that he's stuck at work and my travel visa is in date."

"You deserve a bit of luck," said Charlie. "You work hard enough. Enjoy your trip and we'll see both of you next week."

Cameron closed her screen and went to pack the rest of her small suitcase. The little black and white cat looked at her scathingly. She picked it up and fussed at it fondly.

"I'm sorry to leave you on your own, but you'll be fine. I'll be back on Sunday. All you do is eat and sleep, whether I'm here or not." Still carrying the cat, she walked to the kitchen and checked the automatic feeder. "See? Full."

The cat took this as a call to action, wriggled out of Cameron's arms, and settled face down in the bowl, scrotching happily.

Cameron laughed. "Point made."

•

The cold wind made Cameron's eyes water as she walked towards the local underground station. The hand holding her suitcase was exposed and her fingers quickly became chilled. From the small row of shops rose a tempting smell of baking. She resisted. It was almost lunchtime, but there would be food served on the train and she would be eating well this weekend. She hurried onwards to the shelter of the subway.

After waiting impatiently for the lift down to the platform, Cameron tapped her foot in annoyance at the sight of carriages disappearing into the tunnel. She glanced at the arrival displays: another three minutes until the next one. Still plenty of time to get to St Pancras. She checked her rucksack again for her travel documents. Carrying printed papers was unfamiliar and stressful. Cameron wondered what the point could be, when everything was already recorded digitally and accessible at the click of a switch, the tap of a screen, or the wave of a hand. Regardless, she would not be able to cross the border into France without the right documents in her possession. Archaic, but ultimately effective.

The shuttle arrived and bore her to the north, whirring through the ancient Victorian tunnels of the Northern Line. Arriving at her stop, she allowed herself to be swept along the platform by the crowd, barely casting a glance at the beautiful curve of the roof and the preserved porcelain tiles that lined the walls. The classic décor of the tube network, dating back almost two centuries, might be a historical attraction for the tourists who still thronged around London, but it was part of everyday life for the residents.

Running determinedly up the stairs next to the slow-moving escalator, Cameron arrived slightly breathless in the huge vaulted station. She checked the signs to get her bearings and headed for the international terminal. The queues were already building for the next train, not due to leave for another two hours. Cameron joined the line and tried to curb her impatience. It was harder to travel to her neighbouring country than to cross the world.

Reaching the front of the queue at last, Cameron presented her chip to the scanner. The light glowed green and the barrier slid open. In the background, Cameron knew that this simple wave of her hand had triggered a check against the immigration and identity blockchains, confirming that she was a registered citizen with a right to leave the country. By the time the barrier opened to allow her through, the blockchain would already have an unchangeable record in place, visible to all the authorities, showing that she had crossed the border.

She stepped through the barrier into the limbo between countries and joined the back of the next slow-moving line for French border control. Sensor drones circled the area, some around her feet programmed to probe luggage and detect the latest threats and banned goods, others above her head surveying the growing lines of travellers. The minutes ticked by as she neared the row of desks; still plenty of time.

"Bonjour Madame," said the blue-uniformed officer cordially. "Your papers, please."

Cameron fumbled with the unfamiliar documents, used to shortcutting the whole identity process with a simple wave of her hand. The officer scanned her ID slowly, glancing over to his colleague as he did so.

"T'as ramené le casse-croûte ou tu sors pour manger?" he asked.

Cameron blinked uncomprehendingly, then realised he was not talking to her.

"Je sors mais j'ai des courses à faire," replied his colleague.

The officer grunted and turned back to his work, directing Cameron to face the camera. The biometric scan matched her records: another green light.

"Your visa?" he asked, peering at her.

"Oh, yes, sorry." Cameron produced a second document, slightly crumpled.

The officer frowned as he took it, and spent some moments smoothing the creases before carefully reading the details.

"You are aware this will need to be renewed within three months?" he asked.

"Yes, this is just a quick visit to see a friend," replied Cameron.

"This is all your luggage?"

"Yes," Cameron glanced down at the suitcase.

"You will be working in Paris?"

"No, purely leisure."

The officer grunted and pushed the paper into his scanner for final validation. All in order. Cameron breathed a sigh of relief, retrieved her documents, and stepped over the line into French territory.

"Merci Monsieur," she said tentatively. It had been a long time; her French was rusty.

Behind her, the border guard looked up as a commotion began at his colleague's desk. He abruptly closed his position off, eliciting groans of protest from waiting travellers. Cameron walked onwards to the departure lounge, relieved. She felt a disturbance in the air above her head, close enough to ruffle her hair, as security drones rushed down towards the source of the noise.

Behind her she heard raised voices. "Un sans-papiers. Monsieur, veuillez m'accompagner au bureau." Someone trying their luck with an expired visa, or more likely a fake bought for the journey and not synced to the identity blockchain. They may have been cleared to leave England, but they would not be entering France. There was a scuffle and more shouting, but Cameron kept moving. Not her problem.

Checking the station clock, Cameron realised there was still enough time before the train departed to grab a coffee and check her forums.

She settled in a comfortable seat in the corner of the departure lounge, drink in hand. There were no notifications to speak of on her screen, apart from a message from Nina complaining that her aunt was not coming to see her. She fired a reassuring note back to say all was well and that she would be there next week. Next, a quick call to Ben, which diverted to voicemail. Cameron updated him on her expected arrival time and dropped the connection.

The wallscreens flickered as a new announcement appeared. *"Boarding will commence twenty minutes before departure,"* it read. The English text dissolved to be replaced by: *"L'embarquement commence vingt minutes avant le départ."*

Cameron flipped her screen open again and quickly navigated to her threat intelligence forum. She could drop in and get quick update before boarding.

"Hey guys," she typed.

"Hey SimCavalier," came the replies.

Good, there were some regulars online. As she scanned the user list she also saw Ross's profile pop into life.

"Hi RunningManTech," she typed. "Thanks for dropping in."

Ross responded with a thumbs-up icon.

There was still plenty of discussion and speculation on the expanding revelations from the Calton Global hack. The downstream breach found at Hardy's seemed to have been mirrored across the global supply chain.

"How is Calton Global and the HackerTracker?" asked Bordegiciel.

"The HackerTracker is almost up to date," replied Cameron. "Check it out. I've put in everything we know about Calton so far, and I'll get these latest reports added when I have the chance."

"Have any of you identified the original attack pattern for these breaches?" asked Ross. "It's unusually co-ordinated."

There was a chorus of speculation, but no concrete evidence emerged from the group. Interesting, thought Cameron. The way the data thieves had broken in at Hardy's was still eluding her team, and it looked as if the same was the case across all the supply chain businesses and the specialists working on the problem.

"Off topic, guys," typed Cameron, "but we think we've picked up an unrelated theft. Some new datasets which sold to a buyer on Eden. It isn't something that's been flagged up before. RunningManTech, can you upload?" She waited for Ross to add details of the design files Sandeep had found, and the sale that he had caught by a lucky chance of timing.

"Old-school commercial espionage," Ross commented. "Anyone recognise it?"

"Merde," said Bordegiciel concisely. "I think I know what this is. I come back to you." The user disconnected.

"That was fast," typed Cameron. She glanced up at a rustle of movement in the lounge. The wallscreens now showed the message *'Embarquement en cours'* and a queue was building.

"I have to go," she typed. "Catch up later."

She disconnected and rolled her smartscreen away into her pocket. There was no point rushing, her seat was reserved. The queue started to move, and eventually Cameron stood up and strolled to the door. Her chip was enough to pass boarding control, one stage of the process that was not bloated by bureaucracy. Approaching the gleaming silver carriage with its clean blue, white and red livery, Cameron felt a rising excitement. Even this short trip across the channel reignited a love of travelling that had been with her since childhood. She smiled to herself and stepped aboard.

•

Cameron gazed out of the train window as it sped through the flat landscape of northern France. To the west, fields stretched to the horizon, interspersed with small settlements and church spires. Forests of tall wind turbines, their blades turning steadily in the wind, stood out against the darkening sky. It was only mid-afternoon, but clouds were gathering, and the remaining rays of bright sunshine highlighted the slender white towers. Lights blinked on the turbine spindles, alerting rare air traffic to the hazard. There must also be a system to deter drones from passing too close, she thought idly. Her mind drifted for a moment to the potential for such a system to be compromised: likely to be a simple hack, but what could be the payoff? Knocking drones into turbines would be a target for mischief more than a terrorist or ransom attack. Cameron filed the thought away for future reference.

For a moment, she reflected on the hydroelectric power station attack that had cost so many lives in northern Italy just five years earlier. The communities downstream from the alpine dam had had no warning when the floodgates opened. The court case was still rumbling on, squeezing every last cent of compensation from the power company whose lax network security and refusal to acknowledge a ransom threat had led directly to disaster. It was easy to see cybercrime as just an inconvenience, but the human cost could be high.

Cameron's sombre reverie was broken by neighbouring passengers exclaiming and pointing at the window. She looked outside again and saw the dramatic silhouette of Amiens cathedral, high on its hill.

The landscape flattened out again as the train sped onwards. The rain had not yet arrived, and the fields were a hive of automated activity. Cameron recognised agribots rolling through the crops, lower slung than the ones that tended the vines in her native village. They fertilised and weeded, measured the humidity of the soil and maintained the right level of nutrients. Their micro-management programming helped the farmers to maximise production and to compensate in some small way for the changes wrought by a warming world.

Gradually the villages turned into towns, and industry replaced agriculture. They passed anonymous grey factory units too fast to make out the detail of the unfamiliar logos emblazoned on the sides of the buildings. The solar panels on the factory roofs were dull. There would be very little electricity produced from the sun today.

As the train approached the Paris conurbation, Cameron was surprised to see a wide, bustling waterway many times the scale of the Victorian canal close to her village. Huge flat boats were tied up in twos and threes at the riverbank in the middle of a small town. Cameron saw cliffs rising behind the houses, and even caught a glimpse of tiny, well-tended gardens on the decks of the barges before the train swept away into the suburbs.

Barely two hours after boarding the train in London, Cameron stepped out onto the grimy platform of the Gare du Nord and made her way towards the metro. She paused to study the unfamiliar signs, searching for her route out to Ben's office at La Défense. She'd planned it to the last detail on the train but as the crowd buffeted her she couldn't quite recall the line she had to take, and she was reluctant to stop and pull out her smartscreen. At last she pinpointed her destination, out to the east on the very edge of the city, and moved on towards the maze of tunnels.

As she walked briskly along in the press of travellers Cameron heard the hubbub of advertising panels trying to keep up with the fast pace of passing consumers. One sign switched languages as she approached, addressing her in English. Her foreign chip had triggered a regional setting. 'Free aperitif tonight at Le Moulin, metro Pyramides…' Cameron didn't break stride. Behind her the sign smoothly changed back to French: 'Apéro offert ce soir au Moulin, métro Pyramides…'.

Finding the right platform at last, Cameron scrambled down the last few steps as a rush of air heralded the arrival of her train. The carriage was packed, and she struggled to squeeze on with her small suitcase. Unfamiliar sounds and smells washed over her as she braced herself against the sharp acceleration of the train. The walls rushed past and the powerful shuttle hurled itself towards the next station, decelerating just as abruptly as it had started. Cameron was buffeted from all sides as passengers disembarked and others squeezed aboard, the last few running to leap through the gap as the doors closed. She wasn't used to travelling in rush hour in her own city, let alone a foreign capital. The freedom to work wherever and whenever she wanted was, she realised, a luxury.

Her stop came up quickly and she stepped off the train with a sigh of relief. Following signs to the street level, she glimpsed a familiar figure in the fading daylight. There beyond the barriers stood Ben. For a frustrating few moments she struggled to locate the scanner which would release the gate. Ben's amused grin did not help. Finally, the barrier popped open. She flew through the gate, dodged his kiss, and thumped him on the shoulder.

"Not funny, Ben," she said with a scowl.

Ben laughed. "It was. The great cyber warrior defeated by technology."

"I could have hacked it faster," she replied. She smiled, relenting, and kissed him. "What's the plan?"

"We're meeting up with some of the local team for drinks. Very important to observe the Friday night apéro tradition." He glanced at his wristband. "We have time to drop your case at the hotel. Come on."

He took Cameron's free hand and they walked briskly along the crowded pavement. Although the chatter around them was accented and unfamiliar, the rest of the surroundings seemed all too generic. Autocars glided silently along the broad avenues. Weak sun glinted on the sheer glass sides of towering offices, apartments and hotel buildings. Commercial drones flitted around on delivery runs, dropping out of sight as they accessed chutes and balconies and reappearing without their loads. Security drones patrolled the streets and cameras were keeping a watchful eye on all the comings and goings.

Differences started to emerge. As they crossed the road, Cameron noticed that the passing autocars were taking the right lane, not the left. The delivery drones were a different shape, elongated to accommodate fresh baguettes. Behind the glistening skyscrapers lay high buildings of pale stone, elegant but ancient, with white painted windows and intricate ironwork decorating small balconies. A pair of police officers weaved seamlessly through the crowd and it was a moment before Cameron realised they were on rollerblades. Guns glinted at their hips, a public statement of power and control.

Ben turned sharply into a small lobby. The security guard at the desk nodded to him. "Bonsoir Madame, bonsoir Monsieur."

The elevator took them up to the twentieth floor. Door 2049 opened to reveal a large, comfortable room which was indistinguishable from a hundred thousand other hotel bedrooms across the world. Cameron walked to the window and pulled back the curtain.

"Not a bad view, is it?" said Ben, behind her. He pointed over her shoulder. "There's the Eiffel Tower," he indicated a beacon to the right, "and up there on the left, on the hill, that white dome, that's Sacré Coeur."

The city sparkled below them, the crowds of commuters ensuring that streetlights stayed on as dusk fell. Cameron's attention was drawn to a dark patch, almost hidden behind the Eiffel Tower, which stood out against the brilliance.

"What's that?" she asked.

"It's the new Tour de la Cité," replied Ben, soberly. "The memorial they're building on the island in the river."

Cameron stepped back from the window. "I'd forgotten," she said, distressed. "How could I forget?"

"I know," said Ben, hugging her. The devastating floods a decade ago had ripped through the heart of the city; the death toll had shocked the world. As the waters receded and the head of the Zouave reappeared under the Alba Bridge, devastating explosions from fractured pipes tore through the ancient island in the Seine. The cathedral of Notre Dame, that had withstood perils for nine hundred years, could not be saved.

"They've managed to keep some of the windows, haven't they?" asked Cameron.

"Oh, yes," replied Ben. "The plans look beautiful. They've incorporated the Holocaust memorial, too, and there will be gardens all around." He glanced at his watch. "We'll be late. Let's go."

•

Susie stood in the doorway of the office and tapped her foot angrily.

"Are you coming or not?" she asked. "The others are waiting, and they've booked you a ticket for the show."

Ella looked up from her screen, irritated. "No," she said shortly. "If you want to go, then go. I'm staying here. Cameron asked me to trace these funds through the exchanges, and I think I'm on to something."

Susie pleaded with her. "Cameron isn't here. She's gallivanting around Paris with her bloke. It's the weekend. Take a break."

Ella shrugged. "You know the job. It isn't a nine-to-five. I want to get this finished."

"So, the job means more to you than I do," replied Susie, upset. "That's nice to know. I won't wait up." She turned on her heel and walked out of the office door.

"Susie…?" It was too late. The door had closed behind her.

Ella sighed. Her concentration was broken, and she was desperate to regain the thread of the painstaking search. She loved the exciting leaps of intuition that were leading her through the cryptocurrency maze, and a night out with Susie and her friends would be more frustrating than enjoyable. She had hoped Susie would understand.

Ella stood up and stretched, aware she had been sitting for too long. Coffee? Yes, some caffeine would help. She looked long and hard at the coffee machine. A latte. Some syrup. A comfort drink with a sugar hit.

As she sipped the warm, sweet coffee, Ella reflected that working with the team was easier than working alone. Susie wasn't likely to come back to the office this evening, and Ella would not seek her out. Hopefully she would calm down by tomorrow. Cameron was away for the whole weekend. Joel had plans with Martha. Ross was at a training session: he might call by later, but he hadn't promised anything. Sandeep had mentioned he was going to visit his mother up north: he'd left at lunchtime to avoid the rush.

She picked up her screen and called Noor. There was no answer, but moments later an alert showed an incoming call.

"Ella? What's up?" came Noor's voice, concerned.

"Nothing, really," replied Ella. "I'm still in the office. Wondered what you were up to? I'm on a roll with this forensic work and wondered if you want to help."

"I'd love to," said Noor happily. "I'm supposed to be having dinner with my mum and dad, but they've invited another useless man along to try and match me off, and I wanted an excuse to get out of it."

Ella laughed. "Pleased to be of service. Get yourself back down here. I need your academic brain on this one."

She returned to her screen, refreshed, and resumed her digging. She had not progressed much further when an alert appeared on the large wall screen.

"Anyone in?" came a voice.

"Pete?" replied Ella.

"Hey, Ella," said Pete, the screen flickering into life. "Glad someone's working."

"It's Friday evening, Pete," chided Ella. "What did you expect?"

"Devotion to duty," replied Pete seriously. "Dedication to the cause." He laughed. "And someone to talk to."

"I'll be here for a while yet," said Ella sympathetically, "and Noor is on her way back in. She's avoiding her parents. Want to help out?"

"Definitely," said Pete. "My boys came in to see me today. I got them to bring as much of my kit as they could. I've been doing some digging of my own. I'm following a hunch, and it's looking good."

Ella's interest was piqued. "Are you searching through the Eden transactions as well?"

"No," replied Pete. "I'm more interested in what's going on with the Calton Global supply chain. Multiple attacks on different actors in the blockchain? It's possible but it would take a huge amount of co-ordination, even more planning than we saw with Speakeasy."

"What are you thinking?" asked Ella.

"What about a single attack with multiple outcomes?"

"Ohhhh," breathed Ella. "That's smart."

Pete grinned broadly at her from the screen, enjoying her reaction. "You said it. So, are we on?"

"Let's roll," Ella replied. "Music, maestro?"

"Try this one." Pete tapped on his screen and a playlist link appeared. Ella opened it, and music rang around the office. Pete pulled on his headphones and gave her a happy grin. It was good to be working again.

•

Ben and Cameron peered into the small bar. It was full of people clutching drinks and chattering loudly. A few of the clientele had spilled out onto the small pavement tables, undeterred by an autumnal chill in the air. Cameron stood on tiptoe and looked over the heads of the assembled company. Drinks were being served from a busy counter that stretched the length of the end wall. She braced herself to push through the crowd, but before she could move a man appeared and greeted Ben warmly.

"Bonsoir Ben, ça va?" he asked, shaking Ben's hand.

"Fine thanks," replied Ben. "Sébastien, this is Cameron. Cam, I've been working with Sébastien and his team this week."

Sébastien extended a hand to Cameron and shook it firmly. "Mademoiselle, enchanté. You want a drink?" Without waiting for an answer, he caught a passing waiter. "Deux ponches," he said, then corrected himself. "Non, trois." He waved three fingers at the waiter who nodded and disappeared into the crowd.

Two of Sébastien's colleagues joined them, drinks in hand. Cameron stayed quiet, smiling politely and listening to the mix of French and English discussion. Ben seemed to understand some of the chatter, but Cameron was struggling to pick up more than a few words. She looked around the little bar, taking in the tiled walls, the bright mirrors, and the dark wood and leather. No screen charging docks or service drones in this place. Not even a screen on the wall. Old traditions maintained.

The crowd parted like the Red Sea as the waiter returned with a small tray held high above his head. Cameron eyed the three drinks suspiciously. Clear liquid and a chunk of lime. Sébastien handed her a glass and she sniffed at it. Recoiling slightly, she looked enquiringly at their host.

"Un ti'ponch, Cameron," he said. "Rhum from the Caraïbes and a little cane sugar. Santé." He raised his glass and tapped it against Cameron's, looking her straight in the eye as he did so.

Cameron took a cautious sip. Strong but sweet.

"How do you manage to import this?" asked Cameron curiously. "Surely the costs are prohibitive."

"Mais non," laughed Sébastien. "The islands rise high above the sea, so the cane harvest is safe. They are part of France so there are no taxes. We stay with tradition."

"In all things," she observed. "This bar is beautiful. It must have barely changed in decades. As for the paperwork they need at the border – is that traditional too?"

"Ah, Cameron," replied Sébastien, "bureaucracy was invented by the French. It is our word. And for the rest, computers can never be completely trusted." He shot a rueful glance at Ben. "Bordel de logiciel. Bloody software, you say."

Cameron blinked. "What was that?"

"Bordel de logiciel," repeated Sébastien. His colleagues laughed.

Bordel de logiciel. Bordegiciel? Cameron's mind was racing. This was too much of a coincidence. Was it possible that she had been speaking to Sébastien on her threat intelligence forum that very day? If so, it was highly possible that the stolen design files they found for sale on Eden had come from Ben's company. That fitted with Ben's comment that the problem he was dealing with was in her line of work. What had she stumbled upon here?

Ben looked at her expression and frowned. "What's up?" he asked in a low voice.

"Tell you later," she replied. She took another sip of her drink and smiled innocently at Sébastien. "You're right. So many things can go wrong with software." She raised her glass. "Cheers. This is lovely."

●

Ella pushed her chair away from the desk and stamped in frustration. Noor looked up from her work, startled.

"I just can't find the next link in the chain," said Ella. "I know it's there."

"It's getting late," said Noor. "Shall I order some food? We can think through it while we eat."

Ella sighed and nodded. "How are you getting on?"

"Quite well, I think," said Noor. "I might have managed to link some of the payments back to their real-world recipients. I've been following the Eden transactions out to more transparent cryptocurrencies. Some of the wallets are in regular use and I've matched day to day transactions with known real-world activity. A few people in the UK, some in Europe, a couple in Asia, and a lot in the Americas."

"Which payments have you linked up?" asked Ella, curious.

"Small ones," replied Noor. "I don't want to make too many assumptions, but it looks as if these have been made from a larger pot of data sale proceeds."

"The people who commissioned a hack paying the people who carried it out?" suggested Ella.

"Maybe," replied Noor, "but normally that kind of transaction would be at arms' length. You'd buy services from the marketplaces. This is more like a direct distribution of profits. Salaries, almost."

"Interesting," replied Ella. "Right, let's get some food and talk this over." She paused. "I wonder how Pete's getting on?"

The screen was dark but came to life with a single tap. Pete's face appeared on the screen, headphones on, bobbing gently to the music and oblivious to his watching colleagues. Noor sent him a quick message, and he looked up, startled.

"Hey there," he said. "I was enjoying myself. How are you doing?"

"We're making progress but we're hungry," replied Ella. "How about you?"

Pete glanced away, checking the time. "It's coming together nicely," he replied, "but I'll be chased back to the ward soon. If I send you what I've found so far, do you want to follow it up?"

"Give us a quick run-down, and we'll share our finding too," said Noor. "We might be able to help each other."

"Okay," replied Pete. "I've been digging into the smart contracts in the supply chain. We have access to all the UK members of the chain to audit their security, so I've been running some penetration tests on the business rules that are encoded in the blockchain."

"That's an interesting approach," said Ella. "We've been looking for the usual human error breaches in each client."

"I know," replied Pete, "but it occurred to me that all the nodes on the blockchain have copies of the ledger and the smart contracts. Every smart contract is a series of rules, accepting or rejecting new data entries, or releasing automatic payments, or triggering the next transaction in whatever process is being managed."

"Have you picked anything up?" asked Noor.

"I think I have," said Pete proudly. There was a twinkle in his eye that they hadn't seen since his accident.

"Spill the beans," said Ella, impatient.

"I don't know where it was inserted, but there is a business rule sitting in the main smart contract template which shouldn't be there." He paused for dramatic effect.

"And?" said Noor.

"It interrogates the database of the oracle – the place where the input comes from, like a supplier confirming receipt of some goods – and sends packets of data out to a third party every time the contract executes." Pete smiled broadly. "There's the breach. It's a slow drip feed. It may not even have originated at Calton Global. They are simply the biggest node on the chain and picked up the data loss first."

Ella was speechless. Noor found her voice first.

"That's fantastic," she said. "It might explain why they are struggling to find the source of the breach at Calton. It could have come from any other node."

"It's probably still going on," warned Pete.

"Yes, you're right," replied Noor. She turned to her screen. "I'll get straight on to their teams and let them know. You are a star, Peter Iveson."

"I'm glad my brain is still working," replied Pete. He yawned and rubbed his hand across his face. "I'm tired, though. I'm in no state to pull an all-nighter."

"You get yourself back to the ward before they come looking for you," said Ella sternly. "We can take it from here. Cameron will be happy. I'll drop her a message."

Pete nodded. He was obviously exhausted. "Give her my best. I'll talk to you all on Monday." He reached forwards and the screen went black.

Ella watched Noor, who had connected to the Calton Global teams and was chatting animatedly. She waited patiently for their reaction. Finally, Noor turned to face her, smiling broadly.

"They're re-checking Pete's findings at their end," she said, "but once they've confirmed with us we can broadcast to all the teams working on the supply chain. We can close down the breach and start looking for the real culprit."

"Brilliant," replied Ella. "I've sent Cameron the details, but she hasn't come back to us yet." She looked at the clock. "It's getting late. Food?"

Noor shrugged. "Don't you want to get home?" she asked.

"Not really," replied Ella. "I don't have any plans and there's just me and the goldfish anyway. Susie's out with some of her friends and I won't see her until Sunday. You?"

"I can stay at my brother's place if we work late," she said. "He only lives half a mile away."

"Are your parents cross about you missing dinner?" asked Ella, curious.

"They'll survive," said Noor. "I'm not going to play their traditional games."

"What do you mean?" said Ella.

"I confuse them," said Noor, simply. "My brothers and my little sister are all married and settled and bringing up children. I chose to study, then to work, and I haven't found the right man yet." She sighed. "The last person in the family to have their marriage arranged was my great grandmother in Malaysia but my parents seem determined to introduce me to every single man that crosses their path. It's annoying more than anything. In their own way they think they are doing the best for me."

Ella nodded in sympathy. "We all need our freedom to choose." She changed the subject abruptly. "You studied history, didn't you? What was your doctorate?"

"Ethics and outcomes of state-sponsored digital surveillance," replied

Noor with a grin. "That's how Cameron found me. She picked up on my research and offered me a job."

"Wow," said Ella. "Impressive." She jumped as an alert pinged on her screen. "Ah," she continued, "Cameron got the message. She says congratulations."

"Good," said Noor. "Do we call it a night or carry on?"

"Food," said Ella decisively, "and then let's try and identify the owners of these smaller wallets. If we can match up enough real-world data, we may be able to put names to some of the people who've had a payout from this job."

"And the big player?" asked Noor. "Are you any closer to tracing the bulk of the cash?"

"I need to sleep on that one," replied Ella.

4: CITY OF LIGHT

Ross swung his bike onto the pavement and stopped by the low wall outside his house. The morning sun was shining on the building, highlighting the dusty windows and dilapidated brickwork. He frowned as if seeing it for the first time. How could he have neglected his home this badly? It was time he took the place in hand. Shocked by the recent events and energised by a good early training session, he was ready to get started and blow away the cobwebs of his old life. He wheeled the bicycle into the store at the side of the house, locking it away carefully, and walked the few steps back to the front door.

He dug into his training bag for the key and turned it in the old lock. A sensor simultaneously responded to the chip in his hand and triggered the second seal. The door swung open. He left it ajar and strode determinedly towards the kitchen window, opening it so that a welcome current of air began to blow through the musty house.

Leaving his bag on the table, he stepped into the short corridor that led to the rest of the house: his bedroom, the bathroom, a small sitting room, and his grandmother's old room. The floor of the corridor was bare, the carpet removed a couple of weeks earlier during the forensic work. There was still a tear in the wallpaper, and Ross looked at it critically before reaching out and tugging at the loose flap, pulling a strip of dark paper clean from the wall. It was a satisfying feeling and he grinned to himself. Why not start on the refurbishment right now? He peeled another strip from the wall, exposing the pale plaster beneath.

He was engrossed in this pleasurable destruction when an alert sounded on his smartscreen. Incoming call. He glanced at the caller identity display and was surprised to see Cameron's avatar. Wasn't she away for the weekend? Tapping the screen to set up a speaker call, he carried on with his work while they talked.

"What are you up to this early?" asked Ross.

"Following up some intel," came Cameron's voice quietly. "Ben's asleep."

"You're not supposed to be working," said Ross, amused. Cameron sometimes found it hard to take time off.

"I know," replied Cameron, "but you're not going to believe this. I met one of the forum guys last night. Bordegiciel."

"Really?" said Ross, pausing in his quest to remove all the wallpaper. "He's been pretty active recently."

"Very," agreed Cameron, "and I know why. He's been chasing a suspected data breach, and we confirmed it for him."

"The designs that you and Sandeep spotted going out on Eden?" guessed Ross at once. "They were his?"

"Spot on," said Cameron.

"Why just a suspected breach?" asked Ross. "Surely they knew what was going on?"

"Yes and no," replied Cameron in a whisper. "Their design files were corrupted. That's why Ben's been working away from home. He's one of the senior engineers at the company so he's been called in to check through everything. Bordegiciel, Sébastien, thought it was an attack rather than an innocent software glitch, and by finding the files we proved him right."

"I'm convinced that was a theft-to-order," said Ross. "What does he think?"

"We haven't discussed it in any detail," replied Cameron. "I'm going to try and speak to him today."

"I thought you were having a romantic weekend away?" asked Ross, amused.

"That's why I'm hiding in the bathroom right now," said Cameron. "Ben wasn't too happy when we started talking shop over drinks last night."

"What do you need from me?" asked Ross.

"Can you keep an eye on the forum?" she replied. "Sébastien may post there for help. And if you hear anything from your shady connections about the buyers, that'd be interesting."

"Sure," replied Ross. "I'll check in from time to time. Is this going to turn into official Argentum business?"

"Very likely," replied Cameron smugly. "We are the best, after all." She paused, and Ross heard the faint sound of another voice in the background. "Got to go." The call dropped.

Ross turned back to his half-stripped wall. The paper wasn't coming off so easily now. The job needed to be done properly. He strolled through to the dark sitting room where his computers sat, one for regular work, and the other for access to his 'shady connections'. He switched on the regular machine and activated its voice control.

"Find local decorating services," he ordered. Within moments, the screen filled with advertising videos, tiled and flickering in the slightly gloomy room. Too much information.

"Filter by quality rating, five stars, more than ten reviews." The display shifted and changed, but the screen was still covered. Ross sighed.

"Value for money rating over ninety percent." The tiles changed and grew larger; there were now only a few options available.

Ross opened the curtains and the window to let in both light and air and looked critically around at the space. He turned back to the computer, thinking about the changes he wanted.

"Quotations please: strip and replace existing decoration throughout and replace flooring with power tiles." He tapped on the wall between the sitting room and the unused bedroom. It echoed. "Remove partition," he continued.

"In progress," responded the machine. "Would you like to link your cleaning account to this enquiry?"

"No," he replied curtly. If he had a cleaner bot, the floorplan of the house could be uploaded to the service providers. "Base the quotations on a sixty square metre footprint with kitchen, bedroom, bathroom, corridor, living room." Ross didn't trust the cleaner bots. They gathered too much data for his liking about a building's layout and the residents' habits.

The quotations would take a while. He ran a finger along the windowsill and looked critically at the dust. Perhaps he did need a bot after all. He could probably hack it to stop it sending data back to base. Right now, however, his priority was to get the place straight and take the opportunity to re-configure and upgrade the house systems.

He took a deep breath and opened the door to his grandmother's old bedroom. He had barely entered the room since she died, other than using it as a dumping ground for spare sports equipment and computer parts. Although the clothes and linen had long ago been taken for recycling, there was still a familiar scent in the air which took him back to his troubled youth. On the walls hung static paper photographs, his grandparents on their wedding day, his mother as a baby. There was even one of himself which had been printed specially to add to the collection, a smiling toddler gazing slightly off-camera and clutching a cloth rabbit with long floppy ears. There were no pictures of his father.

He picked one dusty frame from its hook. The paper behind was bright and dark, a contrast to the faded colours of the rest of the wall. Ross gazed long and hard at the happy family group. His mother looked very young, squinting in the sunlight, her unruly blonde hair tamed by a band with huge round ears and a pink spotted bow. Behind them rose slim turrets capped with blue pointed roofs, and crowds of people were just out of focus in the background. Ross's grandparents were probably a little older he was now, in their early thirties. He wondered if his mother had a copy of the picture and whether she would ever want this one if they met again. Casting around in the junk he'd stored in the room, he found a large box. One by one he took down the pictures and placed them carefully together inside it. It was time to make this home his own and build memories that did not rely on the dead and departed.

An alert sounded from the other room. Leaving the box on the floor, he went through to check the computer. The first quotations were coming through. In a corner of the screen, he also spotted a message on the threat intelligence forum. Bordegiciel was online.

Ross slid onto the chair and typed a greeting. "Hi. I hear you met a mutual friend?"

"Salut, RunningManTech," came the reply. "Yes, a good surprise."

"How can I help?" asked Ross.

"Question," typed Bordegiciel. "I finally trace the source of the breach and the bloody malgiciel. Ever seen anything like this? I upload the code."

"I'll take a look," replied Ross. He watched as lines of code scrolled up the screen, then typed out a message to the whole group. "Is there anyone else out there?"

There were a few half-hearted thumbs up from other forum members, but as Ross had expected the group was quiet. It was too soon for the Americas, too late for the Far East, and too early on a Saturday morning for many of the Europeans.

"I'll let you know if anything in there looks familiar," typed Ross. "Are you seeing our mutual friend later?"

"I hope so," replied Bordegiciel. "Perhaps for a drink."

"Good," typed Ross. "Say hello from me."

He signed off the forum, but not before downloading the file. That would give him something to play with later once the momentum of tidying and clearing the house had worn off. He went back to the old bedroom and resumed his task.

•

Pete wheeled himself into the cubbyhole that he had claimed as his own and switched on the computer. His head was fuzzy this morning. The cocktail of drugs that was supposed to be healing his legs and preparing his body for the stem cell treatment seemed to be affecting his sleep and his thought processes.

He pinged a message to the office but there was no response. Too early for them, he guessed. He considered hopping onto one of the forums he followed, but his heart wasn't in it. Best to concentrate on the job in hand, then get some more rest.

Pete re-opened the connection to the audit client's node on the Calton Global blockchain and dug down to view the source code of the smart contracts. These snippets of programming administered all the transactions throughout the chain. The contracts themselves were hard coded, immutable, doing their job in the background. Pete's interest lay not in the code itself but in the history of its inclusion in the blockchain. Somehow, someone had introduced a new step in the supply chain processing. The fact this had gone unnoticed meant that they were likely to be working inside the network. Tracing the source of this extra step would give all the teams a starting point for finding the people behind the hack.

He worked slowly, his head starting to ache. Periodically he pinged the connection to the office but there was still no reply. Deep in thought, he failed to register a rise in volume in the corridor outside and rushing feet.

The door crashed open and he looked up, startled.

"Mr Iveson," said the nurse breathlessly. "You need to come back to the ward."

"Okay," replied Pete, confused. "Let me close down."

He quickly sent his findings and a note to his colleagues. They could pick up where he left off. He was feeling so bad now that he was almost relieved to be called away. Carefully he closed the connection and switched off the machine, locking it securely. The nurse was hopping from foot to foot, agitated.

"What's up?" asked Pete as he wheeled back out of the cubbyhole.

The nurse shook her head. "Can't say right now. Just make your way back." She dashed away down the corridor.

Pete looked around. The main door out to the rest of this hospital from this section, normally wide open, was firmly closed. A red light flashed above it. Staff were moving quickly from room to room and under the relentless efficiency of the ward team there was an air of barely concealed panic. He made his way slowly towards the bed he had called home since leaving intensive care, his head still spinning from digging deep into the Calton blockchain. He hoped that the rest of the team would follow his train of thought; it was annoying to be interrupted. He was sure he had come close to the source of the rogue contract before the nurse had broken his concentration.

The small side room held three beds, each with their own private space. It had been Pete's home for the last two weeks although other patients had come and gone. He nodded to his neighbour, an older man with an annoying tic and a habit of snoring. The third bed was empty. The previous occupant, whose persistent cough had disturbed his sleep during the night, was no longer in residence.

Pete swung himself wearily onto his bed. He was glad he'd been fit enough before the train crash to be able to manoeuvre well with just his upper body strength. He couldn't wait for the stem cell treatment to start and restore him quickly to full fitness. He missed work, he missed scuba diving, and he missed his home.

"What's going on?" asked his neighbour.

"No idea," shrugged Pete. He wasn't in the mood to talk. He pulled his smartscreen from his pocket, still thinking about the work he'd been doing, but changed his mind and laid it on the bed next to him. He wasn't feeling well at all. Closing his eyes, he felt himself drift away into a confused dream of clanking chains and flashing swords, scrolling lines of coloured code and bundles of data incongruously wrapped and beribboned beneath a Christmas tree.

More activity close to hand woke him once more. He heard the ping of a medical scanner and concerned voices.

"Mr Iveson?" came a familiar voice. The nurse he'd spoken to before. "Peter?"

Pete tried to answer but his mouth was dry, and his throat hurt. He blinked in the light and the ceiling swam before his eyes.

"Don't try to move," came the voice again. "You've been asleep for hours. Your temperature's high. We're just going to give you something to bring it down." He felt a dull ache in his arm and a cough welling in his chest. For a moment he wondered what was going on, but his tired brain could not hold on to the thought. As the drugs took effect he slipped away into a dreamless sleep.

•

Cameron gazed out of the hotel window across the Paris skyline, pretty in the morning light. She sensed Ben draw close to her, taking in the view.

"Where shall we have breakfast?" he asked.

"Anywhere," replied Cameron, smiling. "What do you suggest?"

"Hmm," said Ben. "We could head up towards Montmartre? Let's grab a coffee and a croissant on the way and stay for lunch up there."

"Sounds good," said Cameron. "What's the easiest way to get there?"

Ben pointed towards the white domes of Sacré Cœur in the distance. "It's too far to walk and there isn't a direct public transport option, but the autocars are frankly terrifying. I don't know who programmed them but they're nothing like the ones we have in London."

"Really?" Cameron raised a quizzical eyebrow. "I think that's worth investigating. Let's take one half way and walk the rest."

"Don't say I didn't warn you," laughed Ben. "We can pick one up outside the hotel."

Gathering their jackets, Ben and Cameron made their way down to street level.

The security guard nodded to them. "Madame, Monsieur, bonjour."

"Bonjour," said Ben confidently.

Cameron just smiled.

The door slid open and the hum of the street assailed their ears. Ben turned to the right, following the traffic, and took Cameron's hand as they plunged into a bustling crowd on the pavement. Autocars were pulling in to a small bay at the side of the road, collecting passengers and whizzing off again quickly. Ben caught a car as it arrived, and they jumped in.

"Buckle up," said Ben, grinning.

The car moved off rapidly, re-joining the traffic and accelerating.

Cameron's eyes widened. "They're certainly quick," she said to Ben.

"This road is all dual carriageway for the next few kilometres," said Ben. "It's very low risk, so they can all move faster. This is nothing, though. The best is yet to come."

The car sped comfortably along a wide boulevard of tall old buildings. The median strip was grassy and planted with plane trees that still held their green leaves of summer. To the side of each of the main carriageways, separate lanes were busy with cyclists, and the pavements beyond were bustling with people. At intervals Cameron saw small squares with statues and fountains and shaded benches on pale gravel. The facades of the older buildings were broken up with balconies and shutters, while on the more modern blocks advertising screens flickered. Cameron recognised some of the brands on offer, and the ubiquitous ads for the big virtual soccer league that were all over London, as well. One of the top teams, the Singapore MerLions, was touring Europe. They were obviously as popular in France as they were across the channel.

The traffic slowed.

"Hang on to your hat," said Ben.

Out of the front window Cameron saw the solid stone of the triumphal arch, the Arc de Triomphe, fifty metres high and two centuries old, standing proud against the white clouds. She gazed for a moment at the carvings that decorated the square top of the arch, then her eyes dropped to street level. What she saw made her laugh out loud. Autocars six deep were whizzing around the arch in an intricate ballet, joining and leaving the dance by any one of the twelve roads which led away from the roundabout. Before she could draw breath, their car made its entrance on the grand stage.

"This is incredible," she said in delight.

Ben grinned. "I thought you'd like it."

They closed in on the car in front and found themselves hemmed in on all sides. Cameron clutched Ben's hand, feeling a thrill akin to the start of a theme park ride. Her heart sang as the autocar made its way steadily three-quarters of the way around the circle. Every moment they seemed to be just millimetres from disaster, but the passengers in the other vehicles were unconcerned. Some were absorbed in reading their smartscreens, others were talking, and in one car Cameron caught sight of a couple in a passionate embrace.

"They've cracked roundabout programming," she said in wonder. "We just took out our roundabouts and replaced them with traffic lights."

"It's amazing, isn't it?" agreed Ben. "It still scares me. The car's proximity tolerance is right at the minimum."

"It feels like we're going to crash any moment," said Cameron. "I know we can't, but it takes a bit of getting used to. Our autocars are all so, I don't know, polite."

The little vehicle extricated itself smoothly from the flow and zipped neatly to its exit. They sped swiftly downhill through the elegant streets. The pavements were bustling with people, the air thick with delivery drones. Cameron breathed a sigh of relief.

Ben pointed up to the rooftops. "They have a network of farms across the city, planted on top of the buildings," he explained. "The food can't be any fresher."

The autocar turned onto the Boulevard de Clichy and a few moments later pulled into a layby. Ben thumbed the payment sensor and jumped out, offering his hand to Cameron. She took it and followed him across the road. Behind them the little car accepted a new passenger and drove off again.

"Breakfast?" said Ben, pointing up a cobbled side street to a small boulangerie and café.

"Definitely," replied Cameron. "I'm hungry now."

The smell of fresh baked croissants wafted from the door and people were standing at a long counter drinking tiny cups of coffee. There was a constant stream of clients coming in and out of the café, tapping a pad at the door to place their order and pay. By the coffee machine a server bot was anchored, its arms moving quickly and rhythmically as it changed filters and served drink after drink without pausing. A second bot removed fresh pastries from the oven and dropped them straight into a basket for customers to choose their breakfast. The host, human, circulated among the clientele, smiling greetings, shaking hands, and exchanging pleasantries and news. As he moved through the café, he picked up empty cups, returning them to the cleaning station where a third machine gathered, sorted and washed them for re-use.

Cameron watched, mesmerised, as a local strolled into the café. He barely paused as he tapped the order screen. The host greeted him, and they shook hands. As soon as the customer reached the counter, his coffee was placed in front of him by the efficient bot. Glancing at the pastry basket, he picked a small pain au chocolate and bit into it, blowing on the still-hot filling. Another customer, a woman, greeted him; they exchanged a quick kiss on each cheek and talked as they finished their coffees. As they put their empty cups down, the host reappeared and wished them a good day. The man left the café only a few minutes after entering, and his coffee cup was already clean and ready to be refilled. The system ran like clockwork, and Cameron could have watched all day.

Ben disturbed her reverie, bringing coffee and croissants.

"Fabulous, isn't it?" he said. "I asked around for the best place to come."

"It's magnificent," said Cameron. "Almost as if everyone was programmed in to the routine."

Ben laughed, but his eyes weren't smiling. "Can you leave work alone for a moment?" he said. He bit into his croissant forcefully.

Cameron looked at him quizzically. "That's hardly fair, Ben," she said. "You as good as told me you were dealing with a cybersecurity problem, and you introduced me to your colleagues." She shrugged. "What was I supposed to do?"

Ben sighed. "I thought we could have a weekend with just the two of us," he replied.

"So did I," replied Cameron, annoyed. "I'm here, aren't I?"

"Yes, but…" Ben's voice tailed off. He looked frustrated. "You only see the breach as a fun problem to solve. I've had to deal with the consequences."

"Oh," said Cameron, taken aback. "I hadn't thought of it like that."

"I didn't think so," said Ben grimly. "You have no idea what it's like being in the middle of the clean-up. A lot of people are going to be affected by this."

Cameron tried to look him in the eye, but he avoided her gaze. She put her hand on his arm. "Tell me what's been going on, Ben."

He finally looked up, his dark brown eyes concerned.

"It's a mess," he admitted. "Whoever breached the systems did untold damage to the files. There are patented designs going back years which are completely scrambled. Pure vandalism."

"And theft," Cameron reminded him. "We found the stolen design files."

"And theft," agreed Ben heavily. "So, in addition to all our designs being unusable, which means we can't supply our clients, there's a good chance that half of our stuff will come onto the market as counterfeits produced by whoever finally bought the stolen files." He sighed. "People may lose their jobs."

Cameron was silenced. She didn't know what to say. Her coffee and pastry sat untouched on the counter beside her, cooling gently.

Ben looked at her ruefully and rubbed his hand over his face. "I'm sorry," he said. "It's been a tough couple of weeks." He picked up his coffee and drained the cup, wincing. "Ugh, cold."

Cameron shook her head. "No, I'm sorry," she said. "You're right. I don't get to see that side of it. I'm just the gatekeeper." She tentatively sipped her own coffee, finding it acceptably strong and sufficiently warm to finish with pleasure. The croissant was still perfect, flaky and buttery. She savoured a delicious bite before continuing. "Ben, do you really mind if we meet up with Sébastien later? It can probably wait. We can talk online."

Ben shook his head. "No, don't worry," he replied. "I think it will help, and I like him. But I want you to myself for the rest of the time, okay?"

Cameron smiled, relieved. "Okay."

When Ella arrived in the office Noor was already working, a steaming cup of coffee on the desk beside her.

"Muffins in the hatch," called Noor, without taking her eyes off the screen.

Ella made her own drink and flipped the delivery hatch open. Sure enough, a bag of muffins lay atop a pile of assorted groceries. She picked the bag out and placed it on a nearby desk.

"What's the rest of the stuff?" she asked.

"I promised my brother I'd get some food in for dinner," replied Noor, "but I ordered it from here and forgot to set the delivery address."

"It's a good thing it didn't squash the muffins," said Ella, taking a bite.

Noor laughed. "Yes, lucky timing." She reached over as Ella passed her the bag and took one for herself.

Ella swung herself into her chair and flicked on the screen. "Where were we?" she asked Noor lightly.

"I've had some more information through from Pete," replied Noor. "He's disappeared now. I think he was called back to the ward. He's made some good progress on the cuckoo in the nest."

"The rogue smart contract?" asked Ella. "That's a nice way to describe it. A cuckoo contract. I like that, Noor."

Noor smiled. "My mother always said I had a way with words."

"What's Pete picked up, then?" said Ella.

"Well," replied Noor, "he's confirmed the details of the contract itself. We know what the rules are that have been coded onto the Calton Global supply chain, and when they activate. I've sent it out for verification, but a lot of the teams are just waking up, and it's the weekend."

"Looks good, though?" asked Ella.

"Oh yes, it's spot on," said Noor. "He's absolutely right. The code is still running and grabbing data but at least we can disable it and end the leak."

"I guess now we just have to find out where the cuckoo flew in," said Ella.

"That's the next step," confirmed Noor. "Pete added a note about it, but it was fairly garbled. Once we have the when, we can look for the where."

"Pete probably isn't feeling well," said Ella. "It's barely any time since he was flat out in Intensive Care. I'm surprised he's up and about so quickly."

"I don't think he's supposed to be working," replied Noor with a grin. "He'll be back in the office soon enough, once the stem cells take and he's back on his feet."

"I feel bad," said Ella, "I haven't been to see him yet."

"I have," replied Noor. "I went down when he first came round. It was a terrible accident. It was very lucky that the train wasn't crowded. They think that the other people who survived in the first carriage only did so because he warned them."

Ella was silent for a moment. "Wow," she said. "That puts it in perspective. Amazing that he's doing as much as he is already."

"He'll be fine," said Noor. "Pete's a fighter. And he's very good at his job."

"Well, let's get on with ours," said Ella briskly. "We need to follow the paths out of the seller's Eden account. Where did all the money go?"

•

Ben led Cameron through a labyrinth of streets, gradually winding higher up the hill. They came to a flight of stone steps lined with iron railings, bright with new paint. Cameron took the steps two at a time, laughing as she caught her breath at the very top.

"You're nuts," said Ben as he reached her, panting himself.

Cameron was doubled up and gasping for oxygen. "Got to... keep in... training," she stuttered, aiming a feeble punch at his midriff.

Ben laughed and hugged her. They turned along a new path, hand in hand, heading towards the great cathedral. As they climbed, the streets narrowed and tarmac gave way to cobbles. Almost under the eaves of Sacré Coeur, they found themselves in a leafy square crowded with stalls and noisy with the chatter of people and bursts of music. Colour assailed Cameron's senses. Pixel art flickered on portable screens against bright static backdrops. Tourists swayed under awnings as they explored the virtual reality of an artist's fantasy vision on a disposable headset. A young man sat immobile while a bot sketched his caricature on a tablet, exaggerating his long nose and thick eyebrows. Seeing the finished picture, he laughed and held out his smartscreen. The bot dropped the caricature to the customer's device and the young man walked away, chuckling.

"Want one?" asked Ben.

Cameron shook her head, smiling. "Not my sort of thing. Come on, let's keep going."

They wandered the lanes for an hour or so, finding hidden corners, street art and quaint shops in unexpected places. Every so often the view opened out and they found themselves looking down to a schoolyard, or into the back of a row of houses. They rounded the corner to the cathedral, coming upon it suddenly for all its size. There was a short queue for the long climb to the dome.

Cameron led the way up the stone staircase.

She paused, concerned. "I hope there's no-one coming down here at the same time," she said. "It's very narrow."

"Don't worry," replied Ben, "it's one-way. You won't meet anyone except the gargoyles."

Cameron laughed and kept climbing. The spiral stairs gave way to straight but narrow flights along the eaves, with tantalising glimpses of the view across the Paris rooftops. The path plunged back into darkness, twisting and turning around the ancient building.

"One hundred," said Ben. "Wait up!"

"You need to get back to the gym," laughed Cameron. "We're barely half way."

Ben groaned, but once he had caught his breath they carried on with renewed energy. In what seemed like no time at all they emerged into the light under the iconic dome.

"The view is stunning," gasped Cameron.

"Walk all the way round," advised Ben. "Full 360 experience."

The balcony of the dome was crowded, visitors shuffling along and taking in each aspect of the view. Cameron slipped on the headset she'd been given at the street entrance and a transparent screen dropped down in front of her eyes. As she looked out onto the Paris streets, labels appeared, pointing out the Pantheon, the Eiffel Tower, and other less obvious landmarks. Tapping the headset to zoom in, Cameron took in the detail of the old Pompidou centre dominating Beaubourg, and the new Tour de la Cité rising in the middle of the river.

Behind her, Ben pulled his smartscreen out of his pocket.

"Cam, look at me," he called.

She turned towards him, smiling, and he grinned back. "Good picture."

Another tourist stepped in, a motherly lady in her sixties. "Here, dear, let me take a picture of the two of you together," she said.

"Thank you," said Ben, handing her his smartscreen and moving to put an arm around Cameron. They both smiled for the picture, and the lady handed back the screen.

"What a lovely couple you make," she said wistfully, before moving on with the crowd.

Cameron looked at the picture. Ben's dark brown eyes and her green ones shone in the light, the skyline behind out of focus. She had to admit they looked good together.

When they reached the exit from the balcony, Ben looked out at the view and then towards the stairs. "One more circuit?" he asked.

"No, I'm done," replied Cameron. "Let's go down. I'm getting hungry."

The descent felt harder than the climb. The old stairs were narrow, worn, and steep. At the bottom, Cameron groaned. "I felt that," she said. "My calves are killing me."

Ben laughed. "Finally back on terra firma," he said. "My legs were dead way before we got down here." He took her hand and they went back into the maze of streets, settling for a small corner café with a simple menu. A roboserver took their order and disappeared into the café, negotiating the uneven pavement and café steps on its three slim, agile legs. It returned with glasses, a pitcher of water, and a bottle of wine that it uncorked smoothly before pouring.

"Cheers," said Cameron, looking Ben in the eye.

"Cheers," he replied.

Cameron took a sip of her wine and sighed happily. "Let's not talk about work just yet. This is too nice."

"I know," replied Ben, "but if we're meeting Sébastien later you'd better know what's been going on."

Cameron pouted, and Ben laughed. "You were the one who was sneaking around making calls this morning," he said with a smile.

"I was getting Ross to do the heavy lifting for me," she protested.

"Fair enough," said Ben, "but we need to talk. This might affect my job."

Cameron was silent. Ben was right. She saw cybersecurity problems as a puzzle to solve, not as a direct threat to someone's existence. Naturally she was aware of the consequences of poor security and opportunistic hacking, but as a strategic matter, not a personal one. She took another sip of wine and nodded at him. "Go on."

"You know we produce engineering designs for printing," said Ben.

"Of course," said Cameron. "Some of your files are on their way to Mars, aren't they?"

"Yes," replied Ben with a smile. "The colonists will be able to print everything from tools and spares for tunnelling equipment to houses, knives, forks and plates. Those original designs look to be unscrambled, at least, thanks to all the contractual protection around them, but we can't be sure they haven't been copied."

"That's something," said Cameron. "I take it not everything was as well covered."

"Bang on," said Ben. "Ironically, all of this happened after the Speakeasy attacks. When the power went down, it caused chaos. Sébastien thinks there was a speculative hack into the European base when the grids were restored and some of our firewalls had been compromised. I don't follow all of his explanation but that's the gist of it."

"That could be the case," said Cameron," but it feels like too simple an explanation. This is more complex than a script kiddie having a bit of fun. I'm also wondering why we hadn't heard about it until now. I mean my people, my network. Not much passes us by."

"Sébastien has been gagged by the management," said Ben. "The official line was that some of the servers crashed thanks to hardware failure, and the disks were corrupted."

"That's a very remote possibility," said Cameron. "Unlikely, though."

"The more I look into what we've lost, the more I agree with you," said Ben. "All the files are there but they're unreadable. Garbled. If the servers had failed completely then we wouldn't be able to access anything at all."

"It all fits," said Cameron. "This explains why he's been hanging round the forum and asking questions about the HackerTracker. I thought he was interested in the Calton breach, but I guess he was looking much closer to home." A thought struck her. "What about backups?"

"Now there's a question." Ben grimaced. "Even I know there are strict procedures in place. They should have been able to restore a normal data loss very quickly. That's what makes this whole situation so odd."

"The vandalism does point to an irresponsible quick-and-dirty hack," sighed Cameron, "but I don't buy it."

"Sébastien was right that this was an attack and not an accident, then," said Ben. "I heard some raised voices in the office yesterday afternoon. Maybe he's finally persuaded the management to take him seriously."

"That would be when Ross uploaded the details of the files we found," said Cameron. "We accidentally proved that there had been a data theft."

Ben raised an eyebrow. "Really? Now I understand why he was so stunned when he finally realised who you were."

Cameron laughed. "Most people are simply stunned that I'm a girl. It makes a change."

Ben laughed too, the tension he felt evaporating at last. A movement caught his eye, and he looked up to see the agile autoserver skipping across the cobbles bearing a basket of bread and two beautifully presented plates of food. He took a sip of his wine as the bot slid the plates expertly onto the table in front of them, placed the bread basket to one side and picked up the wine bottle, refilling both glasses.

"Merci," said Ben automatically.

"De rien," responded the bot, and it trotted away.

"This looks fantastic," said Cameron, picking up a piece of fresh bread and tearing it in two. She dabbed at the sauce on her plate. "I'm hungry now."

"Not much more I can tell you about work," said Ben, sniffing appreciatively at his food. "I suppose you'll be pitching for some business."

"Of course," said Cameron. "Argentum Associates to the rescue. We'll sort you out. What time are we meeting up?"

"Oh, later," said Ben. "Sevenish."

"Good," smiled Cameron. "We have the rest of the day to ourselves."

5: CONTAGION

Cameron stirred in the warm bed. Her whole body felt heavy after a night of deep sleep. It was dark in the hotel bedroom, but a little light penetrated through a crack at the edge of the curtain. As she came round, she took stock of herself. Legs? Aching slightly. She shifted position and felt her calves and quads protest thanks to the previous day's walking and climbing. Head? Fuzzy. Was that entirely due to sleeping late or could last night's wine have something to do with it? Mouth? Dry. Yes, that was the wine, alright.

She opened her eyes and blinked at the single ray of light that was angled straight at her pillow. Dust motes danced in the brightness and she was dazzled for a moment. Gently pulling back the covers, Cameron slipped silently out of the bed and moved gingerly towards a low table bearing a coffee machine.

She felt around it for a switch or pad; there was nothing.

"Coffee," she whispered in a low tone. The machine did nothing. "On? Tea? Drink? Boil? Breakfast?"

"Café," came a muffled voice from the bed.

A green light appeared on the machine and it started to heat up.

"Dammit." Cameron dived back under the covers.

"Defeated by technology again," laughed Ben huskily. "I blame the rum." He yawned and rolled over to look at her. "What time is it?"

"I don't know, and I don't care," replied Cameron. "I need that coffee."

The machine gurgled as it came to the end of its cycle. Cameron clambered laboriously back out of bed and collected two cups from the tray. Handing one to Ben, she took a cautious sip of the other.

"Careful, it's hot," said Ben.

Cameron put her cup down beside the bed and returned to her warm nest.

"Where did we end up last night?" asked Cameron. "I just followed you both blindly."

"The Latin Quarter," replied Ben. "It's easy to lose your bearings around those narrow streets."

"Sébastien seems to know his way around," replied Cameron.

"He lives here," laughed Ben. "I'm sure we could get him equally lost in London. Do you think he'll come over?"

"Possibly," said Cameron. "It depends how things go with your management team. It would be good to work with him to sort this mess out for you. He definitely knows what he's doing, but sometimes it helps to have an independent eye on the problem."

"He seemed happy enough with the idea," said Ben. "So am I, as long as between you, you can get us engineers working again. I'm sure you'll have the whole thing wrapped up and the culprits behind bars in a week."

"It's never quite that easy," said Cameron ruefully, "but I don't think it'll be a problem restoring all the files. It sounds like a case I've dealt with before, and it's likely to be a similar snippet of malicious code that's causing all the damage. The same scripts keep doing the rounds. As for the culprits, it's usually hard to pin the ultimate source of any cyberattack down to one person. Sometimes it's even hard to establish which country it's come from." She paused to pick up her coffee that was cooling to an acceptable temperature.

"Have you ever tracked down a hacker in real life?" asked Ben, curious.

"As a matter of fact, yes, I have," Cameron laughed. "Plenty of them. For example, years ago when I'd just started out in this game I came across a brilliant young hacker who had been getting up to some nasty tricks. He'd been cracking some fairly tight security and earning top coin on the dark web marketplaces for the data he stole and the messes he made."

"What happened to him?"

"He was shaken down by the authorities and spent some time at His Majesty's pleasure," said Cameron. "And then…"

"Then what?" said Ben, mystified.

"Then I went into business with him," said Cameron with a broad grin. "It was Ross."

Ben laughed in surprise. "Poacher turned gamekeeper. No wonder your team has such a good reputation. You see this stuff from all sides." He picked up his wristband and squinted at it. "It's late," he said in surprise. "It's after eleven o'clock. What time is your train?"

"Not until five," replied Cameron. "Let's relax today. We must have walked further than I thought yesterday." She reached lazily for her smartscreen. As soon as she activated it, she sat up, concerned.

"That's odd," she said. "Three missed calls from Aunt Vicky. I hope everything's okay at home." She glanced apologetically at Ben. "I'd better call her back."

She tapped her screen and the call connected. Aunt Vicky answered within seconds.

"Cameron, darling, are you alright?" She sounded flustered. "I've been trying to reach you."

"I'm fine, Aunt Vicky," replied Cameron. "I'm in Paris with Ben. Didn't Charlie say?" She had a cold feeling in the pit of her stomach.

"Oh! How nice," said her aunt. "No, Charlie never mentioned it. Give my love to that nice young man of yours. I'm so sorry to call you when you're having a nice weekend away."

"What's the matter, Aunt Vicky?" asked Cameron, perplexed. "Is everyone okay? You had me worried with all the missed calls."

"Charlie and Sameena and the children are all fine," said Aunt Vicky. "Although of course they are as worried by the news as I am."

"What news, Aunt Vicky?" Cameron was getting impatient. "I haven't been looking at any of the news channels this weekend. What's going on?"

"The flu, darling, the flu. This Grasshopper Flu. It brings back such terrible memories." Aunt Vicky's voice broke. "I wanted to be sure you were alright."

"I'm fine, Aunt Vicky, and I'm up to date with my jabs," replied Cameron. "The Grasshopper Flu outbreak is in South East Asia. It's hardly likely to hop over to Europe."

"But what about the case in London?"

"No!" Cameron was shocked. "Surely not." She digested the unwelcome news and tried to calm her aunt. "It'll just be an isolated case. These things happen and it's nothing to worry about. Was it a traveller intercepted at Heathrow?"

"I do hope so," said Aunt Vicky doubtfully. "They've quarantined a whole hospital, and there are vaccination clinics popping up everywhere."

"Hmm, that sounds a bit more serious," said Cameron. "I know Charlie and I have kept up to date all this time, but we remember..." She tailed off.

She felt Ben at her shoulder. "What's up?" he whispered, concerned.

"Have you had your flu jab?" Cameron whispered back.

"Yes, company policy," replied Ben in an undertone, "especially for business travel."

"Don't worry, Aunt Vicky," said Cameron sympathetically but firmly, "I'll check the news channels, but rest assured I'm fine and so is Ben. Go and enjoy lunch with Charlie. Why not knock next door and see whether

Andy can tell you any more about this? He's a journalist. He'll know all the latest information."

"I tried but he didn't answer. He must be working away, because I could hear Jasper barking at Donald." Cameron could hear a note of distress creeping into her aunt's voice. "What about Nina's chipping party?" she continued. "Do you think it will still go ahead? It's such an important day for them all. She's so excited and she's got her outfit all ready."

"I'm sure it won't be affected," replied Cameron. "The school is very strict on vaccinations and it's highly unlikely that this will spread beyond one case. Don't worry. Go and see Charlie and Sameena, try not to dwell on this news, and have a lovely day. I have to go now, I'm so sorry."

"Yes, of course, dear," said Aunt Vicky faintly. "Call me when you get back to England, and make sure you look after that young man of yours." The line disconnected.

"What was all that about?" asked Ben.

Cameron sighed. She pulled her knees up to her chest and stared into space, brooding over old memories.

"Aunt Vicky is panicking because there's been a reported case of Grasshopper Flu in London," she said, her voice flat. "She's convinced it's the start of another epidemic. This happens with every isolated case that steps off an aeroplane. I'm sure this is the same story."

"I'm sure it is," agreed Ben. "There hasn't been a breakout since the big one. That's got to be twenty years ago."

"Twenty-one years," said Cameron heavily. "She remembers it very well. I was only thirteen, but it changed my life."

"What do you mean?" asked Ben.

"That's when my parents died," said Cameron simply. She bowed her head as Ben gathered her in his arms.

•

Andrew Taylor was not at his home next door to Aunt Vicky in the quiet village. He was hard at work co-ordinating his channel's emergency reporting outside a south London hospital.

"Giles," he bellowed across the crowd of news crews, "have you got those pictures?"

His colleague struggled through the press of bodies, careful to stay out of shot from the live broadcasts that were running for competing national and international news networks. This was hitting the headlines across the world.

"Drone footage is coming through now, Andy," he panted. He looked up at the sky and squinted at the sun that was directly overhead. "All the blinds are down. I don't think we'll get much."

"Anything's better than nothing," said Andy. "Where's the talent?"

Giles nodded at the reporter who was fixing her makeup in the outside broadcast pod.

"They're rolling the big guns out on this one," said Andy, surprised. "Sort that footage out. I need a coffee." He wandered over to the pod and ordered an espresso from the little coffee machine inside. The water was already hot, and on the dispenser tray was a full cup of frothy cappuccino waiting for collection. Andy quickly scooped it up and handed it to his colleague before the new cup dropped into place for his drink.

"Thanks Andy," said the reporter, brushing her blonde hair into place. "This is worrying, isn't it?"

"I thought it was just a storm in a teacup until I saw you here," said Andy. "This isn't my usual area of coverage. I don't do human viruses as a rule."

The reporter smiled at him, appreciating the joke.

"How come you got landed with this broadcast?" she asked.

"A couple of people off sick," replied Andy. "Common-or-garden sick. Not the flu." He took another swig of coffee. "What about you, Bea? You do a lot of health reporting, don't you?"

"I like to cover health and social issues, or anything along those lines," replied Bea. "I studied pre-med before taking a big detour into journalism."

"Why is this story so special?" asked Andy. "I thought it was a big fuss over nothing."

"I'm waiting for the statement from the hospital," said Bea seriously. "Cases of Grasshopper Flu are more common than you think. There are one or two a year coming off long haul flights and straight into isolation before they can do any damage. It's rare that there's such a high-profile response. If the powers that be are pushing for emergency vaccinations, then they must think there is a wider risk than usual. I wouldn't have expected a case here at St Martin's. They're normally quarantined near the airport. Maybe the carrier has been out in the community. Maybe there's more than one case."

Andy and Bea looked up as Giles reappeared.

"The footage is ready," he said, "and they're getting ready for a statement."

"I'd better get down to the front for questions," said Bea, giving her hair a final fluff.

Giles shook his head. "No access for crews. Drones only. They're giving the statement from the steps and we have a twenty-metre exclusion zone. No questions either."

Bea raised her eyebrows and looked at Andy. "I want to hear this."

Andy drained the last of his coffee and dropped the cup into the pod's recycling bin, which hissed as it cleaned and sterilised. "Let's roll," he said.

•

Ross was working up a good sweat clearing boxes and bags from the house. The decorators he'd chosen would be starting in the morning and there was still a lot to do. He moved around his grandmother's bedroom taking pictures of the furniture. He didn't want any of it. He transmitted the images to the local rental company; they'd be along to collect it later. It was easier to rent everything out and collect a regular fee than to spend time finding buyers for the stuff. He would be renting new furniture from them in turn.

Old curtains and rugs and the wallpaper he had already torn down were destined for recycling and incineration. He started a pile in the garden. That would attract scrap drones. Sure enough, as he dumped the last of the rubbish, a grubby grey drone lurched around the corner, struggling to fly level with only one stabilising rotor running. It stuttered around the garden and flew away again, alerting the scavenger drones in its swarm to the rich pickings. The whole pile would be gone in an hour or so. Ross tried not to look too hard at the overgrown garden. That job would have to wait until he'd finished the interior.

It was time for a rest. Ross made himself a drink and turned on the wallscreen, flopping in an old and comfortable chair. The news channel was buzzing with reports of Grasshopper Flu. He wasn't worried. As an athlete he kept up to date with all his vaccinations, staying as healthy as possible.

A blonde reporter appeared on the screen, a tall hospital building in the background. "Concern is growing following the announcement that St Martin's Hospital, here behind me, has been locked down," she said. "Staff and patients are quarantined after Grasshopper Flu was confirmed in a new admission. There are no reports of further cases at this stage, but the public are asked to be vigilant. Symptoms include sudden disorientation, fatigue, and a persistent cough. Free vaccinations are available at all good pharmacies. This is Bea Black reporting live from south London. Now, back to the studio."

St Martin's, thought Ross. That's where Pete was taken after the train crash. The news report spoke of a new admission, though, so it was unlikely to involve him. Ross hoped that Pete's treatment wouldn't be delayed by this fuss. They may not see eye to eye, but Pete was a popular member of the team and always did a good job. He was reliable and traditional, reflected Ross, a solid ex-army intelligence officer who saw the world in black and white. Ross knew that Pete didn't entirely trust him and his shady past, but he had to admit that he was respectful and a good colleague to work with.

His thoughts were interrupted by the next news item. "Police are appealing for sightings of a man wanted in connection with a burglary in North London," said the presenter. An image flashed up on screen. The features of the dead man were clear, and the image had been minimally edited to make it more palatable and alive.

Ross sat up abruptly, shocked. Wanted? Hardly. The police knew exactly where he was, and he wasn't going to give them any more trouble.

The presenter continued. "Anyone with information on his movements over the past six weeks is asked to contact DI Sara Mercer." A contact link flashed up on the screen, then settled in the corner of the picture as the news bulletin moved on, waiting for concerned members of the public to tap through with their eye witness information.

He wasn't disturbed by the picture, although it brought back nothing but bad memories. The implication was that the man had not been identified. If the police were searching for information, they were likely to be digging deeper than Ross liked into the man's prior movements. In most cases he knew that they would try to trace him by phone signals, but as Ross had both the man's devices there was nothing for the police to go on. It would be a laborious job for them to find him by facial recognition and public appeal, but it seemed that was the route they were taking. He had to check the city's CCTV records. Eventually the investigators would find evidence of the stranger's movements, and that risked revealing his previous contact with Ross. The fact that the police hadn't yet come knocking at the door suggested that he still had time.

He had official access to the CCTV system through the Argentum Associates account, but what he had in mind needed to be distanced from work. Thinking through his options, Ross logged on to the computer he reserved for less straightforward purposes and activated a secure, encrypted connection to a shadowy marketplace that he hadn't visited in years. His account, under an old pseudonym, was still active. That was good news.

"Hey," he typed.

"Hey, Piper," came a response. "Admin bot here. Long time no see."

"Long time," replied Ross. "Need an in. Can you help?"

"Where to?" asked the chatbot.

"City CCTV," he typed. It took a few moments for the marketplace admin bot to answer, and Ross could feel himself getting nervous. He wasn't used to dealing on the dark web these days.

"Here you go," came the response at last. A list of items for sale scrolled up the screen. Ross scanned the options. Some were old records, others more up to date, and all came with a price tag. He sighed and picked the best-looking lead, clicking on 'Buy' and transferring the coins from an old Eden wallet.

"Pleasure doing business with you," said the chatbot. "Have a nice day."

Ross logged off, feeling unexpectedly ill at ease. He used to spend all his time surfing the darker side of the web. He didn't realise how much he had changed. But needs must, and this was a situation he had the skills to manage.

The bundle he'd bought was exactly what he needed. No convoluted path to follow, no waiting for a phishing attack to deliver its bounty over time. A snippet of live code was already sitting on the terminal of an unsuspecting City CCTV user. Hopefully this was an open door. He gently poked at the connection and couldn't believe his luck. Although it was Sunday, the machine was live on the main servers. He must remember to give the marketplace a five-star rating for the product. This was a textbook piece of hacking by a skilled operator who knew the value of their work.

Ross started from a birds' eye view of the whole city and zoomed down to the cameras close to his home. He navigated easily back to the day the dead man had approached him in a local coffee shop, weeks earlier. After a moment of searching, he isolated the snippet of recording which showed him ushering Ross into a waiting autocar. He slipped into the database and overwrote the few seconds of incriminating film with an indistinguishable loop. Good. First base covered.

He followed the CCTV trail of the car's journey out of the city to a run-down industrial estate. It would be too difficult to remove himself from the footage of arriving, entering the building, and leaving again, but it was easy enough to mimic a fault in the single camera that was trained on the building. He duly scrambled the recording for a three-hour period. That would be a believable timeframe for a fault to be reported and fixed by drones. He also noted the location of the camera for future reference. He might want to visit that building again in real life.

Ross checked his timer. He didn't want to spend too long in the system. He knew the security protocols on the other side, and while the bona fide user profile might go undetected, he couldn't risk an alert being flagged if the logs were audited. He withdrew discreetly, and sat back, content with his work.

•

Ben and Cameron sat opposite each other at the restaurant window, watching the world go by. Cameron took a sip of water, then picked up a large wine glass and swirled the rich yellow liquid around the sides. She lifted the glass to the light, watching clear drops of liquid streaming down.

"Legs," she said.

"What?" said Ben.

"This wine has good legs," said Cameron. "See the droplets flowing down the side of the glass? It's a strange effect that comes from evaporation of the alcohol. It's supposed to show how good the wine is. Or how strong. Or how sweet... I can never quite remember." She laughed.

Ben swirled his wine around too energetically, putting the glass down with a guilty grin as it threatened to splash over the rim. "That's not how you do it."

The two of them were trying to hold in their giggles when the waiter arrived with the first course. Cameron looked appreciatively at the beautifully presented plate. "Fresh mushrooms," she exclaimed. "They smell gorgeous."

"From the cellar," said the waiter with a half-smile.

"It's a speciality here," said Ben. "They really couldn't be any fresher. It's one of the most famous mushroom farms in Paris."

"The whole city is a farm, isn't it?" observed Cameron. "Vegetables grown on the roofs, mushrooms in the cellars, fruit on the trees. We could learn a lot." She picked up the wine bottle and examined the label. "I'm sure this wine isn't local, though. I recognise the label. They have vines around my village."

"The climate is better up there these days," said Ben sagely. "How long have those vineyards been established?"

"Commercially, only for the last decade or so," replied Cameron. "There's been a private vineyard in the village for more than sixty years, so when producers from champagne and burgundy started looking for new terroirs it was an obvious choice." She looked at the label more closely. "To be fair, this is probably the genuine article from the original vineyards. Yes, according to the vintage this is definitely French."

"What did the village do before wine?" asked Ben. "There are plenty of sheep in the fields even now, aren't there?"

"Mainly sheep and cattle down in the village," replied Cameron. "And cereal crops up on the level ground. The crops have been genetically modified to handle the changing climate, of course, so they are still being farmed. The stock isn't bothered. To be honest, the vines are a great money spinner. The local economy has never looked so good. The village is buzzing."

"How long did you actually live there?" asked Ben.

"All my life, until I moved away to London to study," replied Cameron. "When mum and dad died, Charlie had already graduated and was helping to run the factory. Aunt Vicky moved into the big house to look after both of us. Charlie got to focus on the business and I stayed at school. It made the awful time less awful." She smiled, remembering. "It was a great place to grow up. Fields to run around in, a stream for getting wet and muddy, and a close-knit community. Charlie's kids are very lucky."

"I had race tracks to run around and my dad's old cars for getting mucky," said Ben. "It was a lot of fun and it made me a better engineer."

"From race cars to space?" said Cameron, fascinated.

"Not a huge leap, really," replied Ben. "I was fascinated by having to put things together to make them work. So much of what we use day to day is served up to us without any idea of the detail underneath. How does your smartscreen switch on? How do the autocars run? How do drones fly? Not the tech, not the programming, but the actual parts. How do they fit together in the first place?" He shrugged. "On Mars, people will have to know the basics. I can help with good designs."

"People don't think about how things work," sighed Cameron. "They assume that if it's convenient, it must be okay. If I had a coin for every time we've traced a cyberattack to a dodgy free wifi connection or a neat-looking link... It's crazy how little understanding there is."

"Where do you think the attack on our database came in?" asked Ben.

"No idea yet," replied Cameron. "It'll be something simple that should have rung alarm bells but didn't. Sébastien will find it soon enough." She sighed. "Do I have to go home?"

"You do," said Ben sadly, "but I'll be back before the end of the week if all goes according to plan. When's Nina's party?"

"Friday lunchtime at the school," replied Cameron. "Are you going to make it?"

"I should do," said Ben. "Now, finish your mushrooms. You have a train to catch."

•

Andy was tired of waiting around. Even Bea Black had lost her bounce. They sat slumped in the outside broadcast pod, watching the drone footage on the wallscreen. There was very little to see, and the light was starting to fade. Giles stuck his head round the door. He looked equally bored.

"Andy, Bea, there's a catering van arrived. Want anything?"

Andy yawned. "That sounds like a great idea. I'm hungry." He glanced at the time on the wallscreen. "We've been here for eight hours already. Are they going to tell us anything more?"

"Probably not," said Bea. "But we'd look stupid if we missed a scoop." She gestured at the crowds of press still camped out alongside them. "Let's get some food and see how the land lies." She hopped out of the pod, her smart top contrasting with jeans and practical trainers.

Andy followed her to the food van where a queue was already forming. The smell of fresh fish on the griddle was enticing, and Andy felt his stomach rumble.

"Fish and chips or fish tacos?" asked Bea.

"Fish and chips," said Andy. "I don't get the chance very often."

Bea looked sidelong at him. "Activity monitor doesn't like you indulging?" she asked slyly.

"It shouldn't complain today," replied Andy. "I haven't eaten since breakfast. The insurers don't have a leg to stand on." He bit into the crisp batter of his fish. "Delicious," he said with satisfaction. "That was almost worth all the hanging around."

The two of them strolled companionably back towards the pod, Bea nibbling at the salad on her taco. Andy glanced at the monitor on his wrist. The little LED was still green. He'd gotten away scot free with the forbidden takeaway.

"What are you working on at the moment?" asked Bea between mouthfuls.

"The big Calton Global hack," replied Andy. "There's a lot of data gone astray right across their supply chain. I'm producing education pieces, getting users to change their passwords, that sort of thing."

"Calton Global have a lot of connections into the healthcare sector, don't they," said Bea. "What do you think the implications might be of a big data breach combined with something like an outbreak of Grasshopper Flu?"

Andy looked sidelong at her, impressed. "I don't know. That's an excellent question. Let's talk it over. We could get some content out without waiting for another anodyne statement from the hospital."

They settled back down in the pod, energised by good food and a puzzle to work through. Andy pulled up a mind mapper on the wallscreen and tapped the centre.

"Data breach," he said.

The words appeared in a circle on the screen.

"Let's put all the possibilities down, said Andy. "Giles," he called, "come and join us."

Giles squeezed into the pod, leaning against the door frame.

"Grab a coffee."

"The obvious one straight away is phishing," said Bea. "Using personal data to build convincing scams." She tapped the screen and said, "Phishing". A circle appeared, joined to the original centre circle by a line. In the middle the text read 'Fishing'.

"Good enough," laughed Andy. "From phishing, what do we have? Access to other systems like corporate networks." He added 'hacking' to the map.

"Fraud," said Giles. "Stealing from wallets, ordering goods with someone else's bank details."

"Identity fraud," said Bea. "Not just financial. Defamation? Loss of reputation?"

"That has personal and corporate implications," said Andy. "It's common to hear of people being unable to access any kind of finance because someone else ruined their ratings for them, and there have been a couple of good businesses who've gone to the wall because of malicious attacks and vandalised public profiles."

"All of that just from grabbing addresses and passcodes?" said Bea. "It's the tip of the iceberg. What about commercial data?"

"Let's add another area," said Andy. "Theft of intellectual property." He tapped the screen and a new bubble appeared which read 'IP Theft'.

"Counterfeiting," said Bea immediately. "Machines. Sensors. Medicines. Vaccines."

"That's interesting," said Giles. "What if a drug is counterfeited and floods the market at a low price, but the actual ingredients aren't exactly right?"

"Nasty," said Bea. "That could have huge implications." She turned to Andy. "Out of interest, are any of the compromised companies in the business of supplying the flu vaccine or any of the current treatments?"

"I don't know," he replied, "but I can find out. I sincerely hope there's no link."

"I'm with you there," said Bea. "Now, where else could we look?"

"Who values the data? Who would gain from accessing it?" asked Giles.

"Plenty of possibilities," said Andy. "How about insurance companies? Turn it round. If someone's had a payout for an accident but there's footage of them which shows the claim was fraudulent, then the insurers could claw back the money."

"Private investigators already do that," said Giles.

"I know," replied Andy, "but it makes their job easier if they can just buy the information off the web."

"Blackmail?" suggested Bea. "What if there's some medical condition that a person doesn't want to make public. Ongoing tests, that sort of thing…"

There was a commotion outside the pod.

Giles hopped down to see what was happening and stuck his head back round the door a few moments later. "We're on again," he said. "Another statement. It's the hospital management and someone from public health this time."

Bea re-applied her lipstick, brushed her hair, and stepped out of the pod again, looking every inch the consummate professional.

"Let's see what they have to say for themselves this time," she said grimly.

Behind her, Andy looked broodingly at the growing mind map on the screen. He saved it, sent it to his own smartscreen, and switched off the pod's display. He needed to talk to Cameron.

•

Cameron unlocked the door of her apartment and braced herself for the assault. Sure enough, the little black and white cat hurled itself at her feet. Cameron bent to pick the cat up and it wriggled in her grasp, purring and squeaking in welcome.

"Missed me, have you?" said Cameron, amused.

The cat looked her in the eye. "Miaow?" it said.

"Liar," said Cameron, putting it down on the warm tiled floor. She turned back to the dark hallway and retrieved her suitcase, dropping it with her bag in the corner of the room. She closed the door behind her and surveyed the apartment. It was a relief to be home after the long delays and stringent controls at the border. There seemed to be a lot of panic around this flu case. Cameron didn't want to think about it too much.

An alert flashed on her smartscreen. Andy Taylor had been trying to reach her. She didn't feel like talking to him tonight. She was sure it could wait until the morning.

The feeder was empty; Cameron opened a cupboard and pulled out a box of kibbles. She refilled the bowl, buying the cat's loyalty for another day. What to eat herself? She opened the fridge and stared at its brightly lit but empty shelves. Tonight, she could almost see the attraction of a smart fridge automatically re-ordering whatever was needed. She shook her head. She must be tired. The idea of a smart fridge was still an abomination.

This evening she wanted a delicious, drone-delivered treat. "Order a curry for one," she said clearly to the portal. "Fish. Vegetables. Rice. Bottle of beer."

The portal would parse the vague command into a clear instruction for the best local takeaway, based on its accumulated learning of her preferences for style, sauce and spice. She would have time to empty her bags before the drone arrived on her balcony carrying the warm, fragrant package. Payment was already reserved and would be transferred to the takeaway's wallet as soon as the delivery was complete. Smooth and easy.

Cameron finished sorting her luggage and strolled to the tall glass doors that led to her small balcony. As she reached for the switch to open the blind, she became aware of an unexpected noise from outside. A drone was already waiting, but it wasn't the familiar little insulated bubble that she was expecting from the restaurant. This machine was much larger, filling the tiny space. Advertisements flickered across its shiny hull, interspersed with a standard service message: 'Please confirm receipt.'

Cameron looked it over carefully, then turned back into the room and searched through a drawer to find a pair of gloves. She returned to the drone and examined the goods it was carrying. If this was a genuine delivery using her home settings, it would be waiting for her thumbprint, not a contactless chip confirmation. She wanted to check what it was before accepting the drop.

The contents of the delivery were perplexing. Three pairs of socks. A box of biscuits. A set of plates. A large box of cat food. A cuddly lion.

Confused, Cameron called back to the portal. "Review recent orders."

"Meal ordered from Koh-I-Noor London Bridge, Sunday, 8.05pm, in progress," said the portal. "Sundry purchases from Hedgehog Trading, Sunday, 2.33am, awaiting confirmation of delivery. Sundry purchases from Walway Online Grocery…"

"Stop," said Cameron. "Replay order to Hedgehog Trading."

There was a pause, then the recording of the order came over the portal speakers. Cameron listened in disbelief, then began to laugh. She heard the unmistakeable sound of the small black and white cat, mewing piteously.

"Cancel the order to Hedgehog Trading," she said as clearly as she could, resisting the urge to laugh. A few moments later the portal confirmed the cancellation and Cameron heard the sound of the drone taking off again. That was a new one, she reflected. The portal would require some urgent reprogramming and the providers would be getting an unusual bug report. She'd heard of ultrasonic commands triggering portals, but never a cat successfully placing an order.

Moments later, the little takeaway drone hove into view. Cameron gratefully collected the package, thumbing a pad on the drone to complete the contract. In a blockchain somewhere in the cloud an instruction was created to send the appropriate payment from her wallet to the restaurant. Cameron carried her food indoors and closed the balcony door.

The news was full of speculation about the flu, but very little fact. Cameron recognised the reporter on the snippets of live coverage and guessed that Andy was working on the story. She took a bite of her curry, the spicy aromas familiar and delicious. The bulletin moved on to other stories: an appeal for information about a wanted man, a virtual soccer team touring Europe, results from real world sports leagues. Cameron wondered what the real-life athletes thought of the online players. She knew that Ben, for all his upbringing in high-octane motor racing and his love of the electric circuit, had a lot of respect for virtual racers and the skills that took them to the highest level of their sport. Maybe it differed from sport to sport. She couldn't see the ancient disciplines of martial arts translating easily to a virtual platform without losing the nuances of personal discipline and growth. Online football, on the other hand, was big business. Charlie was a fan, and the children talked about watching matches, although touring as a virtual side seemed to her an odd concept. The players in a single team were often scattered across the globe, and their on-screen avatar would be quite different from the real person at the controls.

She was half way through her takeaway when her smartscreen pinged with another call from Andy. "Evening," she said, swallowing a mouthful of fish. "Have you been working today?"

"Yes, I got stuck with the flu story," replied Andy. He looked tired. "I wanted to run something past you. We've all been bored and started speculating about the possibility of the Calton Global breach to cause problems with protecting against real viruses."

"You have a point," replied Cameron. "Plenty of scope to disrupt healthcare and compromise treatment. Are you thinking of combining stories?"

"Might do," said Andy nonchalantly. "I prefer computer viruses to human ones. If I send over some notes, would you have a look at them?"

"Sure," said Cameron, "but it won't be tonight."

"That's fine," said Andy. "I'm bushed. I should make the last train. Speak to you later in the week. Thanks, Cameron."

"Any time," she replied. The call disconnected. Cameron yawned. It was getting late. She put the remaining curry away in the fridge and curled up on the sofa with the little black and white cat. The coming week was going to be busy.

6: THE CUCKOO CONTRACT

Charlie Silvera sipped his Monday morning coffee and scrolled through the report on his screen. The figures made grim reading. Sales of one of the company's major product lines had halved in the space of a few weeks. He looked up at his sales director and frowned.

"Lee, this is worse than we expected," he said. "They've pulled the whole contract?"

"Yes," replied Lee, the frustration all too evident in his voice. "The account managers did their best, but we couldn't match the lower costs." He reached across and tapped a section of the report, enlarging it. Encouraging upward curves filled the screen. "Our sales pipeline's strong, though. Plenty of new customers to keep things fresh."

"But not enough volume yet to compensate for losing two major contracts in one quarter," said Charlie.

Lee nodded. "Exactly. We've been preferred suppliers across the industry for so long that we're used to a natural rise and fall in demand, but this? It completely contradicts the normal patterns."

"Daniel's and Formula240 had been with us for twenty years," said Charlie. "We virtually developed the specialist bearing component range around them."

Lee nodded grimly. "That's the crux of it. Until recently we were the only suppliers. Suddenly there's a flood of compatible units coming in at an eye-wateringly low price from overseas."

"Compatible? Virtually identical." Charlie shook his head. "If I didn't know better I'd say we'd been hacked."

Lee looked sidelong at his boss. "Really?"

"Commercial espionage at its finest, Lee," replied Charlie. "I've had a good look at these new components, and the specifications are so close that I'm almost certain they've been printed from the same design files. The one thing that concerns me, which should be worrying Daniels and Formula 240 as well, is that the materials are sub-standard."

"That's something I can feed back through the account managers," said Lee. "Focus on our reputation for quality and see if it brings the prodigal clients back through the door again. Where do you think the new suppliers picked up our designs?"

"I don't think it's a leak through our staff or partners," replied Charlie. "There's no sign of any suspicious behaviour on the ground, and our security training is up to date."

"Agreed," said Lee. "I've no concerns on that score. But where do think the data breach could be?"

"I'm not sure," replied Charlie. "Cam's team checks over the system regularly. There's no sign of any attacks getting through our local firewalls, although there are enough coming at us every day."

"What about the remote hosting?" asked Lee.

"Tight as a drum," replied Charlie. "Best reputation in the business. We've also split the designs across different servers. If there's an attack on one server, it doesn't compromise the whole range of products. Lee, am I right in thinking that there's no problem with customers using other ranges?"

Lee considered his customer base. "Yes," he said decisively. "Apart from these two major clients, there are a couple of smaller contracts where the volume has dropped, and it's the same component range." He gave a weak smile. "That's not so bad."

"Oh, it's still bad," said Charlie sagely. "But if we can find a common thread in the contracts we're losing, Cam will be able to join the dots and tell us where we need to tighten up."

"I'll get onto it now," said Lee.

"Thanks, Lee," replied Charlie. "Could you ask Holly to pop in and see me on your way through?"

"Sure." Lee strode out, head high, and a few minutes later Holly, the Chief Technology Officer, put her head round the door.

"Morning, Charlie," she said. "What's up?"

"We have a puzzle to solve," replied Charlie. "I'm pretty sure we've had a breach in the system. There's a chance that some of our proprietary designs have gone walkabout."

"Always possible," said Holly pragmatically, "but I haven't picked anything up. Cam and one of her guys – Susie, was it? – did a routine sweep just a few weeks ago."

"Nevertheless," replied Charlie, "I feel it in my bones, someone has been through our files. Let's eliminate every likely way in."

"No problem, Charlie," replied Holly. "I'll run another check locally, and I'll follow up with the data centre, too. They haven't issued any compromise notices since the last full system audit, though."

"That's good to know," said Charlie, "but what if there's a breach they haven't detected? Can't tell us about something they haven't found, can they?"

"True," said Holly. "It may be worth asking Cameron to visit on our behalf. She has an instinct for these things."

"You're more than capable, Holly," replied Charlie, "but if you want the visit to be at arms' length, fair enough. Do you want to call her directly?"

"Sure, Charlie," said Holly. "I'll see how she's fixed to go up north."

•

Cameron couldn't believe her ears. "Data theft, Holly? Not another one. There's a lot of it about."

At the other end of the call, Holly nodded seriously. "We've been careful and lucky up until now," she said. "I've been back over the systems here with a fine-toothed comb. If Charlie is right, and some of our designs have been stolen, then it can only be the data centre."

"I'm inclined to agree," said Cameron. "You've eliminated phishing attacks on your own systems, and I know how tight they are." She paused, thinking. "Have you audited your supply blockchain recently?"

"Yes," replied Holly. "We've had all-clear checks on the smart contracts and consensus mechanisms in the last month. No dodgy code, no collusion."

"That's a relief," said Cameron. "I'll organise a trip up to your data centre. Can you make an appointment for me? Say Thursday afternoon?"

"Sure. I'll ping you a confirmation," replied Holly.

Cameron put down her screen and turned to the rest of the team.

"It never rains but it pours," she said, with a rueful grin. "Another data theft, this time at Charlie's place, at Watling Automotive. I'll go and check it out at the end of the week. Let's review where we are with Calton Global." She looked around the office. "Noor, want to go first?"

"Okay," replied Noor. "Pete made a start on auditing the smart contracts and found a recent insertion that will have compromised every party, as they all have identical copies of the ledger. We've called it a cuckoo contract."

"I like that," said Cameron. "It has a nice ring to it. Cuckoo contract. Yes."

"Where is Pete?" asked Joel. "He's normally online by now."

"That's true," said Noor. "I didn't speak to him directly on Saturday. He sent all his findings over before I came in. He said that he had been asked to log off and stay on the ward. I guess that was when the flu case was first reported."

"The hospital's in lockdown, according to the news reports," interjected Susie. "I had a booster jab yesterday."

"You're all up to date with your vaccinations, aren't you?" asked Cameron, suddenly concerned. There was a chorus of assent.

"Didn't Pete have a procedure scheduled today anyway?" said Sandeep. "Fixing his legs? I hope it goes ahead, what with all this fuss."

"I think we can let him off," said Cameron with a grin. "He's not supposed to be working at all. He's just been relieving the boredom."

"I picked up on the work he did and sent his findings round the community," continued Noor. "The East Coast teams have confirmed that he's on the right track."

"The Calton breach is going to be the tip of the iceberg on that supply chain," said Joel soberly. "I wonder how many more data bundles we'll see for sale out on the open market."

"Do we have any indication yet where this new contract was introduced?" asked Cameron.

"Not so far," replied Noor. "We're all trying to track back through a maze of IP addresses. The only thing that seems to be agreed is that it is unlikely to have originated at Calton Global itself. It could be absolutely anywhere. Every other node in the blockchain has to be a suspect."

"All the local systems need checking," said Ella. "The companies concerned are duty bound to notify a data breach quickly."

"Every organisation is scrambling to avoid a hefty fine," confirmed Cameron. "Better to spend their money on people like us to sweep and tighten their systems than risk a blemish on their data protection records."

"That'll tie up half the threat intelligence people in the northern hemisphere," said Ross. "Who's paying for all of this?"

"I think I know where some of the money is coming from," said Ella. She sounded amused. "Check this out."

She pulled up Calton Global's website. A banner across the screen was unmissable. 'Are your records safe?' shouted the headline. 'Guard your health and wealth with Calton Global's Safe'n'Sure™ service – less than a coin a week for full protection.'

"Cheeky buggers," said Joel. "Their data gets stolen and sold to all comers on Eden, and they turn around and get their users to pay to check it all."

"Brazen," replied Ella. "It seems to be working, though." She pulled up a second screen: the public records of the Safe'n'Sure payment wallet. Thousands of transactions were already recorded, and the list was growing. "That should cover their infosec fees."

Cameron laughed. "It's ingenious."

"Borderline scamming," said Ross.

"Sure," replied Cameron, "but it pays our bills. Talking of which, Ella, can you update us on the transactions around the data auction?"

Ella turned to her screen and flicked through her notes, refreshing her memory on the progress they had made.

"On Friday night…" she began. Susie coughed meaningfully, and Ella flashed her an irritated look before continuing. "…Noor and I followed the trail of several amounts which were paid out of the balance on the seller's account straight after the auction concluded. The bulk of the proceeds took a tortuous route out of Eden and through some shady exchanges, so that money's proving hard to follow, but we've hit the jackpot with a number of smaller payments."

"You don't mean you've actually found some people?" asked Cameron in disbelief.

Ella nodded, grinning from ear to ear. "The trail was complicated and pretty well hidden, but we've not only found a number of final destination wallets, but we've managed to link some of them to real-world identities."

Joel and Sandeep, who hadn't heard about the latest developments, whooped in delight.

"Brilliant," exclaimed Joel, grinning broadly. "Where did they slip up? Spending it too fast?"

"That's right," said Noor. "We managed to trace purchases on open sites and linked the account user names back to other accounts. We have to assume that most of those user names are aliases at this stage, of course. We don't have much information on the individuals, but it's a start."

"Excellent work," said Cameron proudly.

"Do we have enough to go after anyone?" asked Joel.

Noor was grinning like the Cheshire cat. "Probably. I've actually got visuals on one of them."

"What?" said Sandeep. "One of the wallet owners?"

Noor nodded. "I've established a solid trail from the data sale proceeds, out of Eden, through a couple of exchanges, into the public currency blockchain, and straight to the checkout of a very high-end clothing store."

"Surely someone who's messing around on Eden knows to stay incognito?" said Sandeep.

"You'd think so," replied Noor, "but this guy's account on the store matches a social profile. Either they're both fake, or they're both real. We have pictures. There's a head shot and a few other images." She turned her screen to show Sandeep. "See? He likes his designer gear."

The pictures showed a slim young man with immaculately styled dark hair, dressed in the very latest fashions.

"The social and store accounts are both in the name of Aman Patel," said Noor. "It's a very common name, so it could well be a pseudonym, but I'm sure the images are genuine."

"That's brilliant, Noor," said Sandeep. "Can you triangulate any further? Nail down some locations in his social posts?"

"I'm on it," said Noor. "I've set a search running to retrieve all the instances of the images we have across the network, and to pick up any others through facial recognition."

"Keep digging," said Cameron. "How about the seller and the buyer?"

Ella shook her head. "Nothing yet. The seller's Eden account is empty, and the bulk of the money has gone beyond what I can trace." She frowned. "There's something bugging me, though. I need a bit more time to look at this."

"Follow your instincts," said Cameron. "I trust you. Do we have any clues on the buyers?"

"I picked this part up," said Ross. "They are proving very hard to trace, but they have a lot of data at their fingertips now. I think we need to worry more about what havoc they could cause with that data than who they are."

"Fair point," agreed Joel. "Has anyone started collating the known breaches?"

"The forum members have contributed all the breaches they know to the HackerTracker," said Cameron. "Obviously some of those won't be linked, like the hack Bordegiciel is working on, or this odd report from Charlie." She turned to Susie who was sitting quietly on the edge of the group, scowling. "Could you start working through the information and build a coherent picture of which of those relate to the Calton Global supply chain?" she asked. "It will give us an idea of the scale and the scope of the data that's been compromised."

Susie nodded. "Okay," she said. "I'll build on their intel and see where we are."

"Talking of your threat forum," said Joel, "how was Paris?"

"I had a nice weekend away, thank you," replied Cameron. "It was complete chance that work reared its ugly head. It's always amusing to meet online connections in real life."

"At least you traced the source of the design data that was sold on Eden," said Sandeep. "That's one thing off our list."

"Bordegiciel seems like a nice guy," said Ross approvingly.

"He is," replied Cameron. "I think he was a little surprised to meet me. He's doing a good job, and we're going to help out. I'm speaking to their management team today about formal involvement."

"That's good," said Joel. "Is this Bordegiciel guy freelancing?"

"No," Cameron shook her head. "He's working full time for Ben's company. He's well connected in France, though. If we ever have a cross-border breach to manage, we know who to call."

"What's the plan for this week?" asked Sandeep.

"Plenty to do," replied Cameron. She considered the priorities. "Susie, you're building a picture of the data that's out in the wild, aren't you?"

Susie nodded, her fingers already dancing across her keyboard.

Cameron turned to Sandeep. "Can you start modelling possible uses for that data? I have some good input for you from our friend Andy Taylor over at the news channel. He and his friends were brainstorming potential threats and came up with quite a comprehensive list. I'll ping it over to you. We want to identify the kind of chaos the data could cause in the wrong hands. I suspect the motive for the hack was purely financial, but what will the buyers do?" She looked up at the blank wallscreen. "If Pete calls in," she continued, "get him to help you out."

Ella spoke up. "I want to carry on with tracing the proceeds of sale."

"Yes, of course," said Cameron. "Keep following the transaction trail. Noor, can you keep going with finding beneficiaries in the real world? Stay in touch with the other teams as well."

She turned to Ross and Joel. "We need to redouble our efforts with our Calton audit clients. If the cuckoo contract originated in this country, I want it found."

•

Ross looked around the room, trying to relax. He did not want his discomfort to show. He had never been in this particular building before, but every law enforcement office had the same look and feel wherever it was. Bland walls. Blank screens. Cameras discreetly positioned to capture every nuance of an interviewee's reaction.

His smartscreen lay silent on the table, all networks blocked. The call had come as he was leaving his Tuesday morning training session. He'd been nervous when it connected, but relieved when he was told to take his time. There was no urgency, they said, just some help needed in the ongoing investigation. Cameron had simply shrugged when he called in and told him to take his time. She and Joel could start off the day's visits without him.

He sat quietly, thinking about his long-buried past. The thrill and challenge of hacking, and his surprise when people started to pay top coin for his services. The knock on the door before dawn that heralded his downfall. The short sharp shock of prison, and his unexpected redemption and rehabilitation through Cameron. In retrospect, being caught was the best thing that could have happened to him. He wondered what his old friends were doing now.

The door opened suddenly, startling him out of his reverie. A uniformed man appeared, and Ross recognised the young officer who had delivered his clothes from the house on the night the body was discovered.

"DI Mercer sends her apologies for keeping you waiting, Mr White." He appeared flustered. "Can I get you anything? A drink?"

"Just some water, please," said Ross. It was good to be on the right side of the law.

The officer left on his errand and returned moments later with a large glass. He put it on the table and hurried out as Sara Mercer walked in, neat and purposeful. She gave Ross a professional but not unfriendly smile, and she had a worried air about her.

"Good morning, Mr White," she said. "Thank you for coming in. I hope you're well. Have you settled back into your home?"

"Thank you, yes," replied Ross. "It's been a good opportunity to sort the house out, actually. I've started redecorating." He took a sip of water; his mouth was dry.

"I'm glad to hear it. The burglary must have been a dreadful shock for you." Mercer observed his reactions carefully, and Ross took equal care to show exactly the emotion she expected.

"Yes, it shook me up alright. I always thought it was a good neighbourhood."

"You're right," said Mercer, "it is generally quiet. We're working on the assumption that your home was deliberately targeted. Do you have any idea why this might have been, other than the presence of valuable technical and sporting equipment?"

"No, not at all," replied Ross. "I work in threat intelligence as you know. It's very rare for us to come across the perpetrators in person. Often we have no idea who they are. We just deal with the consequences and try to prevent attacks getting through." He paused. "Surely you would have a better idea than me about this. I mean, who was he?"

DI Mercer glanced down at her hands for a fleeting moment, then regained her composure. "Mr White, I am sorry to say that despite extensive enquiries, we have been unable to identify the deceased."

This was exactly what he had expected after the appeal for information the previous day. He made an effort to sound surprised. "But that's impossible," he said. "No one is anonymous. ID Cards. Biometrics. Chips."

Mercer shook her head. "No chip, although that's not unusual in people over the age of forty. No physical identification. No smartscreen or any identification on the body." She paused. "No fingerprints. No retina scan on file, as far as we can find."

At that, Ross's mouth fell open. He was genuinely lost for words.

"I know," said Mercer. "We have to fall back on old-fashioned methods." She pulled the picture up on the wallscreen. "Mr White, have you ever seen this man before?"

It would be best to tell the truth, or part at least. "I think I have. By the bikes in Hyde Park at the end of the London triathlon. He was hanging around."

"Excellent!" Sara Mercer could not keep the relief out of her voice. "That gives us a starting point and strengthens the motive for theft."

Ross looked at the photograph, and a thought struck him.

"May I have a high-resolution copy?" he asked, his voice deliberately casual. "I could ask around my team-mates, see if anyone else has seen him."

"Yes, of course," replied Mercer. "We've already started appealing for information. Someone out there will know who he is."

She tapped the screen twice and a menu appeared. "Open your smartscreen, Mr White. It should pick up the closed network in this suite."

Ross thumbed the screen into life and sure enough a connection request was waiting for him. He accepted, and the picture appeared instantly. "Thank you."

"No, thank you, Mr White." Mercer paused. "There is some urgency to this investigation which is unrelated to the burglary itself. I must ask, have you been vaccinated against Grasshopper Flu?"

"Yes," replied Ross. "I'm all up to date. It's a requirement for competition."

"Good," said Mercer. "As you had no contact with the body, you were unlikely to be at risk. However, it will soon be announced that the patient currently in quarantine at St Martin's is a forensics officer who dealt with the deceased."

Ross was, for once, genuinely shocked. "Are you saying this burglar was a carrier?" he asked.

"That's still to be confirmed," replied Mercer heavily. "Our investigations are ongoing."

Mercer stood up, and Ross did the same. "My colleague will show you out." She walked smartly out of the room, and the young officer reappeared.

"This way please."

As Ross stepped back onto the pavement he felt mixed emotions. On one hand he was horrified at the link to the flu case. On the other hand, he could not believe his luck, because he now had the key to the stranger's smartscreen.

Half an hour later, Ross settled at his desk in the half-stripped sitting room and fired up the computer. He searched quickly for a specialist printing service. Results crawled across the screen, and Ross gave a grunt of annoyance at the slowness of the connection. The house network upgrade had been long overdue, and he was looking forward to the work being completed.

He scanned down the list, his eyes lighting on a supplier called 3D Transform Me. 'Get the party started. Costumes and custom printed supplies,' read the listing. Yes, that would do. Ross clicked through to the site and opened an account using a throwaway identity, verifying through an old third-party authentication service. He uploaded the image of the dead man, gave a central collection office as the mailing address, and paid for the printing with the dwindling funds in his Eden currency account.

He glanced at the clock. His printing wouldn't be delivered for another few hours. He closed down his computer and called Cameron.

"I'm all done with the police," he said. "Routine stuff, nothing to worry about. Where are you?"

"We're finishing off at Sherman Sensors and heading to Platinum Labs," replied Cameron. "Can you meet us there?"

"Sure," said Ross, "I'll see you shortly."

Sandeep stretched and tore his attention away from the screen that had absorbed him for too long. It was past midday, and he was hungry. He looked around the office at his colleagues.

Ella was frowning, eyes closed, headphones firmly on. Both ears covered meant do not disturb. He didn't want to break her train of thought. He hoped she was getting close to a breakthrough on her hunch and wondered what path her keen financial mind was following.

Noor was smiling to herself as she built a web of data around each person in her sights. She scanned pages and pages of accounts and profiles, occasionally tapping triumphantly on a link or document and drawing it into the growing picture. Sandeep walked over to her and peered at the screen, admiring the results of her research.

"Looking good, Noor," he said.

"I think I've identified another four people, although I don't have much detail about them," she said, "and I'm fairly certain Aman Patel is a real person."

"Are all of them local?" asked Sandeep.

"No," replied Noor. "Aman Patel is here in England, but I'm not sure exactly where. There's one in France, one in Singapore, and two in the States, in Texas and New York."

"Better let the East Coast teams know about the New York one when you have more to share," said Sandeep. The two of them looked across at Susie who was typing animatedly, chatting online with the teams who had just started work, five hours adrift of London.

"How's it going?" asked Sandeep. In answer, Susie swung her screen around with a grin, and Noor and Sandeep scanned her findings, impressed.

Susie's list of compromised databases was growing. The huge supply chain that included Calton Global stretched across the Americas to the west and Asia to the east. It spanned multiple business sectors. Susie had picked up breaches from manufacturers of equipment for the lucrative healthcare market, whose products fed rich data back to base. She had identified records from insurers who tracked smart device use in customers' homes, adjusting premiums for changing behaviour the moment it was detected. Personal activity trackers the world over had always sent anonymous data back to base, but where users linked their devices to social accounts for convenience there were rich pickings to be had. There was even more personal data in the form of images recorded by CCTV cameras and drones operating in hospitals and clinics and stored in a central archive. Voice recordings of medical consultations through portals, dealing with both real practitioners and artificial intelligence, had been kept for insurance and malpractice claims and their content compromised. Sandeep had even spotted a centralised currency exchange on the list. Protect your health and wealth, indeed.

"The scale of this is amazing," said Susie. She typed a quick note to the community and logged off, ready for some lunch.

Distracted by the movement around her, Ella lifted her headphones off and looked across at Sandeep. She looked tired and concerned. "No word from Pete yet?"

"No, we haven't heard from him," said Sandeep. "I hope he's okay. How's your research going?"

"I think I'm getting somewhere," said Ella slowly, "but you're not going to like it."

"What do you mean?" asked Susie.

"My hunch paid off," said Ella. "I haven't managed to trace the actual seller, but what I do know is that the wallets have been active before, and recently." She paused. "Remember the Speakeasy attacks on the banking system? The big profits that were taken from futures trading?"

"Yes," said Sandeep, "we watched the money vanish into thin air."

"The Speakeasy funds passed through the same wallet as the Calton Global proceeds while they were being moved around," said Ella. "I'm one hundred percent certain that the same person or organisation has been involved in both attacks."

Sandeep's jaw dropped. "That's impossible."

"Not impossible, just arrogant in the extreme," said Ella. "Why would they run the risk of using the same wallet twice?"

"Because they don't expect someone with your tenacity to be following all the transactions," said Sandeep. "You've done an amazing job."

Noor nodded in agreement. "Brilliant, Ella," she said. "I wonder…"

"…if there are any small payments coming back out from the Speakeasy funds?" Susie finished the sentence for her.

"Exactly," said Noor. "Ella, let me have the details. I want to see if any of the people I've found are linked to the original attack."

"You carry on with that," said Sandeep. "I'll order some lunch, and Ella, you'd better let Cameron know what you've found."

•

Cameron, Joel and Ross shook hands with the IT chief at Platinum Labs and walked out of the building. The client was based on a large industrial estate to the north of the city popular with large processors and manufacturers. The three of them walked towards the passenger train station, crossing a bridge over the wide canal. Freight barges were loading and unloading at the busy estate dock, robot stevedores accurately plucking goods from the barge holds and depositing them safely on the wharf. Supervisors with smart screens moved through the loading areas, checking consignments and scanning tags to automatically add another step in the supply blockchain. The senders would be able to see instantly that the goods had arrived, and bills could be paid without delay.

"Their operation's pretty tight," observed Joel.

"The barges?" said Cameron, distracted.

"No, Platinum Labs," replied Joel, laughing. "Their security's great. They've put everything we suggested into practice."

"Good client," said Ross approvingly. "It's a shame they got mixed up in the Calton mess."

"They haven't had as bad a time as some of the others," observed Cameron. "Their underlying data was well protected with extra layers of encryption. The cuckoo contract just sent gobbledegook back to the thieves. Sherman Sensors, earlier, though... different story."

"Their data structures are a mess," said Joel. "They are going to be in huge trouble. No proper indexing of personal data across multiple media stores. It would be impossible for them to run a Right to be Forgotten routine for anyone. I'm not sure they know how much data they've actually lost through this."

"I'm glad I missed that one," said Ross, shuddering. "Are we going to be doing any more work with them?"

"Not unless they pay top coin for it," said Cameron grimly, "and they are going to be looking at a hefty data breach fine already. The directors make Joseph Hardy look like a pussycat. Talking of which, "she checked the time, "I want to head over there tonight. I'm really not comfortable with some of the answers I've been getting. I need a chat with Jessie."

"Do you want us to come with you?" asked Joel.

"No, I don't think it needs all three of us," replied Cameron. "Jessie may open up more to me if I'm on my own. Why don't you two pay a quick visit to FitBot and then head home?"

"They're practically by my house," said Joel. "No point you trailing all the way over there, Ross."

"FitBot have already declared their breach and put their house in order," said Cameron. "It's just a quick visit to eliminate them from our enquiries into the source of the cuckoo contract. You'll be fine on your own, Joel."

"I'll head home then," said Ross, inwardly delighted. He would have a chance to pick up his printing and solve a mystery of his own.

•

The collection office barely deserved the name. A stack of secure mailboxes in an unloved corner of a deserted mall, Ross liked the anonymity it afforded. He eyeballed the scanner and a light began to flash on a box high up to the left. He pulled at the door. Inside lay a slim, light package. He pulled it out and closed the door, which locked with an audible click. He tucked the package under his hoodie and strolled away, unseen.

Back at the house, he opened the bag. Inside lay a thin, flexible plastic mask, printed in 3D from the photograph he had supplied. The printers usually made these up for fancy dress parties and student jokes. What Ross was planning was unusual, but not unheard of.

He picked the stranger's smartscreen up from the table. He had thought there would be no easy way to crack the device but learning that the stranger had no fingerprints and apparently avoided retina scanning had given him an idea. What if the screen's biometric lock relied on facial recognition?

Taking a deep breath, he picked up the flimsy mask and held it over his face. He picked up the smartscreen and switched it on, expecting it to once again fade back into standby. He stared at it through the mask, and it glowed into life, revealing all its secrets.

Notifications scrolled across the screen, endless missed calls and messages. Ross navigated to the screen's memory, checking for contacts. There were no names, just a few numbers, some initials, and obvious nicknames. He scanned down them. 'Gracie'. 'Slings'. 'Cowgirl.' 'DJ.' 'Cox.' 'Tintin.' A number labelled 'Fashion Victim' caught his eye, but he didn't know why it resonated. He looked at the call records. The last outbound call on record was to 'Slings'. 'Cowgirl' was the ID on the bulk of the missed call notifications from the last two weeks.

Ross put the mask and the screen down and rubbed his eyes. He ought to hand this over to the police and let them deal with it, but he was afraid that he would end up being implicated in the dead man's affairs.

He sat in the darkening house, thinking.

·

Jessie was waiting in reception at Hardy's when Cameron arrived. Once Cameron had cleared security, the two women headed straight for Jessie's office.

"What's up, Cameron?" she asked, as the door closed behind them. "Please, sit down."

Cameron sat in the spare chair as Jessie took up her familiar place on the other side of the desk. She picked her words carefully, trying not to reveal too much. "We know a lot more about the source of the breach, now." That was true, but she didn't want to mention the cuckoo contract just yet. Her instincts were screaming that there was something not right here. "Sandeep is sure that he's traced some activity through Joseph Hardy's own office," she continued. That was also true. They had picked up evidence of a phishing attack during the audit. Whether it was connected to the cuckoo contract was another matter.

Jessie looked at her ruefully. "Oh dear. I'm not entirely looking forward to telling him."

Cameron smiled. "I feel your pain."

"So, tell me more," said Jessie. "Do we need HR in here?"

"Possibly," replied Cameron. "I'd like to talk to Yasmin, the assistant. You said you'd reset the accounts recently? That Joseph Hardy had given her access to his profile?"

"Yes, that's right," replied Jessie. "He's always doing it."

"There's something more complex going on here," sighed Cameron. "It looks as if her new profile was corrupted. Ironically, the system was more secure when she was signing on as Hardy."

Jessie looked perturbed for a moment, then recovered herself. "That's very odd. I'll speak to the person who reset the accounts."

"It wasn't you, then?" asked Cameron curiously. "It's just that you said…"

"No, no, not my job," replied Jessie. "One of my staff handles that kind of routine management."

"Okay," said Cameron, confused. "You should have mentioned that at the time. I'll let Ross and Sandeep know. It may have a bearing on the final report we submit to the client, and the recommendations we're making on reinforced security protocols."

"I'm sorry, Cameron. I should have thought," said Jessie, apparently unconcerned. She flicked on the screen on her desk and made a show of scrolling through records Cameron could not see. "Oh, gosh, of course, it was Steve." She looked up and shrugged apologetically. "He's left the company."

Cameron was taken aback. Something did not make sense here. Jessie had been unremittingly helpful until now. What had they stumbled upon?

"Could you fix up for me to meet Yasmin?" she asked without missing a beat. "We didn't manage to catch her during the initial audit."

Jessie shook her head. "Sorry, Cameron, she went on leave this afternoon."

"That's a shame. Not to worry," said Cameron lightly. "I'd better head back to the office. I'll review the final report with the guys and come back to you. Please give my apologies to Mr Hardy for postponing our meeting."

Jessie stood up, and at that moment her smartscreen pinged an incoming call alert. She looked down at the notification, and Cameron saw her eyes widen.

"I need to take this call," she said. She opened the door and called out to a passing staff member. "Mo, could you show Cameron out for me?"

Cameron put a hand on her arm. "Are you okay?" she asked. "Is there anything I can do?"

Jessie shook her head. "I'll speak to you later." She closed the door. There was a moment of silence, then Cameron heard her voice carrying distinctly through the wall.

"I thought you were dead."

•

Ross hurriedly disconnected the call and sat back, the mask hanging limp in his hand, his mouth open in shock. Jessie was the last person he would have expected to answer. How could she be linked to the stranger?

7: TRANSFORMATION

Martha sipped her tea, scrolling through the messages on her screen with one hand. She swiped several to delete them. "So much junk!" she exclaimed.

Joel swallowed a mouthful of toast and laughed. "You need to tidy out that mailbox." He gestured around the room. "I'm not touching it. I fixed the house already."

"And a great job you did too," she said, patting his knee. "The wardrobe gave me the right clothes this morning and the cookie jar is unlocked again."

"Did I unlock the cookie jar? I need to recheck the settings," teased Joel.

Martha held up a warning hand. "Don't you dare! You lock the cookie jar and I'll reset your sports packages."

"Playing hardball, huh? Okay, the cookie jar stays."

Martha finished her cup of tea and checked the time. It was still early, and she didn't need to be at work for an hour. She poured another drink and continued scrolling. Joel was deep into the sports reporting, following the latest news of his real and virtual rugby favourites.

"We've got some visitors coming to the farm today," said Martha. Joel gave a half-interested grunt and carried on reading. "They've travelled all the way from Singapore."

At that Joel sat up and took notice. "Really?" he said disbelievingly. "Are you sure?"

"Yes, of course. They're over here for some tour or other and want to study our farming techniques for use in their own economy. They do a lot of environmental work, cleaning the seas and rebuilding the ecosystems. The girls in the office are very excited. I don't know why."

"I think I've read something about this," said Joel, putting two and two together. "There's an e-soccer team touring, and there was an article about their work on re-establishing coral reefs and that sort of thing."

"That explains it," said Martha. "I've never taken much notice of football. I'm interested in how they're managing biodiversity, though. I think I'll learn as much from them as they will from us."

"Sounds like fun," said Joel. "We're still deep in the Calton Global mess. The fallout from the breach is going to go on for months, I reckon."

"Hmm," said Martha, still scrolling through her messages. "How's Ross doing? He's a funny lad, but nice enough."

"Ross is alright," said Joel. "He has his moments, you're right, but underneath that tough exterior he's quite lonely. He doesn't have any family, and he had a difficult start in life. I like him. He's good at his job, too."

"You should ask him round for dinner more often. I'll feed him up." Martha smiled wickedly. "I wonder if we should introduce him to a few of our single friends?"

"Stop scheming," laughed Joel. "Once you get your hands on him you'll have his entire life organised."

Martha pouted in mock disappointment.

Joel sighed. "I'd better get going. Aren't you heading off yet?"

"Almost ready," replied Martha. "I just need to sort this out." She tapped at her screen.

"What's up?" asked Joel, mystified.

"Message from the insurers," replied Martha. "They've had a problem with our account and need me to reset the access codes." She glanced at Joel. "Is this something to do with your work? They're part of Calton Global group."

"Stop!" Joel lunged for the screen before Martha could thumb the authorisation. "Let me see that." He scanned the message, his face grim. "It's related to Calton alright. It's a scam. I wondered when we'd see the first of the phishing campaigns."

Martha blushed. "I'm sorry. I don't normally fall for anything like this."

"It's convincing, I'll give them that," replied Joel. "Don't worry. No harm done. Tell the folks at your work to watch out. There'll be a lot of these scams going round over the next few months, and they have enough data to make the messages look genuine." He stood up and grabbed his jacket. "I'd better go. Have a good day with your visitors."

Joel disappeared out of the front door, and Martha, sighing, collected up the breakfast things and set them to wash.

•

"Bravo!" Sébastien's delight was palpable. "I see them!"

Cameron sat back in satisfaction and grinned at the smiling face on the wallscreen. Between them, they had pulled off a remarkable and rapid piece of digital forensics, searching for traces of the files before they were scrambled. The team had created a benevolent virus which replicated itself across the company's world-wide computer network, scoured the shadows of files on drives in every location, and scurried back to base with the results.

Sandeep pulled up the records he had captured from the original sale on Eden. "Let's check all these off before we get excited," he said. He opened the document in a sharing programme, and at his desk in Paris Sébastien started working down his list of recovered files. He tapped each matching item, and Sandeep watched as the filenames flashed green for a perfect match, or amber for an older version. There were very few ambers, and even fewer gaps. From a useless set of scrambled drives, the company now had restored copies of the designs that had been stolen from them.

"Looking good," said Cameron. "Most of the recovered files are recent versions. What about other records, Sébastien? Was anything scrambled that wasn't stolen?"

"Yes, it seems so," replied the Frenchman. "This is very good, Cameron. I can see many files that are not on your list. The thieves took only the designs that were created for the Mars mission. They covered their tracks by scrambling the rest."

"That's interesting," interjected Ross, who was taking a break from his own work on tracking Calton Global activity. "We reckoned this was a theft-to-order because of the way the sale went through on Eden."

"You're right," said Cameron. "This hacker was targeting specific designs and documents for a buyer. It's a very skilled job. The vandalism on your drives was unnecessary, though. Why would they draw attention to themselves like that? What would they gain from making it obvious that they had breached the company's systems?"

"It's a calling card," said Ross. "They want people in the black hat hacking world to know how smart they are."

"Building up a reputation for good work," said Joel. "Warped, but it makes sense."

Cameron frowned, thinking. She turned in her chair and looked across the office. "Noor? Ella? The accounts you've been tracing. Didn't you say there was a profile in France?"

"There is," replied Ella. "Want the latest details?"

"Please," said Cameron.

"Why should they be in France?" asked Sébastien from the wallscreen.

"A hacker could be anywhere. Attacks are flying across the world all of the time. We will never know who did this."

"Just a hunch," said Cameron. "It's something we should keep in mind. For now, let's finish up the contracted work. We can speculate on who did it on our own time. We've recovered the files. How are we doing on the mechanism of the attack?"

"We've found evidence that malware was introduced when some hosting system specifications were changed," said Sandeep. "It was cleverly designed to migrate to a load of unmonitored connected devices."

"Where did you find it?" asked Cameron.

Sébastien laughed. "It was hiding in the bathroom, Cameron. We have very smart washrooms. Smart toilets, smart showers. I did not think to scan those dumb systems."

"Hah. The Paris Pissoire Plot," Ross cackled. "I like it."

Joel fell about laughing.

Sandeep carried on with his explanation. "When activated, it targeted a specific tag that was on all of the Mars design files. It looks like there was a second penetration of the system to capture the tagged files, then the malware executed its final routine and scrambled everything."

"There's a lot of inside knowledge there," said Ross. "I agree with Cameron. There is a local aspect to this."

"Not necessarily," replied Sébastien. "The Mars design files have been shared with our clients. The hosting system changes were a standard upgrade. The suppliers of the smart devices would have held details of the connection specifications."

"A good researcher could find all of that out regardless of their location," said Sandeep. "Although, I still think you need to dig further into who had access to all that information and see if there are any unusual coincidences."

Sébastien sighed. "Bloody software. I will get to work. Thank you, all of you. SimCavalier, RunningManTech, I will speak to you on the forum soon."

"Any time, Bordegiciel," replied Cameron. "Any time," echoed Ross.

The connection to Paris terminated and the picture on the wallscreen faded.

"Nice work," said Cameron. "That was a quicker job than I expected."

"It made a refreshing change from ploughing through all the Calton Global audits," said Sandeep. "Good to have a break before hitting Hardy's tomorrow. Talking of a break, who wants coffee?" He gathered the cups from his colleagues' desks for cleaning and checked the store cupboard. "Huh, running low on supplies. Shall we go out instead? Could head to Clarey's?"

Susie glanced out of the window. "It's pouring with rain. Let's just order in. Drones don't mind getting wet."

Joel laughed. "A bit of rain won't hurt you. I don't mind what we do, but I'm hungry."

"Ordering in sounds good," said Ross. "I hope it dries up later. I've got a big training session this evening and it'll be miserable if it's still wet."

Sandeep pulled up the regular delivery menus on screen. "Pick your favourites, folks."

Within a couple of minutes, the orders were placed. The team collected coffees, made calls and checked personal messages, relaxing after a long morning's work.

After a short wait, there were noises from the delivery chute. Joel pulled the hatch open and the scent of hot food wafted around the office.

Cameron was tucking into a huge slice of pizza when she was distracted by an alert on her smart screen. "I need to take this," she said, putting the food down. "Hello? Adele?"

Noor looked up from her sandwich, startled. "Adele?" she whispered, "that's Pete's ex."

The lunchtime chatter faded and they all fell silent, watching Cameron's body language as she listened to the caller.

"I see," said Cameron. "Yes. Oh, no, how awful." Noor jumped but Cameron gave her a thumbs-up and an encouraging smile. "Yes, that's good news. You've all had a tough few days. Thank you so much for letting me know. Please pass on our best wishes." She put the screen down and turned to her team.

"You're not going to believe this," she said heavily, "but it's not as bad as you might think."

"Pete?" said Noor tentatively. "What's happened? Is he okay?"

"Was there a problem with his treatment?" asked Sandeep. "Is that why we haven't been able to raise him?"

"Flu," said Ross flatly. "It's the Grasshopper Flu, isn't it?"

The others gaped at him, and Cameron nodded.

"Yes. He was – he is – the second case. He caught it from another patient. He was lucky that he was on the ward when he started showing symptoms and was treated straight away."

"Was that Saturday?" asked Noor.

"Yes, it must have been," replied Cameron. "Adele says he's out of danger and improving rapidly." She looked relieved. "I was worried about him."

We all were," said Noor. "The office isn't the same without him. When can we go and visit?"

"As soon as the quarantine lifts," said Cameron. "There haven't been any more cases reported in this country, so hopefully it's a storm in a teacup."

"What about the other guy?" asked Ross. "The copper."

"I don't know, Ross." Cameron shook her head. "I don't know."

•

DI Mercer braced herself for bad news when she heard the knock.

"Enter."

To her surprise, the young officer who was assisting her on the burglary investigation came through the door. "John? What can I do for you?"

"I'm sorry to disturb you, ma'am. We've made some progress on the movements and identification of the burglar."

Sara Mercer smiled. "That's some good news, at least." She relaxed. This mystery was an absorbing puzzle, the kind of thing that had drawn her to policing in the first place. "Tell me more. Have the facial recognition scans turned up definite sightings?"

John nodded. "Oh yes. We've been lucky in more ways than one. It's a long old slog, using CCTV, even though the machines are doing the facial matching. I still can't believe that we don't have any proper electronic tracking for this guy. At least the appeal turned up his landlord. The name on the rental register is an alias, of course. The landlord swears our man had a smartscreen, but we've searched the flat and there's nothing there."

"Keep that fact in mind, John. It's an odd loose end that needs to be tied up. What else do you have for me?"

"We've processed CCTV records for the city centre, key locations around the place he lived, and within half a mile of the house where he was found. The Department of Health investigation has been focused on his recent movements, within a week or so before death. They need to work out where he picked up the flu. I've gone much further back. He'd visited the area near the house more than once, but there's nothing to tie him to the homeowner. We did spot him down in Hyde Park at a triathlon event, as Mr White mentioned, so I assume he was after the sports equipment in the house."

"Never assume, but it's a plausible scenario. What else have you found?"

"Connections. Some unusual people have turned up."

"People we know?"

"Well, this is where it gets interesting," said John. "Most of the recordings we've found show the man alone, but we have a handful of pieces of footage with known criminals. We've used the records we had on file for their movements to widen the CCTV searches."

"Go on," Mercer prompted him, impatient.

"Well, for example, about a year ago, there's this snippet."

He swiped his fingers across his screen in the direction of the wall monitor, which lit up to display a clear recording of two men deep in discussion, leaning on a stone wall by a river.

"Embankment," said John concisely. "That's Derek Grace. Hacker. He was put away eight months ago for releasing a nasty little virus that took out part of the water treatment network."

"I remember that. Okay, what else?"

"We widened our search to include Grace's known movements from our investigation last year, and set the machines to search for both of them together from two months before this meeting up to the date when he was picked up. They appeared again at this business park way out in the sticks."

He swiped the screen again, displaying a still picture of a run-down collection of two-storey office buildings. There were a number of letting agent signs in view, and the trees and grassy areas were unkempt and untended.

"What's there?" asked Mercer, her interest growing.

"Not sure yet," replied John. "There are four tenants listed in the building. All of them seem to be shell companies, nothing trading. We ran a check on all the footage we could get from the camera there. It's a pretty glitchy unit with regular downtime for faults, but we've picked up several sightings of the deceased alone and with three others in the same place."

"I assume we have a warrant?"

"In progress, ma'am." John cleared his throat. "We identified two of the people with him, Dinah Johnson and Colin Xato, both petty criminals who were prosecuted for defrauding their employers. The third was this young woman, but we haven't identified her." Mercer peered at the still image on the screen and shook her head.

"I don't recognise her either. Remind me about the other two. What did we send them down for?"

"One changed some account details to send monies due to suppliers to a private wallet. Clear fraud. The other one? If I recall correctly, he was just a disgruntled employee who made life difficult for the company. He sent some confidential information out to a third party and they bore losses as a result."

DI Mercer gave him a thin smile. "Excellent work."

"Thank you, ma'am."

"You've missed something, though." Her smile widened, and her brown eyes sparkled with delight at her deduction. "John, I told you not to assume anything. A hacker, a fraudster and a data thief? The burglary had nothing to do with nifty sports equipment. Ross White works in threat intelligence, cybersecurity."

John blushed with embarrassment. "I didn't even consider that link," he admitted. "I thought we had the motive."

"I am certain that Mr White is an innocent victim," said Mercer. "If you look far enough back in his history you will find that he hasn't always been operating on this side of the law. In the absence of any evidence to the contrary, though, it would seem that his current white hat activity has made him a target of cybercriminals."

"Innocent until proven guilty, eh, ma'am?"

"Quite. Now, we need to know more about the dead man. Expand the search. Where did he come from, who else has he met with, and what is in the office at that business park. I want to know what circumstances link Grace, Johnson, Xato and the deceased, and why Ross White may have been targeted. What did he have stored in his house? Was this an attempt to frighten him?"

"I'll get onto it straight away." The young officer left the office briskly and closed the door behind him.

A few minutes later there was a second brief knock and the station commander walked in, his expression grave.

Mercer felt a sense of foreboding.

"How are you, Sara?" he asked soberly.

"How's Ivan?" she countered.

Her boss looked terrible. He sat down and put his head in his hands.

"I'm so sorry. We've had bad news."

"No." said Mercer. There was a knot in her stomach and her head spun. "Oh no. That's awful." She felt tears welling up as she digested the shock. "I can't believe it. Are you sure?"

The superintendent nodded. "His brother called. They've been at the hospital most of the day. There was nothing more they could do."

"I can't believe it," repeated Mercer, wiping her reddened eyes. She sniffed. "He was so unlucky. It could have been any of us in that house. If the body had been there another day, the virus wouldn't have been live. If only he'd had his jab." Sara was angry now. "Why didn't he? Why wasn't he vaccinated like the rest of us?"

"He'd missed them before," said the superintendent heavily. "We haven't had an outbreak for two decades. He must have thought it could never happen to him. The chances were so remote."

"Where did this come from? Grasshopper Flu is confined to South East Asia."

"The Department of Health is right on top of it and I hear they're making good progress."

Sara gave a hollow laugh. "They are as much in the dark as we are about the deceased. It's an uphill battle to link him to anyone."

"Let's stay as positive as we can," said the superintendent. "They're working with the French authorities now that a case has been confirmed there, so we may get some new evidence to piece together the story here. At least there have been no other cases reported in this country, apart from the other patient poor Ivan infected at the hospital."

"Any word on him?" asked Mercer.

"Apparently he's responding well to treatment," her boss replied.

Mercer bit her lip as a new flood of tears welled up, grieving for her friend and wishing in her heart of hearts that the places had been reversed.

"You may be interested in a coincidence," added the superintendent. "This hasn't been made public, but the man's name is Peter Iveson, and he's a colleague of your burglary victim."

•

Andy Taylor watched the news coverage with a sense of sadness. The death of the first patient had been announced a few minutes earlier. He felt for the man's family and friends, but it was an unnecessary death. Bea Black was still on the story, exuding appropriate sympathy while keeping her piece to camera tight and professional. She was an excellent reporter, and Andy enjoyed working with her. He wasn't sorry to be off the story, however. He had far more interesting research to do, following up on the problems that the Calton Global hack could present for the public, and a juicy piece of news had just crossed his desk.

He pinged a message to Cameron. She picked up the call quickly and flashed a grin at him. "Hi Andy, how's things?"

"Good, thanks," he replied. "Sad news about the flu victim."

"Yes, terrible," agreed Cameron. "Good to hear that the second case is recovering."

Interesting, thought Andy. "Anyone you know?" he asked innocently.

Cameron laughed. "No comment." Something in her voice confirmed Andy's suspicions. "Keep your speculation to yourself," chided Cameron in a mock-formal tone. "I'm sure the patient's family and friends would appreciate privacy at this difficult time."

"Noted, Cam," replied Andy. "That isn't why I called you. I've picked up on some of the Calton Global fallout and wanted to run it past you."

"Excellent," said Cameron. "We've seen the first phishing attacks today. High quality, too. The buyers have made fast work of turning the data round to scams. What's your angle?"

"There's been a surge of thefts reported from bank accounts and crypto wallets," replied Andy. "I know there's always a steady level of fraud going on, but I think there may be a common thread here."

"Tell me more."

"Anything related to cash is normally secured on several levels, isn't it? What you are, what you know, what's the other one?"

"What you have," replied Cameron. "ID card, chip, unique code, note from your mum."

"Yes, right. So, it looks like all this set of thefts has been triggered through faking the biometrics, the 'what you are' element, to change account details, and then logging on and clearing whatever funds are stored there."

"Changing account details isn't unprecedented," said Cameron. "There have been cases of phone numbers being changed to intercept authentication codes for decades. Faking biometrics is a new twist, though. I reckon you're right about it being related to Calton Global. I'm guessing there is a hot market for creating fake fingerprints."

"I bet there is," replied Andy. He made a note on his desk. "I'll look into that. The reports are interesting. It's the depth of detail and the consistency in the features that have changed that caught my eye. The public's wise to most of the usual scams, and the providers, especially where money's involved, have learned to be careful. It isn't just biometrics, either. We've got cases here where they're catching out people who've set their accounts up to authenticate with a code and a fingerprint through their devices. You'd think that combination would be impossible to get around."

"That's more unusual," admitted Cameron. "Two attack vectors. Usually biometrics plus a unique code would be as secure as anything. We're compiling a list of the breached datasets. If you can get me more on these reports, we'll see if any of the victims match stolen records which include biometric data."

"Thanks Cameron. Appreciate it." Andy dropped the connection, and Cameron returned to her lunch.

•

"Good luck with your training, mate," called Joel.

Ross gave him a grin. "Thanks, but luck has nothing to do with it. I'm ready for this one." He left the office and collected his bike from the lockup at the bottom of the stairs. It was early enough that the roads were still quiet, and the rain had stopped. His tyres splashed on the wet tarmac, and he took care not to slip. That would be a disaster with such an important session to come.

Instead of heading straight to the athletics club, Ross made tracks for his home. He hadn't been entirely straight with Cameron and the team. He did have an important training session with the national team coaches, but that was hours away. There was a problem he had to deal with, and he wasn't sure how he was going to solve it.

The stranger's smartscreen. It had seemed like a good idea to take the screen. His own details might have been recorded on it, and he didn't want anyone to connect him to the dead man. He had made a serious mistake in the recent past, opening himself up to blackmail and compromising his work and his training. While he wasn't in any way responsible for the death, it had been a relief to know that the man was gone and the evidence with him. If the truth was to come out, it would end his hopes of representing his country, and lose Cameron's trust and a job he loved. There had been too much at stake.

It could have ended there. If he had disposed of the screen straight away, then no one would be any the wiser. He cursed himself for giving in to his natural curiosity. If he hadn't placed that call to the 'Cowgirl', then as far as anyone who found the screen was concerned, it would have seemed to have lain unused since the man's death. He wished he had left it to the police to trace Jessie.

No use wishing. He had to destroy the screen, to put it beyond reach and hope that the call was never traced. A plan was forming in his head.

The first thing to do was to erase everything on it as completely as possible. Ross cycled up the path to the house and swung his leg over the bike, dismounting fluidly. He popped the lock on the shed and wheeled the bike in.

The decorators were hard at work in the house. Ross picked his way through the kitchen, cursing. He'd forgotten that they were due to relay the floors this afternoon. The main room was a hive of activity with humans and bots cleaning, tiling and painting. His bedroom was still untouched and piled with equipment that he had cleared from the sitting room before they started. Ross ducked his head through the door.

"Need to pick something up for work," he called.

A couple of bots swivelled towards the noise, and one of the humans glanced up and waved. "No problem. We're ahead of schedule. We'll wrap up here in an hour or so, and we should be done by tomorrow night."

Ross went into his bedroom and closed the door. He rummaged in a drawer and pulled out the stranger's smartscreen and the burner phone that he had taken from the body. He started with the burner, hunting for settings to first encrypt then wipe the data. It was a simple process, as he'd expected with a simple device. He prised the phone apart with a small screwdriver and systematically removed all the components, careful not to drop a single piece on the floor. The final stage could wait until the decorators had left.

Next, the main smartscreen. Unearthing the mask once again he unlocked it with ease. He scanned through the information held on it, wondering whether he should save it for future reference. It seemed like a good idea, although warning bells sounded about having hold of incriminating evidence. He chose to compromise, bundling the data out to an anonymous storage account. It took him a little longer to find the encryption method for the device; it was a newer model than his own and the settings had been substantially revised.

There was a knock on the bedroom door. "You alright, Mr White? We're off now."

Ross opened the door, making a show of yawning. "Sorry, I almost dropped off there. Late night last night."

"You want to have a look at the work so far?" asked the decorator. There was a note of pride in his voice.

Ross sighed. "Sure."

He had to admit it was a tidy job. The corridor was finished and the tools and boxes in the kitchen were tidy, ready for the next day's work. The newly extended main room was only half done, but still lighter and brighter than he ever recalled.

"Looking good," he said approvingly. "You're sure you'll be done tomorrow?"

"Yes, no problem," replied the man.

"Great," said Ross. "I'll get the furniture delivery organised. Thanks."

The decorator nodded happily. "See you tomorrow, Mr White." He strolled out to the garden where his young assistant was waiting, two little bots gliding in his wake, and closed the door as he left.

Ross looked around the kitchen at the tools and boxes, and an idea began to form in his head. He picked up a hammer and weighed it thoughtfully in his hand. That would do the trick. Returning to his bedroom, he collected all the components from the burner phone and one by one he smashed them. Those chips wouldn't give up their secrets in a hurry, he thought with satisfaction.

The main smartscreen was another matter. He checked that the encryption had run, then wiped the whole device. Taking it apart was harder. The screen was thin and flexible, designed to roll. There were no easy joints to attack, and the components within it were super light. Ross examined every inch of it, then threw it aside, cursing. He checked the time. It was getting late, and he couldn't be late for this training session. In desperation he took the hammer to the screen. It seemed to make little impact, but he could hear encouraging cracks and faint crunches. It had certainly ceased to function. That was something.

Now to dispose of the pieces. He could easily discard the fragments of the burner phone, but the main screen was more difficult. As he gathered his training gear, he mulled over the problem. Could he risk disposing of it in the waterways? He reckoned it would be impossible to recover any data, even if it eventually turned up in a water treatment works or a beach clean-up. It was worth the risk. He replaced the heavy hammer in the decorator's toolkit, washed the screen with soap and towelled it dry to remove any fingerprints, and carefully stowed it in his bag. The tiny shattered pieces of the burner phone he wrapped in paper and popped in his pocket.

Ross doubled locked the door of the house and pulled his bike back out of the shed. He set off to the athletics club. As he passed through the park, he paused occasionally to tip a few phone fragments into the wayside rubbish bins. One down, he thought to himself as he tipped the last handful away and disposed of the paper. He would deal with the other screen later, under cover of darkness and away from his usual routes.

He arrived at the club in good time. There was a buzz about the place.

"Good luck tonight," called a training partner, holding up his hand.

"You too, Adebayo," he replied, returning the high five. It was time to focus, to forget about the mistakes he had made in the past and concentrate on the here and now. This was his chance to prove himself, and perhaps to make it onto the world stage.

•

"Haven't you had that chip sorted yet?" asked Cameron, seeing Jasvinder struggling with his apartment door.

"I thought I had, but it keeps going on the blink," he replied, frustrated. "I may have to get it replaced."

"That might be your best option," said Cameron. "It's very rare for them to fail, but it does happen. It only takes five minutes to swap them over. I've heard it hurts a bit to extract one, but the newest chips are tiny."

"I'll have to get it done soon, because my room-mate's going on holiday," said Jasvinder. He looked at Cameron, who was dressed in jeans and a jumper. "Aren't you going to training?"

"Yes, but I'll get changed there. Want to share a car?"

The two of them walked down the stairs to street level. Outside, the early evening was cool, but the rain had stopped.

"It's not that far," said Jasvinder. "We may as well walk."

"My niece is getting her first chip this weekend," said Cameron conversationally as they strolled along the damp pavement. "She's very excited."

"I had mine done at school too," said Jasvinder, dodging a puddle. "We were the first year to get them, officially, although plenty of the older kids already had them."

"I meant to ask," said Cameron, "could you keep an eye on the cat while I'm away? I have to go to a client up north tomorrow, and then Nina's party is on Friday, so I'll be away for longer than usual."

"Sure, no problem," replied Jasvinder. "She's a very cute cat. Anything I need to know?"

"I'll drop you a key," said Cameron. "I'll suspend the automatic access and alarms just in case your chip goes on the blink when you're trying to get in. Keep an eye out for anything unusual."

"What do you mean?"

Cameron laughed. "My portal woke up last weekend when the cat miaowed for food and it ordered all sorts of daft stuff. I haven't had a chance to reset it, so if there's a random drone on the balcony, send it away. I'm not expecting any deliveries."

They had arrived at the gym. Cameron took herself off to the changing rooms while Jasvinder climbed the stairs to the training hall. The room was already filling up; this was a popular class. Cameron scrambled into her karate gi and carefully wrapped her belt around her waist. Some of the black cotton had worn off over the years, and there was a soft frayed section showing white at the knot. She stowed her clothes in a locker and presented her chip to the lock which glowed green, confirming that the chip's signature had been recorded. She closed the door. It would not open again unless the same chip was used. Simple and effective, but no use with an intermittently failing chip. Cameron wondered if Jasvinder had managed to retrieve his clothes from the locker in the men's changing room yet.

A fast run up the stairs gave her a quick warmup and she took her place in line at the last moment, at the far end of two rows of students wearing a rainbow of coloured belts from white and yellow to brown and black. She and Jasvinder had trained together here for almost three years, and at other classes for much longer. Cameron cleared her mind to focus on the evening's training, taking pleasure in the familiar routine of punches, kicks, blocks and combinations. She concentrated on fractional changes in the movement of her hips and the angle of her shoulders which pushed her techniques from adequate to explosive, marvelling at the power and fluidity that small tweaks could produce.

When the instructor called a break, Cameron realised how thirsty she was. Her muscles were aching with effort, and it felt fantastic. She loved her work, the days spent fighting in a virtual world, but the thrill of this physical challenge was equally intoxicating. She swigged some water and lined back up, ready for more.

•

Ross was over the moon. His training had peaked at the right time, and his coach was delighted. Every test that had been thrown at him he had performed to the best of his considerable ability. He glowed as his teammates surrounded him, clapping him on the back and cheering. All four of the elite group had done the club proud. Ross revelled in the sense of belonging. He was lucky, he reflected, to have such support in his sport and in his work. Perhaps these people were the family he craved, after all. He'd better not blow it.

Showered and changed, he made an effort to join in the post-training social gathering. He usually went straight home, avoiding the crowd. As night fell, though, he took his leave of the group and cycled off on a roundabout route towards his home. It was time to get rid of the last thing that linked him to the dead stranger. Cycling down an unfamiliar path by the side of a canal, he found a secluded spot. He wrapped his hand in a towel and pulled the smartscreen out of his backpack, bending and twisting it one last time for good measure, then dropped it into the canal. It floated. Swearing under his breath, he looked around for a stone. There was a lump of old concrete in the scrubby grass and nettles. He picked it up and threw it accurately at the screen, which sank beneath the surface. He watched in case it bobbed up again, but it seemed to be gone. Ross breathed a sigh of relief and continued on his way home.

8: A GLASS CEILING

Cameron gazed out of the window as the train bore her northwards from London. The flat fields stretching away in the distance reminded her of the journey last week through France, but the hedge and ditch boundaries were closer together and there were more villages to be seen. Patches of woodland and clusters of farm vehicles broke up the land. For a few miles the train track ran parallel with a narrow but busy waterway. There were a few private craft on the canal even though the cool weather of autumn had set in, and small freight barges were making their slow way to town. The ubiquitous wind turbines turned lazily in the breeze, and by the side of the track old farm buildings and abandoned caravans had been turned into little solar farms, selling their power direct to the train company and neighbouring homes. As they passed a patch of marshland, Cameron was surprised by a small flock of geese taking flight. The train was silent, but the clicking of the wheels on the rails had startled the birds. Drainage ditches and raised dykes patterned the fields, keeping the sea at bay. There was no question of surrendering this rich growing land to fish farms; at least, not yet.

Settled in her seat, Cameron allowed herself to be lulled by the gentle movements of the carriage. She closed her eyes and her mind wandered to the work the team had been tackling for the past few days. The visit to Hardy's earlier in the week was nagging at her. There was something odd going on, and while she liked Jessie, she felt she did not entirely trust her. For all his bluster, unpleasantness and old-fashioned attitudes, Joseph Hardy was the more straightforward character.

She shook her head and tried to relax again. No use worrying about Hardy's now. Sandeep and Ross would take care of the forensics, back on site and searching for the exact route of the attack. Ella, Noor, Joel and Susie were making amazing progress tracing the transactions relating to Calton Global and Speakeasy, and the work she had done with Sébastien was starting to unravel the mess at Ben's company. Her only remaining concern was Pete. At least he was making progress thanks to the fast treatment. The hospital had picked up the infection early enough, and despite the treatment he had undergone for the injuries sustained in the rail accident, he still had some protection from his flu jab. He'd pull through.

Cameron was on her way to Charlie's hosting company to investigate a possible case of common-or-garden industrial espionage. Bread and butter work, although she hadn't expected it so close to home. She had managed the security of her family firm's systems for almost fifteen years and successful attacks had been few and far between in that time.

The train turned inland and up to higher ground, approaching the city. Tracks merged from all directions into one wide iron thoroughfare. The view became cluttered with factories, recycling and waste energy plants, food stores, and building yards. A network of roads criss-crossed the industrial estates and the train tracks, driverless goods trailers and passenger shuttles dancing across the lines in perfect synchronicity with the passing train carriages. New apartment blocks and houses jostled for space between commercial units that had originally been built deliberately far from residential areas, but which were now swallowed up by the advancing suburbs. The town stood proud on a hill, away from the dangers of the rising seas, and it was a popular destination for resettled coastal communities. Tall cranes rose above half-finished buildings, expanding the city to accommodate its growing population.

The train slid smoothly to a halt in the bustling station. Cameron grabbed her bag, hopped off the train, and strode briskly to the exit. There was no underground shuttle network here, and she looked around in vain for an autocar to take her onwards to her destination. This was an old station with little room for traffic so no individual cars were waiting, but small shuttlebuses circulated. Cameron climbed into a passing vehicle which bore her and her fellow passengers to the city centre a few minutes away.

The downtown area was bustling with shoppers. The Grasshopper Flu panic that had gripped London seemed not to have penetrated this northern city, although the popup vaccination booths had a steady trickle of visitors. Glancing at the time, Cameron relaxed. She wasn't expected at the data centre for another hour. This would be a perfect chance to pick up a present for Nina to mark the modern-day rite of passage she and her classmates were about to take. Despite the bright sunshine, the wind was bitingly cold. Cameron chose the shelter of a richly-tiled arcade and strolled slowly at the pace of the crowd, gazing at the bright window dressing. Many windows were purely showcases, waiting for her to place an order with a quick scan of her smart screen. Others were still traditional stores with real staff and a tempting range of goods for sale within. After a few minutes, Cameron settled on a quirky shop selling jewellery and accessories. She dipped through the door from the busy arcade and found herself in a little Aladdin's cave. She quickly discounted the pretty purses for children's coins, richly decorated but barely secure cryptowallet drives, and passed on a range of elaborate feathered hairbands. Something more sophisticated was required. Wandering to a display case at the back of the store, she picked up a necklace of richly polished greens and blues, turning it curiously in her hands to see the turtle motif embossed on the beads.

"Can I help you?" asked the assistant.

"What is this made of?" asked Cameron. "It's very pretty."

"Oh, it's beautiful, isn't it?" replied the young man. "It's sea-gold: plastic."

"Wow," said Cameron, impressed. "How is it made?"

"All the reclaimed material is compacted, dyed, cut and polished," he replied. "You can see the deep swirls of colour, here, and here." He pointed out the rich variations in tone.

"Is it local?" asked Cameron.

The young man reached for the necklace. "May I?" he asked.

Cameron nodded and handed it to him. He pulled a small scanner from his pocket and passed it over the necklace. The scanner screen lit up, responding to an identifier embedded in the material.

"Reclaimed from the Sulu Sea in January last year," he said. "Processed in Sandakan, Sabah, Malaysia." He smiled. "The variety of plastic waste towards the equator gives a far better finished product for jewellery than our local sources. The artist is from round here, though. Her workshop is only a few miles away."

"Thank you," said Cameron. "I'll take this, and the matching bracelet."

"Certainly, ma'am," said the assistant. He scanned both pieces and Cameron thumbed the payment authorisation. The young man wrapped the jewellery, and Cameron stowed the little package in her bag.

Outside the shop, the crowd had thinned out. Emerging into daylight from the arcade Cameron realised the wind had dropped. The sun was warm on her face, and it was turning into a fine day after all. Hopefully the weather would hold for Nina's party tomorrow.

Rounding a corner, Cameron came upon a stand of autocars. Time to get to work. She hopped into the closest vehicle and gave the address. The car pulled silently off towards the outskirts of town.

•

Ross struggled to compose himself as Jessie walked into reception. He coughed and covered his mouth, irrationally fearing that she had glimpsed his face beneath the mask in the few seconds of their call. Sandeep greeted the girl warmly, unaware of Ross's discomfort.

"Come through," she said, ushering them down the corridor towards Joseph Hardy's office. "The old man's out today, and we're flat out working on upgrades so this is the only place I can think to put you. I'm sure he won't mind. Can I get you a drink before we start? Ross?"

"Oh, uh, yes please," said Ross, coughing again. "Dry throat. Sorry. I had a long training run this morning. It was very, uh, dusty."

"There's water in the office," said Jessie. She led them through to the plush room from where Hardy ran his empire and gestured towards the desk. "I've set up everything we need. How do you want to do this?"

"Thanks, Jessie," said Sandeep apologetically, "but we really need to work alone on this part of the investigation. Water would be great, and I would love one of Olivia's special coffees."

"Sure," replied Jessie, apparently unruffled. "I understand. I'll leave you to it. Call me if you have any questions." She strolled out of the office and the door closed behind her.

Ross's ears pricked, listening for the outer door of the management suite to close. It did so, but not before he heard the distant thump of Jessie hitting the wall of the corridor in frustration. He smiled to himself.

"What's so funny, Ross?" asked Sandeep, puzzled.

"Jessie," he replied. "I don't think she's too happy about leaving us to work on our own." He looked enquiringly at Sandeep. "Do you have any concerns about her?"

Sandeep frowned, surprised. "Not really," he said. "She's always been very helpful." He glanced appraisingly at Ross. "What do you know that I don't?"

"Nothing, really," lied Ross. "Call it instinct if you like. I don't think she's as straightforward as she seems. Bear that in mind while we're digging into this breach. Don't assume anything."

Sandeep nodded. "Understood. Right. Where do we start?"

Ross pulled up a chair and flopped into it, folded his hands behind his head, and stared up at the ceiling, thinking through the task. "First off, we need to run through all the access logs. We're looking for anything unusual related to the mess around system permissions. It could be significant, or it could be a smokescreen."

"I'll set up a routine to scan them." Sandeep flexed his fingers. "Out of hours activity, anything going on behind the scenes. Did Cameron manage to interview the assistant when she came to see Jessie the other day?"

"I don't know," replied Ross. "I don't think so. She hasn't logged anything in the case files. We keep missing that girl, don't we?"

"I'm sure we'll see her today," said Sandeep. "Let's see what the audit throws up."

"Sounds good." Ross straightened up in his chair. "I'll run a comparison of activity week by week before and after the first known data dump."

"Do we have the timestamp for the first transaction which used the cuckoo contract?" asked Sandeep.

"Not yet," replied Ross. "Pete was working on it." He sighed. "It would make the raw analysis easier, but I want to dig deeper into the breach itself. I really want to know who's behind this."

"Why are you so interested in this one?" asked Sandeep. "It's tough to pin this scale of cybercrime on real people. Nation states, maybe: people, rarely."

Ross slumped back in the chair again. "I know, but this one smells odd." His scalp crawled as he remembered the dead stranger. 'Smell' was a bad expression to choose. He tried to explain his unease to Sandeep without giving away any secrets. "Usually there's a buzz around the infosec community when this kind of attack goes down. Plenty of speculation, and some clever educated guesses about the source. This time? It feels different. I don't know if it's anything to do with the work Noor and Ella did on tracing a real individual. Somebody somewhere is frightened." Ross shook his head, clearing bad memories.

Sandeep was taken aback. "I haven't picked up on any of that," he said. "I think you're being a little over-dramatic. It's a routine breach. We'll nail down the access point, it'll be human error as usual, and we might be lucky enough to identify the bad actor at state level, maybe better." He looked sidelong at Ross, who was still staring pensively at the ceiling, and tried to change the subject. "What's the main motivation for this one? Money, I guess, from the sale of data."

"Probably," said Ross, giving in to the welcome distraction. "It was below the radar for a while, so it didn't have much entertainment value, and there's no ideological cause that would benefit from the hack."

"Competitors?" Sandeep suggested.

"Unlikely," replied Ross. "The breach Bordegiciel's dealing with, on the other hand, was almost certainly someone taking out the competition. This isn't specific enough. It could be someone showing off their skillset, of course, as it's a complicated piece of work, but I would have expected to hear the boasting on the web and there's been nothing."

"I guess we'll pick up some clues today," said Sandeep, nodding at the machines humming quietly in the corner of the room.

"You're right," said Ross, swinging out of his chair just as the door behind him opened. A junior staff member appeared carrying a steaming cup and a plate of cookies.

"Coffee!" said Sandeep. "Excellent. Thanks." He took the cup gratefully and sniffed at it. "Ahh, that's good."

The youngster smiled. "Just call if you want some more." He left the room and closed the door behind him.

"Caffeine, check, snacks, check." Ross grinned. "You ready?"

"Ready. Let's get started."

•

Cameron's taxi drew up outside the compound in a crowded suburb of the city. Surrounded at a distance by a mix of residential and commercial estates, the data centre was an unassuming dark brick building, smaller than she had expected. She settled the charge on the autocar's meter and stepped out into the sunshine. The wide area around the building was landscaped, looking more like a small city park, with grassy dips and contours, bushes and flower beds. Cameron wasn't fooled. She spotted two drones floating discreetly in the air, and high spec cameras on the building itself. The small access gate which blocked her path through the garden was locked, and Cameron pressed the call button. Her appointment had been booked by Holly earlier in the week; she was expected.

"Chipped?" came a voice.

"Uh… yes," replied Cameron.

"Please present your chip to the sensor."

Cameron did as she was told, extending her hand to the pad on the gate frame.

A light glowed green and the voice said, "Thank you, Ms Silvera. Please come in."

The gate popped open. Cameron walked briskly towards the building's main entrance. Cameras tracked her progress, and from the gatehouse a guard watched her arrival. There was another pad on the main door that lit up when it sensed the chip embedded in her hand. The door opened, and Cameron stepped into the hallway. It seemed dim after the bright sun outside, and it took a few moments for her eyes to adjust to the soft lighting.

"Good afternoon, Ms Silvera," said the uniformed guard. "Let's run you through security, please?" He slid a reader across the counter and Cameron pressed her thumb to it. There was a brief pause while the thumbprint was reconciled to the data chip, and the guard nodded. "Thank you. Now, your bag?"

"I won't need it." Cameron went to hand the bag straight over the counter, but the guard stopped her.

"I need to check it through x-ray, even if you leave it here in the secure storage," he explained. "Just pop it on the conveyor and empty your pockets, please."

Cameron did as she was asked, smiling to herself. It was always good to test security procedures to the full, and so far, the data centre was playing it by the book. She passed through the body scanner without incident, retrieved her pocket screen, and settled down in a small waiting room. A few minutes later a member of staff peered around the door.

"Watling Automotive? You'll be Cameron, right?"

Cameron opened her mouth to reply, but the young man continued without a pause. "I'm Jeremy. Follow me."

Brusque, thought Cameron. Very sure of himself. She stood up meekly and trailed behind Jeremy as he navigated the labyrinthine corridors of the data centre. They arrived at the door to a well-appointed meeting room with large wall screens, and he gestured to her to sit.

"Now, how can I help you?" he asked.

"Let's start by bringing up the server records for Watling Automotive, please," said Cameron clearly. "Access and maintenance schedules. Power consumption charts." Jeremy stared at her, and Cameron sensed his confusion. "Reports of all the attacks your system has stopped in, say, the last six months for a start. We may have to go back further."

"Now wait a minute…" began Jeremy.

"I will want to check out the server in the data hall as well," she said firmly.

"I don't think we can allow that," said Jeremy, affronted. "I can assure you everything is in order."

"We can start here with the records," said Cameron, "but I will still need access to the server. When this appointment was booked, it was made very clear the kind of information I would need. If it was simple assurances and generic reports that we wanted, I wouldn't have come all the way up here from London to see you in person."

"I know that Watling reported a data theft," said Jeremy, "but we've looked into it, and there is no evidence of any breach. Nothing gets through our systems. You must know this company's reputation for information security."

"Oh, I do." Cameron smiled at him sweetly. "You're the best. That's why the company hosts its data with you. I also know that the best can still be compromised, and I have reason to believe this has happened. Now please get me the information I need."

Grudgingly, Jeremy tapped at his personal screen and a monitor on the wall lit up with scrolling information. "Access and maintenance records," he said, swiping quickly through the data.

"Stop," said Cameron. "Just bring up the files, and I'll work through them. Can you get me a coffee?"

"I can't leave you with these records on your own," said Jeremy.

Cameron sighed. She wished this was an official visit as Argentum Associates. She rarely had to fight for data when her client was desperate for a problem to be solved.

"Right. Help me with this search, then. Let's start with all the physical maintenance to our server. I want cross-reference to fault reports and visitor logs."

"I'll need to clear it with my boss," muttered Jeremy.

"You do that," replied Cameron. She sat down and looked expectantly at the boy, who disabled all the screens before leaving the room and closing the door firmly behind him.

Cameron sighed. The youngster would learn a hard lesson about assumptions once she'd finished here.

A few minutes later Jeremy was back, looking shamefaced, with a colleague in tow. The new arrival greeted Cameron apologetically.

"I'm sorry, Ms Silvera, the detailed requests that accompanied your booking never reached my office," she said. "I'm Kess, Kess Mgbeke. If you'd like to follow me, we can visit the data hall now. Jeremy will source the records you requested while we're gone."

"Thanks, Kess. Please call me Cameron." She turned to Jeremy. "I'm sorry to be so firm with you, but I have a very limited time for this visit." He didn't meet her eyes. She looked at Kess. "Shall we?"

The two women walked down the corridor to the data hall. Kess opened the heavy door to the hall and a blast of cool air hit Cameron's shoulders as they walked in. She shivered and looked up to the air vent, then exclaimed in surprise as she saw a smooth glass ceiling, and dimly above it lights and movement.

"What's up there?"

Kess looked up and smiled. "I come in here so often that I forget our history. Two hundred years ago, this building was a brewery. We're down in the barrel store. The building fell into disrepair after the original owners moved out, and it was refurbished and converted into a conference centre – this was part of the auditorium. When the company bought it, we converted most of the naturally cool lower floor into the data hall, but we still use the conference room above for staff and board meetings. It's very attractive. There was a whole host of original features that we had to preserve."

"So, you glassed over the roof of the data hall, giving it some natural light," marvelled Cameron.

"This is a very nice place to work," said Kess. "I used to work in a new-build centre. It had no soul. This is different." She led Cameron through the stacks of servers. "Here, this is the Watling Automotive dedicated stack."

Cameron stood and looked carefully at the server, her eyes scanning every detail of the installation. She pulled out her screen and made a few notes. Cabling tidy. Server racks as expected. Cards in place.

"Thanks, Kess." She checked a file on her screen. "It all looks to be in order. Tidy job. I need to have a look at the maintenance records, though. There have been a few changes to the configuration since the kit was installed."

"I'll make sure Jeremy gives you all the help you need," replied Kess.

"And coffee?" asked Cameron. "Could he fix that too?"

"I'm sure he can manage that," replied Kess, laughing. "He's young, that one, and he needs to learn a little humility."

Cameron smiled in rueful agreement. They left the light, cool data hall and headed back down the dim corridor to carry on their work.

•

"How's it going?" Ross jumped as the office door opened and Jessie appeared. "Do you guys want lunch?"

Sandeep looked up lazily from behind a screen. "Hi, Jessie. Lunch sounds good." He stretched his arms up and yawned. "Ross? You hungry?"

Ross was frowning, following lines of data as they scrolled rapidly up the screen. "Sure," he said, without looking up. "We'll join you, Jessie."

"Uh, I need to see you through the building, Ross?" said Jessie, amused.

Ross sighed, tapped the screen to pause his analysis, and stood up.

Jessie looked from Ross to Sandeep and smiled. "Ready, boys?"

"Yeah, whatever," said Ross, irritated at losing his train of thought. "What's on the menu today?"

"I don't know, but Olivia's in the kitchen so it'll be delicious," replied Jessie.

There was an irritated edge to her voice the Sandeep hadn't heard before. He filed it away for future reference and followed Jessie down the long corridor towards the canteen. Ross trailed behind, preoccupied. Sandeep knew better than to disturb him, so instead he caught up with Jessie. As the two of them passed the organisation chart on the wall, Sandeep suddenly stopped, a question leaping into his mind.

"What's the doppelganger called?"

Jessie blinked and turned to look at Sandeep. "What?"

"Joseph Hardy. He's retiring, yes? His doppelganger, his digital twin. What's it called? Does it have a name?"

"Why?"

"There's nothing on the chart here. Look… Chairman, Joseph Hardy. Assistant, Yasmin Hardy. No mention of the twin."

"Good question, Sandeep," said Ross, catching up with them. "What do you call it, Jessie? You must deal with the doppelganger. You're head of technology."

Jessie's initial shock did not go unnoticed, but she recovered her composure instantly. "Doppelganger? He spun that story to you? It's just a bot that does the day to day stuff when Hardy's not around."

Ross raised a sceptical ginger eyebrow. "Really? He made it out to be way more important. Out of interest, Jessie, who's in line to take over when Joseph Hardy retires?"

"That's nothing to do with you," said Jessie icily. She stalked off up with corridor.

Ross and Sandeep exchanged puzzled looks.

"She's really rattled," said Sandeep under his breath. "What's going on?"

"I don't know," replied Ross, "but we need to find out more about this doppelganger."

After running to get through several sets of security doors before they closed, Ross and Sandeep caught up with Jessie in the canteen queue. She was back to her usual sunny self, chatting to other colleagues ahead of them. Sandeep scanned the day's menu, desperate to lighten the atmosphere.

"This looks good. How about the fish tacos, Ross? You fancy getting some to eat at the desk?"

"Good idea," replied Ross. He tapped Jessie on the shoulder. She spun around, faking surprise. "We're going to get some tacos and carry on with our work."

"I'll have to escort you back to the office," she replied.

Ross detected a hint of relief in her voice, and a guarded undercurrent to her otherwise friendly manner. He made no sign of having noticed, and simply smiled at her. "Thank you."

Jessie left them at the door of the office with a cursory smile. Sandeep settled into his chair and inhaled the scent of the fish tacos appreciatively. "Mmm. These are good." He bit into the warm tortilla with relish.

"You have a point about the doppelganger," said Ross between mouthfuls. "Hardy said to Cameron that the twin could pretty much run the company. Is he under the illusion it's more autonomous than it actually is…?"

"…or does Jessie genuinely not know its capacity," finished Sandeep.

Ross shook his head. "There's a third option. Jessie's lying."

Sandeep looked at Ross. "I think…" he said slowly, "I think you may have something there."

Ross nodded. "Let's go to work."

•

Cameron pored over the activity reports while Jeremy sulked in the corner. There was nothing unusual in the server logs, nothing odd coming up in the access reports, and the company's response to daily attacks was robust and effective. Frustrated, she pushed her chair back and ran her hands through her short dark hair.

"Found anything?" asked Jeremy.

Cameron wished she could wipe the smirk of his face. "Not so far, Jeremy," she said through gritted teeth.

She turned to the next set of records. Power consumption. She scrolled rapidly through the data set, paying little attention to the detail. She felt deflated, disillusioned, and useless. She was wrong, she reflected agonisingly. There was no data breach. She was over-sensitive and narrow-minded, always jumping to the conclusion that there must be a technical answer to every question. The flood of new components on the market was simple coincidence, new businesses lighting on the right solution by chance and making their own way in the world. If Watling Automotive had finally had its day after a long and distinguished history…

Her wallow in self-pity was brought to a halt by a question from Jeremy.

"What's that?" He pointed at the screen.

Cameron's jaw dropped. The figures for power consumption on a single server from the stack showed a barely discernable increase. The usage didn't drop back down to match the other data sets. At the highest point, that one server was using more power than any of the others.

"Yes!" shouted Cameron, her heart singing. "That's it. It's very subtle. I'm not surprised you didn't pick it up."

Jeremy stared at the figures. "We should have. We track power usage and flag any changes outside the usual tolerances."

"Server by server?"

"No, stack by stack," said Jeremy quietly. "A fluctuation like this in a single server wouldn't be enough to trigger an investigation." He looked Cameron in the eye, contrite. "I'm sorry. You really know your stuff."

Cameron nodded. "No hard feelings. Tell you what, can you get me a hot coffee and I'll dig deeper into this." She grinned at him, relieved to the core, vindicated. All that was left was to work out how it had been done.

As Jeremy scurried happily off to the coffee maker, Cameron scanned the server details. She picked through the original installation, the maintenance records, and her own observation of the stack, checking each component off the list. New graphics cards. Upgraded cabling. Extra racks. Faulty components replaced. Sitting back, she checked her notes one more time, elated. There was an anomaly. She had been right all along.

Jeremy pushed the door open and carefully laid down a tray of coffee and cakes.

"I thought you might need a snack," he said. "Did you find anything else?"

Cameron grinned at him and took a sip of her coffee. "Yes, I did. I'm going to need another chat with Kess, and a look at the visitor logs for the whole centre."

Jeremy left his coffee steaming on the table and dashed out to find his boss. The two off them returned to find Cameron scanning through new data on the wall screen.

"That's the centre's visitor log," said Jeremy surprised. "I didn't set that up for you."

"You didn't," confirmed Cameron. "I accessed it through the Watling account login. You have a vulnerability there. I don't know if it's related to this breach, but it's a hole you should plug." She took a bite of cake.

"Can you bring me up to date, Cameron?" asked Kess.

"Sure. The server stack contains an extra network card, or something masquerading as a network card, anyway. The card is sending data straight out of the building and sucking extra power to do it. You need to shut it down right now, and if your CCTV records are in order we might be able to identify the person or people who installed it." Cameron finished the last morsel of cake, wiped a few crumbs from her chin, and took a swig of coffee.

Kess looked at her in awe. "I'm impressed. I looked you up, Cameron. I'm glad to know you and I'll give you all the help you need. What range do you need for the CCTV records?"

"I can narrow it down to within a few hours," said Cameron. "Once the power consumption starts to rise, we know the card is installed. Can you bring up recordings for the twelve hours before that?"

"Sure," replied Kess.

"Here's the visitor log for that window," said Cameron, gesturing at the screen. "Anything jump out at you?"

Kess and Jeremy scanned the list.

"Nothing unusual," replied Jeremy. "Looks like there was a board meeting during the day, and a couple of callouts from the regular out-of-hours contractors during the night."

"Are there names on the logs?" asked Cameron

"Not on the callout appointments," said Kess. "They tell us the company but not the individual contractor. The individual details will be in the gatehouse records, and I'm fairly sure even the SimCavalier can't hack those." She looked sidelong at Cameron.

"What did you say?" asked Cameron, startled.

Kess winked at her conspiratorially, and Cameron frowned. Inside, her stomach was churning. She worked hard to keep her SimCavalier identity secret. How could Kess have made the connection? 'I looked you up', she'd said. Where? Who knew?

Kess sensed her discomfort and moved on hurriedly. "Let's start with the night visits." She pulled up the CCTV records and scrolled through to the night in question. "Here's the first arrival at the gatehouse." A short red-haired girl appeared on the security footage, passing her bag through for scanning.

"I know her," said Jeremy. "It's Elaine. She's here pretty regularly."

"Let's see where she goes," said Kess. They followed her progress through the deserted corridors to the data hall, where she moved to the far side of the room. For twelve minutes she worked on a single stack, then left the hall by the same door through which she had arrived. Corridor footage and recordings from the gatehouse showed her checking back out of the building and disappearing into the gloom.

"She's in the clear," said Cameron. "She's nowhere near the Watling server and all her time is accounted for on camera. Next visitor?"

The film flickered as Kess forwarded through blank footage. "Here you go," she said at last. "The second callout was close to midnight."

A young man appeared on the screen, passing a bag through security. He was tall, slim, and dark, with a certain elegance about him.

Cameron sat up, hairs prickling on the back of her neck. She glanced at Jeremy. "Do you know this guy?"

Jeremy shook his head. "Never seen him before. There are always different contractors coming and going, though."

Kess tracked the visitor along the corridor, where he paused for a short while to check his screen, head bowed. The centre seemed to be deserted save for clusters of cleaner bots roaming around the floor. The man moved out of range of the first camera as he entered the data hall, and Kess switched to a new feed. The recording showed a clear picture of the man as he walked through the door, and Cameron saw his face for the first time. She stared at the screen, shocked, as she heard Jeremy's voice say, "I think this is our guy. He's opened the Watling server stack."

There was no doubt in Cameron's mind. The face on the screen matched the profile picture of the man Noor had traced. It was Aman Patel.

•

The young policeman didn't show any signs of recognition when Cameron gave her name. She was comfortable with being anonymous for once. As far as he was concerned, she was representing a client of the data centre. Argentum Associates meant nothing to him. Cameron knew that once the reports were processed the national cybercrime unit would be in touch with her, but for now she was content to give all the credit to Kess and Jeremy.

Interview over, Cameron sat alone in the conference room, mesmerised by the winking lights of the servers in the data hall beneath the glass floor. Her screen alert sounded, and Noor's profile flashed up. She must have received the message.

Cameron grinned and accepted the call.

"Cameron, you are joking?" came Noor's astonished voice. "Aman Patel has turned up in the real world?"

"No joke, Noor," replied Cameron. "Unbelievable. It seems he used the same name to sign in to the data centre. It shouldn't be too hard for the police to trace him."

"Have you told them about our work?" asked Noor.

"Not yet," admitted Cameron. "I think he's a part of something much bigger. I want to find out more about his connection to whatever group is behind Calton Global."

"It's odd that he turned up hacking into your brother's company data, though," said Noor thoughtfully. "Are you sure it's a coincidence?"

"Oh yes," said Cameron. "I think he's just a black hat for hire. This breach goes back months, before the Calton leaks." A thought struck her. "Can you do some more digging through his wallets, Noor? See whether he got paid for this job, and if so what was the source of the funds."

"On it," said Noor. "I'll let you know what I find."

"It's late," said Cameron. "No rush. I'm not working tomorrow, anyway. I'll be at Charlie's all weekend. Let's pick it up on Monday."

"Okay, Cameron," replied Noor. "Have a lovely weekend." She went to disconnect, then stopped. "Have you spoken to Ross and Sandeep yet?"

"Not yet," said Cameron. "How are they getting on at Hardy's?"

Noor laughed. "Ross is very cross. I don't think he's found what he's looking for yet."

"Oh, he will," said Cameron. "I think it'll be well hidden, and he'll kick himself, but he'll find the trail. I'll call him when I get out of here."

Cameron dropped the call as Kess arrived, fresh from giving her statement. She looked tired and worried, but she gave Cameron a beaming smile. Cameron gave her a crooked grin in return. She was still rattled by the ease with which Kess had identified the SimCavalier.

"All done," said Kess. "They have our statements and the evidence to back them up. It seems there is even a partial thumbprint on record at the gatehouse – not enough to identify the man for sure, but it will help."

"That's brilliant." Cameron tucked her screen away into a pocket and stood up. "I'd better get going. I've missed three trains already and it's getting late."

"Of course," said Kess. "You must go. Thank you for all your help. It's been amazing seeing you work." She paused and looked up at Cameron, taller than her by half a head. "You are who I think you are, aren't you?" she asked, a note of doubt creeping into her voice. "The SimCavalier?"

Cameron chose her words carefully. "Why would you think that, Kess?"

"Well, you know, people talk on the forums," replied Kess. "Everyone thought it was the man on the news reports last year, but it wasn't, was it? The story just went away without any explanation."

There's a good reason for that, thought Cameron, cursing her now-friend Andy Taylor for his journalistic prowess. He had almost blown her cover on his news broadcast, and only a chance meeting at a family party had averted disaster.

"Are you so sure that the man on the news isn't the SimCavalier?" asked Cameron, curious to find out more.

"Oh, I'm sure," said Kess firmly. "I've seen your picture online, and you ran rings around us."

"A picture of me?" asked Cameron.

"Yes, yes, definitely you," confirmed Kess.

Cameron felt the colour drain from her face.

Kess put her hand to her mouth, shocked. "Oh, Cameron, I'm so sorry. You didn't know?"

Cameron shook her head. "Kess," she said in a low voice, "I can't – I won't – say whether it's me, or the guy on the news, or anyone else. Just please, don't share your theory. Stop speculating on identity and leave the SimCavalier to work in the shadows." She sighed. "I have to go. It was good to meet you. Thanks for your help."

She walked out of the conference room and the door swung closed behind her.

Kess remained seated, staring at the lights of the data hall, thinking.

9: RITE OF PASSAGE

The queue was not moving. Ben looked at the time and sighed. He had expected border control to be a breeze this morning, but everything was running late, and he was cutting it fine for the party. His scheduled train had already left but he wouldn't need to re-book. The security procedures had been tightened up to the extent that all the comfortable departure lounges were closed and passengers were simply being herded onto the first available carriages as soon as they passed security. Once he was through he would be on his way.

Staff walked up and down the line handing out masks. Ben declined. It seemed an over-reaction to the new case of Grasshopper Flu, the first infection reported in France for years. His vaccinations were in order and he knew the chances of infection were slim. They must still be working out the source and spread of infection, he reflected.

In front of him, people were being turned away at regular intervals and directed to pop-up booths for screening and vaccination. Neither the French nor the British authorities were taking any chances. The queue shuffled forwards a few paces and he found himself in sight of the border control kiosks. Checking the time again, he relaxed. He would be on the next train, with luck.

Ben's papers were all in order and his medical record scan came up with a green light straight away. The guard nodded him through without ceremony and Ben broke into a run towards the platform. He jumped through the nearest open door of the train with plenty of time to spare and looked around for a seat. He had to walk through two more carriages before he eventually found a place to sit.

The train pulled off, leaving passengers milling around on the platform outside. It quickened as it left the extended Paris suburbs and sped smoothly across the flat fields of Picardy. He would be in London in two hours. His train to Cameron's left from a different station ten minutes' walk away. He could always take the transit pods, a permanently rotating string of little cable cars which rose high above the Library and linked the two stations. It was a pretty way to travel, but perhaps he'd better walking. He could do with the exercise, and today the forecast was dry.

The carriage windows darkened as the train dipped into the long undersea tunnel. Ben pulled out his screen and connected to the national networks, catching up on the latest news. The first flu case had ended in a fatality, he noted soberly. No wonder the authorities were taking precautions. There was an underlying air of panic on the social forums; as he'd thought, the source was still unclear, but the web was rife with speculation. He turned to other stories. A celebrity had been outed as a tobacco addict by the hottest gossip column in town. A politician was fighting for his career after disclosures about his financial affairs. An insurance company was under fire for cancelling policies overnight after their customers' undeclared health conditions were published. One of the more serious channels was blaming this flurry of stories on a data breach at Calton Global. Ben recognised Andy Taylor's name in the production credits.

The train drew in to St Pancras and Ben hopped out. The queues to cross the border in the other direction snaked around the upper floor of the building. He strode smartly past them towards Euston Road, relieved. He would reach Cameron on time after all.

•

Nina was nervous, decided Cameron. She pulled her niece close to her for a hug. "You look fabulous," she said. "Are you looking forward to it?"

They were in Cameron's peaceful attic room at the top of the old family farmhouse. Sun streamed through the south-facing dormers, but a few gusts of wind rattled the solar panels outside on the roof. The attic was still Cameron's domain, although Nina, growing fast, coveted the space to hide away from her younger brother and sister. She was almost Cameron's height now and developing her adult curves. The last twelve years had flown by, reflected her aunt.

Nina looked down at her new clothes, dressed to the smartest heights of pre-teen fashion. "Thanks, Aunty Cam," she replied. "I can't believe it's today." She paused. "Does it hurt?"

Cameron laughed and ruffled her hair. "Barely a scratch. Chip tech has moved on since I got mine." She held out her hand. "See here? The fleshy bit between my thumb and my index finger. If you squeeze hard you may be able to feel my chip."

Nina gave her aunt's hand a tentative stroke. "I daren't," she said.

"I can't feel it," laughed Cameron. "Try harder."

Nina pushed at the muscle. "Is that it? It's just a tiny little bump."

"Yes," replied Cameron, "that's it. Yours will be even smaller, and it'll hold more data." She looked critically at Nina. "You have had the big talk about what to hold on your chip and what to keep separate, haven't you?"

"Of course we have," replied Nina. "Loads of times." She looked at her aunt curiously. "What do you use yours for?"

"Holidays, mainly," said Cameron. "My chip holds the hash of my identity so that border security can check me against the main blockchain. It's set up for fitness metrics and medical triggers as well."

"You mean, all you can do is go abroad and count your steps," said Nina, nonplussed. "What about paying for things, or locks, or controlling screens, or gaming, or sensory augments?"

"Not if I can help it," said Cameron grimly. "I don't want to wave my hand in the wrong place and discover I've bought half the store or have to sit completely still to watch a movie. As for augments, listening to colours always struck me as a bit silly."

Nina giggled nervously, not sure if her aunt was serious. "Now that I'm in senior school, we have to use ours to get into the buildings and pay for lunch. We've had to use temporary cards and fingerprints up until now."

"That's different," said Cameron. "If your school or work makes you use your chip, they should have run all the security scenarios first. Even back in my day we used biometrics in the canteen. Fingerprint, usually. But for your front door at home? That's different. Did I tell you, one of my friends got locked out of his apartment the other week? He had to come home from the gym in his karate kit, too, and all his clothes were still locked away in the changing room."

Nina laughed, some of the tension of the morning melting away.

"Is everyone in your year getting a chip?" asked Cameron, curious.

"No," said Nina, rolling her eyes. "There's one boy whose family won't allow it. None of them have chips. He doesn't have a screen, either. He's weird."

"There are plenty of people as old as me and your mum and dad who don't have chips, and they manage perfectly well," said Cameron.

"He's still weird," said Nina with finality. "I'm looking forward to having my chip. I'm going to have loads of fun trying out all the extra things you can do with a chip on the forums and games. It'll be cool, and it'll annoy Dilan."

Cameron tried not to laugh. "Don't wind your brother up," she said sternly. "And be careful. Call me if you're ever worried about what or who is reading your data." She glanced at the clock. "It's almost time to go."

"Is Ben coming?" asked Nina.

"He should be here any moment," said Cameron, crossing her fingers behind her back. "He's coming all the way from Paris for the weekend."

"I like Ben," said Nina. "He's funny. He's very nice and he makes me laugh. I hope he gets here in time."

"He'll be here." Cameron picked up her bag and dug inside it. "Before we set off, I have a present for you. I'm not sure if it'll go with your outfit, though." She handed Nina the little package.

"Oh! What is it?" Nina unwrapped the paper carefully to reveal the sea-green turtle necklace and bracelet. She held the beads up to the light and they sparkled and glimmered as the sun caught the polished facets. "They're so pretty." She flung her arms around her aunt and gave her a tight hug before scampering down the attic stairs. "Mum, Dad, look what Aunty Cam brought."

Sameena was on the landing, brushing her hair in the long mirror that hung on the wall. She turned and smiled at her daughter. "Let me see? Oh, yes, that is lovely." She looked up at Cameron who had followed Nina down the stairs. "Is it sea-gold? It's beautiful. A real grown-up present."

"I love it," said Nina. "Where's Dad?"

"He's gone to fetch Aunt Vicky," replied Sameena. The sound of the front door opening, Roxy's excited barking and voices in the hall indicated that Charlie's mission had been successful. "Here they are now."

Nina ran down to meet them, and Vicky could be heard exclaiming over the gift.

"I'm glad she likes it," said Cameron. "It's a special day for them all."

"I feel old," laughed Sameena. "It's not just because Nina is so grown up. We didn't have anything like this when I was her age. It feels like a combination of, I don't know, school prom, speech day, and teenage vaccinations. It's very odd." She looked questioningly at Cameron. "When did you get yours? I had to get one when my work changed the access systems over to chip-only, but that was after Nina was born."

"Earlier than you," said Cameron. "I was still at school, but it wasn't common among my friends. I was curious about them, and I had a chance to get one. The technology was well established, even then. There were cyborg artists before I was born who experimented with senses and perception. The armed forces have used chips and ID tattoos for decades, and anyone coming through refugee identity programmes would have been chipped and recorded on the identity chain a long time ago. I can't believe how fast we've come around to chipping kids at school, though."

"Does the security worry you, Cameron?" There was a note of concern in Sameena's voice.

"Nothing is ever completely secure," said Cameron, pragmatic as ever, "but it's always the human factor that makes the difference. A chip can be hacked, but the information on it is cryptographically hashed. A quantum computer would be capable of decoding the hash, but it's extremely unlikely that quantum processing time would be applied to a hacking a teenager's microchip." She laughed. "Ironically, the widest adoption of chips was for access to workplaces, and that's one of the easiest things to clone."

"Will Nina be safe?" Sameena whispered.

"She's a sensible girl and she's aware of what goes on around her," replied Cameron reassuringly. "She will be fine. Don't worry. Our parents were just as concerned about us using social media and talking to strangers through online games, and we've turned out okay."

"You're right, of course," sighed Sameena. "But please keep an eye on her."

"I will."

The two of them started downstairs as the front door opened again, and Cameron heard a familiar voice. "Anyone home?"

"Ben! You made it. Nina will be happy." Cameron gave him a welcoming kiss.

"I got held up at the border," said Ben. "They were doing all sorts of additional security checks for flu jabs, in and out of the country, and the trains were delayed. There's a real panic on. I know there are only two confirmed cases here, but they've just picked one up in France as well."

"Better safe than sorry," said Cameron seriously. "I wonder how it's spreading? I'm guessing that they haven't traced the source."

"That's what it looks like," said Ben. He changed the subject quickly. "Have I got time to change my shirt?"

Sameena glanced at the clock. "If you hurry, Ben. We need to be in town by one. I'll go and check that everyone is ready to leave."

Cameron led Ben back up to the attic room. He emptied his bag on the bed and pulled a slightly crumpled smart shirt from the pile. "Will this be okay?"

"You look great whatever you're wearing," smiled Cameron. "It's fine."

As Ben pulled off the old t-shirt he'd worn to travel, Cameron was distracted by an alert on her computer. Urgent message from Ross on an old account that hadn't been used in years. That didn't bode well. She cursed.

"What?" came Ben's muffled voice.

"Nothing," she replied. "Work stuff. Ross has terrible timing."

"You'll have to answer to Nina if you hold everyone up," said Ben, his dark eyes twinkling with laughter. "Go on. I'll cover for you. Five minutes."

Cameron slid onto her chair and opened the message. "*We're finishing up here.*" Ah, she thought. They've finally traced the cuckoo contract. Odd that he contacted her this way.

"Can't talk right now. Nina's chipping. Later?" she typed.

"*Sure thing,*" came the reply, but it was followed by rapid stream of text which filled the screen, scrolling rapidly.

Cameron's attention sharpened. Why was Ross dumping data straight to her without a word?

Another message appeared. "*Heading home now. All done. Speak later.*" The connection dropped.

Torn between her family and her colleagues, Cameron grabbed her screen from her pocket. Four missed calls from Ross. She placed a call to Noor.

"What's going on at Hardy's?"

"Cameron? You're supposed to be on holiday today. Ross and Sandeep are still over there."

"I think they're on their way back. I had a message from Ross." Cameron's fingers hovered over the keyboard, ready to send the data dump to Noor. She paused. Why would Ross have sent it to this obscure account and not direct to the company over normal channels? Had he picked up on a security risk at Argentum? She lowered her hands.

"When you see them," she continued, "let them know I'll call later for an update. If you're all at a loose end, why not do some housekeeping on the office systems?"

On the screen, Noor raised her eyebrows, but she said nothing to betray her understanding of the wider implications of the suggestion. "Great idea, Cameron. We'll do that. Have a good afternoon."

"Thanks, Noor. Speak later." She disconnected the call on her screen, and as a precaution she saved the data dump from Ross and took the computer offline.

"Cameron!" called Ben from the landing. "You good to go?"

She scrambled down the stairs. "All set," she said brightly.

Ben wasn't fooled. "What's happened?" he asked.

"Nothing. Just a bit of a mystery," she said, trying to make light of it.

Ben put his hands on her shoulders and looked into her eyes. "They can look after themselves. They don't need you to solve every problem that comes along. This is your time." He kissed her on the end of her nose and ruffled her hair.

She felt like a teenager again. Meekly, she followed Ben back down the stairs and out of the house to the waiting car.

•

Ross and Sandeep had spent the morning drilling down through the systems at Hardy's. Elation at finally pinpointing the cuckoo contract responsible for worldwide chaos had turned to frustration.

"I'm still not happy about the insertion point," said Ross. "It's too neat."

"What do you mean?"

"Hardy's assistant clicks on a malicious link in an innocent-looking message. Neither the message nor the click have been stopped by any of the firewalls or security systems. This code – complex stuff – drops into exactly the right place because the assistant is using Hardy's profile and had access to all the systems. Lucky hacker. Textbook mechanism."

Sandeep shrugged. "It hangs together. It doesn't make Jessie look good, though. As CTO she should have been on top of the profile and security systems." He dropped his voice. "There may be a case for negligence. Does she know how much trouble they're in?"

Ross said nothing. He couldn't explain what he knew about Jessie without implicating himself. He desperately wanted to get out of the building and away from her, but there was another loose end to tie up.

"What about the doppelganger?" he asked. "You were at the first meeting with Cameron. What did Hardy say about it?"

Sandeep thought back to the day they started the Calton Global investigation. "He said…" his brow furrowed. "He said that decision making had been deferred to the digital twin." Sandeep frowned and looked at Ross. "But Jessie played it down, yesterday. She made it sound like a glorified chatbot."

"A chatbot with no name, and no discernible system presence."

"Well, yes," Sandeep was getting uneasy. "We haven't found any activity on the internal systems that could be attributed to the doppelganger. If it really was running the company, we'd see it all over these audit trails like a rash."

"What if it was?" insisted Ross. "What if the twin's identity is linked to Hardy directly? He has previous for letting his assistants use his profile." A terrible thought struck him. "Have you ever met Hardy's assistant?" he asked casually, trying to keep his voice level.

"Yasmin?" said Sandeep. "I can't recall. Was she in reception when we came the first time? I've seen her photo."

"If she's Hardy's assistant, surely she'd be based in this management suite," said Ross, puzzled. "Where's her desk?"

He looked around the room, and by chance out of the corner of his eye he caught sight of a faint LED glow fading to nothing in the corner. He tapped Sandeep on the shoulder and pointed discreetly at the place where the light had appeared.

"I'm sure Yasmin works in the main office," he said levelly. At the word 'Yasmin', the light glowed again. The two men fell silent and exchanged horrified looks. There was something in the room that was live and reacting to their voices, and crucially to the trigger word 'Yasmin'.

It was time to get out.

Sandeep was the first to regain his composure. "I guess we're done here," he said jovially. "I was hoping for an early finish."

"I'll give Cameron a call and let her know the score," said Ross, reaching for his screen. "Human error as usual." The call went unanswered; he tried again, three times.

"We can do the final report for Calton from the office," said Sandeep. "Have you saved the details to our system?"

"Just uploading now," said Ross. His fingers flew over the keyboard. He sent the audit findings to the Argentum system, but also opened a connection to an old private account of Cameron's. It was a long shot, but he had to try and get the vital details out.

A message came pinging back. *"Can't talk now…"* Without losing a second, Ross dumped all the data he could find on 'Yasmin Hardy' straight to Cameron.

It was done. *"Heading home now,"* he typed, and he closed the connection.

"Let's go," he said to Sandeep. They gathered their belongings and marched smartly out of the management office and up the short corridor to reception. Sandeep knocked on the door, and a confused staff member opened it.

"Didn't Jessie call through to you?" he asked innocently. "We have to head off now. Can we sign out?"

"I haven't spoken to her," she said, confused. "It isn't a problem, though. She may be in a meeting. I'll log you out of the building and let Jessie know."

The door opened. Ross and Sandeep walked out to the street without a word to each other, relaxing only when they were out of sight of the building.

"It must have listened in on everything we did," said Sandeep wildly. "What the hell is going on there?" He looked at Ross. "Your instincts were spot on. Jessie must know about Yasmin. This is bigger than Calton Global, isn't it?"

Ross nodded soberly. "I'm afraid it is. Let's get back to the office. I want to run a check on all of our systems." He flagged down a passing autocar, and they jumped in.

•

Cameron, Ben, Charlie, Sameena and Aunt Vicky joined the crowd of parents and extended family in the school hall. A hubbub of voices echoed off the high ceiling, and Cameron strained to hear the conversation. Ben had given up trying to follow Aunt Vicky's reminiscences about Cameron and Charlie's schooldays and was gazing around the room. Thick curtains hung at the tall windows that lined either side of the hall, and at the far end steps led up to a raised stage. It was an old room, with some history behind it. On the walls between the windows were mounted static dark wood plaques, elegant gold lettering recording decades of sporting prowess. There were no screens in sight. Ben suspected it had barely changed since Aunt Vicky had herself been a pupil at the school.

Gradually he picked out the trappings of mid twenty-first century technology. Here, a discreet camera. There, beacons tracking the movements of pupils around the school. Several paintings, on closer inspection, turned out to be convincing images on ultra-thin wall monitors. The school had gone out of its way to simultaneously preserve the past and embrace the future.

Nina and her classmates were nowhere to be seen. They had all been shepherded away to another part of the school to receive their new chips. A group of older students circulated with drinks and nibbles for the crowd. Ben suddenly realised how hungry he was. His morning croissant had been a long time ago, and it was already past lunchtime. He picked up a handful of small sandwiches and ate them in two mouthfuls, earning a mock scowl from Cameron.

There was a rise in the volume of the chatter as staff members began to file onto the stage. "Please take your seats," came an announcement. The massed crowd moved awkwardly between the rows of chairs set up facing the stage. The front three rows were empty, intended for the students.

Ben sat down next to Cameron. She took his hand and squeezed it. "It's funny being back at school," she whispered.

"Shh," replied Ben reprovingly.

The muttering in the audience faded as the headmaster took the stage. He smiled at the assembled families. "Welcome to our school. I am delighted to see so many of you here today, supporting your sons and daughters, nieces and nephews, and grandchildren. It is an important day for these children, marking a rite of passage into the adult world. Without further ado, please put your hands together for the Class of '47."

He led the applause as a side door by the stage opened and the students filed in to their seats. Cameron spotted Nina easily, already half a head taller than most of her peers. There was a clear look of relief on her face underneath the studied pre-teen pose.

Once the students were settled, the headmaster called for silence and continued his address. "Many of you are of my generation and older. We grew up without the technology that these young people take for granted. There are some who hark back to the good old days when all we had were smartphones, tablets, and hand-held games. I ask you all instead to look forwards to the good new days. Your children have their future in their hands." He spoiled the joke by giving a thin smile to the audience.

Cameron winced.

"That was terrible," whispered Ben as the head droned on. "I came all the way from Paris for this?" He earned a poke in the ribs from Cameron, and an automatic disapproving stare from Aunt Vicky, which softened as soon as she realised it was Ben talking. He could do no wrong.

The head finished his speech with a flourish, and scattered applause broke out. He waved the audience into silence again. "Thank you, thank you. I am delighted to introduce our special surprise guests for today's celebration. Please welcome to the stage... Harris Amsyar!"

There were shrieks, cheers and wild applause from the children. Cameron looked at Ben who shrugged, none the wiser. Three men entered the hall from the side door. Two sat down, but the third, a handsome boy with a huge grin on his face, high fived the front row of students on his way to the stage. The cheers redoubled. "Settle down," pleaded the head ineffectually as the applause continued.

"Who are they?" whispered Sameena.

"No idea," replied Cameron.

"E-soccer," muttered another parent on the row. "My son loves it."

The over-excited youngsters calmed down at last and the guest began his talk. To Cameron's surprise, there was very little about sport. The young man talked passionately about work to preserve the re-seeded rainforests, clean the seas, and build coral reefs. She thought about the necklace and bracelet that she had bought for Nina. There was a renewed sense of purpose about the planet, a realisation that they had come too close to disaster and that it was up to them to make amends.

The headmaster came back to the stage to conclude the event. "Harris and his colleagues will be with us for a little while longer if you have any questions. Please could you make your way through to the exhibition of students' work."

The Silveras waited for the bulk of the crowd to leave the hall before standing up. Ben's stomach was growling. "I'm starving," he whispered to Cameron.

"Half an hour and we'll be out of here," she whispered back. "The kids' party starts soon. We'll say goodbye to Nina, and Charlie will pick her up tonight for the family dinner." She smiled as Nina loped into view, unconsciously elegant with her long legs. "Hi sweetie, how was it?"

"Oh wow, Harris Amsyar, I mean, how amazing?" Nina was grinning from ear to ear.

Cameron laughed. "I guess you like him? It was an interesting talk. I meant the chipping, Nina. How was it?"

Nina made a face at her. "It wasn't so bad. Jonasz screamed like a girl and Samir nearly fainted. It was really funny." She waved her hand, showing off the reddened patch between her thumb and forefinger. "All done."

"Has anything been programmed in yet?" asked Charlie. "Cameron, could you make it buzz when she needs to do her chores?"

Nina shot her father a filthy look. "Our identity hashes are on, of course, and we've all got some credit to use at the party. No programming chores, Dad."

"I'm sure I can write something cunning for you," said Cameron, deadpan. "I could sell it to other parents, too. I'd make a fortune."

"Sounds good," agreed Charlie. "We can retire on the profits and Nina will look after us. Deal?"

"No deal," said Nina, laughing despite herself.

"Can we leave you now?" asked Sameena.

"Sure, Mum, unless you want to see the exhibition." Nina was trying to be offhand, but Sameena knew her daughter.

"Why don't we walk through the exhibition on our way out?" she suggested. The others nodded their agreement. "Nina, are you coming with us?"

Nina shrugged, but she was obviously pleased. "Okay. Don't laugh. Some of it's quite good."

They joined the crowd moving slowly through the exhibition, which wound around a large room with partitions for extra wall space. Cameron gave the immersive 3D drawings no more than a passing glance but lingered over artwork in traditional pencil and pastel. Ben ignored the carefully reproduced flowers and landscapes and homed in on the technical designs, exchanging nods and laughs with Charlie as they turned virtual models around to see all the details. Sameena and Aunt Vicky followed Nina's nonchalant lead as she led them to the film section. Cameron came around the corner just in time to catch a short video of a very familiar dog playing tag with a unicorn.

"This yours?" Nina nodded.

"Nice CGI," said Cameron approvingly. "How did you get Roxy to run in the right direction?"

"I threw a lot of balls," replied Nina. "It took ages."

"Never work with children or animals," said Charlie, approaching with Ben. "Good work, Nina."

"That's very good," said another voice.

Nina blushed a deep red, and Cameron turned to see Harris Amsyar and his entourage emerge from the crowd. Nina was lost for words and simply nodded mutely. Cameron could tell she was both embarrassed and delighted at being singled out.

One of the men who she did not know gave Cameron an odd look. "Have we met?"

"I don't think so," replied Cameron, confused. She turned to Nina and put a hand lightly on her shoulder. "Excellent video, Nina."

"I agree," said Harris. "The animations are great. You could start a unicorn soccer league, yes?"

Nina was still star-struck but managed to squeak out a "Yes."

There was a ripple of sympathetic laughter around the room from Nina's friends who were watching in awe.

For a moment the three men spoke together softly in a language

Cameron didn't recognise. She automatically listened for snippets of words. One man seemed to be called Raj, the other she couldn't make out. Harris put out his hand to Nina who shook it, her eyes wide. "Nice to meet you, Nina. Maybe you could join me on my private fan forum?"

Cameron could see the shock in her niece's eyes as she nodded dumbly. A nice gesture, she thought, but something to keep an eye on.

The three men moved away, and the crowd closed behind them. Nina was immediately swamped by a group of squealing friends. "Wow, Nina, you talked to Harris Amsyar." "What did he say?" "Isn't he cool?" "Isn't he gorgeous?"

Charlie tapped Cameron on the shoulder. "I think this is where we bow out." He caught Nina's attention. "We'll head off now. Enjoy the party. I'll pick you up at six."

She nodded and was borne away by her chattering friends. The five adults followed the crowd to the door and emerged in the parking lot where a line of autocars were waiting.

•

The Argentum office was in uproar. Noor had started deep scans of all the systems as soon as the warning came through from Cameron, and Ella, Susie and Joel had closed down all their work as a precaution. When Ross and Sandeep walked through the door, the place was a hive of activity.

"Do we have a story for you guys," said Ross.

Sandeep started towards the coffee machine, but Noor raised a warning finger.

"Let's all take a break," she said. "Coffee at Clarey's?"

The six of them trooped out of the door and down the stairs. Outside, the main road was bustling with Friday afternoon traffic. They followed a familiar path down a warren of small side streets to their favourite coffee shop. The barista welcomed them.

"Usual, guys?"

"Thanks, Adam."

They settled at a large table in the back corner of the shop. Susie and Ella grabbed one sofa, Ross and Sandeep the other. Joel settled in a large armchair. Noor pulled up a comfortable stool and looked quizzically at Ross.

"Okay. Spill the beans."

Ross and Sandeep looked at each other, and both started to talk at once.

"We couldn't find the assistant…"

"Jessie was acting really strange…"

"I thought, what's the doppelganger called…?"

Noor held up her hands. "Stop! All we know is that one minute you're digging for the source of the cuckoo contract, and next you're both back here with your tails between your legs. Did you finish the job? Sandeep, talk to me."

Ross was obviously itching to speak but held his tongue.

Sandeep took up the tale. "We knew that the cuckoo contract was inserted through Hardy's, and it was just a question of finding the route. It could have been an internal job or someone hacking in. One of the real grey areas was the profiles for Hardy's assistants. He kept giving them his pass codes and access rights and Jessie kept having to shut them back down again."

"Sandeep made a real leap yesterday, although we didn't realise it at the time," continued Ross. "He asked Jessie about the doppelganger and she was really offhand. Rude, almost."

"Yeah," agreed Sandeep. "Ross has this thing about Jessie. He doesn't trust her. That moment was when I realised he might have a point." He broke off as the coffees arrived.

"Two latte, two americano, two cappuccino." Adam put the heavy tray down in the middle of the table. "I brought you some cookies. You look like you need them."

"Good thinking," said Joel with a broad grin, reaching for the plate. "I meant to ask," he continued, "did you get your wifi fixed?"

"Yes, Susie came round and sorted it all out. We've got the best coffee shop connection in the whole city now."

"And the most secure," interjected Susie. "I thought that would be a good idea, seeing as we seem to be using this as a second office."

The café door opened, and Adam left them alone to deal with the new customers. It was mid-afternoon, and people were starting their weekends early.

Noor turned back to Sandeep, cookie in hand. "Carry on."

Sandeep shrugged helplessly. "We found exactly what we were looking for. Evidence that Hardy's assistant clicked a malicious link in a message. Human error giving access to some unknown bad actor to insert the code. Everyone at Hardy's is in the clear, apart from tightening up their training. Although, to be fair, they could expect some serious comebacks for neglecting the security on the accounts to enable the hack in the first place."

"We found what they wanted us to find," said Ross. "We've been pushed in that direction from the start."

"I don't get it," said Joel, puzzled. "Sounds legit."

"It does," replied Ross. "Completely possible, and the most likely scenario. Human error wins again. But it's a cover. We've surprised them by tracing the breach in the first place, and…" He paused, reliving the shock of the discovery.

"And what?" asked Joel, impatient.

"Hardy's assistant isn't human."

"What?" said Noor, aghast.

"Jessie talked about a string of interns taking the assistant role," explained Sandeep, "and there's a Yasmin Hardy on the organisation chart near the canteen. We never twigged that we hadn't seen her in the flesh. We just took it for granted she existed. I mean, why wouldn't you?"

"Yasmin is the doppelganger," said Ross. "There's a portal in Hardy's office. I think it was listening to everything we did in there."

There was a stunned silence around the table. Ella was the first to speak.

"You're saying that the cuckoo contract may have come from within the company."

"In a nutshell," replied Ross. "An AI can't click on a malicious link. That's been planted in the access records for the fictional intern. I'd need to dig back into the system to prove it."

"I'm not going back there," said Sandeep flatly.

"You don't have to," replied Ross with a rare smile. "I dumped all the data I could find over a separate connection to a private account of Cameron's."

"Blinder, Ross," said Joel. "I guess they'll know you've done that, though."

"I tried to cover my tracks. I don't think they'd have any reason to go looking. Not yet, anyway."

"Aren't we missing the point here?" asked Susie. "We can be pretty sure that the cuckoo contract actually originated at Hardy's. That puts this AI and Jessie firmly in the picture as bad actors. Do we need to involve the police?"

"That's Cameron's call," said Noor, "but yes, we need to start pulling our evidence together. I can work on preparing a dossier."

"The other thing we need to do is check all the office systems," said Ross. "I don't trust any of the contact we've had with Hardy's, or anything to do with the Calton Global breach. We have to make sure that our own systems are not being spied on."

Joel drained his coffee and picked up the last cookie. "What are we waiting for? Let's get started."

Back in the office Ross pinged another message to Cameron, but there was no response. "She's not picking up," he said, frustrated.

Noor looked at him sympathetically. "She's with her family, and we really can't bring that data into our systems yet." An idea popped into her head. "Why don't you go and work from home?"

Ross brightened. "If you don't mind?" There was a chorus of agreement from the rest of the team. "Let me know when we can talk, and I'll let you know what I find." Going home would give Ross the chance to have some frank conversations with forum members, and with other connections that he didn't always mention to his colleagues.

The transport network was busy and slow. There was a constant stream of people going into the underground station, and all the buses were full to bursting. Ross cursed himself for leaving his bike at home. He had expected to be at Hardy's all day. Now, he would be happy never to see the place again. He walked briskly across the bridge and onwards through the City, glad to be out in the fresh air. It would be quicker on foot for the first couple of miles, and a good warmup for his evening training session.

Once clear of the crawling traffic in the crowded city centre, the buses out to the north seemed to be running smoothly. Ross jumped on a shuttle that eventually dropped him at the end of his road. He felt a note of pride when he saw his house, the garden newly tidy and the old air of neglect swept away. The key turned smoothly in the old traditional lock, and his chip deactivated the more modern security systems. Inside, his home smelled fresh and clean. Smart tiles had replaced the eclectic mixture of old carpets and had erased any lingering trace of the dead man. Light, bright walls made the rooms feel bigger and more welcoming. The old partition wall had gone, opening up the stuffy lounge that he had rarely used, transforming it into a comfortable room that reflected his own tastes. New furniture created a generous workspace in the corner of the room.

Ross grabbed a drink and settled down at his computer. He was gratified to see that Cameron had finally replied, but she was offline again. He dropped another message to say he was ready to talk. She would come back to him when she had time.

Next stop: the threat intelligence forums. Ross found some lively discussions going on. The rogue contract was old news and had been confirmed by all the groups working on the Calton Global hack. The latest developments had yet to break, and Ross was not about to mention the mysterious Yasmin on an open forum, even one as security conscious as this. He spotted Bordegiciel's handle come up in conversation and pinged him a private message. He felt as if Sébastien was almost one of the team, and it would be good to bounce ideas off him.

On a separate machine, its connection as tightly encrypted and secured as possible, Ross navigated his way to quite a different community. It was time to call on the group that Cameron and Joel referred to as his shady mates. If there had been any whispers about Yasmin, Jessie, the dead stranger, or any of the recent wave of data thefts, they would be circulating in the darkness. He logged in with an identity from his past life and started to search.

10: THE ADMIN

As they walked through the front door of the old farmhouse, Cameron glanced longingly up the stairs.

Ben sighed. "Go on," he said, "get back to work."

"Do you mind?" said Cameron quietly.

"I just wish you could leave the job at the office," he replied. "I see little enough of you as it is at the moment."

"I'll be as quick as I can," she promised, feeling wretched. "I just want to find out what's happened and why Ross dumped that data on me."

Ben shrugged helplessly. "I know you need to do it. Don't worry. I'll be here." He followed Charlie into the sitting room, and Cameron climbed the stairs alone to her attic.

She started with a call to Ross, but he didn't pick up. Concerned, she called the office, and Noor answered immediately.

"Fill me in on the latest, Noor," she said. "Where's Ross?"

"He's probably on his bike," replied Noor. "He's gone home to follow up on some work. Can I call you back, Cameron?"

"Sure." Puzzled, Cameron dropped the call. Less than a minute later, her screen alert pinged, and Noor's ID flashed up. "What's going on?" she demanded as soon as she picked up.

"I had to get out of the office," replied Noor. "We weren't sure if the place has been compromised. Joel is doing a final sweep now: it's looking okay."

Cameron couldn't keep the surprise and curiosity out of her voice. "Why the sudden panic?" They had security protocols in place for any suspected breach of the tightly locked office systems, and it sounded as if the team had executed them perfectly.

"There's been a development," said Noor cryptically. "Did you get some files from Ross?"

"Yes," replied Cameron. "Let me have a look at them." She switched on her computer, careful not to reconnect with the network, and scanned the files that Ross had dumped over to her. "What's the story with this 'Yasmin'? Isn't that old Joe Hardy's latest floating assistant?"

"That's what we all thought," said Noor. "Are you sitting down?" She gave Cameron a fast rundown of the surprise encounter that had spooked Sandeep and Ross. "They got out of there as fast as they could," she concluded. "There is a good chance that everything they talked about or accessed while running the audit has been recorded, at the very least. Hopefully the files Ross dumped will give us some idea of this doppelganger's capabilities."

Cameron was stunned. "That's beyond anything we could have predicted," she said. "I was convinced that the breach was a third-party action, dropped into the systems at Hardy's through a neat bit of phishing. I had no inkling that they were actually the culprits."

"Yes, the phishing route was the obvious answer, and someone set up all the right evidence for Ross and Sandeep to find. This new development was a surprise for all of us. We decided it would be safest to run our security routines. We couldn't run the risk that the office systems were being watched."

"You did the right thing. You all did." Cameron's mind was racing, absorbed in the puzzle. "It explains why the biometrics were bypassed for this 'Yasmin'. She isn't a real person."

"We couldn't have guessed," said Noor. "This is one of a kind."

"If the office systems are all clear, can I send over these files now?" continued Cameron. "You should take a look and see if any activity jumps out at you."

"Not yet," said Noor. "Let us finish up. You could send them back to Ross. He's doing some research of his own." She paused. "Cameron, this is a police matter, isn't it? We know that the cuckoo contract originated at Hardy's, and Jessie has to have been involved."

"Oh, Jessie," sighed Cameron. "Something didn't feel right last time I visited her. I would never have guessed how deep this went." A sudden thought made her blood run cold. "Noor, do you think there's any connection between the Speakeasy money and Jessie?"

"That would be too much of a coincidence, surely?" said Noor. "I'll talk to Ella, see if there is anything we can link up. I'd be surprised if we find anything."

"Nothing else can surprise me now," replied Cameron grimly. "And yes, you're right. We need a full dossier for Calton Global and evidence for the police."

"I'm on it," said Noor. "Don't you worry about it, Cameron. You go and enjoy your family time."

"I'm not worrying," replied Cameron. "I'm jealous. I want to get to the bottom of this as much as you." She kicked the desk in frustration. "Dammit, Noor. If it wasn't for Nina I'd be there like a shot."

"And Ben?" Noor reminded her. "And your brother? They all need you too. The world will not end if you step off the treadmill for a day. Send the files to Ross, and we will keep you up to date with anything we find."

Cameron took a deep breath. "Okay. I'll set the wheels in motion with law enforcement, too. If I think of anything else, I'll call you."

She ended the call to Noor and placed another to her connections in the cybercrime unit. All she could give them right now was a brief insight: the breach and their suspicions around Jessie and the company founder's digital twin. That task complete, she turned to the last thing on her list. Her frustration at being away from the team while they tackled a problem gave way to guilt. She should be downstairs celebrating and relaxing, not up here working. She chose to compromise and spend another few minutes making sure that everything she could do to help was done. Then she would tear herself away from the puzzle and become the attentive aunt once more.

She was about to place a call to Ross when he called her.

"Cameron? You got the files?"

"Hi. Yes. I'll fire them over. It sounds like you had an interesting day."

On the screen, Ross laughed. "You could say that. I tell you, when I saw that light, it was a scary moment. Evil bots and spies. Who would have thought it?" He sounded more amused than scared.

"Are you doing some digging?" asked Cameron. "Checking in with your shady mates?"

"Maybe," said Ross with an uncharacteristic grin. "You never know what rumours are rife beneath the surface."

"Yes, well, you be careful out there. We don't want you getting into trouble."

"Me? Never."

He's happier than he's been for a while, thought Cameron. Ross could be serious and moody; the lightness in his voice was new. She hoped it was a good sign.

"Did you ever come across the TrustCentre hackers on your travels?" she asked, suddenly recalling a conversation on the forums with Bordegiciel and some of the other members of her online group.

"Yeah, once or twice," replied Ross. "They're not around much in the murky depths. I think they're going very straight these days. I heard they were working in security for a large firm that can keep an eye on them. Why do you ask?"

"No reason," said Cameron, wondering herself why the connection had been made in her head. "I guess they were the last people arrested for a substantial data theft."

"They're nice girls," said Ross defensively. "They were never mixed up in anything this bad. They just got a little over-enthusiastic with some firewalls." He thought for a moment. "I might have a word with them. I wonder if they could recall any of the interested parties crawling around at the time of the hack?"

"That would be useful, I think," said Cameron. She looked at the time and frowned. "I have to go. Is there else anything you need from me?"

"No. I'm good," replied Ross. "You get back to your family. I'll take it from here."

"Keep me updated," pleaded Cameron.

"Sure. I will." Ross disconnected the call and Cameron switched off her computer, sighing. Time to be the adoring aunt. She stood up, yawning, and made her way back downstairs.

Charlie and Ben were deep in discussion in the sitting room. Cameron put her head round the door to let them know she was finished, then followed raised voices to the dining room where Dilan and Tara were setting the table for dinner. Cameron stepped in to resolve the argument between brother and sister. Just seven, Tara could be fierce.

From outside came the sound of a car door closing and Nina calling farewell to a friend. As a special treat, an autocar had been ordered to bring Nina and some classmates home, saving Charlie the journey back into town.

Nina burst through the front door, glowing with pleasure. She could hardly contain her excitement, hopping from foot to foot. "You'll never guess who came to our party, Dilan!"

"No idea," said Dilan dismissively.

"Harris Amsyar," replied Nina, a quaver in her voice.

Dilan stared at his sister. "Really?" he said sceptically.

"Really," said Nina. "Really, really, really. I got pictures!" She grinned at her brother with a mixture of delight and triumph.

"Tell me, who exactly is Harris Amsyar?" asked Cameron, still mystified by the hysteria at the school.

"He's only the best virtual soccer player in the whole world," said Nina, swooning.

"He's okay, I suppose," said Dilan dismissively. "Piotr Brzinski's much better." He returned to his task, putting out forks and cups.

Cameron detected a note of jealousy. "He seemed pleasant enough," she said. "Why was he talking about rainforests and coral? What is he doing in town?"

Nina sighed. "He plays for the Singapore MerLions. He's just the most amazing player, ever…" she tailed off.

Dilan snorted with derision.

"He's the MerLions captain and centre-forward, Auntie Cam. He has a really big online channel. I think loads of people like him because of that and not because of his football."

"I see," said Cameron. "So, Nina, do you like him because of his football or because of what you watch on his channel?"

Nina was too excited to be deflected. "It was really cool to see him, Auntie Cam. He's not much like his football avatar but we all know him from his real-life shows. Everyone in my year is on his channel." She blushed. "I used the access codes he gave me for the private fan community. They checked my chip at the party and it authenticated okay, and now I'm waiting for final approval from the admin to join."

Cameron raised her eyebrows but declined to comment. She was surprised that Nina's membership required chip authentication, but that kind of security would keep fake accounts at bay in the community. She would have a quiet word with Charlie to keep an eye on Nina's interactions with that group. "Is he from Singapore?" she asked instead. "Their players are based all over the world, aren't they?"

"Oh yes, he lives there," replied Nina, "but all the MerLions are on tour. It was on the news. The whole team has flown in to Europe. Well, apart from the players who actually live here, of course." She sighed. "It's so inspiring."

"The whole team?" Cameron raised an eyebrow. "That's some serious carbon offset. What have they been doing to earn this kind of trip?" Realisation dawned. "Ah, that's the link to the environmental work, isn't it?"

"That's part of what he does on his channel," said Nina. "He talks about the football, of course, but there's loads of stuff about them travelling around and helping with the rainforests and the sea."

"That makes sense." Cameron smiled sympathetically. "I bet Mr Willmott didn't anticipate you and all your friends swooning over the poor boy. It sounds like a party to remember." She thought back. "Who were the other men? Was one called Raj?"

"No idea," said Nina dismissively. "Not players. Probably management." She looked at Dilan, who shrugged.

Cameron saw Nina rub her hand unconsciously. "How's the chip feeling?" she asked.

"It's a bit sore," admitted Nina. She held up her hand to the light, peering critically at the slightly inflamed skin. "It was fun to pay for our drinks and snacks at the party with just a wave, though." She looked at the table, set neatly for eight. "I'm hungry. When do we eat? Mum?"

Nina disappeared through the door to the kitchen. Dilan and Tara glanced at Cameron, who cast a critical eye over their efforts to set the table. She nodded, and they scampered off, chores complete, eager to play while they had the chance. Cameron followed her niece to the heart of the house where Sameena and Aunt Vicky were putting the finishing touches to a celebratory meal.

"All done, Cameron?" asked Sameena.

"Yes and no. The table's set, if that's what you mean, but there's a lot going on at work. Everyone says I have to leave them to it, but I can't resist a mystery."

"Everyone is right, dear," said Aunt Vicky. "You need to take a break sometimes."

"I'm doing my best to be hands off, but it's so frustrating," replied Cameron. "If I need to sneak off and answer calls I'll be as discreet as I can. Do you need any more help, or shall I take Roxy out?"

"That's a good idea," said Sameena. "Go and wear that dog out for half an hour. Take Dilan and Tara. Nina, do you want to help me or go for a walk?"

Nina, lounging on a comfortable chair, groaned. "Can't I just stay here? I'm tired."

Sameena narrowed her eyes, but Aunt Vicky was too quick. "Oh darling, you must be exhausted. It's been an exciting day. You just curl up there and save your energy."

Cameron caught a flash of triumph crossing Nina's otherwise demure face. She smiled to herself. Aunt Vicky had always had a soft spot for the girl.

Cameron picked up Roxy's lead from its hook and walked back through to the hall. "Dilan, Tara, do you want to come for a walk?" There was no reply, but she heard the sound of feet on the stairs, and at the magic word 'walk' Roxy had appeared from nowhere and was leaping around. She stuck her head around the sitting room door. Ben and Charlie were still deep in conversation, comparing notes on the common ground of engineering, printing, and design theft. "I'm taking the dog out. Want to stretch your legs?"

"Good idea," said Ben.

Charlie shook his head. "I'll stay here. I have a couple of things to do."

Cameron, Ben, Dilan, Tara and an excited Roxy left the house and headed up the lane. The day was cooling rapidly, and Cameron shivered in her thin jumper. They walked some way towards the centre of the village, then turned away from the main street and up a side road towards Aunt Vicky's house. As they approached her garden, Roxy barked and struggled, and Ben grabbed the lead from Dilan who was having trouble holding onto her.

"It's that bloody cat again," sighed Cameron.

"The legendary Donald?" asked Ben, pulling Roxy close. "I've heard a lot about him."

Donald was occupying the width of the pavement outside Aunty Vicky's house, a malevolent pile of ginger fur, lounging with his eyes fixed on another cat on the opposite side of the road. There was a tense standoff. Further up the street, Cameron spied Andy, Aunt Vicky's neighbour, hanging onto his own dog as he tried set out for an evening walk. He waved.

"They won't budge, either of them, and Jasper's terrified of Donald," he called.

Donald looked languidly at Jasper and blinked his yellow eyes, before turning back to his opposite number. The dog whined.

"These two have been going at each other for weeks," said Andy. "I don't know why, and I wish they'd stop." He pulled ineffectively at Jasper's lead.

Cameron took matters into her own hands. She marched up to Donald and scooped him up in her arms. He wriggled in protest, but she hung on to the furry bundle as he twisted desperately in her firm grip. The cat on the opposite pavement took its chance and slunk away into the bottom of the hedge. The coast was clear. Ben and Roxy passed in one direction, Andy and Jasper in the other.

"Not going to the pub?" asked Andy.

"Sameena's got the dinner on," replied Cameron. "It was Nina's chipping today." She tightened her grip on Donald, who growled in protest.

"Ah, of course it was," said Andy. "That reminds me, I was hoping to do a feature on school chippings. Would you be able to cover the security aspects – anonymously, of course?"

"Sure," replied Cameron. A thought struck her. "Andy, I ran across someone yesterday who recognised me from a photograph and linked me to my handle. Do you know of anything that's slipped into the public domain?"

"Not at all," said Andy, "but I'll keep my ear to the ground. I'll give you a call about the feature next week if that's okay with you." He grinned at the struggling cat. "I'll get Jasper out of here and let you release the beast." Andy marched off down the road with a much happier dog by his side.

Cameron watched as Roxy pulled Ben out of sight towards a footpath over the fields. She held Donald up, two hands around his chest, and looked him in the eyes. "I'll have you for a rug, Donald. Behave yourself." He scrabbled at her with his back paws, wriggling to break free. She let him go and he shot off across the road in pursuit of the neighbouring cat, but his quarry was out of range.

Cameron followed Ben and the children to a narrow path and a stile. She clambered over and jumped down to the thin grass on the other side of the fence, thankful that the weather had dried up. This was a muddy walk in the depths of winter. Roxy was off the lead, barking happily and chasing a ball thrown by Tara. Ben was walking slowly, waiting for her, watching the two children running around happily after the dog. She fell into step with him and he hooked his arm into hers.

"How's it going?" he asked. "Everything okay at the office?"

"Not exactly," replied Cameron. "How does a rogue artificial intelligence and a criminal data breach sound?"

Ben winced. "You've had a worse week than I have." Roxy ran up with the ball in her mouth, and Ben grabbed it and threw it as far as he could across the field. The dog and both children chased after it.

"It's settling down, surely?" said Cameron. "We've been working closely with Sébastien. I thought all the files had been recovered, or did we miss something?"

"Oh, they're all there, alright, just in the wrong places. There's a lot of housekeeping to be done." Ben smiled at her. "Good work, Cam. I don't know where we'd be if we'd lost everything for good. Out of a job, probably."

"I've been talking to Sébastien on the forums," said Cameron. "There are a lot of people digging around on his behalf to find out where the attack came from. We know a lot about the mechanism, but not about who triggered it, or where from. We'll track it down between us."

"At least our hack doesn't have a mad AI involved," observed Ben. "Are the guys sure about that? I thought all artificial intelligence was built in line with the international code of ethics."

"Yes, well, a code of ethics is great as long as everyone sticks to it," said Cameron scathingly. "It was fine when AI was the preserve of scientists in high profile companies with only the best interests of humanity at heart. There were always going to be villains hiding in volcano lairs who could take the technology and do what they wanted."

"Fair point," said Ben. "I suppose everything is designed for good, but people take the tools and repurpose them for mischief and mayhem."

"I like that," smiled Cameron. "Mischief and mayhem. Malice, too. Anything which relies on the moral compass of the user is a risk from the start. Eurgh!" She broke off suddenly as Roxy came bounding back looking very wet and muddy and leapt up at her enthusiastically. "You've been in the stream, haven't you, you horrible dog."

"Oh no," said Ben, trying not to laugh. "I think the kids have, too." He was struggling to stay serious as Dilan and Tara appeared, their clothes filthy. Tara was carrying what looked like one of her shoes, although it was hard to tell with the mud that was caked on it. She was giggling uncontrollably. Dilan looked more contrite. He guessed they were in trouble.

"What happened?" asked Cameron sternly, glaring at the pair of them.

"I just threw the ball for Roxy," said Tara innocently.

"It went in the stream," said Dilan, "and Roxy followed it in."

"I chased Roxy and I didn't see the mud," Tara continued. She wasn't laughing any more. She looked sadly at the muddy object in her hand. "My shoe got stuck."

"I tried to pull her out," said Dilan, "and her shoe came off, and I went to get it and I slipped over."

"Roxy got the ball, though," said Tara, brightening up. Hearing her name, Roxy wagged her tail and then shook herself violently, water flying everywhere. Ben jumped out of range, but Cameron caught the full force of the spray.

"Oh, good grief," said Cameron. "Let's get you home and cleaned up for dinner." She picked up the soggy ball that Roxy had dropped at her feet and carried on through the field to a gate at the far end where the footpath continued towards the house. The children trailed behind her, Tara picking her way carefully in her sock. Roxy bounded around them unconcerned. As they reached the gate, Ben, who had been following at a safe distance, clipped her lead back on.

Arriving at the house, Tara hopped along the gravel drive, squeaking in protest every time she put her unshod foot down. Cameron went straight to the back door, kicked off her shoes, and disappeared indoors in search of warm towels. She came back with Sameena, who sighed at the sight of her two younger children. "Well?"

"It was an accident, Mum," said Dilan, staring at his feet.

"Mum," said Tara pleadingly, "we didn't mean to…"

"It is done now, Tara," said Sameena. "Dinner is nearly ready, and I expect you to be clean in double quick time. Strip those clothes off out here and wrap yourselves up. Cameron, can you wash these horrors? I will deal with Roxy."

Cameron marched the disgraced pair up to the bathroom.

As soon as they were out of earshot, Sameena doubled up with laughter. "Oh, Ben, can you believe the state of them? It is so hard to be cross."

"I know," said Ben, laughing himself. "The secret is safe with me." He looked at Roxy, who sat wagging her tail. "Want some help cleaning this daft dog?"

Sameena gave him a grateful smile. "Thank you, Ben. Let's get her tidied up." She fetched a brush and started working on Roxy's wayward curly coat, which was drying and matting quickly.

Ben brought a bowl of water. "We can't have you spreading mud through the house," he told the dog sternly. Roxy offered up a paw, her tail beating a happy tattoo on the concrete yard.

Hearing the noise, Nina floated through the door from the kitchen, screen in hand. "Oh Roxy, what have you done, you mucky baby," she cooed. The tail speed doubled.

"Not tired any more?" asked Sameena, a slight edge in her voice.

Nina looked at her innocently. "I'm fine now, Mum. When are we eating?"

Exasperated, Sameena gestured at Roxy. "Do you want to carry on with this while I finish cooking?"

"No, Mum. Sorry, Mum." The screen in her hand pinged and she brightened up. "Oh! It's Yasmin the admin! I've got into the fan forum. Cool." She disappeared back into the house.

Ben looked at Sameena, half smiling. "Almost a teenager, isn't she?"

"Oh yes," replied Sameena with a sigh. "So close. She's full of herself. I'm sure I was just as bad at her age." She gave Roxy's coat a last brush and stood up straight, groaning. "There, you silly dog, you're all done." She smiled at Ben. "Thank you for the help. Now, let's eat."

•

DI Sara Mercer was working mechanically through the file of routine tasks that awaited her at the start of her Friday night shift. She wondered whether she should have taken some leave; she wasn't part of Ivan's family, but they had been close colleagues, and his death had affected her more than she liked to admit. The pain was hard to bear. Perhaps it would be eased by solving the mystery of the dead man who had killed her friend.

She worked her way down the list. Some kids had been reported playing dodgems with autocars, trying to override the safety margins to crash into their friends. There were complaints of minor damage and a lot of noise, backed up by headcam footage from an outraged citizen whose peace had been disturbed. A spate of minor burglaries and thefts from under the noses of security bots pointed at a gang of opportunistic thieves operating in the area. The cybercrime unit had a tipoff from an A1-rated reliable source about a data theft, but without any serious detail to back it up. A street tobacco dealer had handed over a private key to access details of his suppliers in a deal for leniency. All in a night's work.

Her coffee was going cold. She picked it up and went to the nearby kitchen area, rinsing the old drink away and requesting a new one from the machine. "Cookie?" suggested the saccharin-sweet voice of the refreshment dispenser. Sara gave in immediately, her willpower at rock bottom. "Chocolate chip."

Hot coffee in one hand and soft cookie in the other, she made her way back to her desk. She sat back and closed her eyes for a moment, then took a welcome sip of the drink. It was going to be a long shift.

The caffeine hit sparked something in her mind. Cybercrime. Cybercrime? Hackers. Ivan.

With a burst of renewed energy, she scrolled back to the report that she had scanned moments earlier. Data theft, mechanism identified. Concerns over one Jessie McCoy, an employee. Something about a doppelganger program.

Mercer disregarded the note about a doppelganger and focused on the human. How would you arrest a piece of software, anyway? She started digging for detail. Her search routines spread out through a web of databases, seeking every snippet of information. As the machines worked their magic she sipped her coffee and nibbled at her cookie. She was no longer tired.

•

Ross was in his element and happier than he had been for years. He lounged back in the new chair at his desk, the room behind lit softly by a tasteful selection of rented lamps. Music was playing, a mix favoured by the team when they were cracking open malware. On the table sat a large bottle of water and a real treat, a small glass of whisky. Both computers were active, their screens glowing. On one, under his handle of RunningManTech, he was chatting with familiar figures in the threat intelligence forum that Cameron had set up. Bordegiciel had dropped in and was in an expansive mood after a couple of drinks with colleagues, and the East Coast teams were awake, working hard, and looking forward to their weekend. On the other, where he was known simply as The Piper, he was reacquainting himself with some older friends. The TrustStore girls, the shady character who pulled off the Westminster hack and still hadn't been apprehended, and a few avatars from his former life that he didn't entirely trust.

He was hunting for clues and news and sightings, listening for whispers of a cybercrime syndicate and an artificial intelligence gone rogue. He was not disappointed.

"Speakeasy was a good payout for a few people, Piper," came one comment. "Big business."

"Gracie was mixed up in that, wasn't he?" asked another member. "Haven't seen him here for a while."

"He's inside," said another. "There's people digging for his treasure trove right now. Can't keep security updated from a cell."

"I heard the payout wasn't as big as expected." Ross dropped the bait into the forum, chumming the waters for the sharks that circled in the depths.

"No shit. And we know why." The poster was a stranger to Ross, a new face who must have joined in the time that Ross had kept his distance from this crew. "Plenty people should have had more. SimCavalier messed it up."

Ross held his breath. He hadn't expected Cameron's handle to come up in this conversation, but if he was looking for the bad apples, this was a fair indication that he'd found one.

"You can't blame one guy for closing down the job," protested a TrustStore girl. ShellPixie was her handle. Ross had always liked her.

"SimCavalier is no guy," replied the stranger.

An image popped up on the screen, and Ross jumped. He was glad that no one on the forum could see his reaction. The picture was clearly of Cameron.

"Hey, a white hat girl," typed ShellPixie, needling the stranger. "She'd beat you any time, KingKatong."

An argument started, and Ross distanced himself, posting a clip of a man eating popcorn and refraining from comment. He kept the forum open and went over in his head what he'd learned. He had confirmed the team's suspicions and his own absolute certainty that there had been some kind of syndicate sitting behind the Speakeasy attack months before. They'd mentioned Gracie, a name he had found on the dead man's smartscreen. All useful to him, but he could never disclose it without implicating himself. Most urgently, though, Cameron's cover had been blown. He went to call her, but there was no response. Cursing, he sent her a message to call him as soon as she could.

The chatter had tailed off and it looked as if KingKatong was no longer online. Ross ventured a new post.

"Stirred up a hornet's nest there," he typed, adding an embarrassed face.

ShellPixie responded with a series of icons – a laugh, a shrug, a bee, a bunch of flowers. "Don't worry about that guy," she typed. "He's always picking fights. Good to see you, Piper."

"You too, Pixie. Long time. Hey, you hear anything about this big data breach?"

"Calton Global? It's been like shooting fish in barrel. So much data, so little time."

"I thought you were going straight?"

ShellPixie returned the embarrassed face. "I get bored. A little phishing here, a little contract hacking there. What else is a girl to do?"

"You should behave yourself. Try knitting." Ross picked an appropriate clip to make ShellPixie laugh, then asked another question, hoping to stay casual. "Who's the winner with Calton, Pixie? Our friend KingKatong?"

"Oh, yeah, I think so, and more. Same people being cocky all over the forums when Calton Global and Mars Attacks broke."

"Mars Attacks?"

"Where have you been, Piper? Some big deals have been going down. You're missing out."

"I can see that," replied Ross, thinking quickly. "Had to keep my head down for a while. Where do I go for the lowdown?"

"You want to get in with Yasmin the Admin," replied ShellPixie.

"I'll do that," replied Ross, his mind racing. "Pix, I have to go. It's past my bedtime. My hot chocolate is getting cold. You look after yourself, you hear?"

"Sure, Piper. Talk again soon."

Ross logged out and severed the connection. He picked up the whisky glass and drank the shot in one gulp. Yasmin the Admin. A link between Calton Global and the attack in France. What the hell was happening?

•

DI Mercer put down her cup as the search results came in. The suspect in the cybercrime unit report wasn't known to the police, so there was nothing on the internal files. She seemed to have been suspiciously cautious online, too. Mercer sighed. An absence of evidence was circumstantial at best and useless at worst. All the Jessie McCoys that the first pass found were red herrings, living in far corners of the country.

The second set of searches had been widened to include the company where McCoy worked, the location of the reported doppelganger. There were standard team pictures published around the web, but they meant nothing to Mercer. Press releases had no images of the girl and no commentary on her activity. Company information was brief and stereotypical. Mercer shook her head and scrolled on.

A third set of searches spread the net further, exploring data related to the company but posted by others. Mercer took another sip of coffee and grimaced once again at a mouthful of cold liquid. She scrolled through page after page of complaints about pay and conditions, pictures of team nights out, wedding parties and socials. She sat back in her chair, flicking aimlessly at the screen as pictures flowed across it. An image caught her eye as she scrolled past and she came back to study it. Why was it interesting? The main group was smiling at the camera, four people arm in arm. Behind, others were standing and talking with glasses in their hands. "Works do," it was captioned. "Tech team doing it in style." The four subjects were all men. In the background, though, there was a woman with her back to the camera. Something about the way she was standing recalled another picture. A CCTV image of a woman and a man entering an office in a deserted business park.

If that was Jessie McCoy, then she could be linked to the dead man.

DI Mercer felt a rush of emotion, and the tears came. She was a step closer to finding why Ivan had died.

11: CONNECTIONS

Pete sat up in his familiar bed on the main ward and watched the rain streaming down the window. The weather had apparently turned while he was in intensive care, and they were well on their way to winter. He felt better than ever, but he was still shocked to discover what had knocked him for six, and devastated to hear about the death of the other man.

A doctor approached. He looked tired and dishevelled, but he was obviously glad to see his patient on the mend.

"Welcome back to the real world. You've been lucky. If you're going to collapse with a bout of Grasshopper Flu, a hospital is the place to do it."

"I'm feeling a lot better," croaked Pete, surprised how weak his voice felt.

"You're doing great," replied the doctor, "but you still need to get your strength up. There may be some media attention. Half the news channels in Europe are camped in the park outside."

"Any visitors? Have my boys been in?"

"Not yet. The hospital is still locked down, but it won't last much longer. It looks as if the fast vaccination response has closed down any risk of an epidemic here."

"That's great to hear." Pete lay back wearily on the soft pillows. "Thanks for everything, Doc."

"Don't mention it," said the doctor with a wry twist in his voice. "We'll all be glad to get home. The staff quarters are pretty cramped." A nurse appeared in Pete's field of vision, tapping at her wrist in the universal sign of 'time's up'. "I'll leave you to rest. I know your medical history: you'll be ready to finish your original treatments in no time at all."

The doctor got up to leave. "Your family should be in as soon as the quarantine is lifted. You have messages from some colleagues, too."

Pete nodded gratefully.

As he lay quietly, listening to the rain, he reflected on the hours and days before he fell ill. He turned the mystery of the Calton Global breach over in his mind, wondering how far the investigation had advanced. He felt a twinge of excitement at seeing the outcome, and regret at missing the fun. Gradually he dozed off, dreaming of an everlasting chain of transaction blocks swooping and dipping in a glittering dance.

•

It was a lazy morning in the Silvera household. Cameron lay in bed sipping coffee and listening to the rain beating on the pitched roof of her attic room. The sky outside the window was dark with heavy rainclouds, and as the year faded the temperature was dropping fast. Beside her, Ben was reading, his smartscreen casting a faint glow in the dull daylight. There were noises coming from downstairs. The younger children were up and about, settled in the family room with their breakfast and streaming their favourite programmes. Nina was undoubtedly asleep, and Charlie and Sameena were enjoying a rare Saturday without children's activities.

Cameron stretched and glanced over Ben's shoulder at his screen. "Anything interesting going on?"

"Not a lot," replied Ben. "No mysterious dead bodies, no high-profile hacks, no more flu cases, in this country at least." He brightened up. "There's news from the Mars mission, though. They've started broadcasting from base camp."

"Recognise any bits of kit in the pictures," asked Cameron.

"Oh yes," replied Ben. "It looks as if our 3D designs are doing the job."

"I'm curious," said Cameron, "why do you think the designs were scrambled and stolen after the mission took off? If someone wanted to disrupt the operation, then they would have attacked long before."

"Purely commercial," said Ben with a shrug. "Space research is big business on Earth. We have to capitalise on the patents within a few months, before the designs are released into the public domain. There will be counterfeits coming through any day, and if it wasn't for you and Sébastien and all the team, we would have been helpless." He smiled at her affectionately. "Nice job, Cam."

Cameron took the compliment graciously. "All in a day's work. Another money-spinning hack, another coin for the good guys."

"Are all these hacks about money?" asked Ben.

Cameron nodded. "Most of them. You do get political attacks, and a few that are purely driven by ego. There are a good number of annoying cases where it's just a kid having fun, but yes, money is generally at the root of everything. For plenty of people, hacking is their way out of poverty. It's amazing the services you can buy off the shelf."

"Was our breach just a talented kid in a slum, then?"

Cameron shook her head. "I don't think so. It was someone who knew exactly how much the designs were worth. They sold for a lot of money. There's no reason why the code shouldn't have come from a contractor, but the social engineering, the complex execution of the breach…" She tailed off, frowning. "It's a money-making machine."

"It's a business."

"It is." Cameron raised her hands, exasperated. "I thought we weren't going to talk about work this weekend? Now I can't get this out of my head." She threw back the covers and stood up, and chucked her pillow at Ben, who caught it, laughing. "I need a shower."

Twenty minutes later, dressed and refreshed, Cameron made her way downstairs. Charlie was already up and stacking logs beside the fireplace.

"It's turned cold. We might be needing this later."

"Honestly, Charlie, you have enough power to heat the whole house without that."

"The solar panels are worthless in this weather," said Charlie defensively, "and the village turbines have been on the blink recently. I'd rather keep what power we have to amuse the kids." He nodded at the children, glued to their cartoons, and smiled wickedly at his sister. "Including you. I'm sure you need all your kit running smoothly for when you sneak off to work."

"You just like building fires," retorted Cameron, ignoring the jibe.

"Guilty as charged. It makes the room more cosy, though, and it's our own wood, after all." He carried on happily adding to the pile.

Cameron shook her head in mock despair and went to find more coffee. She met Nina in the hallway, also heading to the kitchen in search of breakfast.

"How's the hand?"

"It's sore, but it'll be okay," yawned Nina. "Aunty Cam, can you set up some functions for me?"

"Sure. We'll start with an alarm clock and work from there."

Nina gave her aunt a filthy look and stalked into the kitchen. "It's Saturday," she said loftily over her shoulder.

"Cameron, that is a good idea." Sameena had followed her daughter down the stairs. "We need to decide what chip apps you are allowed, young lady."

"Most of the standard ones for teens are already installed," said Cameron. "I read up. We can enable and disable them from your screens."

"Not hers?"

"Not yet."

"Thank goodness for that." Sameena's relief was palpable.

It must be hard for her, thought Cameron, to see Nina growing so independent.

Nina herself was already curled up with her screen in a comfortable chair in the corner of the kitchen, munching on a slice of toast, but she jumped up as her mother and aunt entered the room. "What would you like for breakfast?" she asked. "I can make pancakes?"

"That would be lovely, dear," said Sameena, taken aback. "Thank you." She set to the task of making coffee.

Nina started bustling around the room, gathering ingredients. She deftly opened and closed the fridge quickly enough to stop it talking, then waved her hand casually across a sensor on the wall. Cameron smiled to herself as the family recipe book projected its first page onto the work surface. Nina swiped through the pages until she found the right one, checked through the list to make sure she had everything she needed, and started mixing. "Mum," she said casually as she stirred, "Lucy is having a sleepover tonight. Can I go?"

Sameena sighed. "You should have asked before now. It's a bit short notice, Nina. Who else is going?"

"I'm sorry, Mum, but she only invited us last night. It's me, Rose and Magda." She flipped the pancake over expertly, timing it to perfection.

"The usual crowd," said Sameena. "Does Lucy's mother know about this?"

"Of course," said Nina. "Look, there's Lucy's message on my screen. Please, Mum."

"I suppose so," replied Sameena. "Yes, you may go."

Nina grinned happily.

Cameron winked at her. "Those pancakes had better be good." She picked up two cups of fresh coffee and went in search of Ben.

•

Andy Taylor dragged himself out of the house and through the rain towards a waiting autocar. He cursed the producer who had left him with another weekend job to cover. He was not looking forward to spending a wet day stuck outside the hospital in a broadcast pod, even in the company of the lovely Bea Black.

As he clambered into the little car, he was surprised to see two pairs of yellow eyes under a large sheltered bush. As usual, Donald the cat was surveying his domain from the driest vantage point, but he had company. He appeared to have reached an agreement with the black cat from over the road, who was perched at the very extreme of the dry area, tolerated if not welcomed to the cosy shelter. Andy laughed and glanced back to his house where Jasper was standing at the front window. The poor dog was in for some trouble when the weather cleared up, assuming this uneasy feline truce held.

The autocar swept out of the village up the long lane that led to the main road. Many of the golden leaves had fallen from the trees and water was running down the side of the road, the land drains choked by the autumnal bounty. The brook that ran through the village would be full, thought Andy. He hoped there wouldn't be a repeat of the flooding that had caused problems for his lower-lying neighbours last year.

It was a slow but clear run to the station, and Andy ran to catch the early train up to London. Sitting in the carriage he checked his messages, preparing for the day's broadcast. There was a balance to be struck between tributes to the dead officer and relief at the recovery of the other patient. He was almost certain that he knew who the latter would be. It was only a matter of time before the names were released, and he hoped that he was right. It would be a great scoop for his channel and make up for the wet, early start.

As the train swept into the northern suburbs of the city, the high arch of the old football stadium barely visible through the rain, his screen pinged. New release from the hospital: the official word on the identity of the fatality and the survivor. He read the message and had to resist punching the air in delight. Was it too early to call Cameron? There was no doubt that she would be able to fix him up with an exclusive interview with Peter Iveson, Flu Survivor. He placed a call anyway and was mildly surprised when she answered within a few seconds.

"Cameron? Andy."

"Hold on," came the muffled reply. There was a pause, then Cameron came back on the line. "Pancakes," she said succinctly.

"I won't keep you from your breakfast," he said, amused. "They've released the names of the two flu cases. You could have told me it was Pete. I'd guessed anyway."

"Sorry, Andy," said Cameron lightly. "I suppose you want an interview? I'll see what I can do. I haven't spoken to him yet, but I hear he's up and talking."

"Perfect. You read my mind. It would make a long day very bearable."

"No problem. While you're hanging around doing nothing, can you dig for clues on my handle leak? I really need to know more."

Andy cursed under his breath. He'd forgotten. "I hadn't forgotten," he said quickly. "I'm on it."

"Great, thanks Andy. I'll call you as soon as we hear from Pete. I'll tell him you're outside. I'm sure that if he has to speak to any member of the press he'd be happiest with your team."

"Thanks, Cameron. Enjoy your pancakes." Andy dropped the call and logged on to an internal news channel system. He needed to start by checking all the images of Cameron that they held securely in their e-vaults. The search routines would kick in to cross reference those images against the world wide web, from sites in the light of day down to the depths of the dark web. It would take a while.

The routines hadn't returned all the results before the train arrived at Euston, so Andy stuffed his smart screen into his bag and walked briskly down to the old underground system. A shuttle took him straight out to towards the hospital a few stops away. He wearily climbed the short flight of steps to the street level. The rain had redoubled, and he looked around in vain for an autocar. There were none waiting, the charging rank empty. Grumbling, he pulled his jacket up around his ears and trudged down the road. On any other day he would have been happy to walk the few minutes to the hospital, but there was something about the sudden change from the dry, warm autumn weather to this cold, heavy rain that depressed him. The days were getting shorter and what passed for winter – the chilly, wet season – was upon them with a start.

Bea Black greeted him at the outside broadcast pod. She and Giles were huddled in the small space drinking coffee. Andy shook the excess water off his coat and climbed in, warmed by the sound of the drinks machine whirring. "It's vile out there."

"Think of the overtime," said Giles. He didn't look happy at all.

"I may have some good news," said Andy. "How about I fix up an exclusive with the surviving patient?" He sipped his fresh coffee and gave Bea a wide grin. "No promises, but when he's ready to talk I think we can get him on the line." He looked at Giles. "He's one of Cameron's team."

Giles' mouth fell open and he stared at Andy. "No. Really? Which one."

"The big bald guy. Remember?"

"I do, but I don't think I knew all their names. I would never have made the connection."

"Nice one, Andy," said Bea. "Any good angles we can pull in? Set up some decent questions for me, will you?"

"I'll have to run anything like this through Cameron, but we may be able to broaden the interview out to the data thefts. He's bound to have been working on those."

"Human virus to tech virus. I like it." Bea paused. "Have we started seeing any fallout from the data yet?"

"A few juicy stories," replied Andy. "Some of the gutter press have been spending money in the deep recesses of the web."

"Ah, yes, the tobacco addiction and the financial revelations," said Bea. "I bet there are more where they came from."

"Tip of the iceberg. Let's see what we can work into this piece. A few dire warnings wouldn't go amiss." Andy pulled out his screen and fired off a quick message to Cameron. She probably wouldn't come back in a hurry, but she might have some input for him.

Next to him in the cramped pod, Giles opened up the thought map they had created days before. He began working through the scenarios for use of the stolen data, picking out good sound bites for the day's broadcasts. Bea settled down to work on outline scripts. The mobile unit was a hive of activity, providing a distraction from the drumming of rain on the roof.

Andy's screen pinged. Cameron had replied to his message. "Good news," he said to Bea. "She's spoken to Pete. He's able to do a short one to one, remotely of course. Cameron has sent over some simple personal security tips to add to the piece, too."

They all jumped at a knock on the door of the pod.

"We're up," called the cameraman, who had been sheltering with his team in the equipment unit. "Press conference."

Bea grabbed an umbrella and a hairbrush, nodded at Andy, and scrambled out of the door, ready to face the public.

Andy turned back to his screen. The routines he had set running an hour ago had finally returned some results. He opened the file and groaned. The images were all too familiar: close ups of Cameron taken from his own surveillance of the team, back when he was searching for the mysterious SimCavalier and had not made the connection between the legend of cybersecurity and his own friend's kid sister. He'd initially thought that the SimCavalier was Ross. He laughed ironically at the memory. Someone had obviously worked it out faster than him, and Cameron's identity was out in the public domain.

He checked the files again. No, not entirely public. His scraping routine showed that the images were located deep in specialised forums, on anonymous chatrooms, in dark web gossip. This was not a good thing, he reflected. There would be people there who were excited to put a face to the handle, who recognised her work and looked up to her as a hero. There would be others who would be delighted for a very different reason: target acquired. Cameron could be in grave danger.

Andy placed another call to Cameron. She had to know what he'd found. She didn't answer. He cursed under his breath, sat back heavily and stared into space. For all his promises to keep her safe, it was his own work that had finally revealed her to the world.

The pod door slid open and revealed Bea, rain dripping from her umbrella and a big grin on her face. "We're done," she said happily. "Quarantine lifted, wards reopened. Apart from that last interview you promised me, we're ready to go."

Andy pulled himself wearily to his feet. "Giles? How are you doing with those questions? I'll have to send them over to Cameron for checking."

"Here you go," said Giles, pinging a file across to his boss.

"Thanks," said Andy. He bounced them straight to Cameron with a note: "*Questions for Pete. I need to talk to you about something else. Call me.*"

This time she replied straight away. "Questions look good to go," she chirped happily. "What's up, Andy? I can't talk for long."

"Hold on." Andy nodded at Bea. "You're okay to use those questions. I need to sort something out." He stepped outside the pod, sheltering his screen under his jacket, and ran for shelter in the larger equipment truck. "Are you still there, Cameron?"

"I'm here. Do you have some news?" She giggled. "I know you have news, you're the news channel. You know what I mean."

"Yeah. Not good news, though. I'm sorry, Cameron, but I've traced instances of at least one of the images we took on surveillance. I haven't found out how it leaked, yet. I don't know how it was linked with you."

"I didn't realise they were still stored on your servers," replied Cameron. "Why the hell didn't you delete them?"

"Automatic archiving. We have to keep all our materials for a certain time for regulators. I'm sorry, Cameron."

There was silence. Andy felt wretched. Finally, Cameron spoke.

"Nothing you can you do, Andy." She sounded calm, but Andy recognised an undertone of anger and frustration in her voice. "Too late now."

Andy took a deep breath and continued. "Cameron, the searches returned all sorts of dodgy sites. Some deep dark chatrooms. I'm worried about you. There are some nasty people out there and you have been a thorn in their side for years. Take care, won't you?"

"I'll be fine, Andy. I appreciate the warning and the apology, but what's done is done. Don't worry about me. There are plenty of people who have my back."

"Always, Cameron." The call dropped, and Andy leaned against the side of the truck, brooding. Through the rain he saw Giles approaching, camera in hand, lens protected with a bag.

"They're on their way out," he called. "Let's go and get some pics."

Andy nodded wearily and looked around the truck for a hat, umbrella, hood or anything to protect him from the weather. The downpour showed no signs of slowing. Finding a discarded baseball cap, he pulled it low over his head. Better than nothing. He followed Giles through the park to the hospital gates where the staff were starting to emerge.

•

"I've told you before, stop bringing every waif and stray home for lunch." Noor was furious, and letting it show. Her eyes flashed as she confronted her parents in the kitchen, but she kept her voice low. The visitor sat in the other room, oblivious to the argument that was brewing behind his back.

"Get in there and talk to him, Noor," said her father firmly. "Your aunt introduced him to us and he seems very nice, very clever. You will have a lot in common."

Bursting with anger but at the same time conscious of her family's standards of behaviour, Noor bit her lip. Even as an adult, she didn't want to cross the line with her parents. "How does she know him? What's the story?"

"He lives near her. She sent us a message when he came to London and asked us to welcome him."

"Why do you need me?" asked Noor, and instantly regretted it. This was not the time to pick a fight about her marital status, but the words were said now.

Her mother looked pained and her father flung up his hands. "You are still on your own. Look at your brothers and your sister. They've all started their own families and moved forwards. You must think about settling down. When do you meet people in your job? You work too much. We're trying to do what is best for you."

Noor opened her mouth to retort, to say that she was happy on her own, and did not need a partner to complete her. She thought better of it and chose the path of least resistance to keep the peace. "Okay. I'll stay for lunch. Then I have to go." She turned on her heel and stalked out of the room.

Composing herself, she admitted privately that she was curious about the visitor. No one travelled so far across the globe for fun these days. She could only just remember visiting her relatives in Malaysia as a child, and they had certainly not been over to England to return the visit for more than two decades.

She fixed a smile on her face and walked into the living room where the visitor waited. "Selamat datang," she said politely. "Welcome. I'm Noor."

The visitor extended his hand. "I'm Tenuk. Nice to meet you. Your aunt has told me so much about you."

"All good things, I hope." Which aunt, she wondered?

"Of course," said Tenuk with a smile. "She said I should call in to see you and your family. She also said you and I have some interests in common."

"Really?" Noor raised an eyebrow.

"Yes. You were a student of history? That was also my field of study."

Noor was genuinely surprised. She had expected the link to be tenuous at best. Perhaps he really did know her family well.

"That was some time ago," she said modestly. "I haven't worked in the field."

Tenuk laughed. "Neither have I. Back at college I spent more time on e-sports than on history. I followed my heart, not my head."

Realisation dawned. "Oh! You're with the MerLions tour." That explained how he had been able to travel. Noor had very little interest in sport, but with three soccer-mad brothers and a raft of nieces and nephews she could hardly miss the fuss being made over this club.

"Yes," Tenuk ducked his head. "I don't play – I was never good enough – but I work with the management team. We have been to sports clubs and schools, doing photo shoots and publicity, and all the interviews – so many channels. I am looking forward to going home to Singapore."

"You live in Singapore? How fantastic." He knows Auntie Fatima, then, surmised Noor.

"I do, in Katong," replied Tenuk. He changed the subject quickly. "Where in Malaysia is your family from? Your aunt never said."

"My mother's family are all in Kuala Lumpur," said Noor. "Only my mother and Auntie Fatima moved away. My dad is English, although going back to last century his family came here from Iraq."

The door opened, and Noor's father appeared, smiling broadly. "You two seem to be getting on well. Lunch is ready."

It was a strange meal. Noor found Tenuk to be good company. He was quick witted, friendly and funny. Her mother kept pushing for news of the country she had left behind as a teenager, and he answered her questions as well as he could, although the differences between his native Singapore and neighbouring Malaysia were stark. He was better informed on family news, and it seemed that he and Auntie Fatima really had been neighbours for some years. Noor's father was trying hard not to gloat. She could tell that his over-active imagination was already planning the wedding.

It was with mixed feelings, therefore, that she finally took her leave of her parents and their guest. "I'm so sorry," she said. "I have a friend to visit in hospital."

"Nothing serious, I hope?" Tenuk sounded concerned.

"Actually, yes," replied Noor. "He was in isolation with Grasshopper Flu. Quarantine has been lifted now, so we're allowed in."

"Grasshopper Flu? That's bad. We have it in Singapore. One of my own colleagues on this tour fell ill in France."

"I heard there was a case in Paris," replied Noor. "I'm sorry to hear it was someone you know. How are they?"

"Responding to treatment, I think, but it is a worrying time."

"I'm surprised that you haven't all been vaccinated," said Noor's mother.

"Most of the group have," replied Tenuk. "A few of us have some natural immunity. I have never been vaccinated, and I have never been ill, although I have been in contact with sick people."

Noor stood up. "It was lovely to meet you, Tenuk. How long are you going to be here in England?"

"Alas, only a few more days."

Across the table, Noor's father tried to hide a scowl.

"We have almost completed our work," continued Tenuk. "I will be sorry to leave."

"You must come again," said Noor's father hurriedly. "Come for dinner next week."

"I can't do that," replied Tenuk, "but I would love to stay in touch with you."

Noor nodded. "Certainly." She opened up her smartscreen and

dropped her details to him. He seemed harmless enough, and it might keep her parents at bay in their hunt for a son-in-law. She was determined to live her life her way, and a little misdirection would make things easier.

"Goodbye, then, Tenuk. Safe journey."

"Goodbye, Noor. Until the next time."

•

Andy stood in the pouring rain and watched the staff streaming out of the hospital. The quarantine around the affected wards had been lifted, and there was a mass exodus of people returning to their homes and families, ready for a shower and a quiet meal. Giles was snapping away with his camera, hoping to get some decent images despite the terrible weather and low visibility. Behind them the packed press area was starting to clear as teams moved off site. Bea's pod was going nowhere. They were waiting for the promised interview.

Watching Giles at work, Andy was reminded of Cameron's request.

"Do you remember the stakeout on Argentum Associates?" he asked.

Giles gave up trying to snap images of tired nurses and turned to his boss.

"Sure. Why?"

"All the images are still archived on our servers, aren't they? I mean, they haven't been shared anywhere?"

"They're stored on the servers, sure, but all our syndicated channels have access to the whole media library," said Giles.

"Can we tell if they've been accessed?" asked Andy, cursing under his breath. He'd forgotten about the depth of data sharing through syndication.

"It's not hard to check," replied Giles. "Do you want me to have a look?"

"Yes. I ran a search this morning and some of our images are out in the wild. Not the ones we broadcast, either."

Giles looked sidelong at him. "Andy, you do know we're a news channel, right? We make money from sharing all of this stuff with our partners."

"I know, but someone has made the link between the pictures you took and the real identity of the SimCavalier. We agreed on anonymity." Andy looked pained. "I'm duty-bound to keep that promise."

"I can see you'd be in trouble if that's the case. I wouldn't want to cross her," replied Giles. "Let me check the file metadata. It won't take long."

The two of them trudged back to the pod. The grass underfoot had turned to mud, and puddles had formed where other press teams had been. Everything was damp. Shut inside the pod, dry and warm, Bea was preparing to patch through to Pete on the ward for her exclusive report. Andy looked pleadingly through the window at the coffee machine, but Bea shook her head.

"Let's get some food," he suggested to Giles. "I haven't eaten since breakfast, and it's way past lunchtime."

"Starving," agreed Giles.

The two of them went in search of a food truck in the rapidly emptying park. Ever considerate, Andy picked up a sandwich for Bea, and they headed back to the channel's encampment hoping that the broadcast was finished. Sure enough, equipment was being packed up, ready to join the lines of departing press.

"Thanks, Andy." Bea took the slightly soggy package out of his hand and unwrapped the sandwich, biting into it gratefully. "Where did the time go?"

"How was the interview?"

"Excellent," replied Bea. "He's in pretty good shape considering what he's been through. A bit croaky, but he got through all the questions. It was a great exclusive. There were some jealous crews out here, I can tell you."

"Are we done?" asked Giles.

"We're done," replied Andy. "Bea, get yourself home. Giles, can you get back to the office and check those images? See which partners have accessed them." He turned to the technical teams. "Let's pack up and go."

•

DI Sara Mercer was back on shift and digging deep into all the reports she could find from the cybercrime unit. The research absorbed her, numbing the pain of her loss. From the moment she first linked the new suspect to their old footage, she had guessed there must be more. She trawled through every cybercrime record she could find, building a picture of the people behind the attacks. Of course, there were tens of thousands of attacks happening daily; the world was awash with internet crime, malware, phishing, social engineering, and playful sprites looking for trouble. The cybercrime unit was overwhelmed with reports that had no solid perpetrator, whether the attack came from black hat experts coding for chaos or casual script kiddies launching stolen routines without considering the consequences. Sara Mercer was following the minority, the reports where there had been a criminal identified and prosecuted. How many could be linked to the dead man? How much of his life could she uncover, and would that lead to the source of the virus?

She found more evidence to link Jessie McCoy to both the new report and the man in the morgue. It was probably enough for an arrest without waiting for the full file. She pinged a message back to the cybercrime team; Jessie would be in custody before she finished her shift.

Derek Grace came up more than once in her searches. He had been identified, tried and convicted, and had also visited the office building with the dead stranger. The warrant to search the office was in place, and the visit was planned for the next day. Sara was staying on shift just to take part. She was looking forward to that job, deeply curious about what they might find.

A new file from another force caught her eye. An arrest in the north of England had been flagged up to the national cybercrime unit. She scanned the file. Aman Patel, 28, charged over impersonating a hardware engineer and tampering with a server in a secure data centre. He had been released on bail pending a hearing. Could this be related in any way?

She called through to the main office. "John? Could you run a search?"

John looked at the images, frowning. "It's heavy work running facial recognition without any kind of geographical fix," he replied. "How do you know he has anything to do with our man?"

"Call it a hunch," said Mercer. "Why not run a quick scan on that office building, and, say, King's Cross Station? Last six months?"

"I'm pretty sure he isn't in any of the office footage," he replied, "but I'll try the King's Cross concourse. It's a long shot, though. Don't we have phone records for this chap? It would be much easier to triangulate signals to pinpoint his movements in London, assuming he's been visiting here, and then run the facial recognition scans."

"Of course," said Mercer. "That makes a lot more sense. I'll get the force to send them through."

"Have we had anything useful from the landlord?" asked John. "I guess there was nothing useful from the search of his apartment."

"Not really," replied Mercer. "We haven't turned up any equipment or phones, if that's what you're thinking." She pulled up a series of images on her screen. "Here you go. Basic personal items, clothes and toiletries. There was a decent wallscreen and an apartment portal. The portal is under interrogation, but there's nothing incriminating coming out of it. He used it mainly for ordering takeaways and streaming e-sports and movies. He seems to have been a sports fan. He had a couple of pictures on the wall and a big MerLions mascot."

"MerLions? Great team," said John, grinning. "I follow them. They're touring, you know. My kid brother got to go to one of their live sessions. They played a friendly against the Salford Legends in front of thirty thousand fans. He said it was a real eye-opener. All the players were there, hooked up to the system, and the game play was cast in 3D right in the middle of the arena." He shook his head. "It sounded amazing."

"It seems strange for an e-sports team to tour," said Mercer, amused. "If they can pull crowds of that size to an event then I can see why they would do it, but surely their players are better known as avatars than as real people."

"Not the MerLions," said John proudly. "They have video channels dedicated to the players behind the game. They're household names and recognised in their home countries. There are a couple of African players who are leading on the water education project. The Singapore-based players do some great environmental work all around South East Asia..." His voice tailed off and he stared at Mercer. She made the same connection, and the blood drained from her face.

"South East Asia has an epidemic of Grasshopper Flu," she said flatly. "I want to know all about this tour."

John looked ashen. "The case in France? The news channel reported that it was a traveller who fell ill coming into the country. The MerLions have been all over Europe."

"Get onto it straight away. Find out who the casualty in France is, who he works for, and where he's been. Let me know what you find. I'd be surprised if the Department of Health hasn't already made the same connection. Get hold of their report."

"Do you think that might be the source of this infection? And linked to our man?"

"No question about it," said Mercer grimly. "It's too much of a coincidence. I think we're finally getting to the truth."

12: ENTRAPMENT

Jasvinder struggled to fit the unfamiliar key in the lock, but it turned without a hitch and the door opened. A flurry of excited squeaks heralded the arrival of the little black and white cat, hungry and eager for company. It paused when it saw Jasvinder, expecting Cameron, but relaxed as soon as he made his way towards the food cupboard. Weaving around his legs, the cat purred loudly. Jasvinder stopped and scratched its ears. "Stay still, cat. You nearly tripped me up there. Do you want feeding or not?"

He found the box of food and measured out a portion into the bowl. The cat had buried its face in the food and was scrotching happily before he had straightened up. He laughed at the pure joy emanating from the little animal.

"You were hungry, weren't you," he said. "Don't worry, I'll leave you some breakfast when you've finished that."

He flopped on the sofa and opened up his smartscreen, launching the game that was currently keeping him absorbed in idle moments. He noted that he had managed to sell one of his virtual long Samurai swords for a profit in the marketplace. That would give him enough credit to pick up a new short sword and shield for the next fight in the game. His avatar navigated through the fantasy world with ease, picking up tools and credits at every turn. He was so deep in the game that the cat startled him, jumping up on the sofa for a little attention. He turned and snapped a picture to send to Cameron, to prove that the cat had been fed. He was sure that the creature would plead starvation as soon as she got home.

A sound from the balcony surprised him, then he remembered Cameron's warning about stray drones with unwanted packages. He laughed at the cat who had frozen still in the middle of grooming, one leg over its head. Its eyes were wide and its ears flat.

"What have you ordered this time?"

The cat glanced at him, wide eyed, and bolted for the bedroom, tail fluffed up with adrenaline.

Jasvinder shrugged and went to the balcony doors, feeling for the familiar style of latch which secured all the windows in this block, including his own. He knew that Cameron had disabled the alarms for him. The apartment was three floors up and unlikely to attract casual visitors. The rain had finally stopped, and outside he could see the patient winking lights of a delivery drone, bright in the darkness. He opened the door and crouched to see what it had brought.

He sensed rather than saw the dark shape that swung at him. He rolled backwards through the doors and jumped smoothly to his feet without thinking, the shock helping years of training to kick in. For a moment he reeled as his brain caught up with his muscles. Was it another cat? A passing drone? Surely it wasn't a human.

A second later a figure crashed through the balcony doors and Jasvinder raised his hands in front of him and stepped one foot back automatically, flexing his legs ready to fight or fly. He moved backwards and sideways under a flurry of blows, blocking frantically as he twisted to avoid tripping on the sofa. He saw the glint of a blade.

Stepping sideways out of its path, he hit the arm away from him. He followed up with a blow to the back of the man's head, harder and stronger than he intended. Taking advantage of his attacker's momentary disorientation, he kicked low and accurately at a knee and the man collapsed to the floor. Jasvinder stamped firmly on the hand that held the knife. The man let go with a cry of pain and Jasvinder kicked the weapon away. It slid under the sofa.

He tried to hold the man down, but he was twisting and turning.

Jasvinder shouted at the portal, "Police!"

The portal wasn't coded to respond to his voice in normal circumstances, but it would recognise the heightened emotion and the standard emergency command. That would override authorised voice patterns to respond to anyone in need and bring the police to its location.

"Please stay calm," came a voice through the speaker. "Law enforcement services have been alerted and will reach you shortly."

Jasvinder was almost unbalanced as the man struggled beneath him. With his good hand he was flailing under the sofa, trying to reach the knife. Jasvinder started to wrestle the man's arm away, but he was too strong. Thinking quickly, he grabbed at the damaged hand instead, pulling backwards, trying to control his assailant on the floor. It worked. As the man turned in pain, Jasvinder managed to get a strong grip on him and a knee into the small of his back, pinning him to the floor. Every time the man struggled, Jasvinder simply pulled on his hand.

There was a buzzing from the direction of the window as the police drone arrived, hovering above the decoy on the balcony. Jasvinder smiled tiredly at it, knowing that the scene was being recorded. He didn't dare let his grip slacken, though, until he heard real voices in the hall outside.

"It's open," he shouted. In a ludicrous moment of clarity, his first concern was to avoid damage to Cameron's front door.

The officers held the man down and allowed Jasvinder to stand. He was still full of adrenaline, but he could feel that he was coming down fast.

"There's a knife under the sofa," he said quickly as he saw the man's arm flash out.

"Oh no you don't, my son," said a burly officer, lifting the man bodily from the floor. His colleague ducked down to check and nodded.

Jasvinder sat down on a nearby chair, suddenly weak. He watched the man being handcuffed and bundled out of the apartment by two large policemen, while another officer sent a small scene-of-crime robot under the sofa to record and recover the knife. The stillness and quiet as the officers went about their work was enough to reassure the cat that it was safe to come out. Jasvinder smiled with relief as a curious furry face peered around the door of the bedroom. The cat trotted up to him and jumped on his lap. He who feeds me is my friend, he thought. Calm now, he was ready when the attention turned to him.

"Now, sir, would you like to tell me what happened here?"

•

It was past midnight, and Ross was still working, plumbing the murky depths of the hacking underworld. On the other computer, safe in the shallows, Bordegiciel was also online, chatting on a direct message link. The idea that the theft of his company's Mars mission designs had been one operation pulled by a wide cybercrime syndicate had sparked his imagination. Ross wasn't about to invite Sébastien to the world that lay beneath: he was far too straight. Instead, he kept him updated on what he had learned, an explorer relaying messages from the void.

"Hey, RunningManTech, how do you stay secure down there? Don't they know who you are?"

"Different handle, different place. Have you ever heard the saying, 'He who pays the piper calls the tune'?"

Bordegiciel sent a shrug.

"In the old days, people paid. I was the piper, they called the tune. I'm still known as the Piper down there."

Ross flipped back to the other screen where ShellPixie had just pinged him a private message.

"Want some entertainment?" it read. "KingKatong is on the forum."

"*Thanks, Pix,*" he replied. "*I won't be visiting.*" He wasn't going near that forum again, not while Yasmin the Admin was in charge. It could be an innocent coincidence, but the name sent shivers down his spine. He wanted to know more, and opened a chat window. "What's he ranting about this time?"

"Still fixated on our girl," she replied. "I'm so made up to find SimCavalier is one of us. You ever come across her?"

"Heard the name, of course, but never crossed paths," lied Ross easily. "I always assumed it was a guy, too. Sorry, Pix."

"Hah, don't worry, I made the same mistake. Whoever she is, KK has it in for her. He's normally okay. He's a laugh when he's in a good mood. We don't coincide too often. I guess he's in a different time zone. It's odd for him to be on this late, and he's shouting about some kind of operation going wrong. It's not often the big guys lose out on a hack."

Ross filed that one away to pass to Cameron, but he had other questions for ShellPixie. "It's good that someone stands up to them, I guess," he ventured. "Pix, what do you know about Mars Attacks? Who called that tune?"

"Ah, Piper, we miss you. I heard some strong rumours about the Kalahari space program buying in resources. I know of five separate jobs, all hitting Mars mission suppliers."

Ross was stunned. "Where'd they get the coin for theft-to-order on that scale?"

"I've heard there's a big counterfeiting operation out there in the desert. They use the things they buy in for themselves and recycle the data back out for profit."

"You ever done a job for them, Pix?"

"One or two small things, but the rest is way out of my league. I'm independent. I'm not part of the syndicate. I don't want to go down that road."

"There's hope for you yet." Ross sent a gif of an angel, and a laughing face.

"What about you, Piper? Want some of this action?"

"No. I have other ways of putting bread on the table. I won't go back." He paused, then carried on typing. "Good to see you, Pix. Stay in touch. Let me know what you're doing. And thank you."

"Any time, Piper. Any time."

The chat window closed. Ross turned to the other computer. He had some news for Bordegiciel, and he needed to send Cameron a warning.

•

The message alert pinged a dozen times, and Cameron's second lazy morning ended abruptly. Relaxing for a rare few hours, she had been easily persuaded to set a full Do Not Disturb lock on her smart screen. After all, the people she cared about most were around her, and she didn't expect any calls. At the staccato tone of multiple messages, she sat up, startled, and beside her Ben was roused too.

"What's going on," he asked, surprised.

"No idea." Cameron scrambled out of bed and grabbed her screen. She scrolled through the notifications, her eyes wide. "What?" she exclaimed. "Ben, the police have been calling. And Jasvinder. And Ross."

"What's happened?" asked Ben, concerned.

She sat heavily on the bed, resisting the urge to call people before reading what they had sent. Jasvinder's message first, worried for the cat. Jasvinder knew her well enough and had sent a photograph. She relaxed.

"The cat is fine," she read, "but someone broke in to your apartment. I kicked his ass. Thank you for all the sparring practice. Police have been trying to reach you."

Cameron didn't know whether to laugh or cry. "*Just got this,*" she typed back, "*will call you ASAP. Are you okay?*"

She turned to the police messages and called them without delay. Yes, there had been a break-in. No, nothing had been stolen. Yes, her friend was unhurt but may have a few bruises. The apartment was secure, she was told, and the cat was in the care of her friend downstairs. Forensics had some work to do on a drone that was still on the balcony. Could Cameron, at her earliest convenience, come to the station and assist them with a statement and hopefully with identification of the suspect who was being held in custody. This afternoon would be ideal, they suggested firmly.

Cameron put her screen down and turned to Ben. "Back to London," she said ruefully.

He nodded, unsurprised. "We can stay at my place while they do what they need to do at yours." He got up and started to pack up his things, while Cameron headed downstairs to tell Charlie and Sameena the news.

"It's a shame you can't stay for lunch," said Sameena. "It's been a lovely weekend despite the rain. Nina will be sorry to miss you."

"I'll call her later," said Cameron. "We really have to go. I'm so sorry."

"No, it can't be avoided," said Charlie. "Dreadful news. Was it a random burglary, or do you think you've managed to annoy someone in your line of work?"

"Unlikely," replied Cameron. "You know yourself how hard I try to keep my personal details safe. Although…" she tailed off. "There may have been a leak. I'm following it up. I'm sure it's not connected."

Charlie gave her a serious look. "Be safe, Cam. Sometimes you underestimate your importance."

Cameron smiled at her brother. "Thanks, Charlie. Can I ask you a favour? There aren't many trains running today. Can I take your car? I'll send it back as soon as we get home."

"Even better, why don't I take you myself?" Charlie brightened up. "That way I can be sure that you get home without any drama. I'll be back in time for lunch if we hurry."

"Brilliant. Give us half an hour to get ready." Cameron scampered upstairs to the shower, and Charlie grabbed Roxy's lead to take the dog out for a quick walk in the weak sunlight that was finally penetrating the rainclouds.

•

DI Mercer's shift had finished, but she wasn't planning on going home. She wanted to see this investigation to its end, to find out what was in the remote office building, and where the connection lay between the dead man and the MerLions. The Superintendent found her still in her office, drinking a strong cup of coffee while it was still hot, and purring with pleasure over a report that had come in from their colleagues south of the river.

"What have you got now?" he asked.

"Pure gold," said Mercer. "A man was arrested last night at an address near London Bridge. He entered an apartment and attacked an innocent visitor to the property. The visitor was well versed in martial arts and he subdued the intruder until police arrived."

"Good for him," said the Superintendent, mystified. "What's the connection?"

"The apartment is the home of Cameron Silvera, owner of Argentum Associates, employer of Ross White. The intruder has been identified as one Jun Kai Lee, a Singapore national whose records show he is a security operative with Bay Promotions, the organisers of the MerLions

European tour." She finished with a flourish and sat back, sipping her coffee. Her dark eyes danced.

"Does that prove a link between the dead man and the MerLions?" asked the Superintendent, pressing for more.

"We don't have proof of the direct link yet, but we've received details of the French case of Grasshopper Flu, including the patient's phone records. John is running facial recognition scans for the dead man now that we have some geographical and timing data to narrow down the search. The cybercrime link was already established through the historical connections, and as an added bonus we've managed to link our stranger with a young man arrested up north for data theft. This Argentum bunch are at the top of their game in cybersecurity. It's a clear triangle of connections. White and Silvera have almost certainly been targeted because of their involvement in thwarting cyberattacks."

"Good. What's your next move?"

"We're actioning the search warrant on the office building today," replied Mercer, "and I think we have enough evidence to detain Jessie McCoy on suspicion of aiding and abetting data theft."

"Excellent work, Sara." Her boss smiled sadly. "Ivan would be proud of you."

•

The plush family autocar swept Charlie, Ben and Cameron down the broad highway towards London. Inside, the three of them were howling with laughter.

"There was poor Andy on top of the ladder clearing his guttering," said Charlie, "and he had nowhere to go. Donald had climbed all the way up behind him and was wittering at a bird on the roof. Andy couldn't come down because the bloody cat is so huge that he was blocking the step. It was lucky that Roxy and I came along the road or they'd have been up there for hours."

"How did you get him down?" asked Cameron.

"I thought Roxy might scare him off the ladder, but she's a coward. She won't face up to Donald. I climbed up and grabbed him in the end." He raised his hand and showed a fresh scratch. "War wound. Andy owes me a pint tonight."

"That looks sore." Cameron examined her brother's hand critically.

"It's fine. Sameena sprayed it. I can't feel a thing."

Cameron glanced at the time. "Nina may be awake by now. I'll give her a call." She picked up her screen and tapped Nina's number, but the call rang out. No reply.

"Still asleep? It's late. She should be on her way home by now." Charlie frowned. "Lucy's mum is normally very good at keeping those girls in order."

Ben spoke up. "What did Ross want, Cameron? Did you check his message in all the excitement?"

Cameron put her hand to her mouth. "No. I completely forgot." She scrolled through the notifications again. "I'd better call him. This makes no sense."

Ross took a few rings to answer. "Morning, Cameron," he yawned. He looked tired. "Late night, sorry. Did you get my message?"

"I did. What's going on?"

"Plenty. I've been talking to my shady mates. You need to watch your back, Cameron. Someone out there knows who you are and doesn't like you much. The handle's KingKatong. Ring any bells?"

"No, not at all," said Cameron, horrified. "Look, Ross, something happened last night that may be related. My apartment was broken into. I'm on my way back to London to talk to the police."

Ross was obviously shocked. "That's crazy, Cameron. What a good thing you weren't there. Although, come to think about it," he continued with a grin, "you'd have taken them down, no problem."

"I didn't have to. One of my training buddies was feeding the cat at the time. The intruder is in custody."

"Nice one." Ross nodded in approval. "I have some other juicy gossip for you. For a start, Ben's company wasn't the only Mars mission supplier to be hacked recently. Rumour has it that a setup in southern Africa commissioned that and others. It sounds like there is a big syndicate deep down in the dark taking orders for some juicy thefts, attacks and general mayhem."

"I'm not surprised," said Cameron. "All the evidence Ella and Noor gathered was pointing that way. How do you think Joseph Hardy's doppelganger fits in to this?"

"Yasmin?" said Ross with a shudder. "I don't know why, but I think it's right in the middle of everything we've been dealing with over the past few weeks."

"Ross, are you training today?" asked Cameron.

"Yes, but much later. Shall I meet you after you've been to the police?"

"Good idea. Call me when you're ready." She disconnected and stared at Ben and Charlie. "Did you get all of that?"

The two of them nodded soberly. "What are you mixed up in, Cam?" asked Charlie. "Where is this going to go?"

She couldn't answer. She looked helplessly at her brother and her boyfriend and realised that both were assuming that they had to keep her safe. "Don't worry about me," she said earnestly. "It will be alright."

They didn't look convinced.

The car continued in silence. They had reached the leafy garden cities that marked the current outer limits of the ever-expanding capital. It was dull and cloudy outside, the early sunlight gone.

They all jumped when Charlie's phone rang on the car's audio. They heard Sameena's voice, panicky and urgent. "Charlie? Nina has gone."

"Pull over," Charlie shouted at the car. It ducked onto the hard shoulder and stopped. "Sameena, what's happened?"

She was beside herself. "I called Lucy's mother because I couldn't reach Nina. She said that she put Nina in an autocar herself to send her home, but there's no sign of her or the car."

"Which autocar company?" asked Charlie, aghast.

"One I hadn't heard of. Yascars. Lucy's mother said it was a new one. I can't find anything about them. I don't know who to call."

Cameron gasped, and Ben took her hand. Charlie was pale, the blood draining from his face. On the screen, tears were rolling down Sameena's cheeks. She wiped her eyes with the back of her hand. "I don't know what to do."

"I'm coming back now," said Charlie, shaking, "and you need to call the police." He looked at Cameron. "I'm sorry. This is more important."

Cameron nodded, shocked, her mind churning. "Wait," she cried. "I set up her chip yesterday, Charlie. I set up her location services." She scrabbled at her screen. "I was going to give you access today. Look!" She turned the screen around. Blinking slowly in the middle of a map was a small pink marker. "That's her."

Charlie didn't hesitate. "Patch that through to the navigation, Cam. Sameena, I am going to get our daughter. Be strong, love." He turned to his sister and Ben. "Buckle up," he said grimly. "Emergency mode," he barked at the car. The vehicle set off on its new course at speed, transmitting a priority signal to other autocars on the road which pulled over automatically to let them pass.

Cameron called Ross. "Change of plan. Can you grab a car and follow us? Track my screen. I think my niece is in danger and that Yasmin is somehow involved." He nodded, but Cameron didn't give him a chance to reply before hanging up. She brought the map back onto the screen and the three of them watched the blinking dot as the car sped onwards.

•

Mercer stepped into the back of the police vehicle and sat with the rest of the search team. She was excited to know what they might find at the office building. The car set off slowly through the light weekend traffic, navigating out towards the location that their investigations had pinpointed. After almost an hour of driving they reached a small business park. Blank office windows reflected the grey clouds in the sky. A small grove of wind turbines stood behind the buildings, the blades still. There was barely any breeze. Solar panels on the south-facing pitches were dull, and weeds grew in clumps where the builders had landscaped the park, but the owners had failed to maintain it. Only a few of the buildings bore signs, the rest almost certainly empty.

"This is the place," said John with absolute certainty.

Mercer recognised the building from the CCTV images. She looked around, and sure enough there was a battered camera on top of a streetlight overlooking the office.

There was a small sign outside the target building. Holding up her screen, Mercer zoomed in on the text. Bay Holdings (Singapore), it read. She almost laughed out loud.

"This is definitely the place."

The team organised themselves quietly, making ready to approach. As they were poised to open the doors of the vehicle, the operator held up a warning hand. "Wait. Stand down."

What now?

"There's been a development," continued the operator. "Missing person report. Control has been tracking the parents who are tracking the child by chip. They look to be heading in our direction. ETA three minutes. Control is patching through the data now."

On the vehicle's briefing screen, a dot appeared, closing in rapidly on their location.

Mercer acted quickly. "John, jump out and intercept them round the corner. If there is anyone in that office, we don't want to have the public rock up and disturb them." She looked at the operator. "Do we have a name for the missing youngster?"

"Yes ma'am. Nina Silvera, aged twelve."

Mercer winced. "Oh, no. Poor kid. I don't like the way this is all coming together. Is she related to Cameron Silvera? That's an unusual name, so it's very likely."

There was a pause as the operator made a cursory search. "Niece," he said succinctly.

John came back into view, followed by four adults. She stepped out of the vehicle and greeted them.

"Mr White," She exclaimed, surprised, as she shook hands with Ross.

"Ben," said Ben, extending his hand in turn. "and this is Cameron."

"Ms Silvera, in any other circumstances it would have been a pleasure to meet you," said Mercer. She looked at the older man, obviously Cameron's brother. "You must be Nina's father. I am so sorry to hear about your daughter's disappearance."

"You moved fast," said Charlie. "Thank you for coming so promptly. How did you get here before us?"

"Pure luck. We have a warrant to search that building." She indicated the shabby office. "It looks as if you have tracked your daughter to that same location."

"What are we waiting for," said Charlie. "Let's get her out."

"We're ready," said John. "If you could wait here, please."

"Can I come with you?" asked Ross. "I think I can help. You may come across something unexpected in there."

DI Mercer's attention sharpened. "What do you mean?"

Ross took a deep breath. "You know about Hardy's?" He had to assume that Mercer was fully aware of everything that had happened. She would have seen the report that Noor had passed to the cybercrime unit.

"Yes, Mr White. We have Jessie McCoy in custody," she replied.

It was Ross's turn to look surprised, but he pressed further. "You know about the doppelganger as well?"

Mercer nodded. "Yes. Perhaps you should come. Stay behind the officers."

They approached the building quietly and quickly, passing with only a short delay through secure doors to a featureless, cream-tiled lobby. They could hear voices.

"It's okay, we're not going to hurt you," said a woman's voice.

Ross glanced at Mercer.

"Doppelganger?" she mouthed.

Ross shrugged. He had never heard the AI speak.

The next voice took his breath away. "We wish to speak to your aunt. She will be here soon."

There was a whimper. Nina. Ross's heart went out to her and he felt the anger rising inside him. They shouldn't have involved a child. He saw Mercer nod and the door burst open. Inside was a windowless room, sparsely furnished with just two chairs and a table. A slim dark girl was sitting on one chair, her arms pinned behind her back. A wallscreen was glowing but there was no picture. A man stood in the corner of the room, mouth open in shock.

It was over in a moment. Nina was released and bundled out of the room to be reunited with her father. Handcuffs clicked on the man in the corner. Ross stared at him, furious.

"Hardy," he spat.

Mercer looked liked the cat that had got the cream. "Joseph Hardy?"

The man nodded, flushed with anger.

"I'm arresting you on suspicion of kidnap and aiding and abetting the theft of data." She looked up at John. "Take him away."

There was a shout from one of the officers. "Out the back!"

Ross heard a scuffle and running feet, but a few moments later slower steps returning to the building announced that the quarry had fled.

Mercer turned to Ross. "Well, Mr White. Thank you. You presented a real mystery, and you've helped us to solve it in the end."

"It isn't the end," said Ross. He approached the monitor. "Hello?" he whispered. There was no response. "Yasmin?" whispered Ross again. There was a faint blue glow on the screen.

Mercer's eyes widened.

Ross acted fast. He swept his hand over the screen and expertly opened the settings. The glow faded and the system powered down.

"It's okay," he said aloud. "No one there now."

"It was listening?"

"Oh yes. Yasmin was right there with us all the time. Gone now." He tapped at the dormant screen, thinking. "Let's make sure. Come with me."

They went outside, past a distressed Nina in the arms of her father and aunt.

"I got in the car and the doors just locked," she sobbed. "I tried to call you and my screen wouldn't work."

Ross caught Cameron's eye. She glanced at the building and he nodded. She knew he was dealing with Yasmin. Ross scanned the outside walls carefully and eventually found a discreet cable leading to the main web connections.

Mercer understood straight away. "John, get some wire cutters."

The connection severed, Ross rebooted the system in the office. He scanned through the screen's history, digging into the detail of its connections, and smiled in satisfaction at the haul of data.

"Here you go," he said. "A lot of these will be fake, but they are the recorded IP addresses of every connection to this screen. If you check, I think you'll find that last one traces back to Hardy's." He flashed a rare smile at Mercer. "This is the end."

•

Of course, it wasn't the end of the war, Ross reflected much later, but it marked the end of a battle. As they sat outside the courtroom waiting for the verdict on Joseph Hardy's activities, they pieced together the events of the past few weeks.

"How is Nina coping," asked Noor sympathetically.

Cameron looked unusually vulnerable for a moment. "She's much better. I never told her that her chip was compromised. I managed to completely reset it."

"How did they get her details so quickly after the chipping?" said Andy, mystified. "I understand what you say about the car, that as soon as it confirmed her identity it took her to Yasmin, but how did they manage it?"

"The MerLions private fan forum," said Cameron flatly. "She said she'd had to authenticate membership with her chip. I assumed it was a security feature on the community. I should have checked."

There was a sound of clicking heels on the marble floor of the old courtrooms as DI Mercer approached, neat and smart. "Ms Silvera, Mr White. It's good to see you all. I'm glad you could come today. I think they're ready to start."

Pete stood up, tall and steady. His legs and his lungs had healed and he was enjoying life again, but he knew how much the Grasshopper Flu had cost this woman.

"DI Mercer," he said, extending a hand. "It's good to meet you at last. I'm so sorry for your loss."

Sara Mercer shook his hand and he saw the pain that was still raw in her eyes. "Thank you," she said softly. "I do miss my colleague." She sighed. "You were very lucky, Mr Iveson. Of three cases, here and in France, you are the only survivor."

There was a respectful silence, which Ross broke. "Did you manage to link the cases?" he asked.

"Oh yes," replied Mercer. "The patient in France was positively identified meeting with the man who broke into your property, Mr White. And of course, Ms Silvera, with the man who broke into your apartment, too."

"What about Jessie?" asked Cameron.

Mercer gave a thin smile. "She has been very helpful. The kidnapping shocked her to the core. She had a lot of inside knowledge about the network of hackers and their activities but seems to have been completely unaware that her own boss was at the head of the operation."

"Everything leads back to Hardy, doesn't it?" said Sandeep. "And Yasmin. What have you done with Yasmin?"

"Yasmin," repeated Mercer with a sigh. "She is quarantined on a single secure server. Her…" She stumbled and corrected herself. "Its case is now with Parliament. Is it sentient? Would switching it off violate its rights? Would that, in effect, be murder?"

"Tough call," said Joel pragmatically. "I wouldn't want to be the one that makes it."

The doors of the courtroom opened and Mercer straightened her skirt. "Let's go."

•

Tenuk stared out of the aeroplane window into the darkness. He had mixed emotions going back home to the cool tunnels of Singapore. He had never expected to come so close to the SimCavalier, but his hastily executed plan to entrap her using her niece had backfired terribly and delivered his English network co-ordinator straight into the hands of the British law enforcement agencies. He had lost two valued senior colleagues, first Hardy, then his fellow countryman who had succumbed to the viral scourge that stalked South East Asia. There had been the usual wastage of contractors on the operation, of course, but there were always unscrupulous hackers ready to take their place for the right price. He sighed. On the other hand, he had met an extraordinary woman who lightened his heart. He wanted to get to know her better. Tenuk opened up his screen and started writing. "Dear Noor…"

ACKNOWLEDGEMENTS

Thanks are due once again to David Morton of www.itsw.com who keeps my flights of technical fantasy in check. Plenty of people have encouraged me through writing this second adventure. I'm grateful for the advice and experience passed on by established authors Gillie Hatton, Samantha Hayes, and David Brin, and thanks to all the friends who read Bitcoin Hurricane and surprised me by asking for more tales about Cameron and her team. Finally, thanks to Xavier, Gaelle and Loïc who have gamely put up with me disappearing with my laptop when inspiration strikes.

Many of the locations in this book are real or close to reality, others imagined or disguised. There is a real data centre in the north of England with a glass ceiling. It lies in an old chapel close to the site of a now-vanished brewery, and the flickering lights, seen from the conference room above, are as mesmerising as Cameron finds them here.

TANGLED FORTUNES
SIMCAVALIER BOOK THREE

1: NORTHERN LIGHTS

Daniel peered over the edge of the ditch, moving as slowly as possible to avoid the attention of the security scanners and motion detectors that lined the site. He tugged at his heat-shielded body suit, trying to relieve the irritation of patches of material that were sticking awkwardly. The stealthy, sweaty crawl through the network of drainage channels that criss-crossed the salt marshes had been harder than before. The weather was turning after an uncharacteristic cold snap and the coast basked in a burst of springtime warmth. Now that the sun was setting it was cooler at last, and sharp shadows cast by the surface infrastructure of deep mine workings shielded Daniel's hiding place from human eyes. This was the perfect time of day to make his move, when cameras and infra-red scanners could barely detect him, and the human night shift workers were arriving to take over from tired colleagues. He stiffened as a surveillance drone caught his eye, then relaxed as it passed him by without a jitter. His cover was good.

A commotion a few hundred metres further along the perimeter startled him. Someone else hidden in the marshes had not been so careful. Hunkering down in his ditch, Daniel heard the whine of drones and the shouts of a guard. His own rapid heartbeat was echoing in his ears. The noises faded quickly as the chase moved away from his hiding place. Tonight was his lucky night.

He risked lifting his head, his features in shadow and the hood of his suit pulled tight over his forehead. The landfill site rose above him, once an abandoned grassy knoll overlooking the sea, now torn open on the promise of fortunes to be mined. From the tall steel frames, deep drilling rigs sought compacted materials and extracted valuable gases. On the surface, huge scanner robots quartered the area in search of more recently dumped treasures, their heavy tank chassis and caterpillar tracks leaving imprints in the soft ground and their headlights casting other-worldly beams of light across the ravaged landscape. In their wake scurried swarms of burrowing miner ferrets, tiny but powerful machines taking their cues from the myriad sensors in the roving scanner bot and diving down through the tangle of decades-old waste to retrieve ancient electronic devices, broken glass, discarded metal and lost heirlooms.

Daniel watched carefully as one of the huge vehicles approached his hiding place. He breathed steadily as it filled his vision, confident in his positioning from months of practice. Sure enough, as it reached the perimeter of the current mining area it turned smoothly away from him, moving back up the hill. He was close enough to hear the rustle of the accompanying swarm of miner ferrets as they gyrated and burrowed behind the scanner, emerging fully laden and scurrying to deposit their finds in the vehicle's trailing hopper. He relaxed, surprised to feel tension melting from his shoulders.

A breeze blew across the disturbed landfill and the sickly-sweet smell of rotting garbage and methane assailed his senses. He gagged and wrestled briefly with a rising nausea. This was not the time to get sick. There was work to do.

Reaching for a dark waterproof pouch slung around his body, Daniel pulled at the fastenings and carefully reached inside to find his own captive ferret. The movement woke it from sleep mode, and he set it down carefully on the lip of the ditch. The little machine sat ready, a faint LED blinking on its rump. He tapped it gently and the ferret set off across the uneven ground. It crossed the perimeter and joined the swarm, undetected. Burrowing with its fellows, it tapped into the same tangle of data which led the swarm to rich pickings, but unlike the others, it trundled back towards Daniel every time it surfaced.

Tonight's haul was typically varied. Daniel lingered over a discarded silvery ring, still bright after years starved of oxygen, before dropping it into the pouch for safekeeping. A clutch of crushed aluminium drinks cans glinted in the moonlight and Daniel fretted until they were safely gathered, afraid as always that a ferret going in quite the wrong direction would be picked up by cameras and singled out for investigation. The cans must have been destined for recycling years before but dropped by accident into a landfill collector. They could be smelted easily, and the metal re-used. A dozen mismatched audio pods, earpieces from cordless headphones dropped carelessly over the years, would add to his growing collection. He was keeping those safe until there were enough to make it worthwhile for someone to recover and sell the hidden neodymium.

The last find of the evening was an ancient computer hard drive, encased in a large and unwieldy plastic housing. The ferret struggled to drag it back to its master, catching on tufts of grass, and Daniel held his breath as it approached. That would be enough for now. He disabled the ferret and tucked it back into the top of the now-full pouch, watching the rest of the swarm drift away in pursuit of the scanner robot. The big vehicle crested the top of the hill, following the rest of the machines that had already disappeared to another part of the massive site. The light it cast faded as it moved to quarter the next sector on its round, and Daniel lay back in the ditch, content, looking up at the dark sky. As his eyes adjusted, he saw the familiar constellations twinkling. The night was clear and cooling rapidly. It was time to go, but on the edge of his vision Daniel was stilled by a glimpse of colour in the sky. Waves of green light washed the far horizon as he gazed in wonder. The Northern Lights were putting on an unforgettable show.

It was late when Daniel arrived home. The house was in darkness, but as he pushed the door open, he felt a rush of warmth and heard an animated voice, snatches of conversation, and low laughter.

"Michelle?" he called. There was no answer. Daniel switched on the light and put the pouch containing the ferret and its finds on a low table. He stripped off his body suit, cursing as he hopped and kicked to loosen the grip of the material around his foot. Finally free, he dropped the stinking suit on the floor and slumped gratefully onto the battered, threadbare sofa. Raising his voice, he called again. "Michelle?"

The voice from the other room quickened, the conversation obviously ending, and Daniel heard movement. The door opened and his cousin appeared, bundled up in warm pyjamas, her dark hair messy.

"You're back late," she said, yawning. "Everything okay?"

"Security was tight," replied Daniel. "Someone else was picked up by the drones just along the perimeter." He shivered. "It's cold out there now, and the sky is incredibly clear. I saw the Northern Lights, Shell. So beautiful."

Michelle gave him a wry smile. "Sounds fabulous. I'm glad you're okay. Any idea who they caught?"

Daniel shook his head. "I was deep in my ditch. I didn't see much. I'm sure we'll hear on the grapevine."

Michelle walked towards the sofa and Daniel hurriedly swung his legs off the cushion and kicked the discarded suit out of her path. She flopped down beside him. "What did our little ferret pick up this time?"

Daniel leaned over to the table and grabbed the pouch. "Here," he said. "Have a look."

Michelle took it from him, holding it at arm's length. "Ugh, that stinks," she complained, wrinkling her nose in disgust. She fumbled at the fastenings, opened it, reached inside, and pulled out the ferret. Daniel took it from her.

"It needs more juice," he said. He stretched across to the charging pad, cleared a space among a scattering of other devices, and put the ferret down carefully. Its LED light flicked on.

Michelle dug deeper and pulled the bulky plastic case out of the pouch, turning it in her hands.

"Is this what I think it is?" She fumbled with the catch and popped the housing open. Inside lay the hard disk.

"Not bad, huh?" said Daniel. "The case seems to have protected it. It looks like just another piece of landfill plastic."

"That may pay our rent," replied Michelle. She looked thoughtful. "Don't get rid of it yet, unless we really have to. Let me have a go at interrogating it first. You never know what might be stored on there."

Daniel laughed. "You can take the girl out of hacking, but you can't take the hacking out of the girl. I'll try and hook it up for you. It's probably wiped, or corrupted, or both."

"This is just like Christmas, but smellier," said Michelle with a giggle. She pulled out the cluster of cans and set them aside, then dug down into the corners of the pouch. "What's this? A ring? Nice." She ran her fingers around the inside. "It's hallmarked," she said. "And there's a stone."

Daniel took it from her. "Well spotted. It's clear – it could be a diamond. I thought the metal was silver, but I'm not so sure. I'll have to check the mark."

"Platinum?" said Michelle speculatively. "That would be a good night's work."

"It would be an amazing night's work if it really is platinum," replied Daniel. "As for the other stuff, the cans should get a decent price straight away. I found a few audio pods as well, but I don't think we have enough to sell on yet." His smile faded, sober for a moment. "Good nights like this are getting few and far between, and the security is tighter all the time. It's not really a sustainable lifestyle choice, Shell."

"I heard they were advertising for a lot of new staff on the industrial parks," suggested Michelle. "They're getting on with decommissioning a reactor at the power station, and some of the chemical plants are shutting down for a major maintenance cycle. The money's good."

Daniel gave Michelle a sidelong look. "My security records will probably need reviewing. You've covered your tracks here, haven't you? No one will link you to this address?"

Michelle nodded. "As far as the authorities are concerned, I'm a long way away. I'll do a scan on your records and make sure nothing odd gets thrown up." She stood up decisively. "I want a hot chocolate. You?"

"Oh, yes please," replied Daniel, shivering despite the warmth of the sofa. Michelle headed for the kitchen, and Daniel leaned back on the cushions and reached for his smartscreen. He scrolled through notifications and news until he found the snippet he was searching for.

"Found it," he called. "The chemical plants are all short-term shut-down contracts. The power station jobs look more interesting. They're looking for security staff and electricians." He read further. "How about this, Shell? IT networking and cybersecurity." There was a snort of laughter from the kitchen. Daniel smiled to himself. "That would be the perfect job for you," he insisted, struggling to keep a straight face.

"Don't be silly," Michelle shouted over the sound of clattering mugs, amused. "Why don't you have a quick shower," she continued. "You stink."

Daniel jumped up from the sofa, reinvigorated by laughter. "You're right. Give me five minutes." He picked up the suit and carried it away with him to the bathroom.

Ten minutes later he emerged, wrapped in his favourite MerLions hoodie and sweatpants. Michelle was sitting in the kitchen. "Come and get your chocolate," she called.

Daniel joined her at the table and took a sip of his drink. "That's good," he sighed. He pulled out his screen and brought up the list of jobs again. "Let's have another look at the options. Are you sure you don't want to try for one of these?"

"There's no way I'd get close to the IT jobs, even if I tried," said Michelle. "Even I would struggle to fake the level of detail they need for a new security clearance, and it wouldn't take them long to identify me." She gazed blankly into space, thinking. "Making sure you can get a job, no problem. For me? I'll keep trawling for contracts wherever I can find them."

Daniel looked sidelong at her. "Be careful, Shell. Don't get mixed up in anything dodgy."

Michelle smiled innocently. "Of course not. Trust me."

•

Noor Khawaja stepped carefully out of the taxi and looked up at a wide banner stretched across the front of the hotel: 'CyberFest Annual Awards'.

A steady stream of autocars disgorged smartly dressed passengers onto the pavement. Taking a deep breath, Noor joined the throng, passing under the old portico and into an elegant, opulent lobby, a reminder of the hotel's rich history. She looked around, hunting for familiar faces, and quickly spotted Pete head and shoulders above the crowd. She battled her way across to the mirrored alcove where her colleagues were gathering. Pete waved to her as she dodged around groups of chattering delegates and waiter bots bearing canapés and champagne.

Cameron and Ben had already arrived, she saw, as had Joel and Martha. Ella and Ross were deep in animated conversation, pausing only to allow a passing bot to refill their glasses. Noor watched as Ella hesitated over a tray of sushi, scanning it with her smartscreen to check the sustainable source of the tuna. She nodded, satisfied, and she and Ross each selected a piece.

"Noor, you look fabulous." Susie grasped her hand, wobbling slightly as her impossibly high heels dug into the thick carpet pile.

"You too, Susie," said Noor warmly. Susie really did look fabulous, a vision of gold shimmers and a long skirt split to mid-thigh. Noor looked critically at her own more conservative outfit in the mirror.

Pete caught her eye and winked. "You won't be the one breaking an ankle tonight," he whispered.

"That's not nice, Peter," scolded Noor. She looked him up and down. "You've scrubbed up well. This is quite the event, isn't it?" She glanced around at the assembled group. "Where's Sandeep?"

"He's coming now," said Pete, pointing over the crowd. Sandeep was strolling towards them, neck craned as he admired the ornate vaulted ceiling. He bumped into a waiter bot that ducked and rebalanced expertly, not a drop spilled.

A bell rang over the clamour of the crowd and people began to move more purposefully towards the banqueting hall. Cameron looked up. "Time to go," she said. "Anyone know where our table is?"

"Halfway down on the right-hand side," said Ross. He gave her a sidelong look and decided it was safe to tease. "Tucked away in the shadows, just as the SimCavalier likes it."

Cameron scowled at him, and Ross laughed. "I'm impressed you're out tonight," he said. "See, being well known isn't all bad."

Cameron shrugged and gave him a resigned smile. "I don't think I have a choice these days. We're among friends, though, and it should be a fun night." She took Ben's hand. "Come on. Let's do this."

The crowd swept them along through the doors of the hall, and they settled at their table. A green light flashing on the tabletop scanner indicated that the immediate area was clear of listening devices and network bugs, and that smartscreen communications outside the hall were disabled. Above them a swarm of camera drones circled, recording the event under strict conditions. Cameron watched them carefully to confirm that her privacy settings were being observed. She was sure that whatever happened she would never shake the habit of keeping a low profile, and as she looked around the banqueting hall, she quickly realised that she wasn't the only guest shy of publicity. The camera drones were moving in a complex pattern around the room and avoiding several tables altogether. Cameron spotted some familiar faces whose work on cybercrime she knew and respected. She relaxed visibly for the first time that evening. Ben's eyes met hers, and he raised his glass in a silent toast.

•

High above them, hundreds of nano satellite swarms sat in low earth orbit. Sensors scanned the landscape as it rotated steadily below, feeding petabytes of complex data back down the line to huge storage clouds, ready for the machines to sift and analyse. Artificial intelligences would learn from patterns hidden deep in the data, defining what was expected and normal and identifying new trends and deviations as they occurred. It was one such satellite swarm that passed over the east coast of Russia as the earth heaved and rippled outwards from a central point. The accompanying electro-magnetic pulse reached the swarm in a fraction of a second, rendering the tiny satellites useless and adding to the litter of space junk which circled the planet.

The sudden loss of a data feed sent automated systems searching in vain for meteor activity, but the reports from the next swarm to pass the site escalated the event to red alert. The atmosphere showed heightened radiation readings and temperature changes. The contours of the landscape had shifted, vegetation was scattered, and sensors showed water table evaporation. Alarms started ringing through the upper echelons of friendly and hostile powers. Diagnostic routines whirred into action, and the spike in activity triggered news bots to deep dive the data set. As coded alerts spread out from the data centres the overwhelming response was shock and horror, for all but certain parties who felt quiet satisfaction at a job well done and a long-term project reaching a major milestone.

Andrew Taylor's notifications lit up his screen as he relaxed at home, sprawled on the sofa with a glass of scotch in hand and enjoying an old film which had popped up on his recommendations. His first glance was lazy, resigned. Surely Giles could deal with any breaking news. At the second look he sat up suddenly, dislodging Boris the tabby cat from its cosy spot on his lap. The cat shook itself and stalked off, twitching its tail. Andy ignored it, scrolling through the automatic alerts from the bots and more detailed messages from Giles, busy in the news channel offices, with growing concern.

"Mute," he barked at the wallscreen. The film images continued to flicker, and in the sudden silence he placed a call to his assistant.

"Evening, Giles," he said. There was no need for any preamble. "What's the mood out there?"

"Evening, Andy," replied Giles. "There aren't any mainstream reports live yet. No one's claimed responsibility but – wait." He paused. "There's been a strong denial from North Korea and a statement has just come through from the Kremlin as well."

"I'd be very surprised if any nation state was behind this," replied Andy. "My best hunch is that it's linked to the cyber attack on that Chinese power plant last year."

"I agree," said Giles. "They still haven't worked out who was behind that, but there are a few insurgent groups in the frame."

"Well, if it is, I think this'll be the first non-state nuclear test since the Aum doomsday cult in Australia. When was that?"

"Mid-1990s," said Giles quickly. "I've already checked the files."

"Good lad. Have you got a piece ready to go?"

"Just about," replied Giles. "It's still a bit thin."

"Can you give me fifteen minutes?"

"Sure."

"I'm going to try and get a quote from Cameron. She's out at the CyberFest shindig but I'm sure I'll be able to get her attention. That'll give us a strong angle ahead of the other networks. I'll come back to you before you go live." He cut the line without waiting for a reply and placed a call direct to the London hotel that was hosting the industry's most prestigious awards dinner.

•

Robot waiters sped into the banqueting hall bearing the first course, and the volume of chatter in the room rose over the chink of cutlery. Cameron forked up a bite of the terrine, locally produced fish pressed with vegetables from the hotel's own rooftop gardens. She savoured the fresh taste and watched her colleagues around the table with fondness. Ross was in his element, basking in the glow of the team's award nomination and posing for photographs with a star struck fan who had recognised him as a leading triathlete. Joel was chatting easily with Sandeep, and Pete and Noor were deep in conversation. Susie had snapped a picture of the elegantly presented plate and was now eating in silence, her face betraying no emotion while Ella and Martha laughed over a shared joke. Cameron sighed inwardly. The friction between Ella and Susie had been bubbling for some time, but both were valuable team members. She didn't want to lose either of them over a failed relationship.

"You're looking very serious," said Ben. "You should be having fun. Relax. Everyone is having a good time."

"They should be," said Cameron. "They're a hell of a team, Ben." She took a swig of her wine. "What makes you think I'm not relaxed?"

"You're jumping every time a drone flies past," he said, "and that's my drink you just finished."

Cameron looked at the empty glass in her hand and the full one on the table and laughed. "Touché." She reached to the middle of the table, grabbed a bottle of white from the cooler, and poured Ben a refill. "There you go," she said. She nodded towards Susie, who was sitting next to him looking lonely. "See what's up," she said, "I'm hungry."

Ben turned to talk to Susie who brightened gratefully. Cameron finished her food and gazed thoughtfully at the empty stage where the awards ceremony would take place. She was jerked out of her reverie by a smartly dressed staff member who appeared discreetly at her shoulder.

"Ms Silvera? Urgent message for you." He held out his ID card and Cameron glanced at the details. There was no point trying to verify the card here at the table with no web connection to the identity blockchain, but everything seemed in order, and at this event of all things, any possible security breaches would have been anticipated and stopped dead.

"If you could come with me?" He gestured towards the foyer.

Mystified, Cameron slid out of her chair and followed the man to the main door. The swarm of camera drones swerved to avoid her, but no one else seemed to notice. As soon as she moved clear of the communications block, she felt the faint vibration of her smart screen in the pocket of her dress as notifications streamed in.

"What was the message?" she asked.

"A gentleman by the name of Andrew Wilson," said the concierge.

"He said that once you were connected you would know why he called." The man gave Cameron an almost imperceptible half-bow, an anachronistic touch which seemed to fit with the opulence of the old hotel, then returned to his desk.

Cameron pulled her smartscreen out of her pocket and looked around for somewhere to sit. She ruled out the bar stools – impossible in that dress – then spotted a high wing-backed armchair by the ornate stone fireplace. She sat down and began to scroll through her screen. The notifications were coming from obscure forums and from a few automated early warning services that she followed, and it took her a moment to make sense of the story they were telling. As the pieces fell into place, she felt a mounting sense of horror.

Her screen flashed with an incoming call signal and she accepted instantly.

"Andy?"

"Cameron."

"What's going on?"

Andy sighed. "Reports have just started coming in. I wondered why you weren't on the line straight away, then realised that connections must be locked down at your dinner. I probably know as much as you. There's been an underground nuclear detonation in eastern Russia, somewhere near Vladivostok and the borders with China and North Korea. The details are sketchy, but this has to be connected."

Cameron nodded vigorously, forgetting they were on a voice-only call. "You're right. The uranium that everyone suspected was stolen in China. We thought at the time that the cyber attack on the power station was intended to open the doors for thieves. I guess we were right."

The hubbub of voices from the banqueting hall rose over the clatter of plates as the first course was cleared. "What do you need from me right now?" asked Cameron.

"I needed a sense check more than anything," replied Andy. "We're going live on the news channels in a few minutes. If I could quote you, anonymously of course, that would be a real bonus. If the offer still stands of an interview with one of the team then we can work that into a longer piece tomorrow."

"Sure." Cameron paused, getting her thoughts in order. "How about 'This is evidence that lapses in cybersecurity practice can have terrifying consequences in the real world. Information security teams across the world are working together to improve public safety.' Okay?"

"That'll do for starters," said Andy. "Can I say where you are?"

"Of course you can," replied Cameron with a laugh. "Everyone who is anyone is here tonight. They can have fun guessing who your source is." Delicious scents were wafting from the hall as the main course arrived. "I have to go."

"Thanks Cameron, I owe you, again," said Andy gratefully. "Speak to you tomorrow."

Cameron pocketed her screen and headed back to the table. Ben looked at her enquiringly as she slipped back into her seat. "It was Andy," she explained quickly. "He had some breaking news." She caught the attention of Ross and Joel on the other side of the table. Seeing the expression on her face they stopped chatting and eating, and the others followed suit.

"There's been a nuclear test in Russia," she said as loudly as she dared, trying not to let her voice carry to the surrounding tables. "That's all I know, but Andy thinks…"

Ross finished her sentence for her. "… that it's the Chinese uranium." He gave a low whistle. "So that's what last year's power station cyber attack was about. You were right. Anything from the South East Asia teams?"

Cameron nodded. "There are some messages flying around the forums, but I didn't have time to look at them in detail. At first glance they were generally speculation and shock rather than anything useful. I don't think there is anything we can do for now." She picked up her knife and fork and attacked the plate of food in front of her, hungry despite the news.

"What did Andy want, apart from acting as the message service?" asked Ben.

Cameron finished her mouthful of food. "Oh, he needed a sound bite for the news channel," she said nonchalantly. "I gave him something he could use."

Ross laughed and raised his glass to her. "Well done, Cam, I'm proud of you. You're a natural for the media."

Cameron grinned at him. "Anonymous quote, Ross. You can do the big interview tomorrow if you like."

"Seriously?" Ross gaped at her and laughed. "You actually mean that, don't you?"

"Deadly serious," replied Cameron. "Go ahead. I trust you to keep all of our secrets." She took another bite of mushroom, rich and smooth.

The noise level around them rose, and Cameron spotted staff speaking discreetly to other tables, and several people hurrying to the door.

"Looks like the word is out," said Joel. "Good for Andy getting the scoop on the story."

"I was expecting something like this," chipped in Noor. "Did Andy say where the explosion was?"

Cameron shook her head. "Not exactly. He said it was near the border with China and North Korea. Does that make sense to you, Noor?"

Noor nodded. "That all fits. Sandeep and I picked up some interesting traffic after the power station systems were compromised, and there were odd references to Vladivostok and some small settlements in the sparsely populated areas nearby."

"We published all the details," said Sandeep. "Our reports were included in the full analysis of the attack at the time. I thought the authorities on the ground would have taken it more seriously, but maybe the evidence wasn't strong enough for them."

The news was beginning to spread. Some voices were raised in shock, but others were as unsurprised as the Argentum team.

Ben turned to Cameron. "This doesn't bother any of you, does it?" His voice was shaking. "The first illegal nuclear detonation in half a century and all that worries you is the paper trail. You're probably already working out the business you'll get from it."

Cameron stared into his brown eyes, confused and hurt. "I do care, Ben. I just... it's something we expected might happen. It's one of the possible outcomes that we mapped months ago. It isn't a surprise, and we can't do anything about it. Don't you understand?"

Ben gazed long and hard at her without speaking, then looked away. Cameron felt a knot twist in her stomach.

"Ladies and Gentlemen!" The compere strode onto the stage, and the hubbub of voices faded. "Your attention please! Most of you are aware of the news reaching us from Russia this evening." At the back of the stage a screen lit up. "We'll go to the emergency news broadcast," he continued, "and then move swiftly to tonight's awards ceremony."

Cameron turned away from Ben and composed herself, watching maps and stock footage play out the drama on the big screen as best they could. She smiled to herself as the presenter quoted her words and she heard murmurs of approval around the room. She'd hit the mark.

At the next table she heard a long-term rival muttering, "Who on earth could have given them a quote so quickly from here?"

Ross overheard the same comment; he caught Cameron's eye and winked. She tried not to laugh. It would not do in a room that was absorbing the news.

The short bulletin ended, and conversations re-started, hesitant at first but growing in volume and warmth. There was nothing that the assembled professionals could do right now.

"We're going to be busy in the morning," said Pete quietly, a twinkle in his eye. Once the story got out, a wave of paranoia about cybercrime would likely fuel new enquiries from panicked organisations and double checks from existing clients.

Ben said nothing, but Cameron could sense a chill.

A human host passed by the table, checking that the waiter bots had refilled the empty glasses. Determined to break the ice again, Joel launched into a long and involved tale about his rugby club's last annual dinner, gesturing expansively and drawing his colleagues in as he recounted a scurrilous series of unfortunate and drink-fuelled antics. Waiter bots cleared the main course plates and brought dessert, apples harvested from the urban orchards and stuffed with dried fruit, an imported luxury. The noise level rose again as the crowd relaxed, and Joel reached the climax of his story to howls of laughter from Pete and Ella, feigned shock from Susie and Noor, and a none-too-gentle clip around the ear from Martha. Even Ben was grinning, and Cameron gave him a sidelong glance, catching his eye. He sighed and patted her knee. "You're all the same."

The compere took to the stage again. "Here we go," said Ross. "What's first up?"

"Best Cyber Startup," said Sandeep.

The centre of their table lit up with a projection of the categories and shortlisted nominees. Sandeep waved his hand towards the display and caught the top of a bottle of wine that had been sitting incongruously in the middle of the list. He grabbed at it, fumbled, and knocked it over. A red stain spread over the tablecloth, obscuring most of the projected details. He shrugged. "Sorry."

"No problem," said Joel. "We can get more. Waiter!"

The category winner was announced, and a group of eager youngsters took to the stage, hugging each other and clapping back to the politely applauding crowd.

Cameron peered at the table display, trying to make out the words as the wine stain spread. "Urban Cyber?" She looked up at the stage, squinting slightly. "The guy in the middle there is good. I don't recognise the others."

The winners left the stage and the ceremony moved on through a series of awards for innovation, collaboration, and education. Cameron's hands were sore from clapping.

"Our final award of the night," said the compere grandly. "This award recognises the Cyber Team of the Year. The judges had a hard job choosing from a shortlist of outstanding candidates," – Pete started to snort and managed to turn it into a cough – "but the winner is... The team from Argentum Associates, for their work shutting down the Speakeasy ransomware and managing the subsequent 'Hurricane' series of attacks."

His words were drowned out by cheers from the Argentum table as the team got to their feet. Filing up onto the stage, they looked out at the room, seeing only the first few tables as the lights blinded them. In the darkness of the hall, they heard cheers from Ben and Martha. The compere held out the trophy, a curiously angled 3D print of a globe banded by network connections. There was a pause. Ella nudged Cameron, who was half-hiding behind Joel as double insurance against unwanted photographs. She nudged Joel, who glanced at Ross and nodded. Ross looked at the rest of his teammates before stepping forward to take the award, smiling for the camera drones as applause rang around the room.

2: PASAR AND THE PIPER

Michelle was already awake and sitting in the kitchen when Daniel struggled out of his bedroom, rubbing his eyes.

"Morning, Shell," he yawned. There was no answer. Michelle was deep into a book, listening through discreet audio pods which linked to the apartment's hub, and slowly eating a slice of toast.

Daniel wandered over to the kitchen counter and put his hand to the kettle. It was lukewarm. His cousin must have been up for a while. He topped up the water and flicked the switch. While he waited for it to boil, Daniel rummaged in the cupboard and pulled out the last of the teabags and a box of cereal. He found himself a clean bowl and filled it to the brim with flakes.

The kettle steamed, whistled briefly, and clicked off. Daniel made a pot of strong tea and took it to the table. "Shell?"

She jumped, startled. "Off," she chirped. "Sorry, Dan, I didn't hear you come in. I've been up for ages." She picked up her mug and took a sip. "Ugh. Cold."

"Want a fresh one?" asked Daniel.

"Yes please. Have you heard the news?"

Daniel emptied Michelle's mug into the sink and rinsed it. "What news?" he asked, as he took the milk out of the fridge and sniffed it cautiously. He tipped a little into each of the mugs and poured the rest over his cereal.

"There's been an illegal nuclear test in Russia."

Daniel turned around in shock. "Really? Has anyone been hurt?"

"No reports so far," replied Michelle. "It was an underground explosion, and there hasn't been a major fallout alert."

"Do they know who's behind it?"

"No. There's been nothing announced. I don't think anyone has claimed responsibility. Most of the speculation is around where the uranium came from to build the bomb, and I think I know."

Daniel poured the tea and gave Michelle her mug. "Tell me," he said, taking a spoonful of cereal.

"Well," said Michelle, sipping her tea, "there was a contract on the marketplace, oh, two years ago at least. The work was spearfishing, a really specific, directed attack on a target to drop malware in exactly the right place. It was linked to a trojan build aimed at some archaic systems, and a bunch of other really shady things as well. Everything about that contract screamed 'nuclear power station'. It was well paid, too."

"Please tell me you didn't get involved."

Michelle smiled ruefully. "I'd have loved to. It was a really interesting challenge. I thought about bidding for the work, but it was very soon after I got into trouble for hacking into TrustCentre. I was still keeping my nose clean for the authorities and it would have been too much of a risk."

"Getting sensible in your old age," said Daniel approvingly.

"Oh, I don't know about that," said Michelle with a wicked grin. "I was thinking about those job adverts you're looking at. I'm sure I can help you out with them."

"Shell…" Daniel pleaded. "Really?"

"Don't worry," she said. "I wouldn't lie. There's no point faking any serious qualifications, but we can certainly get your application through all the pre-screening bots."

"And there I thought you could set me up as a top scientist and land the really good gig," laughed Daniel.

"Don't be daft," replied Michelle. "You know fine well that you can put down whatever you want on the form, but as soon as the company goes to verify the details, they won't match without the private key to show you own the original certificate."

"I know," said Daniel.

Michelle looked thoughtful. "If you're missing something specific, I could have a look at the Eden marketplace. I'm sure there are hashed records and private keys out there which have been stolen from databases and dodgy apps and ended up for sale."

Daniel shook his head, laughing. "It's not worth it, Shell. I was joking. I'm trying to keep you out of trouble, not get you in it."

Michelle pouted. "It's not totally illegal to buy from Eden. Well, I suppose that technically, depending on what you buy, it probably is, but this is low-level stuff. You know Eden's one of the nicer places on the dark web and it's not like I'm doing the hacking." She laughed in turn. "It's probably the same degree of mischief as ferreting in the landfill, now, isn't it?"

"Fair point," said Daniel. "But there's no point landing the job and not actually being able to do it."

"I'm not going to give you a doctorate in chemistry," laughed Michelle, "but I bet there are a couple of training certificates that you never got around to paying for."

Daniel nodded ruefully. "You're right, there are probably two or three which would be useful, but I'm more worried about you. You have more reason to be careful. What about the coding jobs you've been doing? Are they all above board? Nothing dodgy like that power station hack?"

"Mainly legit," said Michelle with a shrug. "I'm still doing some threat analysis work for Thorney Solutions. That was one of the conditions I agreed to after the TrustCentre hack blew open. It's quite fun picking apart other people's code. For, well, other things, it depends on the commission. Nothing can be traced back to here, though. I'm very careful."

Daniel stood up and dumped his empty mug and bowl on the countertop. "Okay. I'll have a look at the jobs and work out what I need. It won't hurt to have a helping hand with the recruitment algorithms, either." He yawned again. "First, though, I need to deliver those cans to the collector and find out more about that ring. I won't be long."

"Later, then," replied Michelle, waving her hand languidly as he left. "Play," she ordered the hub as she settled back to her book and took a sip of tea. In her head, as the words washed over her, she was already thinking about the task of getting Daniel his new job.

•

The Argentum Associates office was unusually quiet when Cameron arrived at the top of the stairs. The lights were on and a shadow betrayed Sandeep lurking behind his screen, but there were no other signs of life. The alarm on the delivery hatch chirruped loudly and Sandeep groaned.

"That'll be breakfast," he said, his voice unusually hollow.

"Want a coffee?" asked Cameron brightly, with a little more enthusiasm than she actually felt.

She wandered over to the kitchen area. The coffee machine had started automatically as soon as the office was unlocked. Now it was hissing triumphantly, brewing complete. Cameron pulled open the adjacent delivery hatch and extracted a warm bag, freshly dropped by the bakery drone.

"What do we have here?" she asked, peering into the bag. "Bacon rolls? Breakfast tacos? That must be some hangover."

Sandeep gave her a pained look.

The door opened and Joel walked in, sniffing the air appreciatively as the rich scent of coffee and hot food wafted around the office. He was followed closely by a grinning Ross bearing the trophy, and Susie and Ella, both looking happy but subdued.

"Oh dear," said Ross, with a grin. "Tough night, Sandeep?"

"I've had better Fridays," replied Sandeep ruefully.

Ross looked around the office, thinking. "Where do you want the silverware, Cameron?"

She took the trophy from him and examined its unusual angles critically. "Well, it's certainly original." She tipped it upside down, looking for clues. "Ah, here we are. Printed from reclaimed stainless steel. Designed by... No, I can't read the name." She glanced around the room and her eyes lit on a shelf opposite the door. "Why don't we clear out all those old cables and converters and put it there?"

"We might need them one day," protested Susie indignantly.

"They've been there for years," replied Ross. "We've never used them."

"At least you could box them up," suggested Sandeep. He raised his hand to cover a yawn. "Susie's right. The moment we throw them all out we'll get a job which really, really needs a hard-wired connection to some old kit."

Ross sighed, defeated. He cleared a space on the table and pulled the tangled nest of equipment down carefully, coughing as the dust flew.

"Why does every cable go into storage nicely wrapped and come out looking like a demented spider has been at work?" he asked, pulling hopelessly at the end of an old network connector.

Sandeep sighed and struggled out of his comfortable chair. He nudged Ross aside and started digging into the pile, methodically separating the different weights and lengths of multi-coloured cabling.

Cameron brushed the remaining dust and debris off the shelf and put the trophy in pride of place. She stood back to admire it. "That'll do nicely," she said.

Joel had taken over the coffee duties and was filling mugs and organising a plate for the food. "Are Pete and Noor on their way?" he asked.

"I haven't heard from them," said Cameron.

At that moment, a clattering on the stairs heralded Pete's arrival.

"Sorry I'm late," he said. "Slept in. It's not like me." He looked up the trophy in pride of place on the shelf and nodded approvingly. "That looks nice."

Noor appeared in the doorway behind him, out of breath. "Sorry, Cameron. I had a call from a friend in Singapore and lost track of the time."

Pete cocked an ear and gave her a sidelong look. "The young man your parents like?"

Noor blushed. "Yes. Him."

"Tenuk? You've been chatting to him for a while now, haven't you?" said Ella, digging for news.

"He's nice enough, but he's just a friend," said Noor defensively. "Anyway, he's thousands of miles away on the other side of the world and I'll probably never see him again."

Ella gave her a conspiratorial smile. "Is he at least useful for keeping your parents at bay?" she asked.

Noor laughed. "He is. They haven't tried introducing me to any more 'suitable men' since we met. Win-win."

"Did he talk about the nuclear test?" asked Cameron. "It will be a lot closer to home for him."

"It's huge news over there," replied Noor. "Tenuk said he remembered the Chinese cyber attack and he had wondered if it was connected. He sends his congratulations on the award, by the way."

Cameron frowned. "That's nice of him," she said. "Noor, I'm still not comfortable with his connection to the MerLions, after everything that happened."

Noor looked at her sympathetically. Cameron's family had recently been put in great danger by a gang of determined cyber criminals linked to the MerLions. The memory was obviously still raw.

"He was cleared of any involvement. That should be enough, surely," replied Noor softly. "What happened was terrible, but Tenuk knew nothing about it." She walked silently to her desk and put down her bag.

Sandeep hurriedly placed the breakfast plate on the table in an attempt to lighten the atmosphere. "There've been quite a few enquiries this morning for security checks," he said. "Shall we go through them?"

"Sure," sighed Cameron. "Hardly a surprise. What've we got?"

The team settled down around the table, steaming mugs of coffee in hand. Any tension between Noor and Cameron evaporated as they slipped into their professional roles, working methodically through the messages from old clients and new connections concerned by the reports from Russia.

"Most of them are nuclear power stations," said Sandeep, bringing the list up on the screen. "Hardly a surprise. Who wants what?"

"There's no real point going back to the plant in Kent," said Joel. "We swept that three months ago and their procedures are spot on. They've almost finished decommissioning the first reactor and the core will be sealed tight by the middle of next year."

"Could you do a couple of day's consultancy, just to reassure them?" asked Cameron.

"Okay," said Joel, "but it's like taking candy from a baby. The power station is sitting on a man-made island now that the marshes have flooded. There are no easy routes in for people who shouldn't be there and no fixed connections to the web. Plus, all the staff who are left on site have been there for years and we've done all their training."

"Better safe than sorry," said Ross. "Would you go down there again?" Joel nodded.

"That's one off the list," said Cameron. "What else have we got?"

"I can help with the plants over on the Severn Estuary," said Susie. "I did some network management for them in my old job and I know the head of IT and cybersecurity. I'll need to refresh my security clearances but there won't be a problem."

"That's great," said Cameron brightly. "I'm happy for you to handle the job on your own."

Susie shook her head. "I'd rather go in with a partner. It's a huge site."

"I can come with you, if you like?" said Ella.

"Is that okay?" asked Susie.

That's fine by me," said Cameron. She felt a knot of worry dissipating that she hadn't known was there. Arguments within the team worried her, and here at least it looked as if harmony had been restored. "Do you think you need anyone else?"

Ella shook her head. "We can probably cover the work between us."

"Good," said Cameron. She scanned the rest of the list. "There are a couple of enquiries from France," she said, pointing. "We can pass the details over to our connections there. Noor, can you get in touch with Sébastien or one of the local infosec teams?"

"Of course," replied Noor.

"What about this one up in the North East?" asked Sandeep. "That's not far from where my mum lives."

Pete pulled a map up on his screen. "I've always wanted to go up there," he said. He pointed to a cluster of small islands a little way north of the location Sandeep had indicated. "Check this out. The Farne Islands. I've heard the scuba diving around there is excellent."

Noor laughed. "Really? Isn't it cold?"

"No colder than the Channel," replied Pete, shrugging, "and from what they say, a whole lot more interesting. Is there enough work for both of us, Sandeep?"

"Definitely," replied Sandeep. "It isn't a client we've worked with before. I'm not sure why the enquiry's come to us."

"Hmm." Noor's fingers flashed over the keys as she searched. "According to this, the firm they were using went out of business two years ago. The principal retired."

Cameron peered over at Noor's screen. "Ah, that makes sense. We've had a couple of other clients come to us through his recommendations. It's been a while since he closed so they'll need a full review and security sweeps. You two should be able to handle it but let me know if you need reinforcements."

Ross was making notes. "Right. Pete and Sandeep will head north. Joel, you can sort out the client in Kent. Can you go over to the Norfolk coast as well?"

"Sure," said Joel. "These won't take long."

"Good," continued Ross. "Ella, Susie, West Country. Cameron, you and Noor and I can support everyone from here, can't we?"

"That makes sense with your triathlon finals coming up," agreed Cameron. "Sandeep, is there anything else we can pick up?"

Sandeep scrolled through the messages. "Not really. I think we have enough to be going on with."

"Right," said Cameron. "Let's get these visits set up. They're all preventative, so we have some planning time before we go on site. Noor, pull out the full report on the Chinese cyber attack so that we can reference the original methodology when we're working with these new contracts."

"Yes, sure," said Noor. "I'll review and update the checklists as well." She was back to her cheery, competent self, any awkwardness over Tenuk forgotten. She set to work collating, researching, and preparing the team for their next challenges.

Cameron leaned back in her chair and looked at Ross. "That leaves you and me. Are you ready to face the cameras?"

"Bring it on," said Ross with a grin.

Michelle settled at her computer and gathered her thoughts. She opened a secure connection and tapped her way to Eden, her favourite marketplace on the dark web. Her credit here was good after a series of small but highly successful contracts whose details she had not shared with either Daniel or her bosses at Thorney.

"Search recruitment algorithms," she ordered. There was a momentary pause before the results returned. She listened to the list and nodded in satisfaction. The tools she would need to test and refine Daniel's profile were almost certainly available. Some deeper research was now required to be sure which of the systems was being used by Daniel's prospective new employer.

Start with the people. The power station's website yielded a list of senior managers. A little extra digging through a standard search engine revealed some meeting notes and calendar entries for the human resources director, saved on a third party app outside the plant's systems, which mentioned several colleagues. She opened a useful tool that gave her an anonymous overview of a popular professional networking site and cross-referenced the names. This eliminated one potential contact who had moved jobs but lined up two more targets.

What software could they be using? She pulled up a summary of all the available recruitment packages, but there were too many to work through. She thought for a moment and parsed the command carefully. "Filters on: UK data storage; four- and five-star rating; more than, uh, five years since full release." She was reasonably confident that a site which needed top level security would be using an established software provider and keeping its data firmly within the national borders.

"Twenty results," said her search app.

That might be good enough. Michelle set off a deeper scan of the target individuals, searching for a correlation between the experience they claimed on their professional profiles and the software brands on her shortlist. It took almost a minute for the results to come back, and she tapped her fingers on the desk in frustration. It was worthwhile. She now had just two possible software packages that appeared on both lists and featured prominently in the tools for sale on Eden. That would be enough to test Daniel's application against the filtering algorithms and make sure he made it through to the interview shortlist. She also had full details of five people to target if she needed to be certain of the package they were using.

She was distracted from her task by the ping of a notification. 'New posts on the Pasar community.' Michelle caught her breath. That forum had gone quiet months before, when Yasmin the Admin suddenly went offline and rumours spread that she was not one of the twisted but talented human hackers who frequented the forum, but an artificial intelligence gone rogue. What could have sparked up this new activity? The timing was too much of a coincidence. It had to be related to the nuclear test.

Michelle was intrigued to see what was happening, but she was torn between the light and the dark. If she was going straight, she had to walk away from the opportunities that Pasar offered: the high value, high risk contracts, and the thrills that came with dancing undetected through a connected world and finding its weaknesses. If she was going straight, she would ignore the call. She would stay in the shallows and dabble in low level mischief. She would help Daniel to succeed and continue to rely on his support. She would accept the crumbs of work from her hard-nosed commercial employer. For all her talent, she knew that the management at Thorney Solutions regarded her as just another statistic, a tick in the box of their diverse workforce.

Reliance on others. The thing she had fought against all her life. That was the tipping point. She took a deep breath. "Go to Pasar."

•

While Ross was repacking his training bag, Cameron sent a quick message to Andy. "Where do you want to meet?"

The response came straight back. "Head over to the city studio. I'm at Ruler, Ridge, Robot."

Cameron pulled up the map to check the location reference and nodded to herself. It would be a good half hour walk across the river and up through the city, but it offered a chance to blow away the cobwebs from the previous night. In any case, the morning was fresh and dry, and it would take almost as long to get there on the tube.

"Do you know where we're going?" asked Ross.

She dropped the location to his smart screen. "Yes, one of the studios. I don't know why they need you to come in. Surely they can record from anywhere?"

Ross shrugged. "It depends what Andy wants to do. The sound and lighting will be much better than recording remotely. They'll be able to put it live on the spot and cut it into the later bulletins more easily." He glanced at the map. "I'm training this afternoon. I can go straight from the studio to the track if that's okay with you?"

"Of course," said Cameron.

Ross picked up his bag and followed her out of the door and down the stairs.

They reached the busy bridge across the Thames, and as they left the shelter of the Shard a stiff breeze buffeted them. Cameron pushed her hair out of her eyes, which were watering slightly. "Bracing," she commented.

"It's good for you," laughed Ross. "That was a fun evening, wasn't it?"

Cameron nodded and answered back with a grin, but her reply was lost in the wind as they battled to the middle of the bridge. Beneath them the water of the Thames rippled, and a cluster of small boats moored by the shore bobbed up and down. She was beginning to regret the choice to walk, but soon enough they were across the river and into the elegant streets of the City of London. The wind dropped abruptly, and she ran her fingers through her tangled hair in a vain attempt to tidy it.

Ross looked up at one tall, wide cream-coloured building that stood out from the rest, bathed in the spring sunshine. High windows gazed down on the street below, and stone statues on the façade were glowing like the gold upon which the bank had been founded.

"We should pop in and see Sir Simon Winchester," said Ross. "After all, it was that job which put us onto the Speakeasy ransomware in the first place."

"I heard he's retiring," said Cameron. "Handing over the reins to a new chairman."

"Surely he's not at retirement age yet," said Ross, surprised.

"I thought that myself," Cameron agreed. "Maybe it's a shrewd career move. I hope he's been snapped up by the regulators. They could do with some experience of digital security and cryptocurrency management. The bank will miss him, though. He's one person whose experience should be preserved."

"Don't get me started on doppelganger intelligences," said Ross with a shudder. "It's all very well training something up for supported decision making, but it's next to impossible to predict how an AI will turn out if it's left to its own devices. You of all people should know that." He stopped abruptly and turned to look at her. "Are you alright, Cameron?"

Caught by surprise, Cameron's eyes widened. "I'm fine," she said quietly, dropping her gaze. There was an uncomfortable pause, then she carried on walking.

Ross sighed, frustrated, and followed her. They crossed a busy road in silence and walked through the grounds of St Paul's cathedral, its dome shining in the sun. Cameron smoothly dodged an excited group of small dogs scampering through the small park in the care of an overloaded Walkies robot. Ross scrambled to avoid tripping on their leads as they charged past him.

The two of them emerged unscathed onto one of the busy main arteries running north-west through the legal district. A constant stream of silent autocars moved slowly in each direction, outpaced by pedestrians and bicycles, and liveried high security drones darted in and out of offices high above their heads, managing the flow of pre-digital papers as they moved between courts and lawyers. The bastions of tradition in the legal profession had embraced the new world of technology in most areas of the law, but they kept hold of history in their own unique way.

The passing traffic was virtually silent. A background hum of music and conversation competed with the shouts of workers on a nearby building site. They were busy refurbishing one of the old office blocks from the turn of the millennium, bringing it up to date with its own solar and wind power linked to the local microgrid, rooftop drone landing and charging pads, delivery chutes, and layers of insulation against the changing seasons.

As they reached Chancery Lane and turned to the north, Cameron stopped and looked at Ross apologetically. "I'm sorry. There are a few things bugging me, and I'm trying to deal with them. I didn't realise it was so obvious."

"Don't worry," said Ross. "It's not that obvious. I've known you long enough to see that there's something wrong. Do you want to talk about it?"

Cameron shrugged. "I don't know. I'm not really ready to talk about it." She paused and looked up at the half-timbered façade of a nearby building, her eyes unfocused. "I still feel responsible for what happened to Nina. If I didn't do this job, no one would be in danger."

Ross sighed. "I wondered if that was it." He looked at her earnestly. "Cameron, you love what you do, and you're brilliant. No one blames you except yourself. Everyone who was involved is banged up, including the rogue AI. The MerLions have gone home. Nina is fine. The danger has passed."

Cameron looked at him steadily. "Do you really believe that?"

It was Ross's turn to lower his gaze. He wanted to believe that not only was the world safe for Cameron, her family, her friends, and her colleagues, but that his youthful involvement in the darker side of cybercrime was forgotten. He knew that it was never going to be so simple.

"I wish I did," he said, "but at the very least, we are all safer than we were. Isn't that enough?"

Cameron shrugged. "It'll have to do. Come on. We'll be late."

A few minutes further up the road they arrived at a tall building with an imposing glass façade. The nearest revolving door started turning as it sensed their approach, drawing them into a light, bright colonnaded atrium. Natural light streamed in through great windows that stretched from the ground to the roof high above them. Elevators were zipping up and down between floors, but there was no one to be seen. Cameron spotted a series of large screens mounted on the wall. Advertisements flickered on one, and she was amused to watch its confusion as the simple AI controller detected the two visitors, identified their interests from publicly available data, and tried to serve up appropriate marketing messages for two very different audiences, mixing adverts for training supplements with shots of vineyards. After stuttering a little, it settled on a promotion for a popular chain of coffee houses. A safe compromise.

Another screen showed the rolling output from the news channel, and two more listed the companies who had offices or hot desks in the building. All the upper floors were occupied by small businesses: artists taking advantage of the natural light, service companies who needed the central location. The news channel's studio was down in the basement, soundproofed and secure.

"Over here," called Ross. He had found an appointment pad on the deserted reception desk. He tapped his way through a series of questions, presented his identity chip to the scanner, and an access card popped out of a dispenser. Cameron did the same. Their cards allowed them through the barrier and a trail of lights appeared in the floor to guide them to their destination.

Andy met them at the top of the stairs. "Perfect timing," he said. "Let's get you set up, Ross." He led them down to the studio complex. "This whole building was all broadcasting once, before you were born," he said, gesturing up the light well to the high balconies of the upper floors. "It was too costly to keep the whole building running. The studios down here still come in handy, though."

A door opened and Giles appeared. "Hi Cameron, hi Ross." He looked at Andy. "Are we all set?"

"Almost," said Andy, pinning a small microphone to his lapel. "Is this thing on?" he asked, frowning.

Giles nodded and handed a second mic to Ross.

The studio itself was surprisingly small. Ross relaxed into his chair. Andy smiled and glanced at the camera. There was a pause and a green light flicked on.

"Ross White, thank you for joining me," he said warmly. "A lot of our viewers will know you as a successful British team triathlete, but when you're not competing, you're a consultant with leading cybersecurity agency Argentum Associates. As an infosec professional, what is your reaction to the news of last night's nuclear test?"

"Well, Andy, we've been expecting some kind of incident ever since a large cyber attack was perpetrated two years ago on a Chinese nuclear facility undergoing decommissioning."

"How are the two connected?" asked Andy, prompting him gently.

"The cyber attack literally opened the doors to the site," explained Ross. "It enabled a physical penetration of the power station. Although there were no reports of a theft at the time, it was hardly a leap to assume that uranium might be the target."

"Would the hacker also be a thief?"

"The attack laid the foundations for thieves to operate," said Ross. "Of course, it's extremely unlikely that one single cybercriminal would be responsible." He picked his words carefully and continued. "An operation of this magnitude would involve contributions from many different people who probably have no connection to each other. Different strategies, different attacks, all aiming towards a single goal. What is more interesting is looking up the chain from the individuals to the agencies who commissioned the work, and the clients they answer to."

"So, there is a hierarchy of cybercrime?" said Andy. "Can you tell me more about these 'powers behind the throne'?"

"Sure. The frontline cybercriminal, the developer, is rarely the instigator of mayhem on this scale. There are viruses and malware circulating all of the time which come from small operations or even sole developers and cause a fair amount of trouble, but something as complex and co-ordinated as this operation or, say, the Speakeasy attacks, is more likely to be managed by an umbrella organisation on behalf of a client and involve work commissioned from freelance developers."

"Cybercriminals for hire," said Andy.

"Very much," replied Ross. "In our work at Argentum we see a lot of this fragmented approached. Cybercrime outsourcing is extremely common, and there are plenty of developers for hire. There's an old saying: 'He who pays the piper calls the tune.'"

He stumbled over the last words and a cold chill washed over him. Outwardly he hoped that he looked completely calm. Inwardly, he was horrified. It had just slipped out: a clue to his old, shady persona. He had to hope that no one would make the connection. Ross kept smiling and covered his discomfort with a cough. He did not dare look at Cameron.

Andy hadn't noticed anything. "That's a fascinating insight, Ross," he said. "Thank you." He swung to face the camera, which zoomed in for the summary. "The picture forming around this illegal nuclear test is becoming increasingly complex. A network of freelance cybercriminals and thieves, and a mastermind in the shadows. In our next broadcast, we speak to counter-terrorism experts to find out more about the known activists and insurgent groups who are likely to be commissioning these global agents of unrest."

The green light flicked to red and Andy unpinned his microphone. "That was excellent, Ross," he said. "You're a natural. Will you come on again?"

"Sure," said Ross lightly. "No problem."

•

Michelle worked through the growing thread of posts that had lit up the once dormant forum. The news of a nuclear explosion was a shock, of course, but she knew it was one logical outcome of the work that had been done years ago. What horrified her was the air of celebration among some of the forum members. She had always suspected that a number of her contacts were hardened cybercriminals, and their revelry confirmed it.

"Very good work," typed one character she recognised of old. Mìmi Māo was usually online early in the day. Michelle was sure she was based in China but would never have connected her with the power station attack until now.

"How did they get the goods out?" asked another old hand, known to everyone as the Monkey.

"There's a full write-up coming," posted a third familiar user.

Michelle's jaw dropped. She had known Cloverleaf on the forums for years, although she had barely been active recently. They'd helped each other out on knotty script problems and had even spun up a few low-level hacks together. Why was Cloverleaf mixed up in a job as high profile as this? Panicking, Michelle scrolled through the list of active forum members. Who else might she have misjudged? She was unsurprised to see that King Katong was online and shouting his mouth off. She did not trust him at all. She looked for the Piper and felt a rush of relief when she confirmed that he hadn't visited the site since before Yasmin the Admin disappeared. She liked the Piper. They had become friends over the years and seemed to be living in the same time zone. She had always wondered who he really was.

An insistent pinging indicated a private message.

"ShellPixie? Is that you?"

"Hey, Mimì," Michelle replied cautiously. She debated whether to offer congratulations but could not bring herself to do it. She settled for typing a feeble, "How are you?"

"I'm fantastic, Pix. One big payday today. How come you weren't in the team?"

"Too much on at the time," replied Michelle. "I missed the boat."

"There's more coming," typed Mimì. "Plenty more. Keep following King Katong. He's taken over from Yasmin and he knows how to put a team together."

Michelle shivered. "I'll do that, thanks." Not a chance, she reflected inwardly. "I have to go. Catch you another time."

She logged off and sat in silence, her head spinning.

•

Tenuk was sweating profusely from the humidity of the early evening. He had walked only a few hundred metres from the shuttle and the cool tunnels of home were beckoning. It had been a very long day. A warm breeze stirred the palm trees which lined the street, but it offered no relief from the sweltering temperatures. There was a rustle and a shriek close by as a small troupe of monkeys swung past, scavenging for treats in the elegant gardens of the Katong elite. They had struck lucky. Tenuk dodged a shower of snacks which fell from the sky as the thief spilled the bag it had snatched from an unattended table. He heard an angry shout and the clatter of a broom handle as the victim chased the last of the monkeys away. The troupe swung up onto the high balconies of an adjacent apartment building, undeterred, but pickings were scarce up there. Less than half of the apartments in the block were now occupied, and the empty properties were falling into disrepair as the rain forest gradually encroached on the city. The human occupants had started to move below ground, expanding cool underpasses and subway tunnels and establishing a new subterranean Singapore.

By the time he reached the entrance his shirt was soaked. He took the steps two at a time down to the new street level. As the cooler air hit, he shivered involuntarily, but it put a new spring in his step. The street below was busy with pedestrians and an electric shuttle purred slowly along the side of the tunnel carrying passengers and goods. The tunnel widened out into a broad hallway, the underpass of a large intersection in the city above. At one side a group of older citizens were practicing Tai Chi, oblivious to the crowds that hurried past them.

As Tenuk passed the group, an elderly lady turned towards him, the spell of her concentration broken. He recognised his neighbour, who had taken him under her wing when he moved to the tunnels. She raised a hand and greeted him with a warm smile. "Salamat patang, Tenuk."

"Good evening, Auntie Fatima," he replied politely. "How good to see you."

"You look tired," she said. "You have been working hard." She patted his hand. "And my niece," she continued, "are you still friends?"

"Yes, Auntie." He smiled. "I actually spoke to her this afternoon."

"Oh!" Fatima's eyes danced. "That's good. Noor is a lovely girl." She stepped out of the way of the Tai Chi group as they moved slowly and precisely through their evening routine. "I'm so glad you managed to meet her and my sister when you were in London. Do you think you will be travelling back there soon?"

"I really don't know," replied Tenuk. "It depends on so many things. We have to decide where the next MerLions tour will go, but I don't think it will be Europe."

"I see," said Fatima. "That is a shame." She picked up her shopping bag. "I'm going home. Will you walk with me?"

"Of course, Auntie," said Tenuk. He put his hand out to take the bag, but Fatima shook her head with a smile.

"I'm not as old as all that," she scolded gently. "My grandmother was still climbing the mountain to collect pineapples when she was seventy-six." She smiled to herself at the memory. "So, young man, tell me all about your travels. You are very lucky to be able to cross the world. I would love to go to London, but I have no way of making enough carbon credits for a flight."

They walked slowly with the flow of commuters towards home. On a normal day people would be chatting and laughing as they returned to their families, but today they seemed subdued and there was an atmosphere of unrest pervading the normally settled community. As they approached the next intersection the crowd grew thicker, and there were raised voices. Moving closer, Tenuk saw hastily constructed banners and a figure standing on a fruit box, declaiming wildly. He heard snatches of the rhetoric, preaching doom and destruction in the wake of the nuclear explosion. He shepherded Fatima through the press of bodies and towards their sector. Surveillance bots would be on their way to disperse the crowd and he did not want to be nearby when that happened.

They emerged into a quieter street lined with apartments cut into the side of the tunnel. Tenuk saw Fatima to her door and climbed the stairs to the higher level that he called home. He approached his apartment cautiously, senses heightened and alert for anything unusual. There was no sign of anyone watching. A discreet scanner on his wrist glowed a reassuring green: no new devices detected. The automatic lock clicked open, and he thumbed a second security device that released the door. All was well.

Inside, he stripped off his sweat-soaked corporate shirt with the prominent MerLions logo and dropped it on the tiled floor. He poured himself a long cold drink from the fridge and sat down, stretching gratefully. He could afford a rest, but the day was not yet over. In the corner of the room lurked an array of screens, his window to another, darker world. He sighed. Since the news had broken of the nuclear test, he had barely stopped working, in the real world and in the virtual one. He had no doubt that as soon as he switched on his connection he would be overwhelmed by notifications. They could wait another ten minutes. Meeting Fatima had put him in a reflective mood, thinking about Noor. He liked her a lot. He wasn't sure that she felt the same way.

Maybe he could work some magic to build up Noor's carbon credits so she and her family could fly over and visit. The MerLions had plenty of corporate credit but he had very little of his own to share. Puzzling over the problem, he picked up his smartscreen and searched for offset sharing services. It seemed easy enough to transfer carbon credits as a gift, but he would still have to acquire them from the corporate account. That wasn't likely to be a standard feature of anyone's software. He was going to need an expert on the case.

Tenuk switched on the main screens and braced himself for the wave of messages. Sure enough, alerts began to stream up the side of the display. He ignored them. Instead, he navigated to the familiar Eden marketplace and set off a new search. How could credits be diverted from the corporate account, laundered, and deposited in an individual's wallet? If there was no service already available on Eden, Tenuk was sure he could find someone to commission for the work. It was straightforward enough, a little low-level fraud which would relieve the company of a tiny fraction of the credits they earned from cleaning plastics from the seas. Literally a drop in the ocean.

There were no off-the-shelf solutions coming back, so he placed an advertisement under an alias. He had plenty of time to wait and a lot of work to do. Logging off Eden, he went back to the stream of message notifications which were still coming through for other sources. Most of them were irrelevant, repetitive conversation threads, which he scanned and then discarded. There were several reports from ground zero of the nuclear test. There had been no human casualties and the site seemed to have been chosen carefully to avoid significant ecosystem damage. He had to hope that the forecasts of fallout patterns were accurate and equally benign. Overall, however, it had been a slick operation. Tenuk was impressed.

The most interesting messages he left until last. There were several enquiries from potential clients in troubled countries, tentative explorations of the services he offered. He smiled to himself. There was more than enough work here for the talented developers on Pasar. There would be more paydays to come.

3: CHASING WRAITHS

Daniel tightened the last tiny screw on the ferret's outer casing, tapped the power button, and crossed his fingers. He'd returned from a damp and disappointing night of scavenging with little to show for his efforts other than a length of copper wire, the ferret's only find before its systems were shorted by a water leak. Now dry and its seals re-greased, the little machine sprang happily back to life.

"Done it, Shell," he called. "All fixed."

"That's great," she replied from the other room. "Although hopefully you won't have to go rooting in the landfill again."

Daniel switched the ferret back off, stood up and stretched. "Have you found everything we need?" he asked, walking through to where Michelle sat at her computer.

"Possibly," she said. "Here, have a look through this set of certifications. It'll be easier if you read them yourself. Select the ones you want."

Daniel leaned over her shoulder and scanned the list. "I'm still not sure whether to go for the electrician job or security," he said. "Either way, it looks like everything I'm missing is right here." He scrolled slowly through the list.

"I researched their recruitment systems," said Michelle, "and I found out more about the hiring process. I think you'll have a better chance with the security job."

"It's a very senior position, though," said Daniel doubtfully. "I'm not sure I'm good enough."

"Of course you are," said Michelle fiercely. "You've had bigger jobs than this before. Your references are real enough and you know what you're doing. I'll make sure you get onto the shortlist. Easy."

"Yeah, I guess you're right," said Daniel. "The money's better, too. How are you getting on?"

"Oh, there are a few interesting jobs coming through the network."

"Which network, exactly?"

Michelle pouted. "I'm being very sensible." She avoided thinking about the offers she'd received on Pasar. There were rumours circulating at Thorney Solutions that the cyber law enforcement community had

had enough. The NCA and GCHQ and MI5 would be coming for all the people involved in the uranium theft and nuclear test. It was going to be dangerous for everyone concerned. She had to stay away.

"Good." Daniel straightened up and looked at the clock. "I'm going to head into town. I'll take that copper wire and the audio pods through to the collector and get that ring checked out. I want to drop into the dive shop as well."

"You can't afford to buy any more gadgets," warned Michelle. "Goodness knows we came close enough to selling the gear you already have."

"I'm just looking," said Daniel. "The season's starting, and I may get some work from them, or at least some free dives. You know, showing tourists around the best sites, that sort of thing."

"See what they say," said Michelle. "Before you go, can you hook up that old hard drive to the test machine? It'll have to go through the write blocker."

"Oh, sure, I'd forgotten." Daniel dug through a box of wires and connectors until he found a likely looking adapter. He plugged one end into the drive, and the other into Michelle's blocker kit. This linked in turn to a small computer that was gathering dust in the corner of the room. Booting up the old machine, he waited patiently as it ran through its slow, steady start routine. He checked that the speakers were working, then bent and put his ear close to the hard drive. There was a faint whirring.

"Sounds like it's turning," he said, satisfied.

"Good. I should be able to image it from there."

"Need anything else?"

"No, you get off to town. Have fun." Michelle moved over to the old machine and brushed her fingers over the keys. "Let's see what you are," she murmured, already lost in thought.

Daniel walked through rows of terraced houses towards the bus stop. He glanced at the timetable display on his watch and broke into a run, rounding the final corner as the shuttle drifted silently into view. He was in luck. There was already someone waiting, and it was indicating for the stop. He slowed to a jog and arrived neatly at the door as it opened. The shuttle was already half full, and the other passengers watched Daniel incuriously as he walked up the aisle and slid into an empty seat at the back. The hum of gentle conversation resumed. This line ran into the centre of town from the park and ride at the edge of the urban district. Most of the people who used it lived deep in the rural heartland of the region, farmers and villagers from the moors and hills where communications were still patchy and autonomous vehicles were unreliable and dangerous. They left their old cars and vans in a sprawling parking lot and completed the journey by bus. Some would take the chance to recharge their car batteries there during the day for free. Others could refuel their ancient petrol and diesel engines at the gas station, customers of last resort taking advantage of low prices from an excess supply.

The shuttle bus left the rundown terraces and passed through more affluent suburbs. The houses here were larger, with neat frontages and gardens. They passed a schoolyard; it was morning break time and Daniel could hear the shouts of children playing. The road curved towards the sea front, houses giving way to shops and restaurants and amusement arcades on one side and the beach stretching out on the other. High tide was still a few hours away and a wide expanse of sand was exposed, but it was almost empty. Despite the bright sunshine, a brisk wind meant that the beach was chilly. A few figures could be seen in the distance, walking dogs, or simply enjoying the bracing sea air.

Daniel followed the rest of the passengers off the bus at the terminus and made his way to a side street. The terraced houses here were taller and more elegant than those in the suburb he'd come from. Hidden among the cluster of good family homes were overgrown sheds and old garages where merchants dealt in scrap and collectibles from dubious sources. Daniel checked that no one was watching and slid through an anonymous garden gate. He was hidden from both the street and the house by trees and bushes. He circled an old rockery, then ducked down through a door into a tiny Aladdin's cave of glittering metal and piles of junk.

"Morning, Daniel." The collector knew him well by now. "What have you got for me today?"

"Morning, Gibson," he said, pulling the wire out of his pocket. "Not much. Just a bit of copper and a handful of audio pods."

Gibson took the wire from him and peered at it critically. "That's a good find," he said. "Most copper wiring used to get picked up by scrap merchants and recycled before it had a chance to reach landfill." He picked at the remnants of its plastic coating. "Let me clean this up and weigh it for you."

"I'll wait," said Daniel amiably. He sat at the door of the tiny workshop and watched the man work. This had once been an air raid shelter, built by the residents as an insurance policy against careless wartime bombing raids. The chemical plants of the estuary had been obvious targets and the local communities were all too aware of the risk of collateral damage. As far as Daniel knew, this Anderson shelter had never been used in anger. It had been repurposed by Gibson, its metal frame hiding his clandestine hobby from prying scanners.

"Rum business that explosion last week, eh?" said Gibson as he worked. "Glad it was nowhere near us."

"It could hardly have been further away," said Daniel with a shrug. "Nothing to worry about."

"I'm not so sure about that." Gibson stripped the last of the plastic away and held the wire up to the ceiling light. "We're all connected. The world is smaller than you think."

Satisfied with his work, he weighed the finished twist of wire. Daniel dug the audio pods out of his pocket and handed them over.

"Every little helps," said Gibson, tipping the pods into a bucket with hundreds more. "That all seems to be in order." He held out his smartscreen and Daniel checked the transaction. It was a good price. He nodded and accepted the handshake on his own screen. The payment was complete.

Slipping back out into the alley behind the terrace, Daniel closed the garden gate quietly and retraced his steps to the main street. There was a shop he knew along the strip that sold trinkets and keepsakes, and the owner knew enough about jewellery to manage a thriving pawn operation under the radar. Daniel stepped into the shop and browsed casually through the displays, waiting for two lingering shoppers to leave.

Once they had gone and closed the door behind them, Daniel approached the counter. He fished in his pocket and produced the ring.

"Can you tell me anything about this? I found it when I was moving an old chest of drawers that used to belong to my grandmother."

The woman took it and turned it slowly in her hands. "Someone will have missed that," she said. "Let me have a closer look."

She peered at it, muttering to herself. "White metal, clear stone… Those clasps are a bit shaky." Picking up a tiny fibre optic camera, she scanned the stone and the hallmarks on the inside of the ring. She straightened up and swung a small screen around so that Daniel could see the images she had collected.

"Let's see what we've got," she said. "This hallmark is nice and clear. I haven't come across the maker's mark before but look here at the orb and these numbers."

"999," said Daniel "What does it mean?"

"It means that your grandma managed to lose a pure platinum ring."

Daniel couldn't stop the grin which spread across his face. "Really?"

"Yes. You need to take care of this. I can arrange a professional valuation if you like. It needs repairing, though. The stone is barely held in, and if one more clasp goes, you'll lose it."

"How much would it cost?"

"Repair and valuation?" The jeweller made a few calculations and quoted a figure. Daniel's face dropped.

"I can't really afford that at the moment," he said.

"Well, in that case take good care of it and come back when you're ready." She reached under the counter and produced a small box. "Here, this will be safer than keeping it loose in your pocket."

"Thank you," said Daniel. "I really appreciate it." He tucked the ring safely into the box and closed it carefully. "I'll be back when I can."

His final stop was further along the seafront where the beach narrowed, and the road began to climb up the cliff. The market day shoppers rarely came up this far. At the very end of the seafront terrace, two properties had been knocked together. On one side a bay window held a colourful display of diving equipment and pictures of blue seas, exotic fish, and shipwrecks. In the corner of the display hung an old ship's bell. A plaque showed it had been retrieved from a local wreck, the HMS Nottingham. The other side of the dive centre was given over to a garage and workshop. A bright orange rigid inflatable boat on a trailer was half visible through the garage door, and music was playing.

Daniel bounded happily into the shop, a bell announcing his arrival. The owner appeared from the adjoining workshop, wiping his hands on a towel. He raised a sardonic eyebrow in greeting.

"Daniel, good to see you. It's been a while."

"It's been too cold," laughed Daniel. "Don't tell me you were diving all winter?"

"There's no such thing as a cold dive, just the wrong kit. We broke the ice on the old quarry on New Year's Day. You should have joined us."

"You're mad."

"Maybe." He deadpanned for a moment, then gave Daniel a crooked grin. "It was pretty dull, but it blew away the Christmas cobwebs. The best bit of a New Year dip is the pub afterwards. The weather's warming up nicely now, though. We'll be back out on the wrecks soon enough."

"Sounds good to me," said Daniel happily. "Any chance of some guide work this season? I don't know how much free time I'll have, but I want to get back underwater, that's for sure."

"Well, as you can see, we are knee-deep in tourists," – he gestured around the empty shop floor – "but it'll start to get busy over the next few weeks. I'll find something for you to do." He paused. "If you're not busy right now, you could help me out with the electronics on this boat. I think there's a crossed wire fouling the sonar."

Daniel grinned happily. "Sure."

•

The train pulled quietly out of Paddington Station. Susie leaned back in her seat and closed her eyes.

Ella gave her a gentle kick on the ankle. "Drink your coffee," she said.

Susie groaned and sat up reluctantly. She reached towards the tall cup on the table in front of her. The train jolted as it crossed the points, and Ella shot out a hand to steady the drink before it spilled. Susie took the cup from her and sipped it cautiously.

"Mmm. Hot."

"What do I need to know about this site?" asked Ella.

"It's like any other," shrugged Susie, blowing on her drink. "All the same challenges around data protection and minimising human error. The physical security is super tight, of course. You'll have guessed that from the amount of information they needed to issue passes for this visit."

"What are the systems like?"

"Old but serviceable," said Susie shortly. She took a mouthful of coffee and looked around the carriage. There was no one in the adjacent seats, but the tell-tale tapping of a keyboard betrayed another passenger close by. "Let's talk about something else."

"Fine," said Ella. She looked out of the window at the fast-receding London suburbs.

"What's the matter?" asked Susie. "You've been in this business longer than I have. You know the score," – she lowered her voice – "with eavesdroppers."

Ella shot her a wounded look. "I know my job. I don't see much of a risk in here."

"You're cross about something else, aren't you?"

"Now that you mention it, where were you all weekend?"

"I was out. It was Lin's birthday, remember?"

Ella made a face. "I don't like that crowd. I don't know why you hang around with them all the time."

"They're my friends," said Susie with a shrug. "You used to come out with us, remember?" She turned away from Ella and hunkered down in her seat, sipping her cooling coffee, and scrolling through messages on her smartscreen.

Ella sighed. Susie was right to be cautious about talking on the train. That was an unforgiveable slip-up on her part. She felt ill at ease. It was true that she didn't socialise with Susie as much as she could now. The constant talk of fashion and celebrity gossip wore her down. Ella had found a new circle of friends who shared her intellectual passions. For all she liked Susie, the writing was probably on the wall for their relationship.

Her smartscreen vibrated. It was Cameron.

"Hi Ella. Are you and Susie on your way?"

"Yes, we sorted out our security clearances first this morning. We should be there just after lunch."

"Great, I'll confirm with the client. Let me know when you're able to talk freely. Noor's picked up some new information about vulnerabilities which you need to know about."

"Okay," said Ella. "What kind of things are we looking for?"

"Later, Ella. Too many ears." Cameron ended the call.

Frustrated, Ella thrust the screen in her pocket and stood up. "I'm going to see what they've got in the buffet car," she said to the back of Susie's head. "Want anything?"

"No thanks." Susie didn't look up from her game.

Ella sighed. "Are you sure? We'll have to get straight to work when we get there. This is your only chance of something to eat."

"Okay." Susie unfolded herself from the seat.

Ella led the way down the carriage. The train was half empty, but there was still a queue at the snack counter. A screen on the wall was playing the news channel for waiting customers, showing satellite images of the devastated Russian landscape interspersed with stock pictures of the nuclear power station at the centre of the original theft, and a stream of punditry and speculation.

"Look, it's Ross!" Sure enough, there was a snippet of Ross giving a pertinent and non-committal soundbite.

"He's getting very good at all this media stuff," said Susie admiringly.

"He's had some training from national athletics," said Ella. "He knows how to handle the press, although Andy's not exactly going to give him a hard time."

Absorbed in the coverage, they didn't notice that the queue was moving quickly.

"What can I get you, ladies?"

Ella jumped. "Ah, sorry." She glanced at the small display. "I'll have a cappuccino, please, and that chicken sandwich."

"Coke, please, and I'll have the cheese roll," said Susie. "And two slices of carrot cake," she added.

The girl behind the counter packed the food efficiently in a paper sack and handed it to Susie, who started back up the train. Ella tapped the payment terminal and gingerly picked up her hot coffee cup. Now to get back to their seats without accident or incident.

Ella turned away from the counter but stopped as the screen caught her eye again. Now the news channel was showing scenes of protestors gathered outside a generic industrial site. The caption on the screen credited the footage to a location in Japan, another power station. The scene flicked to an aerial view of mountains, forests, and lakes, zooming in to shadowy figures, masked and laden with guns and ammunition. Could these be the people behind the attack? Ella shivered. If these insurgents and survivalists had graduated to nuclear weapons, then she and her colleagues were shouldering a greater burden than ever before: responsibility for people's lives.

•

Ross took the stairs two at a time, buoyed by the adrenaline of another live interview with Andy and Giles. As he opened the office door there was the sound of laughter.

"I am not helping you to carry all of that," Sandeep was saying, trying to keep a straight face, and failing miserably.

Pete looked wounded. "It's not much. Just the basics." He gestured helplessly at a very large and tightly packed bag. "Dry suit, undersuit, hood, gloves, mask, fins, snorkel, regulator, gauges, buoyancy jacket, reel, torch, knife, bag, dive computer, watch, compass, camera. I can hire the rest."

"It weighs a ton!"

"It's good for you."

"I'll take your suitcase, at least that's on wheels."

"Deal."

Ross watched the exchange with amusement. "You need to find a more lightweight hobby," he said.

"You're not telling me you pack much less," said Pete. "Where do you put the bikes? In your handbag?" He laughed and dashed around the desk away from Ross, straight into the path of a foam rugby ball that Joel launched at him.

Ross grinned at him. "You can run, but you can't hide." He jumped towards Pete who ducked and swerved.

Behind him, Noor grabbed her mug from the desk and dodged out of the way. "That's enough," she said. "Watch my coffee!"

The laughter subsided. Ross flopped into his chair and put his feet up on the desk. "I can't leave you alone for a moment," he said, wiping his eyes. He looked around. "The girls are already on their way to site?"

"Yes," replied Noor. She glanced at the clock. "They should be on the train by now – and so should you two," she continued, glaring at Sandeep and Pete.

"Almost ready," said Pete. "The taxi will be here any minute. I wanted to collect all the up to date reports over a secure connection."

"Where are you staying?" asked Joel. "With your mum, Sandeep?"

Sandeep shook his head. "No. She's in Newcastle, which is miles away. We'll base ourselves near the site, a bit further south. I've found a bed and breakfast that looks okay."

"It's near a dive centre, too," said Pete happily.

"You do know you're going up there to work, don't you?" said Joel.

"Of course, but there's no reason for me to come back to London this weekend," replied Pete. "The boys are with Adele. I'm simply making plans to amuse myself while Sandeep visits his mum. All work and no play makes Pete a dull boy."

Sandeep's smartscreen buzzed. "Taxi's here," he said. "We'll be off." He picked up his backpack and manoeuvred the two suitcases to the small lift on the landing.

Pete lugged his dive bag across the floor and dumped it on top of the other bags.

"Have a good journey," said Ross with a wave as the two of them disappeared down the stairs. He turned to Noor. "There's a lot of new information to absorb, isn't there?"

Noor nodded. "Once I started following up on the original report, there was a huge amount of additional research to collate."

"Hardly surprising," agreed Ross. "The threat potential is enormous."

"It's not just human error, either," said Joel. "The physical threats are high too. There are constant attacks going on."

"Most of them get picked up and stopped in short order, though," said Noor.

"Tell me about it," said Joel. "There have been plenty of things that we've worked on which would have caused havoc if they'd got through."

"And a few which did cause havoc," said Noor.

"True," said Ross. "But we've managed to contain most of them." He leaned over and tapped a link on his screen. The latest download from Noor's research opened and Ross scanned the contents. "There's just so much stuff here. It's going to take a while to nail down the relevant information."

"I'm working on it," said Noor, quietly confident. "I've set up a classification system and I'm cross-referencing everything that I can. This piece about the spearfishing attack, which we now think started the chain of events in China, is a good example. It was traced to a broadly local source quite quickly, thanks to some neat OSINT work triangulating domain names and IP addresses with Chinese government records. That made everyone think that it was someone with a personal grievance, but now we can be fairly sure that it was just one part of a distributed attack, and the fact that this particular one got through is just coincidence. I then checked the style of the code with some of the other malware which has come across our radar, and there is a strong correlation with elements of the Speakeasy ransomware."

"Cybercriminals for hire. No real surprise," said Ross, making a mental note to do some digging around more unorthodox sources. "How does it help?"

Noor grinned helplessly. "I have no idea. All I know is that there is a pattern emerging, and someone actively producing malicious code in China has been careless enough with their security that their activity can be traced to a region hundreds of miles across. It isn't conclusive by any means, but it's one tiny piece of the jigsaw."

"Interesting that you've managed to correlate that much information," said Ross thoughtfully. "Noor, do you think there's enough depth of data in Cameron's HackerTracker to run some more tests?"

Noor's eyes lit up. "Oh yes, why not. Those records go back at least ten years and she's been very thorough. Can you two develop algorithms based on the processes I've followed?"

"Sure," said Joel.

"When are you going down to Kent?" asked Ross. "I have to be at the track in an hour, but if you need to sort out that client first, I'll make a start on the programming later."

"I'm not due there until tomorrow morning," said Joel. "I can make a start with some test samples this afternoon. Is it worth bringing transaction data into the mix? We've got plenty of information on ransomware payments and commissions from previous crimes that we've never matched up to perpetrators."

"Yes," said Noor. "I'll add that to the pile."

"What about all these files on insurgents and unstable states?" asked Ross, opening another folder. "What have we got here? Venezuelan rebels, Wyoming Militia, Indonesian terrorists, Catalan republicans, Congolese anti-corruption activists... Where do all of these fit in?"

"I don't know yet," said Noor, "but this was a carefully planned, well financed, long term plan. Someone, somewhere, commissioned and financed the original cyber attacks, the theft of uranium, and the work to conduct this test. We have to consider all the possibilities."

Joel gave Ross a sidelong look. "How about your shady mates, Ross? This would be a good time to use them."

Ross gave him a crooked grin. "I was ahead of you there," he said. "I'm thinking through some people on the fringes that I can contact. I don't want to get pulled into that circle again, but I'll find out what I can." He paused as a thought struck him. "You could help too, Noor. What about your chum in Singapore?" He held up a hand as Noor started to protest. "Wait, yes, I know you say he wasn't involved. But he was very close to the action and some of his immediate colleagues were prosecuted for the attack on Cameron's apartment and the kidnap of her niece."

"He had no idea what was going on," said Noor defensively.

Ross flung his arms up in frustration. "Honestly, Noor, I find that really hard to believe. He may well be squeaky-clean, but don't you think that he will have seen and heard things that could be, what did you call them, tiny parts of the jigsaw?"

Joel nodded. "He's right, Noor. If Ross is looking up his dodgy connections, the least you can do is ask some hard questions of your MerLions man."

"Fine." Noor was visibly upset.

"Look, it's nothing personal," pleaded Ross, angry at himself for losing his temper. "You're doing an amazing job. I know I couldn't make sense of all this data, and you're just slicing through it, but we can't leave any possible leads hanging. Please, Noor."

She nodded. "Okay."

"Good." He swung his legs off the desk and picked up his training bag. "I'm off to the track. I'll see you tomorrow."

Joel picked up Noor's empty coffee cup. "Here," he said gently. "Want a refill? We'll have all your searches working before he's broken a sweat."

Noor nodded, mollified, and buried herself in her work.

•

Cameron put down her smartscreen and stared into space, thinking. Her concentration had been broken by an unexpected call from a senior connection in the cybersecurity world. The community's response to the emerging threat was gathering pace.

She picked the screen back up and started again with the latest report that Noor had sent her. The work they had done two years earlier on the original breach and suspected uranium theft had been updated and enhanced as more information came to light. She struggled to make sense of the whole picture of disparate incidents that seemed to be linked. All the new vulnerabilities that had been identified would have to be checked and patched by her team and others across the world. The hints of individuals emerging from the background were as frustrating as they were tantalising. Try as she might, she could not hold the shape of the global threat in her head. It was incomplete, its final form eluding her.

Frustrated, Cameron swung her legs up on the sofa, lay back, and gazed at the ceiling. Seeing an opportunity, the small black and white cat jumped up onto her stomach and started to knead ecstatically.

"Ow!" An enthusiastic claw had gone straight through Cameron's thin top and into her skin. She pushed the cat down onto her lap and it squeaked, offended. Cameron scratched between its ears and the purring and kneading started again.

"Want a coffee?" Ben appeared from the bedroom, hair damp from the shower. He yawned. "I'm not cut out for these odd hours."

"Coffee would be great. Are you having breakfast or lunch now?

"Brunch."

"Fair enough. What time did you come to bed?"

"About six o'clock this morning," replied Ben. He busied himself with the coffee maker. "Just as soon as the Americans went to bed, the Russians woke up. They all want new satellites deployed literally overnight, to replace the ones that were destroyed and to double their surveillance capacity."

"So much for a peaceful weekend," sighed Cameron.

Ben frowned. "You've been just as bad. You've been completely distracted since this news broke. In fact, you were distracted long before that. What's going on, Cam?"

She gestured at the files on the screen. "What do you think?" she said shortly. "There's a lot to do."

Ben gave her a strange look. "Calm down, Cameron. I was only asking."

The coffee maker hissed and spat the last few drops into the jug. Ben grabbed two clean mugs and opened the fridge. "You're almost out of milk," he said. "You really need a smart fridge."

"No chance," said Cameron. "The portal does its job well enough."

"Milk added to your next delivery," said a disembodied voice.

Ben laughed, poured the coffee, and set the mugs down on the small table. "You're trying to solve all the world's problems again, aren't you? You're trying to atone for something that wasn't your fault." He shook his head. "It's not up to you to fix this. We're all doing our part."

"I'm sorry," said Cameron, contrite. "I know." She sat up and moved the protesting cat off her knee. It slouched off to find a warm nest in the bedroom.

Ben sat down beside her and folded her in a hug.

"I don't deserve you," she said, her voice muffled in the sleeve of his shirt.

"You're right," he said sternly. "Drink your coffee."

The pause and the caffeine cleared Cameron's head a little.

"I've been staring at this stream of reports for three days," she said. "Layer upon layer of analysis and speculation. There's something underneath that I can't get to grips with. Something big."

"Is it really your job to dig that deep?" asked Ben. "Why can't you just treat the symptoms?"

"Treating the symptoms is the day job. The more I know about the roots, the better we can be."

"I think there's more to it," said Ben shrewdly. "You've always dealt with hidden figures. You chased wraiths online. You're starting to see that there are real people doing this, and real people are getting hurt." He fixed her with a penetrating stare. "Do you actually think you can go after these criminals yourself?"

Cameron met his gaze. "Yes."

"No, Cameron." Ben stood up and walked to the window, looking out onto a jumble of brickwork and rooftops and slate grey skies. "That's a step too far. You're out of your depth."

"It's something I need to do," she replied quietly. "I won't be on my own. I've been asked to join an international team."

Ben turned and stared at her. "Why didn't you tell me?"

"Because I haven't given them my answer yet."

"You didn't think it was worth discussing?"

Cameron shook her head. "I'm not ready to discuss it."

"This isn't something you can decide alone, Cameron. It affects the people closest to you." Ben finished his coffee and put the mug on the countertop. "I have to go. We're working on the final designs for those satellites. I'm going to be pretty busy for the next few weeks, and I might have to travel."

"Ben…"

"When you're ready to talk, let's talk. We've both got a lot of work to do." He dropped a kiss on the top of her head. "I'm sure you'll make the right decision." He picked up his backpack and opened the door. "I'll see you later."

Cameron watched the door close behind him, her stomach churning. She was afraid that she was driving Ben away, distracted by the present threat and by the sense of responsibility she still felt over the attack on her family. She was in danger of being overwhelmed, but she didn't feel she could burden either Ben or her brother. There was only one thing for it. She needed to go and see Aunt Vicky.

•

Tenuk rubbed his eyes and reached for his drink. He'd managed only a few hours of sleep in the past four days. The nuclear test had thrown plans for the latest MerLions team tour into chaos. The authorities in North Korea, recently so flexible, had withdrawn permission for the historic visit. If he'd known the location that the clients had chosen for this demonstration of power, then he could have influenced the decision on where to take the team this year. The inconvenience and extra workload gave him perfect cover, but it was taking its toll on his clandestine activities. He was struggling to keep up with the streams of notifications on all the different channels.

Client enquiries were flooding in. He read through five new ones, rejected three, and replied to the other two quoting the high price that his network could command for its services. He dealt with some queries from previous quotes, drawing the prospective clients closer to a decision. Once they committed to working with him, he could pass them back up the line into the higher levels of the Syndicate to be processed.

New confirmed contracts were arriving from Syndicate administrators, bundled into anonymous individual work packages whose real intention was heavily disguised. These would be advertised to members of the Pasar community and others like it. In most cases the developers would have no idea where the code they produced would be used. The network of skilled cybercriminals controlled by Tenuk and his peers ranged from village kids across Asia to unemployed Russian trolls, coders in the favelas of Rio de Janeiro, and bored high school dropouts across the world. They didn't care about any high-flown cause: they wanted the money and the economic freedom to change their lives.

Tenuk had always believed that the opportunities he provided for people outweighed the disruption wrought by the cyber attacks they perpetrated. He saw himself as a philanthropist, a champion leading people out of poverty. As he sipped his drink, he was surprised to find a knot of doubt buried deep in his mind. The messy business in London must have affected him more than he thought. He had been comfortable in his virtual world, hidden here under the streets of Singapore. The disorder of the real world and the behaviour of some of his associates had caused a tremor in his self-confidence and conviction. He suddenly wanted to talk to Noor. He checked the time; she would be working. It would not be a good idea to call.

Tenuk needed some air to clear his head. He locked the screens and left his apartment, heading for the nearest exit to the surface. The streets were quiet. There was still a partial curfew after the most recent Grasshopper Flu outbreak. By contrast, the night-time birds and insects were in full voice. He walked towards the river, seeking a breeze to relieve the cloying humidity. A brown shape scampered across the road. A rat? No – an otter. It slid into the water and floated on its back, gazing at him. Clutched in its paws was a Koi carp. Tenuk laughed to himself. The otter had ignored the hunting grounds of the bay and chosen the easy pickings of a garden pond. Tenuk could just imagine the reaction of the owner when they realised their prized collection of fish had been raided by the local wildlife.

In the distance Tenuk could see the lights of the busy port. Work never stopped here at the crossroads of the east. Ships were lined up out at sea, waiting their turn in a berth. There was a faint clang of port machinery as containers were offloaded to the docks or stowed on new vessels for the next leg of their journey. Most of the port was automated, machinery humming and robot stevedores organising the containers in a balletic dance too complex for the eye to follow. Despite that, the ships floating in the moonlight gave Tenuk a timely reminder of the human, physical world beyond a computer screen.

Refreshed, he headed back towards home. He dodged a curfew patrol out of principle, although his immunity certificate was up to date and easily verified. He slid back into his apartment unnoticed. Back online, he closed the stream of client enquiries that was overwhelming him. Instead, he dropped onto the Eden marketplace, where he checked the response to his recent advertisement for work on the carbon credit transfer. There had been some interest, and he picked out the best proposals to review later. He recognised some of the handles from the Pasar community, but he was confident they wouldn't make the connection between his Eden personal account and his professional image on Pasar.

Time to go and visit that community. Although many of the developers he contracted knew nothing about the underlying projects to which they contributed, this group were different. There were some very bright people on there, and they were more than capable of pulling together the threads in the advertised work and building a picture of the whole. He'd relied on Yasmin the Admin to manage them, an artificial intelligence which was more than a match for the strong characters. Yasmin was gone, confined to a local server in England while successive courts argued over the sentencing of a virtual being. Now it was down to Tenuk to keep the Pasar community under control.

He had some new jobs to distribute, but he was more interested in gauging the mood of the group. They'd been ebullient when the news of the nuclear test broke, and it was obvious that the bigger fish in the pond knew exactly what their role had been. It was even possible that some of them had guessed who the main client was. Something on the scale of a nuclear explosion could be narrowed down to a disgruntled nation state, of which there were very few now that North Korea had fallen into line, or a high value breakaway group. Tenuk mulled over the client for a moment. He knew exactly who they were, and he also knew that they had not yet paid the final instalment for the work. There was still time, of course – the contract required payment within seven days of the successful test – and Tenuk hoped that there would be no unpleasantness.

He logged into the community and scanned down the list of active members. After long association with the group he had some idea of the time zones each member lived in, although not their exact location. Sagikkun, the trickster, was there; so was Mìmì Mão. The Monkey was nowhere to be seen. It was too early for Cloverleaf and the others who he suspected were scattered across North and South America. Around forty of the elite developers were there, chatting and boasting. Tenuk frowned as he scanned their messages. They were all getting far too friendly. It was time to remind them who was boss. He took a deep breath and joined in.

4: SNAKE RIVER

After three days of tinkering, Michelle was getting frustrated with the salvaged hard disk. The solid plastic case had protected its control electronics well from water damage, and the old motor and heads seemed to be intact. She had succeeded in imaging it, keeping the original disk intact while she examined its contents, but there was very little to see. It didn't make sense to her that the disk would have been cared for so well, before being discarded, if it had been blank.

Daniel had transcribed the fragments of labels that remained on the disk and the casing, in the hope that it might provide some clue to its origins and age. Maybe one of her online connections could help.

Looking for a distraction, Michelle flicked on the radio. The news channel was still talking about the explosion. It would take something really big to displace that from the headlines for the next few days and weeks. They had some cybercrime pundit talking about the methodology of an attack. She listened carefully. He seemed to know his stuff, and his description of a hierarchy of cybercriminals for hire, unaware of the end use for their code, was uncannily accurate. However, this job had been different.

She thought back to the contracts that had been advertised on Pasar two years earlier. There had been the usual smattering of malware required and a phishing campaign to plan. One job had asked for the penetration of seemingly unconnected software systems, from meeting apps and social media to cargo schedules and tax records. Media influence and messaging had been a large part of the work. Michelle also recalled seeing specifications for several complex applications, work for a group, not an individual. She had joined the dots, realised that all of the pieces were probably connected to something big, and avoided entanglement with any of it. The cybercriminals for hire were no longer independent. They knew they were part of a team. They knew what they had done. Yasmin the Admin and King Katong had created a many-headed monster, and it was starting to run wild.

She moved back to her main machine and dipped into the communities and chatrooms that she liked to frequent. She made a cursory search of the Eden marketplace, but couldn't narrow down what she needed closely enough to find an off-the-shelf analyser for an apparently empty disk. In passing she checked on the proposal she'd put in for the carbon credits job. Last time she had looked, it was under consideration by the buyer. According to marketplace rules they should be making an offer within the next few hours, and no news was good news.

The Piper was the obvious person to ask for advice on penetrating the hard drive. They had built up a friendship over the years and she trusted his skills and instincts. She hadn't heard from him for a while, and he didn't seem to be active in any of the usual forums, but she dropped a message for him to pick up if he came by. She wondered for a moment if he was lurking in the Pasar community. She hadn't been back since the news of the nuclear test had come through. Could it be worth checking for the Piper on there?

Reluctantly she logged in and scanned the activity. King Katong was shouting his mouth off as usual. He was always angry, but she had long since stopped caring about his rants. Cloverleaf and several of her erstwhile friends were online, but she didn't want to hang around in that group. There was an undercurrent of radical action and risk taking emerging, and she had no wish to put herself or Daniel in danger. The jobs that she could get through there may be highly paid, but that only reflected the high risk of being associated with something like the nuclear power station breach. It wasn't worth it. She left as quickly as she had arrived.

Back in the shallows of the web, an alert pinged. Michelle smiled to herself. Her message had been read. Sure enough, a few seconds later, she received an invitation to join a private voice chat. She smiled to herself. Piper was one of the few people she trusted enough to have a real conversation.

"Pix! Good to hear from you. How long has it been?"

"Too long, Piper. How are you doing?"

He sighed. "Busy with the day job." He paused. "Pix…" There was a note of caution in his voice. "You weren't involved in this Russian mess, were you?"

"No," replied Michelle firmly. "You?"

"Not a chance." He sounded relieved. "I'm glad we got that out of the way. You said you needed some help? What's up?"

"Oh, nothing much," she said. "I've been clearing out some old cupboards and found a hard drive. I can't get it to play nice."

"It's booting okay? No physical damage?"

"Yes, I hooked it up via a write blocker and imaged the contents, but I can't read the data at all."

"Hmmm. How old is it?"

"I don't know," she admitted. "My cousin found it in an old box from our grandparents." That was as close to the truth as she was going to go. "Decades, certainly. Daniel transcribed the label that was on it. Here, I'll send you the file."

"Daniel?"

"My cousin."

"Oh, okay."

Was that a hint of jealousy? Michelle's stomach did an unexpected backflip. She had always had something of a soft spot for Piper, but it had never occurred to her that the feeling might be mutual. She was probably mistaken. It was just good to hear his familiar voice again.

His voice. That thought had triggered was niggling at the back of her mind.

"Pix? I don't have the file yet."

"Sorry!" She hit the button, pushing the thought away.

"Got it," he said, a moment later.

Michelle heard him whistling under his breath while he scanned the details.

"It's not much to go on," he said finally, "but I'll see what I can find."

"Thanks, Piper," she said. "If it turns out to be something interesting, I'll share my buried treasure with you."

"Arrrr," he laughed. "Look, Pix, I have to go. It's been good talking to you again. I'll be in touch."

"Bye, Piper. Take care." Michelle disconnected from the chat. The flash of intuition she had had during the call was eluding her, but one thing stood out. She knew the Piper's voice from somewhere in the real world.

Another message alert startled her out of her reverie. "Congratulations," said the mellifluous voice of the Eden admin bot. "Your bid has been accepted."

Michelle whooped, her voice echoing around the empty house. The buyer liked her approach and had accepted her top price without question. Their luck was changing. She wondered how Daniel was getting on with his interview.

•

The company's logo covered an entire wall of the small interview room. The other three were a clean dull, corporate grey. There were no windows, and the ceiling light was slightly too bright, showing up a neglected dust ball in one corner of the tiled floor.

"Your certificates all check out," said the hiring manager, scrolling through a list of documents.

Daniel sat up straight and smiled. So far so good. Michelle's wizardry had helped him to sail through the automated selection algorithms and landed him on the shortlist, and between them they had picked out the right set of qualifications to help him through the final interview.

"Tell us more about your experience with large site security." The man paused, ready to take notes.

Daniel nodded confidently. The certificate in the interviewer's hand might not have been acquired in the usual way, but he knew the job well enough, albeit from both sides of the fence.

"Sure," he said. "I've worked with a full range of boundary systems including physical barriers, tethered and free drone surveillance, CCTV, and intelligent threat assessment for risk mitigation." The local landfill could do with some more of that, he reflected. The ditch system across the marshes was popular with scavengers. He had lost his train of thought and coughed hurriedly to cover the hesitation. "Um, sorry. I've also managed continuous shifts in several settings."

"Thank you. You've completed training on the latest incident management guidelines?"

Daniel wasn't sure if this was a statement or a question. He couldn't remember whether he'd submitted a certificate for this. He certainly hadn't done any such training, but it sounded important. He decided to wing it.

"Yes."

The interviewer smiled, and Daniel thought he looked relieved. "Good. You were quick off the mark, then. You didn't include certification in your application pack."

Ah. Very new guidelines, then. "Uh, no," said Daniel. "I finished the course online after I sent in my application. I haven't had any certificates yet."

"Okay." The man scanned his screen and nodded. "I think that's all. If you could forward that certificate as soon as you can, we'll add it to your records. We'll be in touch. Thank you for your time."

"Thank you. I, um, look forward to hearing from you. Soon. I mean, thank you." Daniel stood up and tripped on the chair as he turned. He hobbled to the door, trying not to curse at the sharp pain in his foot. Balanced again, he turned and gave the interviewer what he hoped was a professional and friendly smile and walked out with his head held high.

Outside he hesitated, unsure for a moment which way to turn. If he got the security job, he reflected, one of the first things to do would be to improve the signage and the management of visitors to stop people wandering around the building. A door further down the corridor opened and two men appeared, deep in conversation. The tall, bald, white one glanced at him as they passed. Daniel paused for a moment and followed them. Sure enough, they were headed for reception. The three of them arrived at the barriers together. The two men paused to talk to the receptionist and Daniel waited politely behind them.

"You're off early," she said with a smile.

"We thought we'd have a stroll through the town," said the short Indian man.

"That won't take long," said the receptionist with a laugh. "I thought you were from around here?"

"Newcastle," he replied, shaking his head. "I've never been down here before."

"I've heard the diving is good along this coast," said the tall man. "Is there a club or a shop nearby?"

"You want to visit Slater's at the far end of the beach," interjected Daniel.

The tall man turned to look at him.

"You dive?"

Daniel nodded. "When I can."

The man grinned at him and extended a hand. "Pete. Good to meet you."

"Daniel. You too."

"And this is Sandeep," Pete continued, indicating his colleague. "We're new on the site. Do you work here?"

"I'd like to," said Daniel. "I've just had an interview." He handed his visitor pass to the receptionist, who scanned it and nodded to him.

"You're good to go," she said.

The barrier popped open.

"Mind if we tag along?" asked Pete, as he and Sandeep followed Daniel through the door.

"I can point you towards the town, but I'm heading home," said Daniel. "If you go to the dive shop, just mention my name. I generally go out as a guide for tourist groups."

Pete gave him a wide smile. "Fantastic. I've heard some good things about the coastline here. You've got some good wrecks as well, haven't you? I brought all my kit."

Sandeep gave him a sidelong look. "Everything but the kitchen sink," he said drily.

Daniel laughed. "You've heard right. Some of the wrecks are pretty far down, but there are a few good ones at an easy depth. There are some shallow, rocky reefs here, and of course further north we take trips up to the Farne Islands which are fun on their own. Those islands and rocks caught a lot of old ships out, and there are still a few relics to dive all up the coast from when there were wartime sea mines along here a hundred years ago."

"Sounds great," said Pete appreciatively. He eyed the clouds. "We just need the weather to turn. Thanks, Daniel."

A bell rang on the bus stop, alerting potential passengers to the shuttle's arrival. Sure enough, a few seconds later it appeared in the distance.

"This'll take you straight to the market square," said Daniel, "and just keep heading north until you find it."

"Slater's, yes?"

"Yes."

Sandeep stuck his arm out and the shuttle glided to a halt. "Hope to see you again, Daniel," he said. He followed Pete onto the bus, and Daniel turned and headed towards home.

Michelle was waiting for him at the end of their street.

"How did it go?" she asked.

"Good, I think," said Daniel. He hooked arms with his cousin, and they strolled slowly back towards the house. "The paperwork was all in order. I have one more certificate to send in, and to be honest, I'd better do the course as well. It sounded important."

"You think you got the job, then?"

"Maybe. I hope so." He glanced sidelong at her. "What have you been up to this afternoon?"

"Oh, this and that," she said airily. "I got another freelance commission while you were out."

"We're on a roll," said Daniel proudly. "What is it? I hope it's above board."

"Oh, pretty much," said Michelle, crossing her fingers behind her back. "It's a bit of work on carbon credits."

"That sounds safely dull," said Daniel with a laugh. "See, it's not that hard to behave. Are they paying well?"

"Oh yes," she replied with a roguish grin. "Very well indeed. I haven't worked with them before, and they've already sent a down payment."

"That's fantastic!" Daniel turned and looked at his cousin in admiration. "Nice one, Shell."

The clouds parted and a shaft of sunlight warmed their faces. They splashed happily through a series of shallow puddles left by the afternoon rain.

The stillness of the afternoon was shattered by the sudden roar of an engine. Daniel jumped to the side of the path, dragging Michelle with him. A trail bike sped past, skidding on the wet surface and sending up a spray of dirty water. It disappeared around the corner at the end of the short terrace, closely followed by a second, larger machine. There was a cacophony of barking from the local dogs, woken from their afternoon snoozes by the unexpected noise.

"Idiots," shouted Daniel after them. "Shell, you okay?"

"I'm fine." She ran her fingers through her hair, tugging at the tangles. "Those were petrol engines. What are they doing down here?"

"Daft kids. They'll soon be picked up." Sure enough, there was the whine of police drones overhead, and Daniel looked up to see an interceptor pelting along in pursuit at rooftop height. It followed the route the bikes had taken into rough ground, and the fading noise of the bike motors stopped abruptly.

At the end of the street, Daniel and Michelle turned in the opposite direction along the boundary between the inhabited terraces and the wasteland that stretched towards the landfill and the industrial sites. There had been many more rows of houses here once, home to a large local workforce. As the plants automated their processes and work moved away, the community had declined. A short row of three or four dwellings remained intact in the middle of the uneven scrub, traces of an adjoining building remaining on the flank where the other homes in the terrace had been torn down. They looked empty, dark windows gaping, but Daniel could see one with a shiny communications aerial on its roof. Although isolated from the rest of the village, someone was still connected to the rest of the world.

Michelle sniffed the air. "That's a strong scent. What is it? Honeysuckle?"

Looking around, Daniel spotted an unruly plant clambering over a partly collapsed brick wall nearby on the wasteland. Its bright gold and white flowers were lit by the sun, and a heady sweet smell was rising from them.

"Looks like it," he confirmed. He wrinkled his nose. "It's a bit strong for me."

They had reached their house. As Michelle stroked the entry pad to open the front door, Daniel paused. His smartscreen was vibrating.

"It's them!" He picked up the call and turned away. "Yes. Yes, I see." There was a long pause. "Fantastic. Thank you."

He turned to Michelle, grinning from ear to ear. "I got the job, Shell! I start on Monday."

She threw her arms around him. "I'm so happy for you, Dan. How about a takeaway tonight, to celebrate?"

"Great idea. Our luck is changing, Shell. We are on our way back up."

•

Cameron gazed across a landscape of familiar fields as the hired autocar swept down the country lane towards the village. It was still only mid-afternoon, but cloudy skies threatened rain and the colours of the rolling grassland were lost in the dim light. At the bottom of the hill the taxi slowed to take a sharp bend and passed the house where she had grown up, and where her brother and his family still lived.

"Aren't you staying with Charlie as usual?" asked Andy, sitting across from her in the autocar. They had bumped into each other on the train travelling up from London, both heading for the same place.

"Of course," replied Cameron lightly. "No point stopping here, though. I want to pop in and see Aunt Vicky first."

Andy smiled at the mention of his feisty neighbour. Aunt Vicky was a local legend, her cat doubly so.

"You haven't been up for a while, have you?" he said. "She'll be glad to see you." He looked sidelong at Cameron. "Have you been avoiding everyone?"

She shrugged. "I've been busy." She looked out of the window again, her eyes unfocused. The taxi approached the village green then turned to the left up a small hill towards a cluster of houses.

Andy raised an eyebrow and said nothing.

Cameron turned to face him. Coming back to the place she thought of as home tended to bring her professional guard down and made her more vulnerable. She hated it, but Andy had hit a raw nerve and she was suddenly upset.

"Okay. Yes. It was my fault that Nina became a target for the cybercriminals that I should have stopped. Is that what you wanted to hear?"

Andy opened his mouth to protest, but the taxi had pulled up at its destination and Cameron jumped out without another word, grabbing her overnight bag from the luggage bay. Andy thumbed a sensor to settle the tab and climbed out after her. She was already halfway down the path to Aunt Vicky's front door.

"I'm sorry," he called. "And it wasn't your fault, any of it."

She half-turned towards him and gave him a weary smile. "Thanks," she said. "Let's grab a drink tomorrow, shall we?"

"Sure, Cameron. Take care." Andy headed for his own front door, the next cottage in the small terrace. He skirted cautiously around a puddle of ginger fur that was blocking his path. Donald the cat had a penchant for ankles, and Andy did not want to attract his attention.

Aunt Vicky emerged from her house and gave him a cheery wave, then greeted her niece with an all-encompassing hug and drew her into the house. Andy sighed. Cameron needed some family time. He hoped that Vicky would help her to find her confidence again.

"Sit down, darling. I'll put the kettle on."

Cameron snuggled into the corner of the old sofa, breathing in the familiar scent of the house, and letting the faint sounds of the countryside wash over her. As she tuned in to the birdsong, the bleating of sheep, and the distant whirr of delivery drone rotors, she detected some scuffling in the garden outside. Donald must be on the prowl again. Cameron poked her head above the windowsill and peered out. Sure enough, her aunt's enormous and notorious ginger cat was now sitting in the middle of the lawn, eyes fixed on a small brown shape. It was a bedraggled mouse, apparently Donald's latest catch, and it was still moving. As Cameron watched, the mouse stood up on its hind legs and lashed out at the cat's nose, boxing for its life and squealing loudly. Donald recoiled and made ready to pounce again but was distracted by Aunt Vicky emerging from the back door.

"Donald! Don't you dare bring that mouse in here!"

The spell was broken. The mouse took its chances and ran under a nearby flowerpot. Donald glared at Aunt Vicky and slouched off into the shrubbery in search of new entertainment. Cameron smiled to herself. The mouse lived to fight another day, and Donald had been taken down a peg or two. She felt some of the tension melt away. She had been right to come back to the village at last.

Aunt Vicky bustled in and set the tea tray on a small table.

"Now, dear," she said, pouring a cup and adding a dash of milk, "tell me your news. I don't want to know about work. I want to know how you are faring in yourself." She handed Cameron her tea and looked her in the eyes. "I've been worried about you."

Cameron took a deep breath. "I feel wretched, Aunt Vicky," she admitted at last. "Business is booming, we're incredibly busy, all our clients love us. I'm keeping fit. Ben has been working in London again. I should be happy."

Aunt Vicky nodded sagely. "You should be happy, but you're not."

"Exactly. It's as if I'm watching myself. I'm using all my emotions up on making sure other people are alright. I can't remember the last time I was really happy. Intrigued, challenged, absorbed in what I do, yes, but not... happy." She looked down at her tea, lost in thought.

"You haven't taken a break at all, have you," said Aunt Vicky. "You used to be here every other weekend and heading off on holiday as soon as you had the carbon credits saved up."

"I haven't wanted to stop," admitted Cameron slowly.

"You haven't given yourself time to heal," said Aunt Vicky quietly.

"I didn't think I needed to."

"I heard what Andy said when you arrived. You seem to think that because your invisible cybercriminals came out of the woodwork and tried to harm you and your family, that this was somehow your fault."

"You're saying it isn't?"

Aunt Vicky sighed. "I can see how easy it is to blame yourself. If you didn't do the job you do, no harm would have come to the people you love. But the world is not that simple. If you didn't do the job you do, we would all be at greater risk."

Cameron looked away towards the window. The rain had begun, drops of water running down the glass.

"You're saying that this is the price of success?" She gave a hollow laugh. "It's not like it said on the tin."

"No, Cameron. It's the way the world works." Aunt Vicky sighed. "There is a capricious side to life. However careful we are, things can go wrong."

"So, it doesn't matter what I do. I can't protect everyone."

"Oh, darling, you are very low, aren't you? I was going to say that there is an equal chance of life surprising us with great things when we least expect them." She took Cameron's hand in hers. "You and Charlie have always excelled at surprising me, in the best ways."

Cameron squeezed her aunt's hand. "Thanks."

"I mean it, dear. How long can you stay here?"

"Everyone is out on site with clients," replied Cameron. "I can stay all weekend. Ben is working and the cat has more food than she can manage."

"Good," said Aunt Vicky. "You need some time to relax."

"Not just that. I need time to think." Cameron sighed. "I've been asked to take on a new contract. Part of an international consortium. We're taking the fight to the source. We're looking for the paymasters." She looked pleadingly at her aunt. "Help me to decide what to do."

•

"Noor? Ross?" Joel pushed the door open cautiously. As he expected, there was no one in the office. All the screens were dark, and the only light came from outside, around the edges of the window blinds. There were several layers of security in place around this office, and the first person to arrive had to disable the final checks. It was so long since he'd been alone here that he stumbled over the key switch that started the disarming process, and the system finally acknowledged his identity with seconds to spare.

As Joel moved into the room the ceiling lights flicked into life and the coffee machine started to boil. He chuckled to himself. He'd forgotten that Sandeep had added that to the list of essential processes at office start-up.

He flopped into a chair and wondered where his colleagues were. Ross was probably training, he reflected, but Noor was usually around well into the early evening. He checked the security logs. Noor had left almost an hour earlier. He pulled out his smartscreen, and she picked up almost instantly.

"Noor? I'm in the office."

"I thought you were down in Kent," she replied, puzzled.

"I've done everything I could do," he said with a shrug. "I managed to stretch it out to a third day, just, but the site is as tight as a drum. I came back through to finish off the reports so I can take the day off tomorrow."

"I'm at home," said Noor. "I'm mainly dealing with cybersecurity teams in Asia at the moment and they are all ahead of our time zone. I've been in very early for the last few days and I need some sleep."

"What about Ross?"

"He's running. You know he has a competition coming up soon."

Joel blinked. "Of course. European championships. I'd forgotten."

Noor laughed. "Joel, where is your head at the moment? This is not like you. Did you say you have tomorrow off? In that case go and enjoy the weekend and I'll see you on Monday."

"I'll file the report first so that Cameron can bill the client."

"Cameron is away for the weekend as well," said Noor. "She's gone to see her family. Monday will be fine, Joel. Go and relax."

"Okay." He gave Noor a broad grin. "Have a good sleep. Let me know if you need me."

Joel didn't want to leave straight away. Martha would still be at work herself, and it would be silly to leave the reports hanging for three days. He prepared a coffee and checked in the cupboard for snacks. He could tell that everyone was on site. There was a packet of biscuits unopened on the shelf, which he claimed with a cackle of triumph.

He started to work methodically through the notes he had uploaded remotely, but quickly found himself distracted and staring into space. It was too quiet. He was used to the hustle and bustle of colleagues and the bickering and chat that made the job fun.

"Play Radio Polly," he ordered, and the office portal obliged. Music rang around the room and Joel started drumming his fingers happily on the desk to the complex rhythm. This was more like it. He bent to the keyboard again, re-invigorated.

Joel was so absorbed in his work and the hypnotic melodies of the music that he missed Ella's first call, and only noticed his smartscreen vibrating on her second attempt.

"Volume down," he shouted at the portal. "Hi Ella. What's up?"

"Joel? Are you out? Sorry!"

"It's okay," said Joel. "Off!" he ordered. The radio was silenced. "I'm in the office. Just finishing off the reports on Kent."

"Was there anything to find there?" asked Ella.

"Nothing," said Joel. "Clean as a whistle, which is exactly what I expected. I guess they're happy knowing that, and Cameron's happy to have the business. I'm off to Norfolk on Monday to do the same."

"Have you got time to look at some odd stuff we've picked up here?" asked Ella.

"I thought you and Susie were on top of things," said Joel. "It should be just as straightforward as Kent."

"That's what we thought," replied Ella. "It isn't. I'll put Susie on. She can explain."

Susie's face appeared on the screen. "Hi, Joel."

"What's up?" he asked, puzzled now.

"Well, I haven't been here for a couple of years, and I worked on the network security last time I was here, with my old job, and it was all fine," she said. "But since then they've overhauled some of the hardware and software. They didn't need to do it; the old systems were perfectly robust. It seems like an unnecessary expense."

"How bad is it?"

"It's a bit of a mess. Some of the configuration's changed. There are components and sensors here that I haven't seen before. They claim that the work was just to bolster security, but it's way over the top."

"It may still have strengthened the systems, of course," said Ella. "We can't tell from the little we've seen."

"I know, but I want a second opinion. Can you have a look, Joel? Please?"

"Sure," he said. "I'm not in the office tomorrow, though. What have you got that you can send me now? Specs, systems diagrams? I'll see if anything looks amiss. I'll do some research from here."

"I've sketched out the new configuration," said Susie. "I'll share it now on the secure connection."

"I'll have a look. Will you join me on the vis deck?" He moved across the office to the visualisation deck, sat down and grabbed a lightweight headset and glove from the rack. At first, he could see nothing, but a faint ping signalled the start of sharing and Susie's sketch came into view. Joel blinked, taken aback.

"That's a bit of a mess, isn't it?"

"Yes." Her voice was coming through his headset now. "The more I dig into it, it looks as though the existing system elements have just been mucked around, but those changes hide a new element. Look."

Joel watched as the diagram spun around and a node lit up.

"Here, I've highlighted the section that concerns me."

"Talk me through it, Susie."

"Okay…" She took a deep breath. "The main external firewalls for the connected services in the installation are using non-standard software. The documentation we've seen suggests that some contractors recommended it over the existing tried and tested services. There are testimonials from other organisations, really big names, and some hints of military connections."

"You don't trust the paperwork."

"Not in the slightest," replied Susie. "Apart from anything else, one of the quotes is from a client of ours, and I'm ninety percent sure that they are not using this software."

"Hah, I'll check." Joel read the brief spec that Susie had attached to the diagram. "I can safely say I saw nothing like this in use in the Army, either. What's the company called?"

"Snake River Security," said Susie.

"Never heard of them."

Ella chipped in. "On the face of it, the firewall is doing its job. Of course, it's only significant for the connected servers, and they mainly handle admin and finance functions and links to academic research."

"True," said Joel, "but we know that even access to those areas could open up vulnerabilities in the main plant. It was one of the routes into the Chinese facility."

"I know," said Susie, "but as Ella says, it's doing its job. We've run some tests and it seems to be as tight as a drum. It's the paperwork around it which is making me twitch."

"Fair. What else?" Joel swung the diagram around idly, peering at the intricate 3D construct. "Is there new hardware here?" He scribbled a highlight.

"Yes, they've added new servers and cabling in the air gapped system within the plant and upgraded a lot of the monitoring sensors since I was last here."

"It's not a bad thing," said Joel. "You wouldn't even worry about it if you weren't on edge about the firewalls. How much testing have you been able to do on the plant's air gapped network?"

"Not a lot," admitted Ella. "We've been concentrating on penetration tests for the externally connected systems which sit just behind the firewall and reviewing processes and staff training. We've confirmed that there is no easy way of jumping from the connected systems to the closed systems."

"I only started looking at the air gapped hardware because I found more documentation from the same people who put in the firewall," said Susie. "This element I highlighted before" – she spun the diagram around again – "it shouldn't be there. It doesn't form a logical part of the network."

"What does the documentation say?" asked Joel.

"Just another server," said Susie with a shrug, "but every function is already accounted for."

"Could be a backup?" said Joel.

"Possible, but everything is already fully backed up off site, as you'd expect."

"Does the existing backup mirror that server?" asked Joel.

Susie hesitated. "That's it! That's what's wrong. It's been staring us in the face. It's not backed up."

"If you're right," said Joel. "It doesn't have an operational function on the network. So, what is it for?"

"That's the million-coin question, isn't it," said Susie. "Thanks for your help."

"No problem." Joel checked the time. "I'll leave a note for the others to dig deeper into that contractor. I don't know what you've stumbled on, but there's something very odd going down."

"We'll keep you posted. Have a good evening, Joel."

"You too, Susie." Joel pulled off his headset and returned to his desk. He pulled up his notes on the Kent job and read back through them, checking that he hadn't missed anything. He knew the site and its networks well, and he was confident that there was nothing unusual. There was one thing he could check, though. He picked up his smart screen and placed a call to his connection at the plant.

"Anish? Hi, Joel here. One quick question to finish off my report. Have you ever been approached by a company called" – he checked the name – "Snake River Security?"

He was surprised by the response.

"When was that, Anish? Eighteen months ago? No, nothing to worry about. Yes, I'd be cautious about a direct approach like that as well. Thanks, man. Speak to you soon."

Joel shivered. It might be all be innocent, but something felt very wrong.

•

Ross was sweating freely despite the drizzle that seeped into his clothes and hair. It was humid and unpleasant, the rain giving no relief. He glanced at the dark clouds above. The weather front that had rolled in halfway through his training session was set for the rest of the evening. His teammates, strung out along the trail, were also scowling at the sky. Adebayo passed him as they crested the hill, breathing heavily.

"You're off the pace," he panted.

Ross checked his watch and pushed his tired legs onwards. "This is vile," he replied, catching up to his friend.

"It's a horrible day for the long run," agreed Adebayo. "At least we aren't on bikes."

"Hah, yes, that would be a mess."

They matched each other stride for stride down the slope. The track and changing rooms were in sight now and Ross was ready for a shower and some dry clothes. He pushed for the finish and was rewarded by a nod from the coach, high praise indeed. Ross tucked himself into a sheltered corner by the wall and started to run through his cooldown routine.

"I saw you on the news earlier," said Adebayo, throwing Ross a bottle of water.

Ross caught it and drank deeply. "Thanks. Yeah, we've been busy for the last few days."

"I never knew what you did until now," said Adebayo. "You've never really talked about it."

"For a long time, I couldn't," said Ross. "We're a bit more open about it these days."

"So, you're sort of like the internet police. Do you ever come across real criminals?"

Ross laughed. Adebayo didn't know about his shady past, and he had no intention of revealing his own experiences on the other side of a prison fence. His more recent encounters were more innocent.

"Yes, we do," he said. "We've had some nasty incidents. That's why we tend to stay under the radar. We're not so much like police, though. They have their own cybercrime unit. We're more like puzzle solvers and gamekeepers." And sometimes poachers, he thought to himself.

"It sounds cool."

"It can be a lot of fun."

Heart rate settled and legs stretched, Ross was ready for his shower. They all crowded into the changing room. Ross pulled his clothes and bag out of the locker and glanced at his smartscreen. He'd missed two calls from Joel, and there was a voicemail waiting.

"The girls have found something odd in the West Country. Can you check out a company called Snake River Security when you come in tomorrow?"

The name meant nothing to him. He would certainly follow it up in the morning through the usual channels, but he suspected that Joel flagging it up to him this evening could mean only one thing. He wanted Ross to use his shadier connections as well.

Showered and refreshed, the athletes went their separate ways. It was still raining, and Ross jumped on the first bus that came along, relieved that he didn't have a bike with him today. The journey was slow, a stop-start meander through the suburbs which was very unlike his usual more direct route. It gave him time to think.

All of their focus had been on Russia and Asia for this investigation. Where did this new lead fit in? A quick search for the name threw up more questions than answers. There was no company listing, and a Snake River on almost every continent. One in Indonesia, another in Tasmania, and the largest running across the Pacific north west, passing through a handful of union states and the Wyoming republic. The Indonesian link seemed to fit with the picture they were building. He would have to dig a little deeper when he got home.

Water ran down the window of the bus as it sat waiting for new passengers to board. Looking outside, Ross could see pedestrians hurrying along, some with umbrellas, others with hoods pulled over their heads. The crowd parted around a stranded delivery bot which had misjudged a puddle and ground to a halt. A red light flashed forlornly on its top as it waited for a service drone to come to the rescue.

At the next stop Ross hopped off the bus and picked up another shuttle for the final leg of his journey. It was standing room only and he welcomed the chance to stretch his aching legs. At last he reached his destination, and he was glad to see that the rain had eased. It was only a short walk to his house, and he made it through the door before the next downpour started. He flung his wet, smelly running gear into the washing machine and warmed up some food, then flopped gratefully onto the sofa, listening to the storm that was gathering force outside. He fully intended to start work, but after finishing his meal he sat back and closed his eyes for a moment, and the hypnotic sound of the rain lulled him into a deep sleep.

5: DECISIONS

Cameron slept well for the first time in weeks. She woke to the chirrup of birds calling outside her bedroom window. They sounded alarmed. Cameron peered over the windowsill and was unsurprised to see Donald the cat sitting on the fence between her aunt's garden and Andy's house, his tail twitching as he surveyed the smorgasbord of feathered breakfasts. That would not do. Cameron opened the window.

"Shoo, Donald," she called as loudly as she dared. "Get out of there."

The spell was broken. Donald, alert to anything that might mean food was being served, leaped off the fence and ran towards the door. The birds settled down, reprieved.

It was still early but Cameron knew she would have little chance of getting back to sleep. She decided to go for a walk. Yesterday's rain had passed, and a light ground mist was clearing under the warmth of the rising sun. It would still be damp underfoot, but as long as she kept to the paths and out of the mud, she would be fine. She pulled on her jeans and dug a light jacket out of her overnight bag. Downstairs, Donald was yowling to be let in. She opened the door and he staggered in, giving an award-winning impression of a starving stray.

"You're a fraud," she said sternly.

Donald ignored her and started attacking the carpet. Cameron poked him with her toe, and he stopped and glared at her. How dare she spoil his morning routine?

She filled the cat's bowl and slipped quietly out of the front door. She walked down the hill to the high street and turned toward the village green. It was too early for most people to be up and about, but a lone drone passed overhead, probably checking fences and boundaries for one of the local farmers. Cameron thought of Ben, and the satellites that he designed orbiting unseen above them, gathering minute details about the planet below, and it brought a lump to her throat. She had not seen him since Monday, and they had barely spoken.

Past the village green and up a slight rise in the road lay the village church. Cameron pushed open the gate and closed it carefully behind her. A white stone near the wall marked the resting place of her parents.

What would their advice be? She wandered on along the path, deep in thought, and did not notice the dog walker until she almost tripped over an enthusiastic labradoodle that greeted her as a member of the family.

"Cameron?" came an incredulous voice.

"Charlie!" She jumped, startled, and blushed red.

"What... what are you doing here?" asked her brother.

This was not the meeting that Cameron had planned. "I stayed with Aunt Vicky last night," she mumbled.

"Oh, Cameron." Charlie drew his little sister into a tight embrace. "Why didn't you tell me you were coming? I've missed you."

"I needed some time to think, and I wasn't sure I'd be welcome," said Cameron in a rush of emotion, her voice muffled by Charlie's jumper.

"You are always welcome," said Charlie gently. "This is your home, or had you forgotten?" He hugged her tight. "What's wrong, sis?"

"But when I came before..." She disentangled herself from his arms. "Sameena was very unhappy."

"I know," said Charlie. "She was looking for someone to blame when Nina was kidnapped, but it wasn't your fault. She apologised, Cameron! She's missed you as much as I have."

"Is Nina okay?"

"She's fine. She's taken over most of your attic, though." Charlie tucked his arm through hers. "Come on. Let's walk."

They ambled along the street in companionable silence, watching the dog sniffing and scampering ahead of them as she followed her familiar route.

Cameron's head was starting to clear.

"I'm sorry, Charlie," she said slowly. "I've been an idiot."

He looked at her affectionately. "You took it harder than the rest of us, in the end. I'm sorry too. I should have made more of an effort to check up on you, but you seemed to be on top of things, and busy."

"I've been busy, that's for sure," said Cameron, "but I think I've been hiding. Ben said..." She swallowed. "Ben said I've been distracted."

"How is Ben?" asked Charlie carefully.

Cameron looked off into the distance. "He's okay. He's working very hard. I have to talk to him, too."

"What do you mean?" asked Charlie, puzzled. "You two are still together, aren't you?"

"Yes," replied Cameron firmly.

"That's good. I told you he was a keeper."

"He is." Cameron smiled faintly. "You were right. I only hope that what I'm about to do won't change anything."

"Care to tell me about that?" They had reached an old wooden seat on a grassy spot next to the stream. "Let's sit."

Cameron curled up in the corner of the bench and hugged her knees, staring into space. "Right. I only really made up my mind this morning. I had a good talk with Aunt Vicky last night and that helped to clear my head."

"I'm listening."

"Argentum have been asked to join an effort to track down the cybercriminals behind the nuclear test. There's a very good chance that there's a link to the other jobs we've worked on."

"How is that different to what you normally do?" asked Charlie.

"We'd be working directly with people on the ground who are going after the individuals and the organisations behind this," she replied. "We'll be digging deeper into the individuals who've triggered the cyber attacks and the physical thefts and, well, the nuclear explosion."

Charlie nodded slowly. "The closer you get, the greater the chance that they will fight back."

"Exactly," said Cameron. "This has already happened. We got close to the cybercriminals who were mixed up with the MerLions team, they worked out that I was the SimCavalier, and Nina became a target for reprisals."

"That was accidental," said Charlie. "This time you're deliberately taking the fight to them."

"That's right," said Cameron, "and by stepping up, we invite more trouble."

"What do the others think about it?"

"I haven't spoken to anyone yet, apart from Aunt Vicky. Not even Ben. I hadn't decided myself, and it seemed unfair to have the others decide for me."

"But you've decided now?"

"Yes," Cameron said, relieved. "There. I've said it. I want to do this. For me, for Nina, for everyone who's been damaged by them before."

"You sound more certain about this than I've heard you for a while. Are you sure you're ready for that kind of challenge?"

"I don't know if I'm ready, but I know I have to do it. It's time to stop chasing wraiths."

"Will the international consortium have your back if it goes pear-shaped?" asked Charlie.

"Yes," replied Cameron firmly. "This is a team effort. But regardless, I'll be making myself a target. We've already seen what kind of danger that can bring. I don't want to put my family in the firing line, but I also don't want you to be living in fear of the kind of people who can plan and execute a nuclear explosion."

Charlie looked affectionately at his sister. "That's a tough decision to make, and I think it's the right one. I'm very proud of you. Mum and Dad would be proud too."

Cameron gazed back at him, tears in her eyes.

Charlie patted her arm. "Come on. Come back for breakfast. It'll be a great surprise for everyone to see you."

He whistled for the dog. She appeared from the stream, shaking water everywhere. "Oh, Roxy," he sighed, dodging the worst of the shower. "Let's get you home and dry."

They retraced their steps towards the other end of the village, Cameron's heart soaring. It was going to be alright.

●

The meeting had gone on for most of the afternoon, and Tenuk had had enough.

"We must confirm the new tour now," he insisted. "If we can keep the same dates and change the destination it will save huge effort on revising our marketing and promotional campaigns."

He swiped back through the meeting notes. "There. We have agreement in principle from a majority of alternate venues in North America. Why should we delay?"

The chairperson waved at him to sit. "The MerLions toured in the Americas three years ago," they said. "We have been to Africa and Europe since then. I would prefer that if our first choice of North Korea is no longer possible, we take the options of Australia or India."

There was a murmur of agreement around the table.

Tenuk redoubled his persuasive efforts. "Here, we can guarantee eighty percent of the venues for the same dates. Our global game livestreams can run as planned and we know we have a strong fan base who will jump at the chance of premium, early access tickets. The Indian venues are not available at the same time because of the cricket season, and the timing for the outreach programmes in Australia is wrong."

He glanced at the chair, who nodded, giving him permission to stand again. "Look here," he said, spinning the display around and zooming in to the North American continent. "Three years ago, we toured the east coast. This year, we can access our fans to the west. We have venues and outreach opportunities ready to go in Oregon, Washington, Idaho, Utah and Colorado."

"It's true that we would be visiting a very different market," said another colleague thoughtfully. "You make a powerful case, Tenuk."

The chair nodded thoughtfully. "I have a concern. Some of the locations you propose are bordering on the breakaway states. Have you fully risk assessed our plans in light of the activity of the Wyoming Militia? It would be ironic if we jumped from the frying pan of the recent nuclear incident into the fire of terrorism."

"Yes, it's all here." Tenuk spun a folder onto the display. "Contingencies, guarantees, insurances."

"Time is short," said the chair. "We need a decision from the board. Do we proceed with the North American itinerary or accept a delay and plan for Australia or India? Those in favour of North America" – they counted the raised hands – "and those against."

Tenuk breathed a sigh of relief. He caught the eye of one of his colleagues, another member of the elite team within the MerLions management who answered to the higher power of the Syndicate. He gave Tenuk the ghost of a smile. By sheer luck and determination, they were going to the right place, not just for the MerLions, but for the Syndicate and the cause.

He came out of the meeting on a high. There was a lot of work still to do, of course, but the tour would go ahead according to his plans. He wanted to share the triumph with someone. Noor would be getting ready for work about now, just as he was heading home. It was the perfect time to call her.

She answered at the second ring.

"Tenuk! How are you?"

"Fantastic, Noor. I've had a good day."

"That's great. I'm just starting mine."

"I have some news," said Tenuk. "Our next MerLions tour is going to America. I wish you could join me there."

"You know I can't do that," laughed Noor, "but congratulations. I know you've been working hard to get the decision."

"Where would you travel to, Noor, if you could?" he asked lightly. "Would you come here? Visit your aunt?"

"Visit you, you mean. Maybe. But it isn't going to happen. I'd need more carbon credits than I can possibly collect, just to get on the plane."

"What if I can help?" Tenuk held his breath. "I'm sure that the MerLions have some credits spare?"

"I'm not sure that would be right," said Noor.

"Are you saying you don't want to see more of the world?"

"I do…"

Tenuk could hear the doubt in her voice, and he kicked himself for raising the subject. It would have been better to wait and to surprise her with a gift. He changed the subject quickly.

"What do you have planned for the day?" he asked.

"More research," she replied. "We're still trying to pull together the story around that nuclear test. What's the feeling out there in Singapore?"

Tenuk shivered. It was the first time she had confirmed what she was working on. He had suspected as much. There was a dangerous thrill in this long-distance relationship that made him feel alive. He chose his words carefully. "Everyone's concerned, of course, but there's been no fallout detected, and the government has reduced the threat level already."

"Good. I'm sorry, Tenuk, I have to go. I'll talk to you soon. Give my love to auntie Fatima if you see her."

"Bye, Noor. Speak soon."

He slipped the smartscreen into his pocket and carried on walking along a road thronged with shuttles and pedestrians. Delicious smells wafted around as he approached his favourite hawker market. He was hungry, and he had a long evening ahead of him. He stopped at one stall and picked up a few assorted dumplings, then bought some chicken curry, rice, and sweet, succulent roti flatbread from another. He settled at a rickety table to eat, watching the crowd. High on the wall above the market an advertising hoarding flickered and moved, now showing a montage of the MerLions triumphant e-soccer league win. The American tour would be a success, reflected Tenuk, in more ways than one.

Rested and refreshed, he made his way back to the main street and caught a shuttle towards home. His apartment was cool and welcoming. He changed out of his formal work clothes and settled down in front of the screens. Time to see what was going on in the underworld.

He logged on under an alias, watching and listening. There was trouble brewing, and he knew that as soon as he revealed himself there would be questions and arguments. His alternate avatar was a pangolin, its front paws clutched together in supplication, unthreatening and anonymous.

The problem was clear. The final payment for the work had not come through from the end client, and they were getting angry. Sagikkun the Trickster and Mīmī Māo were there whipping up the crowd, and he was surprised to see the Monkey and Cloverleaf active as well. Those four prominent members rarely coincided. From long acquaintance he had a good idea of the time zones they were in, and the fact that there were Asian, European, and American members online meant that he had a difficult task on his hands.

Tenuk sighed. He missed his AI sidekick, Yasmin the Admin, more than ever. No one talked back to her, she never slept, and she had been ruthless. By controlling the behaviour of the members, she had kept them all safe. The new collaboration between the cybercriminals who called this forum home was dangerous. They knew too much about each other. He was just thankful that they had not yet worked out who the end client was.

The Pangolin slipped quietly offline, and Tenuk steeled himself for a fight.

King Katong was back.

•

Noor was first into the office. By the time Ross arrived a few minutes later, the scent of fresh coffee was circulating around the room and Noor was busy at the visualisation deck, gently manipulating the system diagram that Susie had uploaded the previous night.

"Have you seen this?" she asked.

"No, but Joel messaged me about it." He peered at the display. "That's our rogue server, huh." He turned the diagram around slowly. "Nice work."

Noor went to pour herself a coffee. "Want one?"

"Sure." Ross put his bag down and switched on his screen. "What do you know about Snake River Security?"

Noor looked blank. "Never heard of it. Why?"

"It may be connected. Joel said that the upgrades were carried out by a firm of that name, and that they'd approached the plant in Kent as well. I've never come across them, and that really surprises me."

"Me too," said Noor. "You know everyone." She opened up her own screen and started searching. "There has to be a trace of them somewhere. Leave it with me."

Ross was deep in thought. "It's odd that they targeted those two plants. It feels too random."

"I know what you mean," said Noor. "Have there been others?"

"Let's find out. Can you talk to all the teams we know and get them to make some calls? I'll brief Pete and Sandeep and contact our other clients. I'm going to speak to Susie and Ella as well. I want a copy of the firewall software and more information about that rogue piece of hardware."

"Shall I call Cameron as well?"

"Not yet. Don't disturb her. She needs a break."

"Okay." Noor plunged into her work, following trails through online content, and writing quick routines for deep searching.

Ross tried to call Ella but there was no reply. He left a message for her to call him urgently. Turning to the task in hand, he pulled up the client records system and started to work methodically down the list. He was barely ten records in when Ella rang.

"We're on it," she said without preamble. "Susie's in there with the network manager now. I don't fancy his chances…"

"I need to see all the documentation from Snake River Security," said Susie firmly.

The young network manager glanced at his director, who nodded. Susie caught the faintest hint of an eye roll.

"Uh, what do you need? Invoices?"

"Everything, please, Mason," said Susie. "All the comms, the original proposals, any change notes around the system specification."

"That'll take me a while to collate," he replied. He glanced at the clock. "I can do it next week?"

Susie sighed. "I'm sure it's easier than you make out. You could, of course, just give me access to your CRM system and your network architecture."

"Mason, can I have a word?" The IT manager beckoned him into another office and closed the door.

Ella caught the end of the exchange. She gave Susie a conspiratorial grin. "I don't think he likes you bossing him around."

"He's going to give us what we need," said Susie, determined.

Mason reappeared, sulking. He sat in silence at his computer, tapping through a menu. "Here you go," he said at last. "Temporary access tokens. I don't know what you're trying to do, though. It's all above board."

Susie smiled sweetly at him. "If it was all above board, we wouldn't be checking it, would we, Mason?"

"Let's get started," said Ella, hoping to avoid an argument. "There's a lot to go through."

They both started working through files, dividing the task for speed. Ella was aware of Mason glowering the corner.

"Mason," she said, "I've just found your report on how the Snake River proposal plugs existing problems in the network. It's very comprehensive."

"You know it's a good system," he said. "Top industry standard."

"Let me have a look at that," said Susie, breaking off from her own work. She skimmed down the document, frowning. "I'm not sure I agree with the conclusions here, Mason. What exactly did you assess was wrong with the previous configuration?"

Ella gave Susie a sidelong look. She knew very well that Susie had worked on the original system in her previous job. Hopefully, she could be objective about the changes Mason had recommended.

Mason shrugged. "It was okay, I suppose, pretty standard security setup."

"So why," asked Susie with an edge to her voice, "did the plant change systems?"

"We offered them something better," said Mason defensively.

Susie and Ella both looked up sharply.

"What do you mean 'we'?" said Susie.

Mason looked from one girl to the other like a rabbit caught in the headlights. "Snake River hired me. They got the leads and I did the reports. This was the big job we landed, and I worked on the installation."

"You worked for them? For Snake River?" Susie glared at him.

"Yes. Not for long, though. Once the system was in, my contract with them finished. The plant hired me to manage the network because I know the ins and outs of it all."

"Who else worked for them?" asked Ella.

"Oh, they had a big team," said Mason confidently. "Mainly virtual, of course. They rely on people like me on the ground to manage the clients." He faltered. "Well, relied."

Ella fixed him with a stare.

Eventually he broke the silence.

"I haven't been able to get hold of them for a while," he said in a low voice. "Please don't tell anyone." He put his head in his hands. "There are a few of us, consultants, who still act as tech support for each other. Everyone is in the same boat."

"Everyone?" Susie asked.

Mason looked as if he was about to burst into tears. "There were lots of us recruited at the same time to do business development and installation work. We used to see each other online in team meetings."

"Where were you all based?" asked Susie. "Was everyone in the UK?"

"No, a real mixture," said Mason. "There were a few people in London, head office types. There were people from all over Europe, and Africa too."

"You're still in touch with some of them, then?" said Susie.

"Yeah. The lads in Belgium, Hungary and South Africa mainly."

"Did you meet other people in person at all?" asked Ella.

"When I did the installation, it was me and a lad from Kent and a couple of Welsh girls," replied Mason. "The whole thing was supervised by an old bloke up north. We never met him, though."

"Kent." Ella looked at Susie. "Joel needs to check that."

"There might be a link to Pete and Sandeep's job as well," said Susie. "I'll call this in now." She left the room.

Mason looked pleadingly at Ella. "What's going on? Am I in trouble?"

"Yes, Mason," said Ella. "I think you are."

•

"Shell? I'm going out. Do you need anything?" Daniel stuck his head around the door and watched, mesmerised, as Michelle manipulated blocks of code on her display.

"No, I'm okay," she replied, turning her head towards the sound of his voice. "When will you be back? I thought I'd go out for a walk later."

"I'll only be a couple of hours," said Daniel. "Be careful if you do go out. You don't want to come across those joyriders again."

"I won't go far," she said. "I know my way around."

She heard the front door close, and the house fell silent. Michelle was thinking her way through the carbon credits transfer challenge, mulling over what pieces of code she had written in the past and could repurpose. She opened old repositories, looking for elements to re-use in the build, and listened intently as her screen reader relayed the details at high speed. She highlighted each useful snippet, making the chosen lines vibrate gently on the touchscreen, and dragged them into the new window. She started to feel the structure of the solution in her head. It wasn't straightforward, but she liked a challenge and was more than capable of delivering what the customer wanted.

An hour of thinking and building was enough. The silence was becoming oppressive. She would usually find company online, chatting with friends on Eden, on Pasar, or even on the company's community, but not today. She had no wish to talk to anyone on Pasar, none of her usual connections were active on Eden, and she avoided the Thorney Security chat. She didn't like to mix company business with her more shady contracts.

Michelle saved her work and pulled on her boots. The sun was shining outside, and the scent of the honeysuckle was strong. She decided to follow her nose and see if she could find the flowers. Daniel had said they were close by on the waste ground.

She picked her way carefully. Sensors on her belt and on a bracelet around her wrist scanned the terrain and told her of obstructions and dips in the grassland, and any danger overhead from overhanging branches. She embraced the freedom that the discreet devices gave her. A navigator device in her pocket would get her back home from wherever she ended up, but for now, she was following her nose straight to the source.

The smell was almost overpowering, and as she encountered a tangle of leaves and tendrils snaking around a low wall, she knew she had found it. She breathed in the scent and reached out to touch the delicate blooms.

"What are you doing here?" said a gruff voice at her shoulder.

She jumped and twisted towards the man. "The honeysuckle," she stammered.

"Nice, isn't it?"

Michelle's heart was beating fast and she tried to steady her voice. "It's lovely."

"You're the girl from the end house," said the man. He had an old voice and a direct, brusque manner which was at odds with his soft Scottish accent. Michelle wondered why her sensor kit hadn't picked up his approach. He must not have an identity chip, or perhaps he did, and it could not be read.

"I should be getting back to work." She turned back to the flowers to get her bearings and felt discreetly in her pocket for her navigator. She thumbed the Home button, then confidently stepped away from the wall to retrace her path. The navigator's vibrations would keep her on track. She kept her hand on the device in case she also needed its alarm.

"You're blind, aren't you?" The voice had moved. The man was in front of her now.

Michelle felt a rising panic and a touch of anger. She should have been safe exploring within a few steps of her own house.

The next time he spoke, the man's voice softened a little. "I'm sorry I scared you. I live here. Angus. I'm not out much. I wanted some of the honeysuckle too. Wait."

Michelle heard him moving away from her. She stood quite still. There was the sound of leaves rustling and snipping.

"Here." Angus tucked bunch of flowers and leaves into the crook of her arm.

She flinched at the unwanted contact.

"You're only about three metres from the path. Want some help?"

"Thanks, I'm okay." Her belt sensors checked the ground in front of her and she moved forwards without hesitating. A gentle buzz nudged her slightly to the left, and sure enough within a few steps she reached the cracked pavement and knew exactly where she was.

"Nice to meet you," called Angus.

He must still be standing by the wall, she realised. He hadn't followed her. Michelle felt some of the tension leave her body. "You too," she replied politely. She reached her front door without incident.

Once inside, she started shaking. She dropped the flowers on the floor and curled up on the sofa, hugging her favourite soft cushion. She was still there when Daniel came back.

"Shell? What's all this on the floor? Are you okay?" He sat down beside her and gave her a tight hug. "What happened?"

"The honeysuckle. I went to find it, and there was a stranger out there on the wasteland."

"Oh, Shell." He sighed. "That's where the flowers came from, then?"

"Yes. He cut them and gave them to me."

"That was nice, I guess?" said Daniel doubtfully.

"It was freaky," said Michelle, shivering. "He said he lived there."

Daniel's brow furrowed. "Where? By the honeysuckle?"

"I guess so."

"That must be the house in the middle of nowhere," said Daniel. "I wondered who lived there. In two years, I've never seen anyone at all."

"Angus. He said his name was Angus. He knew where I lived."

"I might just pay him a visit later," said Daniel. "Do you want a drink?"

"Cup of tea?"

"Okay." Daniel got up and headed to the kitchen. He put the kettle on and dug in the cupboard for a jug, which he filled with water. "Where shall we put these flowers?" he asked, collecting them up from the floor. "It's a shame to throw them away."

"Anywhere you like," said Michelle. "How about on the windowsill?"

"Sure." Daniel tucked the last snaking tendril into the jug and set it down carefully. "Try not to brush too close to it."

"I can smell it from a mile off," said Michelle. She was starting to feel much better. Now that the shock was wearing off, she was more intrigued than frightened. "I wonder who he is?" she said thoughtfully.

"The only way you'd know there was anyone living over there is the aerial on the roof," said Daniel. "There are a few houses in what's left of that row, but I think the rest are empty. He must have been there for years."

"Gran never mentioned any other neighbours," said Michelle.

"No," agreed Daniel. "The rest of the terraces there were knocked down more than ten years ago. I always wondered why there are still some standing. I suppose whoever it was who lived there refused to move."

There was a whistling sound from the kitchen. The kettle had boiled. "How about that cup of tea?" said Michelle with a cheeky grin.

"You're back on form, aren't you," said Daniel. "The tea will be here directly, ma'am. Would you like cake with that?"

"What a good idea," said Michelle, stretching languorously. "See to it, butler."

Daniel snorted with laughter. "At your service." He busied himself in the kitchen

Michelle's thoughts returned to her coding puzzle. Now that her head had cleared, there were some parameters she needed to check with the client. She hopped up from the sofa and went through to her computer in the other room. Navigating back to Eden, she dictated a message in the secure contract chat. The client was offline, and she didn't expect an instant response. She searched for the Piper, but he was away too. She wondered how he was getting on with the mystery of the salvaged hard disk. It sat silently on the desk in the corner, unwilling to give up its secrets.

"Shell! Come and drink your tea."

"Coming." She closed the connections. The job could wait a little longer.

•

"You're staying all weekend, aren't you, darling?" Aunt Vicky looked concerned. "It's so nice to see you. You can't rush straight back to London."

Charlie put his coffee cup down on the table. "You need a break, Cameron. Stay until Sunday at least."

"Now that I've made up my mind, I have a lot of things to organise," she said. "I need to talk to Ben as well."

"You can do whatever you need from the attic like you used to," said Charlie. "It'll save you hours of travelling. We can boot Nina out for a couple of days. She won't mind."

"Why don't you ask Ben to come up here and join us?" suggested Aunt Vicky.

Cameron looked from one to the other. "Okay," she said. "You win. I'll ring Ben first and then get to work."

She climbed the stairs to the first floor, then opened the door to a second flight of stairs which led to her attic. Correction – no longer hers. She had given up the precious territory to her niece, now fourteen. It would be nice to reclaim it for a short while. Sun streamed through the south facing dormer windows and Cameron gazed out onto the familiar landscape of rolling fields and trees. It was nice to be home.

She settled in a comfortable chair and called Ben. He answered immediately.

"You're ready to talk." It was a statement, not a question. He peered at the screen, looking past Cameron's face to the room behind. "You're at Charlie's?"

"I am. I needed to clear my head, and it seems to be working." She felt a lightness that had been absent for a long time. "I miss you, and I'm sorry. Will you come up here too? Do you have time?"

"I'd love to," said Ben. "I can't get away tonight, but I can come up tomorrow. So, what was your decision?"

"I'm going to do it. I'm caught between the devil and the deep blue sea. I think this is the only way to protect everyone in the long term."

Ben nodded slowly. "I think you're right. It had to be your decision." He smiled at her, his eyes crinkling affectionately. "I need to get back to work, but I will see you tomorrow. Love you."

Cameron ran a finger across the screen where his face had been. She knew how close she had come to losing him. She hoped that the course she was set on would not divide them again.

Time to brief the team. Ross and Noor had confirmed they were ready in the office. Susie and Ella, Pete and Sandeep were calling in from their client sites. She hadn't heard from Joel. His day off had been booked weeks ago. He would join if he could. She took a deep breath and opened up the call.

"We're already on the case, Cameron," said Ross once she had outlined the task. "It isn't a big stretch from the work we've been doing."

"I agree," said Ella. "How is this really different from tracing something like the Snake River lead?"

Pete chipped in. "I get it, Cameron. This new consortium is going after the threat before it emerges. We're on the offensive now. We'll be visible."

"That's right, Pete," said Cameron. "We may become targets ourselves. After the attacks on my apartment and my family last year it took me long enough to decide whether I was ready to take this on. If any of you are uncomfortable, we'll protect you as much as we can. If the majority of you decide it's too much, I'll decline."

"I'm in," said Pete immediately.

Next to him on screen, Sandeep gave a thumbs up. "Me too."

"Of course," said Ross, "and I have some ideas."

Noor nodded. "I'm okay with it. It's a real opportunity to make a difference, and I'm sure it will be no more dangerous than our other work."

"Ella? Susie?" Cameron waited for their answers.

"I think I'm in," said Susie slowly.

"You're not afraid to go on the attack," said Ella. "You've been giving Mason a hard time."

Susie shot her a confused look. "Just doing our job. But, yes, I think you're right to do this, Cameron, and I'll help if I can."

An alert sounded and Joel joined the call. "Got your message, Cameron," he said. "Whatever you're planning, count me in."

"Good timing, Joel," said Cameron. "Thanks for the support. I guess that's a yes from all of us here. I'll get things moving."

There was a chorus of agreement, and Cameron ended the call.

Time for the final step. Cameron opened up a secure message service and found the original request. "I'm in," she replied, "and I have a team behind me."

The response came quickly. "Fantastic news, SimCavalier. We need your talents. We'll hook you up with your connection on the ground. Her handle is Cloverleaf."

•

The kayak grated on the narrow shingle before sliding into the clear water of the lake. In the distance, Cloverleaf could see a patrol boat passing and she paused, knowing that sudden movement would attract attention. She held tight to the back of the kayak. A series of light ripples from the boat's wake made it bob and shift in the water. The patrol disappeared from view, moving further up and across the lake towards the mountains that rose like a sheer wall on the other side. Cloverleaf grabbed her paddle and hopped into the kayak. This window of opportunity was too good to miss.

It took only a moment to push out of the shallows. The lakebed dropped away quickly here. Her paddles bit into the water as she sped across an exposed channel to a maze of little wooded islands. These extended for a few miles down the edge of the lake, inaccessible from the shore. The way was blocked by marshland, thick woodland, and bears, which protected the wildlife from casual intrusion and hid other activities from prying eyes. As she passed into the shelter of the first island, she stopped suddenly, the water slapping against the side of the kayak. A bear had indeed emerged onto the lakeshore, probably coming to catch fish in the cool light of the dawn. It was a rare sight and despite the danger she was in she revelled in the encounter. The bear ignored her. It jumped into the lake, splashing after its prey, and emerged triumphant, shaking water off its fur. After a last look around it headed away from the shore and into the woods.

Cloverleaf picked up her paddle again and carried on through the familiar channels between islands, aiming for her hidden camp. It was thoroughly camouflaged and had served her well for the past year. She pulled her kayak up onto the rocky shore, careful to pick a new landing place each time to avoid tell-tale tracks that may be visible to passing kayakers or observation satellites. She slipped into the undergrowth and emerged into a clearing. Everything was as she had left it. The solar cells picked up just enough daylight here under the trees to keep her equipment charged without giving away their presence. A communications antenna snaked up one of the taller trees. She remembered the exhilarating climb to set it in place, and the thrill of being so high in the canopy that she was at eye level with an osprey's nest a hundred metres or so away on a neighbouring islet. She occasionally saw the birds as she paddled back and forth, cruising high above the lake, their wings outstretched on the breeze.

Rummaging through her backpack, she pulled out a cereal bar and a water bottle and sat back in the old camping chair. She didn't have long to wait before the call came through.

"SimCavalier?"

"Cloverleaf. It's good to meet you."

"You're going to help me take these people down." It wasn't a question.

"Yes, I hope so," replied Cameron. "Tell me what you need." In her sunny attic room, half a world away, she started to take notes.

•

"How are you getting on with Snake River?" asked Ross.

Noor was scrolling listlessly through the results of her searches. She sighed. "I've got a few things, but nothing current or helpful."

"Let's have a look," said Ross.

"Okay. I'm going to need more coffee, though. Are there any biscuits left?"

"I think so," said Ross, rummaging in the cupboard. "I'm sure there was a whole packet, but I can't find it."

"Joel was in here last night, wasn't he? I bet he snaffled them."

"You're probably right," said Ross. "Would you like a sandwich or something instead?"

"Oh, good idea," said Noor, looking at the time. "I didn't realise how late it was."

Order placed, coffee in hand, they settled down to look at Noor's results.

"Snake River was registered as a company here," she began, "but it's a shell, owned by an overseas conglomerate."

"Directors?"

"Just the one. Appointed when the company was formed, resigned when it closed down less than a year later. I've tried to trace them, but it's a cloned identity. Dead end."

"It doesn't say a lot for the plant's due diligence if they handed a fat contract to a dormant business," said Ross wryly.

Noor shook her head. "It's more complicated than that. Snake River's a throwaway brand. It was splashed all over a fancy website with high profile directors and advisors. That's vanished too, of course, but I found the domain name registration and an old cache of the site online. Have a look."

Ross scanned the pages and gave a low whistle. "Some big names on here... I recognise most of them. Heavyweight experts."

"Exactly," said Noor, "and I am willing to bet that none of them actually knew their profiles were on this site. It would be easy enough to spoof a deep fake of any of these for video calls with the client."

"What about the parent company?" asked Ross. "Any clues there?"

"Not yet," said Noor. "The domain registration is interesting, though. I managed to cross-reference the owners with other sites. There are at least six of the same style that I've found already, using different brands, of course. High profile local experts, similar services, and no longer running."

"This is gold, Noor. Where are they all?"

"Everywhere. Mainland Europe, Indonesia, India, Japan, Canada." She threw up her arms in frustration. "But they're all fakes. I'm really struggling to get past the illusion."

There was a muffled thud which startled them both, and the alert on the delivery hatch pinged.

"Lunchtime," said Ross. "Let's take a break and think about it."

They spread out on the comfortable chairs in the corner of the office and ate in companionable silence. It was a chance to think.

"Where did you say the parent company was based?" asked Ross, scooping the last of his chicken salad out of the tub.

"I didn't," said Noor. "It's another tangle of fakery, but I'm beginning to think it's somewhere in South East Asia." She took another bite of her sandwich.

"Have you found any social accounts at all? They'll have had to build some sort of credibility beyond these fancy websites."

"Actually, yes," said Noor. "You're right. All of the brands had profiles, and they were heavily used. There was a lot of bot traffic and cross-amplification, but of course too much auto-posting gets you banned, so there is plenty of real engagement among the clever algorithms as well."

Ross grinned triumphantly. "How about we take those profiles and run the posts through…"

"… a geolocator!" Noor finished. "Brilliant."

Ross hurried over to his desk and loaded up his favourite tracker software. "Send me all the profile URLS," he said.

As they watched, the software started to extract the details of each post made on the accounts. Pins began to appear on the map.

"Indonesia," said Ross, satisfied. "Look at that cluster growing around Jakarta."

"Korea, too," said Noor. "All the pins in Seoul are within a couple of blocks of each other."

"London," said Ross. "Right on our doorstep." He zoomed the map to its highest level of detail and felt a shiver down his spine. "Literally."

Noor looked at the screen and gasped. The main Snake River account had been posting from outside the offices of Argentum Associates.

6: CLOVERLEAF

"It's pure coincidence," said Joel. "This is a busy part of London."

The team, minus Pete and Sandeep, were gathered in the office. Cameron's enthusiasm had returned after her time in the village. The results of the geolocation were up on the viz deck for all of them to study.

"There must be thousands of people passing our door every day," said Ella. "Didn't Mason say that there was a Snake River team based in London?" She took a bite of her muffin.

"The company was registered to an accounting firm near here," said Noor. "That doesn't mean much, but there may have been an in-person visit at some stage."

"It might be worth following up the date and time of that post with the accounting firm," said Cameron. "It's a long shot, but you never know what it could uncover."

"I can do that, if you like," said Ella. "I know most of the firms around here."

"Thanks, Ella," said Cameron.

"More coffee?" asked Joel. The others shook their heads, and Joel went to pour himself another cup. He came back bearing the remaining muffins and grabbed one for himself before the rest were claimed.

"That's quite a hotspot around Rio," he said, gesturing at a forest of dots on the South American coast.

Ross swung the map around. "That's just a small one," he said. "I'm far more interested in these other clusters. Jakarta. Seoul. Singapore. Half the posts on the accounts worldwide came from these locations, regardless of where people thought they were."

"Media farms," said Susie knowledgeably. "They'll have been hired to run all these accounts, and probably created a lot of shadow profiles supporting and amplifying the brand. I bet if you analyse the responses to the posts, you'll pick up plenty of fakes from the same location."

"I took a closer look at a sample from each of these locations," said Noor. "Here, if we look at Jakarta, you can see very clearly that there are two hundred or so individual cells, all posting about the same volume of content. If you're right, Susie, we will find more." Noor shifted the view to street level, showing the half-drowned buildings of the abandoned capital. She homed in on the run-down neighbourhood where most of the pins had landed. Apartment blocks and homes jostled for space, paint peeling from the walls, and rooftops bristling with communications masts.

"It's quite the cottage industry," said Cameron.

Noor nodded. "I know it's not ethical, but it's work, and it's keeping these people out of poverty."

"The pattern in Korea is quite different, isn't it?" said Ross, intrigued. "Fewer posts, but with one central hub. Is that an office building, or a large residential block?"

Noor shook her head. "No. Look." She zoomed in. "It's residential, but the area is affluent, and the homes are large and spread out. I think there has been one person, or a small group at most, running a mixture of automated scripts and real posts, and the variations in location have simply been an individual responding on the move. Look. There have been some from this coffee shop, and others from the market."

Joel looked sceptical. "This is all too obvious. Anyone who knows what they're doing will make sure they can't be geolocated."

Ross shook his head. "Location data creeps in from the most unlikely places. They'll be careful, of course, but I bet not one of us can say we are completely untraceable. There'll be an app, a service, something they use regularly – and the network itself will help to fix them in place. I helped to write this tracker. You'd be amazed at the metadata it picks up."

Cameron grinned. "I bet. You're the trickiest of us all, Ross."

"I'll take that as a compliment."

"How sure are we of this location?" she asked. "I think we can safely say that Susie and Ella's work uncovering the Snake River link, and your research on it, shows that there's been a sustained and deliberate attempt to compromise several nuclear installations. The social posting is part of the jigsaw. I don't know how close this individual might be to the main perpetrators, but I want to flag it to the consortium so that they can pick them up for questioning." She turned to Susie. "I think we need a word with the lad at the plant, as well."

"Mason?" asked Susie.

"Yes, Mason. He may know more than he thinks. You two are going back down tonight, aren't you?"

"That's the plan," said Ella.

"Can you organise a conference call?" said Cameron. "I want to hear what he has to say for himself."

"If we're all done, I need to get off to Norfolk and do some checks," said Joel.

"Sure," said Cameron. "Look out for Snake River and any of the other brand names that Noor uncovered. I wouldn't be surprised if they turn up in the strangest places."

"I'll see what I can find out with the accounting firm," said Ella.

"Great. If I don't hear from you before, I'll talk to you tomorrow," said Cameron. "Susie, what are you up to?"

"I'm working on the revised system configurations. I'm sure there will be a hole in the firewall, but I haven't found it yet."

"Good hunting," said Cameron. "Noor? I need you to be my eyes and ears. Keep a look out for any unusual activity around the brands you found. Oh, and see what you can find out about the Wyoming Militia."

"Wyoming?" Ross frowned. "I thought we were focusing on South East Asia."

"Wyoming," confirmed Cameron. "Snake River, Ross."

"It isn't the only one," he protested.

"No," agreed Cameron, "but there's been a development. Have you ever encountered the handle 'Cloverleaf'?"

"Yes, a long time ago," said Ross. "I remember that name from the Pasar community."

"I thought you might have. We need to talk. I want to you to go back into the underworld. There's work to do."

•

Tenuk put the latest round of new contracts online and waited to see who would bite. The flurry of enquiries that had come through after the test had been turned around very quickly by the Syndicate's administrators. He put a lot of thought into where he advertised the opportunities this time. Some innocent scripting, he posted on Eden. Media farming and deep fake videos, he could assign directly to the experts who had done such a good job with the last contract. Jobs involving serious manipulation or downright illegal site penetration he would advertise to a select group within Pasar. For the original contracts, Yasmin the Admin had tried to avoid the hardened cybercriminals building up too detailed a picture of the end project. It had been patently unsuccessful, and Tenuk had a new plan. Tonight, he had a surprise for the community. Rather than try to fight the team that was forming, he would encourage it – at their own risk, of course.

The usual suspects were online despite their varied time zones. Waiting for payment of their fees made them hungry. He invited Sagikkun, Mîmî Mão, Monkey, Cloverleaf, and a dozen others to a private breakout room. This was a place where the chosen few could step a little way out of the shadows. They spoke through voice changers and relied on cartoon avatars to represent them, but they were present and accountable in the room.

Tenuk clicked his avatar onto the virtual stage.

"Good news!" he began. "Your efforts have been rewarded. The final payment for your work is being transferred to your wallets."

There was a flurry of excitement. The avatars that disguised the members flickered and danced, animated by emotion. Tenuk waited. The transfers should be running through network confirmations now. Sure enough, after a breathless minute, the first response came from Cloverleaf.

"Received. Good work, King Katong."

"Here, too," said Mîmî Mão.

"They took their time," complained the Monkey. He was never happy.

Tenuk smiled to himself. If he could take advantage of the mood, he might regain control of the group. "I know that you have pieced together the details of this job, and I recognise your worth as a strong team. I must caution you that being so close to each other, you must be more careful. If one of you is exposed, we risk others falling with you."

"We know the risks," said Cloverleaf shortly.

"Good," said Tenuk, "because you have a job to do now, as a team. The client is pleased and is launching phase two of their operation. The sleeping dragons are to be woken. The client needs to obtain raw materials for a second demonstration."

"At last," said Mîmî Mão. "Are we to wake all of them?"

"No," said Tenuk. "The client has been very specific. Just the European locations, and of course only one penetration needs to be successful. The down payment will be split between you all now, the balance on completion."

"What is 'completion'?" asked Cloverleaf. "Surely they don't plan to detonate a nuclear device in Europe?"

"Theft of uranium leading to a readiness to detonate is sufficient," said Tenuk. "A demonstration of power to achieve their political ends." As he spoke, he thought of Noor. It seemed more important than ever to bring her to Singapore, to safety.

"I need you all to sign a message to confirm your participation," he continued. There was a murmur of assent. Tenuk watched the ledger as the encrypted messages trickled in. The signatures were now fixed in time, an irrefutable commitment to the job, verifiable through the blockchain by the Syndicate and its clients.

"Thank you all," he said. "Your detailed briefs will be delivered in the usual manner. Stay safe."

The avatars flicked out one by one as they left the breakout room.

"Sagikkun, wait up," he said. "I have another job for you if you want to take it. There's some more media work. Do you want a slice?"

"Sure, I can handle that."

Tenuk sent the specification to Sagikkun's mailbox and received a signed acceptance by return. It would be a straightforward job. Sagikkun was an expert.

Alone in the room, Tenuk breathed a sigh of relief. He had them all right where he wanted them, back under his control. There would be no more trouble.

•

Pete and Sandeep arrived at reception just a few minutes after Daniel.

"Morning, Dan," said Pete cheerily. "First proper day for you, isn't it?"

"Yes, induction all morning and then straight to work," replied Daniel. "You enjoyed the dive on Saturday, then?"

"It was decent. Thanks again."

"Where did you get to?" asked Sandeep.

"We went up north to the mouth of the Tyne," said Daniel. "There's a pair of nice old wrecks up there, one on top of the other."

"That's unlucky," said Sandeep.

"Not as unusual as you'd think," said Daniel. "Have you ever dived yourself?"

Sandeep shook his head. "It's never really appealed. I'm not keen on water."

Pete laughed. "One day, Sandeep, one day."

The receptionist handed over their passes. "Thank you," said Sandeep. "We'd better get started."

"Have a good day," said Daniel, waving as they disappeared into the maze of corridors behind the barriers. He didn't have long to wait. Soon he was being ushered in the same direction by the HR manager. After what seemed like hours of fingerprint and retina scans, regulations to read and accept, and contracts to sign, he was finally introduced to the senior management.

His new boss was surprisingly young, and Daniel suspected he'd never worked a security shift in his life.

"Daniel, I'm Brandon. Head of Operations. It's good to have you with us. We've arranged a full tour for this afternoon so you can get your bearings on the site. You have access to site plans, resources, and schedules. I'll have my assistant take you through all the nuts and bolts of the systems, and when you're ready we'll introduce you to the staff."

"Will the outgoing security manager be doing a formal handover?" asked Daniel.

"Uh, that may not be possible," said Brandon.

Daniel sighed inwardly. He had known there would be a catch. The money was too good. "What do I need to know about the history of the role?" he asked carefully.

"It's been complicated," said Brandon. "The original site security manager, who had been with us for decades, retired quite suddenly two years ago. You will be the, um, fourth person to take the role since his departure."

"Fourth?"

"Yes. Originally the deputy manager stepped up, but he moved on to a different site very quickly and we had two interim managers in quick succession. The job had obviously become too big for one person, so we split the role into site security, which you'll be taking on, and IT security, and I oversee the two branches. We promoted two promising candidates from within the existing team. You'll meet the IT security manager later. Julia. She's been in the post for six months, like your predecessor had."

Brandon paused.

Here it comes, thought Daniel.

"I'm sorry to report that he left suddenly following a security breach, and there is an investigation ongoing. We thought it best to recruit externally this time."

Out of the frying pan and into the fire. Daniel smiled confidently at Brandon. "That's disappointing to hear, but I like a challenge."

Brandon looked relieved. "Good. I'm glad that's out of the way," he said, without explaining anything at all. He looked at the clock. "It's almost lunchtime. Come and meet the other directors."

"Can I ask a couple of questions first?" said Daniel. He wasn't going to let this bombshell be swept under the carpet. "What was the security breach, and who is investigating?"

"We don't know the full details yet," said Brandon, obviously uncomfortable talking about it. "There was a perimeter breach near the shoreline, that much we know. It's especially sensitive considering the recent incident in Russia. You'll meet the investigating team, obviously."

"What about the cybersecurity firm who're working here?"

"Argentum? No, they're not involved."

"Don't you think they should be?"

Brandon was taken aback. "Why?"

"These things go hand in hand," said Daniel. "The breach which led to the theft of uranium used in that nuclear test was triggered by a series of cyber attacks."

"The investigators have it in hand," said Brandon stiffly. "And Julia will be on top of things, I'm sure." He gave Daniel a shrewd, appraising look. "I think you are going to do just fine."

Relieved, Daniel followed him to the boardroom for lunch. After that start, he felt he could handle anything.

Pete and Sandeep were holed up in their designated office, trawling back through the system specifications with all the new intelligence from their colleagues ringing in their ears.

"Puts a whole new slant on things, doesn't it," said Sandeep as he scanned through another folder.

"It's doing my head in," said Pete. "If I drink any more coffee I won't sleep tonight."

"I know what you mean," said Sandeep. "Honestly, these records are all over the place."

"If I was the suspicious type, I'd say that someone was trying to hide a sneaky job like the one Ella and Susie picked up on," said Pete wryly. "Actually, I think it's just incompetence."

The door opened and a woman entered, short and purple haired. "Are you two coming for lunch?" she asked.

"Hi, Julia," said Sandeep. "Yes, we're more than ready."

Julia glanced at the screen. "If you're working through those files, I'd say you need a stiff drink. That whole period is a mess. I don't know what they were doing. Angus wasn't great at record keeping, but the people in between were dreadful."

"You were working here, though?" said Pete. "I know you only took over as IT manager recently, but you must have had some influence."

Julia shook her head. "It was a strange time. I kept my head down and worked, did what I could on the side lines, and built my team. It paid off in the end."

Sandeep closed his screen. "I'm starving," he said. "Did you mention food?"

Locking the office door, the three of them strolled out of the admin block into fresh air. There was a garden of sorts between the buildings. A few tables were spread around a lush grassy area, and the sun was shining.

Pete stretched gratefully in the warmth. "Let's have lunch out here," he suggested. "Look, there's someone leaving now."

"You grab the table and I'll get the food," said Sandeep.

He was back within ten minutes carrying a heavily laden tray. "This should keep us going," he said, placing it carefully on the table.

"Where's Julia?" asked Pete.

"She had to go. Last minute invitation to lunch in the boardroom. Apparently, she's meeting the new site security manager."

"Daniel?"

"Daniel." Sandeep unwrapped his sandwich and started to devour. "He's a nice lad," he said between mouthfuls. "Did you find out anything about him?"

"Not really," said Pete. "He lives with his cousin. He was a bit vague about what he was doing before this, but that may just be him being security conscious."

They tucked into their lunch, enjoying the early summer sunshine.

"I don't fancy spending the whole afternoon going over more of those files," said Sandeep grimly. "How about a walk? How far can we go around this site?"

"I don't know," said Pete with a conspiratorial grin. "Shall we find out?"

There was no one left in the garden now. Pete sorted their rubbish and dropped the cartons into chutes for recycling and composting.

"Which way?" he asked.

"Let's follow the perimeter," suggested Sandeep.

They took a narrow path that traced a line parallel to the high metal boundary fence. On one side of the path the grass was well tended. The other side was wilder, marking the start of the marshland that extended out beyond the fence towards the seashore. Pete shielded his eyes and peered across the expanse of tufted grass and salt ponds. "Look, is that a curlew?"

Sandeep squinted. "The bird with the long, curved beak? Is that what it's called?"

Pete shook his head in mock despair. "What are we going to do with you?"

No more than a couple of miles away, the marshland gave way again to industry. A mass of metalwork, shining pipes and tall, narrow chimneys rose from the ground: the neighbouring chemical park. Beyond that, in the far distance, they could see the brown and purple of the high moors.

They were not alone on the perimeter path. It was a popular route around the site in fine weather. Everyone they passed had the same reaction to the newcomers. They would smile, then frown, glance at the prominent visitor badges Pete and Sandeep both wore, then smile again. Security was part of the culture. More than once a uniformed security guard stopped to scan the badges and match them to the retina scans on record.

"They're good," said Sandeep after the second check.

"They have to be," said Pete.

The path drew them towards the sea. The huge concrete bulk of the main reactor building stood right on the shoreline, casting a narrow shadow onto the water in the early afternoon sun. The tide was high, and water lapped almost to its edge.

"This isn't where you were diving, is it?" asked Sandeep.

"No! Further south, towards the moorland. There's nothing interesting to see here, and you don't want to be anywhere near the inlet channels, or the outfalls for that matter."

The path ended abruptly, and the fence curved in towards the building. Pete looked longingly out at the sea, and grinned as he spotted a familiar sight.

"Check this out. The seals are having some fun." Two curious heads were poking out of the water some way off. Their skin shone in the sun, and Pete could make out soulful eyes and glistening whiskers. They disappeared under the gently rolling waves, reappearing further out, swimming playfully around each other.

Sandeep was looking further down the perimeter, beyond where they had stopped. "Pete?" he said. "What do you think is going on down there?"

Half a dozen people in fluorescent jackets and hard hats were clustered by the fence. Drones hovered, holding a protective barrier in place, and the people were examining the sensors on the fence and scanning the ground around it.

"Routine maintenance?" suggested Pete.

Sandeep shook his head. "Doesn't look like it. Wrong type of drones, and too many people."

"Excuse me, gentlemen, if you could move along?" The security guard was almost as tall as Pete. She ran a quick scanner over their badges. "Your host should be with you. Julia, is that right?"

"Yes," said Pete. "She was called away to a meeting. I didn't realise the grounds were restricted."

"Not restricted as such," said the security guard with a smile," but we like to know where all our visitors are."

"What's going on?" asked Sandeep, nodding towards the distant group.

The security guard looked unconcerned. "Rabbits. It happens remarkably often. The little swine dig under the fence and chew through the wires." She pointed to a discoloured patch of ground further up the path. "That was about six months ago. I came down here on patrol and found one poor creature fried and a couple of others hopping around on the grass."

"How do they get under?" asked Sandeep. "Surely the fence goes down quite a way?"

"Sections of it do," she replied. "They seem to get lucky and find the gaps. They're very determined. We have rabbits all over the site if you know where to look."

They walked together up the path until another guard came in sight. Their companion signalled to him. "I'll leave you to make your way back," she said. "Nice to meet you."

"Rabbits?" said Pete, once she was out of earshot.

"Rabbits, my arse," said Sandeep. "I suppose we'd better be getting on with those files." They trudged back towards the administration building under watchful eyes.

•

Cloverleaf crossed the pitted road at its narrowest point. This was the most dangerous part of her day. She had visited her island encampment before dawn, first to show her face on the Pasar community, and then to send more data to the SimCavalier. Now she was on her way back home, her kayak safely hidden half a mile up the lakeside. The road was the only place where she might be exposed. If challenged, she could legitimately claim that she had gone for a morning stroll, and she had a bowl of freshly picked berries in her hand as the perfect alibi. Today was quiet, no armed patrols to be seen. The skies were clear, too. The autonomous militia drones ran to an apparently random schedule, but she had overseen their training. It had been easy enough to teach them to avoid this location at certain times of day.

Confident that she had not been seen, she slipped under the cover of another grove of trees and emerged behind her house. She skirted the swing and the fire pit and hopped up onto the wooden deck, opened the screen door and slipped into the kitchen. All was quiet. She set the coffee machine running and mixed up some pancake batter.

The scent of the pancakes drew an audience. Audrey appeared, still in her pyjamas and clutching a teddy, corkscrew curls floating around her head in a shining dark cloud.

"Mommy?" she yawned. "Can I have huckleberries with mine?"

"Coming right up. I've just picked them."

"I didn't hear you go out."

"I was very quiet. I wanted you to get your beauty sleep."

Audrey set her teddy on the table and scrambled up onto her chair. "What are we doing today?" she asked.

"Well, today I have to work," said Cloverleaf, "and you are going to Bonnie's."

"Good," said Audrey with a big smile. "Will I get to help with the horses?"

"I should think so." Cloverleaf put the pancakes on the table. "Syrup?"

"Yes."

"Yes, what?"

"Yes, please."

"Good girl." She carefully poured a swirl of syrup over the pancakes on her daughter's plate, then over her own. They ate in companionable, sticky silence.

"Wash your hands, clean your teeth and get your stuff," said Cloverleaf. Audrey clambered down and bounded happily off to her bedroom, while Cloverleaf finished her coffee. If they had to get out in a hurry, she reflected, Audrey would miss the life she had here. She hoped that her daughter would understand.

Boots and backpacks on, they left the house. Bonnie's place was on the way to headquarters, and Cloverleaf dropped Audrey at the gate. She scampered happily into the yard with Bonnie, barely giving her mother a backward glance.

Twenty minutes later, Cloverleaf arrived at the compound. There were two guards lounging outside the main entrance, sunglasses on, automatic weapons at the ready. They thought they looked so cool, she reflected, but their mismatched combats and oversized ammo belts betrayed their amateur survivalist roots. She kept the thought buried and smiled blandly at them, waiting for the gate to open.

Inside, there was an unusual amount of activity. She spotted a colleague rushing down the corridor.

"Hey, there. What's happening?"

"Hey yourself. Briefing at oh nine thirty. Didn't you get the message?"

Cloverleaf cursed and pulled her smartscreen out of her pocket. Sure enough, there were the notifications. She was lucky to have made it in time.

The large open-air auditorium in the centre of the compound was almost full. Cloverleaf squeezed onto a hard bench at the back, deep in the shadows. She knew exactly where this was going. She prepared herself to act patriotic. The thrum of the music began, stirring the crowd, building up to a big entrance. Firecrackers burned along the front of the stage, and the backdrop of the blood red bison against white mountains billowed as if blowing in the wind. The guard of honour strode onto the stage and took up their positions, rifles poised. The crowd was stamping and clapping, the noise overwhelming.

"People of an independent Wyoming... Your leader!" Everyone around Cloverleaf stood and cheered. She managed a half-hearted "hurrah" which turned into a cover-up cough and avoided any more shouting by sipping at her water bottle.

As the noise died down, the man on the stage smiled thinly at the audience. "Thank you, thank you. Today is a great day for our cause. Today we have announced to the world that our people, our scientists, delivered the successful nuclear test recorded in Russia last week."

The cheering redoubled. Cloverleaf coughed and drank, exchanged sympathetic glances with people, and listened intently. She wanted to catch every nuance of this statement.

"We have shown the world what we can do," he continued. "With the help of our allies and supporters, we are preparing the next demonstration of our strength."

More cheering. Allies, supporters – and mercenaries, thought Cloverleaf. As one of the mercenaries, she wasn't necessarily complaining. She had built up a healthy nest egg of untraceable earnings through Pasar, enough for her and Audrey to start a new life when the time came.

"Europe will tremble when we unveil our next nuclear device. The world will have no choice but to meet our demands."

All her suspicions were confirmed. The end client for the Syndicate, whose work had been passed down to the Pasar cybercriminals, was indeed the Militia. She had suggested as much to the SimCavalier, but at last she had solid evidence. The cheering and stamping redoubled. Cloverleaf hoped that no one would start shooting. When the first crack of a firearm sounded nearby, she sighed. She felt sorry for any birds in the vicinity. It was about to get dangerous in the skies above the compound.

"Are you okay?" Her boss was at her elbow.

"I'm fine," replied Cloverleaf. She put her hands to her temples. "A headache, is all."

"Head over to the office and take some Tylenol," said her boss sympathetically. "All this noise can't be helping."

Cloverleaf escaped gratefully. Not only did she get to avoid the hyped-up crowd, but by sheer luck she had the chance to obtain some highly prized intelligence, and she now had the whole context. She knew exactly what she wanted. She had pieced together most elements of the cyber kill chain that had led to the theft of the uranium, thanks to her involvement in Pasar and few lucky guesses. She was secretly proud of the quality of her contribution to the whole. She had long planned to get her hands on all the files held by the Militia, but this morning's mention of a 'sleeping dragon' by King Katong, and the final confirmation in the leader's speech that yes, the Militia was behind the test, added to the urgency. She needed to find the deployment plans and details of the physical aspects of the attacks that were not part of the Syndicate's contract. She had a good idea where they would be, and she was ready.

Five minutes, she thought to herself. Give me five minutes. That's all I'm going to need. It was all planned out. Crossing her fingers, she grabbed a colleague's distinctive baseball cap and went straight to the server room. She flashed a cloned card at the security pad and thanked her lucky stars that the Militia were so careless that they required no biometrics. She pulled the cap down to hide her face. Anyone casually glancing at the terrible footage on the cheap CCTV cameras would easily mistake her for the owner of the real card she had cloned. She was inside within twenty seconds and went straight to the server that she knew contained the files she wanted. She pulled a storage device from her pocket, something she always had at the ready, and plugged it in. It was a risk, but she would likely be able to doctor the server's access records after the event. There wasn't time to be choosy. She simply copied everything. Time was ticking away. Three minutes. Another sixty seconds passed before the light on the device glowed green. She pulled it straight out and headed for the door without missing a beat. She put the cap back in place on her colleague's desk and hid the storage device deep in her backpack. Four and a half minutes. She grabbed the bottle of Tylenol from a shelf and sat down at her desk, head in hands. Four minutes, fifty seconds. The door of the office opened, and her colleagues walked in, chattering loudly, buzzing from the rally.

"How are you feeling?"

Cloverleaf groaned theatrically. "Terrible. The Tylenol hasn't kicked in yet."

"Why don't you go lie down?"

"I'll be fine," she said bravely. "Maybe a drink would help?"

"Of course. Go sit in the coffee shop for a while."

"Yes, ma'am." Cloverleaf nodded gratefully and stood up. She didn't have to fake the shaking in her limbs. She left the noisy office behind, and went to sit quietly until the adrenaline wore off and the enormity of what she had just done sank in.

•

Noor's patience with the complexities of Snake River in all its guises had finally snapped, and she had gone to visit one of her brothers for a break. Joel was on his way to Norfolk, and Susie and Ella had left for the West Country. Cameron and Ross finally had the chance to talk.

"Will you go back onto those forums? Can you bring the Piper back?" Cameron was pleading with him, but Ross was torn.

"I haven't been on there for a long time," he said, "and to be honest, I feel better for it."

"Have you abandoned the Piper? Are you always RunningManTech online now?"

Ross decided honesty was the best policy. She'd be able to check. "No, the Piper is still around. I lurk on Eden some of the time. It's a good place to pick up useful intel. But Pasar? I don't want to go near it."

"Okay." Cameron accepted defeat. "I can't ask you to do it if it's going to compromise you."

"I may have another way to get in," said Ross slowly. "There's someone I know who I think is still active. It wouldn't arouse as much suspicion as me pitching up out of the blue."

"Want to share?"

"No. Not really. Trust me."

Cameron nodded. "You know what you're doing. Let me know if you need anything."

"I'm going to head home," said Ross. "It's safer to go online from there."

"No training today?" asked Cameron.

"Rest day," said Ross happily. "We're back in the pool tomorrow morning, though. An early night will do me good."

"You cycled in today, though?"

"That's not really training," laughed Ross. "I'll take it easy on the way home. Are you staying here?"

"Yes," said Cameron. "I need to work through the data that Cloverleaf transmitted, and then I'm meeting Ben for dinner."

"Enjoy yourself. Say hi from me."

Ross extracted his bike from the storage room at the bottom of the stairs and swung out onto the road home. He weaved through the evening traffic, enjoying the sunshine, arriving home far quicker than he expected.

Before he asked ShellPixie for any favours, he had one to do for her. He sprawled on the sofa with a drink and opened the details of the hard disk she had found. The partial label was a good place to start, and he was surprised that it yielded fast results. He scrolled through a few pages of original images and found a very close match. It was odd that she hadn't done that already, he reflected. He narrowed down the hardware to around forty years earlier, give or take a few years. It probably wasn't much older, and it may have been discarded quickly as computer technology had gone through rapid improvements over that time. He collated all the information he could find on the make and model, looking at the specifications of the disk and the firmware it ran. Pix had said that she couldn't see any data on it, but there could be several reasons for that. It was time to eliminate all the possibilities.

Ross logged in to Eden and searched her out. She was lurking in a chat room, and as soon as she got his message, she took her leave of the group and opened a private channel.

"Hi, Piper! How are you?"

"Doing well, Pix. Good weekend?"

"Okay, thanks."

"I've been having a look at that hard drive. I have a few things you can try."

"Brilliant," she replied. "I've been puzzling over it."

"I found a match for the label," said Ross. "I think it dates from 2010 at the latest. I know you said that you can't see any data, but here are some ideas to work through." He dropped the list onto the chat box, and at the other end he heard a strange squawk from Pix's audio, almost like a speeded up recording. Strange.

"That's great," said Pix after a pause. "Thanks, Piper."

Ross took a deep breath and tried hard to sound casual. "Hey, Pix, have you dropped into the Pasar forum recently?"

"I'm trying to steer clear of that place," she said, "but yeah, I do keep an eye on it. Yasmin the Admin's gone. Did you know that?"

"Yes, I knew," replied Ross. He knew far more about Yasmin than Pix would ever guess.

"King Katong is trying to run it these days, but if you ask me it's out of control."

"What do you mean?" asked Ross.

"There was a flurry of big contracts a couple of years ago," she said. "I took one look at them and walked away. It was all high security stuff, and I was trying to stay out of trouble after TrustCentre."

"How is that relevant?"

"The nuclear test, Piper. I went back in when it happened. I was sure that those contracts were all related, and I was right. They were celebrating. Cybercriminals for hire. You know, like the man on the news said…" her voice tailed off uncertainly.

"Uh, yes," said Ross. "I know who you mean."

"Piper, you're not… No, ignore me. It's just that, well, you sound very alike, and he really knows his stuff."

"Really?" said Ross with a nervous laugh. "Your own voice always sounds different to other people."

"I suppose so."

Ross could tell she was unconvinced, and he hated himself for lying to her. "Pix…" He couldn't continue.

"He who pays the piper calls the tune," said Pix flatly. "That's what he said. It is you, isn't it?"

Ross bowed his head.

"Yes."

7: REVELATIONS

"What will you do?" asked Ross.

"Piper…" Michelle was lost for words. "I didn't set out to dox you. It was a shot in the dark."

"It's my own fault," said Ross. "I got careless."

"I won't tell anyone, if you don't tell on me."

"What do you mean?"

"I don't think it would be too hard for you to find out who I am," said Michelle with a nervous laugh.

"The TrustCentre hack, right?" said Ross. He ran a quick search of his private files to refresh his memory. "There were four people arrested. Two are in jail. I'm fairly sure you're not one of them."

"Logical, yes."

"That makes you either Iniko or Michelle. I'm going to take a wild guess here…"

"Do you need to phone a friend?" she giggled.

"You must be Michelle. ShellPixie."

"My real-life friends call me Shell," she said.

"Let's stick with Pix, on here at least. No more slip-ups."

"Okay, Piper."

Ross felt the odd sensation of despair turning to elation. His initial fear at having been identified had given way to the comforting sense that he had found a friend who had as much to lose as he did if she were to be identified.

"Are you really a triathlete?" she asked. "And a cybersecurity consultant?"

"Yes," he said. "They both keep me out of trouble."

"I can see why you don't want to go back to Pasar," she said. "That is not the place to be if you're trying to avoid entanglements."

"It would be work," said Ross hurriedly. "My boss asked me to keep an eye on it, but you're right, it's a risky place to be. I don't want to take the Piper back in and I can't set up a new avatar. I'd have to go back through the whole qualification round again and they wouldn't trust a newcomer."

"I can lurk for you," said Michelle. "I mean it. I don't want anything to do with the contracts they're pushing out at the moment, although to be honest they're worth a fortune, but I know a few people on quite well and it wouldn't be too strange if I called in from time to time."

"Would you really do that for me?" Ross asked.

"Sure," said Michelle. "As long as you help me with this hard disk."

"Deal," said Ross with a laugh. "Do you want to give me access to the imaged files?"

"I really want to solve the mystery myself," she said, "but it's a headache swapping out software. I'll sort that out for you. Not right now, though. I have other fish to fry."

"Okay, Pix. No problem at all. Talk to you tomorrow?"

"Sure, Piper. Take care."

The connection dropped, and Ross sat still in the silence of his house, looking at the shafts of evening sunlight cast onto the wooden floor. There was an unaccustomed lightness in his heart. It was an odd feeling.

Restless, he wandered outside and sat on the low wall that divided his small garden from the pavement. The sun was still warm, a welcome relief after a few days of rain showers. The sky was busy with drones, from takeaway deliveries at roof height to traffic scanners flying high over the road network. People passed him on their way home from work, alone and in twos and threes. Some he recognised as neighbours, nodding a greeting as they went by. An elderly lady who had been friends with his grandmother stopped to chat.

"It's young Ross, isn't it?" she said. "My, you have grown up, haven't you?"

"Hello, Mrs Khan," he said politely.

"I saw you on the telly," she said approvingly. "Your gran would be proud. You were a right scamp when you were little, but you've turned out well."

There wasn't much Ross could say to that. She was right on all counts. He smiled and shrugged, embarrassed.

"Very well, considering," she continued, reminiscing. "Your dad was a rum character, you know."

His attention sharpened. "What about him?" he asked.

"Well, he always had some scheme on the go, didn't he?" She tutted disapprovingly.

"I don't know," said Ross. "I don't remember him at all."

"Maybe just as well," she replied sagely. "Lovely to see you, young man." She trotted off down the street without another word, her shopping trolley following behind her like a faithful dog.

"Uh… bye." Ross was nonplussed by the exchange. He hadn't thought about his estranged father for years. He couldn't recall anything about him, that was for sure. Neither his mother nor his grandmother had ever spoken of him, although he had overheard arguments that he knew involved the man. He didn't want to know about him. It was no use digging up the past.

The sun had dipped below the horizon and it was cooler in the shadows now. Ross made his way back indoors, reflecting on an unexpected evening.

•

Tenuk left his apartment as dawn broke. Shuttles were already running silently along the main road towards the bay, half filled with early commuters. There was a slight breeze lifting the humidity of the city and he chose to walk for a while. It was good to be outside, where the smell of breakfast cooking mingled with the heady scent of flowers from living walls and planters. He was about to spend yet another day in a sanitised, air-conditioned office and he needed some time in the real world.

He was still feeling very pleased with his handling of the Pasar coders. It had been remarkably easy to bring them onside. The Syndicate would be happy with the progress his community was making. Activation of the second phase of the project would occupy only the core members, those who had been involved in the original Chinese cyber attacks and had helped to build the different elements of the sleeping dragon. He still had a balancing act to achieve in keeping the rest of the forum engaged and interested, not to mention his own private project. The hacker he had contracted was making good progress on the software for the laundering of corporate carbon credits.

It was getting warm. Tenuk reached a bus stop at the downtown end of the East Coast Road and decided that was enough walking for the day. He hopped on the next shuttle to arrive.

"Tenuk! Good morning." It was a colleague, both from the MerLions and from the murkier world of the Syndicate. "You're some way from home."

"I felt like a walk," said Tenuk. "It gives me time to think."

"There is much to think about," nodded his colleague. "The sleeping dragon awakes."

Tenuk glanced around nervously. "It will be good to go back to America," he said, changing the subject smoothly.

"You worry too much," laughed his colleague.

Tenuk shook his head and stayed silent.

The shuttle swept along the highway around the bay and into the core of the city where skyscrapers reared up into the sky. They joined the throng of commuters on the street. It was noticeably more humid now and the air conditioned lobby of their building came as a relief. They took the elevator to the higher floors and emerged in the MerLions headquarters.

"We can talk in here." Tenuk led the way into an empty meeting room. He pulled out his smartscreen and scanned briefly for bugs, as he did each day out of habit.

"We've been commended for bringing the next MerLions tour to North America," said his colleague. "It was all your work, of course. Congratulations."

"The Syndicate has become concerned about the creditworthiness of the end client," said Tenuk carefully. "This is the most valuable contract they have ever handled, and it may be important to have people on the ground."

"Is all the hardware in place for the next phase? Is there, in fact, a dragon to wake?"

"We must trust that the other subcontractors have done their work," said Tenuk. "It is out of our hands, and we cannot know for sure until the moment comes." Unbidden, a picture formed in his mind of a closed box, the state of its contents unknown until observed. Schrodinger's dragon. He struggled to keep a straight face. It would do his hard reputation no good at all if he laughed.

His colleague nodded slowly. "That will be a moment to savour." He looked at his watch. "I have to go." He left the room and the door closed behind him.

Tenuk could hold it no longer. His comedic vision of a dragon from a childhood cartoon poking its inquisitive snout out of a box was so much at odds with the coming reality. He leaned on the window, ignoring the splendid view across the bay, and laughed until the tears ran down his cheeks. The stresses of the past few days melted away. It was all going to work out.

•

Daniel left the house early. Michelle was still in bed, but awake and drinking tea. She had been up very late working on one of her contracts. He hadn't enquired too closely about it, and he hoped she knew what she was doing.

The sun had not yet hit the wasteland and the honeysuckle was in shadow. Daniel scanned the terraced house in the middle of the rough ground, but there was no movement to be seen. He picked out more details: the mast on the roof was new, and there were a few older aerials visible, rusted and broken. There was the jagged outline of razor wire or glass protecting the top of the boundary wall. Perched incongruously at one corner was what looked like a garden gnome, but on closer inspection it turned out to be a statuette of a monkey in a blue and white striped shirt – the Hartlepool football mascot. He shook his head and carried on walking towards the plant.

He was first through the door of the security office. He worked out how to run the coffee machine and sat down, gathering his thoughts. He wanted to start by looking back at the turnover of managers in the past two years and dig a little deeper into the most recent departure. What was the security breach that Brandon had mentioned?

With perfect timing, Brandon himself walked through the door.

"Daniel! You're in early."

"I thought I'd get a head start today. There's still a lot to learn."

Brandon nodded. "I have some time before my first meeting. What do you want to know?"

"Let's start with the last security manager. You were going to tell me about the breach."

"Ah, yes. This is a very odd story. We've had some problems with rabbits getting under the perimeter fence."

Daniel was taken aback. This was not what he had expected.

"Rabbits?"

"Yes, rabbits," said Brandon. He was quite serious. "They burrow in and out of the site from time to time. We thought that we'd plugged all the gaps and then had another incident two weeks ago."

"Get a better guard dog?" suggested Daniel. "What's this got to do with my predecessor?"

"He was arrested out of work hours for an unusual misdemeanour," said Brandon. "He was picked up by a security detail in the marshland around the landfill site. You know it?"

"Yes, I think so," said Daniel carefully. "What was he doing there?"

"He was carrying a mining ferret and some recovered metal. Hardly a fortune, but it all counted against him. He was charged with theft and trespassing and he admitted it straight away, of course."

There but for the grace of god go I, thought Daniel. There was a good chance that he had witnessed the man's arrest himself.

"How does this tie in with the rabbits," asked Daniel. Brandon gave him a quizzical look, and the connection dawned on him. "It wasn't rabbits?"

"Exactly. These mining ferrets are strong enough to disentangle metal from the landfill, and that's enough to break through deep fencing, as well. When we looked closer at the burrow under our perimeter there was clear evidence of a breach. Rabbits can't chew through metal however hard they try."

"Ingenious," said Daniel. "But what could he have gained from breaking into his own site? You're sure it was him?"

"Yes," said Brandon sadly. "Forensic analysis of soil samples, fence damage and burrowing patterns confirmed it was the same ferret."

"It doesn't add up," said Daniel, shaking his head. "He had a good job, so there was no need for him to be scavenging. How is the investigation going?"

"Slowly," admitted Brandon.

"Is there a way to talk to him?" asked Daniel. "I think we need to ask him a few more questions."

"I think you're right," said Brandon. He looked at the clock. "I have to go. When I'm free later I'll introduce you to the inspectors and arrange a meeting." He gave Daniel a look of approval. "Well done. You're off to a good start."

•

Susie thumped the desk in frustration. "This is doing my head in."

"Let me take a look," said Ella. She leaned over and scanned the code that Susie was reading.

Ella's hair swung forward, tickling the side of Susie's chin. Susie inhaled her familiar scent and sighed. "We need to spend more quality time together," she said wistfully.

"What do you call this?" joked Ella, nuzzling Susie's cheek.

"I missed you this weekend," said Susie. "I never asked. How was your retreat?"

"It was fun," said Ella. "More relaxing than I expected. I was a bit sceptical, but it was good."

"I wish I could have come with you," said Susie. "It was a shame there were no spaces left."

"I know," said Ella. "Next time?" She turned her head and her lips brushed Susie's forehead. She turned back to the screen and pointed at a line of code. "Is that what you were looking for?"

"Oh! Yes." Susie gathered her thoughts. "This software is horrible to analyse. No comments, and the indentations are all over the place…"

"It's clever, though," said Ella. "It looks nasty, but there are some elegant touches. That little spying subroutine, for instance."

"The one that tries to send traffic data to some Snake River servers? It's an old trick and it's badly executed. The code doesn't do anything." Susie closed the screen down. "Honestly, I give up. I'm beginning to think this is all a red herring. There aren't any gaping holes in the firewall, although it certainly looks like they tried to do something shady." She looked at the clock, then across the room to an empty desk. "Where's Mason? Don't we have a meeting scheduled with Cameron?"

"He's supposed to be organising access to that odd server in the air gapped network," said Ella. She checked the time. "I'll go and see if I can find him. Why don't you talk to Joel and see if he's found anything in Norfolk?"

"Good idea." Susie briefly squeezed Ella's hand. "I'll see you back here."

They both went their separate ways at the door, Susie to find some privacy for calls, and Ella on the hunt for Mason. When Susie finally got through to Joel, she was surprised that Ross answered. She could hear Joel's deep laughter in the background.

"What are you lot up to," she asked. "I can't see anything. Turn the camera round!"

"Some things are best left unseen," said Ross, with an uncharacteristically light laugh. He turned the camera anyway. They were in the office. Joel was standing precariously on a counter, reaching out across the ceiling to a small rugby ball that was jammed in the corner of a light fitting.

"Careful," came Noor's voice. "Don't break anything."

"He'll be fine," said Ross.

"I wasn't thinking about him, I was thinking about the lights," retorted Noor.

The office door opened in the background and Cameron walked in. Joel stopped moving, as if stillness would camouflage him. When he realised what he had done, he started laughing again.

461

Cameron simply shook her head. "What do you think you're doing?" she asked.

"Retrieving lost property," he said as his fingertips reached the ball. He grabbed it triumphantly, wobbled alarmingly, and clambered down with no ill effects. As he landed on the floor the lights flickered. He looked up, alarmed, but the flickering stopped.

Cameron spotted the open screen. "Is that Susie?" she said. "How are things going? Is Mason with you?"

"Not right now," said Susie. "I haven't seen him this morning. Ella's gone to find him. He was fine yesterday, though. She spoke to him when we got down here last night."

"Let me know when you're ready."

"Sure," said Susie. "I actually called to talk to Joel. I thought you were in Norfolk?"

"Yeah, that was the plan," said Joel. "I had some stuff to do with Martha this morning, so I'm going now. I came in to get the latest from Noor."

"Something new?" asked Susie.

"Possibly," said Noor. "I'm not sure it's going to help you, though, Joel. I've picked up some more activity in South East Asia – specifically Singapore – and we're waiting for news on the Korean media farm, aren't we, Cameron?"

"Singapore again," said Ross to no one in particular.

"Don't start," said Noor. "It isn't anyone we know."

"The consortium has been having trouble with the Korean authorities," said Cameron, "but from what I can gather they're going in tonight, local time."

"I might have something," said Susie, "but I don't know how it fits."

"Go on," said Cameron.

"There seems to have been an attempt to include some polymorphic code in the firewall software. It would give us a hole in the network security if it was properly written. I'm sure it's useless but I'll send the details through. Maybe you'll find something similar in Norfolk, Joel?"

"Thanks, Susie," said Joel. "Now I know what I'm looking for, it'll be easier to find."

"I'd better get back," said Susie. "I wonder if Ella's tracked Mason down yet?"

"Call me as soon as you get hold of him," said Cameron.

Susie ended the call and went back to the main office. Ella was there, but there was still no sign of Mason.

"How's Joel doing?" she asked.

"He's not there yet," said Susie. "He was still in the office. I caught up with Noor and Cameron as well. Noor's found more links to Singapore, and Cameron says the media farm in Seoul is finally being raided tonight – that's any time now, I suppose. It's quite exciting being in the middle of all of this."

"It'll be interesting to see what they find in Korea," said Ella. She looked around. "I don't think there's much more we can do right now. Shall we get some lunch?"

"Sure," said Susie with a smile. "I could do with clearing my head. Let's go."

•

Cameron, Ross, and Noor were sitting high above street level on the café's roof terrace, enjoying the sunshine. The blustery winds that had been blowing along the Thames for the last few days had died down and they basked in the still warmth.

"It's good to get out of the office," said Noor. She looked around. They were the only customers up here, and the café was in any case their regular haunt. It was safe to talk.

"You've been flat out, haven't you," said Cameron sympathetically. "I can't believe the amount of information you've managed to add to the files. The consortium is lapping up every detail, believe me."

"I hope it helps," said Noor. "The more I dig, the more I find."

"It all helps," said Cameron. "We should have some more data coming through from Cloverleaf. I'll be speaking to her at two o'clock." She looked at Ross. "You said you'd come across her before. What do you know? I want to double check her story."

"She's been active on several of the main dark web marketplaces for a few years now," said Ross. "I've seen her on Eden, but we haven't really talked. She was definitely part of Pasar, the community which was run by Yasmin the Admin. I got the impression back when I lurked on there that she was involved in some of the bigger jobs that were going down, but she was always more pleasant than some of the others. I'm sure that what she's telling you is straight down the line."

"Have you been back on to Pasar yet?" asked Cameron.

Ross shook his head. "I think it's too risky. I do have a connection who lurks there, though."

"Someone you can trust?" asked Noor.

"Yes. Very much."

"If you're sure, I'm good with that," said Cameron. "I'm all for staying in the shadows, even if we can't manage it all of the time. Anything new to share from your 'connection'?"

"A lot of things are just confirming what you learned from Cloverleaf directly," said Ross. "King Katong is still in charge." He looked at Noor. "Another Singapore link. You can't ignore it."

She scowled at him. "Drop it, Ross."

"I'm starting to build a picture of the type of contracts that have been put out," continued Ross, "and they align with the attacks that we documented on the Chinese power plant. I don't think there's any doubt that a large part of the work was done through this group."

"Good," said Cameron. "This all fits. Use your judgement, of course, but if you can tie up any of Noor's research with leads from that marketplace, it'll help." She reflected for a moment. "Would it be useful to make this 'connection' of yours official? Pay some expenses, that sort of thing?"

"That would be nice," said Ross. "I think sh – they – would appreciate it."

Cameron raised an eyebrow at Ross, who had blushed uncharacteristically.

"Okay." She was interrupted by an alert from her smartscreen. She grabbed at the device and opened the encrypted message. Noor and Ross watched in silence as she scrolled through, frowning.

"I don't believe it," she said furiously. "How the hell…?"

"What's up?" asked Ross.

"The Korean raid." Cameron swore loudly. "They spend three days faffing about with the authorities, they finally get what they need, and they miss their target."

"What happened?" said Noor bleakly. "Did we get it wrong?"

"Apparently not," said Cameron. "They've found a lot of equipment and evidence that points to a media farm, so it was the right place. There were signs that someone had left in a big hurry, so quickly that they didn't have time to wipe the records."

"They were tipped off," said Ross.

"Looks like it," said Cameron.

"But how?" said Noor. "There were only a few people who knew what was being planned."

"And when?" added Cameron. "They seem to think they missed the target by minutes. If they'd known about the plan, surely they would have gone much earlier?"

"Cloverleaf?" asked Noor.

Cameron shook her head. "She didn't know anything about this."

"The consortium has a leak," said Ross bleakly. "Nowhere is safe, Cameron. We're going to have to be careful."

"Dammit." Cameron pushed her plate away. Her appetite was gone. "It was always a risk." She stood up. "I need to get back to the office to take Cloverleaf's call. I hope she's got some good news for us. Are you coming?"

Ross gulped down the last of his water. "Yes. I'm meeting Andy later to do another interview. The media can't seem to let go of this story."

Activated by their movement, the robot waiter glided across the terrace and started to clear the table and straighten the chairs. Noor followed Cameron and Ross down the stairs, ready to dive back into her research.

Back at the office, Cameron settled down to wait for Cloverleaf's call. Sure enough, on the dot of two, the connection sprang into life. They exchanged codes to verify their respective identities. All was well.

"Good morning, SimCavalier. How are you today?"

"Afternoon, Cloverleaf. We're fine. Do you have anything new to report?"

Cloverleaf laughed softly. "Oh yes. Transmission incoming. Brace yourself. There's a lot here."

Cameron watched as a stream of data started to appear on her screen. Files and folders began to pop into view, one after the other.

"I'm sending you everything I managed to copy," said Cloverleaf. "There's three terabytes of data coming through. Should take about fifteen minutes to complete."

Cameron stared at the files. "This is amazing, Cloverleaf. How did you manage it?"

"Pure luck, SimCavalier, and not before time. You saw the Militia claimed responsibility for the nuclear test, I guess?"

"Yes."

"Right up until yesterday, I wasn't sure that it was really them."

"We had them as favourites," said Cameron, "even though the explosion was in Russia. After all, if you're going to test a nuclear device, you want to do it as far away from Yellowstone as possible."

"Yeah, you're so right," Cloverleaf gave a hollow laugh. "They're moving to the second phase. They're activating an attack in Europe. I've given you all I know about the Pasar connection. I hope these files will hold the keys to the physical side."

465

Cameron was rocked by the news. The threat was real, and she was in the eye of the storm.

"Are you still safe, Cloverleaf?"

"Yes, so far."

"What do they want?" asked Cameron. "I've never really understood what drives the Wyoming Militia. Why are they waging war on the world?"

"They're fanatics, pure and simple," said Cloverleaf. Her distaste was palpable. "They like their guns and their oil, and they see global decarbonisation as a threat to their liberty."

"How did you end up in there?" Cameron asked, curious.

"I picked the wrong guy. We moved into the community, we had a kid, it was all good until I realised how radicalised he was."

"You couldn't leave then?"

"No way. I left him, but I couldn't get out of the Militia. I had nothing and my kid was safer here. That's changed. That's why I'm helping you. We need a way out when the time comes."

On the screen, the last few files popped into view. The data transfer was complete.

"That's done, SimCavalier. I gotta go." She ended the call.

"Stay safe," Cameron called into nothingness. She looked up at Ross and Noor, who had been listening intently. She turned the screen around so they could see the list of files and folders. "We have work to do."

•

Daniel had hardly stopped all day. He came in from a lengthy tour around the full site perimeter to find a message from Brandon. The investigators would be ready to talk to him tomorrow. He put the appointment into his calendar and started reviewing shift patterns and reports, but his concentration was slipping. He needed a break.

Where could he go? He wandered out into the corridor and saw another door ajar. Pete and Sandeep's temporary office. He knocked on the door and went in. Julia, his counterpart in IT security, was with them.

"Hi, Daniel," Pete said with a welcoming smile. "How's it going so far?"

"Lots to take in," said Daniel, "but so far, so good."

"What can we do for you?" asked Sandeep.

"I was coming for a chat and a change of scene," said Daniel, "but Julia, I'm glad you're here too. I wanted to run a few things by you all."

"What kind of things?" said Julia.

"I'm not sure yet," said Daniel. "Look, you know the power station attack in China, the one which led to the theft of the uranium? That was a mixture of cyber and physical crime, wasn't it?"

"Yes," said Sandeep. He didn't need to elaborate.

"I've been talking to Brandon this morning," Daniel continued, "and I'm up to speed with the recent breach. I know that I'm focused on physical security and you're running IT, Julia, but I want to be sure we're working together. I'm afraid we'll miss something otherwise."

Julia nodded. "Of course. I've been focused on managing systems until now," she said, "but it makes sense."

Pete was looking from one to the other. "Rewind. Dan, did you say there had been a breach? We've been here more than a week, and no one's mentioned anything."

"It wasn't anything to do with the IT systems and security," said Julia defensively. "There was no reason to bother you with it."

Sandeep and Pete exchanged exasperated glances. "Julia, you'd be surprised," said Pete. "We were going to propose a physical penetration test on top of the systems and network reviews, and it sounds like you need one." He turned to Daniel. "What's the story?"

Daniel glanced at Julia, who nodded. "As far as I can gather," he said, "there was a perimeter breach using a ferret. The security manager was caught scavenging with the same ferret, which is why he's gone and I'm here. That's basically it."

"What's a ferret?" asked Pete.

Daniel laughed. "Don't you get these down south? The landfill's being mined for precious and rare earth metals. There's big money involved. They're harvesting gases from the deep compacted layers, and they scan the rest with huge metal detectors to pull out anything valuable."

"Oh, those," said Pete. "The drone swarms that do the digging. We call them rats."

"Rats and rabbits," said Sandeep. "Or rather, not rabbits at all. I'm going to take a lucky guess and say that the breach was on the south-east corner of the site just where the marshes meet the sea."

"How did you know that?" asked Julia.

"We went for a walk when you were in your board meeting yesterday," he replied. "We were turned back by security, but there was a lot of activity down there. I wondered if it was an underwater breach, but this ferret sounds more likely."

"It's possible to re-programme the drones," said Daniel. "People have been known to slip their own ferret into the swarm and collect metals themselves."

"There you go, Julia," said Pete. "The perfect combination of cyber and physical risks."

Daniel could see that she was unhappy at being called out, and he had to keep the peace.

"Julia, I really need your help," he said. She rallied a little. "I'd like to know more about the previous security managers, especially the original guy. You've been here for a long time, and you know everyone."

"Well, yes, I suppose I do," said Julia, mollified. "Here, let me pull up the records." She went through several layers of authentication, exchanging credentials with the personnel database. "This is the abridged record. You need to talk to HR if you want anything more detailed."

Daniel looked over Julia's shoulder at the screen. "Paul Charles White? That was the old security manager?"

"That's right," said Julia.

There were several photographs on file. The first was of a pale man in his late thirties, burly and frowning. The gallery showed his journey towards retirement. In the last picture, his hair and bushy beard were turning to grey.

"Did you know him well?" asked Daniel.

"As well as anybody," replied Julia. "He was an odd character. He didn't let people get too close to him."

"Good at his job, though, by all accounts."

"Oh, yes." She nodded. "He was here for twenty-five years, all the way through the decommissioning of the old reactors and the new build, so he'd seen the site at every stage of its development. He was very handy with computers as well."

"Brandon said that he left suddenly," said Daniel. "Any idea why that was?"

Julia shook her head. "It was quite unexpected. When I joined the staff, fifteen years ago, he was talking about retiring early. He said he had a nest egg put away for his old age. Then he just dropped the subject. I always wondered if he'd lost his money when the South American economies crashed. That caught quite a few pension firms out." She looked kindly at Daniel. "Before your time, I expect. You were probably still at school."

"He wasn't quite at retirement age when he left, was he?" prompted Daniel.

"No, a few years short. I don't think he retired completely. He mentioned that he had some consultancy to keep him going. He stayed just long enough to put in the new computer system and hand over to his replacement."

"New computer system?" said Pete. "Julia, we're still working through the files, and they're a bit of a mess. Most of what we've seen of the network has been in place for much longer than two years."

"Oh yes, we don't chop and change lightly around here," she said. "There was a very specific addition to the system which came with strong industry recommendations and the directors decided it was needed. He managed the installation, and then he left. I heard he was going to earn more for part time consultancy than he had in this job."

"I have to ask you this, Julia," said Pete. "Does 'Snake River' mean anything to you?"

"You've found the file, then?" said Julia. "Yes, it was a Snake River firewall system. That's who Angus went to work for."

"Angus? Who's Angus?" said Daniel.

"Oh, yes, how silly of me," laughed Julia. "When he joined the staff, apparently, there were already two Pauls in the office. He was from Aberdeen, so..."

"Aberdeen... Angus?" Daniel finished for her.

Pete and Sandeep groaned in unison.

"He didn't seem to mind," said Julia. "It suited him. He was always gruff and bullish, but he meant well."

"Wait... Where did he live?" asked Daniel.

"I'm not sure," said Julia. "Down towards the old colliery, I think. He didn't move house for all the time he worked here. He's probably still there."

Daniel laughed. His suspicions were confirmed. "You're not going to believe this, Julia, but he's one of my neighbours. I know exactly where he is."

"We need to speak to him," said Sandeep.

Pete shook his head. "No. We have to talk to Cameron first." He looked at Daniel. "This is sensitive stuff, and it links to something our colleagues are working on. I can't tell you too much yet, but I'd appreciate it if you don't approach this Angus chap just yet. Please don't mention our conversation if you see him."

"Don't worry," said Daniel. "I've never spoken to him. My cousin met him by chance last week. He's something of a recluse."

Julia nodded. "That's Angus alright."

"About that testing I mentioned," said Pete. "I strongly recommend that we do a full physical penetration exercise. Are you two senior enough to authorise it?"

Julia shook her head. "As it would come out of two budgets, and Daniel's barely got his feet under the table, it will have to be Brandon."

"Okay. We'll send you a proposal in the next half hour. If you could clear it with him today that would be great, but please don't let it go any further. The fewer people who are aware of the testing, the better. We'll be bringing in some other colleagues to help."

Daniel's head was spinning. "Okay. Julia, help me out. What do we do now?"

"I'll sort it out, don't you worry." She gave him a genuine smile. "You're switched on. I think we've chosen well. Come and join me for a cup of tea. I want to get to know you better." She ushered him out of the room.

Pete looked at Sandeep. "Snake River. I'm not really surprised. I'm just gutted we hadn't found it before."

"Susie found it so easily in the West Country because she knew the original system," said Sandeep. "We were coming in cold, and I think the files have been messed up deliberately to hide the brand from casual eyes."

"Let's get cracking now, then. We need to confirm it's the same setup as the girls found in the West Country. If it is, we have a serious conspiracy on our hands."

•

Susie disconnected from her call with Joel, and her screen rang again almost immediately. It was Cameron.

"I've just heard from Pete," she said. "They've identified some Snake River software up in the North East as well, and they're checking the air gapped network for anomalies. This is serious stuff. You were really on the ball to pick it up, Susie."

"Thanks, Cameron," she said, enjoying the praise. "I've spoken to Joel as well. I guess he talked to you first?"

"Yes, he did," said Cameron. "Norfolk is an outlier, though. They reverted to their original configurations after installation, so I think we can be comfortable that the plant isn't compromised."

"It's us and the North East, then. Are you sure there are no others?"

"As sure as I can be, for this country at least. I've passed all your findings through the cybersecurity networks to my connections, and so far, there are no similar cases."

"What about the people Mason mentioned, his friends in – what – Hungary, South Africa, what was the other one?"

"Belgium," said Cameron absent-mindedly. "Is Mason ready? I need to talk to him. He probably knows more about this than anyone else."

Susie shook her head. "Ella's been out to look for him again. He should be here." There was a noise in the corridor outside. "That's probably them now."

The door flew open and Ella collapsed through it. "It's Mason," she cried breathlessly. "They've found…"

"What, Ella? Are you okay?" Susie put down the screen, still connected to Cameron, and rushed to her side.

"They've found a body in the water. It's Mason. He's dead." She collapsed onto a chair and started to cry.

8: SUSPICIONS

"Ross, wait up!" Andy ran up the stairs to reception. Ross had paused at the door and was checking something on his smartscreen. He turned and looked Andy straight in the eye.

"You've just heard the same news," said Ross.

"Want to do another interview?"

Ross looked doubtful. "I'm not sure I can. We have people on the ground at that power station. Ella and Susie were working there. Argentum is too close to the action."

Andy looked disappointed. "I understand. The local outside broadcast team are on their way there. It's being treated as a tragic accident, but of course any incident at a nuclear plant is going to be under the spotlight right now."

"You'll have to make do with the footage we've recorded," said Ross. "We covered enough generic cybersecurity for you to repurpose it. Will that do?"

"It'll have to." Andy was a good journalist, and he took care of his sources. He would not dare to cross Cameron or any member of her team, mainly out of fear of his next-door neighbour. Aunt Vicky would protect her niece at all costs.

"I'll be in touch as soon as I'm able to help," said Ross. "I'd better get back to the office." He disappeared through the revolving door with a wave and jogged off down the street. Andy sighed and went slowly back down the stairs to the studio where Giles was waiting.

"No interview, then?" he asked.

Andy shook his head. "Not for the moment. It's still too sensitive. Pick some good soundbites out of the recordings we've just done, and we'll cobble together something with the local reports. It'll have to do."

"Here's what we have already," said Giles, switching on the feed.

"…a statement from the power station's management confirmed that the dead man was one of their employees. Police are tracing his next of kin." The camera panned across the scene, showing a tent erected at the shoreline. A walkway above was taped off.

"What do they reckon?" asked Andy. "Did he topple off that gantry?"

472

"That's the theory they're putting forward at the moment," said Giles. He shrugged. "Accidents happen."

"Yeah," said Andy, "but they rarely happen at a place like that, and the timing is too coincidental."

"I know what you mean," said Giles. "There's too much going on with the Russian explosion, that statement from the Wyoming lot, and now this."

"Exactly," said Andy. "What are the odds?" He turned back to the screen and started to work through the footage, frame by frame, frowning.

•

Ross took the stairs up to the office two at a time. Inside, Cameron was running a team meeting on the big screen. Susie was there, looking pale but determined. Pete and Sandeep had joined from their northern outpost, and Joel from Norfolk. Cameron flashed Ross a quick, stressed smile and waved her hand towards the coffee machine. Ross took the hint and refilled her mug. He caught Noor's eye and she nodded gratefully. He brought her a mug as well and sat down with her to catch up.

"What's the latest?" he asked quietly. "I got all the messages."

"Susie's been interviewed by the police already, and Ella is still with them," said Noor. "They've moved very quickly."

"Hardly a surprise," said Ross. "Anything else I need to know?" Noor shook her head, and Ross moved into camera shot, giving the team a thumbs up, and listened to Cameron.

"I think we have to focus on what Mason was able to tell us when you spoke to him last week," she was saying.

Susie nodded. "I agree. There isn't much more we can tease out of what we have. I still want to have a look at that server, but I'm not sure we'll get access now."

"It's unlikely," said Cameron. "We were only engaged to review their procedures, and you stumbled on the new firewall and hardware configs because you knew the old system."

"Pure luck," said Susie.

"You made your own luck," said Cameron, "It was a good job. Now that the whole site is under investigation, though, there's very little point doing more than a final report and handing over to the authorities."

"I'm not sure that Ella will be up to that," said Susie. "She's very upset. She came across the security guards just as they found him there in the water. She's had a dreadful shock."

"You are more than capable of writing it up yourself," said Cameron, "but I understand you want to take care of Ella. Why don't you both come back here as soon as you're able, and you can work with Joel and Noor to get it finished."

"Yes," said Susie. "Thanks, we will."

"In the meantime, I want to dig into the things Mason said about the Snake River installation," said Cameron. "What did he tell you, exactly?"

Susie looked for her notes, but Ross was ready. "He said he worked with a lad from Kent, a couple of Welsh girls, and an old bloke 'up north' that they never met."

"That's what I was thinking of," said Cameron.

Pete raised his hand. "Cameron, I think we have something. It seems the old security manager here took early retirement and moved on to a consulting job with Snake River."

"An old bloke up north," said Ross. "What are the chances?"

"I'd say they're high," said Cameron, "and that brings me to something else. Pete, Sandeep, you were talking about testing?"

"Yes," said Sandeep. "We're waiting for signoff on a physical test. We should have it before the end of the day."

"I'm really concerned about a perimeter breach they've had, " added Pete. "It was land based, but it got me thinking about uranium theft. You can't really pick the stuff up and walk out with it."

"No," agreed Cameron. "The Chinese theft was definitely 'bots or drones getting through once the security systems were compromised. It's the only way, really."

"Exactly," said Pete, "but where do the 'bots come from? Land or water? It would be easier to hide them in the sea."

"Good call," said Cameron. "Pete, can you look into that in more detail?" She turned to Joel. "How do you fancy a trip up north?"

Joel shook his head. "I need to pass on this one. I'm sorry."

Cameron nodded. "Understood."

On screen, Susie frowned, puzzled.

"Well," said Cameron. "I haven't done one of these tests for a while. Looks like I'll be joining you in the north, lads. I can do some anonymous digging into our mystery man at the same time."

"You get all the fun," complained Ross.

"This one's mine," said Cameron with a grin. "Haven't you got some training to do?"

"Yeah, I suppose so," said Ross.

"You suppose so?" Joel laughed. "You're in the European Championships, man. Double down on that regime."

"I'll be doorstepping you for some of Martha's home cooking," retorted Ross.

"Anytime," said Joel.

"I'll hold you to that."

On the screen behind Susie her office door opened, and Ella appeared. Cameron was shocked to see how upset she was. She quickly flipped Susie's feed into a private channel and addressed the rest of the team.

"We'd better wrap up there. Sandeep, Pete, let me know as soon as you get that signoff. Joel, you'll be back here by the end of the week, won't you?"

"There's not much to do," said Joel. "It'll be Thursday, tops."

"Great," said Cameron. "When you get back, I want you to try and find the Kent connection to Snake River. I know it's a tiny loose end, but every little helps."

"I guess Noor and I just plod on with all that data from Cloverleaf," said Ross.

Cameron could tell he was frustrated not to be getting more involved in the thrill of the chase. "I'm sorry, Ross," she said. "You need to be here in London. You said so yourself."

"We'll be fine," said Noor. "There is a huge amount to go through. Susie and Ella can help when they get back as well."

"Talking of which," said Cameron, "thanks all, I have to go." She closed down the main chat and took her smartscreen off to the corner of the room to talk to Susie and Ella privately. She needed to take care of her team.

•

Ross arrived home tired and out of sorts. He needed a distraction, something out on the edge. He was bored with the endless analysis of someone else's daringly acquired data. He wanted to be part of the action. The sporting success that he had always wanted was stifling his day job, and he found himself longing for the illicit thrills of cybercrime.

He would resist the worst entanglements, of course, but he considered for a moment dropping onto Pasar. No. That was a terrible idea. Instead, he logged in to Eden and scanned the usual places for any sign of ShellPixie. She might have news.

She wasn't online, but Ross found an alert flashing in his inbox. She had sent him a link to access the imaged hard disk. That would give him something to do while he waited for her. He started to work methodically through the image with the tools at his disposal, seeking clues to its content. Although there were a few file names visible, none could be opened. Surely that wasn't the end of the story?

It occurred to him that there were plenty of places on a disk where data could be left behind by accident or hidden deliberately. Pix had said that the disk had been carefully encased and undamaged. Someone had valued it, and probably knew what they were doing.

After a frustrating hour of analysing the disk image for clues, it was time for a break. There was still no word from Pix. Ross shook himself and went to the kitchen. He made some food and grabbed a drink from the fridge, stepping outside for a moment for a breath of the cool night air.

Refreshed by the break he had one more try, and this time he spotted what he had been missing all along. The physical and logical geometry of the recovered disk was different to the original specifications. Ross hashed the firmware and compared it to a hash of the original file he'd downloaded from a historic computing site. They didn't match. The disk firmware had definitely been altered. He was working through the details when he was startled by a voice.

"Piper?" Pix was online. "How's it going?"

"Hey, Pix," said Ross. "I've got good news, and bad news."

"What's the good news?"

"I think I know what's going on with your disk."

"Ooh! That's exciting!" she said. "What's the verdict?"

"Most of it's blank," he said, "but I'm willing to bet there is some hidden data. The firmware has been messed with, and the geometry has changed."

"Oh!" Pix immediately understood what he meant. "Some of the tracks may be hidden, along with the data inside them."

"Exactly," said Ross. "And I have a copy of the original firmware."

"Fantastic," she said. "I can reflash the drive, and that should restore access. It'll only take a second."

"I'll send that over now," said Ross. "There are a few documents that I can see on there as well. I can't open them directly, but there's a good chance that they've simply been renamed."

"They've changed the file extensions, have they?" said Pix.

"Yes, it's an old trick. Shall I work through those and see what I can find?"

"Sure. I'll get started on the forensics."

Pix muted her feed. Ross scanned through the rest of the disk's contents. He worked methodically through the files, and finally yielded some results. There was a photograph of a middle-aged couple standing in front of a building with dark grey stone walls and tall windows. Another showed a dog sitting on a hearthrug, and there was a blurry image of a baby asleep in a hospital cot. A text file contained a list of web addresses that led nowhere. An old spreadsheet showed several columns of random numbers. Ross recognised one column as date serial numbers. He converted them to a readable calendar format and found a range of references from 2009 to 2025. They had been right about the age of the original disk.

Pix's feed went live again.

"Piper? How are you doing? Found anything exciting?"

"Not much. A few websites that don't exist, a list of numbers, and a photo of a dog. What about you?"

"Nothing yet," she said. "The routines are running but I don't know how long this is going to take. I have something I need to work on. Can we pick back up on this tomorrow?"

"I don't know if I can bear the suspense," said Ross, grinning, "but sure. Tomorrow night, I am all yours."

•

Cameron poured two large glasses of wine and handed one to Ben. It was still light outside, and the double doors to the small balcony were open. The cat was sitting contentedly in a patch of fading sunshine, watching the birds who wandered and pecked on the roof of the adjoining building just below.

"You're looking much better," said Ben approvingly. "That weekend in the village was exactly what you needed."

"It was lovely to see everyone again properly," said Cameron. "I'm glad you came up."

Ben slipped a hand around her waist. "It was worth it to see you settled again. You've been carrying the weight of the world on your shoulders, haven't you?"

"I think it's still there, but easier to carry," said Cameron. "I never stop worrying about my family, and my team, and you, but you were right. Once I talked about it, it seemed less of a burden."

"How's Ella?" asked Ben.

"I think she'll be alright," said Cameron. "She and Susie seem to be getting on well again and Susie is supporting her. They'll be back in London by tomorrow night, and that will help."

"It proves you right, doesn't it?"

"What do you mean?"

"This is a dangerous game that you're playing." Ben tucked his chin onto her shoulder. "I think I need to look after you better."

"But you're busy," said Cameron. "You said last week you might have to go away."

"I thought so, and last week was nuts, but I don't have to go far." He stood up straight and smiled at her. "I've managed to stay in England, at least. I'm going to meet with some satellite operators up in the North East."

Cameron spun round. "What?"

"The North East," he repeated. "I'll only be a few hours away. Why?"

She started laughing, holding her glass away from herself in an effort not to spill it. "That's too funny," she gasped.

"Come on, Cameron, what's the joke?"

"I was going to tell you that I have to go away for work… to the North East."

Their eyes met and Ben started laughing too. "You're kidding," he said. She shook her head, her green eyes sparkling with excitement. "Well," he continued, "I guess we'd better look at the map."

The arrival of a delivery drone on the balcony interrupted them. The cat shot indoors, tail bristling, and disappeared into the bedroom. Cameron took their wine glasses to the table while Ben collected the boxes of hot food and sent the drone on its way, delivery complete. A strong scent of garlic wafted through the apartment as Cameron opened the first box.

With a glass of wine in one hand and a slice of pizza in the other, she gazed at the map on the apartment's wallscreen while Ben highlighted the different sites he was visiting.

"Your meetings are all within thirty miles of my work," she said thoughtfully. "Where are you staying?"

"I haven't booked anything yet," said Ben.

"Because of the work I'm doing, I don't want to stay in the same place as Pete and Sandeep," said Cameron. "What if we found somewhere between the two? See, there's even a train line connecting all the dots." The portal was listening. It lit up the track on the map.

"Find accommodation between Newcastle and Middlesbrough," Ben ordered.

Pins started dropping onto the map.

"Filter by available connectivity," said Cameron.

Half the pins in the green inland areas disappeared.

"Hotel?" asked Ben quietly.

Cameron shook her head. "I need space to work and good connections. I don't want to compromise security."

Ben understood. "Show apartments and self-catering only," he ordered. More pins vanished. "Five-star reviews."

Cameron glanced sidelong at Ben. "Hot tub," she said.

He raised an eyebrow.

There were now only six results left. Cameron sipped her wine and picked up another slice of pizza. "Display as a list with photographs," she said through a mouthful of cheese.

Ben fetched the wine bottle from the counter and topped up their glasses. "The third one down looks nice," he said. "The location is perfect for both of us."

Cameron scrolled through the photographs. "There's enough room for me to work, and it's close to the station." She looked at Ben. "Shall I book it through to Sunday and invoice your boss for half?"

"Yes, no problem," he said. "It's way below my usual rate."

Cameron tapped the payment and reached for her glass. The confirmation came through before the wine touched her lips.

Ben raised his own glass in a toast. "To the North," he said.

"To the North," she replied. "This will be quite some adventure."

·

Tenuk was feeling uneasy. Yesterday's warning had come through just in time, alerting the group to a late-night raid on an address in Seoul. Sagikkun had disappeared shortly thereafter and his media farm had gone dark. He had been a stalwart of the Pasar community since Tenuk took his first tentative steps into management for the Syndicate, and he would be missed.

At this moment, he would be missed specifically for the vital work he was doing. He had created an invaluable resource of virtually undetectable and self-managed fake personas whose influence stretched across social channels and into the mainstream media. Their sophisticated bot voices had been silenced, halving the online activity at a stroke. The client would not be happy. Tenuk was not happy, either. Replacing someone with that level of skill would be difficult, and even if the personas were not compromised, he was not convinced that they could be retrieved from backup and reactivated without Sagikkun.

With all this distraction he had neglected the personal project running on Eden. He logged on and was surprised to find that his contracted coder was online. He found it easy to extrapolate likely time zones from activity and had been sure they were in Europe. It was after midnight there.

"ShellPixie, good to see you. How are you progressing?" he typed.

"Pangolin, it's going well," his contractor replied. "I'm running sandbox tests now."

"Don't delay. I need a transfer mechanism in place this week."

"This week? There'll be an extra charge."

"Add it to the contract," typed Tenuk. The cost mattered little. He needed to get Noor out of harm's way.

"Okay. I'll be in touch." The coder left the chat.

Tenuk ignored the rudeness. Whoever they were, if they were in Europe, they might cease to be a problem. He turned to Pasar. As he expected, the atmosphere was heavy. News of Sagikkun's disappearance had travelled fast and there was a palpable undercurrent of fear in the uproar.

"You were all warned," he posted. He felt as if he was shouting to be heard over the throng. "Do not underestimate those who would try to stop our work." The SimCavalier for one, he thought grimly. His people should have dealt with her when they were in London. It had been a squandered opportunity.

His plea went unheard. His elation at bringing the group under some semblance of control had been premature.

He tried again. "Mimi. Cloverleaf. Join me in my office." He opened a breakout room and after a moment two familiar avatars popped onto the screen. They could talk privately here.

"I will pass you some of the work Sagikkun was to have handled. If you accept, payment will revert to you. Any problems?"

Cloverleaf's avatar raised its hand. "I have some challenges. I must decline. I can't take on any more tasks."

"Thank you." He closed her link to the room without another word. "Mimi?"

"Yes, I can help. What do you need?"

"Activation of the swarm."

"Understood." The transaction was fast and set the agreement in stone. Mimi left to start work. She would be hunting for clues to

Sagikkun's progress to date on code repositories in the depths of the web and researching the task in hand. He trusted her to do a good job. Mimi was loyal, talented, inventive, and hard-working, and without scruples. She was a perfect team member. She had been earmarked for future opportunities in the Syndicate, and Tenuk was looking forward to watching her progress.

Satisfied that the Militia contract would be fulfilled despite Sagikkun's untimely departure, Tenuk turned to the other work of the Syndicate. There was plenty to do.

•

Noor's model of the network surrounding the nuclear explosion was starting to test the limits of the office visualisation suite. Ross walked around it, peering critically at certain nodes, poking at others.

"This is pretty impressive, Noor," he said. "Let's work through the details and find the next hole in their defences."

"Okay…" She took a deep breath. "The centre of the model is the Chinese theft, and we now have a really good picture of everything that led up to it. This cluster here" – she swung the model around – "is all the recorded cybercrime which fed into the breach, and down here is what we know of the physical attack." She moved to the other side of the display. "Between the theft and the explosion, we now know that there was work going on to replicate the successful breach methodology in other locations."

"Snake River," said Ross, nodding.

"Yes, Snake River. That activity gave us way more intel than I think the cybercriminals would have suspected."

"It was incredibly complex, wasn't it?" said Ross. "They had to put together a front for the organisation that was convincing enough to get through supplier due diligence and have real people on the ground to get hardware and software through the door."

"Exactly. A really big job with a lot of actors involved," said Noor. "Now then, this is where it starts to get interesting. I've managed to trace common threads back from this interim work to the original cyber attacks."

"Huh, nice," said Ross. He poked at a node on the model. "What's the back story to the Korean media farm?"

"Whoever was running that, their fingerprints were all over the code in the Snake River firewall."

"Really?" Ross was impressed. "How did you figure that out?"

"When the location was raided on Monday, it seems that although the people involved had been tipped off, they didn't manage to empty or lock down their servers. Yesterday the consortium dumped all the code they could find for us to look at, and I ran it through our analyser against the copy of the firewall that Susie got hold of. It came back with a seventy percent style match."

"Very good. But there's not much more we can do with that lead. It's a dead end. What else do we have to go on? What about the intel from Cloverleaf? Are there any more locations to target?"

Noor looked uncertain. "Well, yes. I haven't completed the searches."

"What do you have so far?" pushed Ross.

"The Indonesian media farm was just that," said Noor. "They've started up again with some new campaigns, and I've traced a large number of fake personas submitting articles to well-respected sites supporting the anti-decarbonisation movement."

"Amplifying the message from the Wyoming Militia," said Ross thoughtfully. "Good stuff, Noor. What else?"

"Nothing recently in London," said Noor, "although I did find some more traffic from last year. I wonder if Ella managed to speak to those accountants?"

"I'm not sure she did," said Ross, flicking through the files. "She and Susie are due back in London this afternoon. Let's see how she is tomorrow. What else have we got?"

"There are spots all over America, but that's generally re-posts of the same messages by supporters, I think."

Ross sighed. He knew she was avoiding the issue. "Singapore, Noor. You mentioned that there was activity in Singapore."

"Yes, there was. I haven't gotten around to it yet."

"Okay," said Ross. "Tell, you what, I'll have a look at Singapore while you carry on with the data from Cloverleaf. I know you've barely scratched the surface of what she sent us."

"That's a good idea," said Noor.

Ross could hear the relief in her voice.

They settled to their work. Ross pulled up the location data from the social posts that they had analysed and homed in on the Singapore records. He was in luck. Some of the posts already held location data stripped from other applications on the devices that had been used. He found some outliers by painstakingly working through to identify the IP address of the individual mast where the connection had been routed. Others he managed to match to high traffic sources that could be communities or corporations. There was plenty of data to go on.

Ross glanced up at Noor. She was absorbed in Cloverleaf's data, methodically sorting and categorising the details. He knew that she thrived on bringing order from chaos and finding connections and meaning in information.

He dropped the work he had done onto a mapping tool and looked at the clusters of posts. Most pins were centred on the downtown core of the city-state. Others were scattered around the suburbs.

Following his instinct, and hoping that Noor didn't look up, he looked for the head office of the MerLions. Sure enough, there it sat at ground zero, in the centre of the largest cluster. There could be no question that someone in that block was part of this activity. Ross was unsurprised. His encounters with the cybercriminals who hid behind the front of the respectable e-sports team had almost destroyed him. He had no sympathy for anyone in that group. He hoped for Noor's sake that Tenuk wasn't one of them.

How could he broach the subject? She was very touchy about any suggestion that her friend was caught up in the Pasar community. He decided to give her enough information to come to her own conclusions.

"Hey, Noor," he said. "I've run the analysis on the Singapore traffic. There's a big downtown cluster, but I can't get any further forward. Shall we take a look at it together?"

"Sure," she said. "Throw what you've got into the model." She stopped what she had been doing to examine the map. "Interesting," she said. "I wonder what's in that block. Is it residential? Offices?"

"No idea," said Ross innocently. He waved a hand at the random markers of outlying locations. "What about these?"

"There isn't any coherent pattern," said Noor, "although it's almost as if they are the spokes of a wheel. There's a common hub. Is it several people commuting to downtown, and making a few posts on the way home again?"

"Could be," said Ross. "I hadn't thought of that."

Noor zoomed closer to the map, overlaying a street view. She opened a search box which displayed a knowledge graph, an aggregation of everything the crawlers could find online about the highlighted spot.

"Big building," she said. "It says here there's a hawker market in the basement and a shopping mall on the first three floors."

"There's a Durian fruit company in there," said Ross, "and a major finance house."

"Lawyers," said Noor, "and look, a software company. That's interesting." She took a note of the name. "Can you do a bit of digging, see what they do?"

"Of course," said Ross, crossing his fingers.

Noor scrolled further through the information about the building. "Oh, no!" she said. She had found it. "I don't believe it. The MerLions have offices there." She looked at Ross, pleading. "Surely not."

"I don't know," said Ross. "I really don't know if they have a connection to all of this."

"The company doesn't," she said, almost as if trying to convince herself of the fact. "Maybe there is still a rogue element in there." She swallowed. "Should I talk to Tenuk? Do you think he could help?"

"Don't say anything to him yet," cautioned Ross. "We don't want to compromise him." Or compromise our own investigation if he's involved, thought Ross privately. "I can take the MerLions if you want, and you look into the others," he offered.

Noor shook her head slowly. "No. We can work together on this."

She looked at the map again, following one of the spokes east out of the downtown hub. There was a marker in the Katong suburb, and it was hovering close to the home of her Aunt Fatima. Tenuk was her neighbour.

"Innocent until proven guilty," she said.

Ross could hear a shake in her voice. She was starting to doubt her friend.

•

The train from the West Country glided silently into Paddington station, and Susie and Ella climbed out onto the platform. Across London, the train bearing Cameron and Ben pulled out from King's Cross, slipped through the tunnel under the canal, and gathered speed as it passed through the leafy suburbs on its way north.

"Are you sure you'll be okay going home on your own?" asked Susie, concerned. "I'll come with you."

Ella shook her head. "It's only a few stops. I'll be fine." She yawned, although it was only mid-afternoon. "I'm so tired. I'm going to go to bed. I'll call you later." She put down her bag and drew Susie to her in a clumsy hug. "I'm sorry."

"Don't be sorry," said Susie. "You've had a real shock. I'm going to drop into the office. It's almost on my way home." She squeezed Ella tight and kissed her on the cheek. "Take care."

They went their separate ways to the tube lines, Ella going south and west to home, Susie to the east and the City. The carriages were already crowded with people going into London for the early evening, and Susie hoped that Noor and Ross would still be in the office.

She was in luck. She met Ross at the door on his way to training.

"Noor's still working," he said as he swung his training bag onto his back. "I've got a serious session this evening otherwise I'd stay. She's done some great stuff with the threat modelling." Ross looked at Susie. "Are you sure you're okay?"

Susie was touched. He wasn't normally the type to worry about how people were feeling. "I'm good, I think. Ella's still in a bit of a state. I'm more worried about her than about me."

Ross nodded. "You take care of yourself. I'll see you tomorrow."

Susie trudged up the stairs and found Noor staring at a huge and complex 3D model that filled the visualisation deck.

"Wow," she said, "that's extraordinary."

Noor turned and gave her a weary smile. "Thanks, Susie. A lot of what is on here has come from your work, you know."

Susie approached and examined it critically, tracing gossamer threads between her contributions and a much wider network of connections and locations and actions. Mason's picture was there. She sighed sadly.

"Want to talk about it?" asked Noor.

"Yes," said Susie emphatically. "Yes. Is there somewhere we can go for a drink?"

"That," said Noor, "is a very good idea."

Susie left her bag in the locked office and they walked down the busy main road to an old coaching inn. The beer garden outside had some secluded corners where they could be sure not to be overheard. This spot was a favourite of the team in summer, while indoors in winter the wooden beams in the ceiling of the bar gave it a cosy feel. On a Wednesday, the beer garden would be less than half full at this time. Sure enough, there was plenty of room.

A roving drone waiter placed a bowl of snacks on the table and took their order. A human waiter delivered their drinks minutes later. Susie grabbed the chilled glass of wine gratefully and took a mouthful. "I needed that," she said.

"Cheers," said Noor, taking a sip of her beer. "It's been an odd few days, hasn't it?"

"Oh, boy." Susie realised it was the first time she had relaxed since Mason had been found. She had been focusing so much on Ella that she hadn't had time for herself. "Where do we start? I'm worried about Ella. More to the point, I'm worried about Ella and me. I hardly see her out of work. She has a whole new set of friends, and I don't know if she's the same person anymore."

Noor looked down at her drink and shrugged helplessly. Susie realised that perhaps she was not the only person who needed someone to talk to.

"That's not good," said Noor. "I have something similar. I thought I knew Tenuk, and I like him more than I let on. I almost thought that one day I'd be able to go out to Singapore and see him again. And now, with the things we're finding out, I'm not sure he's who I thought he was."

They looked at each other helplessly. A drone bobbed into the alcove.

"More drinks," said Susie quickly, "and a sharing platter."

They had a lot to talk about.

•

Ross finished ahead of the rest in the time trial, and his coach beamed at him. "You're on fire tonight," he said happily. "I haven't seen you cycle so well for ages. Go and cool down." He turned to greet the next athlete. "Tomasz! Great time."

Tomasz joined Ross on the grass as he ran through his cooldown stretches. "Looking good," he said. "Are you coming for a drink?"

"No, thanks," said Ross. "I have some stuff to do."

He was ready so quickly that the last stragglers were still coming in when he emerged from the changing rooms, hair damp from the shower. His coach let him go and he headed home with a spring in his step. There was someone waiting for him. Not in the real sense, of course, but ShellPixie – Michelle – would be online, and he hoped that she had found something in the hidden tracks of the mysterious hard disk.

He was not disappointed.

"I think we've hit the jackpot," said Pix. "I've got something. Encryption strings which may be addresses, and keys."

"Keys?" said Ross. "Like wallet keys?"

"Exactly like wallet keys," said Michelle. She could hardly keep the excitement out of her voice. "Piper, I think we've found a stash of cryptocurrency."

"Buried treasure," said Ross. "There may be nothing there, of course, but oh, Pix, this is amazing."

She laughed. "I know. Are you ready? Let's start digging."

Michelle pasted the first of the addresses into her browser. It opened a block explorer and displayed a list of transactions that were linked to the wallet. "Litecoin," she said happily.

Ross looked down the list of dates and amounts with rising excitement. "Wait. I've seen these." He opened the spreadsheet that he had found. "Here we go. There's a sterling value and a conversion, then that first movement. Is it a transfer from an exchange into a private wallet?"

Michelle checked the address from which the funds had been sent. "Yes," she said. "Quadriga."

"Isn't that the one that was stripped bare and everyone lost their money?" said Ross, remembering his history.

"That's the one. It looks like these funds were clear of it before anything happened."

"What else have we got?" asked Ross.

They worked steadily through the list of addresses. Some led nowhere, defunct tokens that had been issued to back speculative, failed projects.

"Shitcoins," said Michelle dismissively. "It looks like they had a good holding of early investments, but most of them have died a death."

"That fits with this spreadsheet," said Ross. "I'm starting to see patterns. There was a lot of activity around 2016, 2017 but although the coins are still there, they have no value at all."

One discovery caused Michelle to squeal in excitement. "Dogecoins! Legendary! These will be worth a bit."

"It looks as if they were mined," said Ross. "See, if you explore the record, they've collected the block rewards. They're early, too."

"It'll cause a stir if we move them," said Michelle. "We need to be careful."

"Any Bitcoin?" asked Ross. "That would be something."

"Not so far," said Michelle. "I'd be very surprised if we don't find any. This is an early adopter who knew what they were doing."

"I wonder if there's anything in the images," mused Ross. "There could be more data hidden in plain sight."

"Steganography," said Michelle. "Good call."

"I've got a stego decoder here," said Ross. "It won't take long."

"Why don't you check the last of these addresses, as well," said Michelle, sending him a list of random strings. "I'm going to try and match up the private and public keys we've found so far. It's going to be trial and error."

"There's no need to move any of the coins," said Ross. "Someone may be watching those wallet addresses. I know I would be."

"But how else will I share my buried treasure with you?" asked Michelle roguishly. "Oh – wait," she said. "Is that the time? I have a tight deadline for a client. I'm going to have to go."

"Okay," said Ross. "It's late for me too. You go and work. I'll talk to you tomorrow. Night, Shell."

Michelle was touched that he used her real name. "Goodnight, Ross."

She ended the call and turned back to the carbon credits software she had been testing. Everything seemed to be going well. She sent the test results to her client and waited for a response, toying idly with key pairs in the meantime.

Eventually the Pangolin responded. "This is excellent, ShellPixie. Exactly what I need. Will you be able to supply the final version in time?"

"No problem at all," she replied.

There was a payday coming, in more ways than one.

It was close to midnight. Michelle was still wide awake, but she thought it would be unfair to race ahead with the cryptocurrency wallets without Ross. She decided instead to drop in to Pasar. There might be some snippets of information to carry back to him.

Tenuk had a growing list of urgent work for his community to complete. He scanned the active group. Who else could he trust to pick up the slack? As he looked down the list, he spotted a handle he knew, incongruously out of place. ShellPixie. They had just spoken on Eden. What was that coder doing here on Pasar?

A quick check on their history showed that they had been a frequent visitor for years, although rarely active. He'd never noticed them before. There was talent there, for sure, and a drive to make money. Perhaps they could take some of the load.

"Hello, ShellPixie," he messaged. "I don't think we've ever chatted. How are you today?"

Sitting at her desk in the silence of the night, illuminated only by the glow of the screen, Michelle froze in horror. She did not want anything to do with King Katong. This was the worst that could happen.

9: CONNECTIONS

The cottage was all Cameron could have hoped for, stone built and standing on a slight rise with a view down the bank towards the sea. She woke to light streaming through the curtains and thought she had overslept. A glance at her smartscreen told her otherwise. Of course, they were much further north here, and the sunrise was earlier than in London. The dawn must have broken before five, and it was now almost six.

Ben had been asleep, but her movement disturbed him, and he began to stir. He opened his eyes and a shaft of sunlight caught them, turning their deep brown almost hazel. He blinked. "Is it time to get up?"

"Don't worry," said Cameron. "It's early."

Ben raised his head and peered through the crack in the curtains. "Nice day for it," he said, collapsing back onto the pillows.

"Coffee?" asked Cameron brightly. Without waiting for an answer, she slipped out of bed and made her way to the unfamiliar kitchen. She had made sure that they had what they needed for breakfast.

Ten minutes later she returned triumphantly with coffee mugs and pastries. Ben was sitting up and reading through some notes.

"Working already?" she teased.

He put his screen down hurriedly. "No, nope, not me."

They sat chatting, sipping coffee and basking in the sunlight.

"What time do you have to leave?" asked Cameron through a mouthful of pastry crumbs.

"I think I have to be at the station for eight," said Ben. "It's very odd not having a train every five minutes like in London. What about you?"

"I'll come down with you. I want to get my bearings, and there are a few things I have to collect to do this job."

Ben glanced at his screen. "We've got plenty of time.".

"I know," said Cameron. "It's like being on holiday. I needed this. I'm glad we came."

"So am I."

Cameron couldn't shake the holiday feeling as she walked into the town. Golden sands stretched down the coast and out to sea. It was low tide, and the damp sand glistened in the sunlight. But for a cool wind that whipped Cameron's hair and made her huddle into her jacket, the beach could have been plucked from a documentary on the Caribbean. A few shops and cafés on the seafront were already open and bustling with people. She watched, learning the rhythm of the place. To the south she could see the bulk of the nuclear power station. Beyond it and slightly inland, a suspiciously rounded hill with steel infrastructure on it betrayed a landfill site that was evidently already being mined for its hidden fortune. In the distance rose the slim chimneys and fat cooling towers of the vast chemical processing site, flares visible even in daylight. Her eventual destination was the nuclear plant, but she had some groundwork to do first.

She picked a small, busy café and ordered a pot of tea. She planned to be here for a while. There was an empty table. She slid into the seat nearest the wall and put her back down underneath the chair. A little device inside was primed to set up a strong rogue wifi signal, drawing traffic from the café's customers through Cameron's own access point and capturing data. She busied herself with her smartscreen as the tea brewed. The café was busy. Two men in matching company logo tops approached her table.

"Mind if we sit here?" one asked.

"No problem," said Cameron, smiling and nodding, giving off the aura of someone friendly but busy.

They sat, drank their coffee quickly, and left. Another customer took their place, then another. Cameron listened to everything around her, gathering intelligence. She fiddled with her screen, sipped her tea, poured another cup. The customers in the café came and went. An alert on her screen told Cameron that the first goal of the morning had been accomplished: her pirate wifi had captured login credentials from several devices. It remained to be seen what exactly she'd caught in the net.

The second task she had set herself was harder. Although identification methods varied from site to site, people still tended to carry prominent ID cards that gave instant visual reassurance that they were where they were supposed to be. These were backed up by biometrics and chips, of course, but the visibly reassuring ID card had persisted for decades after it was technically obsolete. Half of the people in the café were wearing cards clipped to their pockets and belts or slung around their necks on lanyards. While apparently idly messing with her smartscreen, Cameron had photographed as many cards as she could capture. The camera was particularly high resolution. She was looking forward to seeing the results.

She had been nursing an empty pot of tea for long enough now, and the crowd was thinning as shifts started in the neighbouring sites. It was time to move on to the next stage and take a good look at the plant perimeter. Cameron left her bag hidden under the seat and carried the cup, pot and milk jug to the counter. She smiled at the girl who was tidying up.

"I'm visiting here," she said. "Is there a good walk I could take along the coast?"

"Oh, yes," replied the waitress. "There's a path all the way down the beach and through the dunes as far as the power station. It's very pretty." She pointed out of the window and across the road. "See that sign? That's the start. It tells you all about the wildlife. Seals and birds and things."

"That's perfect," said Cameron. "Thanks for the tea."

She crossed the road and peered at the sign. The coastal path was clearly marked, and a shifting 3D display showed the flowers on the dunes at each season, wading birds on the marshes, and birds wheeling. She tapped an option on the sign and was plunged into an underwater scene where kelp swayed in the current and a grey shape darted past, turning playfully. She returned to the map and scanned a code with her screen. The data she loaded would keep her on track along the path and give her an augmented reality view of the scenery. Visitors would be guaranteed to see seals and rare birds, even if they were not actually there. Cameron hoped that she might see the real thing.

She started along the seafront, beach to her left and shops to her right. The town was still busy, but the people thronging the pavements now were older citizens going to the market, and young parents fresh from dropping their children at school. The path veered off towards the beach, following the sea wall, and she left the bustle behind. The beach stretched out before her, and the tide was coming in.

Cameron couldn't resist straying off the path and onto the sand. She found it hard going as her feet sank on each step, but it was a delicious feeling which took her back to her childhood. She pulled off her shoes and wiggled her toes in the cool sand. Memories of trips with her parents and her big brother flooded back, tinged with sadness. They had lost their parents in the pandemic when Cameron was barely a teenager. The melancholy threatened to overwhelm her, and she realised that she hadn't quite shaken off her distracted, negative state. She pushed the thought away, bottling it for later, and kept moving towards the dunes that rose ahead.

As she drew closer, the loose sand became more compact and more than once she stood on a stone or a twig underfoot. She sat on a patch of scrubby dune grass and put her shoes back on, then called the café to say, innocently, that she might have left her bag there. They would keep it safe, still sucking data from any passing device, until she collected it.

She tucked her smartscreen back into her pocket and gazed out to sea. The silence was absolute. That was when she heard the girl.

She was hidden in a dip in the dunes. She looked quite young, but as Cameron approached, she realised she was older, mid-twenties perhaps. She had been crying. She looked up suddenly and her head turned towards the intruder, but her eyes were partly closed and unfocused.

"Who's that?"

"My name's Cameron, but I'm sure you know that." Cameron had spotted the girl's vision sensors, a wristband and a belt. They acted as her eyes, scanning the terrain underfoot and hazards overhead. If Cameron was not mistaken there would be a chip sensor there too, feeding information about the people she met through the discreet audio pod that she wore.

"Yes," said the girl. "How did you know?"

"I recognised the sensor kit," said Cameron. "I'm sorry to disturb you. I was just out walking." She looked at the girl. "Are you okay?"

"Yes," she said. "I mean, not really, but... I'm sorry. It's nice to meet you, Cameron. I'm Michelle."

"You live around here?" asked Cameron.

"Oh yes, just back over the dunes," said Michelle. "I needed some fresh air. I had some things to think about. Look, thanks for asking, but I'm fine. Enjoy your walk."

"I will, thank you." Cameron skirted around her and carried on along the path towards her goal.

•

Ross arrived in the office and was surprised to find Ella already at her desk. There was no one else around.

"Ella, how are you doing? I wasn't expecting you in today."

"I'm fine," she replied. "I'd rather be working, to be honest. It keeps my mind busy."

The huge 3D model that Noor had built was turning slowly on the visualisation deck. Ross tapped it idly. "Impressive, isn't it?"

"Amazing work," agreed Ella, joining him at the model. "She's brilliant at making connections. I can't believe the level of detail on here."

"Where is Noor, anyway?" asked Ross. "She's usually first in."

Ella shrugged. "No idea." She turned away and went back to her desk. "How's the report coming along?"

"I'm waiting for Susie," said Ella. "She started doing it and I don't have access to the file."

Ross wondered for a moment what Ella had been working on if not on the report.

She answered his unspoken question. "I've had another look at the Snake River connections. I've arranged to meet with the accounting firm this morning." She looked at the time. "I may as well start walking over there now, if that's okay?"

"Good idea," said Ross. "Let me know how you get on."

As Ella opened the office door to leave, Noor appeared.

"Morning," she said brightly. "If you're looking for Susie, Ella, she's on her way."

"I'll see her when I get back," said Ella. She scampered down the stairs and out to the street.

Noor poured herself a cup of coffee and joined Ross at the model.

"I had a good think last night." She took a deep breath. "I still want to believe that Tenuk isn't involved in this, but there are too many coincidences. I'm going to talk to him."

"Thanks, Noor," said Ross. "You've always stuck up for him, but I think you're right to make sure."

Noor nodded but said nothing. She went to her desk and busied herself with some half-finished tasks. Tenuk would still be at work. She wanted to wait until later when he was home.

Ross cleared Noor's model from the deck and spun up another that he had been working on. "I've been looking at Cloverleaf's data," he said. "I'm starting to build up a picture of their plans. They didn't have Snake River when they attacked the Chinese power station, and I wanted to know why it's so important this time."

"You need to run all this past Susie," said Noor. "She's very good, you know. We went out for a few drinks last night and had a good chat."

"I was going to wait for Ella to get back," said Ross.

Noor shook her head. "It's Susie you want. I'm not sure what's going on with Ella, but Susie's not happy."

Ross raised his hands, laughing. "I can't keep up. I'm not getting involved."

"Coward," teased Noor. "Here comes Susie now."

"Good timing," said Ross as she walked through to door. "Apparently we need to talk about Snake River. I have a lot of data from Cloverleaf. Maybe you can help me make sense of it?"

"Sure," said Susie. "I'm all yours."

•

Cameron clambered over the dunes and finally caught sight of the perimeter fence of the nuclear power station. The fence was imposing even from a distance. It ran down the side of the site all the way to the sea, and the tide was low enough for Cameron to see that it continued into the water. At intervals, drones were tethered to the uprights, scanning the immediate area, and feeding audio and video directly back to the plant. On the other side of the fence Cameron spotted human security guards passing by on a regular circuit. Physical security was as tight as she expected, then.

On the map the coastal path ended here, but the track continued. It turned away from the sea and tracked the line of the fence at a distance of about a hundred metres. Cameron followed it, glad of the capricious breeze that sprang up and gave her an excuse to pull her hood over her head. She took an intense interest in the flora and fauna of the dunes, using her screen for a rich augmented experience while simultaneously recording details of the perimeter security. The software had been very well done, she admitted to herself. At one point an alert directed her attention to the skies where a peregrine falcon had been detected, its tag giving away its position. She was stunned at the speed it travelled.

On the landward side of the plant lay a complex warren of laboratories and administration buildings, low buildings that had been extended in all directions over the years. There were more people moving around here. Cameron decided to retrace her steps. She didn't want to attract attention just yet.

The girl, Michelle, was still in the dunes, but was now lying on her back in the sunshine. She looked more relaxed. Cameron considered skirting past her but realised she would already be aware of her presence.

"Good walk?" asked Michelle.

"Yes, thank you," replied Cameron.

"See anything interesting?"

So many things, thought Cameron. "There was a peregrine falcon overhead," she said.

"Fastest creature on the planet," said Michelle. "Are you on holiday?"

"Yes," said Cameron without skipping a beat. "My boyfriend is working near here. Actually, I should get back. I need some shopping and drone deliveries aren't working very well."

"They have very low capacity for home delivery drones around here," said Michelle. "Connectivity is patchy, so they aren't terribly reliable. We're okay down here on the coast, and in town we have ground delivery 'bots as well, but once you get up to the moors it's a struggle."

"I'd have thought with all the industry around here that the connections would be good," said Cameron.

"You'd be surprised," said Michelle. "They hog what bandwidth there is and leave crumbs for the rest of us."

Interesting, thought Cameron. This girl knows her tech. She wondered who she worked for. It wasn't the time to ask. She would come off as too nosy, and memorable. That was the last thing she needed, at least until her tests were complete.

"I have to go," she said. "Nice to meet you."

"You too," said Michelle. She settled back onto the dune, her face bathed in sunlight, smiling.

Cameron collected her bag from the café, thanking the owner profusely, and bought what she needed at the market. Alongside local food and racks of clothes there were repair booths where smartscreens, personal drones and computers were fixed and enhanced, a thriving second-hand games license stall, and a pile of assorted bric-a-brac. Cameron browsed through the selection and was surprised to see an old games console. She was sure she had had the same as a child.

"This is an old classic, isn't it?" she said to the stall holder.

"You have an eye for quality, madam," he replied. "Nothing but the best recovered goods here."

"Recovered from where?" asked Cameron.

The stall holder gave her a curious look. "Official landfill salvage," he said. He turned the console over and showed her a hologram embedded in the casing. "Certified."

"Does it work?" she asked.

"I couldn't say. It's a real collector's item, though."

"Thanks," said Cameron. "I'll pass."

She caught the train back towards the cottage with a few minutes to spare. When she arrived at the local station, she noticed that the car park contained not only autocars on charge, but old cars and vans that had not been there this morning. These were commuters who lived somewhere without enough data to run autocar navigation safely. It had never occurred to her that such places still existed. That was one of the reasons that Ben's work was so important. Some of his 3D designs may be on the way to Mars, but others orbited earth as part of the complex communications network that kept the planet running and its population connected.

The cottage lay only a few minutes' walk up the hill. Cameron let herself in and settled on the deck overlooking the sea, thinking through her next move.

•

Tenuk scanned the participants on the forum. There was still no sign of Sagikkun, and he had not been active since the raid. He had to accept that the legendary Korean hacker had gone. Mìmì Māo had passed through earlier in the day but must now be hard at work on the deployment phase of the sleeping dragon. There was very little time left.

Who else? The circadian rhythms of the community suggested that the Monkey should be making an appearance about now. Sure enough, that avatar suddenly flicked from red to green. Tenuk was pleased to see him, a real elder statesman of the cybercrime world.

The Monkey was not in a good mood.

"You're going through with it, then, Katong?"

"If you mean the waking of the sleeping dragon, Monkey, then yes, everything is proceeding as planned."

"It's a hare-brained scheme and you know it," said the Monkey scathingly. "The clients have more money than sense."

"You laid its foundations," said Tenuk smoothly. "Your work was exemplary."

"Ach, I took the work because it was interesting and I needed the money," said the Monkey. "It was only later we all figured out what you were up to."

"You're a true mercenary," said Tenuk.

"Thank you," growled the Monkey.

"If you're so concerned, why are you here?" asked Tenuk. He was tired of the Monkey's attitude.

"I'm keeping an eye on things," he said enigmatically. "Now that you've lost one of your sites, and mainland Europe is out of the running, that leaves one possible target. Let's say I have a vested interest in what happens there."

"Why do you think we have lost a site?" asked Tenuk.

"News travels fast," said the Monkey. "I recognised that kid they pulled out of the water."

Tenuk was momentarily lost for words. The Monkey was a lone operator on the forum. He wasn't one of the core of troublemakers that he had struggled to keep under control, nor was he lurking on the fringes, like ShellPixie. He was known, respected, and utterly independent. How would Yasmin have managed him?

"There is still work to do," he said, trying to appeal direct to the Monkey's wallet. "I can allocate you some high commission work."

"Maybe," came the response. "I'll get back to you."

To Tenuk's frustration, the green light flicked to red. To make matters worse, an alert popped up for a priority communication from the Syndicate. He logged out of the forum and onto another secure platform. Changing between Pasar, Eden, MerLions and Syndicate business was making his head spin.

The news from the Syndicate was unexpected. One of their undercover agents, the same one who had warned of the raid in Korea, had new intelligence. There was a spy in the client's camp who had fed data containing plans for the coming attack to the consortium who sought to stop it. Steps were being taken to destroy the leaked data and prevent it being analysed and interpreted.

The spy's codename was Cloverleaf.

Could it be a coincidence? 'His' Cloverleaf was responsible for building some of the very systems that were being deployed in the attack. 'His' Cloverleaf had been an agreeable and diligent member of the Pasar community for years. They had never given any indication of knowing about the end client. They'd just done the work and done it well. Could they be one and the same?

Another alert sounded. Noor was trying to reach him. Much as he wanted to talk to her, this was not the time. He had too much to deal with. He cancelled the call.

•

Cloverleaf checked the uplink and settled back in her camping chair. The air was cool this early in the morning and mist rose from the lake. On her way to the camp she had seen signs of activity from beavers on the lake bank and deer coming down to the water. It was going to be another hot day, and the wildlife was taking advantage of the misty morning. The dark peaks of the mountains beyond soared into a clear blue sky. Cloverleaf looked in vain for the distinctive white patches of glaciers that had still been visible when she moved to Militia territory, but there were none to be seen. They had melted for good.

The SimCavalier came online a few minutes late, apologising profusely. "I'm off-site," she said. "I had trouble setting up a secure connection. How are you doing?"

"I'm okay," replied Cloverleaf. The adrenaline rush of a few days earlier had faded. "I guess we're into the endgame now. I'm getting ready to run."

"We'll keep you and your daughter safe for as long as possible," said the SimCavalier. "At the moment, there's no reason to believe you're in danger. The data you sent us is being processed by a tight group of people that I – we – trust."

"I don't trust anyone," said Cloverleaf. "No offence, ma'am."

"None taken."

"You say we're safe right now," said Cloverleaf, "but there's always a risk of being found out. The consortium promised me a way out in any case. Is that happening?"

"Yes, it is," replied the SimCavalier. "There are plans in place to bring you out as soon as you need to run."

"That's good to hear. What do I need?"

"I've just had emergency codes through from the consortium," said the SimCavalier. "I'm sending them over now. We've got both your chip IDs for fast retrieval when the time comes. The message says to pack light."

"Yeah, I guess we'll be leaving a lot behind."

"I'm sorry."

"Don't be. All the good memories are saved, and the rest we can rebuild."

"I'll help any way I can."

"Thank you," said Cloverleaf. "That's real sweet of you. I have to go. Talk to you tomorrow."

She closed down the comms unit with care and left the camp tidy. The paddle home was uneventful, and she made it into the kitchen with seconds to spare before Audrey woke.

"Can we have pancakes again?" asked the little girl.

"No, honey. Eggs today. We're all out of pancake mix and there are no huckleberries left on the bushes."

Audrey pouted. "Pancakes are better."

Cloverleaf cracked two eggs onto the skillet while Audrey watched. They sizzled gently. Once they were cooked through, Cloverleaf slid them expertly onto Audrey's plate. "Sunny side up, ma'am, just as you like them."

"I have a surprise for you," she continued. "Would you like to go on a camping adventure?"

Audrey tried to answer through a mouthful of eggs, then nodded hard instead, her eyes bright with excitement.

"Okay. This is going to be a secret and special adventure. You mustn't tell anyone about it. I'm going to surprise you one day, very soon, and we'll just go. That means that every day, you need to put the special things in your backpack that you want to take."

"I have to bring Teddy," said Audrey. "He'll enjoy camping."

"Yes," said Cloverleaf. "You definitely need to bring Teddy." That was one thing she couldn't do without.

"When are we going to go, mom? Where are we going?"

"I don't know," she said lightly. "That's part of the surprise. It depends when I finish my work. I have a lot to do at the moment, but as soon as there's no more to do, then we'll be off."

"Can we pack now? Please, Mom?"

"Sure. We have time this morning. Let's see how much we can fit in your bag." She cleared the empty plates away and followed Audrey into her bedroom. They needed to be ready. She could trust no one.

•

Cameron was thoughtful when she closed the call with Cloverleaf. For all the danger that Cameron feared, Cloverleaf and her daughter were far more vulnerable. She had to do everything in her power to protect them.

There was nothing that could be done right now, though. She needed to concentrate on the task in hand. It was all related. Anything she could do to help secure this power station would mean one fewer opportunity for the Militia to cement their position.

She started to sort through the intelligence she had gathered this morning. The images of the power plant were very clear, and it put Pete's description of the place into context. She needed to explore the southern boundary to the marshes as well, but that could wait.

The images she had captured in the café and along the plant's northern perimeter were excellent. She had high resolution copies of the front and back of several ID badges which would be enough for her to construct her own mock-up. She had also accessed the data held by the badges. She would be able to print a passable copy that would return a genuine data set if scanned. The data wouldn't entirely match the fake badge, of course, but she was trusting to a combination of human error and AI blindness to pass muster.

Her rogue wifi hotspot had captured some surprising results. Despite the stringent security protocols of the site, two people in the café had exposed details of their work network. Cameron compared the stolen credentials to the badges and found two matches. These people warranted more research.

She called Ross.

"What's up? Are you having fun?"

"I thought you'd like to do some digging for me," she said. "These two" – she pinged over the details – "sat in a café this morning with their ID badges dangling in my face and their network access codes ripe for the picking."

Ross chuckled. "How careless. I can probably get details down to their inside leg measurements and last grocery order, if you want."

"Anything that will help me get in the door," said Cameron.

"Sure. What angle are you using?"

"I don't know yet. I'm thinking along the lines of extreme flattery. Maybe a media interview?"

"You could easily claim to be a researcher for Andy's channel," suggested Ross. "I'm sure he'd back you up, no questions asked."

"That's a great idea," said Cameron. "Brilliant. Will you call him, or shall I?"

"Let me dig through these profiles first," said Ross, "then you'll have a better idea of the cover story. Give me an hour or so."

"Okay. How are things in the office? Are the girls back in?"

"Yes, they are. Everyone's out at the moment, but Susie and Noor were apparently together last night, and Ella was back in this morning. She was first in the office, actually."

"Really?" said Cameron. "I'm glad she's back on form, but she was very upset about that chap who drowned."

"She said she wanted to keep busy," said Ross. "She went off to the accounting firm that we'd linked to Snake River, and then arranged to meet the others for lunch."

"Joel's due back today as well, isn't he?"

"Yes, he should be in this afternoon. He's finished up with Norfolk and he's tracked down the guy in Kent. They've got a meeting later."

"I can't wait to see what you get out of him," said Cameron. "Dig deep on that reference to 'an old bloke up north'. I want more details on him, and on the management team that Mason claimed were based in London."

"Right-oh."

"Is there anything else?"

"Yes, one more thing," said Ross. "Noor and I finally bottomed out the Singapore locations on the social posts. You'll be unsurprised to hear that the MerLions headquarters was right in the middle of the action."

Cameron sighed. "How did Noor take it?"

"Quite well, in the end," said Ross. "She's been trying to reach her mate all morning but he's not answering. I'm going to add our findings into the big model now."

"Good stuff. Thanks, Ross."

"No problem," he replied. "I'd better get on with these profiles. I'll call you back."

It took him less than an hour to uncover everything they needed.

"These two are great," he said. "They're as unsubtle online as they are in real life. Their current personal login credentials are up for sale in five different breach stores, and they aren't using extra authentication for half the accounts they've registered to. Their company logins are protected, but of course you've captured the underlying network settings already, haven't you?"

"Yes," said Cameron. "I'm not touching those. I'll just add them to my report and make sure Pete and Sandeep flag it up to the powers that be. Where do these characters figure in the plant personnel?"

"One of them is a scientist and the other one is in human resources."

"The scientist might be more interesting given our cover story," said Cameron thoughtfully. "If we arranged to meet near the labs, I'd have access to more of the site, but I'll be up against serious health and safety practices and hypersensitive staff. On balance, probably the other one, but I'm not sure if an interview with HR is a plausible line."

"That was what I thought, too," said Ross, "so I did a little more digging on him. Junior personnel officer by day, DJ by night, and he really fancies himself."

"I know exactly who that was in the café now," laughed Cameron.

"Good call. That's our target. I guess you have some more juicy details for me?"

"Oh, you bet," said Ross. "I'm sharing the files now."

Cameron opened the first note and giggled. "I'm going to have trouble keeping a straight face," she said. "Can you call Andy and get some legit contact details we can use just in case this character checks me out. I bet he won't, but we only have one shot at this."

"Will do," said Ross. "I have to head off to training. Joel's back if you want a word."

"I'll call him later," said Cameron. "I want to set up this meeting first. Enjoy your training and talk to you tomorrow."

"Good luck," said Ross with a smile as he ended the call. Cameron was going to have fun with that one. He was almost jealous.

He hadn't been entirely straight with Cameron. There was a training session scheduled this evening, but his first priority was Michelle. She had left a message asking for help. Ross tidied up the day's loose ends, had a quick chat with Andy to secure his help, and left Noor, Susie, Ella, and Joel to their own devices.

The roads were busier than usual. There had been demonstrations all week, triggered by the Wyoming Militia announcement, from both decarbonisation supporters and detractors. Today's march by the Petrolhead movement had smuggled some fossil fuel powered vehicles through security and fired them up in the middle of Whitehall. The stink of exhaust fumes hung over the city. The demonstrators would be wiped out by the fines, thought Ross, but he was sure that someone waiting in the wings would bankroll them to carry on.

He dashed into the house. It was already past the time he had promised Michelle he would call, and he had news. Thankfully, she answered at the first ring.

"Hi, Ross."

"Hi, Shell."

Ross was taken aback to see that she had dropped the avatar and her camera was on. She had her back to the light, all the same, but he took in the silhouette of her face. This was a new level of trust. Slowly he reached for his own camera and unblocked the lens, hand shaking. His image changed, and he thought he could make out a smile on Michelle's face. She had her hand to her ear, listening to something through an ear pod.

"What's up?" asked Ross. "Is everything okay?"

Michelle shook her head. "Not totally. I think it's something we can deal with, but you know how I was lurking in Pasar? The big guy spotted me. He asked me to take on some work. I couldn't really say no, could I?"

"Not easily," said Ross. "Why do you think he picked on you?"

"I don't know," said Michelle. "I can hazard a guess, though. I think he has too much work and not enough coders."

"Overstretching themselves? It's possible. Why, though?"

"There are a few big names out of action," said Michelle.

Ross pricked up his ears.

"Sagikkun has vanished overnight, and he'll be a big loss from what I could see of his work."

"Wait," said Ross slowly, "any idea what he was working on?"

"Oh, he had a big reputation for media. Troll farming. Fake personas, videos, that kind of thing. You must have seen him on Eden as well?"

Ross punched the air in delight, then remembered he was on camera. Michelle didn't react.

"Did you have something to do with Sagikkun vanishing," she asked slowly.

"Maybe," said Ross. "Team effort. Who else is slacking?"

"The Monkey hasn't done much since that first wave of contracts, from what I can gather. He was on the forum when the test happened, and he was part of the gang celebrating a big payday, but I don't think he's picked up any of Katong's new jobs. I haven't seen anything allocated against him."

"That's two big players out of the picture," said Ross thoughtfully.

"There are fewer people on the forum altogether," said Michelle. "It went dark for a long time, between Yasmin the Admin going offline and this nuclear test happening."

"You're right then. He doesn't have the capacity to fulfil the jobs. What's he asked you to do?"

"It's low grade stuff," she said. "He's not going to trust me with anything big."

"Everything fits together," said Ross. "What's the job, Shell?"

"Automating some Nmap tests on a network they've specified. Checking over and over which hosts are up and responsive on the network."

"What are the conditions for a successful test?" asked Ross.

"A positive response from a specific host," said Michelle.

"Interesting," said Ross. "You can't hack a host which doesn't exist, so maybe they have something ready to roll when it responds."

"That fits," said Michelle.

"You were right to take the job," said Ross. "Are you okay now?"

"Yes, I think so. It was a bit of a shock when he messaged me. I took some time out today, went offline for a bit."

"That was the best thing you could have done," said Ross. "I use my sport for that. What about you?"

"I went and sat on the sand dunes and listened to the sea," said Michelle. "It was peaceful. There was hardly anyone around."

"Sounds amazing," said Ross. "No such chance here in the middle of the city."

"Hey," said Michelle suddenly. "What about testing one of the key pairs from that hard drive? I think I've matched up most of them. We should have access to the wallets."

Ross couldn't stop himself grinning. "Not just those wallets. You'll never guess what I found in those images."

"Bitcoin?" said Michelle incredulously. "Really?"

"Yep," said Ross. "Not a whole one, but enough. We can't move any of it, though. The community will spot us straight away if we even touch it."

"Let's just sign a message. That shouldn't attract too much attention."

"It will, believe me," said Ross. "We need to pick a cryptocurrency that isn't mainstream but will still be confirmed by the network. What've you got?"

"There's a bit of Ethereum Classic," she said.

"That'll work. What's the message? You're hardly going to say, 'Shell Was Here', are you?"

"Of course not. What's the top headline on the news channel today?" asked Michelle.

"Let me see," said Ross, scrolling to his feed. "Petrolheads Face Fines for Whitehall Stunt."

"That'll do." In the darkness of her room, Michelle tapped away at her braille pad, the screen reader squawking in her ear. "It's gone. Get yourself to the blockscanner and see what you can spot."

It was a few seconds before the transaction was confirmed, and Ross realised he had been holding his breath. "Got it," he said. "It worked! Congratulations. You have now proven ownership of that wallet. Get in, Shell!"

Michelle whooped with excitement. "This is amazing, Ross. This could be, well, life-changing."

"How much crypto are we talking altogether, Shell?" asked Ross.

"It's quite the treasure chest," she replied, "but I'm worried that the pirate who buried it will come back."

"They'll never find us," said Ross. "This is ours."

In another place, an alert pinged on a grimy smartscreen. The impossible had happened. A lost wallet had been accessed. The pirate's treasure was found, and he wanted it back.

He opened one of his own new wallets, accounts he had set up after his hard disk had been lost. His savings were starting to accumulate again, but they would never reach the sum he had allowed to slip through his fingers. He sent a fraction of a coin back to the address that had been reactivated, along with a message of his own.

"This is mine. I will find you."

10: ENEMIES AT THE GATE

Tenuk ran through the final checks on the software he had bought from the Eden marketplace. This coder was talented, that was for sure, and he was glad to have secured their services on Pasar as well. He made the final payment from his private account and left a glowing five-star review. Now he had to deploy it quickly before circumstances sent him far away from the MerLions headquarters. There were specific credentials to input for the main carbon credit account, and those could only be sourced in person. He had been planning this for some time. He locked his screen and left his desk, walking purposefully through the office towards the central hub that connected all the departments.

His destination was the tour logistics section where they planned the intricacies of the team's itinerary, from meet-and-greets to meals, hotels and flights. He headed for desk at the side on the room, and the clerk's face lit up and he approached.

"Tenuk, what can I do for you this time?"

He had been going backwards and forwards to the same girl for weeks, building a trust relationship that he was about to cash in.

"Just one more little thing, Sophia," Tenuk replied. "I would have messaged you, but I'm leaving very soon, and I wanted to stretch my legs."

"I could do with a break myself," said Sophia, stretching tiredly. "Re-organising this tour has been hard work. I have a performance review this afternoon as well. The timing is terrible."

The timing was perfect, but Tenuk murmured his sympathy. "I need to double check the carbon offset figures for all the interstate travel," he said. "There's a complex model for flexing the itinerary based on local conditions, and I can't quite get the offset to balance. Could you pull up the details?"

"Of course." Sophia opened her password manager and selected the system credentials, then confirmed the login with a tap of her chip.

Any moment now, thought Tenuk.

"Sophia!" It was her manager calling from across the office.

"Oh, no, already?" she turned to Tenuk. "I'm so sorry, I have to go." She was torn between two senior managers and unsure what to do.

"I can find what I need," said Tenuk. "You go on." He smiled and waved across the office at Sophia's manager. This seemed to reassure her.

"Please log out after you've finished," she said, relying on the assumption that her manager must know what was happening, and vainly grabbing at a last thread of good security.

"Of course," said Tenuk smoothly. "Don't worry."

Using Sophia's administrator access to the system it was the work of moments for him to set up some fake credentials for his own use. Although there would be no way to hide that her login had created them, it afforded her some protection. The movement of credits would not be attributed to her and he fully intended to delete the new account as soon as he had what he wanted. If he worked fast, the fake ID would be gone before it was noticed, and the question would never be asked. They would not miss the credits, and the accounts would balance once he had massaged the interstate journeys the team was due to take.

He was careful to collect the data he had originally asked for, as the query would be recorded. He logged off safely, leaving Sophia a note of thanks, and made his way back to his desk. Once there, he lost no time. He fired up the fake account, linked it to his new software, and let it run. All he had to do now was wait.

He finished off the last work-related tasks on his list. His flight was scheduled for later in the evening and he was packed and ready. There were some loose ends to tie up on Pasar, but that should not take too long if the right people were online.

Noor had tried to call him again. He was not ready to talk to her yet. He wanted to surprise her with the news that, if she wanted, she could come to Singapore or even join him in America. He hoped that she wanted to come. He was afraid that she would not.

The routine finished. He checked the results. All the credits he wanted had been transferred and the software had started on the complex process of cleaning the metadata attached to each token, transferring them repeatedly around the network, obfuscating their nature and pathways, until they could be reallocated convincingly to the new wallet he had set up. The MerLions wallet had barely a dent in it. Tenuk killed the fake account and covered his tracks, said goodbye to his colleagues, and made his way home.

Pasar was a hive of industry. Everyone was getting on with their allotted tasks and the code repositories were filling nicely. Mimì Māo was storming through the workload, ShellPixie's first scan results were in, and Cloverleaf had uploaded some neat routines. Tenuk was still not convinced that 'Double Agent' Cloverleaf and 'His' Cloverleaf were the same person. He kept moving. He was looking for the Monkey and was relieved to see a green light against the username.

"Monkey."

"Katong."

"I have a job that needs your special skills," said Tenuk.

"I'm listening."

"It has come to my attention that certain cybersecurity operatives are getting too close to our operations. I need you to interrupt their work and relieve them of any data they may have acquired. It may require physical intervention, although you must try to avoid confrontation."

"The money had better be good."

"It is." Tenuk transmitted the details and the rate for the work and waited patiently.

"I'll sort it." The signed agreement came back moments later.

"Excellent," purred Tenuk. That should be dealt with by the time he arrived in America. He had one more call to make. He wanted to be sure that Noor would not be in any danger if the Monkey's plans went awry.

•

Ben and Cameron left the cottage very early. Ben was travelling up the coast to visit a flagship space site, and Cameron wanted to take a look along the southern boundary of the plant before meeting her mark. They parted at the station, the north and southbound trains passing within minutes of each other. The car park was virtually empty at this time of the morning but there were some early commuters on their way to work from further afield.

Half the passengers got off in the town centre. The rest must work in the chemical park or further south in the ribbon of towns that followed the river inland. Cameron hopped off at a halt, barely more than a short platform, which gave access to the wildlife reserves on the marshes. Paths coastwards led to a viewing platform over a sand bar where seals lazed in the sun, and to hides for birdwatchers. On the other side of the tracks the marshes gave way to the slopes of the landfill. Cameron saw huge vehicles quartering the site, scanning for treasures like the games console she had found on the market. Behind each of them a swarm of little burrowing drones leapt and scurried, calling to mind a picture buried in her memories of birds following the plough on village farms. She could make out the hopper of the nearest vehicle gradually filling with finds untangled from decades of waste. It was mesmerising.

It was also smelly. A gust of wind bore strong odours of methane and rubbish which made her nose wrinkle in disgust. She shook herself out of the reverie and turned her attention to the landscape between the tracks and the coast. She followed the nearest path and soon found herself at a hide overlooking a small pond. Out of curiosity she ducked through the door. It was dark, but she found the shutters and opened them, giving her a view of a lonely pair of moorhens outside. The light fell on some information displays – old school posters – and a board which showed that in the last week a pair of Canada geese had been seen on the pond. Cameron was about to leave the hide when some debris on the floor caught her attention. Snippets of wire. Lost screws. A discarded circuit board. On closer inspection, the nooks and crannies at the edge of the hide held other similar rubbish. She looked up and around the hide. There were no lights or electric points, a deliberate design that ensured the hide remained unobtrusive to the wildlife. It was an odd place for a workshop, and it looked as if it had been used by a number of people over time. She didn't want to disturb the find and instead took pictures from several angles. They were very close to the plant perimeter here, and her security instincts were screaming.

She closed the shutters and left the hide, shutting the door carefully behind her. She stood contemplating the perimeter fence in front of her. It was still imposing and bristling with security drones. They would register a walker going to the hide as normal activity, and she didn't want to do anything to alert them. From her vantage point her eyes followed the fence towards the sea. There was a cordon of some kind nearby on the inner perimeter. She wanted to know more, but it could wait.

Cameron made her way back to the halt. Halfway there, she saw the northbound train sweep past. There wouldn't be another one along for half an hour. She had time to wait, but the idea of being downwind from the landfill was not a pleasant one. Instead, she took the path that ran alongside the tracks for the whole length of the route. It was only a mile or so to the power station gates and the day was still cool. Several cyclists passed her, and she met a walker on their way down towards the nature reserve she had just left.

She stopped just before the main gates and turned into a small settlement of narrow terraced streets, lonely on the very edge of town and surrounded by wasteland. She was looking for somewhere to brush her hair and tidy up for her meeting, but there were no shops in evidence. She stopped instead in a bus shelter and used her screen as a mirror. The area was very run down. Weeds pushed their way through paving slabs and there was graffiti on most of the walls that she could see. Cameron peeked into the yard of one of the houses and noticed that, in sharp contrast to the bright hanging baskets by the door, the garden bench was chained to the wall. Close by, a dog barked.

An information display on the shelter lit up, announcing the arrival of a shuttle to town. Cameron decided to ride the bus the remaining distance. In minutes she found herself facing the main gate. She took a deep breath and walked in, head held high.

•

The morning meeting was in full swing. Joel, Noor, Ella, Susie, and Ross were gathered around the table, and Pete and Sandeep were on screen. The smell of coffee permeated both offices, and an argument was raging about the quality of breakfast.

"You'd be amazed at the bacon sandwiches up here," said Pete, lifting an enormous hunk of bread towards the camera.

"What even is that?" asked Ella.

"They call it a stottie cake," said Pete. "It's a giant bap."

"Bap?" said Joel. "You mean a cob."

Sandeep laughed. "I grew up eating stotties. They're very special." He raised an eyebrow at the camera. "Local delicacy. What are you all having?"

"Only the finest London croissants," said Ross. "You know, a hearty traditional English breakfast."

"Have you seen Cameron yet?" asked Joel.

"Not yet," said Sandeep. "She said she'd see us later. We're keeping our heads down. The less we know, the better."

"I did some digging for her yesterday," said Ross. "Her way in is sorted. She's probably at the door now."

Pete grinned. "I can't wait to see how far she gets."

"How is the rest of the work going," asked Ross.

"We're almost done," said Pete. "We've compared the Snake River installation with the software Susie and Joel identified at their sites, and we have a match. We've done what we can to tidy up the network and bring the security protocols up to scratch."

"One more job to do," said Sandeep. "We're getting access to the server today."

"You have a rogue server there too?" said Susie. "One that isn't on the backup?"

"Yes," said Pete. "I know you never got access to the one you found, and when we started comparing systems, we realised we had the same thing."

"One abandoned machine that's been forgotten about is hardly unusual," said Ross, "but two makes me think that they're related." He turned to Joel. "Did you find anything in Norfolk?"

Joel shook his head. "Nothing there, although there was a report that a hardware review had resulted in some kit being discarded. There's no way of telling if that was the same thing."

"If it was intentional, surely there was always a risk that the machine would be thrown out?" said Noor. "How could someone rely on it being in place for activation?"

"Let's not forget there were more than three of these things," said Ross. "Our friends in Europe and South Africa have tracked down the plants that Mason mentioned, and they've all cleaned up their installations. I don't know if they were part of the plans, but they've gone. Your box up there in the North East is probably the only one left."

"That's not exactly reassuring," said Sandeep. "It tells me that we're right in the firing line for whatever is being planned."

"You may be right," said Ross soberly.

"No, I don't think we're in too much danger," said Pete. "Do we have any indication at all from the Cloverleaf files as to the structure of a physical attack?"

"We're still working through them," said Noor. "Joel, you picked up something last night, didn't you? What was that?"

"Yeah, wait…" Joel scrolled through his notes. "There's something here about drone swarms."

"Rabbits?" said Sandeep, looking quizzically at Pete.

Pete shook his head. "That was one incursion and it only breached the perimeter fence."

"Not land based," said Joel. "Water."

Everyone looked at Pete.

Sandeep broke the silence. "Well," he said, "it's a good thing you lugged all your diving gear up here."

Pete grinned broadly. "I think Daniel and I have a job to do."

●

Cameron was laying the flattery on with a trowel, and her mark was lapping it up.

"This is fantastic material," she gushed. "I'm so glad to be able to meet you."

"And you," he replied, preening. "I wouldn't normally be able to bring you in to my work setting, but I insisted. My music is essential for your feature. It would be a tragedy if your audience lost the chance to discover me."

"It's important that your talent is recognised," she said, hoping she wasn't being too over-the-top. "I hadn't realised that you were based up here. It was pure chance. I wish I'd been able to see your set live, but I'm running to a very tight schedule."

"So I understand," he replied. "How much longer do we have?"

Cameron made a show of checking the time. "It's later than I thought," she said, standing and gathering her things. "I must run. I have a train to catch."

"But of course," he said. "Let me show you out."

They followed the corridor towards reception. Cameron had already worked out her exit.

"I need to use the loo before I leave," she said. "Would you mind?"

"Not at all," he said. He took her hand and kissed the back of it. She felt her skin crawl but kept the smile fixed in place. "The reception desk is just around this corner. If you could hand in your badge on the way out? I'm so excited for your feature."

Cameron escaped gratefully into the Ladies'. The first thing she did was to wash her hands thoroughly. She stayed in the room as long as possible to make sure that the coast was clear. No one else came in or out. She changed her muted, professional top for a more bohemian look, pulled her short hair up with a flowered band, and hung her newly printed ID badge on a bright lanyard around her neck. On a decorative top pocket, she had hidden a camera to record her passage around the offices, building evidence to present to the client. It was time to play.

Stepping out of the door she walked briskly back along the corridor, away from reception. She dipped back into the room where she had just had her meeting and picked up a bulky chair. This she carried towards the first secure door. Her ID card would stand up to basic scrutiny, but

512

it wouldn't grant her access to anything. For that she had to rely on the misplaced kindness of others. Sure enough, within minutes someone arrived behind her as she apparently struggled to manage the chair and present her card to the reader at the same time.

"Here, let me help you," they said, glancing at her badge and opening the door.

"Thank you so much," said Cameron, manoeuvring through into the next section of the corridor. She marched off confidently, although she had no idea where she was going.

She dumped the chair in the next empty room she passed and stole a quick glance at an evacuation plan on the wall. It told her everything she needed to know about secure doors and department locations, and she snapped a picture. She wanted to avoid HR at all costs, although she suspected that her interviewee was so wrapped up in himself that he would completely fail to recognise her. The security office would be a poor choice as well. That left the labs and the accounts offices.

The plan seemed to show a breakout room at the entrance to the lab complex, and there were no secure doors in the way. It turned out to be a comfortable lounge area with a coffee machine and a tray of cake laid out. It must be someone's birthday. Cameron poured herself a coffee, took a piece of cake, and sat down at a table in the middle of the room. She watched, listened, and learned as people wandered in and out on their breaks. One person dumped a pile of paperwork on the table next to her and went to get their coffee. Cameron turned suddenly as if to say hello and knocked the pile, scattering documents on the table and the floor. She apologised profusely and helped to gather them up, filming the content as she did so. They chatted idly, passing the time of day. Cameron finished her coffee and took her leave from this new, unsuspecting friend. Time for more exploring.

The accounts office lay behind another security door, but this time she managed to follow a group of people who were coming back from their break. She moved through the office, leaning over desks, and asking questions about equipment. Acting the role of the IT help desk was second nature.

One clerk called her over, asking for help on a login. She tapped away with expert hands and frowned theatrically. The problem was clear to her – a file on the desk was pressing on the keyboard and fouling every attempt at entering credentials – but she muttered and fiddled with cables, and finally declared that the unit was faulty and would need to be replaced. She unplugged everything and left the clerk sitting at an empty desk.

That would be enough to make the point, she decided. Time to come clean.

She returned to the original meeting room where she had begun her journey and pinged a message to Pete. When he, Sandeep, Julia, and Daniel arrived, they found Cameron lounging in a chair with another cup of coffee in hand, the stolen computer on the table and the film of her travels playing on the screen behind.

Pete and Sandeep broke into spontaneous applause. Julia looked furious, and Daniel simply laughed.

•

Noor was surprised by the call. Tenuk avoided contacting her during work hours, and it was late in the evening for him. She moved into the private booth in the corner of the office to chat, her mind swirling with questions and misgivings.

"I'm on my way to America," he said. "I'm waiting at Changi for my plane right now. I realised I hadn't spoken to you. I'm sorry. I've been so busy."

Noor was taken aback at the apology. "That's okay, Tenuk," she said. "We've all been busy. I tried to call you a few times."

"I know," he said, contrite. "I've been working very late on the arrangements for this tour. Changing the entire thing to run on a different continent was a real challenge."

"It must have been. When does the team fly out?"

"Another week," he said. "I'm going ahead with some of my other colleagues to do final preparations. I'll be glad to get out of the madhouse."

This was the Tenuk she liked and remembered, the friend she made before suspicion was cast on members of the MerLions staff and he became tainted by association. If he had called her at home, she might have weakened. Here at work, the pale grey walls and plain desk and chair reminded her that she had a job to do.

"It sounds more like a holiday than work," she said with a nervous laugh.

"It will be a nice break from the routine," he replied happily.

Noor took the plunge. "Tenuk, I need to ask you something. We've uncovered some evidence of connections between the MerLions office and the people behind the nuclear test. I wondered…"

"Do I know anything about it?" Tenuk sounded concerned. "I'm glad you asked. No, I haven't seen or heard anything suspicious. There was a big cull after the incident in England and I was sure that any bad actors had been weeded out."

"That may not be the case," said Noor firmly.

"That's very serious," said Tenuk. "I'd better flag it up to my superiors. I can't do much from America, but I'm sure they'll take any action that's needed."

"Thanks, Tenuk," said Noor. "I really appreciate your help." She paused. "Out of interest, do you have any colleagues who live close to you? Anyone who makes the same commute?"

"I can't think of anyone," he said, puzzled. "There is one colleague who lives at the city end of the East Coast Road, but that's quite a way from my place. Why?"

"Just a question that came up, but I think you've answered it. Not a problem."

"Noor," he said, wondering whether it was wise to broach the subject now, "did you think about travelling? Coming to Singapore, or even to America?"

"You know I can't do that. I don't have the carbon credits. We discussed this before."

"I know we did." He took a deep breath. "Noor, what if I told you I can get you as many carbon credits as you need? Right now? If you give me your offset wallet address, I can send them to you."

"What?" Noor was completely thrown. "How?"

"Consider it a gift from the MerLions," said Tenuk.

"You can't do that," said Noor flatly. "Carbon credits are provenanced. You're not telling me that the MerLions have added me to their approved user list?"

"I found a way to circumvent the usual processes," said Tenuk.

"Tenuk, no," said Noor. "Honestly, I appreciate the gesture, but what were you thinking? What have you done?"

"They won't miss them," said Tenuk, throwing caution to the wind. "Noor, please."

"I don't understand you sometimes," said Noor. "On one hand you're working to keep the MerLions free of any dodgy business, and then you go and steal from them."

"It's hardly stealing."

"It is."

Tenuk was kicking himself. He had crossed an invisible line in their relationship, and he wished he could take everything back. He tried another tack. "Noor, I'm sorry. I was thinking of you. I wanted to keep you safe. The threats that have been made by the Wyoming Militia frightened me."

Noor softened slightly. "That's very sweet," she said, "but we're dealing with that threat on our own terms."

"I didn't mean to speak out of turn," he said. "Why don't you take some time out to think about it? You need a break as much as I do. Get out of your office and clear your head."

"I'm too busy for that." In the background Noor could hear an announcement. Tenuk's flight was boarding. "I have to go, and I think you do too," she said. "Have a safe trip."

"Be careful, Noor." He ended the call, angry with himself that he could not have made the immediate warning more explicit. He hoped that the Monkey would capture what he needed without endangering her.

Noor emerged from the booth looking troubled.

"What's up?" asked Ross.

Susie gave her a knowing look. "Tenuk?"

Noor nodded. "I asked him, Ross. He denied any knowledge of activity at the MerLions, but he didn't give me a good answer about the posts we picked up near his apartment."

"He wasn't expecting the question," said Susie. "You caught him out."

"I wish I hadn't," said Noor quietly. "Part of me wants to believe he's innocent, but I'm beginning to think he's mixed up in it, even at a really low level. There was something else, as well…" Her voice tailed off. She was still processing the revelation.

"Go on," said Ross gently.

"It's a bit of a strange one," she said, blushing. "He keeps asking me to fly to Singapore. I mean, I'd love to, but I can't."

"You'd never stack up enough carbon credits," said Joel. "Martha and I have been saving for ten years to get out to visit my cousins in the Caribbean."

"Exactly," said Noor. "He's somehow managed to lay his hands on a bundle of credits originally issued to the MerLions."

"That can't be legit," said Joel straight away. "What's he playing at?"

"Carbon credits?" said Ross. "I don't know if it's related, but there was a contract on Eden for something like that. I'll have a closer look at the transaction when I get back home."

"However it's been done, I don't like it," said Noor. "There's just too much weighing against him."

"Oh, Noor," said Susie, giving her a hug. "Don't let it get to you. He's not worth it, and we're all here for you."

Noor looked around the room at the concerned faces of her colleagues. Ross, Joel, Susie, Ella. These were the people she trusted, and if anyone was to keep her safe, it would be this team.

"Thanks, everyone," she said quietly. "Let's get back to work." She returned to her model, scanning for connections, and visualising the web of conspiracy, thread by thread.

"Ella," she called after a few minutes. "What did you find out from the Snake River accountants? You visited them yesterday, didn't you? There's nothing on here about them."

"I thought I'd uploaded the file to the main repository," said Ella, coming across to look. "That's odd." She frowned. "Let me see where it is."

"Can you give me the headlines?" asked Noor.

"Not much to report, to be honest," she said. "It was an off-the-shelf company which didn't last. They had to dig deep into the files to find anything."

"Thanks for checking up on it," said Noor. She marked the thread as a dead lead and moved on to the next element on her list.

"I've got a headache," said Ella. "I'm going to walk around the block. I might pop down to the market. Want anything?"

"Yeah," said Joel. "Can you pick up a couple of bottles of that nice pale ale from the brewery stall? I'd order by drone, but if you're going down anyway...?"

"Sure," said Ella. "I won't be long." She disappeared out of the door, and the others returned to their work.

•

Julia had finally calmed down and arranged for the computer to be returned to its place in the accounts office. The ease with which Cameron had strolled around the building without being challenged had shocked her. Security had evidently been lax under Daniel's predecessor. There was plenty of work to be done.

"The problem you have," said Cameron, "is that people assume if you've made it through the front gate, and reception, and the internal doors, then you have a right to be there. None of the people I talked to batted an eyelid."

"Spies rarely sneak around," added Daniel. "You were careful to stand out. Bright colours, confident manner. It was a good exercise. It's given me plenty to work with."

"This was all commissioned because of the perimeter breach, though," said Julia. "You didn't go near that."

"On the contrary," said Cameron. She pulled out her screen and found the photos she needed. "I heard all about your rabbits and weasels."

"Ferrets," said Daniel quickly.

"Yes, ferrets. Just on the other side of the fence, close to where you had the breach, there is a birdwatching hide. It looks as if it's been used it as a workshop to modify electrical equipment. I found a control chip that may have come from a drone. Could that be related?"

Daniel looked carefully at the pictures. "Yes," he said. "The chip is generic but used in the ferrets, and that screw looks the right size for the casing." Julia looked at him oddly. "I repaired a ferret once. I've done all sorts of electrical work in my time."

"What do we think the story is, then?" asked Pete.

"I reckon someone has poached a ferret from the landfill, reconfigured it, and tested the controls by sending it under the fence," said Daniel. "Looking at all the different bits of debris, it's happened more than once."

Realisation dawned on Cameron. "Ferrets. They're the things which follow the big scanners on the landfill."

"That's right," said Daniel. "People steal them and customise them. It's remarkably common. I hadn't heard of people testing them by burrowing under our fence but it's the kind of daft dare that I'd expect."

"Why would the previous security manager be mixed up in it?" asked Pete.

"I may have something there," said Sandeep. "I did some digging. It looks like he had a lot of gambling debt. What if he decided to pay it off with some out-of-hours crime?"

"He's picked up the ferret, customised it, tested it, and then got himself arrested scavenging with it," said Daniel.

"Could it really be that simple?" said Julia. "I thought it was all some kind of dastardly plot to break into the site."

"We don't believe it was," said Pete, "but that doesn't mean there is no dastardly plot. We're looking into theories about the use of underwater drones as well." He looked at Daniel. "The conditions look right for a spot of diving later. What do you say?"

"I'm up for that," said Daniel with a grin.

"First, though, we want to have a look at the server we highlighted on the systems diagram," said Sandeep. "Julia, you were going to take us through the details?"

"Yes, of course," she said. "I don't know why you're so concerned about that one in particular. It's part of the security system that Angus put in, and it's always been reliable."

"What does it do, exactly?" asked Cameron.

"I'll show you, shall I?" said Julia. "Come with me – officially, this time."

She led them to the server room from which the air gapped power plant system was controlled. Inside, she greeted the technician cheerily. The air was cool, and Cameron wished she had brought her jacket from the office.

The target was just another anonymous cabinet in the line. Julia dug a set of keys out of her pocket and unlocked it. She pulled out the keyboard shelf and flicked on the monitor.

"Can you talk us through this stack?" said Cameron.

"Of course," said Julia. "This is the main security stack. There are eight servers in here, and we control them all from this console through the KVM switch."

"Angus configured all of these?" asked Pete.

"That's right," said Julia. The menu appeared. "Here you go." She ran a finger down the list. "This is the one you were asking about. It's a local backup of all the security settings from the other servers. It runs a daily refresh routine then goes back to sleep."

"Unusual," said Cameron, "but not unheard of."

"Maybe that's why it isn't on the main backup," suggested Sandeep. "Why keep a backup of a backup?"

Cameron was deep in thought. "Make a note of all the settings," she said. "There's something we're missing here. The contents of this server are incredibly sensitive." She turned to Julia. "You are absolutely confident of the air gap, aren't you?"

"Of course," said Julia. "You're welcome to talk to the technicians, but it's a secure as they come."

"We will," said Cameron. "Sandeep, can I leave you here to sort that out? I have a call to make, and Pete, you have some diving to do."

•

Ross signed off and picked up his bag. "I'm sorry, folks, I have to go."

"They're working you hard, aren't they?" said Joel. "What is it today?"

"Short training session and a team meeting," said Ross. "We're supposed to be competing in some local events around the country this weekend. It's all publicity."

"You were never shy of that," said Joel, laughing. "Where are you off to?"

Ross shrugged. "I actually don't know. I'll find out this afternoon, I guess."

"Are you coming back later?" asked Noor.

"No," said Ross, "I'll work from home. That'll give me a chance to look into the carbon credits job that I saw on Eden, as well."

"Thank you," she said.

He could see that she was still upset.

"There is one thing that would be useful," said Ross. "Can you push a copy of your model to my remote repository? I know I can't visualise it, but I want to work through some of the connections again in light of the Cloverleaf data. I don't want to mess up your work. We can merge any changes later."

"Sure," she said, tapping some keys. "That's done. Do you want a dump of the data sets you've been working on as well?"

"No, we don't want those going anywhere. If I need anything, I'll VPN through."

"Bye, Ross," said Susie. "If you see Ella on your way out, tell her to hurry up. She's been gone for ages."

"Will do," said Ross. He collected his bike and set off for the club.

"Yes, where is Ella?" asked Joel. "It doesn't take that long to walk around the block." He went to the window and peered out. "Can't see her." His attention sharpened. "Wait, that's odd..."

He was interrupted by a gasp from Noor. "My system is down."

"Mine too," said Susie, jumping up from her seat.

"What the hell?" Joel ran back from the window and hit a panic button on the wall, then frantically stabbed at his keyboard. "Security systems are down." The ceiling lights flicked out and the coffee machine fell silent.

"Power outage?" said Noor in a small voice.

"Get down," yelled Joel. There was a commotion on the stairs. "Under the desks, now!"

Two figures burst through the door. "Server, now," yelled one, brandishing a gun.

Joel gauged his chances of taking the man down. He seemed nervous, and his finger was on the trigger, which did not fill Joel with confidence.

Noor jumped up from her hiding place. "No!" The gun swung towards her and Joel took his chance. He leaped forward and knocked the man sideways. There was the sinister pop of a silencer and Noor screamed and fell. Joel fought both of the men at close range but took a blow to the head and staggered for a moment. The second man took his chance, kicked Joel's knees from under him, and pinned him down.

"Server."

Joel nodded and the man released him, still training a gun on him. Hands held up, Joel moved slowly across the room and started to unplug a device. He stole a glance at Noor, who was sitting up on the floor. She met his eyes and winked reassuringly. There was plenty of blood and she was holding tight to her upper arm, but she was okay, and she knew that the device Joel was giving them was an old backup unit, barely used.

"Not that one." The man gestured towards the blank visualisation deck.

Noor's shoulders sagged, and Joel caught a glimpse of Susie's frightened eyes under the desk. It had been worth a try, but these people knew exactly what they wanted and where it was. He started to detach the device that held the data for Noor's model, moving as slowly as he could. The panic button might have raised the alarm. Ella might come back from her walk. The more time he could give them, the better. It was still not enough. He couldn't draw it out any longer.

He could still fight, though. He turned sharply and ran at the assailants, pushing them off balance. He would risk their itchy trigger fingers. They didn't seem comfortable with the weapons, whereas Joel's army days were fresh in his memory. Finally, his luck turned. There was a piercing scream and the crash of glass. Ella stood in the doorway, one of the beer bottles smashed at her feet.

Joel took his chance. He grabbed at the first weapon that came to hand, the trophy that sat in pride of place on the shelf, and swung it with force and accuracy. The first man went down like a stone. The second ran for the door and slipped on the spilled beer. He tumbled across the landing and went headfirst down the stairs into the arms of a very confused police officer. The cavalry had arrived, and the data was safe.

11: SLEEPING DRAGON

"Are you alright, Mr Bardouille? Your quick thinking almost certainly saved your colleagues from serious harm."

Joel stared past the young police officer's ear and into space. "I'm okay," he said finally. "I didn't even think. It was automatic."

"You served in the army, is that right?"

Joel nodded.

"They were lucky to have you here."

"They shouldn't have needed me," said Joel heavily. "The peripheral security systems should have kicked in before the power went off. And why would our office become a target? It's crazy. Everything is online, all backed up and secure."

"Not everything is on the main systems," said Susie. She was sitting next to him, wrapped in a blanket. "The Cloverleaf data is ring-fenced."

"Cloverleaf?" asked the officer.

"It's some specialist data we've been analysing," said Ella. She was huddled next to Susie in a blanket of her own. "The only copy is here." She indicated the equipment that the attacker had tried and failed to steal.

"No, there's an off-site backup," said Joel. "We would never hold data without a disaster plan."

Ella looked nonplussed. "I meant to say that it's not backed up with the main systems."

Joel looked at her curiously, but was interrupted by an incoming call alert. "It's Ross," he said. "I'll put him on speaker."

"What the hell's happened? Are you all okay? How's Noor?" Ross was beside himself. "I must have missed all this by minutes."

"You did," said Ella tartly. "Isn't that a coincidence?"

Susie glared at her. "I can't believe you just said that."

"Noor is going to be fine," said Joel. "It was a clean shot through her arm and nothing's broken. She was lucky. They could have shot any one of us."

"That's good – I mean, that's terrible – you know what I mean," stammered Ross. "The police pulled me out of the team meeting, and

I couldn't believe it." He paused. "Have you heard from Cameron? She knows, doesn't she?"

"She knows," said Susie. "She got the alert from the office alarm system, and we spoke to her as soon as we could."

"There isn't much she can do," said Joel. "The police'll secure the office until they're done with the investigation."

"Do we have any idea who the attackers are?" asked Ross.

"I didn't recognise them," said Joel. He looked questioningly at Susie and Ella, who shook their heads."

"It's got to be related to Snake River," said Ross. "I honestly can't think of any other reason why we'd be targeted."

"Mason mentioned a team in London, didn't he," said Susie.

The police officer's attention sharpened.

"Exactly," said Ross. "Is it worth talking to the people in Kent and Norfolk, Joel?"

"Good idea," said Joel.

The police officer nodded and made a note. "Do you have contact details?" he asked.

"Sure," said Joel. "As soon as we have our systems back online, I can give you everything you need." As he spoke, the lights flicked back on and a technician appeared with a smile on her face.

"There you go," she said. "They'd closed your node on the microgrid so the system couldn't buy any power, and they'd hacked into the inverter on the building's solar unit and disabled it, so you weren't generating, either."

"Clever stuff," said Ross, who was still on the line. "Whoever was behind this knew what they were doing."

"Even more reason to suspect that it's the same cybercriminals," said Susie.

"Shall I come back to the office?" asked Ross.

"No point," said Joel. "You've got everything you need, haven't you?" He deliberately didn't mention Noor's model. Ella's comment had been a timely reminder that the data they held was valuable, and the fewer people who knew where copies might be held, the better. "You could talk to Andy, though. There's a flock of press drones circling. The police keep dispersing them but they're persistent."

"I'll see what he can do to take the heat off," said Ross. "Are any of you up to giving an interview, if he wants one?"

"Not me," said Joel. "I need to get back home to Martha. She's worried sick."

"I couldn't," said Susie. She was still shaken. "Ella?"

Ella nodded reluctantly. "If I have to. Let me know, Ross. We're going to go and see Noor as soon as we're finished here but Andy can call me."

"I'll be in touch," said Ross. "I have to go and see my coach and talk to Cameron. If she needs me to cancel tomorrow's competition to support the team, it won't be a problem."

"Do you know where you're supposed to be going?" asked Joel.

"Yes," said Ross with a laugh. "A place up north. I'll practically be on her doorstep."

"That could work out well," said Joel. "If she needs you anywhere, it'll be there."

"I want to be down here for you folks as well," said Ross.

"Thanks, man. We'll be fine. You go and race. We're rooting for you."

"Thanks." A teammate appeared behind him, calling him back to the meeting. "Got to go. I'm glad you're all okay, and I'll call Noor and Andy as soon as I'm done here." The screen went blank.

•

Cameron was as white as a sheet when she came off the call. Pete and Sandeep, shocked and sober themselves, waited silently for her to gather her thoughts.

"I guess we know we're getting close to Snake River," she said finally, her voice shaking. "We have to stop these people before anyone else gets hurt."

"Noor is okay," said Pete. "I managed to speak to her while you were on your call. She's waiting to be discharged home."

"Thank goodness," said Cameron. She felt herself welling up and struggled to get the feelings under control. After months of being distracted and numb, the emotions were overwhelming. "We have to stop them now. No one else gets hurt."

"Why did they target the office?" asked Sandeep.

"Cloverleaf's data, and probably Noor's modelling," said Cameron heavily.

"That means someone knew we had the data and that it wasn't being kept in the usual places," said Pete.

"How would they know?" asked Sandeep incredulously.

"I don't know yet," said Cameron. "I really hope that the consortium has a leak. If not, then..."

"If not, it's closer to home," said Pete slowly.

The implications were too awful to contemplate.

"It can't be any of our team," said Sandeep. "Pete and I haven't had a lot of involvement with the Cloverleaf stuff. I couldn't even tell you now where it's being stored."

"Everyone else was at the office," said Pete. "Except Ross, of course."

"I'd trust Ross with my life," said Cameron flatly.

"There's got to be a leak somewhere else along the line," said Sandeep. "But where? Who exactly in this consortium of yours knew about the Cloverleaf data?"

"A few people," admitted Cameron. "We kept it very close, though."

"Have you talked to the police in detail?" asked Pete.

"Not yet," said Cameron. "I'm waiting to speak to a connection in the cybercrime unit. He'll treat the information with the respect it needs."

"What now, then?" asked Sandeep.

"We have to carry on regardless," said Cameron. "The police can do their job, and we'll do ours." She took a deep breath. "Pete, you and Daniel need to get in the water and let me know if you find anything. Sandeep, go and talk to Julia. Explain that there'll be a delay to our final report because something else has come up."

Pete gathered his things quickly and headed for the door. "I'll call later," he said.

Sandeep followed him out.

Cameron relaxed and put her head in her hands. She had a lot to process. First, though, she had to reach Ben and her family before the news got out.

Ben was on the train on his way back to the cottage. "I'm coming down to the town," he said. "I know I can't come to the plant, but I'll be as close as possible."

"I'll meet you in the Endeavour bar at this end of the main street," said Cameron. She needed a break to gather her thoughts and recover from the initial shock.

"Good," said Ben. "I'll see you very soon."

Sandeep reappeared. "No problem with Julia. What do you need me to do?"

"Let's assume that whoever sent those goons into the office knows that they haven't got hold of our data," said Cameron. "It was a stupid move, because now we know they're after it. I want to you get into all our repositories and double down on security. I don't want any dirty footprints on our systems."

"Understood," said Sandeep. "Julia will give me anything I need. What about you?"

"I'm going out for a little while. I need to think through our next moves. I'll be back."'

Cameron signed out of the plant and made her way towards the town. Once outside the perimeter, she called her brother, explaining everything as she walked.

"Oh, Cam," said Charlie as she relayed the news. "Are you okay yourself? I know you'll be worried about your team, but I'm worried about you."

"I'm on my way to meet Ben," said Cameron. "I'm not really okay, but I have a job to do. We have to see this through to the end."

"I know, and I'm proud of you," said Charlie. "You know we all have your back, sis. Take care."

Cameron turned onto the main street of the town and saw Ben coming towards her from the direction of the train station. She was glad he was here with her, but she had a job to do. Her team needed her to be strong right now, and she wouldn't let them down.

•

Pete and Daniel carried out the final checks on each other's diving gear as the boat bobbed gently at anchor half a mile out from the plant.

"What's your plan?" said the boat handler.

"Drop down the shot line here," said Pete, "head due south, circle the area, and come back. I want to have a look at those two bumps you picked up with the sonar. You're sure there's no old wreckage down there?"

"I'm sure," he said. "I know where all the wrecks are around here and there's nothing recorded in this spot." He checked his instruments. "The anchor is at fifteen metres. As you go south towards the features we spotted, you'll get to twenty, twenty-five at the deepest. There's a small rock reef running north-south, and you want to be going east from about fifty metres along."

"I know the one," said Daniel. "It's a nice little reef. Lots of life, and as no one bothers diving around here it's rarely touched."

"You might get some seals, as well," said the boat handler.

"Sounds nice," said Pete, "but remember we're on a mission here. Are you ready?"

"All set," said Daniel. "Fins and weight belt, check. Zips closed. Cylinders full on. Shall I go first?"

"After you," said Pete.

Daniel put one hand over his mask and the other around the gauges that dangled from his cylinders and rolled backwards off the side of the boat. He disappeared in a cloud of bubbles. Moments later he surfaced, waved an okay signal, and swam around to the anchor line on the bow. Pete followed him. They nodded to each other, exchanged thumbs down signals, and disappeared from view.

Pete wasted no time dropping down to the sea floor. He landed gently on his knees, sending up a small cloud of sand. Daniel was right by his side. They both checked their gauges and compass headings and set off to the south, finning steadily side by side. The weather had been settled for several days, and Pete thanked his lucky stars that the visibility was so good. Almost immediately the reef came into view and Pete looked back. The anchor line was visible from here. That would make life easier at the end of the dive.

The little reef was bright with life, sunstars illuminated by the light penetrating the water, and dead men's fingers shining. Pete caught a glimpse of a lobster hiding in a crevice, and a crab scuttled past. He ducked down for a closer look and the lobster waved its claws at him.

At a gap in the reef, Daniel tapped his hand and pointed east. This would be a good marker for their circle around the area. The reef wall dropped down to a sandy bottom at twenty-five metres. They dipped down, and Pete could not resist peering into the nooks and crannies with his torch to see what life was lurking. As they approached the sand, his attention was drawn to an oddly regular outline, but as he tried to reach it a grey shape flashed beneath him and turned acrobatically in the water. Daniel, a little further away, gave him the okay signal and Pete returned it. They hung in the water, neutrally buoyant, watching the seal play. Another one shot through the gap in the reef wall and joined the fun. Then, as suddenly as they had arrived, the seals turned and swam off up the reef, disappearing into the distance. It was a magical encounter, and Pete's spirits lifted.

Daniel started out on the circuit they had planned, and Pete caught up with him. They finned evenly along, scanning the bare seabed beneath them and to either side. Their navigation was good, and very soon they saw the two features they were searching for.

To the casual eye there was little to distinguish them from the dips and hollows of the seabed, and Pete wondered if it they were simply natural formations, but then he spotted the same outline in the sand as he had seen at the gap in the reef. He bent closer to it and gently wafted the sand away. The grains of sand swirled in the water and he paused to allow them to settle. His hand closed on a cable. He beckoned to Daniel. Together they followed it, hand over hand, clearing the sand as they went. It was heading directly for the two bumps. If their intelligence was right, thought Pete, this could be a power feed from the shore. They were too deep here for machines to get enough power from the sun.

Pete paused and tugged at the cable, dislodging the sand from it. Oddly, it seemed to bypass the first feature. He followed it past the first bump and on to the second. Daniel hung back to check the other one.

There was something here alright, thought Pete. A container was buried in the seabed, and the cable led straight to it. Its rounded top was virtually covered in sand, avoiding casual discovery or entanglements with fishing nets and lines. Pete attached a line to the cable at the point where it joined the container and sent up a surface marker. They would be able to find the spot straight away. He had his hand on the top of the container, trying to work out how to get in, when Daniel tugged frantically at his ankle.

Pete turned and saw Daniel's eyes wide behind his mask. He gestured at the other feature and made the unmistakable signs for, 'swim away fast and get back to the boat'. Pete looked past Daniel and saw an exposed spherical metal surface with a spike coming off it. He didn't miss a beat. They both started swimming as hard as they could for the end of the reef.

The anchor came into view and they steadied themselves on the line. It would do no good to rush their ascent. They climbed slowly up the line, hand over hand, venting air as they went. Six metres from the surface they paused, waiting silently while their dive computers counted down to a safe nitrogen load in their bodies. Daniel's computer beeped first, but he waited for Pete to finish his stop, and they surfaced together.

"What did you find, lads?" asked the boat handler as they handed up their weight belts and pulled themselves, exhausted, over the side of the boat.

Daniel took out his mouthpiece. "Sea mine," he shouted back. "Let's get out of here!"

He didn't need to say it twice. They sat on the bottom of the boat, still fully kitted up, as it sped back to the harbour.

•

Ross flung his kitbag on the floor of the kitchen and went straight to his computer. The first thing he checked was that he had access to the copy of Noor's model. All was well there. He checked his messages and picked up a note from Sandeep to say that the data repositories and backups were now running an extra layer of multi-factor authentication. Ross didn't need access to them. He was simply relieved that they were secure.

His first job was to look into the carbon credits contract that had caught his eye on Eden. If it was the same job, then it would be part of the completed archive. He missed it on his first pass through, the search algorithm returning all sorts of odd results, but once he had refined the filters it popped straight up. Commissioned by an occasional user, the Pangolin. Five-star rating from a satisfied customer. The contractor? Ross laughed out loud. It was ShellPixie.

He pinged her a message, and she came back to him almost straight away.

"Hey."

"Hey yourself," she said. "How's it going?"

"Not great," said Ross. "There was some trouble at work." She knew what he did; there was no harm in telling her. "Someone broke in, trying to steal some local storage disks. We think it's connected to Snake River."

"They broke in?" said Michelle. "Overnight?"

"No, broad daylight," said Ross grimly. "Four of my colleagues were there. One's hurt and the rest are in shock."

"Oh no!"

"We've got to stop this conspiracy, Shell," he said heavily. "I don't want anyone else put in danger."

"What do you need from me?" she asked. "I'm still hooked into activity on Pasar. King Katong's gone quiet. He's normally online at this time of day but there's no sign of him. Mìmì Māo is running the show."

"Any sign of Cloverleaf?" asked Ross.

"Yes, she's dropped in," said Michelle. "No word from Sagikkun. The Monkey has been in and out. He's looking for King Katong and he doesn't sound very happy."

"Okay," Ross thought about his next move, then remembered his original question. "Shell, this is probably completely unrelated, but you did a job recently around carbon credits on Eden. Can you tell me about it?"

"Sure," she said, taken aback, "how did you know?"

"Long story," said Ross. "Is this the job you were racing to finish the other night?"

"That's the one," said Michelle. "The client brought the deadline forward and needed it delivered by last night at the latest."

"Any idea why?" asked Ross.

"I'm guessing that they were going to lose access to the account they wanted to, uh, take advantage of," said Michelle slowly. "The software cleans the credits and deposits them to a new wallet. The user has to link it to the target account to collect the credits in the first place."

"That makes a lot of sense," said Ross slowly. "I think I know who your client was, in real life."

"That's crazy," said Michelle. "What a small world!"

"There are a few things that would confirm it," said Ross. "Any idea where your client was from? The Pangolin, is that right?"

"Yes, the Pangolin. Time zone-wise, I'd say South East Asia. They were very careful not to give much away, though. Have you searched their other activity?"

"There isn't a lot to go on," said Ross, scrolling through a search he had just run. "They've commissioned a few jobs, but they're not very active, on Eden at least."

"What language are they posting in?" asked Michelle.

"Good question," said Ross. "All the feeds are translated. Do you think they were talking to you in native English?"

"They were definitely speaking English but with a few odd phrases," said Michelle. "What happens if you disable the auto-translate?"

"On it," said Ross. "Hah. You're a genius, Shell. Their posts are mainly in original English, but there are a few here in Malay."

"There you go. South East Asia," said Michelle smugly. "Malaysia or Singapore. Does that help?"

"It matches what I suspected," said Ross. "I want to know more about this Pangolin, though."

"I've seen the handle on Pasar," said Michelle suddenly. "They lurk there occasionally. I'd completely forgotten about that."

"What?" Ross was caught out completely. "Are you sure?"

"Yes, I'm sure," she said. "It's a really cute avatar. I'd know it anywhere. I don't think they've ever taken a contract, but they pop in from time to time."

Ross was confused and concerned. Noor had always maintained that Tenuk was unaware of the criminal element of the MerLions, and investigations had cleared him of any involvement in the business with Yasmin the Admin. Ross was certain that Tenuk was the person who had commissioned the carbon credit laundering software from Michelle, although he could never prove it beyond doubt. If the Pangolin on Eden and the Pangolin on Pasar were one and the same, then Tenuk knew a lot more than he should.

"Michelle," he asked, "was the Pangolin active on Pasar when Yasmin the Admin was in charge?"

"I don't know," she said. "I think so. I'd have to check through the logs. Give me five minutes."

Ross took advantage of her absence to empty his training bag and grab a drink and some food that his brought back to his desk. He checked his messages and found a missed call from Andy and a note from Sandeep. He would call them both back once he had got to the bottom of this mystery.

Michelle's chat window sprang back to life and her now-familiar silhouette appeared. "Yes, they were," she said without preamble. "The account was authorised by one of the Pasar admins three years ago. Not Yasmin. King Katong."

Ross's mind was spinning. "The Pangolin was active before the MerLions came to London," he muttered, "and King Katong rubber stamped its forum membership."

"That's the odd part," said Michelle. "Katong is really strict on code tests and ratings for new applicants. I mean, all the admins are, but he's especially bad. You're registered on Pasar. What did you have to do to get in?"

"It was tricky to get through selection even ten years ago," said Ross, thinking back. "It was always the place to go for high value contracts."

"Exactly," said Michelle. "So how did our Pangolin end up there, when they haven't done any work in three years, and they had to commission me to write what was honestly quite a simple application?"

"How indeed?" said Ross. "Unless they're very good friends with King Katong."

•

Cameron and Ben emerged from the Endeavour bar and heard the shrill sound of a siren. The barman followed them outside.

"What's that for?" asked Ben.

"It means I'm about to get busy," said the barman with a grin. "Look." He gestured down the road towards the power plant. People were flooding out through the main gate.

"Is it a shift change?" asked Ben.

The barman laughed.

"No. That's the evacuation alert."

Ben looked alarmed. "What do we do?"

"You? Nothing. You're fine." Realisation dawned. "Oh, no, don't worry, that's not the nuclear alert. It's probably a security drill, to be honest."

Ben looked at Cameron. "You should go." She nodded and set off at a run towards the gate.

The barman shook his head. "She'll be back in a few minutes. Do you want that drink now, marra?"

Another klaxon sounded from the far end of the beach. The barman finally looked startled. "That's odd," he said. "I haven't heard that for a while. They're clearing the beach. There must be something in the water."

Cameron came walking slowly back, a few hundred metres ahead of the pack. "Pete just called," she said. "Would you believe they found a sea mine?"

"Ah, that explains it," said the unflappable barman, satisfied. The first customers started arriving. "I'd best get behind the bar," he said, and disappeared inside.

"What do you want to do?" asked Ben. "You can't get back into the plant, can you?"

Cameron shrugged. "I probably could, but I don't need to. Pete didn't just find a sea mine. They also found evidence of something else being stored underwater. He didn't have a chance to see exactly what it was, but it all stacks up with the intelligence that we have. There's an underwater drone swarm ready to go."

Sandeep came wandering up the road carrying several bags. "I brought all of my stuff and all of Pete's, so we can set up anywhere you like."

"Okay," said Cameron. "Is your guesthouse closer than our cottage?"

"Yes," said Sandeep.

Ben looked relieved.

"Let's go," said Cameron. "Pete can join us there." She and Ben followed Sandeep along the front and into the maze of streets inland. "We've got some work to do. Ross can help as well. I want to get into the Militia systems and stop anything being deployed. I reckon that any attack will have to come from there, even if the systems have been developed by Pasar. If we can disable the red button, we're safe."

"How are you going to manage that?" asked Ben, running to keep up.

"We have enough information about the Militia systems from the data Cloverleaf sent us," said Cameron.

"She didn't just dump data, she dumped all the configurations and operating system information as well," explained Sandeep.

"We're going to send Cloverleaf a virus to deploy," said Cameron. "Something that will take down everything that's linked to their systems. Hopefully that will include the deployment trigger. It's not subtle, but it's the most direct route."

They arrived at the guesthouse. Ben brightened up when he saw that it had a small bar and tables in a sunny courtyard. "I'll wait for you all here," he said happily. "Let me know if you need help."

"Thank you," said Cameron, kissing him quickly. "We won't be too long. You could bring drinks? I tip well."

"At your service, ma'am," said Ben with a sweeping bow.

An autocar pulled up at the kerb and Pete jumped out. "I've left my kit at the dive centre," he said. "I got your message."

"Sea mine? Really?" said Sandeep, eyebrow raised.

"Yep. Apparently, they get them washing up all along this coast from time to time. They're left over from World War Two."

"And this sea mine was sitting right on top of what we think is our drone hangar?" said Cameron.

"Practically, yes," said Pete. "It will have drifted there, or it was already in the vicinity and it's been uncovered by wave motion. It won't be there much longer, though. They've called in the Navy's underwater bomb disposal team."

Cameron looked up with hope in her eyes. "They're going to blow it up? That'll take out the drones as well."

"It will, if they're still there," said Pete. "The team has to come from Portsmouth. They'll be a few hours."

"We may not have that much time," said Cameron. "Let's get started."

•

Michelle's automated scanning routine had been running quietly in the background for days, and she jumped when the alert sounded.

"Ross," she called. "The scan's picked up a new open port on the networks I've been targeting."

They had left the chat open by mutual agreement while they worked on other things. Ross had washed his training gear, and Michelle had grabbed a quick bite to eat. Daniel was not home. He was dealing with a security incident at the plant.

Ross was now back at his computer and chatting in another window with Cameron and the rest of the team. He was pulling some old code out of a dark and dusty file that might be useful to scramble the Militia's systems.

He switched chats, muting one and opening the other.

"What have you got?" he asked.

"I think this is what they've been looking for," said Michelle. "It's just opened out of the blue." She sent the details to him.

"slpng.drgn," said Ross. "That's a very odd name."

"Even the most security conscious people sometimes use names which give away what the port does," said Michelle. "What could it be?"

"Slow ping? Sloping? Sleeping? No idea," said Ross. "Can you ping it?"

"Pinging," said Michelle. "Do you want the details?"

"Sure," said Ross. "Every little helps. I'll pass this on to the team."

He switched chats again. "Hey folks, I have something from my friend. She's been scanning a set of ports for a contract on Pasar and she's picked up a newly open one. It's assigned name is slpng.drgn and I'm sending you the IP address now."

"If Pasar wants to know when this port opens, I think we can assume it's important," said Cameron. "Nice work, Ross. You know, I think I'd like to meet your friend."

Sandeep interrupted with a howl of rage. "I don't believe it," he said. "Pete, look at that IP address."

"Oh, hell," said Pete. "It's in the plant. Please tell me it isn't the security backup."

"How can we check?" said Cameron. "We can't go back on site."

"There's still a skeleton staff there," said Sandeep. "That technician will be in the data centre. I'll see if we can get through."

"I can contact Daniel directly," said Pete. "He's back in there managing the situation. What do we need to know?"

"Is it running, is it talking to anything," said Cameron. "Is it still under their control." She turned back to Ross on her monitor as Pete and Sandeep started making calls. "Ross, if this has started, we need that malware ready fast. It doesn't need to be subtle. It could do with a delay in it, to give Cloverleaf a chance to get out to the pickup location, but otherwise we just need to it to break everything quickly. I don't care if it can be fixed in half an hour. It's enough to disrupt and stop the theft."

"I'm on it," he said. "I can put together a kernel rootkit to kill off random processes, and build in a delay. I have most of the code that I need."

534

"That's nasty and I love it," said Cameron. "They won't come back from that in a hurry. Could your friend keep tabs on Pasar activity? Anything that happens in there may be linked."

"I'm sure she can," said Ross.

Pete was looking puzzled. "If it is the server, how did your friend's scan find it? I suppose the air gap has been compromised, but there's still the firewall to get through."

"The Snake River firewall," said Sandeep. "Something in that software has to be dodgy."

"We didn't find anything," said Pete.

"Susie and Ella ran a full bank of tests on the installation in the West Country," said Cameron. "It was as tight as a drum."

"We've done the same here," said Pete. "The only things going backwards and forwards are whitelisted connections. It's very strict."

"Oh, wait, no," said Cameron. "Could it be that simple?"

"What?" asked Pete, puzzled.

On the screen, Ross started laughing. "Hiding in plain sight," he said.

"What?" asked Sandeep.

"Whitelists," said Cameron. "Addresses and applications that want to talk to this system have to be on the list, or they don't get in."

"We went through all of that with our pen tests," said Pete. "It's clean. We know there's a bit of polymorphic code sitting in the firewall software, but it doesn't do anything."

"Inbound connections may be clean," said Cameron, "but have you looked at outbound whitelists?"

"They wouldn't turn up on pen tests from outside the firewall, would they?" said Sandeep. "We never even thought of running one from inside."

"Don't worry," said Cameron. "It's not a standard test. It would take a long time to pick anything up."

"I wonder if the polymorphic code does have a use, then?" said Pete. "What if it adds that server to an outbound whitelist every time it updates?"

"This has been in the planning for years, hasn't it?" said Cameron. "The server updates its security profile backup every day, and the Snake River firewall opens up, regular as clockwork, and lets it connect to an external address whenever they're ready to launch their attack."

"Shall we re-analyse the firewall software and work out how to close the door?" asked Sandeep.

"It's worth a look," said Cameron. "It gives us another string to our bow. Can you access a copy from our files?"

"On it," said Sandeep.

"I'd better get on with that malware," said Ross. He muted and went back to work.

•

Mìmì Māo checked and double checked that everything was in place. She was honoured to have taken custody of the project while King Katong was out of reach. He had messaged her from his Tokyo stopover to check everything was running smoothly. The jigsaw pieces were coming together, and the client was ready to move.

She was waiting for the window of opportunity to open. Tapping her fingers on the table, she looked at the clock. A message alert sounded: ShellPixie was on the forum, and she had good news.

"The scan routine has just come back with a positive result," she said. "Here are the details."

"Ahhh," sighed Mìmì. "Well done. The client will be pleased. The Sleeping Dragon awakes!"

Michelle tapped a note onto her braille pad and sent it to Ross. "slpng. drgn = sleeping dragon." She wondered what the next stage was.

Other Pasar members were arriving the chat. Cloverleaf was there, and the Monkey. Mìmì was grandstanding, and Michelle was taking notes at a fiendish pace.

"We have access to the target, and we will now take control of their security systems," said Mìmì. "Once the doors are open, the client will deploy their drones to gain access and retrieve the uranium safely."

"Congratulations," said the Monkey's avatar. "The hare-brained scheme is working."

"Monkey," said Mìmì sternly, "your attitude is most displeasing. You developed part of the system. You should be proud of your contribution to the cause."

"Cause my arse," said the Monkey. "It's all about the money. Where's Katong got to? I need a word."

Cloverleaf interrupted. "I have to go, Mìmì. Something has come up. Good luck with the final steps." She left the chat.

Michelle kept quiet, listening. She looked around the group, searching for the Pangolin, but there was no sign of them. King Katong was noticeably absent as well.

"King Katong is travelling," said Mìmì. "He will join us again in a few hours."

The Monkey laughed. "What's wrong with video calls? He is such a poser."

Michelle sent another note to Ross, and this time he replied.

"Travelling?" he said. "That's too much of a coincidence. Shell, I think you need to get out of there. We have all we need."

She didn't need telling twice. She slipped away. Mìmì Māo wouldn't notice her go. She had done her job and was no longer interesting. Michelle dropped back onto the chat with Ross.

"I've finished cobbling together this root kit," he said. "Can you take a look at the code?"

Michelle listened intently to the playback of the code. "Sounds good," she said. "I have a couple of suggestions."

Ross edited the file as she talked. She was good. Her ideas were elegant and precise, and they would improve the code's performance. As soon as it was done, he uploaded it for Cameron's final check.

Cameron came back to him faster than he expected. "This is stunning work, Ross. It looks great. I'll get it over to Cloverleaf now and we have to hope it works."

"Great," said Ross. He wondered whether to mention Michelle's contribution. "I had some help," he admitted finally.

"I thought so," said Cameron triumphantly. "I've known you for a long time, Ross White, and I know your code. That little tweak there is genius and it's not your style at all. When this is over, introduce us."

"Okay," said Ross. "I will."

"The show's about to start on the beach," called Pete. "I want to see the detonation. It's going to be spectacular. Sandeep, how's it going with the firewall?"

"I think I know where the hole is," said Sandeep, "but I can't work out how to close it without disabling the whole thing. I don't think we have time."

"I think we've done all we can," said Cameron. "Now we have to hope that either Cloverleaf's software stops the trigger, or the technicians in the power station manage to regain control of the security systems."

"Or that the Navy team blows the drones up," said Pete.

"It's all down to luck and timing," said Ross. "Go and enjoy the show."

•

As soon as the emergency alert vibrated on her screen, Cloverleaf knew the end had come. She calmly stood up from her desk and walked towards the rest rooms where she could check her messages in private. One confirmed the pickup that had been arranged for her and for Audrey. The other was from the SimCavalier. Cloverleaf had one last job to do. The file containing the code she needed came straight through on a standard encrypted message service. There was no time to use the secure comms link on the island, and Cloverleaf would be gone before there was any risk of discovery.

Her first priority was her daughter. She called Bonnie.

"Hey," she said, "Looks like I'll be finishing early today. I promised Audrey a surprise camping trip. Could you get her ready to go, and I'll collect her on my way home?"

Her attitude changed as she walked back through the door of her office. She clutched her stomach and looked pained.

"Are you okay?" asked the supervisor.

"No," she replied weakly. "I feel dreadful."

"You don't look too good. If you're sick, you should go home. Take the afternoon off."

"I will," said Cloverleaf. "Thank you. I'll just finish this job."

The supervisor turned away from her to take a call. "Yes, understood." Cloverleaf heard her say. "Sleeping Dragon is go. Awaiting transmission."

Cloverleaf sat gingerly back at her desk, acting her heart out. The code from the SimCavalier had to be loaded into the main operating system. She made a show of slowly completing the routine task she had been working on while the SimCavalier's code processed. Once it was done, she set a timer on her smartscreen. She had exactly thirty minutes to get out to the pickup point. She closed down her terminal, picked up her backpack, and made her way to the door, whimpering gently and grimacing in mock pain.

"Y'all go get some rest and we'll see you on Monday," said the supervisor kindly.

"Thanks," she said weakly.

Outside the compound she saw a friend on guard duty.

"You're out early," he said, surprised.

"I'm sick," said Cloverleaf, coughing dramatically.

"You're going to miss the big show," said her friend. "They've just called a full gathering."

"Ah, no way," said Cloverleaf. "I'm going to have to watch the feed at home." She coughed again and doubled over. "I think I'm going to throw up."

"Go home and get yourself well," said her friend sympathetically.

"I will," she called as she made her way down the road. As soon as she was sure that it was safe to do so, she broke into a jog. She didn't have much time.

Audrey was waiting at the gate with her backpack on. Cloverleaf had made sure that Teddy was packed, but she double checked, to be sure. She thanked Bonnie profusely and took Audrey's hand.

They walked and jogged towards the lake. "We're going to take the kayak," she explained breathlessly. The wide concrete roadway was clear of patrols and they ducked into the woods. The kayak was well hidden, and Cloverleaf had left another couple of light bags with it containing a few extra clothes and treasures that she wanted to bring.

There were only minutes left. She settled Audrey in the bow and pushed off into the lake. High above them, the consortium's drones fixed on their location and prepared for retrieval.

Mīmì Māo confirmed that the deployment code had been transmitted to the Militia. "The Sleeping Dragon awakes," she announced to the community. She was sorry that King Katong was not there to see the culmination of the project he had worked so hard on. He could not have known that it would come to fruition so quickly. The plant security was open wide. Now they simply had to wait for the Militia to release the drone swarm. Mīmì knew that the leadership would be grandstanding, showing off to their followers. The wait was frustrating, but the client was always right.

Cameron, Ben, Pete, and Sandeep stood on the beach, watching the navy boats speeding back to shore. Their charges were laid, and the detonation was imminent.

In Wyoming, the Militia's leader pressed a ceremonial button with a staged flourish, and cheers rang around the auditorium.

The seaward defences of the power plant failed. Daniel and Julia watched the screens helplessly. The uranium stores were exposed, and there was nothing they could do.

12: CHANGING FORTUNES

Tenuk bowed politely to the cabin crew as he left the plane. The thin air of the Mile High City made him catch his breath. He walked purposefully towards the shuttle that would whisk him to the main terminal. The little carriages glided through tunnels decorated with gold mining picks and pans and plastic dinosaur fossils. He ignored them, instead watching his smartscreen run through its secure connection sequence for this new country.

As he approached immigration, the first notifications started to scroll up the screen. A lot had happened since he was last in contact. He did not trust the connections on the plane, so had chosen to go dark and leave Mìmì Māo in charge. It was good practice for her. He needed a second in command.

"Smartscreen away, please, sir," said the barrier. It would not lift until he had closed the device. Sighing, he put the screen back in his pocket and the bot granted entry to the screening area. His ID, fingerprint and retina scans all matched first time and he was allowed through to the final security desk. Others were not so lucky, struggling to position their fingers quite right on the pads, failing to match their biometrics. The queue for the more intensive screening section was lengthening.

"You here for work or vacation?" asked the border guard gruffly, checking the visa details on his screen.

"Work," Tenuk said clearly. "I hope to have a little time to see the sights." He tried to be as relaxed and natural as possible, knowing that his reactions were being minutely observed by sensors and analysed in real time.

"You enjoy your stay," said the guard after what felt like an endless pause.

"I will, sir."

He was free to collect his bags and go. He pulled his screen back out of his pocket as soon as he left the secure zone and worked through his messages. The most recent updates from Mìmì were exactly what he wanted to hear. Pasar's work on the Sleeping Dragon was complete, and the client had taken control of the project. Better still, the Syndicate confirmed that they had been paid for the work. There was even a message from Noor. Perhaps she had forgiven him?

He settled into the broad seat of an airport autocar that took him to his hotel. There he set up a secure communications relay in his suite, and opened Noor's first message.

The sight of her, pale and bloodied, shook him to the core. There had been an attack on the Argentum office, she said. Tenuk was upset and furious. The Monkey had overstepped his brief, and he himself had failed to protect her.

He would deal with the Monkey later. First, he wanted to speak to Noor. Was it too late to call? It was late at night in England, seven hours ahead of his current time zone.

"Noor?"

"Tenuk." Her voice was flat and sleepy.

"Are you alright? I just got your message."

"No, I'm not alright."

"Your arm? What happened?"

"I was shot, Tenuk. The office was attacked, and I was shot." Her voice shook. "Tell me you had nothing to do with this."

"Why – how – no, of course not," he protested. "Why would you think that?"

Noor took a deep breath. "I believe you are part of the cybercrime syndicate. I think you've been lying to me."

"Noor!" he pleaded.

"Ross made the connection," she said. "I didn't want to believe him, but it's too much of a coincidence."

"I have nothing to do with those... those criminals!" he protested.

"I have to know, Tenuk. Are you the Pangolin, or are you King Katong?"

Tenuk stared at her, dropping his guard completely. The shock on his face was enough for Noor. She lowered her gaze.

"Goodbye, Tenuk."

"Noor..."

It was too late. She had gone.

Tenuk had to take his rage and pain out on someone. Where was the Monkey? He fired messages out in several directions and waited for him to respond.

"Katong."

"Monkey. You have some explaining to do."

"What the hell are you talking about?" he growled. "It's the other way round. I want a word with you."

"I told you to avoid physical confrontation," said Tenuk. "People have been hurt. Did you at least get the data?"

"I haven't got any data," said the Monkey. "I can't get close. They've doubled down on their security."

"The attack on their premises. Are you saying that wasn't you?"

"Hah, I saw something on the news channel. That was them, was it? Why the hell would I go mob-handed into someone's office? There's no bloody point."

"Who else could it have been?" asked Tenuk, half to the Monkey and half to himself.

"Your problem. Are you saying that the contract's cancelled? I want half my fee."

"Yes," said Tenuk absentmindedly. In the background of the call, there was a loud noise and cheering.

"You hear that sound?" said the Monkey. "That's the sound of your hare-brained Sleeping Dragon plan going Kaboom!" He hung up.

Tenuk sat with his head in his hands. Noor knew who he was, and where he lived. She would tell the authorities, of that he had no doubt. The MerLions management would make an example of him to keep their record squeaky clean. There was nothing for it. He was exposed, and he had no choice but to run.

•

It felt as if all the inhabitants of the little town were gathered on the sea front. It was late but still daylight, and everyone's attention was fixed on the water. Many had their screens raised in front of them, waiting to catch the spectacle for instant sharing on their social channels. On the beach, someone in an outsized monkey costume was running up and down, entertaining the kids who had been brought to see the detonation.

"What's that supposed to be?" Ben asked Sandeep in a low voice.

"Local football mascot," said Sandeep, laughing. "Not my team – Hartlepool's. It's called H'Angus the Monkey. Long story. I'll tell you later."

An outside broadcast pod had arrived and launched its press drones high above the crowd. Cameron was watching the sea and listening to updates from the consortium at the same time. Pete was on the line to

Julia and Daniel, with his eyes fixed on the place the Navy team had been operating a few minutes before.

"The technicians in the plant are working to shut down the server," he said quietly to Cameron, aware of the growing crowd around them.

"Cloverleaf's been located at the retrieval point," replied Cameron softly. "She's delivered her package."

Someone in the crowd started a countdown from ten, but it petered out, and the sea was still. In the silence, a faint signal sounded from the harbour where the Navy team had beached. Pete recognised the warning. "Here we go," he said.

"They're reporting disturbances in the Militia zone," said Cameron, but her voice was drowned out by the loud crump of an underwater explosion and the awed gasps and cheers of the crowd. A broad column of water erupted from the sea, rising so high that it blocked their view of the huge wind turbines further offshore. The water column rose higher, hanging in the air for impossible seconds, before crashing back down. The gasps gave way to applause.

Cameron's sharp ears picked up an unusual phrase. A voice nearby had clearly said, "Sleeping Dragon." She and Sandeep both spun around at the same moment, and she caught the eye of a burly man with a bushy beard. They stared at each other for a second. It was impossible not to acknowledge the connection. He disappeared into the crowd.

"You heard that too?" said Sandeep.

Cameron nodded. "Follow him."

Sandeep pushed his way out in the same direction, but the crowd was starting to disperse, and the stranger had vanished.

"Cameron, there's a message from Ross," said Ben. He handed her his smartscreen.

Her shoulders sagged.

"Pete," she said. "Tell Julia and Daniel that reports suggest the launch software was deployed after all. We don't know whether the drones made it out of their hiding place before the mine was detonated."

"They already know," said Pete grimly. "Sensors show foreign bodies incoming, but far fewer than you'd expect. Four or five, only. It looks as if most of the swarm was caught in the blast." He listened intently. "Wait." Another pause, then he punched the air in delight, startling several passers-by.

"Yes!" he shouted. He smiled at Cameron. "The security system has been reset. The defences are solid, and it looks as if they've trapped the drones in the inlet channel."

"Fantastic," said Cameron, relieved. She felt as if a great weight had been lifted.

"Sandeep and I will give Julia and Daniel any help they need now," said Pete. "You may as well get some sleep."

"It's over," said Ben. "You've won."

Cameron shook her head. "Not quite, but everything else can wait until the morning."

"Good," said Ben. "Let's go home."

They caught the last train back up the coast. Night had fallen at last, and they walked hand in hand from the station up the hill to their cottage. It was quiet and dark, and the skies were clear. As they stood together on the deck looking at the stars twinkling above the calm sea, the sky began to glow. Blackness gave way to green and red and gold, and the northern lights danced for them.

•

Cloverleaf held Audrey tight as the autocar sped south. The little girl was asleep, exhausted by the upheaval and the excitement. Although it was after midnight and they had been on the road for several hours, Cloverleaf was still wide awake, turning over the events of the past few weeks in her head. The consortium wanted to debrief her, and she had plenty for them.

The car swept into the underground car park of an anonymous airport hotel. Cloverleaf had dozed off herself and wasn't even sure which state they were in. Had they crossed south east into Colorado or south west into Utah? As the agent ushered them through the deserted hotel lobby to the elevators, she caught a glimpse of a screen broadcasting local news against the backdrop of a capitol building with a golden dome. Colorado, then. Denver. She relaxed imperceptibly.

Access to the upper floors was restricted, and other uniformed agents guided Cloverleaf and a yawning, stumbling Audrey along silent, carpeted corridors to their new temporary home. Cloverleaf wasted no time tucking Audrey into bed, then freshened up with a welcome shower. She would not get a chance to sleep yet. The debrief was too important to leave until morning.

"How much can you tell us about the members of the Pasar community," asked the agent kindly. The suite was comfortable and secure, and Audrey was sleeping soundly in her bed, her tight curls a dark cloud on the white pillow, and Teddy clutched in her arms.

"Handles and possible locations, and the things they've worked on," said Cloverleaf. "I'm sure they don't know that I've defected. I can give you full access under my credentials and you can view the forum archive."

"Fantastic. Thank you, ma'am." The agent made a note. "What insights can you give us on the structure of the community? Is it a standalone group or is there more to it?"

"More to it," confirmed Cloverleaf. "The Syndicate controls the client relationships. I get the impression that Pasar is simply one spoke of the wheel. There will be others."

"Shall we take a look in the community now?" suggested the agent. "We have a VPN set up here."

"Okay." Cloverleaf copied her avatar and access keys from her private files to the agent's machine and logged in.

There was a frantic air to the conversations in the forum, and she quickly realised they knew that the Sleeping Dragon had failed. She had expected King Katong to be online, but he was nowhere to be seen. Something was wrong.

"There's one guy missing that you need to track down," said Cloverleaf immediately. "King Katong."

The agent looked pained. "We're trying," he said. "We found out a few hours ago who he really is and where he lived. He's gone."

"Are you sure you have the right person?" asked Cloverleaf anxiously.

"Yes, one hundred percent," said the agent. "His apartment has been breached and searched and the evidence is overwhelming, even if we can't find the man himself."

"You've clipped his wings, like you did with Sagikkun in Korea."

"We still should have picked up both of them," said the agent. "Hopefully, we can get the others."

"I don't want to spend too much time here on the forum," she said. "Let's get what we wanted and get out." She opened the group archive in a new window and the agent began copying all the data he could find. Cloverleaf lurked on the edge of the conversations. Suddenly a familiar name was mentioned: the SimCavalier.

"The Syndicate's source has transmitted details of the individual known as the SimCavalier," Mimi said. "The contract is open. Compromise, distraction, collusion or termination."

A name, a picture and personal details appeared on the feed. Cloverleaf captured the screenshot before it disappeared. A woman based in the UK, as she had thought. There was no response initially, but then the Monkey stepped up.

"I've seen her," he said. "I know where she is. I'll take it on."

Cloverleaf and the consortium agent exchanged horrified glances. "We have to warn her," said Cloverleaf.

"More to the point, we have to find the leak," said the agent. "How does the Syndicate know who the SimCavalier is? She may be in more danger than we think."

He checked a new alert on his own screen. "I think we have everything we need from here. Everything's been downloaded, and my colleagues are taking the forum down now. It's time to say goodbye to Pasar."

•

Cameron slept late, and Ben was careful not to disturb her. It was only when she finally stirred of her own accord that he woke her gently with a coffee. She looked more relaxed than he had seen her for months.

"What time is it?" she asked, squinting. "It's very bright out there."

"Almost ten," said Ben. "Don't worry, I've been keeping an eye on your messages. I'm a great personal assistant."

She relaxed and sipped her coffee. "Tell me the latest."

"Your morning briefing." He scrolled through the list. "Pete and Sandeep got in about four o'clock this morning from the plant. Everything's secure and they've recovered the trapped drones and disabled them."

"They'll be fun to take apart," said Cameron happily.

Ben was pleased to hear the excitement in her voice. He carried on with the list. "Noor checked in to say good morning. She's sore and stiff and she's very sad about Tenuk, but I think she'll be fine. We had a bit of a chat."

"I never quite worked out her relationship with Tenuk," sighed Cameron. "To begin with it was a friendship which kept her parents off her back about finding a suitable husband. I think she got much closer to him than she will admit. I'll have to keep an eye on her." She took a mouthful of coffee. "What's Ross up to? I want to meet this friend of his."

"He says he's on the way to the competition, and he hopes you'll be coming to support him. Does that make sense?"

"Yes." Cameron yawned. "I suppose I'd better get up."

"If you must," said Ben, "but I'm coming back to bed with breakfast."

"Okay," she said. "I'll stay." She snuggled down into the duvet.

Ben flicked on the wallscreen and went off to get more coffee.

Cameron closed her eyes and let the voices on the news channel wash over her. She heard Ben come back in.

"Look," he said, "it's Ella."

Sure enough, there she was, giving a carefully worded statement about the attack on the office, which had after all disrupted one of London's main thoroughfares on a busy Friday afternoon.

"She's doing a good job," said Cameron approvingly. "Another media star in the making. Is that live or did she record it yesterday with Andy?"

"I think it's a repeat," said Ben. "Yes, look, there's the timestamp."

"Thought so," said Cameron. She flicked the screen off again.

It was closer to eleven o'clock when Cameron's smartscreen alerted her to an incoming call. She reached across and picked it up, carefully answering on audio only.

"Ms Silvera? DS Frost here. Is it convenient to talk?"

"Sure," said Cameron.

"I'll get straight to the point," he said. "Your colleague Mr Bardouille was able to provide contact details for people who might be able to identify the men we have in custody following yesterday's incident."

"Good," said Cameron. "Is there a problem?"

"Yes and no," said Frost. "We have clear positive identification of both men as members of a team running an organisation called Snake River, as you and your colleagues suggested. However, the two people who confirmed those identities both told me, independently, that they have seen other members of that leadership team recently."

Cameron sat up. He had all her attention now.

"Where?"

"On the news channel. One was the young man who sadly drowned in the West Country four days ago."

"Mason?" Cameron was flabbergasted. "One of the actual leaders? We thought he was just a consultant on the fringes."

"It would seem he was more senior than that," said Frost. "It has put a very different slant on the investigation into his death."

"It would," said Cameron. "And the other?"

"This is very awkward," said Frost. "She was one of the witnesses to the attack on your office, and she was in the vicinity when Mason's body was found. I understand she is an employee of Argentum Associates. Ella Stanford."

Cameron's jaw dropped. "No. No, it can't be," she stammered.

Ben, who had dozed off next to her, woke with a start. He took one look at Cameron's face and realised that the idyllic morning had come to an abrupt end.

"The evidence is enough for us to bring her in," said Frost. "Unfortunately, it seems she knew this. We've visited her home and that of Ms Lu and, well, it looks like she's gone to ground."

"But this is Ella we're talking about. She's no criminal. She's well respected, great at her job…" Cameron's voice tailed off. "I need to talk to Susie."

"Ms Lu has been helping us with our enquiries," said Frost. "She's not under any suspicion and she's given us some very useful information."

"I'll call her now. Is there anything you need from me?"

"Not now," said Frost, "but if you can think of any other details which might help our enquiries, please call me."

"Of course." Cameron hung up and put her head in her hands.

"We've found our leak," she said huskily. "It was Ella."

"I'm sorry," said Ben.

"I wonder how much more information has been passed on," said Cameron. "She had access to everything." She swung out of bed. "I need a shower, then I'll call Susie."

Susie looked understandably pale and shocked. She was sitting on an unfamiliar sofa and clutching a large cup of tea.

"I'm at my dad's place," she explained. "I didn't want to stay at home."

"I'm glad you're with someone," said Cameron, relieved. "You've had a hell of a time. Want to tell me about it?"

"Yes." Susie wiped a tear away, angry with herself for crying. "I need to apologise, as well. I knew we had a leak, but I thought it was Joel."

"Joel? Why ever would you think that?"

"Ella said… Ella used to point out that he was missing from meetings, taking days off when the rest of us were working. He didn't want to go north to do the penetration test. She made me think that he was up to something. Of course, when the office was attacked, it was obvious he wasn't, and that's when I started to wonder what Ella was playing at."

Cameron laughed softly. "There's no mystery," she said. "This is still a secret, but you need to know. Martha's pregnant. She's been having a difficult time and Joel's been supporting her. He didn't want to be too far from London."

"Oh!" Susie's face lit up. "That's really lovely. I won't say anything."

"What was the story with Ella? I know you two weren't getting on well."

"No," admitted Susie. "She fell in with a new set of friends very soon after we started dating. At first it wasn't a problem, but she started spending more time with them, and she changed. She became harder, if you know what I mean."

"I do," said Cameron. "I noticed that myself."

"I should have worked all of this out sooner," said Susie.

"There was no way you could have guessed that it went this deep," said Cameron. "Honestly, I'm the same. You were carrying her all the time in the West Country. You did some excellent work there."

"Thanks, Cameron," said Susie. "I can't stop thinking about Mason, though."

"When will we be back in the office?" asked Susie. "I want to work. It'll help."

"Good," said Cameron. "There's plenty to do. I'll see you on Monday. Take care."

•

Tenuk was lurking on Pasar as the Pangolin. He knew that it was too risky ever to be King Katong again but hoped that his other avatar had been overlooked. He wanted to know what was happening.

The great revelation of the SimCavalier's identity did not take him by surprise. He had known for a long time who she was. He was fascinated by the interactions of the members, and Mìmì Māo was getting into her stride as the leader of the pack. The Monkey was his usual unpleasant self. Tenuk was glad to be abandoning his old handle. He might shake off the Monkey with it.

As he watched, the familiar dashboard of the community morphed and changed. Users vanished one after the other, fleeing an incoming attack. Mìmì was one of the last to go; she held on loyally as along as she could. Eventually, only the Pangolin and Cloverleaf were left as the security forces stripped the forum. Tenuk shook his head sadly. 'His' Cloverleaf must have been the double agent all along.

He deleted the Pangolin's account, closed his connection, picked up his unopened bags and left the hotel. America was his oyster. Everything could be rebuilt. It was only a matter of time.

•

The sea front was bustling with day trippers, the drama of the previous

549

night forgotten. Cameron and Ben skirted milling crowds outside the shops and ice cream stands, making their way slowly from the station to the Endeavour where Pete and Sandeep were waiting.

Cameron stumbled on the kerb, and as she found her footing again, she stepped straight into the path of another pedestrian.

"Sorry," she said automatically. The other person did not move. "Excuse me?"

She looked up. Ben was already ten metres ahead, and her path was blocked by the bearded man she had seen last night. His grey eyes bored into her, and she shivered.

The tension was broken by a familiar voice.

"Angus! How lovely to see you. It's been a long time." It was Julia. She bustled up to them and looked from one to the other, confused. "Do you two know each other?"

Cameron recovered first. "No," she said. "Should we?"

"Angus was our head of security for many years," said Julia happily. "Gosh, it must be eighteen months since I last saw you. How are you? This is Cameron. She and her team have been doing some work at the power station."

"It's a pleasure to meet you," said Cameron smoothly, hiding her shock well. She knew exactly who he was now: the 'old bloke from the north' who had led the Snake River installations. She could see the fury and frustration in the man's eyes and couldn't shake the feeling that he knew her secrets, too.

"And you," he said. "Lots of drama last night, wasn't there?"

"Oh yes, Angus," said Julia. "It was rather a stressful evening."

"I thought the Navy boys did well," he said. "They do have something of a, shall we say, a cavalier attitude to explosives." He fixed Cameron with a penetrating stare, and her blood ran cold.

Over Angus' shoulder she saw Ben coming back towards them, and she broke the tension with a shout and a wave to attract his attention.

That was enough for Angus.

"Nice to see you, Julia," he said. "I can't stop." He shambled off towards the marketplace.

"Typical Angus," said Julia. "He's a strange lad but his heart's in the right place." She was talking to empty space. Cameron had disappeared into the crowd in pursuit, and Ben followed. It was no use. The crowd closed around the man, and when Cameron reached the edge of the beach, he had vanished.

"Who was that chap?" asked Ben, catching up to her.

"Dammit, Ben, he's the key to all of this," said Cameron. "I can't believe I lost him."

From a distance, Angus watched them go. He had been close to the best payday he could have wished for from Pasar, and it had been snatched away. There was no point fulfilling his part of the contract now that the other party had defaulted, the community scattered to the four winds by the security services. He would bide his time. One day, someone would pay handsomely for what he knew.

•

Ross stood on the starting blocks at the edge of the lake and waved at the small crowd and the press drones overhead. Cameron and Ben were sitting on a grassy patch, cheering with the rest. It was almost time, and he was well rested and ready to show what he could do. The starter called for silence, and for a moment all that could be heard was the distant noise of a swan calling to its cygnets. At the signal, the athletes dived into the water and thrashed out towards the first buoy. Ross ploughed ahead, flipped onto his back to turn tightly, and struck out to the second marker. The race was on.

"Did we miss the start?" Pete arrived, panting. "We stopped to pick up Daniel's cousin, which took ages because there was a fire on the wasteland near their house, and then the autocar couldn't find this place. We've just had an extended tour of the countryside and I had to recalibrate the navigation system."

"I'm not sure the hire company will be very impressed," added Sandeep, who had followed him.

"They've just started swimming," said Cameron. "Come and sit down. Didn't you bring the picnic?"

"Yes, Daniel's got it," said Pete, gesturing back towards the dusty car park. He looked at the pack of swimmers sweeping past as they headed around the lake for a second lap. "Which one's Ross?"

"The one at the front in the Great Britain cap," said Ben. "He's looking fantastic."

The marshals started to clear a path across the car park to the gate, ready for the athletes to emerge from the water and start on their cycling leg. Daniel made it across to the grass just as the barriers went up. He was carrying a huge coolbag and had a girl in tow.

"Made it," said Daniel happily. "This is my cousin, Michelle. Michelle, this is Pete, Sandeep, Cameron and Ben."

"Hi Michelle," said Cameron. "I think we've met."

"I recognise your voice," said Michelle. "Yes, we met on the dunes."

Daniel looked from one to the other. "Really? You never mentioned it."

"I went for a walk while you were at work the other day," said Michelle. "Cameron practically tripped over me when I was sitting there enjoying the sunshine."

"Here they come," said Ben. "Look sharp."

Three swimmers emerged from the water, neck and neck for first position. Ross was one of them. They dashed for their bikes and disappeared in a cloud of dust out of the carpark to the road, followed closely by the rest of the group.

"Fast changeover," said Pete approvingly. "Right, where's that food?"

There was very little to do now other than wait. Cameron lay back on the grass, her head on Ben's lap. She gazed up at the clouds in the blue sky and nibbled at a sandwich. Pete and Daniel were laughing together and exchanging ever-taller diving tales.

"They do dive training here in the lake," Daniel said.

"No mines?" asked Pete.

"No mines."

There was a flurry of excitement as the first group of elite riders came whizzing back into the car park. They all stood to cheer Ross on as he completed the cycling stage and set off for his run.

"He's doing okay, isn't he?" said Daniel.

"This is his strongest section," said Cameron. "He started out as a runner, back when I first knew him."

"RunningManTech," said Sandeep. "That's his handle online, Daniel."

"Have you ever come across him?" Daniel asked Michelle.

"I don't think so," she said.

Cameron gave her a sharp look. "You're a coder, Michelle?"

"Yes," she said. "Officially I'm on the staff at Thorney Solutions, but they don't send me much work. I do a lot of private contracts."

"How do you code?" asked Sandeep.

"With a computer, like everyone else," said Michelle. "Why do people assume that because I can't see the screen, I can't build the code?"

"I'm sorry," said Sandeep. "That was a really silly question."

"That's okay," said Michelle. "It happens all the time. My clients can't see me, though. They judge me by the quality of my work."

"Ouch, Sandeep," laughed Pete. "That's a burn. What kind of things do you do, Michelle?"

"Custom jobs," she said carefully. "Things that need a bit of imagination. Plenty of boring stuff as well, of course, but I like the challenging ones better."

"Don't we all," said Cameron. "Anyone want a beer?"

They drank and chatted until a commotion from the road announced the arrival of the runners. They were perfectly placed by the finish line to cheer Ross as he led the field home.

Ross waved to the crowd and went into a huddle with his coach. Formalities finally over, he trotted over to see his friends.

"Fantastic, Ross," said Cameron.

"I've never seen you race before," said Pete. "That was bloody good."

Ben clapped him on the back. "Nice one."

"Have you met Daniel yet?" asked Pete.

"No," said Ross. "Hi, Daniel. You've been in the thick of things at the plant, haven't you? I've heard all about you."

"Good to meet you," said Daniel. "This is my cousin, Michelle."

"Hi, Michelle," he said automatically, then paused. Something was ringing a very loud bell. What had ShellPixie said? That her cousin Daniel had transcribed the label on the hard disk. "Wait…"

Michelle reached her hand out to him. "Hello, Piper," she said quietly.

"Shell?" Ross gazed at her in disbelief.

"Do you two know each other?" asked Daniel.

"Yes," said Ross. He took Michelle's hand and squeezed it tight. "Yes, we do." He looked at Cameron. "You know you said you wanted to meet my friend? I guess you already have."

Ross turned to Michelle and whispered to her. She laughed and whispered back, their heads touching. Daniel watched in amazement, and everyone else was silent. Ross and Michelle didn't notice.

The whole field had finished, and a battered podium was being put into place with the photogenic lake behind it. "I have to get my medal," said Ross. "Wait here." He gave Michelle's hand a last squeeze and dashed away.

Pete stood open-mouthed. "Is that our Ross?" he said to Sandeep. "Did someone swap him for a new model when we weren't looking?"

Ross accepted his medal, congratulated the runners up, and waved at the press drones. As soon as everything was finished, he jumped down and ran back to the group.

"Here," he said, putting the ribbon around Michelle's neck. "You can look after this for me. I need a word with my coach."

"Michelle," said Cameron, "did you know?"

"I didn't know who you were when we met," she said. "I've known Ross online for years, but we've done a lot of work together in the last few weeks. He mentioned your name when we were working on the virus for Cloverleaf."

"You know all about that?" said Sandeep. "This is crazy."

"If I'm not mistaken," said Cameron, "you put the finishing touches to that code. It was amazing work."

"Thanks," said Michelle, blushing.

"Did you know who Ross was?" asked Daniel. "Is that why you asked to come with me? You could have said. I wouldn't have minded."

"I know, Dan," she said affectionately. "I wasn't sure if it was him. I'm glad it was, and I'm sorry I didn't tell you."

"That's okay, Shell," he said. "You have good taste. He's cute."

Michelle laughed and punched him playfully and remarkably accurately. "Hands off."

Ross reappeared carrying his training bag. "I don't need to be back at the club until Tuesday," he said. "I'm going to stay up here for a couple of days."

"I suppose you want the day off on Monday," said Cameron. Ross grinned, and Cameron returned the smile. She was glad to see him so happy.

The car park was emptying. Two hired autocars sat at the gateway waiting to bear them back to the coast.

Ross jumped out with Pete and Sandeep at their guest house. "I need to freshen up and buy a toothbrush," he said to Michelle. "I'll see you shortly."

Cameron and Ben's car whisked them back to the cottage, and Daniel and Michelle returned home.

"I'm going to have a shower and get changed," said Michelle as they walked through the door. "Oh, Daniel. This is bizarre. Lovely, but bizarre."

"Wait," said Daniel. He went to his room and emerged with a small box. "Here. You can't wear it until it's repaired, but I think you should have it."

Michelle opened the box and ran her fingers over the smooth platinum. "We've come so far since you found this," she said. "Cameron has offered me a job. I might go to London, but I don't want to leave you."

"Don't worry about me," said Daniel. "It won't take me long to sort the plant out, and there's a chance to do more with this consortium.

554

They need people on the ground as well as you technical folk."

Michelle flung her arms around him. "Our luck has changed, Dan. We're flying. No more scavenging."

He held her tight. "Proud of you, cuz."

•

Cameron and Ben sat in the hot tub, looking out at the sea.

"We've got a lot of work to do," she said. "We may have won the battle, but the war never ends."

"You're ready to face the challenge now, aren't you," said Ben.

"Yes," said Cameron. "I'm not afraid anymore."

"What were you afraid of?"

"I was afraid of losing you, of hurting Charlie and Sameena and the kids and Aunt Vicky."

"I thought so," said Ben, pouring her another glass of bubbly. "I think you'll find they were more worried about you than about themselves."

"I know that now," said Cameron. "And you?"

"You were never in danger of losing me," said Ben.

The SimCavalier's adventures continue in

CRITICAL NEXUS
SIMCAVALIER BOOK FOUR

Read more about Kate Baucherel's work at
www.katebaucherel.com

ACKNOWLEDGEMENTS

Thanks as always to my family, Xavier, Gaelle and Loïc, who are very tolerant of the ever-present laptop, especially as a deadline looms. For the projection of existing tech into the future, once again I'm grateful to CIO and security specialist David Morton who checks that I'm not flying too far from the possible. Thanks also to ethical hacker Tom Johnson for allowing me to use part of his tale of penetrating an office building in a real-life security exercise. This really did include social engineering of a mark, copying an ID badge, drinking coffee with unsuspecting staff and removing an entire computer.

The setting for the story is inspired by North East England. The geography isn't exact, but if you visit you will find wide sandy beaches, marshlands, birds, a landfill, old colliery villages, chemical plants, and a nuclear power station along this coast. The diving is exceptional, and there are seals.

The technical background to Cameron's adventures comes straight from the work that I do on emerging technologies, and the fantastic world of cybersecurity. Many of the threats and technologies described here already exist. Software to track the location of any social channel posts is based on the cree.py application. Steganography, the art of hiding data in other data, is one of many reasons you have to be careful what you download. It is most often associated with hidden data in pictures, and has a long pre-digital history from invisible ink and book codes to hidden meaning in paintings. Nmap is a real scanning tool in regular use. It is remarkably easy to build a picture of someone from very little data through their public digital footprint: be careful what you share. Polymorphic code changes its nature, which causes headaches for antivirus software. That protection works by comparing the hash of the software your computer wants to download with all the hashes they have on record for known malware. If the code keeps changing, the software will not flag it up, which is why it's important to keep your antivirus up to date. A kernel root kit is a particularly nasty piece of malware which has the same rights and access as the operating system. It's hard to detect and has the same rights as the operating system, so it can cause serious damage and can't be easily removed. All of these things exist now, so stay safe!

ABOUT THE AUTHOR

I've been embedded in science fiction since before I could talk. My parents rented their first TV to watch the moon landing when I was a toddler. My first glimpse of the Daleks, hiding behind the sofa aged about four, pulled me into new worlds. I wrote my own Dr Who, Space 1999, Blakes 7 and Tomorrow People stories on an old typewriter in my bedroom. After Star Wars came out (I was nine) more fan fiction and occasional scripts for friends to act out followed.

I graduated from reading Dr Who books and Star Wars novels to Tolkein, Wyndham, Bradbury and thence Iain Banks and David Brin, Terry Pratchett and Neil Gaiman, but all my published writing until 2017 was non-fiction.

The first SimCavalier novel came as something of a surprise, written after a friend suggested that cybersecurity might be less dry as fiction. Cameron Silvera and the Argentum Associates team burst into life in Bitcoin Hurricane. Hacked Future, Tangled Fortunes and Critical Nexus followed, and there is more to come. Along the way, the wonderful team at Sixth Element Publishing launched the Harvey Duckman Presents anthologies, and there are more of my science fiction stories to discover in that series.

In my professional life, I am a writer, speaker, and digital strategist specialising in the application of emerging technologies, with a focus on the use of blockchain and cryptocurrency. My non-fiction books include Blockchain Hurricane: Origins, Applications and Future of Blockchain and Cryptocurrency (BEP 2020) and the What's Hot in Blockchain and Crypto series (2020,2021). In a career spanning more than 30 years, I've held senior technical and financial roles in businesses across multiple sectors including utilities, manufacturing, leisure and software, leading several enterprises through their start-up and growth phases. My first tech role was with an IBM business partner in Denver, back when the AS/400 was a cutting-edge piece of hardware and the World Wide Web didn't exist. I graduated in business from Newcastle University, I'm a Fellow of the Chartered Institute of Management Accountants, and I lecture at Teesside University in both the Business School and School of Computing, Engineering and Digital Technologies. I have a 3rd Dan black belt in karate and live in the UK with my husband and children.

Lightning Source UK Ltd.
Milton Keynes UK
UKHW010709170522
403088UK00004B/924